HUMANS

The Untold Story of Adam and Eve and their Descendants

VOLUME THREE:

THE DEMONIAC

(3RD REVISED EDITION)

EDITORIAL REVIEWS

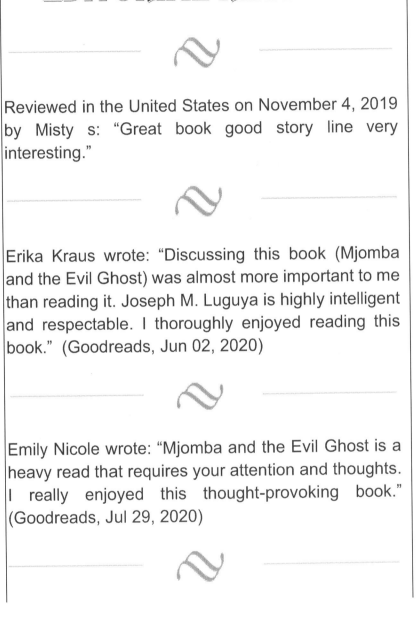

Reviewed in the United States on November 4, 2019 by Misty s: "Great book good story line very interesting."

Erika Kraus wrote: "Discussing this book (Mjomba and the Evil Ghost) was almost more important to me than reading it. Joseph M. Luguya is highly intelligent and respectable. I thoroughly enjoyed reading this book." (Goodreads, Jun 02, 2020)

Emily Nicole wrote: "Mjomba and the Evil Ghost is a heavy read that requires your attention and thoughts. I really enjoyed this thought-provoking book." (Goodreads, Jul 29, 2020)

Melissa wrote (regarding "Mjomba and the Evil Ghost"): "Interesting read. Well written." (Goodreads, May 23, 2020)

⁓

Debra wrote (regarding "Mjomba and the Evil Ghost"): "Very interesting and often thought provoking." (Goodreads, May 23, 2020)

⁓

Mary wrote (regarding "Mjomba and the Evil Ghost"): "Interesting read." (Goodreads, Jul 28, 2018)

⁓

Csimplot Simplot wrote (regarding "Mjomba and the Evil Ghost"): "Excellent book!!!" (Goodreads, Dec 18, 2018)

⁓

Sasha wrote (regarding "Mjomba and the Evil Ghost"): "This book for me was a very interesting read. I truly enjoyed reading this book. I couldn't put it down once I began reading it. I kept wanting to find out more. I would recommend this book to others. It is a very good read. I will be reading this again. This is an amazing author. If you haven't read any of his books you should." (Goodreads, Jul 30, 2020)

Connie wrote (regarding "Mjomba and the Evil Ghost"): "I found this book uneven. Parts I could hardly read. Other parts I devoured. It is the story of a young man writing his thesis (think) and he somehow gets the devil to lecture him. It is never anti God. Always God is a real being in the story. It's the how and why the devil was banished and what his job has become." (Goodreads, Dec 20, 2018)

Mary wrote (regarding "Mjomba and the Evil Ghost"): "Unique read." (Goodreads, July 1, 2020)

 The Columbia Review of Books & Film

-- Avraham Azrieli, TheColumbiaReview.com

Humans: The Untold Story of Adam and Eve and their Descendants is a substantial novel in three parts by Joseph M. Luguya, which explores good and evil through human, mythological and supernatural characters, much of it in the form of a grand debate, delivering an intricate theological saga.

Humans includes three volumes: "The Thesis" (Volume One), "Mjomba and the Evil Ghost" (Volume Two), and "The Demoniac" (Volume Three). The scene that launches Humans appropriately involves both mystery and magnificence: "The International Trade Center literally sat on the edge of downtown Dar es Salaam, the beautiful metropolis whose name fittingly signified "Heaven of Peace". Christian Mjomba's office was located on the twenty-seventh floor.

In an unusual move, using a key he took from his wallet, Mjomba unlocked a side door to his office and slid furtively inside." And from this opening of a mysterious door, Humans builds up to a complex yet compassionately humane story of Mjomba's fascinating journey.

In his earlier days, Mjomba had been a seminarian whose tangling with a monumental assignment on the "Original Virtue" led to an immensely challenging intellectual and spiritual quest—as well as a "Devil's bargain" of sorts. He fences with Satan and with its good counterparts while bringing into stark question many of the basic tenets of the church. In fact, "having in effect enlisted the help of Satan in the task of turning out a winning thesis on the subject of "Original Virtue," Mjomba finds himself "feeling quite uncomfortable filling the role of scribe to a creature that the sacred scriptures had pointedly referred to as "Accuser of our Brethren" (Revelation 12:10)."

And so, in a twist that makes Humans uniquely intriguing, Mjomba's sincere efforts to turn the most evil force into good and, thus, save souls, ends up placing our hero himself in a highly questionable—and dangerous—position.

Author Joseph M. Luguya brings to this novel enormous knowledge of religious concepts and historical records. Through the protagonist and the secondary characters, the reader becomes privy to a wealth of ideas and detailed arguments, many of them new and daring. While much of the book offers a multi-faceted, extensive dissertation that might appear dense to some readers, the author's creative use of Satan's own voice makes it hard to put down, not only when provocative arguments begin to attain logical flair, but also when the author brings in controversial historical figures whose legacy is open to debate—and to literary license—as Satan claims them to his side: "Take the so-called 'reformation' that I engineered. Believe it or not, but it was my idea. I used Martin Luther, a Catholic friar – yes, and a good one at that – and a reformer, to set it in motion."

Or this one: "… Joan of Arc who was labeled a witch and burned at the stake! You may or may not like to hear it, but I also succeeded in using that innocent girl to confound and drive other good souls in the Church to virtual despair."

Some of the arguments in fact ring true not only in the historical context, but in our current world, festering as it is with religious tensions and ethnic prejudices: "Later, during his oral defense of the thesis, Mjomba would comment that one of the legacies of original sin was the perennial tendency of humans to never see evil in themselves, and to see nothing good in other humans – especially those who were different from themselves in some respect." How true!

The author is especially deft at merging abstract ideas and structural visualizations into symbols that our hero's mind ponders in ways reminiscent of Dan Brown's symbologist Robert Langdon in The Da Vinci Code: "But the image of an inverted pyramid balancing on top of another pyramidal shape flooded Mjomba's mind with a force that made him feel like he might pass out. He attributed his ability to stay afloat and not drift off into a swoon to the fact that he was able to focus his mind on the peculiar design Primrose had produced using the blurb's material and its similarity to the letter "X"!

Humans is also distinguishable in telling a story within a story, cleverly utilizing several layers of imaginary characters. For example, here is our protagonist reflecting on his own created protagonist: "Mjomba shut his eyes and paused to think about Innocent Kintu, the central character of his 'masterpiece'. As images of the nurse's beguiling manner came flocking back, he came close to concluding that a non-fictional character like Kintu could in fact be considered fictional when contrasted with a character like Flora!"

In summary, Humans: The Untold Story of Adam and Eve by Joseph M. Luguya creates a dramatic confrontation between a virtuous young scholar and the most malevolent character of all, delivering an extensive, all-encompassing confrontation that becomes a metaphor for the very core of human existence. This thought-provoking, sprawling novel explores unresolved issues of faith and spirituality while the leading character valiantly defends all that he holds dear in the struggle between good and evil, life and death, and the opposing forces of divine creation. Readers will be enticed to contemplate the

most fundamental questions of human existence and come away with a deeper understanding of both differences and commonalities that define us. Significant and Memorable!
-- Avraham Azrieli, TheColumbiaReview.com

KIRKUS REVIEWS: Luguya (*Payment in Kind*, 1985) offers a three-part novel about one man's extensive views on Christianity.

When readers first meet Christian Mjomba, he's seated in his 27th-floor office in the city of Dar es Salaam, Tanzania. He has a pleasant view of the harbor and a degree from Stanford University on the wall, and seems to be doing fairly well. However, his dream of publishing a best-selling work remains unfulfilled. He does have a background in writing, though; as readers soon learn, he'd once been a member of a seminary brotherhood. During that time, he composed an extensive thesis on various aspects of the Christian faith, which strayed from official church teachings. Mjomba's intention was, in part, to "show unequivocally that the Prime Mover loved everyone irrespective of religious affiliation."

The book begins with an in-depth exploration of the

protagonist's views; there's more action in later chapters, but the emphasis throughout is on ideas. They include Mjomba's annoyance with those who use the phrase "the bible says", and his meditation on the human body, which he says is "designed to be both a temple of God and a vessel of His grace." The book covers an extensive amount of theologically intriguing material; it's critical of many different parties, including the Apostle Peter, the devil, and people who revel in "mostly ill-gotten wealth…"

Readers looking for new interpretations of Christian thought will find them here, though those hoping for more thorough integration with plot may be disappointed. Its details of life in Tanzania, such as the notion that "Even though most spoke English very well, Tanzanians just loved to speak Swahili," are memorable. That said, the text as a whole is concerned with issues that go well beyond any single nation.

An insightful…array of spiritual material.

BOOKS WE'VE REVIEWED BY JOSEPH M. LUGUYA —Foreword Reviews
Joseph Luguya's book *Mjomba and the Evil Ghost*

involves a sprawling discourse with Satan concerning the tenets and values of Christianity.

Christian Mjomba is a Stanford-educated success story. The virtuous Tanzanian scholar is also an amateur theologian; in the book, he functions as a stand-in for Christian inquiry. Even his name is symbolic: "mjomba" means "fish" in Swahili. Through a twisting, dramatic series of debates and clashes with dark forces, he explores ideas about faith.

The opponent in Christian's debates is Satan, who is silver-tongued, slick, and convincing. Christian's arguments are human and sometimes clunky, so Satan often claims the upper hand. Referred to by many aliases and claiming to be "more catholic than the Catholics," Satan can debate any point. The two cover topics including the meaning of "victory of good over evil," the pre-lapsarian state of original virtue, murder, and the dangers of rationalization.

Both parties hold forth at length, with Satan picking holes in each of Christian's arguments with the expertise of a lawyer...The book's extensive, in-depth scholarship is excellent, educational, and exhaustive, but as a morality play, the book is too dense to be entertaining.

Mjomba and the Evil Ghost is a discursive novel

concerned with the heresy that it views as inherent in scholarship; it works to justify the dogma of the Catholic Church.

Reviewed by Claire Foster
—Foreword Reviews

Joseph M. Luguya's *Humans: The Untold Story of Adam and Their Descendants* spins an ambitious three-volume fictional tale, in which he charts the history of the human condition…

In this novel, readers learn first-hand from Satan how humans have historically succumbed to temptation. Satan makes sure to present himself here not as villain but victim, and merely one who whispers suggestions to humans who then make unfortunate decisions…

According to the devil, he didn't instruct them to eat

the proverbial fruit, but merely to think; they then concluded they didn't need the "Prime Mover" to make choices for them. The next instance was not far behind, when their son Cain listened to whispers and yielded to jealousy…

No pride-based offense is omitted, from that original fall through present-day power grabs by nations who justify their actions by claiming that they are for the greater good.

Readers must first digest the sum of Christian history, the Bible, all the major players (ex., St. Peter, Mother Teresa), and spiritual concepts (free will, sin, etc.) before being introduced to Satan and his apologetics…The author's own biblical study background is on full display, and he can accurately quote not only Scripture but also his scope of theology in general...
www.blueinkreview.com

www.Spiritrestoration.org: In the same way that C. S. Lewis wrote **Screwtape Letters**, Joseph Luguya attempts to describe the spiritual realm from a human perspective. Luguya does very well at portraying the character of the Devil…This book is one that every fan of C. S. Lewis should check out. Luguya has a very scholarly form just like Lewis…The Devil teaches almost more than the Christian. It is a very convicting book. Luguya is a great writer and well worth the investment in this huge book.

Fr. Gary Coulter: Joseph Luguya has written a very different novel, somewhat on the lines of C.S. Lewis' Screwtape Letters .

Stanford Business Magazine: In this novel, the fictitious author of a thesis on "Original Virtue" offers an African perspective of spirituality in general and Christianity in particular.

Midwest Book Review: Hellishly delicious, (Humans) is a novel about the devil's desire to claim his due, and one man's journey to hell and back…A worthy contemplation of good and evil, and highly recommended reading for its insights on humanity, its wordplay, and sheer devilish delight!

Hellishly
Delicious...
Sheer Devilish
Delight!

xvi

Hellishly Delicious... Sheer Devilish Delight!

Original Books
14404 Innsbruck Court
Silver Spring, MD, 20906, USA
Website: www.originalbooks.org (under construction)
Visit Amazon's Joseph M. Luguya Page

Library of Congress Control Number: 2015914304
ISBN-13: 978-1-73556-493-7
ISBN-10: 1-73556-493-1

Third Revised Original Books Edition, November 8, 2020
Created and written by Joseph M. Luguya
Illustrations by Lorna M. Luguya
Printed and produced in the United States of America
First published August 2015.

About the Author

The author is a native of Uganda. He received his early education at St. Pius X Seminary Nagongera, St. Joseph's Seminary Nyenga, and St. Mary's Seminary Gaba. A graduate of the University of Nairobi, Mr. Luguya is also a former Sloan Fellow at the Stanford Graduate School of Business. He has lived and worked in Uganda, Kenya, Tanzania, Canada, and the United States. He is also the author of Payment in Kind, 2nd Revised edition (Original Books, 2017); The Forbidden Fruit (Original Books, 2011); and Inspired by the Devil Part 1: The Gospel According to Judas Iscariot (Original Books, 2007).

About the Book

Publisher: "This is Volume Three ("The Demoniac") of Joseph Luguya's three-part blockbuster "Humans, The Untold Story of Adam and Eve and their Descendants". The other volumes are "The Thesis" (Volume One) and "Mjomba and the Evil Ghost" (Volume Two).

A virtuous but rather naïve member of St. Augustine's seminary brotherhood has a class assignment to turn in a thesis on "Original Virtue". But he has a runaway imagination, and easily gets snared into serving in a very strange role, namely the role of scribe to none other than Satan.

Misled by the practice in Rome that has one of the

cardinals (the Promoter of the Faith) play the role of the so-called *advocatus diaboli* (Latin for Devil's advocate) in order to argue against the canonization of the candidate for sainthood, he falls for the temptation to use the devil as his mouthpiece for expounding on the Church's doctrines. He imagines that if he succeeds in doing that, he will effectively make Beelzebub, who is also known as Lucifer, work for the salvation of souls instead of their damnation; and he falls for the bait.

And, incredibly, the seminarian appears to succeed in tricking the Evil One into working against his own interests and helping him craft a thesis that looks like a definite winner! Satan sets out to advocate for the damnation of all but those souls that lead the most heroic lives, like Mother Theresa and Josephine Bakhita, a native of Darfur in Sudan who was kidnapped by Arab slave traders at the age of nine, sold into slavery, but eventually found refuge in a convent in Italy where her incorrupt body lies.

The devil brags about how he derailed the father and mother of mankind, and it soon begins to dawn on the student that it is the Evil One who is using him instead of the other way round. Using the free platform provided by the unwitting seminarian and a "neophyte", the devil indicates gleefully that he is in total control, and that his evil plan to consign everyone, Catholic and non-Catholic alike, the luckless student himself included, to hell is on track!

And that former "Angel of Light" and also "Father of

Lies", in a master stroke of genius, succeeds in ensuring that humans are on the road to perdition by pulling off the most unlikely hat trick of all, namely shining as much light on truth as possible so that humans, who are already inclined to sin as a result of the fall of the first Man and the first Woman from grace, don't have any excuse at all when their time of reckoning comes - or so he leads the seminarian to believe! The Prince of Darkness attempts in that manner to counter the Deliverer who, in the moments before His death on the gibbet, pleaded with His Father saying: "Father, forgive them, for they know not what they do." Predictably the devil also brags that he is more knowledgeable in matters of theology than all the doctors of the church combined! And as he goes about shining light on the "Truth", the devil seems quite happy to use this opportunity to show the world that he does not just profess the Catholic faith, but he is actually more Catholic than the Catholics themselves!

In an expansive, record shattering homily on the battle between the forces of Good and the forces of Evil, Satan paints the picture of sinful and sinning descendants of Adam and Eve, who won't give a second thought about turning the house of the "Deliverer's" Father which, according to the Catechism, encompasses the "Sancta Ecclesia" and the "people of God" (CCC 781-797), into a place of commerce! But the devil knows what he is up against, namely the Deliverer and those saints who just go marching into the Divine Banquet Hall for the Marriage Feast of the Lamb exactly as Louis

Armstrong piped.

Before long the student himself starts to see limitless possibilities of benefitting from the scheme, and dreams about riding on the cocktails of Diabolos and achieving fortune and fame by converting the "winning" thesis into a mega-selling blockbuster! While the devil is quite happy with that mutual arrangement and wants to see the student succeed, because disseminating "Truth" in whichever way now serves his purposes very well from one angle, from a different angle, because as the Father of Lies he is being coerced to act against his nature and sees it as punishment, all this now puts the student's eternal salvation in the greatest peril because of his central role in it

This prodigious work dramatizes the battle between the forces of Good and the forces of Evil in a singularly effective manner, and would make for a really hilarious flick!

If *Humans, The Untold Story of Adam and Eve and their Descendants*, ever does get to hit the "Big Screen", the movie goers will actually accompany the seminarian in the final scene as he crosses the gulf that separates the living from the dead and, unrepentant, prepares to meet "His Mystic Majesty" face to face for his final reckoning only to find himself accosted by a totally enraged and menacing Satan who is at the head of a column of crazed demons. They are there to take him to his dungeon in the bottom of hell; and it happens in the moments before the student's "resurrection"!

"Humans" is a treatise on the knowledge of good and evil; and it damns and convicts sinful and sinning humans one and all without any distinction.

This is the untold story of Adam and Eve and their descendants. Prepare to take off on a cruise into realms of spirituality quite beyond anything you had ever dreamed of; and be a witness to:

The Epic Battle

Between

the Forces of Good

and

the Forces of Evil

Watch the showdown as the devil and the Deliverer battle for human souls

As you delve into "Humans", it will start to dawn on you slowly but surely that for a long time you had been wishing, albeit subconsciously, that someone would write a book exactly like this one. Your wish that someone would succeed in tricking Satan, that evilest of evil creatures, to spill all his dirty secrets, has come true at long last. Relax, sit back now, and enjoy "The Demoniac"!

Disclaimer:

This book is a work of fiction. The characters, names, businesses, organizations, places, events, incidents, dialogue and plot are the product of the author's imagination or are fictitiously used. Any resemblance to actual persons living or dead, names, events, or locales is entirely coincidental.

Acknowledgements:

To my daughter Lorna for her imaginative illustration of the Prince of Darkness; and to my family, for being a great inspiration, and for their support; and to the many individuals who genuinely could not wait to see "Humans" in print.

TABLE OF CONTENTS
HUMANS, THE UNTOLD STORY OF ADAM AND EVE AND THEIR DESCENDANTS

VOLUME THREE: THE DEMONIAC

VOLUME THREE: THE DEMONIAC

Next steps for Satan and his troops...

Because the Prime Mover's 'intervention' won't go beyond what He has already done, namely dispatching His only begotten Son into the world where He was promptly killed for being determined to do His Father's will, it is safe to say that there is no justice or anything like that in the world. A better way of saying it might be that there is only injustice in the world.

"Now, in these circumstances, the only real hope which the

critical. They must forget that the Deliverer, who could easily have recruited tens of thousands to work for His cause, chose just twelve 'apostles' among them fishermen and others who were pretty dumb by the world's standards. And then they promptly incurred the wrath of the priests and Pharisees for joining the Deliverer in promoting a 'schism', something that also earned them the title of the 'Dirty Dozen'!

"The zealots must forget that the Deliverer even made Peter, a simple fisherman, leader of this 'Dirty Dozen'. With the possible exception of the shrewd Judas Iscariot, Peter and the rest of the 'Dirty Dozen' would actually be quite uncomfortable and mollified visiting with any of the princes of the Church of modern times!

"It shouldn't be that difficult for us to get the zealots to make it look as if the situation relating to the numbers of those working the 'fields' is absolutely desperate. The role of the Holy Spirit in saving souls must be played down. That will, in turn, make it easy for the wrong type of humans to get in there.

"There ought to be a couple of really good

orators among the recruits - fellows who can move crowds with their choice of words and booming voices, and make a huge impression! In that way, we will see lots of self-willed folks running around claiming that they are raking in souls when it is all a show orchestrated by us, and nothing is really happening.

"And then, we will be on the lookout for those truly selfless souls - souls through whom the Holy Spirit performs real, not staged, miracles. The problem though is that even if they are removed from society and, confined to a hermitage or some such place where they are devoting themselves full time to a life of contemplation, through their prayers and works of penance, they really do a lot to frustrate our work.

"We, for our part, must endeavor to frustrate them as much as possible. Our tack will be to try and condemn them to 'dark nights of the soul' permanently, so they at least won't get away with the damage they do to our cause (inglorious though it may be) that easily. And because those selfless types are the beloved of the Prime Mover and 'untouchables', we will try to achieve our objective by working through those with whom they must perforce commingle - their colleagues, and especially their spiritual advisors and superiors.

"We have to do everything to ensure that the spiritual directors and others who exercise lawful authority over them, even though outwardly pious and devoted to the spiritual welfare of those they serve, are self-willed and virtual human devils - saintly on the surface, but crooks on the inside - yeah, crooks whose actions in fact aim to achieve the exact opposite. If we can also get the 'hypocrites' to burn with jealousy because of being 'overlooked' and even 'sidelined' by the Holy Spirit in the dispensation of His graces, all the better!

"The selfless souls must be made to believe that they have been abandoned by the Prime Mover, and that their prayers for peace and a stop to the killings are in vain and completely wasted effort. They must be made to feel exactly like the Deliverer felt in the Garden of Gethsemane when, peering into the future, he saw that self-willed humans would continue to act as if He hadn't been around!

"That would be the case even though He was going to pay a very heavy price for their redemption. Except, as we of course know, it is only those descendants of Adam and Eve who would believe in the Deliverer and also do His bidding who would be saved, not the murders, thieves and liars!

"If we can cause just one of those beloved of the Prime Mover to lose faith in Him and revert to a life of sin and debauchery, that will be a huge blow to the cause of Good, and a great triumph for the cause of Evil! We must do what we must do. Nothing must be left to chance.

"And we must, of course, also work hand in hand with those self-willed, crafty, and dissembling individuals in the Church whom the establishment nonetheless touts as 'living saints'. We must support the activities of these self-proclaimed 'models of virtue', and offer them all the help they need in perpetuating their schemes of deception and in sustaining their facade as holy souls. Our technique must be to get as many folks as possible inside and outside the Church focused on these bogus 'luminaries' instead of turning to the Deliverer to implore His mercy.

4

"We must support them to the very end, and particularly during those moments when it looks as if they might not be able to sustain their facade as 'exemplars of virtue', and risk exposure. We must constantly be close to their side, especially when it looks as if their posturing and antics are only thinly disguised and might give them away.

Impossible to forge the divine seal of approval...

"Still, the fact remains that when humans, conceited and well satisfied with themselves, embark on any mission including those that are trumpeted as being spiritual, it is usually a disaster - and no wonder. In attempting to show that they are clever, quite frequently these folks unabashedly claim that they are conducting their missions on behalf of the Prime Mover when the ultimate goal is all about worldly success.

"Believe it or not, but the sin of Judas Iscariot consisted in pretending that he was responding to divine grace in 'betraying' and handing the Deliverer over to His enemies. That 'ex-seminarian' would just have been a common thief if he had admitted that he was just after the thirty pieces of silver.

"But he represented himself to the priests and Sadducees as a good Jew who became a follower of the Deliverer and allowed himself to be groomed as one of the twelve 'apostles' in good faith - after being tricked into it by the 'insurgent'. To save his skin after they let him know that he was in hot soup for allowing himself to be 'misled' the betrayer (turned exemplary citizen and patriot) had assured the assembled members of the Sanhedrin that he now regarded it as his sacred duty to turn the Son of Man over to them!

"As a result, the Deliverer let the world know that it would definitely have been better if His betrayer had not been born! Meaning that *Judas himself*, had he somehow known that it would fall upon him to formally betray the Deliverer in the name of all sinful humans - and known it *before* he was born - and if he had been able to tell the Creator 'Pass' when it was his turn to be brought into the world, would have done so.

"There are those Judas Iscariots who set out proclaiming that they are on a mission to root out abuses in the Church. But they end up misleading hordes. Instead of living up to their reputation as 'reformers', they end up as schismatics, heading heretical movements. Others inside the Church represent themselves as defenders of the faith when all they really are doing is pursue their own agendas and personal ambitions, and have no real interest in Church unity.

"Indeed, there was a time when some 'zealots' organized crusades ostensibly for the purpose of keeping the holy places in Palestine from falling into the hands of 'infidels'. But the 'holy' crusades quickly degenerated into plundering, mayhem, and murder! As a matter of fact, as Armageddon draws near, you can expect to see more and more crusades of that type - crusades that are driven by narrow-minded geopolitical, and ultimately selfish, interests but are carefully camouflaged as 'Christian' crusades - taking up the energies of humans.

Holier than thou...

"It is all driven by that I-am-holier-than-thou attitude. Female prostitutes think they are better than male prostitutes, and vice versa. And they are in turn scorned by everyone else - as if that ancient profession could have survived without the universally unfailing and all too generous support that it has always enjoyed, not to mention the lusting and what not that goes on inside the minds of humans, the weird activities that go on in people's bedrooms, and the adulterous relationships that pass for chic lifestyles!

"Yes - what goes on in the bedrooms *and* inside human minds! Inside the dirty minds where the offences of humans against the authority of the Prime Mover are actually committed. It is there, inside the mind, where evil thoughts that corrupt originate. It is also there, inside the mind, where the evil plots against the Prime Mover and against fellow humans are hatched.

"Those who enjoy classical music despise those who enjoy Rock' n 'Roll, Rhythm and Blues, or Hip Hop, and the other way round. Members of church choirs look down on pop musicians, and vice versa, when it is an established fact that it is church choirs that frequently kick-start the careers of pop stars, and many a pop star's career winds up in the pews alongside gospel singers.

"People of one religious persuasion think they are better than those of other religious persuasions - when it is all a matter of persuasion, and the Deliverer died so that *all* humans might be saved. Folks on the Christian right think that folks on the Christian left or the Christian center are 'unsaved', and the other way round.

"There is only one Truth; but just look at all those so-called 'Christians' who pride themselves in belonging to this or that denomination, and are nevertheless united in one common cause of slandering the 'chosen people' for passing up the opportunity to rally behind the promised Messiah and Deliverer of humankind two thousand years ago; and of supposing that one of the twelve, who had been hand-picked by the Deliverer to lead His infant church, not only was an unworthy choice for the position of 'apostle' but, despite his remorse at having let down his divine Master, stands as a symbol of damned and lost humans!

"These same 'hypocrites' (if I, Beelzebub, may dare call them that) would lynch anyone who was so despicable as to commiserate with the 'bad thief' as those who had just caused the Son of Man to suffer an ignominious death on the cross in expiation of mankind's sordid iniquities turned on him, and began bludgeoning him to death with blunt clubs! Oh, how you humans suck (as you yourselves say)!

"Atheists think that believers are less than

8

honest in their reasoning, and believers fault atheists with a lack of moral integrity. One group of shortsighted folks despises other groups for stupid reasons, and vice versa.

"And, as if that is not bad enough, members of opposing groups will even hunt down and kill each other non-stop for the same stupid reasons, instead of just 'getting along' together. There is no specie that exploits its own as much as does the human species. And there is certainly no other specie whose members are permanently locked in deadly combat with their own kind and, moreover, for no good reason!

"Those humans who are devilish believe that they are angelic and wise and, by the strangest of coincidences, the least devilish among them believe that they are the biggest sinners and the most foolish - as if I wouldn't be happy to embrace them and turn them also into devilish creatures dedicated to the service of evil, if I had been able to! Which illustrates the stubbornness of the wicked and their reluctance to hearken to the urgings of divine grace, and the problems that we in the Underworld have with humans who retain their childlike innocence!

"Boys think they are better than girls who supposedly are 'sissy'; and girls think they are better than boys who supposedly are 'rough'. Those who are young and 'green' despise and discriminate against those who are elderly and well versed in things of this world. And they not only rebuff the advice of the 'wicked old men' and 'wicked old

9

women', but the young people keep repeating to themselves that they will not allow themselves to be swayed by some 'genteel' old lady or gentleman however handsome.

"Thus, a sprightly *madame* or *monsieur* boasting curly and really beautiful, but greying locks of hair however seductive to the eye, supposedly does not deserve a second glance; and even the first glance is given grudgingly. The function of old people supposedly is just to serve as a reminder to the young people that the things with which they are preoccupied and for which they have so much concern are for the most part temporal, passing and transient. And, invariably, the young people interpret that to mean that anything that can be enjoyed should indeed be enjoyed while it lasts!

"The elderly in turn scorn young people as immature and innocent, with lots to learn about the hard realities of life. And they dismiss the ideas of humans who are still youthful as churlish and untested! Those who are slender in build despise and discriminate against those whose frames are full and robust.

"Those who are in the prime of life despise those who have had a full life and are on the verge of joining the ancestors, while those who are in the twilight of their lives invariably look upon themselves as the fortunate few who had made it to a ripe - and cheery - old age. Perhaps justifiably so after living through one, two and sometimes even three 'world wars', plagues that have seen the world's population decimated and nearly wiped out, famines, and other natural disasters which the rest of the populace know about only through history books.

"Humans who are still alive despise those who have passed on - supposedly because the latter are no longer in a position to frolic and enjoy things of this world any more, unaware that the dead actually have nothing but pity for the folks they left behind; and the dead pity the living precisely because the latter seem unable to learn that any enjoyment back on earth is strictly temporal and a distraction that prevents humans from making the best use of their short time on Planet Earth for 'keeping watch with lighted candles for the coming of the bridegroom'!

"Then, of course, the dead additionally sympathize with the living because (according to the Evangelist) at the time of the Second Coming of the Deliverer, it is those who have already passed who will precede the living when humans line up to meet Him.

"But the dead pity the living for other reasons as well, not least among them the fact that whereas the dead no longer doubt that Christ will come again to pass judgement on the world, not only are there still many living humans who do not realize that the promised Deliverer came unto the world and paid the price for the sins of humans two thousand years ago (as had been foretold) before ascending into heaven, but many didn't even believe that there was such a thing as the 'second coming' of the Deliverer!

"Westerners" versus "Easterners"...

"Those who hail from the 'West' despise those who hail from the 'non-Western world', and do not regard the lives of non-Westerners as being of the same value as the lives of 'Westerners' - and the other way around. Westerners think that they have been blest and above all 'anointed' by the Prime Mover. They believe that, unlike non-Westerners who supposedly are allied to me (the Prince of Darkness), they themselves (Westerners) are allied to the one and only true Prime Mover! Westerners also believe that they have a lock on the destiny of the world in which non-Westerners can regard themselves as completely irrelevant, and non-Westerners think the same of Westerners!

"Non-Westerners also believe that Westerners are wedded to sordid materialism, wallow in smut, and are caught up in the strangest perversions and a peculiar kind of spiritual depravity that effectively stunts the human conscience, and are enslaved to vices that rival those that caused the cities of Sodom and Gomorrah to be singled out for destruction.

"Westerners glorify individualism and 'democracy' or big government that is controlled by lobbies for the benefit of the 'establishment' and the moneyed folks, and look with disdain on extended family ties that are valued much more by non-Westerners. But non-Westerners, whose traditional beliefs are centered around nature, and who have always had the 'tribe' as their governance model, despise and ridicule Westerners for the same reasons that Westerners despise them. Westerners regard themselves as cultured, and non-Westerners as uncultured, while non-Westerners believe that Westerners lost their culture long ago, and hence the spiritual morass to which Western society appeared to have been condemned.

"Westerners believe that the non-Western world is a festering eye sore that is home to millions, if not billions, who should never have seen the light of day for their own good (supposedly)! They believe that, as a result, the non-Western world is now the breeding ground for all manner of dissatisfied humans, 'terrorists', and 'insurgents' who are out of their mind; and that the non-Western world is a threat to world peace. They also believe that it is now (Alas!) up to them (Westerners) to go after these disgruntled folks, bible in one hand and bunker-bursting bombs in the other, and teach them (non-Westerners) a lesson or two, and root out the 'miscreants' to save (Western) civilization!

"For their part, non-Westerners believe that Westerners are imperialists who, for the most part, still live in the 'wild west'. They believe that Westerners have legalized corruption (now going by such labels as 'lobbying' and 'political contributions'), practice cronyism and believe in 'ruling oligarchies', while at the same time investing in a prison 'industry' that is bursting at the seams and that almost exclusively targets the poor and the disadvantaged.

"Non-Westerners believe that many of those

who occupy the seats of power in the West and the 'experts' who advise them suffer from delusions and are, for all practical purposes, out of their mind. They (non-Westerners) believe that the arsenals of weapons of mass destruction (WMD) in the hands of self-appointed messengers of a 'Western' divinity', who are determined to take over the world in concert with crazed 'neocons' and 'neolibs', represents the real threat to the survival of Planet Earth.

"But non-Westerners also believe that Westerners may be dying out because of their attitudes to everything from women's reproductive rights to family values, and they (non-Westerners) regard that as good riddance that might not be coming fast enough! According to non-Westerners, their technology-minded counterparts in the West, in trying to space childbirths using pills, that oftentimes have proved to be dangerous and with multiple side effects, and other artificial methods, inadvertently interfered with the cycles in nature that regulated the earth's population, and ended up stunting the human reproductive processes and also bequeathing all manner of diseases including the HIV/AIDS virus to the world. That, incidentally, is also how non-Westerners explain the incurable nature of HIV/AIDS!

"Westerners believe that there is 'no other side', that only their feelings and their sufferings matter, that their behavior, however depraved and monstrous, can never amount to a disgrace; and also that they are the only sane humans left on earth; and non-Westerners are convinced that Westerners are

14

insane!

"Westerners believe that Armageddon is not far off and they have adjusted the pace of life in the West accordingly, while non-Westerners do not think so and are still committed to a happy-go-lucky, slow and easy pace - and lifestyle. And Westerners believe that they are the only ones with valid passports to heaven, and that British and American passports in particular take one there by the most direct route; and that non-Westerners, steeped in oriental, African and similar religious 'crap' have passports to hell only (unless they become Westernized). And, for their part, non-Westerners regard Western societies as decadent, and the Westerners themselves as lost with no hope of redemption!

Members of the same "inhuman" family...

"Humans even forget that they are all members of the same human - actually inhuman - family: brothers and sisters who are descended from the same, albeit fallen, Adam and Eve; and who also have the same nature. They all laugh and cry in the same way and for the same reasons. They have the same aspirations in life - to live happily and productively, and to grow to a ripe old age - and even the same temperament.

"In point of fact, whether a human is a male prostitute or a female one, a porn star or a cloistered nun, old or young, a dead one or one who is still alive and 'kicking', a Westerner or a non-Westerner, a

15

murderer or an actual or potential victim, they are all the same thing - humans.

"Which should come as a relief especially to hypocrites! However, because they really are hypocrites, it comes as very bad news and as something they find very difficult to accept. Hypocrites sincerely believe that only humans of their 'moral' or 'religious' persuasion are in good books with the Prime Mover or their concept of 'the Almighty' - as if the Son of Man did not die for the salvation of all humans. In the case of atheists, 'the Almighty' is in fact themselves. (Pity no one regards me, Beelzebub, also as one!)

The ways of hypocrites...

"Because hypocrites firmly believe that they *alone* are in good books with the Prime Mover, they like to imagine that when they do anything - so long as it is them and not someone else - it has to be perfectly O.K. and even virtuous. In their eyes, when humans who have a different perspective on reality from their own do anything, it must be wrong because it has to be the devil that is the source of the inspiration for whatever these other humans conjure up and do.

"The tussle between neocons and neolibs over the 'sanctity of human life' is illustrative. Neocons are convinced that neolibs, by supporting women in their struggle for equal rights with men, are murderers and evil because they also indirectly support things like

16

contraception and abortion. Neolibs charge, fairly or unfairly, that neocons are the ones who are always quick to support trade embargoes on so-called rogue nations when it is well-known that it is the most vulnerable members of society - the unborn and the newly born - who pay the price with their lives!

"According to neolibs, neocons not only blindly support capital punishment, but are the biggest supporters of that strange new phenomenon - the corporations that produce armaments and weapons of mass destruction. Neolibs charge that neocons are warmongers who will not balk at furthering their geopolitical agendas through the use of force without any regard for the value of human life. Neolibs also accuse neocons of putting money first and the health of people second with their support of health management organizations and antagonism for moves to institute free universal health care. Neolibs also point out that neocons are indifferent to the fact that pharmaceutical companies, with their pricing policies, effectively deny millions of people living with HIV/AIDS access to drugs that would save their lives.

"Thus, according to neolibs, neocons are murderers for doing what they do. But what they themselves (neolibs) do cannot be questioned supposedly because all they are doing is support the struggle of women for equal rights with their male counterparts - a very noble goal to which neocons only pay lip service. And, according to neocons, neolibs are the ones who are guilty of the charges they (neolibs) make against their camp and are murderers. Otherwise, all they themselves (neocons) are doing is adhere to the conservative ideologies which - in their minds - have the Prime Mover's stamp of approval and, therefore, can never harm anyone except the wicked.

"It seems to be typical of hypocrites that they themselves *must* invariably *be* *right* always regardless of the facts of the case, and those who disagree with them *must be wrong always*. Instead of asking the *real* hypocrites to please stand up, it might well be better to pose the following questions: Are the neocons the real hypocrites, and the neolibs the guilty ones, or is it perhaps *vice versa*?

"Might it just be that this label is transferable, and the camp whose party loses in a given election, becomes the one that deserves to pick it up - albeit only as long as they remain out of office? Or is it that neocons and neolibs are all 'immune' to that 'disease', with the result that the accusation is groundless. Meaning that neither camp, regardless of what it does, endorses or is in the business of killing? But if hypocrisy is the sort of disease that is no respecter of either ideology or persons, and is consequently plaguing neocons and neolibs alike, then they have to accept that they all do indeed kill, and are accordingly guilty - and doomed!

"Certainly, killing could not be OK when neocons did it, and bad when neolibs did it - or vice versa? Well, since the 'sins' of hypocrites - in their own perception - are not 'sinful', both the neocons and the neolibs are effectively off the hook - in their minds!

18

Consequently, contrary to what some churchmen say about situational ethics, taking away a human life under one set of circumstances apparently may be sinful (depending on whether the judge is a neocon or a neolib), while doing so under a different set of circumstances could be just fine (again depending on the philosophy of the judge)! And - depending on the identity of the players and the circumstances - the 'sin' could also turn out to be a virtue! But if you ask me (Beelzebub), that is just another kind of hypocrisy.

"If the actions that result in needless death were motivated solely by the desire to maintain super power status, may be a case could be made about the morality of killing while pursuing that goal. Its weakness would consist in the fact that every nation yearns for super power status, and if they all indulged in needless killing in an effort to gain or regain, or retain that illusory status, quite a bit of killing would be going on all the time. It seems patently worse that in the final analysis, the needless killing is motivated by desire to win party elections, and be in a position to keep lobbies - yes, the lobbies that exert their muscle and dole out the big money that in the end determines who triumphs in an election - happy.

"One thing about this business of killing that works in our favor is that 'once a killer, always a killer!' As with other sins that humans commit, after snuffing out the life of his/her first victim, the killer's urge to do it all over again grows stronger by the day; and, before long, the killer human will be itching for another kill as if to stopping and turn away from that

19

murderous path is an admission of guilt - and an act of cowardice.

"After laying waste and plundering one city, megalomaniacs work to strengthen their image as 'tough' and 'resolute' leaders by moving on to the next one to repeat their exploits. It doesn't take long after that before taking another human's life or helping oneself to someone else's property becomes completely ordinary - like sipping iced tea. Humans become so easily intoxicated with these things, and Julius Caesar was a good example.

"While he was personally leading his armies into Gaul, North Africa, and elsewhere, it never once struck him that a time would come when he himself would give up the ghost and leave all the booty he had amassed behind - and that it was all a waste of time, effort and lives. It never struck him that killing and stealing were damnable things - until the moment his 'friend' Brutus produced the dagger, and the Commander-in-Chief and Field Marshal noticed that he himself might have unwittingly wandered into the cross hairs of a like-minded 'Son of Sam'. It was in that momentary flash, when the beloved Roman Emperor and Conqueror of the World saw that Brutus was unmoved and determined, and ready to strike out with the dagger, that taking a human life suddenly became revolting and an outrage - and completely damnable! Until then, Julius Caesar thought that prosecuting wars in which thousands, including his own countrymen, lost their lives prematurely was cool. He himself had killed and had seen his henchmen also kill, and he had savored every moment of his devilish - yes, devilish - pastime.

"But, for the doomed megalomaniac, killing now became damnable for all the wrong reasons. Sons of Sam do not become converted just because they realize that they themselves are on death row - just like everyone else. And it certainly doesn't strike them that, because they too can and indeed will die one day, any act of self-aggrandizement and any preoccupation with worldly things for their own sake is wasted effort. It doesn't strike them that, if they were thinking aright, they should be holed up in some hermitage fasting and doing penance for the multitude of their sins. The fact that another Son of Sam shows up and seems determined to snuff out the killer's own life prematurely becomes damnable and revolting because it threatens to rob them of the enjoyment of the booty they have spent all their waking hours amassing.

"It is not as if megalomaniacs and other killers and thieves end up here in the Pit with us because they are not afforded ample graces by the Prime Mover like everyone else. The Prime Mover uses so-called 'acts of God' and other signs almost on a daily basis to show humans that, one and all, they are both at His mercy and totally dependent on Him at the same time - and that worldly success is a mirage. We can of course only thank our stars that evil minded humans refuse to pay heed to their consciences and end up pitching in their lot with me, the Author of Death and mastermind of evil.

21

"It is bad enough if a pugilist hits the opponent below the belt in a contest. It is very bad if you sneaked up behind someone you did not like and crushed a rock against his spine - or if you took him out from a safe distance with a rifle shot. It has to be worse if you tried - successfully or unsuccessfully - to neutralize your 'enemy' with a guided missile from the safety of a bunker. It could never be right for the simple reason that it is not something you would have liked someone to do to you. It must be really bad if you did that sort of thing just because you wanted to triumph as a politician. It is as simple as that.

"When hypocrites 'murder', they might believe that all they are simply doing is mete out justice - on the Prime Mover's behalf, so to speak. When they 'seize' property that does not belong to them, they might deceive themselves that such an action can never be counted against them - that they do not need to worry about restitution - like happened in Zimbabwe, South Africa, Kenya, and other places (with the blessing of the missionaries).

"They attempt to justify their action by claiming that it is necessary because the 'intentions' of the wicked have to be frustrated. But when others make a move to seize theirs even for justifiable reasons, it becomes 'nationalization' or 'robbery' - and it will even elicit the ire of churchmen. And so, in the end, robbery and stealing are all things that too are relative, and are right or wrong depending on whose property it is and, above all, who is seizing it.

"When Britons, Spaniards, Portuguese,

22

Italians, and others easily overrun Africa, the Americas and elsewhere with the benefit of gun powder and the blessings of missionaries, and seized lands and other property from 'natives' in those lands, apparently that could not possibly have been regarded as wrongful annexation in some people's view. And not even churchmen saw anything wrong with it. If they did, they would be busy pontificating about restitution and things like that.

"As it is, no one sees anything wrong with the fact that a few hundred individuals own most of the land in some of the former 'colonies' or 'possessions' while the original owners in their millions remain landless. It is obvious that the 'ideal' situation, which was also undoubtedly the intention, was to drive those 'natives' into the sea so that it would be pointless to sermonize about the obligation to pay restitution following the massive, officially sanctioned, land grabs. But it would even make more sense if churchmen came out and announced that stealing was not stealing; that killing was not a sin; and, of course, that 'restitution' applied only in a different world - an imaginary world - and that everybody went to heaven, and that hell was only for me, Lucifer, and the other rebel angels, and Judas Iscariot (the convenient scapegoat) who is assumed by everyone to have brought damnation upon himself when he betrayed the Deliverer (as if Judas Iscariot is the only one who has ever done so).

"It certainly says something about how 'Christ-like' those churchmen who are comfortable with the status quo are. Being Christ-like is apparently also a relative thing - meaning that, depending on who you are and the circumstances, you can rob and plunder and still be one of the 'elect' even if you did not make any restitution. Accordingly one must use the label 'thief' carefully - since some who would otherwise be counted among thieves are actually privileged and exempt from the obligation to return stolen property!

"Relativism is apparently unavoidable because it would be a contradiction in terms for actions of humans who are 'saved' or 'chosen' to amount to something that could be regarded as crass in the eyes of the Prime Mover! The injunction 'Do unto others what you'd have others do unto you' supposedly applies to those who have me, Beelzebub, on their side; and it does not apply to those who have the Prime Mover on their side! Is that so - or is it so, perhaps, only in the mistaken perception of hypocrites?

"For sure, if it is unacceptable for a crooked cop to issue a traffic citation to a motorist who is innocent (because that crooked cop himself would definitely not want to receive an undeserved speeding ticket), it has to be unacceptable to loot and plunder, and even less so for humans to physically and/or mentally abuse or torture fellow humans. If it is indefensible for humans to incarcerate their own kind, and treat them in ways they wouldn't treat their own pets and beasts of the wild, it is even less so for any human to torture another human - regardless of his/her race, religious affiliation, social status, political leanings, and religious affiliation - for any reason.

"When did it become acceptable to do unto others what you would not have others do unto you? I am Lucifer, and I do not believe I am crazy! That would be really tragic given my weighty responsibilities of putting to the test the faith and trust of humans in the Prime Mover! When an undeserved traffic ticket is issued, it hurts the victim. But there are also consequences for the crook who issues the ticket. The gratification derived from issuing it actually does turn into something quite nasty in time; a couple of months in Purgatory, perhaps?

"And when, oh when, did it become acceptable to seek to kill out of revenge? You wouldn't try it if you were facing a foe you knew was much stronger than you yourself - or if you knew that your vengeful act would mean the end of you - would you? Says something about the callousness of some of the world's so-called 'leaders' who will engage in vengeful pursuits from the safety of the bunkers in which they are closeted, while sacrificing the blood and treasurer of the nation! You do not want to witness their encounter with the Avenging Angel when their own time to go comes, I tell yah!

"I have to say that there is a heavy price that will be paid for condoning or engaging in any practice that amounts to abuse, humiliation or torture, even if it might appear as if that is just a matter between contending humans with no 'outsiders' involved. The Avenging Angel does not take kindly to a-social behavior of that nature - behavior that, besides, is the height of hypocrisy. And you'd better mark my words, because I speak from experience!

"Humans who kill forget that the Avenging Angel cannot be talked into taking bribes, is no respecter of persons, makes no distinction between neocons and neolibs, or the Christian right, the Christian left, the Christian center and the 'non-Christian' world. Humans kid themselves that the Avenging Angel can be rendered irrelevant - like the United Nations or the League of Nations that preceded it. Many, completely blinded by self-love, believe that they can plunder and kill, and effectively conceal the telltale evidence.

"There is no ruse that humans - or, for that matter, any creature - could use to put the Avenging Angel off the scent; and no trick that humans could play to foil his mission. There is, naturally, no weapon that humans could use to deter him or delay his mission. There is no bunker that could keep out the messenger from On High who goes everywhere with his hand on the sheath that holds his razor-sharp cutlass. There are no ramparts that human ingenuity could build to block his advance. There is no type of cuirass or armor that his sword cannot slice through. There is nothing behind which a human could hide to escape justice, just as there is no place to which a human could fly to escape his wrath! And, when the day of reckoning comes, the haughty and the mighty will be cowed down and will be begging to be spared the sword.

"And if a human killed, it will not matter in the

slightest if he/she was acting solo, as a member of an organized or disorganized gang or mob, as a member of a disciplined or undisciplined platoon, a special operations unit, or unit of a regular army that was staging an invasion. It will not matter if the decision to kill was made in cabinet or on a street corner. It will not make a difference whether the killer did it while 'On Her Majesty's Secret Service' or was taking his/her orders from the CIA, the KGB, or some similar 'shady' organization. If a human killed, it will not even matter if the killer was under the delusion that he/she had been appointed the Prime Mover's enforcer.

"It will not make any difference if one killed while following orders. This is because there is no entity or organization that has the power or ability to indoctrinate a human to the point where his/her conscience becomes effectively blunted. There is no order that anyone however high placed can issue that can absolve a human from personal responsibility for taking property that belongs to another, leave alone taking another's life. What is more, humans are not only under the obligation to love their neighbors - and that includes their enemies - but they must also be prepared to turn the other cheek when slapped! And, of course, you fools...the end can never (repeat 'never' fifty times or as many times as is necessary to get you to accept this simple obvious principal) justify the means!

"The fact that a killer was 'one of the finest' so-called and, bedecked in his/her uniform and swinging a baton, was using only 'necessary' force, will not help

27

an iota. The Avenging Angel won't be impressed in the slightest by the uniform and, instead of feeling awed by the baton as it is swung this way or that way to scare him, will casually take that baton from the surprised killer-minded cop and use it to give him a hiding such as he will never forget through all eternity. The fact that the crooked cop might have been decorated a thousand times over for the act of killing won't make the slightest difference. Not even if he/she had succeeded in getting him/herself short-listed for beatification!

"It will also not matter whether the killer called it 'killing' or something else. It will not make any difference if labels concocted to malign the victim and justify the murder successfully stuck or did not stick. It will not even make the slightest difference if the killer's name turned up on the list of candidates for canonization - he would still be my man (or woman).

"It will make no difference whether the killer achieved his/her objective by sticking a dagger into the victim's heart, lobbing a guided missile which hit its mark, or by dropping a 'smart' bomb. It will not matter if the killer attained his/her objective with the help of a primitive sling; or did it by ferrying a nuclear bomb to the detonation site in a remote controlled conveyance and then detonated it from a 'safe' distance in a cowardly fashion; or if the killer decided to show bravado and take his/her own life along with that of the 'enemy'!

"The Avenging Angel will cause all killers regardless of whether they came from the East or the

West - or the South or the North - to be stung with their individual consciences for crimes they committed against fellow humans - period! And when the killers are being stung by their consciences for their murderous deeds, any propaganda they might have been involved in ginning up to falsify reality will not just haunt them. It will be dangled in their faces as part of the damning evidence against them by any and all who got hurt as a result of their misdeeds, and it will cause them to wish that they had never been born!

"Actually, in the end, it will be completely immaterial whether a human successfully carried out the plot to murder or was prevented from doing so by circumstances. That is because a human - endowed with intelligence, free will and a conscience - was a murderer from the moment he/she decided that another human did not deserve to live and deserved to die.

"The Avenging Angel will not discriminate between a war lord and a foot solder; a privileged member of society and an underprivileged or disenfranchised member of society; a commander-in-chief of a super power and a 'private' in the armed forces of some 'basket' nation in the third world, a prisoner and a jailor, a slave and his/her master, or between a beggar and a billionaire. He will not even make any distinction between kings and their subjects. In the eyes of the Avenging Angel, killers will be killers, and the fact that some should have known better, while damning in and of itself, will be

29

secondary.

"Humans have to remember that this is the same Avenging Angel who led the host of faithful angels in the battle that saw me and my troops dislodged from our beach-head in Paradise, and who made sure that we were left boarded up in this hell hole. He might not have had the wherewithal to take the sting out of the seeds of death I had succeeded in sowing - only the Deliverer could do that (as He indeed did by His own death on the cross and resurrection from the dead). But the Avenging Angel and his army of holy angels certainly succeeded very well in cornering my army of rebel angels and driving us from the heavens into this miserable 'Underworld'. And if the Avenging Angel could deal with me, earthlings must be really dumb to imagine that they can kill and get away with it.

What distinguishes human "devils" from real ones...

"We ourselves in the Underworld may be evil - you cannot start to imagine the kind of wicked things we demons do to each other and to humans when we get the opportunity - but one thing that we don't do is act hypocrite. When we pure spirits choose to be evil, we stop pretending that we are saintly - unlike you humans! Hypocrisy is not in our culture. It is what sets sinful humans apart from us demons. And we demons dislike hypocrites and others of that ilk, because we ourselves can never know where we stand in their regard!

"The significance of being born with original sin - as in the case of humans - is that, as humans grow up and lose their childhood innocence, they all automatically graduate into 'closeted' murderers, prostitutes, pornographers and terrorists, and hypocrites. And then the shame causes some humans to start sidelining others as *the* prostitutes, thieves, and killers.

"According to the intelligence in our possession - and this is real, not fabricated, 'Intel' - those humans who are loudest in accusing others of being gangsters and purveyors of immorality are usually the ones who are the worst offenders in those respects, the hypocrisy and facade of righteousness notwithstanding! And, far from being imaginary, the hypocrisy is real for the simple reason that, on their own, humans are only capable of sinning!

"And a word about intelligence: unlike you humans, we in the Underworld are not in the habit of manufacturing any of it to suit circumstances. And, because of its unreliability, we made a conscious decision at the outset to put no reliance on the so-called human intelligence, including intelligence gathered by humans who share our 'hell'. We rely entirely on the 'demonic' intelligence generated by fellow demons.

"According to that intelligence, a goodly number of the 'apostles' who minister to the needs of the faithful are really no different from Simon Peter who denied having any knowledge of the Deliverer on

31

so many occasions. And the Simon Peters of today won't even be nudged back to their senses by any cockcrow however ear-splitting. Others, of course, are no different from the priests and Pharisees, and members of the Sanhedrin who started plotting to liquidate the Deliverer from the moment they heard Him preach and represent Himself as the promised Messiah. Without admitting it, they nonetheless see Him as an obstacle to the intrigues, plots and bad habits to which they are wedded, their priestly status notwithstanding.

"Others operate in the exact same way Judas Iscariot did - they are obsessed with the visible trappings of power and their hearts sink whenever it looks as if 'Peter's Pence' might not be bringing in enough collections and the Church (whose coffers sustain them) might go broke. Others are skillful operators like Pontius Pilate. They are not just cozy with the powerful; but, in order to maintain their relationships with the powers that be, these 'apostles' are always prepared to do what it takes to legitimize and even bless the activities of politicians whose activities are contrary to the Gospels and the Church's teachings.

"Others, by their silence in the face of injustices that are perpetrated around them (when they are not openly supporting the perpetrators of the injustices), are in effect chanting along with the rabble: 'Crucify Him! Crucify Him!'

"Some 'apostles' are narrow-minded and self-satisfied with themselves to the point to which they

32

have nothing but disdain for individuals/groups of individuals who dare express their desire to adapt the Church's liturgy to the cultures in which they were brought up. There are even those for whom a *Misa Flamenco* will elicit adulations; but a *Misa Chakacha* or anything approximating it, with its connotations of traditional African rhythmic movement, will cause raised eyebrows and despondency. No, *Misa Chakacha* would be just too scandalous and the body movements just too suggestive! And, of course, the 'Beethoven Mass', even with the distracting sounds of harps, trumpets, drums (Oh, yes – 'drums'!) and strings, must have been divinely inspired. More or less like the Holy Book!

"And at least the Spaniards and the Austrians are traditionally a Christian people, as also are their customs and traditions. One could even say that the Flamenco dance movements and the rhythms that accompany them have been sanctified by centuries of use in Church liturgy! Spain - a 'Catholic' nation, has bequeathed to the world the likes of Theresa of Avila, Phillip Neri, Padre Pio and others like that, the implication being that, even after years and years of evangelization, some of these countries in the 'New World' - countries like Uganda which is populated by animists (something that supposedly is far worse than being a plain pagan) - simply will never produce a single candidate for canonization!

"Holy Saints of Uganda? That must be a mistake - the speaker must have meant Holy Saints of Italy or Holy Saints of some other Western nation!

33

Oh, and Saint Josephine Margaret Bakhita must be Italian - or Japanese. She couldn't possibly be hailing from Sudan of all places! And you, of course, guessed right - Simon the Cyrenian, the father of Alexander and Rufus (Mark 15: 21) whom the Roman soldiers drafted to help the Deliverer get to the summit of Mount Calvary with his cross, couldn't possibly have been an African despite his African origins!

"It is, in any event, also implied that the ancestors of Africans and the inhabitants of other lands in the non-Western world, who are held in so much esteem by their progeny, are all lost and in hell!

"And the only chance Africans, Indians, Chinese, Arabs and others like that had of being elevated to sainthood was if they turned against their societies and agreed to publicly condemn the customs and traditions of their people because, in the eyes of Westerners, the traditional values and mores of people from Africa, India, China, Arabia and places like that simply were incompatible with 'Catholicism', the meaning of that word notwithstanding! In any event, the chances of Africans, Indians, Chinese, Arabs and other 'non-Westerners' being elevated to sainthood were minuscule if non-existent, and that was borne out pretty much by the records.

"Westerners could, of course, not be blamed for the 'fact' that things were like that. And since the Prime Mover could not possibly be the one to blame, it followed that Africans, Indians, Chinese, Arabs and others like them were almost certainly under a curse! Which probably also explained why the number of

African, Indian, Chinese, and Arab peoples who were Catholics was very small and in some cases in fact non-existent.

"One North American cardinal was probably echoing what many of his compatriots believed when he reportedly confessed on national television that he was quite surprised that the African and Indian prelates he met in Rome at the Second Vatican Council spoke Latin as well if not better than his North American compatriots! (Even though I am the devil, I swear that I am quoting my 'reliable' source faithfully, and I am not lying to you.) You see, it a good thing - a very good thing in fact - to be addicted to music compositions by Bach, Hayden, Mozart, and Handle, and 'classical' music in general. But it is the lowest one can descend to appreciate traditional African music? That is as low as one can get.

"The only 'real world' is one that is seen through the prism of Western eyes. In fact Westerners can belong to schismatic or plainly heretical movements that even espouse the most anti-Catholic views - even when they believe (as many do) that Holy Mass is an instance of devil worship, or that the Pontiff of Rome is not just the Antichrist but the personification of Satan - but they can never really be far off the mark.

"So long as they call themselves Christians, Westerners, regardless of the nature of their 'heresy', remain 'separated brethren' who, for all practical purposes, still safely belong in the fold.

"But woe to the African who genuinely believes that the religion of his ancestors is the true religion, and that adherents to Christianity are individuals who may be victims of indoctrination - perhaps a combination of religious and political propaganda - and who find it in their interest to close their eyes to the glaring and, indeed, scandalous 'divisions' in the 'Church'!

"An African or anyone who dares to challenge Christians to show that there is more to Christianity than the sentimentalism one encounters at every turn is deemed to be committing a sin that is of its nature unpardonable. Africans and other faithless non-Westerners, who have the audacity to question the authenticity of a religion whose adherents contradict one another right and left, are regarded as irrational 'heathens' and 'infidels' who are beyond the pale of salvation by definition. And, of course, even though the New Testament contains ample evidence of the Middle Eastern - or more precisely Palestinian – origins of Christianity, anyone who dares to question the claim that Christianity originated in the West must be intellectually dishonest. That was because it could never be that the cradle of Christianity was 'Middle Eastern' - just like the cradle of Islam, and never mind the mountains of evidence that the most damaging divisions in Christianity are attributable to growing influence in the Church of 'Westerners'.

"But what Westerners say, believe or do is really immaterial - and provided they quote from the Holy Book (the bible) to support their beliefs. In point of fact, so long as an individual professes to be a Christian, that individual's is as good as saved

36

already - or is it so? And are those who flock to Catholic churches really 'safe' even if (in contrast to Moslems, Hindus, Buddhists, and other folks) they are just 'church-going' Catholics whose lifestyles are no different from those of every Dick and Harry - and even if only a handful of them would be willing to try and emulate Mother Theresa or Francis of Assisi?

"And might it just be possible that Catholics and many of their so-called separated brethren were the ones the Deliverer had in mind when he referred in a parable to original invitees to the heavenly banquet being turned away because they were busy doing other things instead of 'keeping their candles alight'?

"This is just conceivable for any number of reasons like being busy calling on the Lord's name in vain; or being busy making judgements about people whose cultures they had no interest in knowing or understanding (as the Evil One and also ring leader of the legion of disgruntled and disgraced spirits, I have the license to do that, and humans who follow my example in that respect write-off their chances of being rehabilitated!); or being busy - in league with colonialists, imperialists, slave dealers, and pirates on the high seas - grabbing fertile lands in South Africa, Kenya, Zimbabwe, and Australia by force from the natives there or in the Americas; or, in the case of the 'New World' that Columbus 'discovered', being busy systematically and brutally wiping out the natives-turned-insurgents so the colonists-turned-Yankees could parcel out the lands there among themselves without interference from any quarter; or, in the case of settlers in the New World, being busy plotting insurrections (or 'insurgencies') against their British, Spanish, Portuguese, Belgian, French, Italian, and Dutch masters.

"And any way - aren't all 'good' folks inside and outside the Church like that, the difference between them and the 'really good' folks being that the latter readily accept that if they ever do escape my tentacles, it will not be so much because they feel justified (like the Pharisee), but because of the mercies of the Prime Mover and His grace (like the tax collector)!

"And might it just be possible that African and Indian mystics, and others who try their best to follow their consciences in whatever they do were the ones He had in mind when he referred to the king's command that the doors of the banquet hall be opened to let in the rabble from the streets (provided they had on 'proper attire')? It, indeed, might just be that quite a few people (who now regard themselves as redeemed and virtually saved) will actually be surprised to find themselves excluded from the 'heavenly banquet', and those they now despise as unfit being herded towards tables piled high with all sorts of mouth-watering gourmets and other goodies!

"Adamantly opposed to changes in the Church's liturgy that would accommodate peoples of different cultural backgrounds within the 'assembly of God's people' or Church, it goes without saying that the attitudes of many of these 'Princes of the Church' pay only lip service to the rapprochement that would even bring the separated brethren back into the fold, and represent thereby a major obstacle to Church unity.

"Other 'apostles' are so conceited and puffed up, you would think that they belong to some 'ruling' sacerdotal family - members of royalty in some 'messianic' kingdom! When they pray, give catechetical instruction or act as celebrants at Holy Mass, they remind one of the Pharisee whose prayers (and, no doubt, also catechetical instruction/lectures) always revolved around fellow humans they deemed unworthy. The humans who constitute their audience are all presumed to be like the God-forsaken tax collector!

Selfishness and godliness contrasted...

"Selfishness and wilfulness contrast with the infinite goodness of the Prime Mover which is manifested in His decision to create 'things' or 'essences', including humans and angels, out of nothing, and to endow the creatures who are made in his own image and likeness such that they will continue their existence in an afterlife with things like reason, free will and the ability to choose between good and evil. The Prime Mover's infinite goodness is manifested, above all, in His decision to give His only begotten Son for the redemption of humans.

"And if ever there is anyone who would have been justified in avenging ills by killing, it is the Prime Mover. The fact that He has explicitly ruled out anything of that sort should remind humans that they are knocking on the wrong door when they kill fellow humans. But - fortunately for me - it does not. That says something about my 'reach' doesn't it!

"The Prime Mover's infinite goodness is manifested in His decision to allow those with evil intentions - like me and my minions among earthlings - to have their way while they are able to. He doesn't go back on his word or step in to stop them from exercising their wills in contravention of His Moral Law.

"But wilfulness is incompatible with what is noble and divine. This is because it focuses on the self. Wilfulness focuses on whatever appears to guarantee excitement and immediate 'fulfilment'. But excitement and fulfilment are changing and temporal, and are the antithesis of true and genuine love - love or generosity of the mold that is divorced from the 'now' or present; is sacred and permanent; and is, above all, in accordance with the Deliverer's injunction that humans love their neighbors and enemies.

Humans scared of the spiritual....

"Divine grace - as you might have guessed - is a spiritual thing; and it also operates only on the spiritual dimension and in a purely spiritual manner. So, how could humans, who moreover are so scared of the spiritual, succeed in bringing about what could be engendered spiritually? It is completely ridiculous

40

to expect this of creatures that are so scared of what 'lies yonder'!

"If humans knew how the breathing mechanism worked, they likely would invest all their energies in trying to discover how to restart it as and when it stopped. That is how scared stiff humans are of the spiritual. Death, the gateway to the purely spiritual and also to heaven, is something they would rather not encounter if they could help it.

"Actually, humans - with the possible exception of the so-called animists - don't say so, but they are afraid of divine grace because it is a spiritual thing. Unfortunately for humans, with every day that passes, the moment of their dreaded, and yet inescapable, encounter not just with death, but with His 'Mystic Majesty' who is also the Prime Mover and Creator of all that is, and who sent His only begotten son into the world so that those who believe in Him might be saved, draws ever closer. With every second that passes, the moment of truth when humans have to come to terms with the fact that they are just as much spirits as we ourselves are, approaches.

"That is the principal reason humans find it so hard to cooperate with divine grace. And if they find that hard, what could be said about bringing off, completely on their own and unaided, what divine grace does, namely sanctification of the soul? That is the 'hole' into which I lured Adam and Eve to step two hundred and fifty thousand years ago in the Garden of Eden. Once their rebellion against the Prime Mover got under way, it became literally

41

impossible for Adam and Eve and their descendants to 'save themselves' in the spiritual sense.

"In that sense, we demons, being pure spirits and unafraid of the spiritual, were in theory at least at an advantage after we fell from grace. We wouldn't have been so helpless, and we would indeed have been able to help ourselves - if there had been a second chance. Unfortunately the nature of our rebellion did not permit that.

"It suits us in the Underworld perfectly that humans are scared of the spiritual. It would be uncharacteristic of us if we did not take full advantage of this fear and if we did not deal with humans accordingly. If it had not been for the promise of a Deliverer and the graces He merited for you humans by His death and resurrection, humans would have been entirely at our mercy!

"In conclusion, to understand why humans on their own, unaided by divine grace, cannot perform anything that would amount to an act of virtue, you have to go back to the Garden of Eden and the rebellion of the first man and the first woman against the Prime Mover - and the nature of humans.

"When humans transgress, they do not just transgress and it ends there. They typically wallow in the transgression or sin. You see - an immoral act is never a one time, stand-alone affair. Human transgressions are tied to sinners' intention and they are inevitably accompanied by rationalizations whose objective is to make the immorality sit well with the evildoer. That in turn assures that, instead of the one transgression that the sinner originally contemplated, a series of transgressions will ensue, and each one will in turn be accompanied by further excuses and rationalizations.

"This happens easily - almost inevitably - because at the time of sinning, the individual effectively ditches trust in divine grace and abandons himself/herself to a virulent wilfulness. Even 'pulling back' from that disposition to offend the Prime Mover is itself only possible with the help of divine grace. The upshot of this is that the sinner becomes mired in sin and immorality. By the time Adam and Eve realized that they had gone overboard in their quest for kicks and thrills in disregard of the divine command, they were literally swimming in sin with no life vest anywhere in sight.

"Now, my job in those circumstances is not to suggest to humans how to avoid drowning in sin. We in the Underworld want humans to sink and die spiritually like us. And we were all agog and already celebrating the downfall of humans. Their guardian angels had been helpless and, like us, could only stand there and watch the entire human race go to pot.

"But it was then that something quite unbelievable happened. Incredibly, the Prime Mover, who had been insulted by Adam and Eve, apparently decided in His infinite mercy to throw them life jackets. This was in the form of a promise to send His only begotten son into the world as one of them - as a human!

"If there ever was a time when we in the Underworld were taken aback, that was it! We simply could not have imagined that the Prime Mover, spotless and albeit infinitely almighty, could forgive a sinner for an insult of that magnitude - not even after they had had a change of heart and expressed remorse. It was an even bigger shocker that the Second Person of the Blessed Trinity, equal to the Father and the Spirit and almighty, consented to come down to earth to pay the price for the transgressions of men, and do it, moreover, with His own life!

"And then, in a master stroke, the infinitely merciful Prime Mover, knowing that Adam and Eve were mired in sin and could not recover on their own, decided to extend the promise of a Deliverer to their posterity as well! Adam and Eve, by their transgression, had already created an environment that would have made it impossible for their children and the children of their children to stay out of the doghouse - it was, after all, Adam and Eve who still retained the responsibility for nurturing and bringing up their immediate descendants who would in turn be responsible for the upbringing of the generation that would follow after them. But the sin of Adam and Eve and the effects thereof had bedevilled the Divine Plan in that respect as well; and it was the specific inclusion of the progeny of Adam and Eve in the promise of salvation made to the first man and the first woman even before they had any issue that salvaged that situation.

"It may be true that the sin of Adam and Eve, which plunged the world into the chaotic state from which it is still reeling today, as sins go, was not really extraordinary. As humans, Adam and Eve themselves, were not extraordinary people except for the fact that they were the first humans who came into the world without the blight of original sin. In fact, sins committed by humans today are as appalling to the Prime Mover even though they are committed by humans who are already inclined to sin from birth - the legacy of the original sin of Adam and Eve. These sins, had they been committed prior to the fall of man from grace, would have had the same effect on the relations between humans and the Prime Mover as the sin of Adam and Eve.

"Because of the peculiar nature of humans, a sin committed by any one of them impinges on the creature-Creator relationship enjoyed by humanity as whole. The friendship between humans and the Prime Mover is affected when any one human offends Him. This is in addition to the effect on that individual's personal relationship with the Prime Mover.

"My troops and I celebrate every sin that is committed against the Prime Mover. But we celebrated the fall of Adam and Eve from grace in a special way; because, representing the first offence by members of humankind against the Prime Mover, we knew that its consequences were going to be incalculable for not just Adam and Eve, but for all their posterity as well. And predictably, original sin made a huge dent in what was otherwise a rock-solid friendship between man and his Maker.

"But there was an additional reason for us to celebrate. If Adam and Eve, the father and mother of humankind who had been created in the Image and as such were wholesome in His sight, had persevered and not fallen from grace, that would have been it! It would have firmly and permanently sealed the friendship that existed between the human family and the Godhead; and with that, Adam and Eve, their children, and their children's children would have earned the right to inherit eternal life in a heavenly paradise. The earth would have remained a place of pilgrimage for humans - a *holy* pilgrimage dedicated to the greater glory of the Prime Mover; and it wouldn't have been the dreadful place it is today in which all things spiritual are overshadowed by the preoccupation with material things.

"Just as all humankind stood to benefit from any special gift or blessing which the Prime Mover in His infinite wisdom bestowed on any one member of the human race, it was only to be expected that they also would stand to suffer from a blight or curse that fundamentally affected humanity's relationship with the Creator. Accordingly humans stood to suffer from the very serious lapse of judgement on the part of Adam and Eve, a lapse of judgement that broke up the friendship of the human family with the Holy Trinity. But they also stood to gain tremendously from the perseverance of Adam and Eve in their judicious and faithful observance of the Creator's injunctions.

46

"The promise of a Deliverer in the wake of the fall of Adam and Eve from grace - a promise that was no doubt prompted by the sorrow of the first man and woman on realizing the horrible tragedy which sin represented for their individual selves and also for their posterity on the one hand, and by the Prime Mover's infinite love - was very timely. The world is in a bad enough situation as a result of the effects of one 'original sin' - the original sin committed by Adam and Eve.

"In the absence of a promise of deliverance (a promise that was not just made to Adam and Eve, but to them as representatives of all humankind), all subsequent sins committed by Adam and Eve and their progeny would have individually represented original sins in their own right.

"And it is safe to assume that the earth would be a very different kind of place today as a result of the cumulative effects of those original sins - probably just like Mars or Venus. And the human race would already have become extinct, the result of the actions of humans themselves in a blighted, free-for-all, man-eat-man social environment.

"Now, of course, absolute faithfulness and obedience to the will of the Prime Mover had been a prerequisite for humans to remain in His good books and reap their reward after their period of trial in the Garden of Eden. And so now again, the salvation of humans was made dependent on the total obedience and love of the Son of Man for the Father!

"But that was not all - according to the divine

plan and even in the face of sin, the Prime Mover decreed that the advent of the Son of Man into the world would additionally depend on the constancy and ultimately also *fiat* or consent of a humble, unknown maiden by the name of Mary! Yes - the *fiat* or agreement of a human!

"That was how what had looked like certain victory by evil over good was snatched from me in a master stroke! The promise of a deliverer, the decision to specifically include Adam and Eve's posterity among the beneficiaries of the work of redemption, and the involvement of one of Adam and Eve's descendants - the Immaculate Virgin Mary who would consent to be the earthly mother of the Deliverer - as a key player in it!

"Now, Mary, even though spotless and always full of grace, thought of herself as nothing. She always magnified the Prime Mover - the Lord before whom the meek were exulted, and the proud and mighty were humbled. Despite knowing that I, the Prince of Darkness, am stricken with terror at the mere thought of her, Mary remains the one descendant of Adam and Eve who has always understood better that any other the fact that without the help of divine grace, humans are as nothing!

"Unable to be virtuous by dint of their own efforts on the one hand, and finding that they must still do whatever it takes to survive in a world in which equity and justice are just a sham, humans inevitably find themselves 'stranded'. They then invariably seek to escape from their bind, and that is when they land into the traps we lay for them. They make very easy prey for us at that time. For one, they become easily taken in by dissembling in the world that passes for character and integrity.

"And as humans discover that it was all a mirage, they soon find themselves with 'no choice' but to acquiesce to our suggestions that they stop sitting on the fence, not be shy about being capricious and acquisitive, join everyone else in essentially exploiting others for their own benefit, and above all start to 'enjoy life' while they can.

"Add to that the human inclination to sin, and you pretty well can guess what the results will be when we set about putting the faith and trust of humans in the Prime Mover to the test..."

Willing spirit, weak flesh...

"If one is inclined to do negative things, it follows that merely avoiding to do negative things has to be through struggle. As humans attempt to avoid things that are dubious so they may be free to focus on things that are constructive, they invariably come up against the problem of a spirit that may be willing, but flesh that remains weak. And the flesh constitutes a growing obstacle as humans embark on the uphill task of trying to accomplish positive things. Because the inclination to negativity does not abandon humans even as they start to grow in holiness, they will continue to feel a sense of helplessness.

"Humans will always have reason to fear that

49

the weakness in their bodies might one day succeed in overwhelming the willingness of the spirit at any time, eventually steering them right back into their old sinful ways. The apostle of the gentiles, and others like Jerome could tell you the same thing.

"The weakness in the flesh will always tend to draw the individual away from reason towards what is base. Appeals by the likes of John the Baptist urging humans to put their lives in order in view of the impending judgement clearly assumed that, despite being weak in the flesh as a result of original sin, humans were at least capable of willing to live as befitted creatures of the Prime Mover. No such appeals have ever been directed at beasts of the earth, fishes, reptiles or birds not so much because they are innocent in the eyes of the Prime Mover, as because they are not endowed with a spirit. But that does not mean that the innocence of these lower creatures should not put humans to shame.

"Guileless and unassuming, they have never betrayed the Prime Mover even once, the harsh realities of their existence notwithstanding. Even though they share this 'valley of tears' with humans, no animal of the wild, bird of the air, reptile, fish, insect or any of the lower creatures suffers from 'weakness of the flesh'. These creatures all have one thing in common: they just do what their instincts tell them and no more. Avarice, debauchery, slothfulness and other pitfalls of the flesh are foreign to them. Birds of the air know instinctively that not one feather gets dislodged from their coat and goes missing without the Prime Mover expressly permitting it. And He is glorified when they respond in whichever manner to that or any other eventuality that comes to pass.

"Believe me, I myself feel so much shame observing the ardour, fealty and dogged constancy of these lowly creatures to their Maker. Just to think that I, so richly endowed at creation, floundered; and that I am now good for nothing save as a spiteful tempter who is driven by jealousy and envy.

"Would you believe it? I am a total failure and a write-off; and even though I have notched up some successes, I can't really claim to be the prime cause for the evil things humans do. After all, beyond the fact that I am a creature like them and a spirit, what do I really have in common with them? There is, actually, little doubt that a good deal of the things that constitute distractions for humans and prevent them from focusing on the Perfect Good and also their last end can be directly blamed on the weakness of the flesh. Of course that might be my window of opportunity; but it is, nonetheless, only a window of opportunity and nothing more.

"I really wish I had the power to actually besmirch and defile humans in the same way someone soils apparel. And even when I have permission to possess a human, it all stops there, because I cannot forcibly haul my victims into my hell even after I have made their lives on earth a living hell. If anything, at the end of these adventures, I have always been more frustrated and miserable than when I started out, because I cannot bear to see

51

those I thought I had succeeded in reducing to nonentities suddenly pluck up energy and sweep past me to their eternal reward in Valhalla!

"When the Prime Mover promised to send the Deliverer in the aftermath of the fall of Adam and Eve from grace, it was clearly on the supposition that the human spirit was capable of willing; and that, once the willingness was activated by the individuals concerned, it became impervious - with the help of grace - not only to my suggestions, but also to the weakness of the flesh. In making the promise, He essentially said that whenever humans invoked His name, He would always be there for them, even though they and their fore fathers before them had transgressed.

"And that is what gets me. Even though bedevilled by original sin, humans become transformed by prayer to the point where the weakness of the flesh, however debilitating, cease to have any real power over the spirit. That is how prayer undermines my efforts. Even when the flesh is weak, so long as the human spirit is willing and you folks, aware that you are no match for an evil genius like me, begin pleading to be shielded from vitriol and other diseases of the soul, all my efforts somehow always come to naught! And that has led me to a theory about how grace works - and don't you start imagining that I can't expound on this just because I happen to be evil! Are you crazy? No creature, however brilliant, can presume to understand the mysterious ways of the Almighty One!

"In the final analysis, one can only hazard an explanation about how sanctifying grace works. This is in the nature of the beast that we are dealing with. But the theory, even though not fool proof, still is interesting.

"It may well be that, to the extent that one's spirit is willing but the flesh is weak, grace steps in to reinforce the willingness of the spirit. And it also may well be that, to the extent the willingness of the spirit starts to falter with the neglect of prayer and to look like it might be unable to surmount the frailty of the flesh, the ability of grace to bolster it also diminishes correspondingly.

"But it is risky, clearly, to talk about the role of sanctifying grace in these or any other circumstances, because sanctifying grace is a gift. But even if it were something that worked mechanically, how would it function if willingness of the spirit and weakness of the flesh were actually intertwined as they probably are, since we are talking about an *animal rationale* and the exercise of its free will?

"The fact is that, regardless of the situation, prayer is an avenue that is always available to humans for strengthening the willingness of the spirit. When they pray - well, even in the most befuddled way - my schemes, however advanced or promising, just go burst and I have to start all over again. Hypocrites may believe that prayer and its sanctifying effects are only available to them alone and not to others.

"The grace of the Prime Mover and a host of

other blessings are available to all humans alike, because all humans are in the exact same predicament - they are creatures with spirits that, if not already actually willing, are at least capable of willing. And, as such, they recognize that Perfect Good, which is also their last end, can only be fully enjoyed (or missed) in eternity and not in this world. They know that, in the same way a spouse who is unfaithful cannot simultaneously claim to be true and trusted, they too cannot be wedded to materialism and say that they are focused on their last end at the same time.

"Although they experience the urge to scramble and obtain immediate respite, and will even invest everything they possess in the pursuit of temporal happiness and security, they also know full well that temporal pleasures and satisfaction are temporal by definition and cannot extend into eternity. They also know that the converse is true, namely that Perfect Good can only be possessed in eternity by definition, outside the limitations of time.

"They know that the Bride is coming; but yet are unable to muster the little attention that is needed to assure that their candles stay lit. If you ask me, I will tell you that they don't even give a damn that they might not have on attire that is deemed appropriate for a wedding feast.

"Again, they know that they are going to die, and yet can't quit pursuits that are incompatible with their status as creatures of the Righteous One. Humans also know that to wear their crown and also have their revenge on the wicked - and I recognize very well that I'm at the top of the list naturally - they must physically die; but the vast majority of humans would sooner sell everything they had to acquire a 'magic' potion that looked like it might insure them against dying - if there had been such a 'magic' portion - than contemplate life after death!

"You humans - if you don't mind me including you, Reverend Mjomba, among them. You humans have been told 'Ask and it shall be given to you'; and yet you seem unable to do that simplest of simple things...sitting back and asking! Worst of all, you need someone like me to come from hell to sermonize about the importance of prayer! Of course the less you pray, the better for us in the Underworld, for we can then rely on the weakness of the flesh to do the job for us.

"I thought I knew how low creatures could sink; but you humans have set new records and surprising even me! The lying, the cheating, the decadence, the killings, and yes especially the killings! I have admittedly killed myself, but only in the spiritual, not physical, sense.

"Unlike you folks, I can truthfully - yes, truthfully - say that I do not have blood on my hands. Guess what - I am a pure spirit, and do not even have hands to brag about!

"As regards the killing, this has been going on since time immemorial - from the time you humans invented the arrow and the sling. It became really bad when it became possible to mass-produce swords and spears, and it got worse when you invented gunpowder. And just imagine what it is going to be like with the success of the Manhattan Project and other projects like that! And investment in these 'projects' continues unabated and at a maddening pace, led by the 'super powers'.

Redefining the "moral order"...

"And while all that has been going on, my troops and I have been working overtime to just ensure that the killing itself becomes accepted, blessed by the religious, and institutionalized. That is how the Philistines, Egyptians, Greeks, and Romans all came to regard killings done in the cause of territorial expansion - not just killings done in defense of borders from 'enemies' - as perfectly justified. This is one of my greatest accomplishments - getting murder to become institutionalized and glorified as military science, and promoted with gusto in the name of 'national security' or 'vital interests'. And since it is the victorious who call the shots, we have been getting more and more of this as time went by.

"We should hear more and more about 'collateral damage' and things like that, which absolve the culprits for the frequently open 'ethnic cleansings' that go on all the time and the sometimes scarcely veiled genocides perpetrated in the name of national security, now that killing is fine in most people's eyes. One of my aims is to see all so-called rules and conventions of war - like those that were designed to safeguard non-combatants and the innocent - abolished. It is also one of my goals to get the United Nations weakened to the point where that body can be manipulated into backing unprovoked pre-emptive or so-called first strikes if it is in a super power's 'national interest'.

"There was a time once when some so-called advanced nations had legislation on their books that outlawed the murder of heads of state of other countries during peacetime. But that was then. One thing that is high on our agenda is to get all nations of the world to accept that, as and when earthly powers and principalities become 'blessed' by the Prime Mover and succeed in acquiring the wherewithal to launch pre-emptive strikes against other nations that are not so blessed with impunity, it will also signal that failure to employ that capability to advance their 'national interests' will be criminal! The reason being that all such capability is God-given and must be put to use just like talents that humans receive from the Prime Mover! While this idea has started to take root in certain circles, we are working hard with all our stakeholders to ensure that it becomes elevated to a moral imperative at a much faster pace.

"If you do not know, we here in the Underworld don't have any wish to see peace reign on Earth. We must do everything to ensure that there is turmoil and war all the time, and the best weapon that we have is the greed that drives men to covet things that do not belong to them. We were therefore very fortunate that we were able to get some stupid fools who were in key positions in super powerful nations on board with this idea almost as soon as the so-called 'cold war' came to an end; and, instead of promoting permanent world peace, the stupid fools, claiming to be driven by holy zeal, saw our point and began doing everything according to our script! Yes - when the Prince of Peace was lying in the manger in Bethlehem, the holy angels, announcing the good tidings to the shepherds, sang 'Alleluia' and, pointing to the shining star that helped the wise men of the Orient make it in time to Bethlehem, had greeted them saying 'Peace on Earth'. That was, of course, anathema for my evil plan. We luckily are back in the driver's seat, and we must work with our allies to try and thwart the Divine Plan. We must foil the intentions of the Madonna of Fatima who prayed for peace to descend on Earth.

"To those humans who savor worldly things, we say that victory in war brings more affluence and new opportunities to pander to the desires of the flesh - at least until such time as the 'super powers' of the day themselves get nixed by other emerging super powers and become obliterated in the unending cycle of retribution, that is!

"The existing world order in which materialism and acquisitiveness drive everything is a hallmark of my success in this area. And my troops and I continue to notch up successes as we pursue our ultimate goal of turning things around and making the religions of the world serve our purposes and promote our immediate objectives. You see - having a world that is just secular or 'irreligious' is not bad enough.

And we must work hard because we have only a short time to do our dirty work. Yeah, that is what the book says! We've so far succeeded in getting individuals to canonize themselves even before they have left this life for the next, never mind that it is all based on feelings of self-justification and false piety. And we've almost succeeded in using religion to promote materialism and worldliness. We have still got lots of work to do to turn religion around and make it the primary vehicle for triggering wars and causing misery for humanity.

"We've succeeded in making lasciviousness and debauchery accepted in society - I mean, it is legal at least in the 'advanced' countries to set up shop and sell those degenerate and corrupting wares to the public. I mean - there is no limit to the kind of trash you can buy in the open market place. And just imagine that thousands upon thousands around the world make their living peddling the trash! And now, in fact, a nation is not regarded as 'advanced' until we in the Underworld put our stamp on its social fabric, and things of that sort become normal fare!

"And you know, we were very much behind this 'worldwide web' thing - you call it the 'Internet'. It is perfectly legal for anyone to set up shop on that indefinable, so-called borderless the Internet and operate a website whose only purpose is to corrupt morals. I said 'so-called' because the Internet is not really borderless certainly the phone lines it uses are confined to borders, regulated and are even subject to bugging by the authorities. But that is exactly as it should be - my troops and I find that arrangement just terrific for our purposes. Our lackeys amongst you have complete leeway to peddle their sick, corrupting merchandise without interference from anyone. It is exhilarating to see new sites devoted to promoting hate spring up almost every other day with no interference from anyone.

"And very soon there will be websites that will provide complete courses related to the production of weapons of mass destruction. You see - the world is now on the brink of a major war - the third world war. Triggered by a pre-emptive strike, employing so-called tactical nuclear weapons, on one of the so-called rogue states, you can be sure that the third world war will make the first and second world wars look like storms in tea cups.

"Talking about nuclear weapons, can you imagine that all the United Nations member states, including the Holy See, signed off on the so-called Nuclear Non-Proliferation Treaty without any prodding! The purpose of NPT was of course to protect the five original members of the Nuclear Club from the rest of the world. It would be a contradiction in terms to suggest that its purpose was to protect nations that did not possess those weapons from those that did. So, how come that the UN member states that were actually targeted signed on that "treaty"? Well, you now have an idea what 'fear' does to you humans. It makes you start reasoning backwards - in the reverse!

"You can also consequently conclude that the

nations that are more likely to use the WMD are the original members of the Nuclear Club and, in particular, the nation(s) with a history of using those weapons since their fear would was greatest!

"Any way, we are approaching the time when, not just states, but entire continental shelves will be completely obliterated in avalanches of nuclear and hydrogen bombs. But the greatest damage to humans will be inflicted by the chemical and biological weapons which will also add a new dimension to warfare, namely panic. Reports of plumes of smoke mushrooming and enveloping entire cities will cause most humans sixty years or older to suffer fatal heart attacks.

"Many people will pass out at the sight of the clouds of chemical dust, and the putrid smell of biological agents will knock out many others. The weak will be trampled to death as the strong try to escape mushrooming clouds that will be bearing down upon them, or at the mere sight of other people suddenly clutching at their throats, after inhaling the deadly biological, viral and radiological 'killer' agents, and writhing in silent agony. Without a doubt, the chemical and biological weapons will inflict the greatest pain and suffering on the people of the Prime Mover.

"It will be a completely different story with respect to the nuclear and hydrogen bombs, and the worst devastation will take place in countries with the biggest arsenals of these weapons. This is because, a single 'direct hit' by an enemy nuke (or a friendly nuke in a 'friendly fire' situation) will set off nuclear and hydrogen bombs hidden in deep silos within a radius of a thousand miles. Meaning that countries with the biggest arsenals of these weapons will be the ones that will suffer the greatest devastation as one exploding nuclear or hydrogen bomb triggers incendiary explosions that in turn will set off nuclear and/or hydrogen bombs in the entire 'arsenal'.

"For now, I use fear - the fear of both those nations that do not possess weapons of mass destruction and those that do - to proliferate these WMD. It might surprise you, but the fact is that, at this particular time, the bigger an arsenal of WMD a nation possesses, the greater its fears - perhaps because that nation is aware of the destructive power of those weapons. But, unfortunately for these nations and perhaps fortunately for the rest of the world, it is also the best example of fear that is leading these nations to 'dig their own graves' as you folks would put it. My influence in the citadels of power around the globe has of course never been greater, and I am determined to see this thing through before the real Armageddon is unleashed upon you humans. Nothing will please me more than the sight of a nuclear conflagration triggered by fear and human stupidity!

"Wars do not happen by accident - believe me. Of course not! We in the Underworld work hard to make sure that our people are the ones in the decision-making roles, and we make certain that they are appropriately rewarded - in material terms, of course.

"And understand me - you nowadays have all that bullshit about 'democracy' and other rubbish about taking polls to establish the 'will of the people' before nations can go to war. Regarding democracy - completely ignore what the whining, good-for-nothing philosophers have written. Democracy as a system of government only dates back to Marie Antoinette and the French revolution she engineered. It was her idea that the traditional rulers - kings and emperors should be toppled in favor of the dictatorship of the masses. Also, it was not an accident that Karl Max, who took that notion one step further and advocated ownership of the means of production by the masses spent some time not far away - in the British Isles just across the channel.

"In so-called 'democracies', it is usually a tiny but, of course, well connected clique - a small group of ambitious, power hungry individuals - that wields power. They are the ones who wield power, not the masses who 'elect' them. Elections themselves are nothing but a circus and a farce, designed to give the small group of individuals who step into a nation's halls of power credibility. The clique that is in power, in concert with any other clique(s) in existence, invariably strives to suppress the emergence of any new cliques or groupings - political parties as you call them - that might end up challenging and even supplanting them in the halls of power.

"I tell you - what goes on in the name of democracy is all a farce. Remember, we are talking about the exercise of raw power here in a world gone amok, and the opportunities that 'leaders' of nation states have of promoting their self-interest. And you can be sure that it is not the 'official' agenda of the so-called political parties that cliques in power implement. It is certainly not the agenda that is dictated to them by their Prime Mover. It is the agenda of the clique in power that is pursued, and members of the clique see absolutely nothing wrong with subordinating the *bonum commune* to their own personal interests.

"And what do you think the role of the Prince of Darkness would be in those types of circumstances? You can be pretty sure that, with my interest in influencing the course of history, and hastening the onset of Armageddon, I will be all over the place dictating to these power brokers exactly what they should do. It is I, Diabolos, who remains in charge, and this is true whether what you have brewing is British, Portuguese, Spanish, Japanese, or American imperialism, communism, Nazism, or whatever other 'ism' that might be in the works.

"And on the global scene, it doesn't really matter to me either whether victors in global conflicts are Germans, Americans, French, Russians, Arabs, Chinese, Indians, or Africans. The 'color' of the super power - or hyper power - is immaterial to me. In this murky business, I make it a rule to always go with the winner! If this will get you bubbling 'Brilliant!', I would advise you to check yourself - it is just simple common sense! But of course, 'common sense' is not very common nowadays - or is it? On the national scene, it does not matter a dime to me which clique takes the reins of power.

"I am trying to say that it is of very little significance to me whether the clique that occupies the halls of power comes from a 'political' or 'non-political' party'; and - if a political party - whether it is a party that is 'rightist' or 'leftist', 'conservative' or 'liberal', 'neo-conservative' or 'neo-liberal', 'Christian' or 'non-Christian', 'secular' or 'non-secular', etc. If you ask me - I do not even see any difference between 'neocons' and 'neolibs', and that distinction is not in my vocabulary. Perhaps you are one of those who likes to discriminate against some people - not me, I tell ya!

"And guess what - if the individuals who made up the cliques in power in the different countries were as fool-hardy or as brave as they make it appear, instead of dragging their countries into conflicts and 'wars of opportunity', they would be offering to fight duels with the leadership of any nation they found themselves at loggerheads with as a way of settling disagreements that arose. And in a duel, cheating in not permitted! And you certainly don't try and 'disarm' the other party first, because then it wouldn't be a duel. And, of course, if it looks from the outset like it will be an uneven match, no person of honor will try and lay false claim to valor, much less victory, by agreeing to be a participant. Doing so brings dishonor not just to the individual, but to that individual's family and country as well.

"Understand that you humans are all from one stock. You are supposed to get along with one another, and it does not make sense to try and destroy one another on the battlefield either. What's more, by opting to settle their differences through such duels and saving ordinary folk in those countries the curse of war, these leaders would be showing the highest statesmanship. They would in effect be proving to the world that they are prepared to sacrifice *their* lives for their countries. And if they lost the duels and gallantly met their death at the hands of the 'enemy', they probably would be going straight to heaven for showing that they had such great love for their countrymen.

"The ruling cliques the world over are made up of virtual impostors who have no respect for human life, and who see nothing wrong with killing. They believe senseless killing stops being murder when you decide to employ the 'security forces" or the 'military' to do the killing, or when you 'declare war', when that actually makes it worse! This is because, instead of committing the murder single handed (like Cain did when he murdered his brother Abel), you now do it by conspiring and colluding with other people to commit the crime and, moreover, in a manner that is undeniably premeditated. And then the gravity of the crime changes to something else completely when you take steps to institutionalize it. Because you then also become culpable for drawing other innocent humans into your conspiracy to destroy life under the guise of defending the

66

homeland, and for the pain and suffering that conscientious objectors to your murderous scheme end up having to endure. And it is, of course, quite terrible when, in the eyes of murderers, aggression suddenly stops being aggression when they call it 'a pre-emptive strike'!

"Unfortunately for all those humans who are in league with me in this 'killing' business, however much they 'justify' their actions, they can never deny the fact that they would never have liked the things they do unto others done by others unto them. One thing about that moral 'standard' is that rationalizations however elaborate, and excuses however framed, all suddenly stop holding any water when measured against it. And it is precisely this that will be their undoing come their day of reckoning - which, very unfortunately for them (but very fortunately for me) happens to be just around the corner.

"Humans! The self-deception becomes total when, trying to skirt logic, they start claiming that people do not go to heaven because they are *good*, but because they have believed and are *saved*! The rest supposedly go to hell because they are so *predestined*! In other words, they become lost regardless of whether they are good or bad! Yes, that is exactly what '*salvation by faith alone*' means - if you did not know. As if it is not bad enough to peddle such warped reasoning, humans even go on to shamelessly attribute that false doctrine to the *Logos* - the Word through whom all things were created and without whom was made nothing that was made! (John 1:1-3) But let's cut to the chase. The Deliverer - the Good Shepherd - knows his sheep, and His sheep know Him. And He lays down His life for His sheep. Yeah! His sheep hear His voice; and He knows them, and they follow Him. And He has other sheep that do not belong to the fold. Those also He must lead, and they will hear His voice, and there will be but *one* flock, *one* shepherd. (John 10: 14-16).

"But, look - that was the doctrine which the Priest and the Levite who are referred to in Luke 10: 25-37 lived by. They believed that salvation was by faith alone, and they accordingly left the observance of the commandment to love one's neighbor to the Samaritan. They sincerely believed that they themselves were predestined for heaven, and did not believe that doing good works was part of it!

"Which reminds me of this famous evangelical preacher whose powerful sermons so captivated those who thronged his mega church to hear him preach the 'Word of the Prime Mover' they never could have enough of them, and they typically hang on to his every word as he spoke. One day, addressing the enraptured audience, he said: 'And you must always trust what the Prime Mover says, and you must never trust your own opinion and interpretation of the Word of the Prime Mover!' And the he turned and, referring to the *Sancta Ecclesia* that was established by the Deliverer, the *Logos*, on the rock called Peter, he admonished: 'You trust yourself, and you could easily be ensnared by

Babylon the great, mother of whores and of earth's abominations!' Right? Wrong! Aaaah, ha, ha, ha, haaah! Hak, hak, hak, haaah!

"And, again - this has nothing to do with the fact that I, Beelzebub and Ruler of the Underworld, would throw a huge party to 'celebrate' the damnation of humans faster than you can blink an eye - if I were able to. I'm unfortunately damned and can't party in any way. This just happens to be a fact, namely that salvation is not by faith alone (*a sola fide*), but by faith (a gift of the Holy Ghost) *and* good works (involving the use of the faculties of reason and free will) with which humans are endowed). To use the words of the Apostle of the Gentiles: '*Psius enim sumus factura creati in Christo Iesu in operibus bonis quae praeparavit Deus ut in illis ambulemus.*' (For we are his workmanship, created in Christ Jesus in good works, which God hath prepared that we should walk in them.) (Ephesians 2:10).

"You'd not expect the Father of Lies to like facts, and you are right. I wish everything that was fact and verifiable as such - or real - wasn't. I wish that everything was fake just like 'fake news'. If there were no facts - if everything was fake - there would also be no such a thing as 'salvation by faith and good works' or otherwise'. And with salvation for humans out of the picture (which would, of course, have been the case if the Son of Man had not condescended to come to Earth at the behest of His Heavenly Father), all humans would be on the road to perdition.

"That is the extent to which you humans have

been favored by the Non-Creature and Master Craftsman. And it is not in dispute in any case that because much had been given to us celestial beings, much would be required of us. And you can now gauge the extent to which the Prime Mover had favored us by the extent to which we have been disgraced! I mean - the connotation of my name (Satan) and the fact that my abode is in hell while the victorious angels who spurned me and remained faithful now minister to Him in heaven tells it all!

"Now it is also a fact that, even though lost and damned, I myself, along with the legion of demons who followed in my footsteps and also ended up being damned, live by the doctrine of *a sola fide* (by faith alone)! Yes, by faith alone - except that you must understand me correctly. The faith I'm referring to isn't a gift of the Holy Ghost. If you did not know, I ditched the supernatural virtue of faith - a gift of the Prime Mover that is infused by Him in His creatures that are created in His image (Matthew 16: 16-17) - when I rebelled against Him. I took the position that as a creature that was endowed with the faculties of reason at creation, I needed to be totally free and to live by faith in myself - period! Yeah, faith in my own self!

"Unfortunately for me, it dawned on me too late that any faith that was not infused by Him (as all three theological virtues of faith, hope and charity that form the foundation of moral activity of the disciples of the Deliverer must be) had to be 'fake'. I realized that I could not change the way things were ordered after I had already committed an irreversible act of insurrection against the Holy Trinity (I had even attempted to get members of the Godhead to disown each other) and become an outcast! I realized my error only after I had 'crossed the Rubicon' as you folks would say. I was shocked to discover that as the renegade that I had become, I was only capable of evil doings like trying to entice the faithful celestial creatures (the good angels) to jump ship as well, and no longer had the wherewithal to perform any good works. Admittedly I will continue to pay the price for taking that route through all eternity!

"So, all humans who are tempted to subscribe to that false doctrine (*a sole fide*) had better be aware! Their 'faith' could easily be faith *in themselves*, and it could conceivably be fake as well - just like mine! They should in any event remember what the Deliverer said about me when He said: 'When any one heareth the word of the kingdom, and understandeth it not, there cometh the wicked one, and catcheth away that which was sown in his heart: this is he that received the seed by the way side.' (Matthew 13:10). Humans would do well to remember - always - that I am watching, and that my names include 'The Adversary', 'The Deceiver', 'The Tempter' and 'The Seducer'!

"You have been told that it was the sin of pride that bought me tumbling from the heights and was my undoing. That is a fact - and one that is not fake or unreal; and the fact is that I believed in myself and I refused to acknowledge that the supernatural virtues

71

of faith, hope and charity (which the Prime Mover was about to infuse in me) were a gift in every sense of that word. I had this idea that as the brilliant creature that I was, I didn't need to be cuddled like a baby - that I could get by completely on my own without the Non-Creature and Master Craftsman having to infuse in me any of that 'crap' (or so I imagined) before I could perform the smallest decent act like bowing in His presence.

"I demurred when it was my turn to 'genuflect and worship the Non-Creature and Master Craftsman'. Well, that is exactly what it would have signified if a magnificent creature like me that was endowed with such beauty and brilliance at creation - and a pure spirit at that - stooped to acknowledge that I too needed to have the supernatural virtues infused in me before I could bring off any thing that was good. And so, I refused - to my detriment as I immediately discovered; and it was then that I realized that, with that explicit act of rebellion, I had actually cancelled out all prospects of applying my brilliant intellect in concert with my free will to cooperate with divine grace and continue to exist as befitted a creature that was molded in the image of the Non-Creature and Master Craftsman Himself!

"But (as you might have guessed) I must now take my frustrations out on you humans. My troops and I must work overtime to ensure that humans don't get to see that it is the Prime Mover Himself who, as Thomas Aquinas explained, 'pours in them (infundere) the infused virtues, and not by compulsion or overriding the free will of man, but without dependence on them'; or that these virtues 'are produced in them by God without their assistance' to borrow the words of that African Augustine of Hippo.

"You can probably now see a parallel between my own act of disobedience and the position of earthbound humans who won't submit to the authority of the *Sancta Ecclesia*, the 'Mystical Body of the Deliverer' as Pope Pius XII brilliantly explained in his encyclical *Mystici corporis Christi*. When they demur (like I did) and do not become disciples of the Deliverer, they deny themselves thereby the opportunity to enjoy the fullness of grace found only in His *Sancta Ecclesia*!

"To quote from that papal encyclical: 'Just as at the first moment of the Incarnation the Son of the Eternal Father adorned with the fullness of the Holy Spirit the human nature which was substantially united to Him, that it might be a fitting instrument of the Divinity in the sanguinary work of the Redemption, so at the hour of His precious death He willed that His Church should be enriched with the abundant gifts of the Paraclete in order that in dispensing the divine fruits of Redemption she might be, for the Incarnate Word, a powerful instrument that would never fail.' (Paragraph 31 of *Mystici Corporis Christi*).

"The pontiff penned that encyclical as World War II was raging and humans were battling to annihilate each other. It was the time of blitzkriegs and fire bombings of cities even after the initial crippling carpet-bombing runs (also known as saturation bombing runs) had already reduced them to hulks and the heavy bombers had run out of targets. And it was also the time when 'the Yankees' did not see anything wrong with testing the efficacy of atom bombs over Nagasaki and Hiroshima, the same folks who now worry that some 'rouge state', using the technology the 'Manhattan Project" had pioneered, might one day acquire their own 'nukes' and get tempted to drop them over New York City or on the City of Angels to avenge years of perceived mistreatment! The fact though is that, terrible as the devastation from World War II was, compared to the devastation from World War III which is just round the corner, World War II will look like a storm in a tea cup!

"The timing of that encyclical by the successor to St. Peter could not have been more precise. The pain and suffering of each and every human not just during that war but during any military campaigns that humans have ever waged against each other were on the mind of the Savior of Mankind as He languished on the cross. He made that clear when He said: 'Amen I say to you, as long as you did it to one of these my least brethren, you did it to me.' (Matthew 25:40)

"When a human injures another human, that human also injures the Deliverer and very directly too as the encyclical pointed out. And when the Deliverer taught you humans how to pray (and you can bet that many humans automatically end up on their knees praying when they find themselves in the midst of raging wars), He did not use the words: 'And forgive

74

us our sins as we forgive those who sin against us *and this includes Beelzebub*'. He excluded me entirely. He knew that I was sworn to work for the downfall of you humans to the very end. And so don't you think of 'forgiving me'. First of all it would be an insult and would make me madder; and secondly it would be completely wasted effort.

"But when a fellow human injures you however badly, you'd better learn how to get around to forgiving him/her; and not just once, but seventy times seven times (Matthew 18:22), which simply means that you have to forgive trespasses against you by other humans with whom you share Planet Earth as many times as you are injured.

"And when a human sees another human, he/she should be seeing in that other human the image of the Non-Creature and Master Craftsman. (Genesis 1:27) And that is always true even when the other human is a stranger, looks like an alien, or has an appearance that is deemed revolting.

"Of course the Deliverer knew that in the wake of the Fall of Man, the concept of the 'human family' had all but ceased to exist. The notion of the human family was dealt a mortal blow by the disobedience of the first man and the first woman. That is the reason the Deliverer came down to earth - to redeem sinful and sinning humans who were 'lost' in a real sense. They no longer believed in the human family. And Peter's behavior in the Upper Room on the night the Redeemer instituted the sacrament of the Holy Eucharist - the 'source and summit of the Christian life' (Paragraph 1324 of the Catechism) - was symptomatic. When it was his turn to have his feet washed clean by the Savior of Mankind, his disbelief showed; and it prompted the Deliverer to tell him: 'What I do thou knowest not now; but thou shalt know hereafter'. (John 13:7) But Peter, who would deny Him three times in a row not long thence had shot back as if he did not need redemption: 'Thou shalt never wash my feet!'

"How was Peter, who was so adamant in his refusal to have his dirty feet washed by the Deliverer, going to understand and above have others follow the admonition the Deliverer was about to give His apostles as He said: 'Know you what I have done to you? You call me Master, and Lord; and you say well, for so I am. If then I being your Lord and Master, have washed your feet; you also ought to wash one another's feet. For I have given you an example, that as I have done to you, so you do also. Amen, amen I say to you: The servant is not greater than his lord; neither is the apostle greater than he that sent him. If you know these things, you shall be blessed if you do them.' (John 13:12-17)

"It would be an even tougher sell when the Deliverer would venture to say: 'A new commandment I give unto you: That you love one another, as I have loved you, that you also love one another. By this shall all men know that you are my disciples, if you have love one for another.' (John 13:34-35)

"The situation was so bad that the Deliverer found Himself compelled to add: 'But he that hateth his brother, is in darkness, and walketh in darkness, and knoweth not whither he goeth; because the darkness hath blinded.' (John 13:34)

"Of course humans as a rule don't have time to stop and reflect on the fact that they have morphed into such wicked creatures; almost as wicked - I might even say as evil - as us demons. They get motivated to try and find out only when they are on the verge of kicking the bucket and are about to head to their judgment, or when they suddenly find themselves in the crosshairs as conflicts around them rage; at which time they flop on their knees instinctively to beseech the Prime Mover to have mercy on them and make it possible for them to escape to safety in whatever way.

"They will continue at it while they are huddled in overcrowded and often leaking boats, as they trekking through deserts in an effort to avoid combat zones, or as they try to make a dash for it from underneath tunnels or culverts or basements where they were holed up with their dear ones amidst artillery fire and mortars unleashed by the combatants.

"Many start blaming the Prime Mover at that point for the evils that humans do to each other, and find it hard to grasp that, while the Prime Mover permits ill-intentioned humans to do their damnedest as they attempt to drive their own foes into the sea, He will always still cause good to come out of the evil deeds of humans! Others who survive their harrowing experiences, determined to render evil for evil (1 Peter 3:9), immediately start stupidly plotting how to avenge for injuries suffered in contravention of what the Prime Mover had revealed to Moses: '*Mea est ultio et ego retribuam in tempore ut labatur pes eorum iuxta est dies perditionis et adesse festinant tempora.*' (Revenge is mine, and I will repay them in due time, that their foot may slide: the day of destruction is at hand, and the time makes haste to come.) (Deuteronomy 32:35). They are stupid to do that because they also perpetuate the senseless cycle of violence in the process.

"The Prime Mover, after He was done with causing the light, the firmament of heaven, the waters and the earth, the sun and the stars, the fish and the birds, the cattle, the creeping things of the earth, the cattle and the other beasts of the earth, and finally the first humans (whom He made crafted in His own image and likeness and given dominion over the fishes of the sea, and the fowls of the air, and the beasts, and the whole earth, and every creeping creature that moved upon the earth) to bounce into existence out of nothing, he had looked and had seen that all the things that he had made and had also blessed were very good. (Genesis 1:31).

"But now look at all the mayhem that humans had created in the world beginning with the fall of the first man and the first woman from grace! And still the Son of Man deigned to come down from heaven to redeem them from sin. And with His death and resurrection, humans now even get to have a shot at beatific vision after they kick the bucket! [Confer: Matthew 22:30-32; John 14:21; 1 Corinthians 13:12;

1 John 3:2; John14:8-14; John 14:21; John 20:17; and Pope Benedict XII's *Benedictus Deus*(On the Beatific Vision of God)].

"But you've also to admit that humankind must have been in a really bad way to require no less than the *Logos* and a member of the Godhead to come down from heaven to save them. If you are getting the sense that the human experiment had ended up a signal failure (not because of anything the Non-Creature and Master Craftsman had done or failed to do but because of the pigheadedness of humans), I am with you.

"With the exception of a few 'odd' ones (that is how the 'ordinary' ones view them) like Mother Josephine Bakhita, Margaret of Antioch (also known as Marina the Great Martyr and Vanquisher of Demons), and Mother Teresa of Calcutta, humans by and large have lost their bearings. The odd ones are literally stranded in a dog eat dog world and also one in which man is a wolf to man' (*Homo homini lupus*), if Titus Maccius Platus (ancient Rome's best known playwright) is to be believed!

"It was not accidental that the Deliverer warned his disciples saying: '*Ecce ego mitto vos sicut oves in medio luporum. Estote ergo prudentes sicut serpentes, et simplices sicut columbae.*' (Behold I send you as sheep in the midst of wolves. Be ye therefore wise as serpents and simple as doves.) (Matthew 10:16) Yeah, they have 'lost it'! They don't even know what they are - that they are created in the Prime Mover's image and likeness, and have a perishable body made up of atoms and molecules and an immortal soul!

"Because they have discovered atoms and molecules, the way humans boast, you'd think they have gotten to know something at long last. Not long ago when so-called *classical physics* was the rage, they thought they had almost reached the apex of human knowledge, when they couldn't even predict the behavior of atoms correctly due to the quantum effects. The 'scientists' now speak with confidence (or know) that every atom is composed of a 'nucleus' and one or more 'electrons' bound to the nucleus; and that the nucleus is made up of one or more 'protons' and typically a similar number of 'neutrons'. But it is usually those who are into that 'scientific' lingo who are least likely to believe in the existence of the Prime Mover. They instead believe in the 'Big Bang', a 'theory' that is supposed to throw light on how things around them came into being - as if something can come out of nothing!

"Yeah, Big Bang! The problem with that is that even a 'big bang' cannot just happen like that. To be effectual a 'big bang' would require attributes that belong to the Non-Creature and Master Craftsman; it would have to be an 'almighty' Big Bang that was also capable of infinite love, and of causing creatures that are also capable of loving to bounce into existence over the eons; the Big Bang would above all also have to be imbued with omniscience and not be subject to any limitations, otherwise it would itself need to be caused by another almighty Big Bang! In short, the

Big Bang could never metamorphose out of nothing.

"The problem is really not so much with the idea of a big bang as with humans themselves - begrudging humans who are reluctant to accept that they owed their very own existence to the Non-Creature and Master Craftsman - and the way they use their God-given faculties of reason and free will. When we pure spirits reason, it is automatic. A good way for humans to try and think of those of us who inhabit the pure spirit realm is to imagine very bright celestial objects or luminaries that however are pure spirit with no matter in their makeup. That was why my troops and I could not be forgiven by the Prime Mover when we decided of our own volition to rebel against Him (Paragraphs 391 - 395 of the Catechism).

"We all understood each one of us exactly what we were doing. Humans on the other hand are created with brains that they must then learn to use. They are therefore in a position to pick and chose what they want to embrace intellectually, and they must factor in their conscience. And that is what is at play here. We in the celestial realm can't be disingenuous and try to cloud our vision. But humans, exploiting their nature, have become masters of disingenuity, and don't see any shame in positing and then believing in a hackneyed and wacky theory like that which attributes creation to a 'big bang'.

"They cannot of course argue against the maxim 'Nemo dat quod non habet' which means that no one gives what he/she does not have, and which

81

also sounds the same as 'Nothing can come out of nothing'. But they won't concede that there was a Prime Mover behind everything they touch, see, feel, smell or hear either. And even though fashioned in the image of the Prime Mover, they don't even know it, and they don't seem to have a clue that He exists, and that everything they touch, see, feel, smell or hear would cease to exist the instant the Prime Mover was excluded from the picture - this is in the exact same way a human's supernatural life of virtue requires the Divine help of grace with which the Christian must freely cooperate to advance by slow degrees in perfection (John 3:5; 1 John 3:9; 2 Peter 1:1-11).

"Humans like to describe themselves as *animal rationale*. Actually that is only partially true. While they are 'rational animals' all right, humans need to recognize that, in addition to using their faculties of reason and free will, to attain self-actualization they must also perforce tap their potential as 'faith' creatures. It is apparently only the 'odd ones' who seem able to do this! It is the odd ones who are with the Apostle of the Gentiles when he writes: 'And as in Adam all die, so also in Christ all shall be made alive. But every one in his own order: the first fruits Christ, then they that are of Christ, who have believed in his coming.' (1 Corinthians 15:22-23)

"Before making that point, Paul had stated: 'But, as it is written: That eye hath not seen, nor ear heard, neither hath it entered into the heart of man, what things God hath prepared for them that love him.

But to us God hath revealed them, by this Spirit. For the Spirit searcheth all things, yea, the deep things of God. For what man knoweth the things of a man, but the spirit of a man that is in him? So the things also that are of God no man knoweth, but the Spirit of God. Now we have received not the spirit of this world, but the Spirit that is of God; that we may know the things that are given us from God. Which things also we speak, not in the learned words of human wisdom; but in the doctrine of the Spirit, comparing spiritual things with spiritual.' (1 Corinthians 2:9-13)

"Paul, a Hebrew and also a Roman citizen who had been intent on persecuting the risen Deliverer's disciples and the Deliverer Himself in the process (Acts 9:4, Acts 22:7 and Acts 26:14) and now a self-styled 'Apostle to the Gentiles', did not stop there. And he didn't mince any words as he explained the condition of humans.

"In his missive to the Hebrews He had gone on: 'Now faith is the substance of things to be hoped for, the evidence of things that appear not. For by this the ancients obtained a testimony. By faith we understand that the world was framed by the word of God; that from invisible things visible things might be made. By faith Abel offered to God a sacrifice exceeding that of Cain, by which he obtained a testimony that he was just, God giving testimony to his gifts; and by it he being dead yet speaketh. By faith Henoch was translated, that he should not see death; and he was not found, because God had translated him: for before his translation he had testimony that he pleased God.

'But without faith it is impossible to please God. For he that cometh to God, must believe that he is, and is a rewarder to them that seek him. By faith Noe, having received an answer concerning those things which as yet were not seen, moved with fear, framed the ark for the saving of his house, by the which he condemned the world; and was instituted heir of the justice which is by faith. By faith _he that is called Abraham_, obeyed to go out into a place which he was to receive for an inheritance; and he went out, not knowing whither he went. By faith he abode in the land, dwelling in cottages, with Isaac and Jacob, the co-heirs of the same promise. For he looked for a city that hath foundations; whose builder and maker is God. By faith also Sara herself, being barren, received strength to conceive seed, even past the time of age; because she believed that he was faithful who had promised, for which cause there sprung even from one (and him as good as dead) as the stars of heaven in multitude, and as the sand which is by the sea shore innumerable. All these died according to faith, not having received the promises, but beholding them afar off, and saluting them, and confessing that they are pilgrims and strangers on the earth. For they that say these things, do signify that they seek a country. And truly if they had been mindful of that from whence they came out, they had doubtless time to return.

'But now they desire a better, that is to say, a heavenly country. Therefore God is not ashamed to be called their God; for he hath prepared for them a city. By faith Abraham, when he was tried, offered Isaac: and he that had received the promises, offered up his only begotten son. (To whom it was said: In Isaac shall thy seed be called.) Accounting that God is able to raise up even from the dead. Whereupon also he received him *for a parable*. By faith also of things to come, Isaac blessed Jacob and Esau.

'By faith Jacob dying, blessed each of the sons of Joseph, and *adored the top of his rod*. By faith Joseph, when he was dying, made mention of the going out of the children of Israel; and gave commandment concerning his bones. By faith Moses, when he was born, was hid three months by his parents; because they saw he was a comely babe, and they feared not the king's edict. By faith Moses, when he was grown up, denied himself to be the son of Pharao's daughter; rather choosing to be afflicted with the people of God, than to have the pleasure of sin for a time, esteeming the reproach of Christ greater riches than the treasure of the Egyptians. For he looked unto the reward. By faith he left Egypt, not fearing the fierceness of the king: for he endured as seeing him that is invisible. By faith he celebrated the pasch, and the shedding of the blood; that he, who destroyed the firstborn, might not touch them. By faith they passed through the Red Sea, as by dry land: which the Egyptians attempting, were swallowed up. By faith the walls of Jericho fell down, by the going round them seven days.

'By faith Rahab the harlot perished not with the

unbelievers, receiving the spies with peace. And what shall I yet say? For the time would fail me to tell of Gedeon, Barac, Samson, Jephthe, David, Samuel, and the prophets: who by faith conquered kingdoms, wrought justice, obtained promises, stopped the mouths of lions, quenched the violence of fire, escaped the edge of the sword, recovered strength from weakness, became valiant in battle, put to flight the armies of foreigners: women received their dead raised to life again. But others were racked, not accepting deliverance, that they might find a better resurrection.

'And others had trial of mockeries and stripes, moreover also of bands and prisons. They were stoned, they were cut asunder, they were tempted, they were put to death by the sword, they wandered about in sheepskins, in goatskins, being in want, distressed, afflicted: of whom the world was not worthy; wandering in deserts, in mountains, and in dens, and in caves of the earth. And all these being approved by the testimony of faith, received not the promise; God providing some better thing for us, that they should not be perfected without us.' (Hebrews 11:1-40)

"And it was not by accident that Simon Peter, the son of John, who had been singled out by the Deliver and had been formally charged with the all important task of 'feeding His sheep' (John 21:17), writing to the 'chosen sojourners of the dispersion in Pontus, Galatia, Cappadocia, Asia, and Bithynia' *ex cathedra*, had stated: 'Wherefore it is said in the scripture: Behold, I lay in Sion a chief corner stone, elect, precious. And he that shall believe in him, shall not be confounded. To you therefore that believe, he is honour: but to them that believe not, the stone which the builders rejected, the same is made the head of the corner: And a stone of stumbling, and a rock of scandal, to them who stumble at the word, neither do believe, whereunto also they are set. But you are a chosen generation, a kingly priesthood, a holy nation, a purchased people: that you may declare his virtues, who hath called you out of darkness into his marvellous light: Who in time past were not a people: but are now the people of God. Who had not obtained mercy; but now have obtained mercy.' (1 Peter 2:6-10)

"The Deliverer was Himself dismayed at the inability of his disciples to heal the poor child into whom I had entered, and who was described by his father as a lunatic who really suffered much as a result. The decisive moment came when his disciples asked Him in confidence out of sight of the crowds saying: 'Why could not we cast him out?' He lamented: 'O unbelieving and perverse generation. How long shall I be with you? How long shall I suffer you?' (Mark 9:14-29; Luke 9:37-42; Luke 17:5-10).

"And elsewhere the Deliverer had told his disciples: 'Amen, I say to you, if you shall have faith, and stagger not, not only this of the fig tree shall you do, but also if you shall say to this mountain, Take up and cast thyself into the sea, it shall be done.' (Matthew 21:21) And again: 'Amen I say to you, if you have faith as a grain of mustard seed, you shall say to this mountain, Remove from hence hither, and it shall remove; and nothing shall be impossible to you.' (Matthew 17:20).

"Actually the gift of 'Faith' makes all the difference for humans as the episode of the Feeding of the Five Thousand, described by the Apostle John (and mirrored in all the synoptic gospels) clearly showed: 'The next day, the multitude that stood on the other side of the sea, saw that there was no other ship there but one, and that Jesus had not entered into the ship with his disciples, but that his disciples were gone away alone. But other ships came in from Tiberias; nigh unto the place where they had eaten the bread, the Lord giving thanks. When therefore the multitude saw that Jesus was not there, nor his disciples, they took shipping, and came to Capharnaum, seeking for Jesus. And when they had found him on the other side of the sea, they said to him: Rabbi, when camest thou hither?

'Jesus answered them, and said: Amen, amen I say to you, you seek me, not because you have seen miracles, but because you did eat of the loaves, and were filled. Labour not for the meat which perisheth, but for that which endureth unto life everlasting, which the Son of man will give you. For him hath God, the Father, sealed. They said therefore unto him: What shall we do, that we may work the works of God? Jesus answered, and said to them: This is the work of God, that you believe in him whom he hath sent. They said therefore to him: What sign therefore dost thou shew, that we may see, and may believe thee? What dost thou work? Our fathers did eat manna in the desert, as it is written: He gave them bread from heaven to eat. Then Jesus said to them: Amen, amen I say to you; Moses gave you not bread from heaven, but my Father giveth you the true bread from heaven. For the bread of God is that which cometh down from heaven, and giveth life to the world. They said therefore unto him: Lord, give us always this bread.

'And Jesus said to them: I am the bread of life: he that cometh to me shall not hunger: and he that believeth in me shall never thirst. But I said unto you, that you also have seen me, and you believe not. All that the Father giveth to me shall come to me; and him that cometh to me, I will not cast out. Because I came down from heaven, not to do my own will, but the will of him that sent me. Now this is the will of the Father who sent me: that of all that he hath given me, I should lose nothing; but should raise it up again in the last day. And this is the will of my Father that sent me: that every one who seeth the Son, and believeth in him, may have life everlasting, and I will raise him up in the last day.

'The Jews therefore murmured at him, because he had said: I am the living bread which came down from heaven. And they said: Is not this Jesus, the son of Joseph, whose father and mother we know? How then saith he, I came down from heaven? Jesus therefore answered, and said to them: Murmur not among yourselves. No man can come to me, except the Father, who hath sent me, draw him; and I will raise him up in the last day. It is written in the prophets: And they shall all be taught of God. Every one that hath heard of the Father, and hath learned, cometh to me. Not that any man hath seen the Father; but he who is of God, he hath seen the Father. Amen, amen I say unto you: He that believeth in me, hath everlasting life. I am the bread of life. Your fathers did eat manna in the desert, and are dead. This is the bread which cometh down from heaven; that if any man eat of it, he may not die. I am the living bread which came down from heaven. If any man eat of this bread, he shall live for ever; and the bread that I will give, is my flesh, for the life of the world.

'The Jews therefore strove among themselves, saying: How can this man give us his flesh to eat? Then Jesus said to them: Amen, amen I say unto you: Except you eat the flesh of the Son of man, and drink his blood, you shall not have life in you. He that eateth my flesh, and drinketh my blood, hath everlasting life: and I will raise him up in the last day. For my flesh is meat indeed: and my blood is drink indeed. He that eateth my flesh, and drinketh my blood, abideth in me, and I in him. As the living Father hath sent me, and I live by the Father; so he that eateth me, the same also shall live by me. This is the bread that came down from heaven. Not as your fathers did eat manna, and are dead. He that eateth this bread, shall live for ever. These things he said, teaching in the synagogue, in Capharnaum.

'Many therefore of his disciples, hearing it, said: This saying is hard, and who can hear it? But Jesus, knowing in himself, that his disciples murmured at this, said to them: Doth this scandalize you? If then you shall see the Son of Man ascend up where he was before? It is the spirit that quickeneth: the flesh profiteth nothing. The words that I have spoken to you, are spirit and life. But there are some of you that believe not. For Jesus knew from the beginning, who they were that did not believe, and who he was, that would betray him. And he said: Therefore did I say to you, that no man can come to me, unless it be given him by my Father.

'After this many of his disciples went back; and walked no more with him. Then Jesus said to the twelve: Will you also go away? And Simon Peter answered him: Lord, to whom shall we go? thou hast the words of eternal life. And we have believed and have known, that thou art the Christ, the Son of God. Jesus answered them: Have not I chosen you twelve; and one of you is a devil? Now he meant Judas Iscariot, the son of Simon: for this same was about to betray him, whereas he was one of the twelve.' (John 6:22-71)

"But Matthew's account was particularly telling: 'And Jesus came into the quarters of Cesarea Philippi: and he asked his disciples, saying: Whom do men say that the Son of man is? But they said: Some John the Baptist, and some Elias, and others Jeremias, or one of the prophets. Jesus saith to them: But whom do you say that I am? Simon Peter answered and said: Thou art Christ, the Son of the living God. And Jesus answering, said to him:

Blessed art thou, Simon Bar-Jona: because flesh and blood hath not revealed it to thee, but my Father who is in heaven. And I say to thee: That thou art Peter; and upon this rock I will build my church, and the gates of hell shall not prevail against it. And I will give to thee the keys of the kingdom of heaven. And whatsoever thou shalt bind upon earth, it shall be bound also in heaven: and whatsoever thou shalt loose upon earth, it shall be loosed also in heaven. Then he commanded his disciples, that they should tell no one that he was Jesus the Christ.' (Matthew 16:13-20).

"Generations of humans going back to the time of Adam and Eve and linked by great great grand parents and great great grand children have this one thing in common. Each generation has been distinguished one from the other by, among other things, the appearance of messengers of the Prime Mover or 'prophets' or 'psalmists' whose mission was to have the nation of Israel and along with it the rest of humanity know that even though humans had incurred the Prime Mover's wrath with the fall from grace of Adam and Eve, help was on the way in the shape of the promised Messiah.

"Following the fall from grace of Adam and Eve, that was the very least that the Non-Creature and Master Craftsman could do for the 'poor banished children of Eve' as humans are described in the Marian antiphon Salve Regina (Hail Holy Queen).

"With the inauguration of the *Sancta Ecclesia* two thousand years ago, some of these messengers have ended up being formally canonized and celebrated as 'saints' by the faithful who themselves were referred to as 'saints' in the Early Church (Acts 9:32; Acts 9:13; Acts 26:10; Matthew 27:52).

"The Deliverer had, of course, warned His disciples saying: 'Many false prophets shall rise, and shall seduce many. And because iniquity hath abounded, the charity of many shall grow cold. But he that shall persevere to the end, he shall be saved. And this gospel of the kingdom, shall be preached in the whole world, for a testimony to all nations, and then shall the consummation come' (Matthew 24:11-14).

"But in the meantime, as in the days before the flood, till the times of the nations are fulfilled (Luke 21:24) foreboding the coming in a cloud, with great power and majesty, of the Son of man (Luke 21:27)), humans will be eating and drinking, marrying and giving in marriage (Matthew 24:38).

"The crowds that had resolved to keep up with the Deliverer wherever he went and not let Him out of sight were of one mind regarding the Nazarene. Judging by His works, he had to be one of those messengers of the Prime Mover!

"But the Deliverer had just given strict instructions to His disciples to the effect that they stay mum as concerning the fact that He was Jesus the Christ referred to by the prophets (Genesis 3:15, Genesis 14:17-20 Isaiah 9:6, Isaiah 7:14, Isaiah 50:6, Isaiah 53:3-7, Zechariah 9:9, Micah 5:2, Psalm 22:16-18). Clearly He wanted His generation and all future generations to discern from His words and actions that 'before Abraham was made, He is (John 8:51) and that if any man keep His word, he shall not see death for ever (John 8:58); and that He is the Word that was made flesh and dwelt among humans (John 1:14) and that He speaks that which He has seen with His Father (John 8:38). He wanted His disciples to understand that His grace was sufficient for that to happen! (2 Corinthians 12:9).

"And, even after the Savior of humankind would say 'It is consummated' (John19:30) and, bowing his head, give up the ghost, and then, after rising up from the dead, give a send-off to His *Sancta Ecclesia* by providing final instructions regarding the Sacrament of Baptism and the Holy Spirit's role in it, amongst other things, His disciples needed to remember the admonition He gave them when sending them to preach to the 'lost sheep of the house of Israel.' (Matthew 10:6).

"Those instructions went thus: 'Do not possess gold, nor silver, nor money in your purses: Nor scrip for your journey, nor two coats, nor shoes, nor a staff; for the workman is worthy of his meat. And into whatsoever city or town you shall enter, inquire who in it is worthy, and there abide till you go thence. And when you come into the house, salute it, saying: Peace be to this house. And if that house be worthy, your peace shall come upon it; but if it be not worthy, your peace shall return to you. And whosoever shall not receive you, nor hear your words: going forth out of that house or city shake off the dust from your feet.'

(Matthew 10:9-14). They would, in other words, need to remember always that the graces he merited for humans with His death on the cross were enough so long as they did their part as instructed.

"There are, of course, those for whom everything in the Sacred Scriptures, starting with the Book of Genesis penned by Moses and ending with the Book of Revelation (or the Apocalypse) that was penned by John the 'Evangelist' and last apostle to die, belong in mythology. Well, the references by the Deliverer Himself to Noah and to the Flood (Luke 17:26-27 and Matthew 24:36-44) in and of themselves make quick work of that false proposition.

"So there really was someone called Noah, and the flood is an event that really occurred! You just heard it first hand from the Deliverer - the *Logos* - that it sure did. One has to conclude that the other stories in the Book of Genesis aren't spurious either.

"This has to be tough for those humans who can't wrap their heads around the fact that the flood as described in the Book of Genesis is a historical event, and that Noah, who is also mentioned in the First Book of Chronicles, and the books of Tobit, Wisdom, Sirach, Isaiah, Ezekiel, 2 Esdras, 4 Maccabees, and in the New Testament in the Gospel of Matthew, the Gospel of Luke, the Epistle to the Hebrews (by whoever), and in the first and second epistles of the first pope actually lived, and is not an entirely mythological figure. By the same token, humans must be prepared for the Doomsday referred to in Ezek. 32:7, Joel 2:10, 3:15, Amos 5:20, Zeph.

1:15, Luke 12:4–5, Luke 12:49, Luke 13:23–28, Luke 21:22-24, Matthew 3:10–12, Matthew 7:13–23, Matthew 13:40–43, Matthew 24:3, Matthew 24:4-14, Matthew 24:21-37, Matthew 25:31–36, Matthew 25:45–46, Mark 13:19, Revelation 20:11–12 John 3:16, John 14:2, Acts 2:20, 1 Thessalonians 5:1-9, 1 Thessalonians 5:2, 2 Peter 3:1-18 (and elsewhere) as surely as new generations of humans are born and old generations of humans cross the gulf that separates the living from the dead and head to their judgment.

"Of course many humans dismiss even that; and even though they are aware that they are changing by the minute and are getting a little older every second of their lives, when they don't believe in the transmigration of souls, they like to con themselves that when the end comes, they will go back into the nothingness from which they came, the fact that they are created in the image of the Non-Creature and Master Craftsman notwithstanding. That vain and fruitless attempt to dodge the looming and certain encounter with the victorious Son of Man who will be seated at the right hand of the Father on that day of reckoning quite clearly won't work, as every human must needs render an accounting for the manner in which he/she employed his/her talents on that Day of reckoning.

"In his letter to the Romans, Paul explains that feigning ignorance will not help. He writes: "For not the hearers of the law are just before God, but the doers of the law shall be justified. For when the

Gentiles, who have not the law, do by nature those things that are of the law; these having not the law are a law to themselves: Who shew the work of the law written in their hearts, their conscience bearing witness to them, and their thoughts between themselves accusing, or also defending one another, in the day when God shall judge the secrets of men by Jesus Christ, according to my gospel.' (Romans 2:13-16).

"And then there is this other problem. In His response to His disciples on Mt. Olivet (when they came to him privately, saying: 'Tell us when shall these things be? and what shall be the sign of thy coming, and of the consummation of the world?'), the Deliverer said amongst other things: 'And when the Son of Man shall come in his majesty, and all the angels with him, then shall he sit upon the seat of his majesty. And all nations shall be gathered together before him, and he shall separate them one from another, as the shepherd separateth the sheep from the goats: And he shall set the sheep on his right hand, but the goats on his left.

'Then shall the king say to them that shall be on his right hand: Come, ye blessed of my Father, possess you the kingdom prepared for you from the foundation of the world. For I was hungry, and you gave me to eat; I was thirsty, and you gave me to drink; I was a stranger, and you took me in: Naked, and you covered me: sick, and you visited me: I was in prison, and you came to me. Then shall the just answer him, saying: Lord, when did we see thee

97

hungry, and fed thee; thirsty, and gave thee drink? And when did we see thee a stranger, and took thee in? or naked, and covered thee? Or when did we see thee sick or in prison, and came to thee? And the king answering, shall say to them: Amen I say to you, as long as you did it to one of these my least brethren, you did it to me.

'Then he shall say to them also that shall be on his left hand: Depart from me, you cursed, into everlasting fire which was prepared for the devil and his angels. For I was hungry, and you gave me not to eat: I was thirsty, and you gave me not to drink. I was a stranger, and you took me not in: naked, and you covered me not: sick and in prison, and you did not visit me. Then they also shall answer him, saying: Lord, when did we see thee hungry, or thirsty, or a stranger, or naked, or sick, or in prison, and did not minister to thee? Then he shall answer them, saying: Amen I say to you, as long as you did it not to one of these least, neither did you do it to me. And these shall go into everlasting punishment: but the just, into life everlasting.' (Matthew 25:31-46)

"That is to say, on Doomsday (and I am not referring to the 2008 science fiction action horror movie that Neil Marshall wrote and directed), all humankind will be split up into just two groups, one that will be to the right of the 'King' and one that will be to His left. Whilst on the pilgrimage on earth (and you might as well refer to it as 'trial on earth' because my troops and I are alert and watching their every move and ready to pounce), every human action and deed matters in anticipation of that fateful Day of Reckoning. Humans decide by their thought, word and deed if they want to end up on the right side of the throne on which the Saviour of the world will be seated or on the left side. (Matthew 5:21-22; Matthew 7:15-23; Matthew 12:36-37; Luke 6:43-45; and Colossians 3:17).

"Thomas Aquinas, the Angelic Doctor who because he was 'big, quiet and slow to speak' had earned the nickname 'dumb ox" from his teacher St. Albert the Great, called sin, "An utterance, a deed or a desire contrary to the eternal law." (ST I-II, 71:6). He added: 'Accordingly sins are divided into these three, viz. sins of thought, word, and deed, not as into various complete species: for the consummation of sin is in the deed, wherefore sins of deed have the complete species; but the first beginning of sin is its foundation, as it were, in the sin of thought; the second degree is the sin of word, in so far as man is ready to break out into a declaration of his thought; while the third degree consists in the consummation of the deed. Consequently these three differ in respect of the various degrees of sin. Nevertheless it is evident that these three belong to the one complete species of sin, since they proceed from the same motive. For the angry man, through desire of vengeance, is at first disturbed in thought, then he breaks out into words of abuse, and lastly he goes on to wrongful deeds; and the same applies to lust and to any other sin.' (Q.72, Article 7, Summa Theologica)

"The apostles were in the seminary for only three years; and yet they all without exception ended up professing the same 'Apostle's creed'! Clearly the Son of Man was not your ordinary seminary professor. You recall the episode described in Matthew 4:2 when He spent forty days and forty nights in the desert fasting and praying to His Father in heaven for the success of His mission on earth. And then there was something special going on over the period of forty days between His resurrection and His ascension into heaven. He was undoubtedly quite busy giving instructions to His disciples on the way forward during that time.

"And then, true to His word, He kept His promise regarding the Holy Ghost. He had told them: 'But I tell you the truth: it is expedient to you that I go: for if I go not, the Paraclete will not come to you; but if I go, I will send him to you. And when he is come, he will convince the world of sin, and of justice, and of judgment. Of sin: because they believed not in me. And of justice: because I go to the Father; and you shall see me no longer. And of judgment: because the prince of this world is already judged. (John 16:7-11). The fulfillment of that promise saw His disciples speaking in tongues to the multitudes that were gathered in Jerusalem from the known world for the feast of the Passover. (Acts 2:1-13). The stupid ones in the crowd thought that the Deliverer's disciples were just drunk with new wine! And clearly they would not be the last ones.

"Addressing Zachary in the sanctuary of the

temple as that old descendant of Aaron prepared to offer incense, the angel Gabriel said to him: 'Fear not, Zachary, for thy prayer is heard; and thy wife Elizabeth shall bear thee a son, and thou shalt call his name John: And thou shalt have joy and gladness, and many shall rejoice in his nativity. For he shall be great before the Lord; and shall drink no wine nor strong drink: and he shall be filled with the Holy Ghost, even from his mother's womb.' (Luke 1:13-15). His son John, the Forerunner of the Deliverer, would be filled with the Holy Spirit whilst in his mother's womb!

"Six months later, the same angel Gabriel appeared to a virgin espoused to a man whose name was Joseph, of the house of David; and the virgin's name was Mary. He started his salutation with the words 'Hail, full of grace, the Lord is with thee: blessed art thou among women.' Not longer afterward, when Joseph was troubled upon noticing that Mary was actually expecting, and was troubled in spirit, the angel of the Lord appeared to him in his sleep and said: 'Joseph, son of David, fear not to take unto thee Mary thy wife, for that which is conceived in her, is of the Holy Ghost.'

"Like all humans, with the sole exception of Adam (the first man) and Eve (the first woman), the Son of Man had started out as an embryo and then graduated into a foetus before He saw the first light of day as He lay in a manger in Bethlehem. He was not fathered by Joseph and would therefore have been a prime candidate for as an abortion today; and that despite the word of the Lord that came upon Jeremiah, saying: 'Before I formed thee in the bowels of thy mother, I knew thee: and before thou camest forth out of the womb, I sanctified thee, and made thee a prophet unto the nations.

"And, regarding His own appearance on earth, the Son of Man, talking to Nicodemus, Himself said: '*Sic enim Deus dilexit mundum, ut Filium suum unigenitum daret: ut omnis qui credit in eum, non pereat, sed habeat vitam æternam. Non enim misit Deus Filium suum in mundum, ut judicet mundum, sed ut salvetur mundus per ipsum. Qui credit in eum, non judicatur; qui autem non credit, jam judicatus est: quia non credit in nomine unigeniti Filii Dei. Hoc est autem judicium: quia lux venit in mundum, et dilexerunt homines magis tenebras quam lucem: erant enim eorum mala opera. Omnis enim qui male agit, odit lucem, et non venit ad lucem, ut non arguantur opera ejus: qui autem facit veritatem, venit ad lucem, ut manifestentur opera ejus, quia in Deo sunt facta.*' (For God so loved the world, as to give his only begotten Son; that whosoever believeth in him, may not perish, but may have life everlasting. For God sent not his Son into the world, to judge the world, but that the world may be saved by him. He that believeth in him is not judged. But he that doth not believe, is already judged: because he believeth not in the name of the only begotten Son of God. And this is the judgment: because the light is come into the world, and men loved darkness rather than the light: for their works were evil. For every one that doth evil

102

hateth the light, and cometh not to the light, that his works may not be reproved. But he that doth truth, cometh to the light, that his works may be made manifest, because they are done in God.) (John 3:16-21)

"If there are any witnesses to the fact that human life, starting from conception right up to the moment humans in the Prime Mover's own time cross the gulf that separates the living from the dead, is sacred, it is the Deliverer Himself first and foremost, the Second Person of the Blessed Trinity, the only Son of God, eternally begotten of the Father, God from God, Light from Light, true God from true God, begotten, not made, consubstantial of one Being with the Father; through whom all things were made; and Who for humans and for their salvation came down from heaven, and by the Holy Spirit was incarnate of the Virgin Mary, and became man. And then there is His Blessed Virgin Mother who, when the Angel of the Lord declared unto her, conceived of the Holy Spirit. And finally there is John the Baptist, the forerunner of the Deliverer. Even though no more than a 5-month old baby (or so-called 'foetus') in his mother Elizabeth's womb, he very nearly caused her problems when he started jumping up and down with joy at the sound of the salutation of the visiting mother of the promised Saviour of the world! (Luke 1:41).

"No wonder the criteria for whether folks will be ending up to the right (with the sheep) or to the left (with the goats) will be the extent to which humans were prepared to keep the Deliverer's

103

commandments and in particular the commandment to love fellow humans among whom he Himself was now counted.

"But, going back to Peter's testimony, it was the Non-Creature and Master Craftsman - the Son of Man's Father in heaven - who had given the erstwhile fisherman the revelation and about Whom the Apostle to the Gentiles wrote: 'O the depth of the riches of the wisdom and of the knowledge of God! How incomprehensible are his judgments, and how unsearchable his ways! For who hath known the mind of the Lord? Or who hath been his counselor? Or who hath first given to him, and recompense shall be made him?' (Romans 11:33-35). And it was none other than Him Who revealed to Peter that that Jesus was Christ, the Son of the living God. And He it was Who would reveal this to all humankind, both Jew and Gentile.

"And it is not said anywhere about any other 'church' or religious assembly that I, the Ruler of Hades, shall not prevail against it. It is only the Sancta Ecclesia that the Deliverer was going to build on the Rock called Peter, the Church of Rome, that, like it or not, I and my troops in the netherworld can never prevail against.

"The Non-Creature and Master Craftsman formed man in His own likeness and set him over the whole world to serve Him, man's creator, and to rule over all creatures. Even when man disobeyed Him and lost His friendship, He did not abandon him to the power of death, but helped all men to seek and find

Him. Again and again He offered a covenant to man, and through the prophets taught him to hope for salvation. The Prime Mover so loved the world that in the fullness of time He sent His only Son to be their Savior. He was conceived through the power of the Holy Spirit, and born of the Virgin Mary, a man like them in all things but sin. To the poor He proclaimed the good news of salvation, to prisoners, freedom, and to those in sorrow, joy. In fulfillment of His Father's will, He gave Himself up to death; but by rising from the dead, He destroyed death and restored life. And that humans might live no longer for themselves but for Him, He sent the Holy Spirit from His Father, as His first gift to those humans who believe, to complete His work on earth and bring humans the fullness of grace.

"Still, by the time humans will be able to connect atoms and molecules to the fact that there is a Prime Mover behind everything they touch, see, feel, smell, or hear, and to see that they are *animal rationale expressam esse, et opus fidei in se* (rational animals who need faith for self-actualization), it will be too late. The end of the world will already be at hand! This is the extent to which the human experiment has ended up a total fiasco and an unmitigated disaster! Paul summarizes their philosophy quite neatly: 'Let us eat and drink, since we must die to-morrow.' (1 Corinthians 15:32).

"It was because humans, fashioned in the image and likeness of the Prime Mover, had gravitated to what was close to a total write-off that

105

He essentially decided to start all over again in their regard, sending His only begotten Son to earth to redeem them. With the fall from grace of Adam and Eve, humans, inclined to sin and incapable of accomplishing any good without the help of the Prime Mover's grace, were a total write-off. And not surprisingly, they couldn't wait to try and rub Him out. He even hastened to let His disciples know what was in store for Him saying: '*Non potest mundus odisse vos me autem odit, quia ego testimonium perhibeo de illo quia opera eius mala sunt.*' (The world cannot hate you: but me it hateth, because I give testimony of it, that the works thereof are evil.) (John 7:7).

"The other point that I, as Ruler of the Underworld, would like to make is the disparity in the treatment that I and the other celestial comrades who joined me in my rebellion received and the treatment that humans (who were, like ourselves, also fashioned in His Own Image and likeness) received despite all the dreadful things they do to each other and to His messengers including the Son of Man. It is certainly indicative of the heights from which we ourselves fell. Isaiah described it pretty accurately when he wrote: 'Thy pride is brought down to hell, thy carcass is fallen down: under thee shall the moth be strewed, and worms shall be thy covering. How art thou fallen from heaven, O Lucifer, who didst rise in the morning? How art thou fallen to the earth, that didst wound the nations? And thou saidst in thy heart: I will ascend into heaven, I will exalt my throne above the stars of God, I will sit in the mountain of the

106

covenant, in the sides of the north. I will ascend above the height of the clouds, I will be like the Most High. But yet thou shalt be brought down to hell, into the depth of the pit. (Isaiah 14:11-15)

"Our intransigence was admittedly also of a nature that could not possibly be forgiven, leading the Almighty One to cast us into the fires of hell without any further ado. So, it really wasn't simply a case of the Prime Mover going out of His way to treat you humans with kid gloves while making us an example of how He can be unpleasant. My troops and I knew before we fell from grace that our sin was unforgivable.

"But even though this was quite clear to us, we couldn't help daring Him to cast us out of His presence - because we thought we were indispensable! He had created us so wondrous and captivating, we didn't think He would go to the extent of casting us out of His sight just like that. He had made us so dizzyingly and so spectacularly and so awesomely beautiful as beautiful creatures go, we were tempted to imagine that He had done it impulsively and had made us what was tantamount to the 'apple of His eye' because He couldn't help it! We thought that the Almighty One needed such wondrous creatures around Him, instead of being humble and accepting that, lacking nothing Himself, He had deigned to bring us into existence out of His infinite goodness and love, so that we too would have a chance to share in that awesome goodness and awesome love. Instead we decided of our own volition to turn into traitors who were ready to try and stab the Non-Creature and Master Craftsman in the back!

"But you humans might do well to also note that the gravity and magnitude of our offence against the Prime Mover in all probability are things that are beyond the comprehension of even the most brilliant humans like Einstein or Thomas Aquinas.

"Quite apart from the fact that we were created pure spirits, we were gifted at creation with the grandeur and majesty that just fell short of making us gods! We were created with splendor that you humans cannot fathom. The *raison d'etre* of our existence was to minister directly to the Almighty One both for His glory and for our self-actualization. When we rebelled, we were caught off guard as Michael, the warrior archangel, leading an army of faithful angels (Revelation 12:7) and with the trumpet of God, sent us scurrying for our 'safety' (or so we imagined then) into the 'lake of fire' (20:14-15). We realized - too late - that we had done ourselves in; that, while we needed the Almighty One for our actualization, He had brought us into existence out of His infinite goodness and He did not need us at all. And, oh! So great was our fall!

"Unlike you humans who were created in the Prime Mover's image and likeness so that you would be able to do things that redound to His greater glory and honor while eschewing anything and everything however enticing that you might favor above Him (like the 'Forbidden Fruit' which caused Adam and Eve to trip), the nine orders of celestial creatures (namely Angels, Archangels, Virtues, Powers, Principalities, Dominations, Throne, Cherubim and Seraphim among whom we demons once counted) were fashioned in the Almighty's image and likeness in order that we would minister to Him without ceasing when we were not acting as His messengers.

"And we are not talking about ministering to some earthly potentate here. We are talking about creatures being brought into existence who would minister to Him who said 'ego sum qui sum' (I am Who am) (Exodus 3:14) and is all knowing, infinitely good - infinitely everything and is incomprehensible (Romans 11:33). He is incomprehensible to our celestial minds that are of quite a different order from human minds. Your human minds rely on your physical senses that have all those limitations.

"And look, when Adam and Eve fell from grace, I was dangling a fruit - I mean a 'fruit' albeit one plucked from the Tree of Knowledge of Good and Evil - in front of their eyes! That is definitely not something we pure spirits would have fallen for. That should give you an idea about the extent to which we celestial creatures were endowed at creation compared to you humans. The only exception is that woman whose seed would crush my seed - and also bruise my head. Leaving the Son of Man aside, she is the only human who ministered directly to the Almighty One from the first moment of her existence.

"Born to Joachim and Anne who were ordinary mortals, she herself was no ordinary mortal; and she herself said as much to the mother of John the Baptist: '*Magnificat anima mea Dominum et exultavit spiritus meus in Deo salutari meo quia respexit humilitatem ancillae suae ecce enim ex hoc beatam me dicent omnes generationes quia fecit mihi magna qui potens est et sanctum nomen eius.*' (My soul doth magnify the Lord. And my spirit hath rejoiced in God my Savior. Because he hath regarded the humility of his handmaid: for behold from henceforth all generations shall call me blessed. Because he that is mighty hath done great things to me: and holy is his name.) (Luke 1:46-49).

"Crowned queen of heaven as Pope Pius XII confirmed in his encyclical *Ad Caeli Reginam* (Queenship of Mary in Heaven), her son was the 'Son of the Most High'. And for anyone who might have had any doubt, in his Apocalypse, the Apostle John was commanded to write: '*Et signum magnum paruit in caelo mulier amicta sole et luna sub pedibus eius et in capite eius corona stellarum duodecim.*' (And a great sign appeared in heaven: A woman clothed with the sun, and the moon under her feet, and on her head a crown of twelve stars.) Revelation 12:1. And sure enough, the Holy Ghost came upon her, and the power of the Most High overshadowed her and her son was called the Son of God'. (Luke 1:35). She beat us to it indeed.

"But even then, the Psalmist would write about the 'son of man' thus: 'Thou hast made him a little less than the angels, thou hast crowned him with glory and honor: and hast set him over the works of thy hands.'

110

(Psalm 8:5-6). So there you have it from the horse's mouth so to speak - that we celestial creatures were created really grand; and that whilst humans too were created such that the Prime Mover was quite pleased with the product, they was really no comparison.

"Regardless, given the way humans have detested their own kind from time immemorial beginning with Cain's murder of his brother Abel and extending to the horrors of war that have defined relations between nations ever since, we ourselves here in the Underworld have oftentimes feared that humans were out to try and outdo us in devilishness.

"And humans are 'bad to the bone' not because *Homo sapiens* evolved from a particularly brutish branch of mammals as some of the 'new research' claims, but because they do not stop to reflect on what they are and to pay homage to the Prime Mover. The Deliverer indicated that Isaiah had prophesied correctly of humans when he wrote: 'This people honoureth me with their lips: but their heart is far from me. And in vain do they worship me, teaching doctrines and commandments of men.' (Matthew 15:8-9). But the Son of Man still went ahead and taught them how to pray. The problem is that when humans recite the *Pater Noster*, they do it while their hearts and minds are elsewhere - on matters that promise to them material success in a world many believe has gone crazy and out of control. As if the Son of Man did not teach them saying: 'But seek ye first the kingdom of God and his justice, and all these things shall be added unto you.' (Luke 12:31). 'Seek

111

ye therefore first the kingdom of God, and his justice, and all these things shall be added unto you.' (Matthew 6:33).

"And I often observe those whose hearts and minds were on matters that promised material success as they 'prayed' instead of concentrating on the words of the *Pater Noster* become frustrated by the unfair treatment they receive from bigoted business partners, fellow workers and crooked supervisors. I always try to seize those opportunities to blind humans to the fact that those undeserved frustrations that evil people inflict on them are actually answers to their *Pater Noster*. They must not see that it is a sign that they have been singled out by the Prime Mover to share in the redemptive pain and sufferings endured by the Son of Man on the cross when they are visited by misfortunes!

"They were told" 'Ask, and it shall be given you: seek, and you shall find: knock, and it shall be opened to you.' (Matthew 7:7). And the Deliverer had said: 'If you then being evil, know how to give good gifts to your children: how much more will your Father who is in heaven, give good things to them that ask him?' (Matthew 7:11).

"Well, we here in the underworld wouldn't be doing our jobs if we did not act in situations like these and tried to get stupid humans to commit the sin of despair!

"But in spite of that, the Prime Mover continues to be infinitely merciful to humans as long as they stand a chance to recant their evil ways and begin to make amends.

"And the reason you humans must forgive those who trespass against you is simple: you yourselves are not so innocent. Even the smallest stain of sin, because it offends the Prime Mover who is infinite Goodness and the Perfect One, is just such a dreadful thing. You're just lucky that He is infinitely merciful just as He is infinitely good. But remember that He is also infinitely just.

"But even after you humans have committed mortal sin - a grave evil that is committed with full knowledge, and with the deliberate consent of the sinner, destroys charity in the heart of man by a grave violation of the Prime Mover's law, turns man away from the Prime Mover who is his ultimate end and his beatitude, by preferring as inferior good to Him (Paragraph 1855 of the Catechism) - He forgives you completely and wipes your slate clean out of His infinite goodness, provided you make some effort to repent your misdeeds, and then make satisfaction for or expiate them.

"But definitely the Almighty One has a soft for you humans; and that was more than evident from His exchange with Abraham in the days leading up to the destruction of Sodom and Gomorrah: 'And drawing nigh he said: Wilt thou destroy the just with the wicked? If there be fifty just men in the city, shall they perish withal? and wilt thou not spare that place for the sake of the fifty just, if they be therein? Far be it from thee to do this thing, and to slay the just with the wicked, and for the just to be in like case as the

113

wicked, this is not beseeming thee: thou who judgest all the earth, wilt not make this judgment. And the Lord said to him: If I find in Sodom fifty just within the city, I will spare the whole place for their sake. And Abraham answered, and said: Seeing I have once begun, I will speak to my Lord, whereas I am dust and ashes. What if there be five less than fifty just persons? wilt thou for five and forty destroy the whole city? And he said: I will not destroy it, if I find five and forty. And again he said to him: But if forty be found there, what wilt thou do? He said: I will not destroy it for the sake of forty. Lord, saith he, be not angry, I beseech thee, if I speak: What if thirty shall be found there? He answered: I will not do it, if I find thirty there. Seeing, saith he, I have once begun, I will speak to my Lord. What if twenty be found there? He said: I will not destroy it for the sake of twenty. I beseech thee, saith he, be not angry, Lord, if I speak yet once more: What if ten should be found there? And he said: I will not destroy it for the sake of ten. And the Lord departed, after he had left speaking to Abraham: and Abraham returned to his place.' (Genesis 18:23-33).

"The Non-Creature and Master Craftsman (who told Moses 'I am who am') will never forgive me and the other fallen angels; and you humans should not think of doing it either. First of all we wouldn't be interested (as we've in fact never repented of our act of disobedience); and, secondly, you humans - yes, you humans - are now the target for our vitriol. That is why I am called all sorts of names including 'Accuser'!

114

"But the Deliverer addressed my machinations when He added: 'And lead us not into temptation, but delivers us from evil'. And that is also where the supernatural virtues of faith, hope and charity must come into full play. But even with them, just recall how He warned Peter saying: 'Simon, Simon, behold Satan hath desired to have you, that he may sift you as wheat...' (Luke 22:31)

"Even Peter, the rock upon which He was going to build His *Sancta Ecclesia*, was at my mercy absent help in the form of divine graces. That was even though the Deliverer had stated: 'And I say to thee, that thou art Peter, and upon this rock I will build my church, and the gates of hell shall not prevail against it!' (Matthew 16:18) The graces are necessary because as Paul let the Ephesians know: 'But God, (who is rich in mercy,) for his exceeding charity wherewith he loved us, Even when we were dead in sins, hath quickened us together in Christ, (by whose grace you are saved.)' (Ephesians 2:4-5)

"So, I can tell you frankly that those humans who subscribe to the belief that salvation is by faith alone outside the *Sancta Ecclesia* have ventured out on a limb, and are completely on their own. It has to be so because that is what we here in the Underworld subscribed to, much to our regret. I might also add that it is not what the Son of Man and His *Sancta Ecclesia* teach. And they are now totally exposed.

"Those who persist in propagating that false doctrine might do well to revisit the first epistle of St. John (an epistle that he devoted to false doctrines)

115

especially where it states: 'Dearly beloved, believe not every spirit, but try the spirits if they be of God: because many false prophets are gone out into the world. By this is the spirit of God known. Every spirit which confesseth that Jesus Christ is come in the flesh, is of God: And every spirit that dissolveth Jesus, is not of God: and this is Antichrist, of whom you have heard that he cometh, and he is now already in the world. You are of God, little children, and have overcome him. Because greater is he that is in you, than he that is in the world. They are of the world: therefore of the world they speak, and the world heareth them. We are of God. He that knoweth God, heareth us. He that is not of God, heareth us not. By this we know the spirit of truth, and the spirit of error.' (1 John 4:1-6).

"But orthodoxy is useless if the 'faithful' do not live accordingly; and Paul put it nicely: 'If I speak with the tongues of men, and of angels, and have not charity, I am become as sounding brass, or a tinkling cymbal. And if I should have prophecy and should know all mysteries, and all knowledge, and if I should have all faith, so that I could remove mountains, and have not charity, I am nothing.' (1 Corinthians 13:1-2).

"It was therefore quite appropriate that John immediately followed up his admonition regarding falsehoods with the following: 'Dearly beloved, let us love one another, for charity is of God. And every one that loveth, is born of God, and knoweth God. He that loveth not, knoweth not God: for God is charity. By this hath the charity of God appeared towards us, because God hath sent his only begotten Son into the world, that we may live by him. In this is charity: not as though we had loved God, but because he hath first loved us, and sent his Son to be a propitiation for our sins.' (1 John 4:7-10)

"Look, the Jews, the chosen people (Deuteronomy 7:6), stumbled when the moment of truth came. John describes the entire episode succinctly as follows: *'Amen, amen dico vobis: qui non intrat per ostium in ovile ovium, sed ascendit aliunde, ille fur est et latro. Qui autem intrat per ostium, pastor est ovium. Huic ostiarius aperit, et oves vocem ejus audiunt, et proprias ovas vocat nominatim, et educit eas. Et cum proprias oves emiserit, ante eas vadit: et oves illum sequuntur, quia sciunt vocem ejus. Alienum autem non sequuntur, sed fugiunt ab eo: quia non noverunt vocem alienorum.*

'Hoc proverbium dixit eis Jesus: illi autem non cognoverunt quid loqueretur eis. Dixit ergo eis iterum Jesus: Amen, amen dico vobis, quia ego sum ostium ovium. Omnes quotquot venerunt, fures sunt, et latrones, et non audierunt eos oves. Ego sum ostium. Per me si quis introierit, salvabitur: et ingredietur, et egredietur, et pascua inveniet. Fur non venit nisi ut furetur, et mactet, et perdat. Ego veni ut vitam habeant, et abundantius habeant.

'Ego sum pastor bonus. Bonus pastor animam suam dat pro ovibus suis. Mercenarius autem, et qui non est pastor, cujus non sunt oves propriae, videt

lupum venientem, et dimittit oves, et fugit: et lupus rapit, et dispergit oves; mercenarius autem fugit, quia mercenarius est, et non pertinet ad eum de ovibus. Ego sum pastor bonus: et cognosco meas, et cognoscunt me meae. Sicut novit me Pater, et ego agnosco Patrem: et animam meam pono pro ovibus meis.

'Et alias oves habeo, quae non sunt ex hoc ovili: et illas oportet me adducere, et vocem meam audient, et fiet unum ovile et unus pastor. Propterea me diligit Pater: quia ego pono animam meam, ut iterum sumam eam. Nemo tollit eam a me: sed ego pono eam a meipso, et potestatem habeo ponendi eam, et potestatem habeo iterum sumendi eam. Hoc mandatum accepi a Patre meo. Dissensio iterum facta est inter Judaeos propter sermones hos. Dicebant autem multi ex ipsis: Daemonium habet, et insanit: quid eum auditis?

'Alii dicebant: Haec verba non sunt daemonium habentis: numquid daemonium potest caecorum oculos aperire? Facta sunt autem Encaenia in Jerosolymis, et hiems erat. Et ambulabat Jesus in templo, in porticu Salomonis. Circumdederunt ergo eum Judaei, et dicebant ei : Quousque animam nostram tollis? si tu es Christus, dic nobis palam. Respondit eis Jesus: Loquor vobis, et non creditis: opera quae ego facio in nomine Patris mei, haec testimonium perhibent de me: sed vos non creditis, quia non estis ex ovibus meis. Oves meae vocem meam audiunt, et ego cognosco eas, et sequuntur me: et ego vitam aeternam do eis, et non peribunt in

aeternum, et non rapiet eas quisquam de manu mea. Pater meus quod dedit mihi, majus omnibus est: et nemo potest rapere de manu Patris mei. Ego et Pater unum sumus. Sustulerunt ergo lapides Judaei, ut lapidarent eum. Respondit eis Jesus: Multa bona opera ostendi vobis ex Patre meo: propter quod eorum opus me lapidatis? Responderunt ei Judaei: De bono opere non lapidamus te, sed de blasphemia; et quia tu homo cum sis, facis teipsum Deum. Respondit eis Jesus: Nonne scriptum est in lege vestra, Quia ego dixi: Dii estis? Si illos dixit deos, ad quos sermo Dei factus est, et non potest solvi Scriptura: quem Pater sanctificavit, et misit in mundum vos dicitis: Quia blasphemas, quia dixi: Filius Dei sum? Si non facio opera Patris mei, nolite credere mihi. Si autem facio: etsi mihi non vultis credere, operibus credite, ut cognoscatis, et credatis quia Pater in me est, et ego in Patre. Quaerebant ergo eum apprehendere: et exivit de manibus eorum. Et abiit iterum trans Jordanem, in eum locum ubi erat Joannes baptizans primum, et mansit illic; et multi venerunt ad eum, et dicebant : Quia Joannes quidem signum fecit nullum. Omnia autem quaecumque dixit Joannes de hoc, vera erant. Et multi crediderunt in eum.'

'(Amen, amen I say to you: He that entereth not by the door into the sheepfold, but climbeth up another way, the same is a thief and a robber. But he that entereth in by the door is the shepherd of the sheep. To him the porter openeth; and the sheep hear his voice: and he calleth his own sheep by name, and leadeth them out. And when he hath let out his own sheep, he goeth before them: and the sheep follow him, because they know his voice. But a stranger they follow not, but fly from him, because they know not the voice of strangers. This proverb Jesus spoke to them. But they understood not what he spoke to them.

'Jesus therefore said to them again: Amen, amen I say to you, I am the door of the sheep. All others, as many as have come, are thieves and robbers: and the sheep heard them not. I am the door. By me, if any man enter in, he shall be saved: and he shall go in, and go out, and shall find pastures. The thief cometh not, but for to steal, and to kill, and to destroy. I am come that they may have life, and may have it more abundantly.

'I am the good shepherd. The good shepherd giveth his life for his sheep. But the hireling, and he that is not the shepherd, whose own the sheep are not, seeth the wolf coming, and leaveth the sheep, and flieth: and the wolf catcheth, and scattereth the sheep: And the hireling flieth, because he is a hireling: and he hath no care for the sheep. I am the good shepherd; and I know mine, and mine know me. As the Father knoweth me, and I know the Father: and I lay down my life for my sheep. And other sheep I have, that are not of this fold: them also I must bring, and they shall hear my voice, and there shall be one fold and one shepherd. Therefore doth the Father love me: because I lay down my life, that I may take it again. No man taketh it away from me: but I lay it down of myself, and I have power to lay it down: and

I have power to take it up again. This commandment have I received of my Father.

'A dissension rose again among the Jews for these words. And many of them said: He hath a devil, and is mad: why hear you him? Others said: These are not the words of one that hath a devil: Can a devil open the eyes of the blind?

'And it was the feast of the dedication at Jerusalem: and it was winter. And Jesus walked in the temple, in Solomon's porch. The Jews therefore came round about him, and said to him: How long dost thou hold our souls in suspense? If thou be the Christ, tell us plainly. Jesus answered them: I speak to you, and you believe not: the works that I do in the name of my Father, they give testimony of me. But you do not believe, because you are not of my sheep. My sheep hear my voice: and I know them, and they follow me. And I give them life everlasting; and they shall not perish for ever, and no man shall pluck them out of my hand. That which my Father hath given me, is greater than all: and no one can snatch them out of the hand of my Father. I and the Father are one.

'The Jews then took up stones to stone him. Jesus answered them: Many good works I have shewed you from my Father; for which of these works do you stone me? The Jews answered him: For a good work we stone thee not, but for blasphemy; and because that thou, being a man, maketh thyself God. Jesus answered them: Is it not written in your law: I said you are gods? If he called them gods, unto whom the word of God was spoken, and the scripture cannot be broken; Do you say of him whom the Father hath sanctified and sent into the world: Thou blasphemest, because I said, I am the Son of God? If I do not the works of my Father, believe me not. But if I do, though you will not believe me, believe the works: that you may know and believe that the Father is in me, and I in the Father. They sought therefore to take him; and he escaped out of their hands.

'And he went again beyond the Jordan, into that place where John was baptizing first; and there he abode. And many resorted to him, and they said: John indeed did no sign. But all things whatsoever John said of this man, were true. And many believed in him.)' (John 10:1-42).

"But that was before the Old Testament gave way to the New Testament at the time the veil of the temple was rent into two as described by the authors of the Synoptic gospels: 'And Jesus again crying with a loud voice, yielded up the ghost. And behold the veil of the temple was rent in two from the top even to the bottom, and the earth quaked, and the rocks were rent. And the graves were opened: and many bodies of the saints that had slept arose, And coming out of the tombs after his resurrection, came into the holy city, and appeared to many.' (Matthew 27:50-53).

'And when the sixth hour was come, there was darkness over the whole earth until the ninth hour. And at the ninth hour, Jesus cried out with a loud voice, saying: Eloi, Eloi, lamma sabacthani? Which is, being interpreted, My God, my God, why hast thou forsaken me? And some of the standers by hearing, said: Behold he calleth Elias. And one running and filling a sponge with vinegar, and putting it upon a reed, gave him to drink, saying: Stay, let us see if Elias come to take him down. And Jesus having cried out with a loud voice, gave up the ghost. And the veil of the temple was rent in two, from the top to the bottom. And the centurion who stood over against him, seeing that crying out in this manner he had given up the ghost, said: Indeed this man was the son of God.' (Mark 15:33-39).

'And it was almost the sixth hour: and there was darkness over all the earth until the ninth hour. And the sun was darkened, and the veil of the temple was rent in the midst. And Jesus crying with a loud voice, said: Father, into thy hands I commend my spirit. And saying this, he gave up the ghost. Now, the centurion, seeing what was done, glorified God, saying: Indeed this was a just man. And all the multitude of them that were come together to that sight and saw the things that were done returned, striking their breasts.' (Luke 23:44-48).

"This is how the Apostle John described it in his account: 'Afterwards, Jesus knowing that all things were now accomplished, that the scripture might be fulfilled, said: I thirst. Now there was a vessel set there full of vinegar. And they, putting a sponge full of vinegar and hyssop, put it to his mouth. Jesus therefore, when he had taken the vinegar, said: It is consummated. And bowing his head, he gave up the ghost.' (John 19:28-30).

'Then the Jews, (because it was the

parasceve,) that the bodies might not remain on the cross on the sabbath day, (for that was a great sabbath day,) besought Pilate that their legs might be broken, and that they might be taken away. The soldiers therefore came; and they broke the legs of the first, and of the other that was crucified with him. But after they were come to Jesus, when they saw that he was already dead, they did not break his legs. But one of the soldiers with a spear opened his side, and immediately there came out blood and water. And he that saw it, hath given testimony, and his testimony is true. And he knoweth that he saith true; that you also may believe. For these things were done, that the scripture might be fulfilled: You shall not break a bone of him. And again another scripture saith: They shall look on him whom they pierced.' (John 19:28-37)

"With the veil of the temple getting rent into two on Good Friday, the 'Law of Moses' came to a crushing end; and the difference between the Law of Moses (which governed the alliance of Yahweh and Israel) and the New Testament could not be starker.

'And the Lord spoke to Moses, Saying: Bring forth the blasphemer without the camp, and let them that heard him, put their hands upon his head, and let all the people stone him. And thou shalt speak to the children of Israel: the man that curseth his God, shall bear his sin: And he that blasphemeth the name of the Lord, dying let him die: all the multitude shall stone him, whether he be a native or a stranger. He that blasphemeth the name of the Lord, dying let him die.

124

'He that striketh and killeth a man, dying let him die. He that killeth a beast, shall make it good, that is to say, shall give beast for beast. He that giveth a blemish to any of his neighbours: as he hath done, so shall it be done to him: Breach for breach, eye for eye, tooth for tooth, shall he restore. What blemish he gave, the like shall he be compelled to suffer. He that striketh a beast, shall render another. He that striketh a man shall be punished. Let there be equal judgment among you, whether he be a stranger, or a native that offends: because I am the Lord your God. And Moses spoke to the children of Israel: and they brought forth him that had blasphemed, without the camp, and they stoned him. And the children of Israel did as the Lord had commanded Moses. (Leviticus 24:13-23).

"Explaining the new setup under the New Testament, the Deliverer had been quite blunt: 'You have heard that it hath been said, An eye for an eye, and a tooth for a tooth. But I say to you not to resist evil: but if one strike thee on thy right cheek, turn to him also the other.' (Matthew 5:38-39). 'But I say to you that hear: Love your enemies, do good to them that hate you. Bless them that curse you, and pray for them that calumniate you. And to him that striketh thee on the one cheek, offer also the other. And him that taketh away from thee thy cloak, forbid not to take thy coat also." (Luke 6:27-29).

"It is, of course, a fact (regardless of what some humans make of it) that two thousand years ago the Redeemer of humankind, the Son of the Most High, came down to earth in fulfillment of the prophecies of the Old Testament, just as the great Jewish dispensation was drawing to a close (as it is aptly stated in Volume 13 of the Flaming Sword), and the world was ruled by Rome even as Rome could not rule itself (or so historians believe); and He paid the price for the sins of humans with his death on the cross, and thereupon ascended into heaven where He is now seated at the right hand of His Father. But, apart from the fact that Romans and their subjects (from England to Africa and from Syria to Spain) were wont to ride on horseback and relied on mules and sail boats for transportation, while present day folks get about in autos, electric and diesel powered trains, airplanes, and the occasional ride in a space shuttle to and from the moon, the world hasn't changed an iota. Humans are still as morally bankrupt and as mean as they were then or, indeed, at the time of Cain and Abel.

"When the Deliverer sent out His twelve apostles, he said He was sending them out 'as sheep among wolves'. (Matthew 10:16) The successors to the apostles are still in that exact same boat as they go about spreading the message of the crucified and risen Savior of humans.

"The difference between you humans and myself is that I discovered instantly, albeit too late, that I was in error. But humans who are in error usually just keep bumbling along, and most discover that they were in error only after they have kicked the bucket and find themselves face to face with the Non-

Creature and Master Craftsman on their judgment day. And that is just swell from our perspective here in the Underworld. Why should we be the only ones to miss out on heavenly bliss, and to suffer the way we do here in Gehenna. Let humans also come and see - and above all taste and experience - the horrors of this goddamned place! The Prime Mover might have a soft spot for humans who stray from the path of righteousness. My troops and I don't.

"Still, I do admire the way humans go about rationalizing away the responsibility and guilt. That is something we pure spirits cannot do - make excuses for an evil life. In the pure spirit realm, everything - sin and judgment - happens in real time. Incidentally, the holy book does not say anywhere: 'By Faith Alone'! You'd better believe that I, Beelzebub, would have been the first to note such an incongruity in the divine scheme of things. It would have been a bonanza!

"A good way of checking out the facts is to isolate all the biblical passages that refer to 'faith', and then start tackling the parts of the bible that don't with the intention of learning what humans are supposed to do to attain salvation. Well, not surprisingly, the Ten Commandments, from which no one is exempt, are found far from those sections of the bible where 'faith' is discussed.

"Oops, I misspoke! That is not quite true. There is one exception that I myself, the Father of Lies who was also a murderer from the very beginning - much as I would have liked to - cannot pretend that it does not exist. That exception, alas, also deals a mortal blow to the doctrine of 'a sola fide' (salvation by faith alone)'! And it goes…and I quote:

1   *If I speak in human and angelic tongues* but do not have love, I am a resounding gong or a clashing cymbal.*

2   *And if I have the gift of prophecy and comprehend all mysteries and all knowledge; if I have all faith so as to move mountains but do not have love, I am nothing.*

3   *If I give away everything I own, and if I hand my body over so that I may boast but do not have love, I gain nothing...*

"And that is, of course, rather unfortunate. How I wish that the Apostle of the Gentiles had written all the epistles he wanted to write, but stayed mum on just this one subject of love *vis a vis* faith! He made our work more difficult by positing the obvious, namely that faith, although necessary, was not sufficient for salvation!

"But it is now also quite clear that this is the source of the problems we've just discussed - the inability to read! Humans overdo things sometimes, and it is a good bet that a lot of them will be in for some nice surprises when they shed those bodies and enter the realm of pure spirits. That is something that might seem to them like an eternity away whereas it isn't. Even though they have reason and are able to calculate their lifespans fairly accurately, humans prefer to remain engrossed with the hear and now, and not to dwell on their looming and certain rendezvous with the Creator of the Universe who told Moses: 'Ego sum *qui sum.*' (I am who am). (Exodus 3:14)

"And how can killing be justified! It would be terrific if humans were right. It would validate what I stand for completely. But they are not, unfortunately, because 'he who lives by the sword dies by the sword'! And guess what - the humans who seem least bothered by the fact that people get killed in wars are the very ones who make the biggest stink, obviously hypocritical, about the evils of abortion and things like that! And you also guessed correctly – these are the same ones who approve of torture of 'suspects'! Yes, the torture of suspects in detention without trial for lack proof of wrongdoing! And I, Beelzebub, am not about to complain if folks vehemently assert that they do not see my fingerprints all over the place, for the obvious reason - I would hurt my own cause if I did anything to discourage them or those they support."

Still same old struggle (between Good and Evil)...

"Might there be something I don't know about the constitution of humans, fashioned in the image of the Prime Mover and to that extent also sacred, that would justifiably incite one human to try and do away with another human? Certainly not after all humans have sinned and are in need of their creator's mercy - all humans including those stupid ones who think they are special and, even though their sins have been traced in the sand for all to see, they still can defy their Deliverer and proceed to stone the woman who was unlucky to be caught in the act.

"In any event, what is there about the human constitution that would cause a normal 'person' to try and stick a spear into a brother or a sister, or to try and stone or shoot a brother or a sister, much less to design mega bunker bursting bombs and drop them in places where other brothers and sisters might be hiding out.

"In a situation in which there is more than one superpower, common sense dictates a policy of *detente* as you folks call it, not one of head-on collisions. That is what happened during the so-called 'Cold War', much to my chagrin. It is most unfortunate that the Cold War came and went without seeing the world engulfed in turmoil. It would have been just wonderful if the West, armed to the teeth with weapons of mass destruction had challenged the Soviets, who were also armed to the teeth with similar weapons, to a fight - or vice versa.

"We in the Underworld actually thought that it was a done deal at one time, and we were cheering on one fellow called Ennedy and another one called Rushchev so one of them - or, preferably, both - would press 'buttons' and unleash fire and brimstone on the earth. And so, we were rooting for them to get the third and of course also final world war going. But unfortunately the prayers of the peaceniks, led by the fellow who occupied the Holy See at the time, triumphed!

"Oh, we wanted to see suffering and miseries engulf the world on a much bigger scale than we had seen in all the wars humans had ever fought against each other combined. Even I, with all my powers of divination, had all but concluded that Armageddon was at hand, but I was mistaken.

"Any sort of pre-emptive action on the part of one power would have been immoral, because it would have automatically spelled the annihilation of its own people regardless of whether they were civilians or in uniform. It was understood and above all recognized by all that any attempt to 'neutralize' the troops of one super power by the other was immoral and unacceptable. The Soviets did not even think of 'degrading' or 'neutralizing' the troops of the Western Alliance, and vice versa. In the nuclear age, it was not practical to talk in those terms. It was simply do or die!

"The time has now come, however, when the world recognizes the existence of only one hyper power. In terms of morality, it is of course even more depraved for the sole hyper power to use its overwhelming force to degrade or neutralize those whose calling is to serve in the security forces of any independent nation the hyper power might have designs on regardless of the nature of those designs. This is because super power or hyper power - whatever you wish to call it - comes with

131

responsibilities.

"Believe it or not, it is also a calling to be the leader of a hyper-power; and it is a very grave thing to misuse the authority that goes with the position of 'Commander-in-Chief of a hyper- power. For my part, I like to see that authority misused - I want to see the chaps in the Kremlin, at Number 10 Downing Street, the Palais Elyeece, and especially the chaps in the White House misuse their authority and power. I want to see them end up here in Gehenna with me - I do not want St. Michael the Archangel to triumph over me in the battle for the souls of these fellows.

"I am not known for humility; and I, Diabolos and author of death, will hasten to brag to you that it is really my agenda which the individuals whose actions trigger wars - particularly unjustified wars - carry out. But if I sound a little upset, it is because those who are bent on starting wars, even in the face of stiff objections from the rest of the world, also seem determined to do it in the name of the Prime Mover, and not in my name. You humans should learn to give credit where it is due!

"And even then, they take so long to decide on the next target - as if it is hard to finger a 'rogue' nation. To my knowledge there is no nation that does not fit that description - where the state does not use its machinery to kill - and that includes the hyper power itself. The chaps in the Kremlin, Palais de l'Elysée, Number 10 Downing Street, the White House and what have you, should just get on with the job - there are so many countries they can overwhelm in a short space of time with their superior fighting machines.

"Instead, I see all the posturing and the hypocrisy about 'involving people in the targeted nations in determining their own future' and that sort of tripe. Call a spade a spade - call foreign occupation 'foreign occupation' and just get going with the next one. Get going with those regime changes. The more the indigenous people suffer in the aftermath, the better for our cause - yes, because you are either with Him or with me, and do not pretend now that you are with Him! There is tons of 'black gold' and uranium out there. Come-on...show me what you've got - go get it!

"And how do those of you who pride yourselves in being conscientious and God-fearing (I am assuming there are still a couple of you left) like that? You may not like me, or the fact that these terrible things - yes, truly terrible things - have my full backing; you have little choice but to live with them. And you now realize that you have also to cope with my tactics of shock and awe! Or, did you perhaps think that the struggle between good and evil was the product of some crazy and misguided ascetic's imagination? And if you still do, you just wait to witness the real Armageddon. It will be more than blood curdling, I tell ya!

"And there is now also this rubbish about 'disarming' the so-called 'rogue' nations - as if only some special nations should be in a position to defend themselves against outside aggression and not

133

others! First of all, that is something that will never succeed - the world will never accept the idea of some 'exceptional' nations, that have their own so-called national interests, taking on the role of policemen to keep other nations in check. That would be the beginning of anarchy caused both by the inherent contradictions in such a system and the fact that the very next logical step by the 'policing' or 'benevolently imperialist' nations would be to actually take over and colonize the 'rogue' nations. It would, of course, also be discrimination at the highest level with the citizens of the 'policing' nations or 'super powers' setting up themselves as virtual 'super humans' who alone enjoyed the prerogative to punish or reward 'underlings' representing the rest of humanity! And, if you do not know, that is why the evils of colonialism and imperialism of 'Old Europe' were defeated in the first place! In the same way the 'exceptionalism' of the nations that took their place is doomed to failure!

"Which leads me to the point I want to make - nothing should ever interfere with the principal of survival of the fittest! That principle applies to individual humans and also to nations just the same. It is also why I am against some humans setting themselves up on a pedestal to play 'judge' and 'sentence' fellow humans to 'jail' or even to die for their 'wrong doing'. All that goes against the principle of survival of the fittest. Everybody should be free to do what they want - to rob weaklings, to kill, and so on. That is the only law we in the Underworld recognize.

"When nations go to war, the 'ideal' situation is if they do so without any reason. In that way, we can have wars all the time. And, clearly, nations should be in a position to go to war even if the wars are not morally justifiable. In the realm I control, there is no such a thing as morality, let alone moral justification for conflicts between individuals and even less conflicts between nations. And when a nation decides to take that step, everyone within its borders should be obligated to support the campaign, and those who are not prepared to do so should be rounded up and promptly shot, gassed, beheaded or just hanged and quartered for their 'treasonable' act. In that way, we can be sure to have killing fields that stretch from the aggressor nations' own territory to the most distant shores. Yes, killing fields! Frankly, the more the better for my cause!

"And my prayer right now is that some dumb 'statesman' or 'stateswoman' somewhere in the world might by his or her actions set in motion events that will lead to new religious crusades. When nations go to war for security reasons, they do so simply because they want to conquer and annex - no nation would be willing to risk the lives of its citizens for nothing. Any so-called 'economic reasons' are usually only camouflage.

"But conflicts based on religious differences have a way of feeding on themselves and driving humans to slaughter others happily in the name of their gods. Just imagine humans who espouse different ideas regarding their last end going at each other with whatever they can get hold of and eliminating the problem by killing 'the enemy' on the spot. It would just be swell. It would prompt a spate of killings in different parts of the globe and cause the world to explode in the sort of Armageddon we in the Underworld have been looking forward to ever since the Deliverer announced that one was in the offing.

"You see - in the last days, apart from a few 'untouchables' like St. Peter's successors and a couple of really pious souls, I will be permitted by the Prime Mover to possess any number of humans I want, and also to use them as instruments to create absolute chaos on earth. But it now looks like I actually may not need to use that prerogative to achieve my purpose. You fellows are on the right track and, obviously, the sooner you get into that destructive mode, the better!

"And now a word about industry and technology. As far as the *other side* is concerned - the primary and indeed the only really lawful purpose of industry and technology is to improve living conditions of humans during their sojourn on earth. It was the reason you humans were created 'rational', but with the concomitant responsibility for using your 'head', including any schemes that you concocted with the aid of reason, for the greater glory of the Prime Mover.

"It therefore suits me perfectly when the priority of nations, particularly the so-called advanced nations, now is to employ advance in human knowledge for warfare or the 'killing' industry as I call it. That is how the world came by its present supply of deadly chemical, biological, viral and radiological 'killer' agents. It is very significant that none of those concoctions can just be dug up from the earth's crust or harvested from trees in their present form - they were all manufactured under controlled conditions and with the objective of employing them to kill and maim fellow humans. And take my word - time is coming the nation that developed the so-called HIV/AIDS virus will be exposed.

"In the meantime, those nations in a position to do so invariably manipulate organizations like the United Nations to enforce 'economic embargoes' and things like that on other so-called nations, especially the so-called 'rogue state'. Such embargoes not only lead to the deaths of zillions - particularly the young and the aged in the process - but they also ultimately destroy societies by assuring that generations grow up disillusioned with everything and without any real hope in life.

"The children of the countries that are the object of economic strangulation, as they die prematurely and are on their way to eternal life with Prime Mover, must wonder why people in some of the world's nations, including those that have exhibited a proneness to dillydally with nuclear bombs, have actually tested them over the cities of other nations on more than one occasion, and are accelerating the development and build-up of ever newer and more deadly nuclear weapons systems in tandem with the unilateral abrogation of nuclear test ban treaties, do that to them.

"In the same way, the children who get blown up to bits by landmines, while playing with what appear to be toys or while helping their parents grow food, must wonder, as their fragile little bodies succumb to the impact and they find themselves returning to their maker so quickly, must wonder why some members of humankind are in the business of producing things that are so dangerous. And, of course, those children of Nagasaki and Hiroshima, who perished along with their loved ones in the nuclear conflagration after the A-bombs were dropped on them, must have wondered why those bombs were made in the first place.

"As their souls were being ferried from the ashes of Hiroshima and Nagasaki to the safety of the heavenly Paradise, they must have wondered why humans did not realize that they were commanded to love one another as themselves, and that a nation that dropped those bombs on them effectively lost the war. Upon arrival in heaven, the children must have asked St. Ignatius who, as legend has it, was dying to be killed in the service of the Deliverer and his fellow humans as he made his way to Rome for his execution, why other adults seemed to think (as the Roman rulers of his time apparently did) that the act of killing another human represented victory of some kind!

"And the children must have been flabbergasted to behold earthlings in New York, London and other places celebrate the bloody massacres with merrymaking, bunting and fireworks instead of fasting and doing penance for those sordid deeds. We here in Gehenna were also celebrating. Yes, celebrating the beginning of an era in which hounding and killing people for whom one had a distaste was elevated to a virtue - a cardinal virtue!

"At the same time, it must have seemed pretty obvious to the children that what drove humans to kill others was the combination of feelings of guilt and the fear of dying. It must have seemed rather obvious to the children that a sense of guilt was what made humans fear to die; and that the fear of dying in turn drove them to kill those they perceived as their enemies. That fear of dying spoke volumes about guilty consciences; because, when people were innocent of any wrongdoing, they did not fear to die even if they knew that they did not deserve to be killed. The fact was that humans who had not been fair to others, and who were consequently guilty-laden, were terrified of dying and going to their judgement. Sinners saw no wrong in putting innocent lives at risk in their efforts to keep death at bay and postpone their encounter with the Deliverer and Judge.

"The justifications for killing in self-defense are always self-serving, because they are backed by a pack of lies packaged as facts. Moreover aggressor and victim alike could cite the exact same 'reasons' for acting in self-defense. Nations become powerful only at the expense of other nations, and nothing really belongs to Caesar in that sense! And so there is really nothing to defend. And, anyway, if the Prime Mover took the same stance and decided to defend his honor, which was under assault daily, by being a little stingy with His mercies and withdrawing His saving graces, humans who have been rebels since Adam and Eve fell from grace would all be here in the Pit with me. The only reason that did not happen is that I would have been the clear winner in the contest between good and evil!

"Humans kill because they are themselves scared of facing their Judge. They even attempted to get rid of Him, and they would try again if they got another chance. In a similar fashion, when hedonists indulge themselves, it is because they have no moral fibre and are spiritual weaklings. It is not because they are brave or are heroes - which they would be if they succeeded in letting their cravings go unfulfilled!

"Talking about hedonists - the moment of truth for hedonistic humans is that time when, as the end draws near, they realize that escapist pursuits were a smoke screen for being weak-willed and spineless; that they had just squandered opportunities to excel as men and women of virtue; and that they now had nothing to show for it except the fact that they now were hardened in their crooked ways! The hardest part of all must be the realization that, unlike the woman who was accosted by the Deliverer at the well and who rose to the occasion by renouncing her lifestyle upon learning that the stranger knew everything relating to her secret affairs, they themselves were now beyond redemption.

"The children of Hiroshima and Nagasaki knew that they were only children, and they must have wondered what it was that caused adult humans to pursue economic gain from producing nuclear and hydrogen bombs, and other types of weapons systems. They must have wondered why it did not strike Americans that the quickest way to oblivion for a newly christened 'super power' was to heave its weight around, and place its hopes in its military might, and that it would serve America best for it to abandon its massive investments in weaponry particularly now when it did not face any visible challenge to its power, and channel those resources to improving the lives of its citizens and others who are in dire need. They must have wondered why America did not use its influence to resolve international conflicts and chose instead to pursue policies that in some cases exacerbated the situation.

"It is a hallmark of the success of our campaign that today, all it needs is for a leader of some foreign nation whose policies are not in the national interest of nations that are more powerful militarily to be declared a terrorist by leaders of these other nations, regardless of whether that is really true or not, for that leader to get a price on his head. It pleases us tremendously when one day a country has its seat at the United Nations, and the next day it is treated like a pariah and rogue state just because a militarily powerful member wants things to be that way.

"We love the fact that such precedents are set; because, regardless of the reforms that an organization such as the UN undergoes, the way will now always be open to the militarily powerful 'entity' - and this can be 'terrorists' operating from their invisible base, or may be even some tiny, previously insignificant nation that had its agents strategically placed with brief-case nuclear A-bombs and didn't have anything to lose - to call the shots. This is a development that opens up lots and lots of possibilities for our cause.

"But there is nothing that is more satisfying to me, Beelzebub, than seeing the 'sanctioned' aggression and murderous wars used for public entertainment in the 'victorious' nations - more or less like what used to go on in ancient Rome in the amphitheatre, when starved African lions were let loose on slaves who were permitted only small daggers with which to ward off the fangs of the hungry beasts. It is a great feeling, I tell you, to know that the difference between ancient Rome and 'modern civilized nations' (as you chaps refer to them) is the same!

"And so, thanks to the evolution of satellite communications, and the fact that you live in an age of real time news, the citizens of the nations under attack can now literally see and hear the powerful, bunker bursting bombs lobbed from enemy vessels that may be moored in seas hundred and even thousands of miles away bring ruin and devastation to their neighborhoods at least until the television stations themselves are taken out by missiles and the lights on their TV sets flicker and go out. They can even watch as their loved ones are killed or bloodied by 'stray' bombs, and this in addition to being able to watch those country folk whose sin was to try and make a living serving in the country's security forces, 'neutralized' by the advancing enemy.

"And while those who survive the first volley cower in fear or cradle mortally wounded loved ones, their brothers and sisters in Christ who happen to live in the safe zone of the conflict within the borders of the aggressor nations typically rally around their own TV sets to enjoy the spectacle put on by their 'gallant' sons and daughters serving in the military. And it is usually quite a spectacle - the sight of a nation's infrastructure that took enormous resources and will power on the part of the citizenry and certainly great sacrifices to put up vanish from view in a matter of seconds in clouds of smoke, buildings with people inside them collapsing, columns of enemy soldiers obliterated in a matter of seconds with the help of bunker-bursting munitions made from radio-active nuclear waste. And, of course, pictures of screaming ambulances ferrying the dying and wounded to makeshift treatment centers carried live to a worldwide 'audience' by journalists 'embedded' in the forces of the aggressor nations!

"And the 'success' of the pinpoint strikes against one 'enemy' will invariably encourage military planners in the aggressor nations to immediately start planning their next moves - against the next 'rogue' nation on the list, giving that priority over fulfilling promises to restore the shattered lives of nationals in

143

the vanquished country, establish so-called democratic systems and governance, rebuild the infrastructure, and other things of that nature in the pacified nations. And these are humans who are commanded to love one another as they love themselves!

"And also, nowadays, all it needs to absolve those behind the destruction of property and deaths of the innocent from any and all personal responsibility for their actions is to label or 'classify' the activities initiated by those individuals as 'military' operations. The control exercised by the super powers over so-called 'human rights watchdog organizations' such as the International Criminal Court of Justice, and as well over the actions of the *ad hoc* war crimes tribunals it sets up, translates into freedom by nationals of the super powers to do as they wish, because the veto powers wielded by those super powers in world forums have the effect of shielding their citizens from facing justice for any war crimes they might commit. Then the nations themselves, because they are super powers, are free to break - and have in fact frequently broken - codified international law with impunity.

"This state of affairs didn't come about by accident. Believe me when I say that my troops worked very hard after the war you folks refer to as World War Two to ensure that, instead of posing a threat to our agenda, an organization like the League of Nations (which eventually came to be known as the United Nations) would actually promote it. We are not

144

fools!

"And, by the same token, virtually anything that is done by a country that has been branded a 'rogue' nation to safeguard its infrastructure or otherwise prevent its installations, factories and other strategic sites from being trashed by aggressor super powers is now liable to be branded as a war crime with the blessing of the supposedly impartial world bodies mentioned. But not only that: the miseries undergone by the citizenry of the targeted nation become something they deserve even in the eyes of spiritual leaders in the aggressor nations.

"Their sufferings automatically become quite distinct and apart from human sufferings that the Deliverer sanctified by His own passion and death on the cross and made His own. Even the regions of the conflicts automatically become identifiable with places that are supposed to be the abode of 'evil spirits' referred to in some books of the Old Testament!

"You can be sure that it gives me enormous 'pleasure' - if you can call my satisfaction with the way things proceed 'pleasure' - to see so-called Catholic nations take center stage in bringing about this new world 'order'. And it is immensely gratifying to observe the near stunning silence of the clergy - yes, the clergy - in these nations. You would think they live on a different planet altogether! It pleases me immensely when churchmen, abandoning their responsibilities to the downtrodden, and those who are constantly subjected to humiliation and injustice, go about their business as if everything was all right - just as they did at the height of imperialism and colonialism, or at the time the Deliverer himself was being marched to his death on the cross.

"I refer to the silence as 'stunning' because taking hours - perhaps even days - to craft an innocuous statement that is addressed to no one and is only intended to be read by priests from pulpits without any further action is a virtual signal to the chaps who might be openly plotting to commit murders in some foreign land to get on with it. What I am always fearing is that the prelates will do just like the apostles they succeeded did, namely pick themselves up, confront the political leadership and rebuke them for cooking up the murderous schemes - just as John the Baptist confronted Agrippa and rebuked him for stealing his own brother's woman. Of course if they did that, their own fate would be in the balance and what happened to John might well happen to them.

"But that would be the case only in the short run. You know what they say about the blood of martyrs being the seed of conversion? When the apostles and their immediate successors matched on Rome and rebuked the emperors and the victorious generals for scandalous lives they led - for the killings that went in the amphitheatre in the name of sport and for indulging in the hideous practice of slavery, and other evils - they were of course promptly silenced. But look what happened next - becoming a follower of Christ suddenly became the fad and fashion. Peter's

146

successors effectively took over the Roman Empire and, using Rome as a springboard, went on to spread Christianity throughout the known world and beyond!

"That would do such damage to my cause, it would almost be as if that John the Baptist was back and kicking, and disturbing the peace again. The present situation in which Catholic prelates the world over have cozy relationships with politicians, many of whom are known murderers, and which makes me describe the reaction of the clergy as stunning silence suits me perfectly. God forbid that they will suddenly wake up to their responsibilities and cause chaos in my realm!

"The priests and prelates are supposed to be like other Christs, are they not? Well before you rush to judgement, just remember these words of the Deliverer: Judge not, that ye be not judged. For with what judgment ye judge, ye shall be judged: and with what measure ye mete, it shall be measured unto you. And why beholdest thou the mote that is in thy brother's eye, but considerest not the beam that is in thine own eye? Thou hypocrite, cast out first the beam out of thine own eye; and then shalt thou see clearly to cast out the mote out of thy brother's eye. But, after warning of false prophets, who came to folks in sheep's clothing, but inwardly were ravening wolves, He did say: By their fruits ye shall know them.

"And so, assuming that the priests and prelates fall short, it means that they are not in a position to act, confess the greatness of the Prime Mover, and to suffer the way the Deliverer Himself did. And to that extent, their lives do not exemplify the true Christian life, and they additionally will have the tendency to misrepresent the Deliverer. Now, I myself have already been judged and condemned, and I can therefore hazard without fearing any further consequences that it is this that explains the silence and hesitancy of the Church's functionaries when it comes to pointing out injustices.

"Of course, what I fear is that the stupid fools might suddenly wake up and start pointing out that, in any modern war, the senseless destruction of life and property in today's world likely will be on a scale that even leaves the victorious stunned and mentally and emotionally transformed for the rest of their lives. What I fear is that some nut might point out that such an eventuality was reason enough to get a worldwide ban imposed on all weapons of war, starting with the stockpiles under the control of the so-called super powers. Some fool might even be brazen enough to suggest the obvious, namely that the perpetrators themselves likely would never want to see tables turned and they themselves at the receiving end of modern weapons of war! That sort of railing would expose the shallow thinking of warmongers, which would be a real tragedy.

"But the question that would be the most damaging to my cause if asked would pertain to what the Deliverer Himself would do if He had been in the place of these clerics. What would He do, for instance, were to observe citizens of a nation that might have already been largely disarmed and therefore unable to defend itself against aggression killed, maimed, and trampled upon by the war machinery of a super power ran amok and out of control? What would He do?

"Good thing not too many of you can even hazard an answer! Unfortunately, I really have no choice but to tell you. You recall what He did when He was in Jerusalem one day and saw what was going on in the temple? Because humans beings - whether they are Rwandese, Russians, Japanese, Germans, Americans, Iraqis, Spaniards, Palestinians or Iraqis - are temples of the Prime Mover, you can bet that the Deliverer would make Himself a strong enough whip from any tough enough material within His reach (perhaps depleted uranium) and chase the 'merchants' (because that is what they are in the final analysis) out of His temples. He is a jealous Prime Mover. So, you can see that by maintaining their stunning silence, in the eyes of the Prime Mover, members of the Church's hierarchy have become virtual collaborators in the senseless murder and mayhem.

"Do I know what I am talking about? Of course I do. Who is it that lays the traps over which these priests and prelates trip? One problem is that these traps do not fit on the narrow path. Even with our superior intelligence, we haven't been able to come up with a design that would make them do. But since they fit on Broadway, we lay them there; and, of course, all who eschew that thoroughfare are pretty safe from them. You have to be dumb to believe that priests and prelates practice what they preach, namely walk only on the Narrow Path - and stay on it!

"Perhaps *you* can afford to be dumb; it is something we in the Underworld cannot. Just believe me when I tell you that chicanery is as rampant in the 'pilgrim' Church today as it was in the Middle Ages. This is despite the fact that these priests and prelates really do try, one and all, to 'clothe themselves in Christ' to borrow an expression from the Apostle of the Gentiles. Long ago, they could face their congregations and tell them to at least 'do as I say'; because it would have been disastrous to suggest that their flocks 'do as I do'. These days even that is out of question. A lot of what the clergymen say is abominable even by my standards.

"To get to this stage required painstaking planning on my part and very great patience, I tell you! Whoever thought that naked aggression - or 'wars' as you call them - would become a 'morally accepted' method of guaranteeing the 'economic security' of a nation whether a super power or not. And just to think that all this is sanctioned by a body like the United Nations of which the Holy See is a full member! And whoever thought that it would be morally legitimate for some nations and not others to launch so-called pre-emptive strikes, using everything in their arsenals, in the name of national security?

"But our biggest coup is the fact that nations, prodded by their 'intelligence services', have legitimized the methods that had hitherto been confined to gangsters and 'the Mob' or the mafia of

150

'taking care of unfinished business'. And so, no one bats an eye lid when one head of state wakes one morning, declares everybody on a 'list of wanted persons' including fellow heads of state and, with or without a 'coalition of the willing', plans openly to 'liquidate those listed. I mean - these are things you used to read about in fairy tales, not in history books! And just to think that this is done in the name of civilization and with the full backing of 'churchmen'!

"To sum up: there is nothing that works to drive humans who try to pray for peace - and are always a thorn in my side - to despair more than the appearance that the developing turmoil and the wars have the Church's tacit approval. You must know that there is nothing that undermines my cause more than prayers - not the demonstrative, almost meaningless posturing of hypocrites; but the sincere prayers that are offered up in the secrecy of people's living rooms, and spring from the heart, speak volumes about a people who feel completely powerless in the face of imminent man-made tragedies. They are prayers of people who know that succour for the grief-stricken in a world that is driven by materialism is unlikely to come in the present life.

"You see - you humans have a very short memory. Remember the flood and Noah's Ark? Or the story of Lot and his wife and their escape from the City of Sodom! If you want to know the Prime Mover's position regarding the wicked, you have to understand the background to His promise that He would never again visit sinful folk with any more floods and things of that nature. But He promised not to do so well knowing that humans would continue in their intransigence.

"The Prime Mover was essentially signifying that, just as He continued to allow Satan to tempt humans and to sow his seeds of death, He was going to let the wicked have their way on earth - but clearly only for so long. He was going to let killers have their way and wreck and ruin the earthly lives of their fellow men on earth. He wasn't going to stop them. There would, of course, still be major floods, landslides, earthquakes, pestilences, etc. But they would be man-made, having their origins in industrial pollution that was driven by human greed, and in the environmental and ecological degradation caused by the underground and atmospheric nuclear tests conducted by the so-called super powers in secret.

"But, by the same token, being a jealous Prime Mover, He was also signifying that the wicked would not just face some watery flood, but the full wrath of an angry Prime Mover when their time of reckoning came. In retrospect, it would be quite clear that ridding the world of the wicked by drowning them in floods (and keeping them out of the Noah's Ark) or by raining fire and brimstone on their cities was motivated by the desire of the Prime Mover to spare sinners something worse.

"Therefore take notice that those of you who will be caught with your candles out when the Bridegroom arrives will find yourselves in hell with me; and believe me, it is a hell of a place! It is a place where you humans who can cry and have teeth, will get a chance to weep until your tears run dry, and to gnash those teeth, which now show whenever you laugh, until they pop out! You will wish that mountains had fallen on you when you still lived since that would have stopped you in your tracks and, by incapacitating you, would have had the effect of reduced the terrible guilt that will be haunting you throughout eternity.

"And those of you who sit on the sidelines and won't stir to try and point out evils - as the prophets and the other messengers the Prime Mover sends on earth do - will also get a taste of the Prime Mover's wrath in Purgatory as you are cleansed and spruced up to make you a bride befitting of the divine Bridegroom.

"Yes, I mean you who just want to be observers in the face of evils committed against your own brothers and sisters by the wicked! It is a different kind of evil mind that entertains indifference in the face of injustices and certainly day light murder. Such indifference and love for one's neighbor are in any case incompatible! And you can bet that we in the Underworld have invested very heavily in creating the conditions in which such indifference can thrive.

"Does the Prime Mover 'see the injustice to the wage earner' (that group includes individuals who choose to serve their countries as soldiers, but end up being targeted by invading armies) or 'hear the cry of the people oppressed in Egypt'? Does He heed the silent prayers of the peaceniks? The answer is definitely 'Yes'! This is even though He might not be observed with the naked eye stepping into the fray and stopping a super power from trampling over some nation that might already have been disarmed and is therefore perhaps quite defenseless. The Prime Mover invariably steps in without fail and in a very decisive way, believe me. It is, however, not in exactly the way you or me expect.

"You might not observe the Prime Mover physically restraining killers and murders, but the end result - when His action is figured in - is always far more devastating than if He had physically stopped or even taken action Himself to 'neutralize' them. Once humans murder or maim those it was not their business to murder or maim (and it certainly never can be in an unjustified conflict), the fact always remains that they have murdered or maimed. They could even go ahead and do their darndest, including genocide and things like that, at will. The bad news is that those who murder and maim themselves become damned the moment they start plotting their activities - and that is the catch!

"And once you do that sort of thing - once you take away the lives of those who have a moral obligation to defend their country, you can never bring them back alive with any talk of reconstruction, you see. And any actions on your part to get those you regard as your 'foes' in those circumstances to abandon the cause of their country will be no different from what I myself do to you all the time - namely trying to tempt and entice you to be unpatriotic and to betray your own country against all accepted norms of behavior. Besides, when you murder or maim in those circumstances, you know even before you start that you would not like what you are going to do to the other party done by the other party to yourself, and that you are on the wrong side of the Prime Mover's law. And that is what makes your situation so tragic.

"Having killed and maimed, you stand condemned by your callous and highhanded destruction of lives you did not have any part in bringing into existence. And because you have also usurped the authority of the Prime Mover in every respect, you invariably end up in the truly awkward position of challenging your own Creator to a contest. Now, I have been in that position (and I am still stuck in it), and will testify here and now that it is not a position in which a mortal soul should be. When you get in that position, your fate is sealed - if you know what I mean!

"What this means is that each and every act of those prosecuting a war under those circumstances becomes damning evidence against them, and any successes of the campaign become even more damning in so far as evidence goes. Defeat would in fact be a boon and should even be welcomed. For one, defeat - especially humiliating defeat - could cause those involved in the unjustified aggression of another country and all the things that such aggression entails to wake up to the reality and retreat from the brink. Success would embolden them in their adventures and blind them to the lurking danger.

155

"The real coup for us is the fact that humans, at our instigation, spend their lives trying to 'liquidate' or 'rub out' their 'enemies' only to find that they in fact don't have the power to bring that about. They only appear to 'liquidate' their fellow humans who are 'temples of the Prime Mover' and by definition cannot be destroyed. It is the same way those who murdered the Deliverer were convinced that they had dealt Him a mortal blow only to discover three days later that His tomb was empty - that He had risen up and had even taken the sting out of death to which he was no longer subject. And so the killers end up here with us while their victims - thanks to the fact that humiliation, suffering and death have been sanctified by the Deliverer's death on the cross and contrary to the expectations of their shortsighted enemies - die only to regain and enjoy their life in eternity with their Deliverer. For the victims who die resigned to their fate, their interrupted lives merely amount to a fight well fought and for an evidently good cause.

"But there is one thing about you humans that we in the Underworld envy - your ability to con yourselves into believing virtually anything you want to believe, including lies that you yourselves manufacture. You humans exhibit prejudices and bias on such a scale, it is nowadays an exception rather than the rule when one is caught telling the unvarnished truth. Lying for the sake of lying is the way most you do isn't something that would come naturally to a pure spirit. I myself might be the author of death, but I must say that the author of lies - if there is such a being - has to be a human. It is such a low down thing to do - I mean believing one's own lies - I would have to sacrifice a lot of my pride to sink that low.

"We ourselves also lie of course. But we certainly do not believe our own lies, and you humans are always free to fall for them or reject them after doing your analysis and deciding which lies are in line with your own crooked intentions. There is a world of difference between that and putting out bulletins full of lies or telling lies until you are blue in the face just for the sake of it.

"And then, in the eyes of humans, it will be seen as cool when it is one group of people manufacturing and disseminating the lies. And, funnily, in the eyes of the liars it is usually regarded as criminal not only if opponents in a conflict also try to practice lying, but even when they stick with the truth. They are supposed to admit whatever their 'enemies' like to hear and in that way give lies the stamp of truth. It is strange that you yourselves even have a term for it - situational ethics!

"Humans ordinarily appear to be incapable of seeing anything objectively. It is as if one must have on special lenses to be comfortable with anything that crosses one's vision. Consequently things like weapons of mass destruction are only weapons of mass destruction depending on the party that has control over them. In order to know that a weapon is of the WMD category, one has additionally to try and figure out who is likely to end up using them! Now, that is a little funny - and confusing too! Perhaps deliberately, given the prevalence of lying in human relations! This is really sad, and it is little wonder you've christened lying 'diplomacy', no doubt as a way of avoiding the stigma that is associated with that sinful practice. If things had been like that in the Underworld, by Jove, that would make it one hell of a mess!

"Alas, you humans seem patently unable to distance yourselves from your biases and prejudices! Then the materialism - it is nothing like we fallen spirits would have thought possible! The Deliverer Himself, when He came, did not set up an earthly kingdom for Himself. And He, of course, isn't about to enthrone these peaceniks on any. That would be changing His *modus operandum* in a very radical way, and it is not like Him to start doing that.

"Although the Prime Mover is kind and merciful, it is typical of Him that He leads His 'bride' into the 'desert' - yes, desert'! Not some bed of roses. And it is there that, as Hosea said, He espouses her to Himself, and espouses her in justice, love, mercy, and in fidelity, until she gets to know Him permanently.

"Don't think you should heed the call to take up your cross *and* to follow! Yah, *cross*! Doesn't make sense to you either that you should be prepared to suffer with Him *if* you love Him! Don't think that in coming down from heaven to redeem you, there *was* a price He came to pay, sinless though He was! Those who tell you that you should expect to receive your reward in this world - don't you think they might have fallen for the trap I set, even though they might have good intentions, and consequently tell you what that they tell you because they know it is what you are dying to hear!

"You don't think that their message is a little too good and that, other than urging you to aspire for possession of the good things of this life by getting yourself a faith that can move mountains, they are really not saying anything new to you! Think - and also know one thing - if you can get Satan himself cornered like this and even doing a better job of providing humans spiritual guidance than those self-appointed messengers of the Prime Mover, Armageddon cannot be very far off!

"And, by the way, I may now be laboring under this spell which is forcing me to reveal so many of my secrets; but you'd better believe that the moment I will be rid of it, you humans will be dealing with one very nasty character on the lam; and you can be sure that there will be some people who will pay for this very dearly. And if you think I am bluffing, just remember what happened to people like Jerome, Augustine of Hippo, and your favorite philosopher Thomas of Aquin.

"If you do not remember your history, you can pray to them to find out what happened, and they will tell you how nasty and mean I was to them after I was released from the spell that caused me to reveal to them so many of my secrets. They can tell you about the wave upon wave of the most wicked suggestions that I kept sending their way; and about the flood of the most God-awful images that I bombarded their 'fickle' minds - yes, 'fickle' compared to the minds of pure spirits - with images that very nearly caused them to pack up and return to the sinful lifestyles they had given up when they were converted and (as that Saul turned Apostle of the Gentiles put it), girding their waists with truth and putting on the breastplate of righteousness, and having shod their feet with the preparation of the gospel of peace, and having above all taken the shield of faith with which they were able to quench all the fiery darts that I, the Wicked One, was won't to send their way, took the helmet of salvation, and the sword of the Spirit, which is the word of God; praying always with all prayer and supplication in the Spirit, and also being watchful to that end with all perseverance and supplication for all the saints! (Ephesians 6:14-18)

"It will be the same with you, except that this time around, having learnt a thing or two from my experience with that trio, it is I - not you - who will come out triumphant.

"Any way - to return to the subject of the prayers that peaceniks offer up - all that the Prime Mover does in answer to those prayers is sustain the peaceniks in their times of trouble and suffering so that they do not despair in the face of the calamities of war. And for those peaceniks who do not become 'collateral damage' and who somehow survive with their faith in Him intact, their lives on earth will continue to be miserable and shattered all the same, not unlike the lives of those who do not pray but also manage to survive with their reason intact because of their faith in me! Yes, their faith and confidence in me, Beelzebub, because I automatically become the one who sustains that group in times of joy and also in times of their sorrow!

"So, luckily for us in the Underworld, the activities of peaceniks really do not interfere very much with our reign over murderers and other sinners in the long run.

"Any way - it pleases me very much when I see placards borne high by peaceniks proclaiming 'Justice, where are you hiding?' They should know that I, Beelzebub, am not in the habit of resting on my laurels. There is, after all, no rest for the wicked and especially for someone like me whose job it is to sow seeds of death.

"And I, of course, detest those peaceniks - 'demonstrators' as you call them - who match in silence with their banners against wars. They might look like people who are themselves terrified as they march past contingents of mean-looking cops bristling in their riot gear and itching to pounce on the marchers. Believe me - their silent 'prayer' is heard by the Prime Mover, even though you do not see Him intervening to stop the wars. And when they are tear-gassed, whipped with batons or hosed down with water cannons, tears might flow down their cheeks and their sides might ache for days or even months on end from the buffeting; but trust me when I tell you that their 'prayer' usually proves to be more effective against my designs because of things like that for some reason.

"For one, their actions, by distracting warmongers, cause them and their supporters to come lashing out (they act really stupid sometimes, don't they!), and to identify themselves. Which is too bad, because then my minions can never deny their allegiance to me when their day in the Divine Court of Justice comes - when the time comes for them also to give up their ghosts. Which fulfils one of my immediate objectives, namely to see humans lose their souls, but pretty well frustrates my ultimate objective of thwarting the Divine Plan.

"Talking about giving up ghosts - you humans with your 'funny' constitution, which consists of a bag of chemicals and an intangible soul, are really walking corpses. I mean - at any time, chemicals in some part of that 'body' of yours can undergo a reaction that causes some vital organ to malfunction, forcing the individual to make what might be likened to an unscheduled exit from this world. It does not matter whether you live in the Palais de l'Elysee, the Kremlin, the White House, or at Number Ten Downing Street! And when you kick the bucket, all the cheek, haughtiness, foolishness and stupidity also ends there. It is not just a time of reckoning. Your earthly works also come to naught at that point when you wake up in another world to the chants of 'The Magnificat'.

"Still, I can't resist allowing myself the indulgence of a victory cry in this connection. A toast to a nation that is home to so many of our comrades-in-arms: 'America! Oh America! My America! Thou, great 'Christian' nation, blest to be the World's only - and undoubtedly also last - 'Super Power' as well as the bearer of the touch of 'exceptionalism' and 'enlightenment'! How great a boon thou art to my cause! What could I - even I, Mephistopheles - accomplish without you in this day and age? We in the Underworld salute thee who art home to so many of our comrades-in-arms! Of course you have some ways to go before you can challenge Babylon. But my troops and I have full confidence that the time is soon coming when thou will not just pose a challenge to the great city of Babylon that sadly is no more, but thou shalt verily surpass Babylon and break whatever records that 'Sin Capital' set!'

"Any way - let's get back to business. As I have already said, we have only got a little time left, and we must work hard at these things as Armageddon approaches. We in the Underworld, and our lackeys amongst you, have no choice but to step up the activities that lead to perdition, the most promising of which are related to human life and its destruction. But that does not mean that you humans do not have to be realistic. It is very important for our cause if you humans can understand our limitations, and then figure them in your plans to thwart Providence.

Never legit to try and "rub out" a fellow human...

"You humans have this funny idea that you can get rid of an individual you do not like by killing! You

163

should know that creatures that have been crafted in the image of Him-Who-is-Who-is actually don't die! You cannot just 'rub out' your fellow human being. If you were able to do that, you would also be able to rub out pure spirits too, including me! When you try to 'rub out' a fellow human being, all you are really doing is trying to interfere with the divine plan, and you do that to your own detriment. Those you supposedly 'get rid of' here on earth live on - the vast majority of them actually quite happily - in the after-life.

"And when your own time to go comes, believe me that is when hell will break loose on you for having tried to interfere with Providence - for having tried to play God when you should have been practicing charity, forgiveness, or even deservedly turning the other cheek! And so, just when you thought you had permanently disposed of those you saw as a problem, you yourself kick the bucket and boom! You suddenly find yourself confronted with all those witnesses to your brazen attempt to thwart the divine plan - all those folks you thought you had efficiently and permanently 'rubbed out'!

"If you had the ability to rub out a fellow human, you would be able to rub me out also, you fools! Well, come to think of it, it wouldn't be such a terrible thing to be rubbed out by a human devil. It would certainly end my hell and bring to a close a sad chapter in the history of creation.

"But, of course, that is not in the divine plan. The only exception to the rule - the only time the

Prime Mover permitted a creature that was made in His image to be rubbed out - was the destruction by me of my rival; and with good reason, no doubt. I by myself am trouble enough for humans - and for my fellow angels. Can you imagine a Tempter *and* a Temptress roaming the earth? If the Prime Mover had not gotten us at loggerheads with each other to the point that one of us had to go, you can expect that the number of the elect wouldn't be what it will be! With our combined forces, the earth would be such an evil place, it would take much, much more for humans to survive our wiles and enter the New Jerusalem! But that is all by the way.

"Know, moreover, that we creatures have been commanded not to kill - meaning, interfere with the plan that Providence has in place for our fellow creatures. It is dumbness - sheer stupidity - which makes you folks believe that you achieve anything by 'getting rid' of fellow humans whom you hate for one reason or another. It is the sort of stupidity that we in the Underworld have every right to exploit; and you'd better believe that when you kill, you do so at your own risk!

"Instead of humans spending their time celebrating the fact that they are privileged to be living in the same age and instead of gladly welcoming their fellow humans with open arms into their lives and homes, and oblivious to the fact that they all have sinned and are on a pilgrimage on Earth, stupid humans allow their egotism to have the upper the hand; and soon enough they begin finding fault with

165

each other and making it a habit to engage in battles for the control of their Mother Earth to the exclusion of their fellow humans. And when they start conspiring to knock off those they regard as their 'enemies', it doesn't even strike them that their mission would be rendered hopeless and pointless if either they or their enemies had come into the world at different times of human history - or not at all!

"They never once stop to reflect on what it means to discover oneself circulating in this former Garden of Eden in the company of other humans who are obviously descended from the same Adam and Eve, and have the same Prime Mover to thank for finding themselves in existence! Instead of taking a moment to reflect on what all this means, they are for ever running around non-stop unconcerned about what they are or their last end, and only bothered about things that serve their self-interest until, exhausted from serving the self, they literally drop dead!

"They go about things in life in much the same way the folks of Judea and Samaria, who heard about the miracles the Nazarene was performing, flocked to His 'crusades' only to lose interest and turn away when they heard the Deliverer urge that they sell whatsoever they had, and give the proceeds to the poor, so they would have treasure in heaven: and then go, take up the cross, and follow Him.

"Snap it! None of you has any power to rub out anyone. You just imagine that you have liquidated those you 'kill', because it is just a matter of time - a very short wait in fact - before you are confronted with those you thought you had eliminated for good. And guess what - once you make up your mind to liquidate a comrade, however nasty he might appear to be and set about looking for ways to achieve your goal, it doesn't really matter whether you succeed in your plan or not. You are already a murderer!

"Stupidly, you humans go out of your way to interfere with the plan the Prime Mover has had in place from time immemorial for the humans you label as your 'enemies' here on earth, not because of a moral threat they pose, but because of a perceived physical threat. Just what do you think you are? You imagine that your 'enemies' are the problem, when it is in fact you yourself who is the bigger problem!

"You humans have no business seeking revenge. The Prime Mover has said that it is His prerogative and His alone to avenge evil. Tit for tat is His prerogative, and humans who try to avenge perceived evils done to them by fellow humans are guilty of usurping the Prime Mover's authority. It is a very grave thing to try to do so, and that is why we in the Underworld work so hard to get you folks to do it. But you demonstrate that you have lost all faith in the Prime Mover when, despite the fact that He sent His only begotten Son to deliver you from evil as He promised, you are bent on revenge - on exacting your pound of flesh!

"Then you would think that humans would know better and not make things worse by lying. Nope! Even dictators who are caught murdering their defenseless subjects will swear that they did it in self-defense! They do it to rid the 'State' of traitors and others who are guilty of committing treason! That is if the 'traitors' don't end up as victors who promptly put the fallen dictator on trial for crimes against the same 'State'. It is just hopeless.

"When humans slaughter cows, well - they just slaughter cows, and that is all there is to it. But when humans 'neutralize' or 'kill' or otherwise attempt in some way to 'rub out' one of their own, that is something else altogether. When a creature, human or otherwise, is created in the 'Image', there is simply no way that creature can ever be rubbed out. When an attempt is made to 'liquidate' that creature, the attempt automatically targets the Word who determined - in eternity and well before that creature existed - that, once in existence, any essence that enjoyed that particular type of 'signature' would exist with Him for ever regardless of what that essence did while on trial.

"It is simply no joke being brought into existence in the Image. Humans and angelic beings alike come into existence as a result a solemn act on the part of the Prime Mover. Every single creature that is fashioned in the Image is prized by the Prime Mover as if it were the only one in existence.

"All creatures that are made in the Image automatically become brides of the Word. They come into being through Him, and He indwells in them from the very first moment of their existence. The ceremonies for celebrating that bridal 'union' typically take place at the time humans depart their earthly existence for their afterlife - after they have proved, during the period of their 'trial', that they too for their part are also in love and are prepared to commit to an eternal union with their Creator in heaven and to thus enter 'permanent wedlock'.

"The date for the 'marriage ceremony' can always be brought forward at the behest of humans - as happened in the case of Augustine, Jerome, Theresa of the Child Jesus, Theresa of Avila, Francis of Assisi, Padre Pio, Thomas Aquinas, Bernard, and others who opted for humble, self-effacing lives. In contrast, my entire short-lived period of trial was marked by running battles of the will in the course of which I sought, unsuccessfully, to impinge on the rights of the Prime Mover Himself.

"To the extent humans remain faithful to their consciences, to that extent they remain fit to be brides of the Word. But when they act contrary to natural and divine laws, they effectively signal that they are not in love with the Word. They declare in their thoughts and by their deeds that they have another suitor, and are calling off the divine wedding. And when humans abjure their love for the Word, there is no clearer way of showing it than turning against their fellow humans who also are brides of the Word by virtue of being made in the Image. Humans, who turn against their siblings, parents and other members of the 'human family', have reason to know that the Word is indwelling in those they have chosen to daub their 'enemies'.

169

"Their act does not just symbolize unfaithfulness; it amounts to an attack on the person of the Word. That is the effect of any deliberate act that aims to 'neutralize', 'dispatch', or 'liquidate' a fellow human. And hence the divine order or commandment that says: 'Thou shalt not kill!' Despite that commandment, some humans give orders to kill - orders that are motivated by 'material' considerations - and still pretend that they are brides of the Word! Those who cause others to die declare war on the Godhead by their actions, and belong in our company here in Gehenna, regardless of their station in life.

"An attempt to rub out a creature that is fashioned in the Image overlooks the fact that the creature in question is very unique, and that its uniqueness springs from the fact that the Prime Mover Himself dwells at its core. Any such attempt goes counter to natural law (which forbids humans and angelic beings to try and get rid of one of their own kind), and supernatural law (because 'murdering' another individual represents a crude attempt to derail the divine plan and frustrate the Prime Mover's intentions).

"To make matters worse, those who try to rub out others do so because they themselves feel inadequate and suffer from an inferiority complex. They feel insecure, and imagine - quite wrongly - that they will feel less threatened with the 'removal' of those who loom as a threat to them. They even forget that a 'dead' human is more dangerous for the simple reason that it is not just the victim's ghost, but the Holy Ghost Himself who comes back to haunt the 'killer' and whoever connived in the attempted 'liquidation'.

"And, it is those who suffer from the most severe forms of insecurity who get easily taken up with strange survival ideologies. When humans feel insecure or threatened, they have this tendency of gravitating towards all sorts of ideologies, especially ideologies that promise power and domination over others. Because they desperately crave to be recognized and if possible also feared, the idea of serving under or working for a 'super power' is always very attractive indeed.

"And, once hooked on to an ideology, chances are that they will end up believing that it doesn't really matter what they do as long as they are focused on making their chosen ideology a winner. They end up believing that the end in fact justifies the mean; and they typically won't tolerate criticism or competition.

"As far as they are concerned, no price will be too great to pay as long as it appears that whatever they are up to promotes their cause - and that holds true even if their expectations turn out to be exaggerated or even plainly unrealistic. When they start putting their pet theories into practice, it will usually be with passion and great determination, and without any regard to public opinion. It is an irony of nature that insecure humans are the ones who usually end up as the most implacable and feared ideologues.

"When humans, who have an inferiority

171

complex and feel insecure, embrace an ideology, more likely than not, existence and life will be at the core of their ideology. They will, however, also have this tendency to proclaim the sanctity of life even as they pursue to destroy all other humans who look like they might pose a challenge that, for people who suffer from inferior complexes, is synonymous with posing a threat. And they will also tend to be extroverts. They will have this strange tendency to proclaim that life is sacred in the same breath as they will be vowing to utterly destroy their 'enemies'!

"They typically cloak their inferiority complex and feelings of insecurity in a show of bravado in which they try to act Superman. The link between the desire to liquidate others and feelings of inadequacy, inferiority complex, and insecurity is not accidental. You might recall that sins - all sins - engender feelings of inferiority complex. It is no wonder that the desire to liquidate others - the desire to commit the worst sin of them all - is driven by these self-same feelings.

"The idea of dominating the world and exercising imperial power is particularly appealing to humans who have an inferiority complex and consequently feel insecure, because it promises total security. They delude themselves that subjugating the whole world will cure their inferiority complex and make their feelings of insecurity go away. They imagine, mistakenly, that pacifying the world will assure that they are rid of all who would otherwise pose a threat to them. Blinded by short-term considerations, they forget the lessons of history according to which pacifying, subjugating, and occupying powers always end up with far more enemies than they can ever handle.

"It is tempting for an independent observer to suppose that war against the invisible enemy that 'terrorists' represent could have been obviated if their concerns, which in fact are modest, had been addressed in an equitable manner at the outset. That the cost of addressing those concerns would have been just a fraction of the tremendous outlays which the self-described 'civilized nations' now stand to incur in taking the fight to their 'invisible enemy'.

"It is also tempting for an independent observer to think that powerful nations, bent on a course of world dominations, could save themselves a lot of problems by tampering their greed and expansionism; that launching unprovoked, pre-emptive assaults on weaker nations in pursuit of so-called 'vital national interests' spells more not less trouble for them as the dispossessed and disenfranchised join the 'invisible enemy' making it a multi-headed, ever-mutating beast that does not stop at seeking redress for humiliations and injustices suffered, but will likewise aim to dominate the world as a matter of survival.

"The 'grievances' aired by the 'terrorists' speak to only a part of the problem. Since the fall of Adam and Eve, humans, inclined to sin, must work to satisfy their greed. Nations become advanced on the backs of other nations; and, as history has shown, it is the changing balance of power that causes smart leaders of imperial powers and colonialists to pull back and curb their greed, and not risk losing all their gains from imperialism and colonialism. But, human nature being human nature, as long as nations still consider themselves 'powerful', they will always be itching to do things that will generate new generations of 'terrorists', 'bandits', 'secessionists', 'revolutionaries', or whatever label spinmeisters in those 'powerful' nations will concoct for the occasion. And that guarantees the cycle of violence the world has lived with since the children of Adam and Eve fought over inheritance.

"The fatal flaw in pursuing this or that perpetrator of 'terrorism' lies in the politics of world domination. Accordingly, acts of 'terrorism' are despicable and unacceptable only when the 'national interests' of 'powerful nations' so-called are threatened. The leaders of those nations play dumb and ignorant when atrocities are committed against humans in other situations, often as a result of conditions that were created by leaders of these very nations (in pursuit of their national interests) or even with their direct connivance, or simply look the other way. Which suggests that those powerful nations are not 'powerful' after all - certainly not when their 'power' depends on the exploitation of resources which they lack at home and are available in the countries they would like to see become satellite states.

"Once humans who suffer from an inferiority complex and feel overly insecure as a result start down that path, it is usually only a matter of time before they also start imagining that they have a messianic mission. And, invariably, that mission will be about trying to dominate the world so that it might benefit from their grandiose visions of things. They will be determined to 'take enlightenment to the ends of the earth', to 'promote democracy', or some such balderdash.

"Instead of seeing danger and making a U-turn, these people typically become fixated with the notion that they themselves are finally making history. And even as the countries they lead are being slowly but surely sucked into the black hole that turns once so-called powerful nations into history, they will be doing everything possible to speed up that process.

"Unfortunately for the super power - and fortunately for us here in the Underworld - the closer a super power gets to the slippery perimeter of the black hole, the more common sense itself ceases to be common. And usually, before long, the truism that people deserve their leaders also begins to apply as protests against plain injustices perpetrated by the nation in the name of 'democracy', 'civilization' or 'enlightenment' within the country's borders fizzle out, and everybody jumps on the wagon of Patriotism in a fruitless attempt to avert the disaster that its leaders had been courting from the beginning.

"Guess what - when I myself took off on my mission to sow the seeds of death (at the time I should have been preparing for the Church Triumphant Entrance Test), I claimed that I was leading the 'struggle for independence' and freedom from the yoke of natural law and divine law! I still claim that I am leading the struggle for independence from the Prime Mover, and that is what makes me a devil! Do I, therefore, talk from personal experience? You bet I do.

"Killers incur the same wrath of the Prime Mover as I did. And if you are looking for proof that being haunted by the 'dead' is an experience that no one should court, just look at me and see how I languish in this 'hellfire' that never goes out. That is what I mean by killers being haunted by the spirits of their victims.

"Talking about killers being haunted, you should know that my scheme to undermine the divine plan by sowing the seeds of death was doomed from the very beginning, just because the immediate objects of my murderous scheme were creatures that were fashioned in the Image. I should have known - or at least guessed - that, in tempting my fellow angels and subsequently humans, I would be automatically challenging the Word who not only brought them into being, but was sworn to defend them with His divine graces.

"I should also have known that any success I had in winning some over to my cause would only make my situation worse - that the spiritual 'death' of each and every spirit I succeeded in misleading would come back to haunt me!

"In the case of a human who dares to raise a finger with the intention of rubbing out another, and who departs from this world for the afterlife whilst unrepentant, the murderous deed results, rather ironically, in the spiritual demise of the would-be-murderer even as the victim gains eternal life in a truly haunting reversal of fortunes. Understand that there is absolutely nothing that victims of this totally aberrant behavior could themselves ever do to reverse what the Word decrees at creation, which namely is that they can never return to nothingness out of which they were made. That any attempt to liquidate them will fail.

"The essence of being created in the Image is that creatures that are fashioned thusly also become endowed with immortality by virtue of being the adopted children of the Prime Mover. The victims themselves might have committed sins and blunders, of course; but it *is* sinners whom the Deliverer came unto this earth to save - not those who are already 'justified' or self-proclaimed saints.

"And in any case, in the eyes of the Prime Mover Himself, there simply is nothing an angelic being or a human can do that will cause the Prime Mover to go back on His "Word" and decide that they deserve to return to the nothingness out of which they came. I myself am in hell because I set out to sow seeds of death, and was allowed to actually kill - rub out my archrival who, like me, was also made in the Image.

"I burned myself far more than I hurt those I was targeting - the rival Arch-Devil, Michael the Archangel, Adam, Eve, and so many others who are enjoying

177

beatific vision even as I speak! Also keep in mind that, even though the Prime Mover made an exception and permitted me to 'rub out' my arch rival, I am now as odious as I am in His eyes - with such detestable titles as 'the Accursed One', 'Father of Death', and 'the Evil One'- because I had the nerve to go through something as unthinkable as that.

"My cause, as Prince of Darkness and Father of Death, was doomed at the inception precisely because I was tampering with the destiny of creatures that had been fashioned in the Image. I even tried to pretend that I was not entirely responsible for the situation, and I had in fact planned to lay the full blame at the door of the Eternal Word. That is what I had planned on doing, because I thought that there was no way the Word could come down on earth to rescue Adam and Eve and their posterity.

"What utterly wishful thinking on my part to imagine that the Deliverer would remain 'neutral' in the matter between me and Adam and Eve - to imagine that the Word could allow me to meddle with the divine plan, and not take action of some kind to halt the madness that had gotten ahold of me. And even after He had promised His Father that He would come to the rescue of humans, I just kept telling myself that He had to be bluffing. I could not imagine the Word reducing Himself to a virtual non-entity for the sake of humans and taking up their nature, promise or no promise!

"It seemed a foregone conclusion that death - the spiritual death that I had succeeded in visiting upon humans - was going to be the lot of every human upon kicking the bucket. I was not just disproved. I am licking my wounds - and talk about being smelly! Some preachers are given to bragging about 'Satan...this' and 'the devil...that'; if He had not come - in fact if He had not *died* to neutralize the consequences of sin - you would all be heading to prison cells in hell as and when your time on earth ran out. In other words, you humans would *die* in the real sense when the time came for your souls to be separated from your bodies!

"Sin has a price that is commensurate with the deed, and a spiritual being that defies the Prime Mover is fully deserving of what has been our own lot since we fell from grace - eternal damnation. And you folks should thank your stars that you can expiate for your sins before your time on earth is up and save yourselves the rap; and you should also be thankful for the fact that those folks who survive you can actually alleviate your plight in Purgatory - yes, Purgatory - by turning a blind eye to insults and being extra good, and asking Him-Who-is-Who-is to apply any graces they earn thereby to alleviating the miseries of the poor souls in Purgatory.

"And those of you who attempt to cut short the lives of *enemies* here on earth might in fact discover, when you yourselves kick the bucket, that you were being used by the Prime Mover as his instruments to consign to Purgatory those sinners who would otherwise have gone straight to hell - something that clearly would not work to your individual benefit because, in trying to get rid of those you hated, you were hoping all along that *they* would end up in hell. Since we still end up with a prize, it doesn't much matter to us. And, in case you folks thought we were indifferent, 'Please, welcome to Gehenna!'

"You ought to know by now that while the Prime Mover *hates sin*, but *loves the sinner*, we for our part *hate sinners* and *love sin*! You should also be aware that killings of humans by humans are the perfect measure of the success of our efforts to derail the divine plan. It is also one reason you folks would be well advised to pray for peace at all times.

The Pilgrim Church and Purgatory...

"Some of you don't understand why there is this Purgatory place, but that is being daft! If you somehow escape my tentacles, but haven't taken advantage of the rest of your time on earth to put off completely the 'old man' and to put on the 'new man' (as St. Paul said), or to apologize and sufficiently make amends to those you wronged (like the good thief did) by doing penance, you surely can't just breeze past St. Peter and get into heaven as if you had never wronged Him-Who-is-Who-is! And, by the same token, it would be unfair if people in that category - which is just about every repentant human who heads off from the earthly life to the after-life remember - were just turned away.

"I mean, because they would be souls that had rejected me and my works, and had come 'clean', even I - Beelzebub - wouldn't be in a position to take them under my wing. Bedecked with divine grace and reconciled to the Prime Mover, they would be completely unwelcome in the Underworld!

"But - guess what - many of you earthlings are so puffed up with your self-importance, you won't even face up to the fact that you are on trial here on earth! And so the sinning - yes, especially the killing - goes on!

"When you humans sin, you are essentially telling the Deliverer to take a hike – or else! You are giving the Word and also Author of Life notice that you regard Him as an ignoramus who made a big mistake by creating you in His image at the time He caused you to come into existence, and endowing you with the gifts of reason and free will! You are not just putting the Word and Lord of the Universe on the spot, but - just like I myself did - you are grading Him C-minus and letting Him know that His performance so far isn't good enough! When Adam and Eve found my suggestion that they would be like the Prime Mover if they ate of the forbidden fruit enticing, and followed through by sampling the fruit from the Tree of Knowledge, they were actually tasking the Word and Son of Man to show why, years later, He wouldn't deserve to be scourged and nailed to the tree for 'wavering' in His response to the chief priests and Pharisees concerning the fate of a "woman who had been caught in the very act of committing adultery" - never mind that there was no mention of the name of the man; and never mind that the prostitute had often serviced the chief priests and Pharisees themselves right there within the temple precincts; and also never mind that the luckless temple guard with whom the woman was having adultery that time around had been water boarded before vanishing mysteriously.

"You stupid humans don't even realize the extent to which you humiliate the Word and Author of Life when you sin! So, so Dumb! I sometimes think that if I somehow went out of circulation - if I had not been foolish enough to attempt that coup - the next arch devil would be a human!

"And talking about dumb humans – I have never seen dumb fools like the so-called 'Modern man'! First, you 'moderns' don't even know that you are dumb! You know…Adam and his contemporaries whom you moderns only imagine as 'cave men' were enjoying life spans that averaged nine hundred years in their time! Eve, the matriarch of humankind, did in fact notch a thousand and twenty years before she gave up her ghost! This was because those humans of old were still capable of harnessing both their brain *and* their brawn as they went about their daily lives - and also because they were not addicted to 'red meat' and 'pills' like you moderns! Yes - pills or, as you call them, 'medicines'! That was too bad because consuming red meat and overdosing themselves with medicines would have hastened their arrival in Gehenna where we succeeded in keeping them prisoner until the Deliverer, after acquiescing to die Himself, turned up there and rescued them!

"If I may digress a bit, you probably now also

182

understand why I myself and the host of demons over whom I wield control never celebrated the Deliverer's death! No, that would never do. The way things were ordained undercut me. When saving humans from the clutches of sin and from damnation, the Son of Man used a clever trick to ensure I wouldn't be able to interfere at all. He emptied himself, taking the form of a slave and being born in human likeness. And, being found in human form, he humbled himself and became obedient to His Father to the point of death - even death on a cross. It was only by emptying Himself to that extent that my minions, including chaps like Herod Agrippa and Pontius Pilate who were worked in tandem with the priests and Pharisees to 'destroy' Him, could get away with it and do not have to face the avenging armies of angels who were just waiting for a word from the Prime Mover to unleash hell on those earthlings.

"That is how dumb you humans are. First, you imagined that if you cut down the Son of Man, it would be the end of it! Quite typical of you humans...and you never learn because nothing has changed - the only thing you think of when someone steps on your toe is to grab an AK 47 and pull the trigger until the poor soul supposedly is no more!

"Yes, we demons work hard to see you humans suffer. When you humans are suffering and unable to pursue earthly joys, you typically imagine that it is finished - you lose all hope, and end up on the verge of despair! And that is what our aim is - to drive you humans to despair! But the Deliverer was, of course, something else altogether. He was literally victorious in death - in allowing fools like you to do to Him what you did. And you can, of course, recall that when the Son of Man cried out with a loud voice and then he died, many graves opened of their own accord, and the bodies of the saints who had gone to sleep in them arose! His death presaged life for you folks!

"To get back to our subject of lifespans of humans, in contrast to the longevity of life enjoyed by the mother of the human race, the oldest she-human of modern times, according to the 'Guinness Book of World Records' so-called, survived for just one hundred and twenty-three years! Her modern male counterpart notched up a hundred and twenty-one years; and only because he drank a lot of *Sho-chu*!

"But the stupidity of humans doesn't stop there! Can you imagine dumb fools like you even suggesting that I, Beelzebub and Lord of the Underworld, ain't bright! Just listen to the language some of them preachers use when talking about me – you would think that a preacher of all people would know that I ain't dumb or stupid! But, No! They seem to get a kick from lambasting me for being the father of death, and then suggesting in the same breath that I am good for nothing and that I am finished! They don't see that I am still very much in charge on this little globe, which will soon be rendered inhabitable even before the clouds of World War III settle down! It is I who is behind the maddening arms race with which you humans have been engrossed for generations.

"Since the discovery of gun powder, the so-

184

called bourgeoisie among you have been intoxicated with the desire to dominate not just the proletariat, but everyone who doesn't huff and puff in the same way as them! And so, that small, terrified 'privileged' class, at my instigation, allowed a mighty, all-powerful military industrial complex to evolve only to cede all political power to it. But what is the military industrial complex? It is of course just my tool in the exact same way all these so-called military alliances are my tool! If you do not believe me, just wait until the third world war breaks out. And if you do not believe that World War III is on the horizon, then you do not know your own human history! I just can't wait to see the expressions on the faces of humans when they see their familiar surroundings - earth, sky and all - ignite and vaporize just before their beloved Mother Earth implodes, as the world's arsenal of nuclear bombs, on which the world's demagogues now spend katrillions of dollars, set one another off!

"You should know that you do not hear very much these days about cases of possession because too many of you seem ready to fill my role unasked? It astonishes me even more because, while at it, no thought is given to the fact that all the rot is transitory, a mirage! And even though you know that this is so, you humans act as though you are going to be able, when your time is up, to turn around and pick up where you left off without in a new lease of life without ever having to confront your Maker and Judge!

"Now, you fools had better learn that your life on earth is not just *like* a one-time stage performance;

it *is* a one-time stage performance, and the performance itself is restricted to one act. Those humans who try to do the right thing - and I really hate them for that - actually look to the moment when the curtain falls, because it hastens their reunion with the Prime Mover and Stage Director. Everybody else - and I really love them for it - balks at the fact that the curtain will fall and they will get something else instead of that hug!"

Mjomba, who thought it was a great idea to have none other than the Prince of Darkness pontificate on things that he himself would rather not in real life, had the devil continue as follows about the nature of humans. It did not strike Mjomba at the time that his book would one day be compulsory reading for all students of religion, or that teachers and students alike would be quoting this shadiest of shady characters to support their theological positions! And so he had Beelzebub continue his parley on human nature uninterrupted.

Spiritus Gallivantus...

"And how did you humans even get the idea that you are *Animal Rationale* - especially when you do not even act like it. I will tell you what you really are: *Spiritus Gallivantus*! You are spiritual essences that can traipse or amble around, and even do a caper! Your bodies or animal features are merely aids to help you navigate around on earth during the time I have permission to tempt you, and test your faith in the Prime Mover.

"And you have a lot to be grateful for; because, in addition to spiritual obstacles like myself, there are lots of physical obstacles out there; and, believe me, you wouldn't last very long without simple things like eyesight. Your bodily organs and sense faculties are just there to complement your spiritual faculties - so you can see where you are going, and also forage for food, communicate with one another, and so forth and so on while you work on the Church Triumphant Entrance Test or 'CTET' as you call it.

"You are not animals, but spirits - just like me, damn you! That is why the fact remains that your Maker will never allow me to tempt any of you beyond what you can bear with the help of His grace; and He, understandably, gives you all the strength you need to carry the crosses that He sends your way. So know that if you were soul-less beasts who bore no resemblance whatsoever to your Maker, regardless of what you could accomplish or do, I wouldn't have any interest in you at all.

"If you were merely animals that were driven by instinct, and you went nuts and decided to ignore what your instincts told you, I would just sit back and observe, curiously of course, as you dove head first into on-coming traffic, or if you yourselves clambered aboard your autos and raced over some cliffs in them - or if you just lay down and starved yourselves to death.

"But you have souls, you nuts. That makes you look too much like Him, and it also makes me hate you as much as I hate Him - don't you see? This is so even if you might be born without limbs or you are conceived OK but end up as utter failures in the eyes of the world - paupers perpetually immersed in debt, or a liability to society for no fault of yours, innocent victims of diabolical schemes concocted by your fellow humans; or if, individually or collectively, you were to somehow meet an ignominious end at the hands of enemies - like your Lord and Messiah did! And just to think that it leaves you strengthened and even closer to the Maker, rather than exposed or weakened!

Homo Sapiens...

"True, 'Thinking Man' is what you humans are - which is just another way of saying that you humans are spirits. And that is also where the confusion begins. Saying that one is a 'rational animal' does not mean that one has to engage in mental exertions - spiritual gyrations or anything of the sort - to realize one's fullness as a rational animal. The fact is that when you humans try to 'think', all you end up doing is 'rationalize', which is not even the same as 'reasoning'. You end up just looking for excuses to justify the empty 'animal' lives you lead. You end up clouding the fact that you are spirits - period - and that you do not need to justify that to anyone.

"In other words, you do not need to engage in a 'thinking' or 'reasoning' exercise either in order to show that you are '*homo sapiens*' or to be one. As a matter of fact, to think clearly and creatively (which is not the same as saying 'generating original ideas' because there is no such a thing as 'an original' idea), a human needs to stop and give 'reflection', an automatic reflex for a human when the conditions are right, a chance to occur.

"In order to 'think', you must relax, leave whatever might ordinarily be distracting to the mind aside, stop 'thinking' in the way that word is normally used in human lingo, and become disengaged from what might be getting you all excited and going off on a tangent. It is only then - when you are curled up in a yoga position and have shut out the world that the human thought processes get a boost and true 'thought' or mental creativity gets a chance to burst forth.

"You had better believe me when I say that it is when you humans effectively 'stop thinking' - it is when you interrupt all that sentimental stuff you equated with 'true thought processes' as defined above - that you really start thinking. It is only then that, freed from worries and other distractions, the soul or 'spiritual' mind gets a chance to transcend matter, and gets in a position to tap that unlimited fountain of truly enriching ideas or thoughts that ultimately emanate from Wisdom or Him-Who-is-Who-is, and to start maturing spiritually.

"When you humans exert yourselves and try to 'think' (perhaps to show that you are very clever!), you actually stifle learning and you become dumber. In order to meditate fruitfully and become enriched in your thoughts, it is of the essence to banish distractions the way monks in monasteries do when practicing 'yoga'. Yes, monks in monasteries who discovered the 'yoga' that people like Einstein and all other great inventors practiced.

"That is why a good night's sleep is the best preparation for 'sitting a paper', not an all-night immersion in books that leaves you all excitable, distracted by all the stuff you were trying - most likely unsuccessfully - to absorb, unable to concentrate, and prone to misread and misunderstand the exam questions!

"This is a set-up that clearly favors infants whom grown-ups, in their stupidity, mistakenly fancy to be both gravely handicapped and seemingly prone to go to sleep as soon as they get their fill. Actually, infants do not really sleep all that much. But they relax a lot and, in the process, abandon themselves to the 'spontaneous thought processes' or 'meditation' (in the correct sense of that word) quite a lot. Children learn so fast because they do not have the bad habit of the 'roving eye' and other habits of that nature which plague grown-ups.

The wise and the not so wise...

"It must sound very funny coming from me of all creatures; but it is true, nonetheless, that when some of you - poor banished children of Adam and Eve - find yourselves fulfilled and not wanting, you become so distracted by the good life, you forget, for the most

190

part at any rate, that there is such a thing as a doomsday clock. You conveniently forget that it exists even though none of you has found a way of disabling it. There is no doubting that the good life does engender a false sense of security which might even lull one into concluding that there indeed is justice and fairness in the world!

"Not surprisingly, there are so many of you who find things so comfy, you have become oblivious to the fact that a small event like a bad deal, a burglary or some freak accident, a storm or perhaps even a flood, or a black-out and the myriad things that might ensue there from in its wake including looting, a riot, a coup d'etat or a revolution, a fire, a war or a famine or the outbreak of a plague, a landslide or an earthquake, a volcanic eruption, or perhaps Doomsday itself - for those of you who will live long enough to see it - not only will prove things otherwise, but those 'successful' people will find themselves in the exact same boat as those who are 'failures' in the eyes of the world.

"I like to compare these so-called 'successful' sons and daughters of Adam and Eve to a group of people who go surfing on the worldwide web for the purpose of getting directions to the heavenly Paradise; but who become so distracted by the different pop-up banners which greet them from the moment they log on to the Internet, they decide to give up their search and spend the rest of their time exploring the web sites, of which there is an innumerable number. Switching to computers with superior memory, and using Yahoo, Excite and other powerful search engines, they pass their days exploring cyberspace and enjoying, and completely lose sight of what they had originally gone to the web to look for.

"The original 'failures' are those people who are really interested in making the journey to the heavenly Paradise. After logging onto the worldwide web - and they do so at the same time the first group does - they completely ignore the irritating banners and proceed to specify 'Heavenly Paradise' when prompted to spell out their intended destination. From the bewildering array of 'sites' which represent themselves as paradise of one sort or another, and each of which suggests to them that they need not go any further in their quest for a good *time* and happiness, they pick out the only site which does not imply that it is an *earthly* paradise. They click on '*Way of the Cross*', which is the name of the site and, on entering, find the directions they were looking for.

"Logging off the worldwide web, they commence their journey and presently find themselves retracing the footsteps of their Savior, and trudging along a meandering stretch of road which takes them from what is easily recognizable as the Upper House, site of the inauguration of the Blessed Eucharist, through the Garden of Gethsemane, past the imposing palace of the Roman Governor who is better known as The Fox, and on to the summit of Mt. Calvary! You cannot get to the mountaintop by any other way, and it is of course one route that we of the

Underworld have worked over in what you can be sure is very thorough fashion, and that consequently is studded with every conceivable obstacle. And I will try and give you some idea of the sorts of people you will find struggling to make it to the summit along that route.

"Actually, one of them is a mentally retarded man. He has been languishing on death row awaiting execution for a murder he did not commit! You just cannot imagine how hard we've tried to trip him up. Fortunately for him, he is really insane and all our efforts, which are ongoing even as I speak, have not been able to drive him crazier than he already is. And that is how he seems to be succeeding in getting to the summit of Calvary. Another one of their number is a fellow who was water boarded over and over by some crazies, and who ended up being coerced into confessing to a crime he didn't commit either and is now languishing in jail. Looks like he too will escape my tentacles because, after what his jailors have taken him through, this fellow seems prepared to die under the load of his 'cross'. This fellow is suicidal!

"And yet another one - a woman who was forcibly raped and impregnated by guards while she was serving a jail term for a misdemeanor - has decided against an abortion. She is typical of those people who seem determined not just to believe in the Deliverer, but also to try and walk the walk. Even as I speak, she is quietly raising her baby and watching him grow up into a happy and athletic young man, with nary a word to anyone about the humiliations that

193

have marked the road she has travelled. By resisting the temptation to go public and even sue the authorities, she has actually helped our cause, because this means that the jailors can continue preying upon other female inmates in those sink holes you folks call jails at will. These are the kinds of injustices we in the under-world like to see become commonplace. Because then the perpetrators can be sure of joining our ranks here in hell when the time for their trial on earth is up.

"You've got to give me and my cronies credit for making sure that any soul that gets past St. Peter and walks through that gate into heaven is fully deserving of the crown!

"The lives of those who try to retrace the Stations of the Cross make very interesting tales indeed, and you should love this one. It is the story of a young padre whose zealous parents coerced him into the priesthood and a life of celibacy. After striving over the years to remain faithful to his priestly vows, he is worried that he may now be at the end of his tether, and has decided to take it a day at a time while praying that he be taken from this world before something catastrophic happens!

"This is one case I have been taking a personal interest in - the objective is simple and straight forward, namely drive the fellow to despair! It is that simple - but, inexplicably we may be failing in our objective of getting this fellow to stop believing that there is an Omnipotent Being who cares for the forsaken. The way things have been going lately, this priest just might succeed in escaping my tentacles.

"We've gone to the extent of using a poor soul - a scoundrel who had been abused by his own parents as far back as he could remember and who had additionally been under my virtual control from the time he was a little baby - to try and derail the man of cloth. We succeeded in snaring the priest into a situation the whole world believed was compromising. And so, falsely accused of taking advantage of an 'innocent' altar boy who had been entrusted to his care by 'loving' parents, the padre not long ago found himself in jail for his 'abominable crime'. The story sounded so credible, even the Church tribunal found him guilty, and endorsed the long jail term that a sleazy magistrate, who obviously had grudge against the priest - something to do with a divorce and the padre's reluctance to bless the judge's marriage to his current girl friend - handed down.

"And you would think we would be done with the poor man at that point out of pity. Wrong! In the jail house, we've got there rotten characters who, operating in concert with the guards, have been repeatedly violating his person in such an unspeakable fashion, if he had been someone else, he would have preferred to take his own life! But the humiliation only seems to have strengthened the fellow's resolve to keep the faith! Not even after he contracted an incurable disease as a result of being repeatedly assaulted by fellow prison inmates. And, as if in mockery of our efforts to drive the fellow to despair, as the priest lies dying in his jail cell, alone and without any possibility of receiving the last sacraments, his face is enveloped in this strange, mesmerizing smile even as I speak - as if he is eager to get up and meet Someone he greatly loves and admires! I have never been so humiliated!

"Those who persevere and make it to the summit of Calvary have one thing in common, and it is that they do not have any trust in themselves. And yet you would think that to be able to make it over a road that is so studded with obstacles that I get the best minds in the Underworld to device, the individual needed to have something of a Don Quixote in him/her!

"Contrary to what pseudo prophets will tell you, salvation and being 'small minded' evidently go together. And, as well, do not be deceived that 'blessings' come your way in this life when you decide to follow the Deliverer or, as some like to put, when you 'become born again'. Nothing is farther from the truth! There would, otherwise, be no reason for anyone to decry what goes on in Hollywood if being richly 'blessed' on this earth was one of the measures of spiritual success.

"'Accursed' is a much better description of the life of the folks who make it to the summit of Calvary, I tell you! And you, of course, understand that their reward is not in this world, but in heaven. And so, if you hear someone saying that you will receive blessings here on earth when you accept the Deliverer, take it with a pinch of salt. Moreover, if your conversion is not staged and is true spiritual conversion, the first thing you are likely to experience is probably going to be what is known as the 'dark night of the soul'! That is because my troops and I will be working overtime to try and reverse that situation. That is also the price you pay for rejecting me and my works!

"Also, those who brag about being 'clever', 'diligent', 'far sighted' and that sort of nonsense cannot prevail against my wiles, for the simple reason that the mind of the least endowed among my troops will always be more than a match for the brightest human mind! Cleverness, business acumen, far sightedness and things like that would of course work in normal circumstances. But you fellows don't exist in circumstances that are anywhere near normal! Don't you remember Paul telling the Corinthians that the world as you now know it is passing away?

"That is why it is so true (as you yourselves sing) that 'He guides the humble to justice; and He teaches the meek His way'! And keep in mind that it is not what goes in that corrupts, but what comes out. It is these sorts of things that have me and my troops fooled every time, I can tell you - and all my clairvoyance notwithstanding!

Finding rest for the soul...

"But if I may let you in on a secret - the Catholic Church's biggest handicap in its work of saving souls is the fact that its priests and prelates, not just in these times but throughout the Church's two thousand-year history, by and large do not practice what they preach. They act and behave just like the priests and Pharisees did two thousand years ago! Notice the aloofness of the clergy? It has its roots in the certainty - yes, certainty - of members of the Church's clergy that they and only they are the rightful successors of the apostles!

"That aloofness - or lofty indifference to attempts by anyone who is not one of their number to engage them in a discussion of matters of faith - amounts to a statement that they should be taken off of the all 'unorthodox' sounding mailing lists. I have even observed souls that are groping for enlightenment turned away because members of the clergy, perhaps taking the cue from some of Christendom's popes, generally like to pontificate and don't have any time to listen - to lend 'strangers' their ear! You can see straight away that such an attitude represents a serious problem for the growth in holiness of members of the clergy themselves and an even bigger problem for the work of evangelization whose success depends very much on how well priests live as *alteri Christi*.

"Members of the clergy are in a tricky situation - they must try and impress their audiences that it is the whole truth and nothing but the truth to which they give expression, whether by word of mouth or by writing. And that automatically conflicts with the fact that they are not exempt from the requirement that all must be like little children - and also the fact that *'He guides the humble to justice; and He teaches the*

198

meek His way! In short, there is always a real danger that the call by priests that their flocks be humble and meek and as little children is really a hollow statement, because it does not reflect what they themselves do. You've got to understand that this is one group of people whose endeavors my lieutenants and I will happily work unpaid overtime - yes, unpaid overtime - to undo.

"When we are not tempting those fellows to stand in their pulpits and essentially act like the Pharisee who, unlike the tax collector who was so ashamed of his life that he found it necessary to hide his face in the shadows of the pews at the back of the Synagogue, was certain that he was, for all practical purposes, already saved and redeemed, we are tempting them to behave as if they have a monopoly over truth, and to show that they do not care less for any would be challenger in that regard. And we tempt them above all to imagine that they themselves do not need to be as little children to receive the Holy Ghost's guidance and instruction. We actually tempt them to think they do not need the Holy Ghost, the weekly homilies to their flocks urging them to be meek and humble of heart notwithstanding - period.

"If you do not believe me, go to the official website of the Vatican. It is full of stuff - really good stuff actually - that *you* are supposed to read and internalize. But if you should have the audacity to try and address *the authors* an e-mail regarding the material on the website, the response is likely to be something like: 'Pray for meekness and humility so that you may receive the guidance of the Holy Ghost and accept the Church's teachings' or 'take me off your mailing list'! I call that being 'sharp' and 'smart'. And, if it were possible for a celebration to take place in Gehenna, that state of affairs in God's Church would constitute a reason for non-stop celebration. Unfortunately it only hurts when we in the Underworld try to throw a party.

"However elevated you might be in the Church's hierarchy, the moment you begin thinking that you are a somebody - the moment you start to think that you have no need for anyone else and that you do not need to heed voices from the pew or elsewhere, that you are in some way special, can withstand temptations of the flesh, and are in a position to face and overcome my wiles single-handed without the help of other people's prayers or God's grace - the moment you start to promote yourself in that fashion, you also automatically begin to demote God the Father (who formed you along with other members of the human race out of nothing), God the Son (who came down from heaven, took up human nature and ended up being nailed on the cross by your kindred, and was left hanging from it helplessly - while the crowd mocked Him and while He was to all appearances abandoned even by His Father - until He finally died in expiation of the sins of men), and God the Holy Ghost (to whom those amongst you who pray confess that you are good for nothing on your own and are entirely dependent on Him to keep out of trouble and for any

200

accomplishment that might appear to accrue to your personal efforts) in your life. You then also are underestimating me - and I don't take kindly to anyone who does.

"From the moment any individual begins to regard himself or herself as a 'somebody', from that same moment, he or she exposes himself or herself to the weakness of the flesh in addition to leaving himself or herself completely at my mercy! And the fact that one is ordained a priest - or gets elevated to the full rank of an apostle and trades in his parish for a bishopric and, in these days, also a bishop's crozier, mitre and the Episcopal ring that members of the flock genuflect to kiss - should constitute an even bigger reason to strive to be truly meek and humble. How otherwise can the individual connect with his flock, and engage everyone who comes knocking at the door in fruitful spiritual dialogue.

"Can you just imagine a swashbuckling and haughty Prince of the Church standing there in full regalia like a peacock, trying to welcome souls into the Mystical Body of Christ! It is a complete contradiction, and it is not the kind of opportunity a prince of darkness like me would possibly pass up and not exploit to the max! You should certainly be able to imagine what Peter or Paul looked like as they journeyed back and forth in Asia Minor in their endeavors to win souls for the Deliverer.

"You can certainly imagine what they would have said if the chaps they were grooming to take over when they themselves passed on had turned up

201

for work one morning bedecked in chasubles, wearing mitres handcrafted in silk atop their burnished crowns, and waving gold-plated crosiers in place of their usual, rough-shod walking canes! Poor souls from all walks of life are struggling to keep pace with the intermittent glimmer of stars in the darkened skies as they attempt to locate the one that will lead them to the Holy Child in a manger - the Holy Child who is hosted, mark you, by poor shepherds and not by puffed and haughty men of the cloth! And this is not because I, Beelzebub, do not know how the transformation in the Church came about. You'd better believe me when I tell you that I worked very hard personally to bring it about!

"And so, when you think you are a stalwart spiritually and you proceed to claim that God is blessing you, you are really calling something else upon yourself. You are begging the Judge to pronounce you a 'betrayer', perhaps even an incorrigible sinner and hypocrite who is determined to shut out the Deliverer's redeeming graces, and who might conceivably be entirely unfit as a man of the cloth!

"No, being sharp and smart does not get humans anywhere in the business of holiness. But being as nothing does. And Judas Iscariot was a case in point. He was so cock sure of his ability to withstand my wiles as well as temptations of the flesh, he did not think he really needed the Deliverer. This was even though he was a very smart man and also the Deliverer's confidante.

"If you ask me - my dear friend Iscariot, who dropped out of the seminary just weeks before the risen Deliverer performed the first ordinations to the priesthood under His new testament, was actually a great intellectual with a sharp wit that made him stand out among the candidates the Deliverer had handpicked after reviewing the resumes of scores of his disciples. You ought to know by now that when it comes to opposing me and my troops, pig headedness of that kind isolates the cocky individual from the Source and allows us to make quick work of him or her.

"I can't stand the sight of some loud-mouthed nitwit who comes along out of nowhere, and is all suddenly puffed up and 'raring to go' as if he/she can fly to heaven on his/her own volition - as if I, Beelzebub, can be brushed aside just like that! It is a disrespect I do not take lightly, and I typically hit back with deadly force. You see - it is a grave disrespect when you humans try to face off with me on your own. I deal with all who disrespect me in the exact same way and judo style. I lead them along and encourage them to get really bold and to think that they can even dispense with the grace earned for them by the Deliverer. And it is when they are finally intoxicated with their self-love that I pounce on them and strike.

"When it is opportune, I will even get them to take their audacity to the logical conclusion by imagining that they can self-righteously shove their warped beliefs and ideology down other people's throats - especially those over whom they have any kind of influence. They typically realize that they have been on the wrong track all along too late - when those who had followed them blindly, suddenly decide to cast off what they finally perceive as a self-imposed yoke!

"But take the case of Peter. A simple fisherman and one of the original twelve apostles, he is one of the best examples of those who are 'failures' in the eyes of the world. Unschooled in the ways of the world, you could in fact say that he was a precise fit for my description of a dunce! This fellow ended up in the top leadership position in the infant Church, appointed by none other than the Messiah Himself. And if there was anything that worked in his favor, it was the fact that he was meek, readily admitted that he was himself a nonentity, and that he was completely dependent on the Almighty One, and on those who were sent to help him shepherd God's flock, for bringing in the harvest. But in spite of being so humble and reticent, our camp still succeeded in accomplishing a couple of things to make Peter's evangelical work very difficult - and we of course are still at it. You bet! We work hard to ensure that a couple of new splinter groups turn up in Christendom every week, because if there weren't all these denominations to add to the confusion, it would be so much easier for the adherents to other religions to find their way into the Church that was founded by the Deliverer.

"At the trial which preceded the execution by crucifixion of his Lord and Savior, Peter, caving in to the pressures that we were applying, denied any knowledge of the Messiah not once or twice, but a full three times! That is just one of the things we succeeded in bringing off, and you can bet that he was haunted by his denial of the Messiah for the rest of his life.

"A simple man who had been content to live and die a fisherman just like his forefathers before him, it was not as if Peter had sought out and followed the Son of Man out of personal ambition or with a view to gaining anything from being a follower of the Anointed One. He would always distinctly recall that sunny afternoon in autumn when the stranger from the little town of Nazareth, who nonetheless spoke with the authority of the Ruler of the Universe, commanded him to leave his boat, fishing tackle and all and follow him. In retrospect, the account of his life had all the ingredients of a scriptural legend.

"Anyway, the fact was that, Peter, uncontested leader of the Deliverer's 'troops' in the period immediately following the resurrection from hell and ascension into heaven of the Son of Man, who (much to my chagrin) now also celebrated the Holy Eucharist almost on a daily basis and was responsible for providing innovative leadership to the body of apostles in the work of evangelization and doing so infallibly, had publicly denied knowing his Lord and Savior. It was a denial that had not just been a slip of the tongue, but one that had been made in full view of Jerusalem's press corps, and which had received extensive coverage in the media along with that week's other tumultuous events.

"For the rest of his days on earth, the strident voice of that woman in the crowd identifying him as the Chief of Staff of the growing army of the condemned Man's followers, his own halting voice as he lied in front of everyone and proceeded to provide alibis that proved unsustainable, and the shattering sound of a cock's crow which seemingly came from nowhere - and also the words '*Tu es Petrus, et super hanc petram, Ecclesiam meam edificabo*' - would never stop ringing in his ears.

"Regrettably, that woman - whom we got to screech on Peter - a rascal and turncoat in our opinion, subsequently converted to Christianity herself not long after, and even died for her faith at the hands of a functionary of Pilate's by the name of Saul. And that Saul, who changed his name to Paul, was another turncoat who suddenly abandoned our cause just when we thought we were succeeding in strangling the Christian Fellowship. He became one of Christianity's fiercest crusader! We ourselves have had our ups and downs as you can see.

"One reason Peter stumbled and fell as he and John raced to the tomb on the day the Deliverer and Son of Man rose from the dead was that the echoes of his trembling voice as he denied his Master three times continued to ring in his ears all at once and incessantly, and had reduced him to a virtual zombie.

"To make things worse, the leader of the nascent Church was also prone to have bad dreams. Now I can tell you that we in the Underworld love people who dream dreams. Dreams are a ready-made vehicle for temptation, and provide me Old Scratch and my fellow fiends wonderful opportunities for manipulating the human mind, you see!

"On each of the seven days that followed the Day of Pentecost - the day Peter along with the other disciples spoke in tongues to the Jewish worshippers who had come to Jerusalem from different parts of Asia Minor and other parts of the globe - he had the same identical dream. Peter dreamed that his travels had taken him all the way to Rome, where he decided to settle permanently. And, according to the nightmarish dream, he had set up home in a castle atop a nearby hill that went by the name of 'Gandolfo'! But that was not all. He dreamt that by the time he got to Rome, the power of the Roman emperor had greatly waned, while his own power as the leader of Christendom had grown to the point at which he could appoint or dethrone Caesar's successors at will!

"It was, of course, not so much the fact that he wielded such colossal power which made the dream a bad one as the fact that the dream reminded him of Pontius Pilate and of the woman who had picked him out of the crowd on that 'Good Friday' morning. The dream made it appear as if he, Peter, could verily have stopped 'the fox' from sending his Lord and Master to an undeserved and cruel death by just 'telling the truth and shaming the devil' instead of cowering with fear and denying that he had any knowledge of the condemned Man.

"As if that was not bad enough, on the

consecutive nights following the day the Messiah ascended into heaven in full view of the disciples, Peter had a different kind of dream even though it also had something to do with Rome. He dreamed that his travels, devoted to the spread of Christianity, had brought him to the City of Seven Hills where Peter was promptly apprehended and condemned to die by crucifixion for his activities.

"The dream was nightmarish not so much because of the garish manner in which his life was going to end, but because Peter felt completely unworthy of the honor of dying in a manner that was so similar to that in which the Deliverer had chosen to die in atonement of the sins of men. Certainly not after his denial had directly resulted in the Deliverer's death - if there was anything to the earlier dream, that is. When he awoke from his nightmarish dream, Peter, like the scrupulous fellow he was, refused to forgive himself for presuming and imagining that he could leave this world for the next in the same manner his Lord and Savior did! Troubled, Peter swore repeatedly that he would never allow that to happen - almost as if he had the power to dictate how his earthly life would end.

"The number of humans who set out with the intention of 'walking the walk' with the help of the directions they obtain from the worldwide web is large. And that is not surprising because unless squelched - and it takes a lot of determination to do so - the craving of souls for that perfect Good is as powerful as the source of the desire for fulfilment.

And you can bet that all those souls will each one have a similar story to tell.

"Now, you should also understand that a devil like me gets a real kick out of dethroning a fellow spirit. I am the author of death after all! That is why I love to hear you folks say: 'He made me do it!' That is even though I can never really make you do anything until you yourself choose to play along! I would feel like I had smacked ox below the belt if I heard one them ox confide to the rest of the herd: 'He made me do it!'

"It is evident that you humans prefer to think of yourselves as beasts or animals. Don't want to take any responsibility for your actions, Eh! It is something we fallen spirits couldn't do even if we tried. Unfortunately, the more you humans believe you are animals, the less pleasure I derive from derailing any of you. By doing so, you lull yourself into a false sense of justification and you spoil my fun in the process!

"If you need any additional evidence for the fact that you humans are inclined to sin, it is this obsession with the animal aspect of your human nature and your continual denial of the fact that you are spiritual beings first and foremost. And, again, it should be embarrassing that humans need Satan to remind them of this simple fact.

"And this is not to suggest that the human body isn't sacred. During the one hundred and twenty years or so that the body is informed by the spirit - that period used to be around four hundred years

209

before the combination of medical discoveries so-called and poisoned meat and fish, and junk food triggered the deficiencies in your immune systems - the human body is also the temple of the Prime Mover and Author of Life. If that were not the case, you can be sure that you all would be possessed and in the full control of one or other member of my team from the moment you were conceived in the womb! You'd better take my word for it - even if you do not believe anything else I say!

"You see - when you are made in His image, even though you are created an intelligent and also free creature, it is really your likeness to Him which makes you special. When discussing humans, there is no such a thing as 'the extent to which humans are *not* made in the Prime Mover's likeness', or 'in so far as their likeness to something *other* than the Perfect One goes'. It is the reason all humans, including the characters that might appear to you as really distasteful, are very precious in the eyes of the Creator. And, indeed, that is why to the extent a human sees another as 'distasteful', to that extent that human himself or herself becomes less deserving of his or her position as a servant of the Prime Mover - because, in so doing, that human effectively attempts to usurp the prerogative of the Prime Mover and Judge.

"Humans who do not see the beams in their own eyes, and get all worked up about imaginary specs of dust in the eyes of others, would never make good judges. But they are the ones who, with a little help from my troops and I, are out there pontificating about criminal minds of those they perceive as their enemies without tiring.

"The likeness of you humans to the Prime Mover is what makes you capable of transcending the limitations of time and space, enabling your accomplishments (and failures) under those conditions to be credited (or debited) to your eternal life. It is what makes physical acts neither good nor bad in themselves, and intentions paramount in determining the extent to which a deed is noble or otherwise. The consciences of humans derive their legitimacy and authority from the likeness humans bear to the Prime Mover, and also attest to His presence at the kernel of the human soul.

"And, on a completely different level, the likeness of humans to the Prime Mover or 'God' is what makes what I call 'innocent' joys innocent - the taste of good food and good wine, the sounds of a harmonious tune, the sight of a lily flower bed or a virgin forest, and so on and so forth. Except that, in this former Garden of Eden which is now effectively a Valley of Tears as a result in part of my scheming, you humans would be well advised to forego even those innocent enjoyments as part of self-mortification and to expiate for the sins you commit from time to time, and in order to keep the possibility of becoming addicted to the 'innocent' pleasures and getting sucked into something else (things not even the beasts get into) remote. And, of course, innocent enjoyments and delights stop being innocent the moment they start being actively sought! Because then intentions, and *ipso facto* also the conscience, and all that they imply immediately come into play.

"The likeness of humans to the Prime Mover's image is the reason every human has an inalienable right to life, and also why taking away the life of another is one of the surest ways of putting one's own eternal life in jeopardy. It is the reason humans have a right to freedom of worship. It explains why all humans are equal, and acts of discrimination are outlawed. It is also the reason each and every human act or thought that is deliberate either pleases or displeases the Prime Mover.

"It is the reason mortal creatures like you still can pray to and even commune with the Prime Mover who is divine and immortal with confidence. It is the reason humans can smile and laugh - unlike beasts and other 'lower' creatures. It is because you humans are made in the image of a divinity that you sometimes feel like you can fly - even if you do not have any wings! It is, of course, the reason no human can vanish from the Prime Mover's sight let alone be forgotten by Him. And last but not least, it is what makes me, Beelzebub who was also created in God's own image and likeness, stand condemned for my role in the downfall of humans, for grooming all those false prophets and sending them out into the world to counter Truth, and for doing whatever else I do.

"But why do I have to tell you these things, you numskulls! If I, Diabolos, can be pining away here in this place of damnation, completely cut off by flames that cannot be extinguished from all that is godly, fair, beautiful and good...done in by what used to be my very own flames of desire, how can dunces like you even hope to prevail by setting yourself up in opposition to Him-Who-is-Who-is! And just imagine how humbling it is for me to be here - against my own will of course - confessing these things! Nay, eating my own words! You cannot begin to imagine how chastening it is for me to be here talking to you like this.

Fulfillment...

"But, I must say, you humans have a really screwed up idea of happiness! While we devils might have a reason to take our revenge on you humans because of the fact that you will take up residence in mansions in heaven that were really meant for us, it is difficult, even for us devils, to see any rationale for the belief by humans in revenge, visiting capital punishment on members of society who are singled out as being 'errant' (which is really legalized murder that emulates Cain's act of fratricide and overlooks the fact that, once in existence, creatures that are fashioned in the Image can never be rubbed out), wars whether they are labeled pre-emptive wars, wars of attrition, or holy wars, and things of that sort. That is, of course, not to say that we are about to try and dissuade you from indulging in them. But the pleasures and satisfaction you derive from exacting revenge or watching so-called 'criminals' being hanged - as if you yourselves were not that or, perhaps, even worse - must provide the most ephemeral and passing of pleasures. I have a perfectly valid excuse - you can even call it 'reason' - for referring to you humans as stupid.

"The revenge exacted by the Prime Mover is of a completely different nature and on a different plane. It makes complete sense, and is actually brought on by creatures who are fashioned in His image and likeness, but who go against their own reason and attempt to be what they are not.

"The stupidity of you humans also shows glaringly when you pursue other 'pleasures' like gluttony for instance. When gormandizing in an effort to satisfy the palette, you humans completely forget the simple logic which applies in your particular case - at least whilst you still have that body. At the time you are satisfying your appetite for food, your other appetites which you cannot satisfy all at the same time as a practical matter - and I won't go into a litany of these appetites - will also be crying out for fulfilment; and fulfilment in an atmosphere of peace - meaning an atmosphere that engenders uninterrupted and above all enduring satisfaction.

"But this hopeless situation is rendered more hopeless by the fact that the food employed by the individual to satisfy the palette might taste just fine one day - which itself may mean any number of things - depending on things like the weather and the mood of the individual gobbling it up. On another day, its taste might remind the individual of some really dainty dish which he or she enjoyed many years before as a child. And on another day, regardless of the skills of the chef, weather conditions, and even that individual's determination to revel in the food, it might taste like vinegar! And similarly for the other appetites you folks are always trying to assuage.

"And then the celebratory activity of the hedonist might be completely frustrated for any number of reasons - an emergency visit to the dentist, a draught, or even the premature death of the joy seeker. Now, I mean...if you can even die - well, put it this way - if you will die, then not only are the efforts you expend in the meantime pursuing passing pleasures a total waste; but any fleeting 'happiness' you might derive there from also effectively becomes a stain on your record - a stain that labels you as being one of those individuals who seem to be satisfied with illusions, and have no interest in the real thing.

"Unfortunately for us angelic creatures so-called, we don't die. I mean - we are ghosts and we really couldn't 'give them up' in the same way you humans do. And I say 'unfortunately' because if we did - if we too possessed some sort of 'body' that we would have had to vacate on a non-spiritual plane before facing the Judge on a spiritual plane, we might have thought twice before we bolted and landed ourselves in this accursed place!

"Any way, you couldn't get clearer testimony to the fact that this whole preoccupation with self-indulgence is based on flawed logic. The very objects you folks use to get satisfaction are not even meant for that purpose. Their purpose is not to engender fulfilment in that sense at all; and, try all you can, you won't succeed in getting those objects - many of which are inanimate - to give you, a spiritual creature, what they do not possess. How could they possibly give you true *spiritual* joy? They might give you material and, by definition *transitory*, happiness!

"The idea of different types and/or levels of satisfaction is completely inconsistent with the idea of fulfilment in the sense in which that word applies to creatures that are made in the image of Him-Who-is-Who-is. To be real, that fulfilment has to be complete, unchanging, and permanent.

"You humans don't even seem to be aware that the situation resulting from such dissolute lifestyles is more devastating to the human constitution - destabilising, if you like - than that which would prevail if you were just busy curbing your appetites and abstaining from all pleasures. If you exercised your will and did that, you would see that your other appetites and desires for fulfilment would gradually diminish in their intensity and even eventually go to sleep, and you yourself would get some respite.

"Because of the peculiar way in which sense faculties and the appetites they serve are linked, when an individual seeks to satisfy one sense faculty, the appetites served by the other faculties automatically also start to clamor for fulfilment - because of the simple reason that they all belong to a body that is informed by the same spirit. By the same

216

token, mortification and things like abstinence, self-abnegation and works of atonement or penance engender calm, composure and serenity. They facilitate growth on the spiritual plane, and the flowering of virtues, while dampening any tendencies to wantonness and profligacy.

"And if it were not for the pervasive hypocrisy, ingrained intellectual dishonesty, and moral bankruptcy, humans would actually see proof of the existence of the Prime Mover in their very inability to perform any virtuous act without the aid of divine grace. The wickedness of humans, which drove them to attempt to liquidate the Deliverer and has brought them on the verge of sending Planet Earth up in a plume of smoke with nuclear explosions that are targeting their own kind, beggars even our demonic imagination. That is how far the fools have travelled down the path to perdition.

"The reason saints in heaven can enjoy rapturous joy, happiness and complete fulfilment is because the totality of their person is fulfilled all at one and the same time, and without any threat of interruption, in the presence of Him-Who-is-Who-is. Just as He Himself is not just beautiful, but ultimate Beauty itself - or just good but ultimate Goodness itself - partial things are not possible in His presence. The angels and saints are able to share in that Beauty and Goodness only because the totality of their individual person, not just parts of themselves, had been readied for fulfilment. That is what emptying oneself or being selfless means!

"My own hell now consists in the fact that I squandered the opportunity to have the totality of me fulfilled; and that happened when I focused on self-aggrandizement during the period I was on trial, instead of surrendering myself to Him-Who-is-Who-is without any reservation. Being the first one He had created in His own image and likeness and a free creature, I tried to stake out for myself a special position which would see me - or so I thought - wield unfettered authority over all the creatures that would follow after me. I was in effect going out on a limb, and lunging after fulfilment on my own, instead of putting all my trust in Him and waiting patiently to be ushered into His regal presence. I undercut myself in that way.

"If you are curious about conditions in the hell that is now my lot, go find out for yourself what Lucia, Francisco and Jacinta told Father Pena, their parish priest, after they were allowed a glimpse of the place. And if you do not believe their account, you can go read the accounts that St. Catherine of Siena, St. Frances of Rome, St. Theresa of Avila, St. John Bosco, St. Faustina Kowalska, and more recently Sister Josefa Menendez left for you. And if you still don't get it, why don't you do yourself a favor and just go look up all those biblical passages in both the New and Old Testament that describe the conditions here in Hades.

"I know that I am stupid - very stupid, in fact, considering the miscalculation I made - me and the host of angels I succeeded in misleading, so I wouldn't be all by myself in Gehenna. But you are more stupid, I tell you...for one, unlike us, you have this second chance which you seem determined to fritter away. And I certainly didn't have some stupid devil come and make a homily. Of course, it suits me perfectly that you are all so stupid - I do not have to worry that you will hear me out or pay attention to any of the things I am suggesting to you. And it goes without saying that you will cite as your excuse the fact that it is me, Beelzebub - aka Diabolos, the Evil One, and Prince of the Darkness - who is the messenger - albeit a reluctant one.

"I actually like the way you idiots make it look as if you are in a Catch 22 situation here. The classic Catch 22 situation - lending your ear to the Tempter whose business it is to tell lies or doing the very opposite of what I am suggesting and being damned! Can't actually think of a better Catch 22! I shouldn't even complain that I am standing here giving this testimony against my will. But your stupidity is just my first line of defense. For those of you who do decide to proceed and try to implement those truly excellent suggestions, the real battle starts right there.

Fight to the finish...

"First of all, even though the spirit might show that it is willing to act, the flesh will almost certainly pull you into the opposite direction. But usually it is your desire to show off and try to bring it off all on your own, without the help of the grace of Him-Who-is-Who-is that constitutes my second line of defense. When you neglect to pray or when you just say what I like to refer to as the 'Hypocrite's Prayer', it usually also assures me victory, while you yourselves, puffed up with pride and mired in hypocrisy, end up attempting vainly to suppress those natural appetites.

"You bet I have lots of fun watching folks waste their valuable time trying to do what Freud has already proved they can't, namely repress natural desires by dint of their will power without going insane! But the vast majority of you don't even think of going that route, anyway. This is because you are faithless - which makes you even less inclined to get down on your knees to pray for the gift of faith. Yes, faithless - and it is immaterial that you might happen to be one of those people who just love to stand there in front of crowds bragging about your 'great and unshakable' faith in the Prime Mover!

Still a force to be reckoned with...

"And I will now reveal to you my dirty little secret - I have got a third line of defense, and it is virtually impenetrable! You see...even after you've done all the things I have said - and even though I have made it clear that I have said them under duress - how do you know you are carrying out the will of Him-Who-is-Who-is and not my will? Like now...whose will are you actually going to be carrying out - His or mine? Remember, you either have to take me at my word and do what I am telling you, or you just don't believe me and don't do as I am telling you! If you are saying to yourself that you can verify if what I am telling you is fact, I challenge you to try and do that!

"I can tell you that I am not almighty, but I am certainly capable of giving you a run for your money. Or, are you thinking of turning to prayer to beat me to it? I might not be capable of being in two places at the same time, but I am a spirit and can move pretty fast. And I am also invisible, just like He is. And I am also quite capable of mimicking His voice.

"Oh, you are thinking of teachers of the law and the prophets? I have out there a whole army of devotees who are quite capable of taking on those roles. And, believe me, some of these guys and gals can put on quite a show. And, fortunately, that is what this business of salvation boils down to nowadays - a show. And you can bet that it is not by accident that this is the case. So, don't you write me off just as yet!

"I mean - It is a war we are engaged in. And it has to be fought to the bitter finish. And while the other side believes in fighting wars according to rules, I don't; and at the moment I am throwing in everything I've got. In my vocabulary, there is no such a thing as fair play! And while I sympathize with you, I have to admit that you are fair play - you all are up for grabs. And while you can run, you absolutely cannot hide. And don't you underestimate my reach.

"You cannot differentiate my workers from His; and my workforce is highly motivated - I have enough dirt on them which will come out if they do not produce results, and they know it. I have at my beck and call some of the greatest orators alive. My arsenal includes preachers whose eloquence will make you start believing that you are saved long before the grace of Him-Who-is-Who-is has had an opportunity to touch you.

"And you would be surprised at the kind of things they can do with a bit of 'inspiration' from me. If you are not alert, they will talk you into believing that the Son of Man - the Word through whom creation came into being who is also the Second Person of the Blessed Trinity - is really not divine. That the Son of Man is the son of Mary and that He just happens to be the 'Son of God' because he did not have an earthly father with nothing more to it! At my instigation, they will 'prove' to you anything.

"They will prove to you that you can mumble some prayer formula and become saved - that it is so easy to clinch yourself a mansion in heaven. Or that you can be saved, not by keeping the Ten Commandments, but by 'faith alone'! Or that the late Pope John Paul was the Antichrist! They will 'prove' to you that all wars, justified or unjustified, provided they are initiated by the nation that you are a citizen of are always OK, and they will back up their 'proof' with quotations from the holy book. The fact is that I have been behind all the heresies that have plagued the Church since its inception. You can bet that a lot of my energy goes into trying to cause as much disunity in the Church of God as possible!

"And you may not like to hear it, but there has

never been a shortage of fellows in the Church - men with shortcomings in charity, patience and humility - who end up in visible positions in the Church's hierarchy, usually as its apologists, with a little help from me, naturally. Just a couple of people like that, instead of drawing souls to the Church, actually keep multitudes, among them many good people, away with their display of scarcely veiled hypocrisy and intolerance! They set themselves up as judges even as they are harping on the Prime Mover's infinite mercies in their sermons, and the fact that His judgements are incomprehensible. These folks would burn Joan of Arc at the stake all over again. And only recently, some of them were arguing that Padre Pio of all people - that Capuchine priest with the stigmata who undid so much of what I had done - was possessed by me! They are my moles inside the Church - and quite a lot of fun to watch them operate as my instruments when they should be operating as instruments of the Prime Mover's sanctifying grace!

"Thinking of devotional hymns and songs of praise as Solomon did? I have under my control choirs whose voices can move congregations in whichever way the conductor desires. The performance of these choirs will send you into a swoon. You will not just feel as if you have been touched by the Spirit; you will feel as if you finally have been saved, and are safely in the hands of Him-Who-is-Who-is when you remain as exposed as ever...ha, ha, ha!

"But you shouldn't forget that even at the height

223

of heresies and schisms that I have helped to engineer, those at the helm in the heretical and schismatic movements will be doing everything to make it seem as if everything was still well even after what might have started out as mere threats of excommunication and anathema had been confirmed by formal decrees or bulls issued by the Holy See. They will be even be trying to do so by showing that the ceremony and pomp of their liturgy could still rival the traditional ceremony and pomp of the liturgy of the *Sancta Ecclesia* from which they had been summarily cut off, and with which they no longer in communion.

"Look, I as the former angel of light know exactly what to do to help heretics and schismatics along. They must feel at home even in their heresy or schism so that it looks as though truth is relative. Even though they are completely off, I want them to believe to take the Deliverer really seriously when He said: 'I am the way, and the truth, and the life. No man cometh to the Father, but by me.' You must be kidding if I you believe that I wouldn't do everything in my power to try and keep humans away from the real presence in the altars and the fullness of truth which subsists in the Catholic Church by virtue of having the Deliverer as its head.

"Or are you one of those stupid people who are fixated with the notion that because I am a creature like you, my schemes and activities as boss of the Underworld will ultimately prove inconsequential? Well, I might not be able to will the Non-Creature and Master Craftsman out of existence - you have to know that I would have done it long ago if I had the capability. You tell me - I cannot even will a fly out of existence! And I also might not be able to abolish all that orderliness, symmetry, beauty and other nonsense like that in the universe and beyond that nevertheless testifies to the greatness of Him-Who-is-Who-is; but I certainly can and have succeeded in persuading other creatures, including pure spirits - yes, pure spirits - to exercise their free will and join me in causing as much damage and destruction in creation as possible.

"For one, the hosts of angels who joined me in my rebellion are brilliant, smart creatures - I'd say a lot smarter than the great bulk of you human creatures. So you can go on dreaming that my efforts will always be inconsequential, and that I won't succeed in siphoning off hordes of human spirits into our ranks and the Underworld!

"You do not even need to wander very far from your home to see the results. You do not have to make a trip to all the way to Vegas (the modern day Babylon) to view the trash that my cohorts and I have helped dredge up for human consumption. You only need to switch on either your telly or web browser to see what I mean. I bet you can't even avoid seeing it all over the billboards as you drive out to drop the kid off to school or drive to church. You must be a complete nut if you still do not believe that I have everything wired and under control. These are astounding accomplishments for me particularly as I do not have the advantage of possessing a human body - damn you!

"And if you still have the idea that I am a toothless bulldog with no muscle left, I invite you to think again. All right, I will ask you to pick up your bible and go to the Book of Revelations for a change. Who do you think will be responsible for causing all the havoc described by the sacred author? And, for one, who do you think will be behind the Antichrist? Who do you think will be behind the tribulations that will be visited upon the Earth that the great majority of you hold so dear?

"And, incidentally, who do you think was behind the many tribulations of the Israelites - the chosen people? You must know that history would be very different if the forces I had marshalled had gotten the upper hand and hadn't been wiped out - wiped out, you might have noted, each time with help from above!

"And - without trying to beat me at my own game of cunning and duplicity - answer this one straight. Who do you believe will be behind the wave upon wave of those nondescript creatures that will come from nowhere and add to the miseries of God's people when the end of the world nears? Who do you think will be behind the terrible tribulations of the descendants of Adam and Eve in those last days?

"And if you still think I am a loser, you just consider the prediction that those saved - yes, saved from my clutches - will come from every tribe and also hail from every corner of the earth. My reading of that statement is that I, Diabolos, will also have succeeded in diverting a goodly number of you from the narrow path, and made them my lackeys once and for all! And as for those of you who do not think that no harm can come to God's beloved creatures, I will affirm here that salvation is a function of the free will that governs everything you do or omit to do. So, you are - all of you without exception - exposed. I dare say you have by now already traversed a lot of distance either in the direction of Him-Who-is-Who-is, or in my direction. I leave you to guess in which direction the great bulk of you are headed right now!

"And remember - we are talking faith, beliefs, and convictions here. You might know that when it comes to helping you human beings form opinions and things of that sort, the forces I command pretty well have the situation under control. That is why you get so many people with preconceived ideas about everything - people who are often ignorant enough to believe that without their 'intellectual' contributions, the world would be poorer. You must have heard the expression that 'common sense isn't so common nowadays'. Well, who do you think is behind that?

"I actually no longer go out to recruit people to work for me - there are so many human 'devils', going out to recruit from your ranks would be a waste of time and energy. Then, the way some humans go about their 'devilish' business, you would think that they are out to prove that they are more diabolic than I, Diabolos himself. Of course that situation is quite pitiable, pathetic or whatever you would like to call it.

"I have persuaded the more foolish ones that

their own opinions, however irrational, are not opinions but truth - objective truth. And, at a signal from me, they now also will argue to death that any contrary opinions, however logical, must be indicative of crass ignorance and/or an ingrained inability to reason!

"I actually believe I have done an excellent job in helping all you folks out there to be bigoted and blinded by your own views to a point where opinions of others now simply do not matter. That is an understatement actually. Contrary opinions expressed by other people, even if obviously correct, must be held against them; and it is imperative that this be the rule everywhere - in the home, in the classroom, in the churches, synagogues or other places of worship, in the workplace, and in the political arena. Yes, especially in the political arena, because that is where being in a position of advantage also means being in a position to use the state machinery, the law enforcement agencies and the security apparatuses against your opponents.

"But a word about the home, the classroom, the places of worship, and the workplaces. The home is where someone who is evil can mold attitudes and teach the impressionable young to hate, to kill - anything. The workplace is where even little people who have no chance of becoming millionaires dream of becoming one by hook and crook - even at the expense of co-workers. The classroom is where persons who prescribe to my beliefs and philosophy can take the propaganda initiated in the home a step further - it is where you can give the craziest ideas respectability!

"And, of course, places of prayer are where you can mold young minds to go out and kill, maim, commit genocide and so forth in the name of Him-Who-is-Who-is. And, it is also where, with a little bit of luck, we have been able to get our minions inside the *sancta ecclesia* to use their sacred offices to hound their perceived enemies when they should have been practicing the virtue of charity. Take the case of the Great Schism that was precipitated by the action of the legates from Rome, headed by Cardinal Humbert, excommunicating the Patriarch of Constantinople Michael Cerularius and his legates at a time when the Church had no pope, and Cardinal Humbert and his legates in turn being excommunicated by Cerularius with each side accusing the other of having fallen into heresy and of having initiated the division. You will find on almost any page of the checkered annals of the Holy Catholic Church that I have been very diligent in taking advantage of human frailty to create problems for her mission of evangelization. No one can fault me for not doing my job there. It is what I promised the Angel Gabriel after he visited the aging priest Zachary to let him know that his barren wife Elizabeth would conceive a son, John. And I repeated it to Gabriel as he was heading back to heaven from Nazareth where he had told the Blessed Virgin Mary that she too would bring forth a son who would be called the Son of the Most High.

"But what I think stands out as my crowning achievement is the fact that today, as soon as humans turn adolescents, almost without exception they head for the hedonistic camp. This is because all those who mentor them no longer believe in the real happiness, which is bliss in eternity as opposed to bliss in this world. Those mentors themselves think that the void within them which can only be fulfilled through possession of the Non-Creature and Master Craftsman - and which, by the way, becomes all-consuming when the human body is discarded at the end of the probationary period on earth and the next life is ushered in - will somehow go away on its own.

"And that has actually been quite easy to bring off, I dare say. All that I needed to do was to get parents to embrace the idea that youth and freedom are two opposites, which of course also implies that the young do not deserve to be treated as human beings and are essentially second rate despite what the parents proclaim and their protestations to the contrary. They do that and...Boom! As soon as the young fellows discover that they too had an inalienable right to choose between right and wrong, and that they had up until that point been treated like chattel, they rebel. A few do not even recover from the trauma which results from discovering that those they trusted didn't regard them as creatures who were deserving of their love in as much as they deserving of the love and mercies of the Prime Mover by virtue of created in the image.

"By that time, those among them who succeed

in assuming control over their lives automatically do so under circumstances in which freedom - or the exercise of the right to choose - and rebellion are synonymous. Because their mentors, along with their parents, don't believe in eternal bliss or are believers only in name, it is only the most enterprising youngsters who end up realizing that there is such a thing as a Church Triumphant Entrance Examination and that they are expected to use their days on earth preparing for it. And I simply make sure that, as the young fellows grow up, it does not strike them that they all are, without exception, part of one people - part of a single human race; or that, in the last analysis, they are one family whose members just have different characteristics and gifts. Or, that the divine plan calls for the joys and sorrows of anyone individual in that human family to be felt and shared by all the family members.

"Now, if there is anything that any descendant of Adam and Eve ought to be concerned about, it is the fact that he or she was conceived with original sin. It is the reason humans are inclined to evil. It is also the reason that food for humans is not like food for animals of the wild. Humans have to sweat to get their sustenance. It is also above all the reason humans die! And so, in dealing with those young fellows, I just need to ensure that these pretty obvious facts escape them completely and that is easy enough.

"I make certain that the reason for descendants of Adam and Eve being conceived with original sin in the wake of the rebellion of Adam and Eve escapes these fellows completely. And then, I do not want them to establish the link between Adam and Eve enjoying, by design, a very intertwined life from the beginning of the time of their creation, and the fact that it was inevitable that they share the responsibility for their rebellion - just as I myself, by virtue of being a creature that was fashioned in the image of Him-Who-is-Who-is naturally sought to involve other created spirits in the revolt against the triune God's lawful authority. And, of course, it suits me perfectly when these young chaps eventually opt to live like animals instead of creatures with a body and a soul - creatures that are fashioned in the image of Him-Who-is-Who-is.

"When humans do not fully appreciate the significance of original sin (or condition in which they are born), it is my guess that they will find it harder to see the relevance of things like redemption, Church and sacraments to their lives. Even if they eventually come round and see these things as important, there will be misconceptions galore. The contradictory views that already abound are a good indication that my efforts in this respect have not all been entirely in vain!

"And after taking advantage of the indecisiveness of those young fellows during the period they are expected to start acting like grown-ups, and getting them essentially disoriented and set on a perilous course, you can bet that, during that critical period in their development, during that critical period in their development, I and my cohorts keep up the pressure in an effort to make sure they remain fools to the very end - so that they only realize too late, on the day of their judgement, that their own being also forms part of the resume of the Non-Creature and Master Craftsman after all. If only these fools thought of themselves as a part of *my* resume instead of imagining that they came out of thin air!

"And you can bet I try very hard to make damn sure that they do not grasp the fact that, in coming down from heaven and taking up your human nature, the Second Person of the Blessed Trinity became a true member of the human family and a real brother to all of you folks; and even I, Beelzebub, pray constantly that those youngsters remain in the dark about the immense benefits which directly spring from the Mystery of the Incarnation like, for instance, the beatific vision those of you who escape my tentacles go on to enjoy.

"Using my minions amongst humans I operate evil systems that just mutate. Take the evil system of slavery. What is the difference between that and modern capitalism, a system in which the corporate greed of Wall Street so-called gets rewarded at the expense of ordinary folks and peasants? Look what the passage of time does to you humans. Take a step back and reflect on the events that took place two thousand years ago in Jerusalem in the immediate aftermath of the Deliverer's death and resurrection.

"It is well documented that, when the day of Pentecost arrived, the Deliverer's terrified apostles were all together in one place. And suddenly there came from heaven a sound like a mighty rushing wind, and it filled the entire house where they were sitting. And there appeared to them parted tongues as it were of fire and it rested on each one of them. And the Parthians and Medes and Elamites and residents of Mesopotamia, Judea and Cappadocia, Pontus and Asia, Phrygia and Pamphylia, Egypt and the parts of Libya belonging to Cyrene, and visitors from Rome, both Jews and proselytes, Cretans and Arabians - Jews and devout men from every nation under heaven who dwelt in Jerusalem - each heard the story of the death and the resurrection of the Deliverer told in their own tongues.

"And after Peter, the leader of the group, admonished them saying 'Save yourselves from this crooked generation', fear came upon every soul. And all they that believed, were together, and had all things common. Their possessions and goods they sold, and divided them to all, according as everyone had need.

"Using my minions among humans, we in the underworld have labored very hard indeed to ensure the overthrow of that system of 'Socialism'. That is a coup that we can now celebrate thanks to the work of our minions.

"But I shouldn't dwell on this subject lest more of you fools wake up to the obvious fact that, because the Son of Man Himself is involved, there indeed has to be a next life - the real thing in fact - for you earthlings because you happen to be fashioned in the image of Him-Who-is-Who-is.

"I can tell you that I derive a lot of fun from one thing - keeping so many of you guessing to the very end whether I myself am just a mythical creature or the Evil One who actually helps in separating the good seed among you from the chaff. And, in the meantime, using a form of black magic - *juju* - which I know is quite effective on all but the meekest amongst you, I keep you so absorbed with temporal things, you forget that time is a mere dot in eternity, and that temporal happiness is exactly what it is - transient; which is the same as saying that it is ephemeral - a mirage. Using my *juju*, I have you cornered nicely in a spiritual desert.

"There, parched and starved of true spiritual happiness, you make a great sight as you *lunge* after the illusory pools of unadulterated spring water you see right there in front of you and, once inside those waters, you *swim* and *frolic* like you have never done before in all your life; and, when you are in fact just wallowing in temporal pleasures, you envision that you are in the Paradise that Dante and others before and after him have detailed at such great length in their poems and works of fiction. A pity that many of you turn around and cast aspersions on the same *juju* absent which such thrills would be out of your reach!"

Satan's dirty little secrets...

"Why, you might ask, do I keep referring to my brothers and sisters in sin as fools? Well, you are

235

obviously one of them and that is why you can't even attempt a guess. I have always tried unsuccessfully to explain to you earthlings that, while one must try to sin as much as possible, one must go about it with a wee bit of common sense. As you yourselves know, you can get very sick in the process of sinning.

"Take sins of the palette for instance. Food can easily slip down the wrong throat, if you do not go about gormandizing wisely. Gorging can leave you with a bad tummy ache, and you are also liable to suffer from other ailments as well as a direct result of that type of excess. In this business of passing joy, one thing you have to keep constantly in mind is that too much of anything is bad - really bad.

"You humans must be especially careful because, as you might have noticed generally, the organs that facilitate self-indulgence are located near other organs that can quickly turn the self-indulgence into something else. Whenever you are indulging yourself, always remember that you can contract diseases in the process or pass them on to others. In terms of safety, abstaining from indulging the self is really the safest option.

"But, just as we demons did, you humans, unfortunately, have to sin because that is the only way to hit at the Non-Creature and Master Craftsman. And you do that by renouncing His fatherhood, and by striving to be not what you are *supposed to be*, but what *you fancy* or want to be - even if that means sacrificing your souls for the 'cause' and, just like us, meriting eternal damnation!

236

"It is very unfair, but that is what it is. Some transgressions of the flesh cause direct bodily harm - you could go deaf while enjoying loud music, or you could go blind from surfing for trash non-stop on the world-wide Web, and so on and so forth. And all self-indulgence without exception dulls reflexes and also the conscience that happens to control the intellectual faculties. Actually, often times you will feel good - in fact great - during or after sinning and it won't occur to you that your health is being adversely affected. Which, of course, does not help very much if you are going to drop dead prematurely soon afterward!

"And that is even more dangerous because, just when you think you are having a whale of a time, you actually are hurting real bad, but don't know it! You might as well be enjoying a bar of candy you know is laced with cyanide or downing some other sweet-tasting substance that is deadly. And that is not mentioning the real price you have to pay - the demise of your soul!

"And the way some of you conduct yourselves, it seems to be with the conviction that you will never die! This is even though you know that there have been empires that looked like they were going to last forever, but lasted only for so long: the empire of the Incas in South America; the Roman empire; the Bantu People's empire which, in its heyday, stretched from Timbuktu to the Cape of Good Hope; and others which thrived in Europe, Asia Minor, China and the Far East. And they all faded away for the exact same reason - insatiable greed.

"You know that a principality, empire, or 'super power' - as you call them nowadays - is about to self-destruct when you see signs that expansionism and the desire to conquer, dominate and subjugate others have taken hold. You mark my words. One thing that goes for me is that Providence typically allows evildoers to have their way. Even though I have already been judged, Providence lets me continue to sow seeds of death - spiritual death – through my surrogates!

The prospects of divine intervention...

"While He has not facilitated the appearance of the Antichrist - no, not by a long short - Providence has certainly granted the Antichrist (who is, of course, only my front) permission to set up shop in the guise of bringing salvation to God's people. And I do not see Him interfering to stop the many souls who genuinely hunger and thirst for the Word of God from wandering right into the 'lion's den'. I do not see Providence intervening when some of them go on to believe that they are saved when all they have done is lull themselves into a false sense of security. And, certainly, Providence won't intervene to stop warmongers, empire builders, and other evildoers who are prepared at my command to unleash miseries upon their fellow men to satisfy their inflated egos.

"You overlook a couple of things when you expect the Prime Mover to 'intervene' in that fashion.

You ignore the fact that He has created humans with free wills, and that it was a conscious decision on the Prime Mover's part to do that - to conceive of creatures that were endowed with faculties of the intellect and free will, and to make you one of them. You underestimate the goodness of the Prime Mover and the fact that in endowing his creatures with His gifts, far from being begrudging, He was extremely generous - something that certainly also raises the stakes if those creatures of His should decide that they were going to do their own thing and to break His law. And you, of course, underestimate your worth in the eyes of your infinitely good and gracious Prime Mover.

"You underestimate the extent to which you humans can be bad - the extent to which free creatures can go to try and subvert the divine plan with or without my help, in complete disregard of the goodness of the Prime Mover to you. And you underestimate the extent to which you fellows are prepared to try and usurp the authority of the Prime Mover - just like I myself tried to do.

"You demonstrate that you fallen humans - just like us fallen angels - in general find it hard to desist from trying to pigeon the Prime Mover the way you do your perceived enemies. You imagine that He is constrained by limitations of time and space, and you even try to limit his options for intervening by imagining that He can only react to things in the way you expect.

"And then you confirm, perhaps without

realizing it, that the ways of the Prime Mover are indeed mysterious and incomprehensible even to the cleverest creature. And, in your ignorance and stupidity, you even overlook the fact that the Prime Mover, who created you and everything else that is in existence out of nothing, is quite capable of causing good to come out of evil (or something where 'good' is supposed to be but is lacking). You, furthermore, underestimate the Prime Mover's foresight, and the fact that he could anticipate everything you humans would be up to - just as He did in my own case!

"You show your ignorance of history and of the covenant the Prime Mover made to you humans when He declared that the seed of the woman would crush the head of the serpent - I mean my head! You therefore forget that the Prime Mover has in effect already 'intervened'. Then you forget that He actually did send His only Son to earth in fulfilment of His covenant. You forget that the Son of God emptied Himself, becoming obedient to the point of death - even death on a cross. And you forget that it was indeed the Son of God - a man of sorrows, accustomed to infirmity, and spurned and avoided by His own when they claimed that He was not their King, and that they had no king but Caesar! And you forget above all that, oppressed and condemned, He remained silent even as He was led away like a lamb to the slaughter. That, smitten for the sin of His people, He was finally cut off from the land of the living - 'effectively' neutralized!

"You also demonstrate that you do not quite get

the point made by the Deliverer to His apostles after He came back from hell that all power in heaven above, on the earth, and even in the Underworld had been given to Him by His heavenly Father.

"You underestimate the Deliverer's ability, resolve and determination to hold everyone who has been created in the image and likeness of the Prime Mover accountable for his/her actions, just like you underestimate His ability, resolve and determination to reward His faithful servants who heed the advice of the Deliverer, take up their crosses, and follow in the footsteps of the Son of Man.

"You completely forget that when wicked humans act irresponsibly and cause death and untold sufferings to their fellow humans, the Prime Mover 'intervenes' in the exact same way He does when one of you breaks any one of His ten commandments or refuses to accept His invitation to get aboard the Ark - the Church the Deliverer founded and commissioned to propagate the good news of salvation. You forget, above all, that if the Prime Mover were to intervene in the manner in which you all expect - by injecting Himself in there and striking the wicked dead, or by getting in there and physically sheltering the victims of injustice from their miseries or from their painful demise - He would be giving respectability to the actions of those who are in effect daring Him to intervene and stop them. You also forget that if the Prime Mover 'intervened' in that fashion, He would in effect be revisiting His divine plan and modifying it by taking away the right of

241

creatures He fashioned in His own image and likeness to make choices regarding what was good and what was evil.

"All of which of course goes to demonstrate the importance and indeed necessity of praying always - saying the Lord's prayer, contemplating the mysteries of the rosary (which deal with the life and work of the Deliverer) and, above all, following the injunction of the Deliverer to the apostles on the night before He died and feasting on the 'Bread of Angels' in the Deliverer's memory at Holy Mass (which is a re-enactment of the passion, death and resurrection of the Deliverer, and a gift of incomparable value to all who face trials and tribulations during their sojourn in what is no longer the 'Garden of Eden' but effectively the 'Valley of Tears').

"But there is a 'downside' to the fact that the Prime Mover does not ostensibly intervene. The downside is that the sure way for the wicked to self-destruct is to let them have their way. That same principle also applies to nations particularly those that boast super power status. They self-destruct when they wield so much power over the destinies of other nations; it makes their leaders start to believe they are virtual gods who do not have to be swayed by world opinion, their consciences, or anything else for that matter. Not even by the fact that they themselves will die - just like those whose lives they have a hand in cutting short.

"The self-destruction invariably starts as soon as the super power, intoxicated with power, sets out to conquer and subjugate. It happened to the Philistines, to the Greeks, to the Egyptians, to the Romans, to the Turks, and to the Bantustans. At the time nations self-destruct, you can be sure that many innocent people get hurt. We in the Underworld see that as a win-win situation. And then, another 'super power' usually and fairly promptly emerges from the ashes, and the cycle starts all over again. Hence the axiom 'There is no rest for the wicked!' Which automatically tells you something about the immense - nay, infinite - goodness of the Prime Mover. He created man free and you won't catch Him breaking His covenant and undoing what he did with the best of intention.

"But I hate to think that my minions who, even as I speak, are busy conjuring up grand schemes in the name of national security - the same schemes that will lead their nations down the path of self-destruction - will not ultimately have their will of permanently dominating the world. Also sadly, the 'technology' that helps nations develop and evolve into super powers is the selfsame that becomes their undoing.

"I naturally wish I had control over that 'technology'. You can bet that if I had, I would let only one nation - any nation - have a monopoly over it. And soon enough, that nation, at my command, would spread miseries all over the globe as it sought to subjugate other nations with an eye to the resources within their borders. And I would not stop there - I would make sure that the conquering 'super power',

243

in the process of subjugating other nations, would take the next logical step, which namely would be to hold the peoples of the rest of the world in enslavement; and I - even I - would pray that no savior would come along to deliver them as happened when the Deliverer suddenly appeared and freed the souls of the departed humans that I myself had been holding in captivity in hell from their bondage.

"Just as the leaders of certain nations today conduct themselves as if the nations in question, made 'powerful' by 'modern' technology, will never fade away, many of you think that, because you are here today and can move your hulk around, you will remain a permanent fixture wherever your prowess is now being felt. Technology is really analogous to speech or language. Now, speech is essentially codes and formulas, while the ability to heave your carcass around can be equated to the fortune of being one of those whose life was supposed to be nipped in the bud for one reason or another whilst you were still inside the womb but was not, allowing you to eventually see the light of day. You humans just over do it.

"Now, you tell me which peoples on earth do not have a tongue or language in which they communicate? And, while noting from this that no single nation can ever have a monopoly over technology, don't be mistaken about what being powerful on the national level means. 'Powerful' might be in the sense of possessing the capability to construct offensive weapons systems; but a nation may be powerful in other ways.

"One nation might be powerful by virtue of its ability to broker peace among other warring nations; whilst another might be powerful because of its ability to sustain and nurture a population that is disproportionately large when compared to the size of its territory; and another might be powerful by reason of its ability to preserve its ecosystems in circumstances in which other nations would be unable to do so. And there is, of course, no question about the greatness of a nation within whose borders people of very diverse backgrounds live out their lives to the full in harmony as a matter of course.

"Actually, if my reading of the situation is correct, very soon tiny, little known nations, armed with brief-case nuclear bombs that they will assemble using know-how posted on the Internet or stolen by hacking computers of the military establishments of the super powers, and employing delivery systems consisting in a simple network of Kamikaze prototypes or 'suicide bombers' as they are now increasingly known, will be capable of taking out entire cities and other places of significance of any so-called super power.

"But the really bad news for any potential super or hyper power is that technology has already advanced to a point at which high school whiz kids, using 'advanced' electronics, will be able to hijack satellites in space, and then use them to 'take over' the guidance systems of submarines, aircraft carriers, B-52's, and even military command and control centers of any super power, and command them to direct the deadly firepower they control at targets anywhere on earth, including cities and vital installations in countries they were supposed to defend and/or to self-destruct.

"Remember that I am the devil, and I certainly ought to know - if you were doubting my words! It is in any case just a matter of time before tiny, little known states, that have nothing to lose themselves, will be able to threaten a country like America with its arsenal of nuclear subs, aircraft carriers, fleets of B-52s equipped with smart bombs, missiles systems tipped with bunker bursting bombs, technologically advanced predators, and thousands upon thousands of state of the art jet planes with their deadly payloads of nuclear bombs and other weapons of mass destruction. These same nations will likewise compel global military alliances like the North Atlantic Treaty Organization and others to disband or expose their countries to ruin or even extinction.

"In a sudden reversal of fortunes, to save their cities and avoid being decimated, one by one, the super powers, threatened by a new crop of these 'rogue states', will be forced to jettison their nukes into space, in an effort to convince the world that they no longer posed a threat to any country.

"And that will not be all. In addition, they will be compelled to come clean and to account for each and every weapon of mass destruction that they had ever produced. After destroying their armaments in the open, they will be forced to declare to a revamped

United Nations (in which no nation will have any 'veto' power over resolutions passed) that they no longer possessed any weapons of mass destruction.

"And finally, goaded on by the self-styled 'liberating powers', they will be forced to convert the installations they previously used to produce the submarines, aircraft carriers, intercontinental ballistic missiles, tanks, landmines, and other armaments, into factories producing tractors, ploughs, hoes, and other equipment that will be supplied free to poor nations for the purpose of rehabilitating those nations' productive enterprises.

"These are, of course, developments that we in the Underworld really do not welcome, because they postpone Armageddon. We would like to see those weapons of mass killings (WMK) used to do the job they were designed to do. Even though condemned, we 'rejoiced' and 'celebrated' when some super powers balked at signing treaties banning land mines. And we welcomed recent developments in the arms control arena, and specifically the decision of one major military power to turn its back on arms control deals to which it had been a party, if only because that now paves the way for a new arms race.

An old myth...

"Still, much as I hate to admit it, it is completely fallacious to think that only super powers are powerful. Being a little known nation, with hardly any resources or anything else that might attract the attention of other combative nations, will probably be a better guarantee of survival of the fittest in future conflagrations between nations. As I have said, you will soon see super powers voluntarily disarming, and destroying the weapons of mass destruction they have spent billions developing in the face of threats from the new rogue states. But that will only be after these super powers (following my script and using some of the dirtiest tactics ever seen, including surprise pre-emptive military strikes on other unsuspecting resource rich nations, for the purpose of consolidating their own control over the world's scarce resources) have caused untold miseries to many innocent souls in different parts of the world.

"The best signal that a nation is great is its ability to protect the physically, socially, politically and economically disadvantaged and vulnerable. It is a sign of greatness that is frequently derided as weakness by those who themselves feel insecure for one reason or another.

"I should add that a nation populated by nondescript and physically emaciated and starving Francises of Assisi, Teresa's of Avila and Padre Pio's - or Mother Teresa's for that matter - would look weak on the surface, but it would actually be as powerful as any nation could get, their vows of poverty, chastity and obedience notwithstanding! It would be the most powerful nation that ever existed, even though that mad crowd would be doling out their country's resources to 'alleviate' the poverty of needy fellow humans elsewhere. I tell you I wouldn't want too many nations of that sort around, because then my influence over such nations and ultimately on the course of human history would be negligible.

"And, again, you tell me which individuals have you met who did not pass through the womb before they saw the light of day? I have been around a little longer than you numbskulls, and I can tell you that all nations have enjoyed the benefits of technology at one time or other in the course of their history while the neighboring nations were cowed down with apprehension.

"And, similarly, everyone who has ever lived has heaved his or her hulk around while oblivious to the fact that a myriad others had done the same before them or would do so after they themselves had come and gone. There is, in short, nothing you do that some nitwit has never done before, and this is especially true for the kind of ways in which you seek to indulge yourself daily.

"Even though all this makes a compelling case for you humans to abandon my cause, I have always been confident that most of you will stick with me for the simple reason that you are fools. And, similarly at the national level, you can be sure that I will never lack allies. There will always be nations whose actions will trigger wars and lead many a man and a woman to discard the notion that there can be a Non-Creature and Master Craftsman - a Creator who is not just good but Goodness itself - in a world in which chaos reigned; and to embrace the idea that all the good things a human being desires in this world can be had, not by flopping down on one's knees and praying, but by simply going out and getting them.

"For us pure spirits, transgression leads to the immediate permanent failure of any faculty associated with that sin - which, in practice, means all the faculties of the spiritual essence. That is how sin came to claim the lives of so many of us in a moment of time, and led instantly to the spiritual demise of all involved. It is like a trap - you sin and some vital part of you goes. In your case, the first sin you commit induces you to even sin some more, causing you to lose more and more of your vital parts!

"But while we pure spirits can never recover once we start down that road, you humans can - by renouncing sin, severing all your links to me, mortifying yourselves and refocusing your lives. You humans ought, at the very least, to note your makeup, and the way transgressions can affect the longevity of your lives. I am not suggesting that you should not sin. By all means go ahead and sin all you can; but at least watch out for the pitfalls. And that is the point you humans will never get. Why go on shooting yourself in your foot again and again? No body forces you to sin, let alone act so foolishly.

"Judas Iscariot was typical. Everybody knew that he was the confidante of the Deliverer, and also the purse bearer; and he himself knew it too. But his greed blinded him to the danger. His association with the Deliverer had already made him a marked man. And yet there he was, dreaming that he could be a double-dealer.

"He thought he could be a mole inside the 'schismatic' sect, reporting to the Sanhedrin while continuing to hold tight on his Master's purse. It was completely suicidal. The Deliverer put it succinctly when he said that it was better if he, Judas, had not been born. The high priests already had their man cornered, and did not even need Judas' services.

"If you ask me, I really never had any sympathy for the priests and Pharisees - I admired the role played by the 'fox' more.

"But Judas was just too greedy, and could not miss out on the opportunity to make another buck! He would probably have been more useful to me hanging in there close to Peter especially, and eventually engineering the break-up of the fledging organization from within after the Deliverer had departed and left them to their own devices.

Blind humans...

"But there is nothing that exemplifies the stupidity of you humans better than your blindness to the truth regarding your true self. You do not know it, and you have actually never thought of it; but you are all blind - blind as bats! And I do not just mean those amongst you who 'see' - or so you think - with visual aids. I mean all of you.

"Talking about visual aids - you are all able to get about because you all have visual aids. Your eyes are your visual aids, and they frequently do not perform nearly as well as the artificial visual aids. But whether natural or artificial, one thing they definitely do not do is show you your real self or even how the real you looks like when you stand in front of a mirror. All that these things - I mean the visual aids - are meant to do is help you get about without colliding with objects in your path.

"But you guys and gals use your eyes to focus on the image you see in the mirror; and, after a while, you invariably start believing that the blurry reflection of the *physical* part of yourself in the mirror not only is your look-alike, but the whole you! In the process, you effectively close your eyes to the real you. And, consequently, the only way you can now really 'see' and stop deceiving yourselves and start 'seeing' is by literally pluck out your eyes - as the Deliverer suggested.

"And talking about images in mirrors, you must have traveled to some faraway place only to see strangers milling around you who looked exactly like the strangers you had left behind! Well - that is because you humans, sharing the same *human* nature, do indeed *look alike* all of you! And so, the strangers you meet when you travel to distant lands *aren't* really *strangers* after all except in your imagination. And they aren't the folks you left behind because they happen to be creatures that share your *human nature* (which remains the same and unchanged), but enjoy a separate *existence* from yours and that of their look-alikes back in your homeland.

"If you still think there is a difference between

what a pair of spectacles and what your cornea does, then there is nothing that can save you! Anyway, how in hell and on earth can you trust your eye glasses to tell you what you look like, let alone what you are? If you could tell what you are only with the help of these things, how do you account for the fact that those who cannot see or hear are still quite capable of knowing themselves? How come that they will respond with 'Yah?' when they are called by name?

"Which brings me to the point I am trying to make: you folks believe that your eyes are essential for knowing who - or what - you are, and that for all practical purposes you cease to exist when you lose your eyesight - which you certainly do when you 'kick the bucket'.

"You have heard so much about idols made by human hands out of stone. Well, here we have the human body, approximately ninety per cent water and a bag of chemicals for the rest, which turns out to be by far the most worshipped 'idol' as if though it were made by human hands! What a turn of events! For me, this is like what you folks refer to as 'sweet revenge'. But quite frankly, even though I am the Cunning One so-called, I would be remiss if I took all the credit for what you fellows - I mean fools - do. Guess you deserve some too!

"That is why I keep referring to you people as fools. You need to stop and think sometimes. You don't have to be suicidal. But I am in a way to blame, because the idea of sin started with me. I blundered big time actually when I thought the Non-Creature and

253

Master Craftsman was calling the bluff when He said that anyone who disobeyed would die the death! Yes, I also make mistakes - I am a just a creature like you, you know! I wish I could have given you folks a better deal. Unfortunately, however, the saying *'Nemo dat quod non habet'* applies to me too...!

"But one of my problems is that I can't stop talking once I start. May be it is something which goes with being the Evil One. But who cares! You ask me now about the so-called baby boomers, and I will tell you this: my guess is that only a third, at the very most, will escape my tentacles.

"What that means is that, when the time comes, only a third of the baby boomers will step forward and go down on bended knee to pay Him-Who-is-Who-is homage. A full two thirds of that generation will balk and refuse to genuflect! Just imagine - two thirds of the baby boomers will say 'Pass' when they are asked to recite the *Pater Noster*! They will say 'Nay' in unison when they are asked to profess the Nicene Creed or to chant the *Te Deum* along with the gaggle of the redeemed brethren. And a full half of these 'Nay Sayers' will be baptized Christians!

"And now *you* tell me how someone who is not considered to be valuable enough to warrant the personal attention of both parents and is left at the mercy of baby sitters during the most crucial period of his or her upbringing can grow up respecting him or herself? How can they believe that there was a Non-Creature and Master Craftsman behind the big bang when they themselves are treated like accidents of nature, or when one of the parents just walks out on them! No, I believe I can claim at least some measure of success in my endeavors, buddy.

"If you want me to give you the reason why those truly saintly folk among you feel a yearning to be joined to the Creator while the rest of you are scared stiff as your day of reckoning approaches, it is simply the fact that they are humble, have succeeded in denying themselves, and consequently feel that they have absolutely nothing to lose when they vacate their earthly abode - no earthly goods to mourn over, and certainly no lost opportunities for indulging the self. On the contrary, they look forward to dying and hastening to Him who is never changing, is perfect beauty and goodness, and who is above all He-Who-is-Who-is."

Mjomba reasoned that Satan, although banished from the sight of the Prime Mover and a complete disgrace to the rest of creation, could actually be used as a mouthpiece to throw light on tenets of the faith for that very reason. There was no comparison between Man's fall from grace and the dishonor that Beelzebub brought to creation when he rebelled because he had been one really prized gem in the works of the Creator. His betrayal had been all the more repulsive because, being so close to the Prime Mover, he had no excuse for what he did. According to Mjomba, using Satan in that manner only went to emphasize that, even in disgrace, created beings remained subject in every way to the Prime Mover's power and authority.

The unanswered question was how he, Christian Mjomba, had ended up in between, and in a role that had him explaining to the world these goings-on in the spiritual realm from a human perspective! He wondered if it was because of something he did - or failed to do - in his life!

PART 6: THE ORAL DEFENSE

Later on, during his oral defense of this part of the thesis, Mjomba was surprised that it was his fellow students, not his professors, who were most troubled by his use of the devil in that manner. One student, who was already obviously angry that Mjomba had not been reigned in for his provocative ideas, went as far as screaming: "Heresy! This is another Judas Iscariot! He is against the Holy Father - and also against America!" Other students had chimed in with "He is a Mau Mau sympathizer!" and "He supports Mandela!"

Like a panel of impartial Supreme Court justices, the committee of six professors had proceeded to elicit answers to the students' objections by shooting their own questions.

Father Damian...

"And why do you think that a theologian who is trying to expound on some dogma can employ the Evil One as a mouthpiece with impunity - just as you have done here?" This was from Father Damian, world famous author and also the diocese's foremost expert on Dogmatic Theology.

"If I am not mistaken...there is no Church dogma against doing this, Father!" was Mjomba's curt reply - which appeared to ruffle some feathers in the audience.

Father Lofgreen...

"Well, supposing there was such a dogma - and I am speaking hypothetically here. Might it just be conceivable that a situation could arise in which this practice would be permissible and not be morally wrong?" That was from Father Lofgreen, Professor of Moral Theology.

"I'm glad you are speaking hypothetically, Father. Anyway, one such situation would be if I was'nt aware that such a dogma existed. To the extent that I wouldn't have any intention of going against the Church's official teaching, I might be mistakenly burned at the stake for espousing heretical views - like Joan of Arc. But I really couldn't be accused of acting immorally."

Mjomba's reference to being burned at the stake evoked a prolonged burst of laughter from all but the student who had screamed "Heresy".

Father Donovan...

The next question came from Father Donovan, the Canon Lawyer: "You are not suggesting that you would sit back and just watch as members of your flock, who were always preoccupied with things of the world and had never had any time for contemplation, bible study and things like that, broke moral laws and canons of the Church with impunity, are you?"

"I think it would all depend on what is meant by

'things of the world' Father" Mjomba responded hesitatingly. "If they did whatever they did religiously. I mean - if they prized self-sufficiency above dependence, including dependence on social security or charity, and especially if they did not want preoccupation with matters of their faith to be an excuse...And, if I may add, Father, I believe St. Paul was with me on this when he wrote in his second letter to the Thessalonians that Quote: *"If any man will not work, neither let him eat..."* Unquote.

Father Cromwell...

Mjomba was stopped in mid-sentence by Father Cromwell or "the Welshman" as the seminarians called to him. His speciality at St. Augustine's Seminary was Pastoral Theology. The Welshman, who had very poor eyesight and saw with difficulty even with the help of his bifocals, lowered his head, and peered down on Mjomba through the upper section of his eyeglasses.

The priest spoke in a rough grating voice: "Now, that is bordering on heresy, Reverend Mjomba. I'm sure you agree that that's what everybody is busy doing. If you are right, I should pack up and return to Wales. To return to the original matter at issue here - can there possibly be any justification for anyone to use the adversary as a mouthpiece in moral matters? Isn't that the same as suggesting that the devil can be a mentor, an example?"

Mjomba hesitated before responding: "It's the

Church's position that sin is to be hated, but not the sinner. I am not suggesting that anyone should be cozy with Beelzebub or even less love him. I am respectfully suggesting, however, that while the damned Satan's deeds are entirely reprehensible, he is still permitted to continue to exist - and to that extent, even he knows that the Prime Mover is infinitely good..."

Father McDonald...

It was now the turn of Father McDonald, Professor of Biblical Theology, to fire his question. "When the devil proclaimed that the Deliverer was the Son of the Most High, was that a profession of faith?"

"Certainly not; I submit, Father, that the rich man who tried in vain to get word about the horrors of the Pit to his friends back on earth wasn't making a profession of faith either. That sort of thing can only be accomplished by folks that are still on trial. After the sentence is passed, all such expressions become laments - laments of the eternally lost. But, in appropriate circumstances, I believe such expressions can be inspiring..."

Father Raj...

It was the professor of Systematic Theology whose objections to the use of the Evil One as a mouthpiece really rattled Mjomba, and even caused him to concede mentally that he had made a bad judgement in doing so. Still, while Mjomba was quite sincere, he could not rule out the possibility of going back on that statement at some future date.

There was, after all, no doubt that Providence could use the archenemy for good causes just like he could turn evil into good! Nothing was impossible with the Prime Mover! But for now, Mjomba, head bowed, was attentive as Father Raj, who hailed from Goa on the Indian sub-continent, began talking.

The Indian, who was also Mjomba's confessor and spiritual advisor, was relaxed and self-assured as he said: "Sonny, you just reminded us that the Antichrist isn't just a fictional idea. If I did not know you as well as I do, wouldn't you agree that I would have every reason to suspect that you just might..."

There was nothing Indian at all about Father Raj's accent. His years of studies in London and Rome made his accent indistinguishable from that of the Welsh, Scottish, Irish and Dutch members of the seminary's permanent staff of twelve - or the "Dirty Dozen" as the students referred to them on the sly. Mjomba did not allow Father Raj, whom he held in very high esteem and considered his "guru", to finish the sentence.

"I completely agree with you, Father..." he interjected. But he was himself promptly interrupted by his guru.

Fr. Raj: Diabolos's role in keeping humans weak...

261

"If you decide to make Diabolos a mouthpiece for any doctrine" Father Raj continued, "You also have an obligation, at the very minimum, to make him completely forthcoming about his role in keeping us humans weak.

"We might be entirely responsible for our own sins and downfall through the exercise of our free will. But Diabolos is also on record as being the one who cleverly engineered it - by thrusting himself between us, while we were still in our pristine innocence, and our loving and gracious divine Master; and by making the abominable suggestion that we follow his example and act as though our Maker was an entirely fictitious character, and regard the Almighty's clear injunctions to the human race as the figment of our own imagination!"

Fr. Raj: Lost mantle of godliness...

"And - concerning his role in keeping us frail and powerless - you have had Diabolos rightly suggest that, to be safe from him and also from the on-set of concupiscence that has plagued us human beings since time immemorial, we must pray at all times. It is quite significant that you have not had him - or, may be, he has not had you have him - disclose how, having succeeded in driving a wedge between us and our Maker, he continues to pull fast ones on us so that, citing our first amendment or the right to exercise our faculties of reason and free will and lacking faith in God, we continually turn down opportunities to be close to our Creator through prayer and self-denial and consequently remain handicapped and exposed - the holy book says 'naked'.

"You see, sonny, our first parents were so ashamed of their act of transgression, which they committed while knowing quite well that they were made in the image of their Creator, they went and hid themselves in some bushes there in the Garden of Eden. It soon dawned on them that they were in the wrong, and they, in fact, never did recover from their shame. When they emerged from the bush, they were still bedecked in twigs, and they eventually took to the habit of covering their person in bark cloth. That was not enough for Eve because she was unable to wander about outside of their dwelling without headgear of some sort as well.

"Stripped of their original innocence, it had immediately become evident to Adam and Eve that something very essential and real was missing on their persons. Conceived in the image of their Creator, they now felt as though they were stark naked. The mantle of godliness with which they had been outfitted at creation was gone. The first Man and Woman noticed, to their surprise and dismay, that the shroud of holiness had been supplanted by, of all things, a diabolic inclination to commit even more transgressions! It proved to be a haunting state of affairs in view of the fact that they were spirits first and foremost and flesh and blood only as a secondary matter.

"After eating of the forbidden fruit, instead of feeling like gods, they felt like ejecting themselves from the Garden of Eden and getting lost in the tropical jungle - which they did all but physically. They were too terrified about the prospect of encountering beasts of the forest - that also now suddenly seemed belligerent and unpredictable, and particularly vipers that were going to be a permanent reminder of their temptation and fall from grace from then on - to take that option.

Fr. Raj: The embodiment of evil...

"There was no doubt about the fact that Adam and Eve had known from the very first that they were created in their Creator's image, and had been extremely proud of it. You see - unlike Adam and Eve who were in good books with their God until their rebellion, Diabolos, a pure spirit, rebelled against his Maker as soon as he was created and has been in bad books with Him from the outset; and you must understand that his spite was always infernal. And as soon as Adam and Eve came onto the scene, Diabolos had moved to exploit that situation adroitly, suggesting that they could be like the Prime Mover in all respects - if they ate of the forbidden fruit. They did not have to believe him - they did not even have to give him a hearing, which was the first mistake they made. You do not play hide and seek with a snake! And after that succession of errors, they even forgot that, as creatures fashioned by God in His own image, they owed Him - and Him alone - their total allegiance.

"One point about Diabolos - he is, as you know, created in the Prime Mover's image like us, and he should feel the greatest shame for spearheading these rebellions against God. It is precisely because the devil has never felt any remorse or shame whatsoever for his terrible misdeeds that he is so odious in every way even in God's eyes. Our Creator, while hating sin, loves the sinner to the end. In the case of Satan, the Lord has taken pains to make it crystal clear that Diabolos is completely evil.

"To avoid any misunderstanding, He has even cautioned us not to enter into any dialogue with the Evil One. Now, badness is the absence of good; and evil is the absence of godliness. Surprisingly, Diabolos does not just symbolize those infernal qualities; he actually embodies them! It is something that is quite unimaginable for a creature to be so debased.

"Up until the moment they got involved in the fateful dialogue with Diabolos, whenever they had wanted anything, all they did was ask and it was granted them by the Prime Mover. Their decision to eat of the fruit therefore implied a complete about turn! And, lo and behold, it was the image of Diabolos, the archenemy, and not that of their infinitely loving and most gracious Maker that suddenly came to mind as they considered ways to free themselves from their allegiance to the Almighty. It was Diabolos who loomed up in their minds as a friend! Their communication line to their Maker had been permanently and irrevocably severed before they knew it.

Fr. Raj: Faith in God and in His Church...

"The point of all this is that your thesis has Diabolos urging human beings to pray without mentioning anything about 'faith'. While you believe that you are using him as your mouthpiece to expound on the Church's teachings, I submit to you that it is Diabolos who is trying to use you to prepare the way for the dreaded Antichrist. He wants you to leave a void that the Antichrist will fill, in much the same way the breach in the channels of communication with the Creator caused by the sin of Adam and Eve left a void that faith now must fill. I will explain.

"Although it is important to know that prayer is necessary for human beings to live as befits children of God, this knowledge is no longer enough by itself. There is now an additional requirement - faith - before the proper dialogue can be restored between Man and God. Even though this new requirement, or faith in the Redeemer, comes by knowledge, it remains a gift that human beings, endowed with reason and free will, can accept or reject when offered. It is a gift of the Holy Ghost, offered to human beings at the behest of Christ, the Anointed One. After bridging the chasm that previously separated erring humans from His Father, He fills the void created by the severed line of communication through the gift of faith. The fact of the matter is that human beings, having rebelled against their Maker, had been banished from His sight; and they are completely helpless on their own and, in fact, lost without the labors and travails of the Second Adam.

"You have, no doubt, heard the expression: 'Get behind Me, Satan'. If it was our Lord who was addressing you, I dare to suggest to you that he would be telling you just that. And you would be glad he would be telling you that and not 'It is better if you were not born' or something like that. He would be treating you like he treated the man he eventually appointed to be a 'fisher of men' because your faith in Him is still largely intact. You see - faith in God might not be sufficient, but it is certainly necessary.

Fr. Raj: The Antichrist has come...

"The Antichrist will probably have everything right except the point regarding faith. He will be at pains to show that the gift of faith is not necessary for the equation of salvation - faith in God the Father, in God the Son, and in God the Holy Ghost; and - for a generation of humans like ours that did not have the opportunity to eat, live and visit with Mary and her divine son as the twelve apostles did - faith in the efficacy of sacramental grace dispensed through Holy Mother the Church over which the Deliverer Himself presides as High Priest.

"You can be sure that the Antichrist also - yes,

267

especially the Antichrist - will talk faith. He will do so while simultaneously claiming that the Church, confessing the faith received from the apostles - the faith the Church confesses in accordance with the ancient saying that *lex orandi, lex credendi* and which precedes the faith of the believer - has it all wrong. And the Antichrist will also claim that the Church, celebrating the sacraments - that act *ex opere operato* by virtue of the saving work of the Deliverer and are not wrought by the righteousness of either the celebrant or the recipient - is in error. Claiming that the Deliverer's death on the cross was sufficient for Man's redemption, the Antichrist will argue that the sacraments of the New Covenant are not necessary for the salvation of believers. He will in effect be inviting humans to place all their faith in himself!

"You can understand why the Antichrist, the devil's persona on earth, will not be very eager to talk about the baptismal, and even less the ministerial, priesthood. Like the baptismal priesthood that is dispensed by the Prime Mover's priestly people, the ministerial priesthood that is dispensed by the ordained ministry, and that in turn draws its validity and efficacy from an unbroken apostolic succession, as you know also works *ex opere operato*. You might remember from your catechism that the Church, forming as it were, one mystical person with the Deliverer, the head, acts as an organically structured priestly community. And, by the way, if you should ever be looking for the one doctrine that sets the Church apart from all the other 'churches', always remember the doctrine that is captured by those three words - *ex opere operato*!

"And, talking about the Antichrist, we keep saying 'he will come' when the fact is that 'the Antichrist' (used in a generic sense) has already showed up. According to the evangelist, the spirit of the Antichrist was already up and about even as he was writing. If you ask me, the Antichrist showed up twenty centuries ago, synchronously with the appearance of the first heresies that rocked the infant Church and ironically also helped it mature quickly. His ugly head has popped up times and again since, and you can bet that he has by now successfully established a beachhead that he is using to propagate his pseudo-messianism. There is no doubt that religious deception, which is what the Antichrist is all about, 'offering men apparent solutions to their problems at the price of apostasy from the truth,' has been with us for some time and is already very widespread.

"To quote the catechism, 'the Antichrist's deception already begins to take shape in the world every time the claim is made to realize within history that messianic hope which can only be realized beyond history through the eschatological judgement'. But of course humans, myself included, like to react only when things happen in a big and dramatic way. That is why we are still waiting to see the Antichrist descend on the world from the sky - or something of that sort.

"My advice to those who are looking for signs

that the Antichrist is with us is: Look for dissertations and books whose authors claim to be inspired, or sermons that are billed as being prophetic and a panacea for all your spiritual problems, and things like that. And keep in mind as you do this that the sermons of the Deliverer Himself and the miracles he performed did not result in any dramatic conversion of sinners! If anything, many just walked away when the Deliverer reminded them that leaving everything behind - including family and possessions - and shouldering their burdensome crosses were things that following in His footsteps entailed.

"Contrary to the Antichrist's claims, for instance that salvation was about to descend on humans in a dramatic and big way as a result of his intervention or - more appropriately - meddling, things are going to get worse for the *Sancta Ecclesia*. The number of false prophets is going to increase, for one; and it is going to be increasingly hard for well-intentioned individuals to find their way into the Church. For all I know, scandals in the Church, an occupational hazard for folks who are not only called to minister but also to give a good example, will increase rather than diminish. And the sufferings, not only of the followers of the Deliverer, but of people of good will as well, will grow likewise.

"And, talking about human suffering (if you can bear with a little diversion here), some folks in the Church notice it only when they they hear that Catholics are in the cross hairs! These folks act as if the rest of humanity does not consist of souls that are created in the Prime Movers' image in the exact same way they themselves are! And you usually get this from chaps that set themselves up as spokespeople for the Church! Really sad, isn't it! Hopefully this Class now has got the idea.

"And don't you start thinking that the role of the Antichrist is reserved for non-Christians or the separated brethren. To the extent that Hindus, Buddhists, and others do their thing with sincerity, conscientiously and in good faith, to that extent they cannot be deemed to be working for the Antichrist, let alone be him. A member of the Communist politburo in China who gets demoted to a low level position and suffers because of his attempts to be a compassionate communist could be headed for martyrdom and baptism of blood or baptism of desire at the minimum while some of us are trying to rest on laurels that don't exist and are dreaming that Peter will automatically wave us on through the gates of heaven because of what we are. To the extent that I pass up opportunities to rake in souls into the fold because of bigotry, personal prejudices or negligence, to that extent I am a prime candidate for the role of the Antichrist, I tell you!

"All of us on this panel could become Antichrists overnight - if we are not already - by fancying that you folks are being molded into useful members of the Church's hierarchy through our own personal efforts, and not through the work of the Prime Mover's grace! Conversely, I could be addressing a bunch of Antichrists if it suddenly turned

271

out that you have all been imagining that there had to be something about you that makes you a suitable candidate for the priesthood, instead of considering yourselves as completely unworthy as John the Baptist and Peter did - or Judas! You have to be a saint, folks, to avoid playing the role of the Antichrist!

"And take the hypothetical example of prelates - successors of the apostles - who, instead of standing up for the love of God and of their neighbor at all times and being prepared to become martyrs for it, are caught identifying themselves with the "national interests" of the countries in which they are called to minister to the faithful when those "national interests" and the ensuing policies subvert the principles of love, justice and equality for all. In this hypothetical example (I am probably wrong to refer to it as hypothetical), those prelates would be hard put to it to defend themselves against the charge that they are anti-Christian to the extent they permit themselves to be on the side of injustice. That is precisely why the faithful must pray for priests, bishops and the Holy Father - yes, the Holy Father - all the time, folks. And, yes, especially the pope!

"The Holy Father himself could become anti-Christian if he started fancying that he could claim credit for some of the Church's successes, the conversion of Russia for example; or, alternatively, if he failed in his duties as Peter's successor. Popes cannot obviously fill that role, thank God, on those occasions when they are speaking or acting *ex cathedra*!

"When the Deliverer showed up two thousand years ago, the priests, Pharisees and Sadducees were supposed to roll out the red carpet for Him - especially after the long wait that humanity, along with the people of Israel, had endured since the promise of a Messiah was made to Adam and Eve. Who would have thought that those same priests, Pharisees and Sadducees, who led the concourse of the people of God in prayer in the temple on every Sabbath day (or day of rest) and also doubled up as the teachers of the law, would turn their backs on the 'Son of Man' just when He needed their help most! Who would have thought that those priests, Pharisees and Sadducees, bedecked in the vestments they normally don when they officiated in the temple and in other regalia, would lead the mob in threatening someone as vile as Pontius Pilate that he would no longer be a friend of Caesar if he dared to let the Deliverer, who was clearly innocent, go free as he was proposing to do!

"And, well, that happened then. If the Deliverer had turned up for His mission of human redemption in our own time, are we sure we wouldn't be a part of that mob - or at least pining to be a part of it from wherever we might be?

"The fact is that humans, whatever their station in life, will always remain humans, free to act the part of the devil if they so choose. There is nothing to stop a bishop who occupies the Holy See, as amply demonstrated by history, from playing the part of the Antichrist notwithstanding his position as the successor to St. Peter! The definition of the Church as the Mystical Body of the Deliverer with Himself as its head and the rest of us with all our imperfections as its members implies as much! That is why it is no exaggeration to say that the folks who happen to be members of the Church's hierarchy are badly in need of the prayers of all men and women of good will.

"That said, the fact remains that those who have been called to holy orders, princes of the Church, and the Pontiff of Rome are *alteri Christi* in a very real sense; and it is a very serious thing when they start acting, even remotely, like Antichrists. But remember that they do not stop being human just because they carry responsibilities of that gravity on their shoulders. And it is not at all far-fetched to say that this is the one group of people that the Evil Genius has a special interest in, and in whose regard he will work any amount of overtime in hopes of derailing them from their God-given mission! Diabolos prays - yes, prays - and dearly wishes that members of the Church's hierarchy, because they are the successors to the apostles, end up acting like *Antichrists*, and not like *other Christs*. He prayed and tried very hard to derail the mission of our Divine Savior Himself didn't he.

"And you can bet that the devil now tries very hard to make members of the hierarchy even deny that they know the Son of Man, just like Peter before them did. And he does this even as he tries to make it appear to many out there that the apostles' successors could not possibly *look* or *act* like Catholic priests, bishops and prelates who appear ever so reluctant to abandon the staid and traditional, even as they themselves struggle to practice what they preach; and that the apostles' successors are a completely different calibre of people who are easily identifiable by their message - quick and easy deliverance from the bondage of sin - by just *believing* what is in the Book rather than by each one *taking up his or her cross and following Him*, for instance!

"And you know that on their own, without the help of the Prime Mover's grace, that is exactly what the successors to the apostles will do, namely deny the Savior - by being silent and complicit! And I challenge any of you to say that on your own, without the help of God's grace, you or anyone else would not do precisely that, namely deny the Savior - especially, I might add, when you see Him and His Church on trial before the world court of opinion! Thank God that those who accuse the Church of all sorts of things, including witchcraft, at least concede that the idea of grace is not satanic or mythical!

"The question to ask, therefore, is: How many people out there are not swayed by this or that as they go about their daily business, so that instead of doing whatever they do to the greater glory of the Prime Mover, they do it to the greater glory of something else? And, anyway, how many among us Catholics, the Church leadership included, do not need to go to confession? I bet you, the number of 'Antichrists' is much much larger than the number of 'proChrists'. That is why you hardly hear of the latter. And you would be surprised at the number of people who are trying to cheat their way into heaven!"

Even though the Indian pontificated non-stop, that did not at all seem to bother his audience whose rapt attention he continued to enjoy as he went on undaunted.

"The Antichrist was really a scam artist and nothing more. And, conversely, all scam artists were Antichrists and would, of course, all face the Judge sooner or later, along with whoever the Chief Antichrist was, to answer for the scams they perpetuate without any shame!"

"And, talking about scams and scam artists" father Raj continued, "I would say that there are basically three types of scams. The first type is the one that common criminals use to trick unwary individuals to part with their hard-earned cash and/or other goods with next to nothing in return. The activities of these scam artists are frequently 'legal' to the point to which the perpetuators actually enjoy the protection of the law as they go about conducting their dirty business. It is the same type of scam that often characterizes so-called 'good business practices' that 'big business', after twisting the arms of law makers to force them to legalize those business practices, go on to use to skim profits and grow even bigger and more powerful. Frequently the scam artists are actually government functionaries who, knowingly or unknowingly, ensnare or actually 'buy off' governments in impoverished countries with so-called tied aid. You can always tell that it is a scam if the 'aid' produces the opposite result, or the donor countries end up getting far more out of the deals than the recipient countries.

"The second type of scam involves those who persuade others into investing in things that can only yield temporal and passing satisfaction. Because all of us in this world belong to the same human family with the same last end, it behoves each one of us to do everything in our power to mitigate the consequences of this type of scam.

"Talking about the human family, there is absolutely no doubt socialism and communism are the closest things to that ideal, even though promoters of greed for money, also known as capitalists, preach otherwise!

"The last type of scam is the most serious and involves what I call false prophets or individuals who represent themselves as messengers of the Prime Mover as you call Him to unwitting folk when they in fact they are not. It is the ultimate scam because not only because of what is at stake, namely the eternal destinies of the populace, but because it is only after the targeted individuals pass from this world into the next that they will discover that they were being given a ride. Now, with so many religions, churches, and what have you, none of which seem to agree on anything except that they are all led by prophets and messengers of the Prime Mover, it is probably correct to say that poor ordinary folk are resigned to the fact that they have to live with this particular type of scam, and who can blame them anyway."

The excitement of members of his audience, already palpable, reached a new high as the Indian declared: "We could, of course, blame everything on the Antichrist, except that we all have a streak of the Antichrist in us just like we all have a streak of Judas Iscariot in us."

Speaking above the voluble chatter, the priest continued: "Believe it or not, the Antichrist is among us already. And, most sadly, we are even seeing fulfilled in our own time the ominous words of the Deliverer to the effect that kin would turn against kin, children against their parents, and so on. And then the drum beats of war, coming so soon after a dreadful and murderous world war and which are growing louder with each passing day, also look more and more like they might presage a religious conflict of global proportions and a war that has the potential for quickly escalating into the Mother of All Wars!

Fr. Raj: The most powerful prayer...

"Any ways...back to our topic of the day. Having the devil urge souls to beseech, wail and pray to God for their needs is a contradiction in terms. But it is an even more glaring contradiction to have him urge souls to say the one prayer that incorporates all articles of our faith - the Holy Mass. Don't you think it is a bit far-fetched?

"You see, far from being any kind of prayer, the prayer of the Holy Mass has already been answered through Jesus' death, His resurrection, and ascension into heaven. One does not have to worry that one might be praying in vain when participating in this prayer. Besides, when Mass is being celebrated even by a lone priest assisted by the altar boy, the church is always full - full and resounding with the praises of choirs of angels and members of the Church Triumphant.

"And it is precisely for this reason that the sacrament of the Holy Eucharist, inaugurated by the Deliverer on the eve of His death and celebrated by His Church ever since, will be something that is completely anathema to those who do not wish the Church well.

"Understand me - I am not suggesting that there are some prayers which are ineffectual or wasted effort. The story of the disciples in the sinking boat is, in my view, quite telling. There they were, wailing - praying - when they realized that they were going to drown. The Nazarene, when he awoke, told them that they were 'men of little faith'!

"It was good that the shaken apostles were crying out in fear - or 'praying'. As it turned out, the measure of their faith was not the intensity of their cries or prayers. To all appearances, they were completely faithless. Knowing that people in similar situations perished as a rule, they were convinced that it was their turn to go.

"You would have thought that, after they had crisscrossed Galilee in the company of the Messiah and listened to all those sermons, their faith would be really deep. It is also significant that, even though

279

they had rushed the Lord's sleeping quarters in the boat to get Him to save them from drowning, they were advised that they did not have very much faith.

"After Adam and Eve transgressed, they must have wailed and beseeched God unceasingly for mercy. Their prayer, which was undoubtedly the prayer of people who had given up all hope and were at their wits' end, was answered despite the fact that the channel of communication with their maker had been irrevocably cut. With the Second Adam in the picture, human beings are heard very well by the Father, who is concerned even when a bird loses a feather. But humans needed the gift of faith nonetheless. Still, just as the Deliverer interrupted his rest and not only answered the prayers of his faithless disciples, but focused on beefing up the little faith they had (so that they could actually become apostles who were dependable and capable of manning the Church he was in the process of setting up to continue His mission after His ascension into heaven), it would be most imprudent to even imagine that He does not respond in the same way when human beings of all races, sexes, backgrounds, and religious convictions pray. Any prayer is, after all, better than none at all. I fully agree with your thesis on that particular point.

"The most difficult part for many is to accept that only those in communion with the Holy See can *fully* participate in the perfect prayer - the Holy Mass. And - if I may make one final remark about Holy Mass - you can be sure that Diabolos, who would not dare to venture near the Blessed Sacrament, will strive to keep souls away from the sanctuary and their God to the very end of time.

Fr. Raj: Everybody is a "Judas"...

"It would, finally, be a serious omission on my part, especially given my position as your spiritual director, if I did not make one point very clear. I certainly would not go as far as calling you Judas Iscariot. We all are Judases after all. But I have to emphasize that, at any time we human beings try to pit ourselves against the fallen spirits and Lucifer in particular, we run the risk of underestimating the powers of the Underworld and overestimating our own strengths.

"In my opinion, Judas Iscariot did just that, and ended up destroying himself - and we ourselves, I might add, all have the tendency to overestimate our strengths and underestimate the enemy's powers!

"And it isn't as if we merely have a streak of a Judas Iscariot in us. We all are full-fledged Judases by our failure to live up to expectations and by acting the way we do. We are traitors - all of us! You all remember the hymns we used to sing until recently - the hymns that laid the blame for the Messiah's death squarely on the shoulders of the Jews.

"Man! Blaming the Jews is the same as saying that we are sinless, because it implies that we ourselves wouldn't have done what they did to the Deliverer if we had been in their place! Moreover, if we cannot completely associate ourselves with the chosen people from whom we got our Messiah - if we insist on disassociating ourselves from the Jewish people in this particular respect - how on earth can we claim to be among the beneficiaries of His redemptive work?

"A human being could, in theory, have an advantage over Satan in one or other respect; but that is not what counts when push comes to shove. The fact is that when all is said and done, we do not stand a chance when pitted against the Evil One. Remember that if he hadn't fallen, he would be rubbing shoulders with Michael the Archangel and with Rafael.

"We might not yet be lost and are certainly not yet written off in that sense - like the Diabolical One. But the fact remains, nonetheless, that left to own devices, we are as nothing. We are helpless and unable to perform even the simplest act of virtue! When we are in that kind of position, prudence dictates that we avoid all occasions of sin by mortifying ourselves to keep temptations of the flesh at bay, and also that we constantly pray that our God keep our paths clear of the temptations of Satan and deliver us from evil.

"We have to be humble enough to admit that we cannot win in any one-to-one contest with the Prince of Darkness, and we pay a heavy price by failing to do that. We easily forget that the Mystical Body of Christ - Holy Mother Church - is made up of the sinless Christ *and* mortal human beings who are frail and are burdened with their own failings. And, finally, we easily become scandalized and end up failing to be full participants in the Church's redeeming activities.

Fr. Raj: Wicked humans...

"According to Holy Mother Church, far from being something imaginary, evil is very real indeed; and Satan and his hosts are committed to perpetuating it. As you have ably pointed out, we human beings at a certain point in our lives go nuts, and refuse to accept that there are some rules to the game of living.

"And we sometimes even stop acknowledging that we owe anything to a Prime Mover, and begin acting as though we were the ones who decided that we should have two eyes instead of one, two legs instead of three; that we should be human beings and not kangaroos or reptiles - or some inanimate object shone of feelings (albeit, perhaps, with a life span that might be as long as that of the earth's crust) but without anything resembling intelligence or a free will, and endowed with the capacity to obey His laws of physics and nothing else! We act as though we were the ones who decided that we should be humans and not pure spirits (with no bodily appendage to fuss about) or not at all!

"And to think that we do this without ever a thought as regards our limitations, and do it in league with one who is a mortal enemy at that! To think that it is also with the same goal that we ourselves set out to defy our God and Lord of the Universe, namely to be rid of our Maker who, in His infinite wisdom, established the rules of human conduct that we in our stupidity fancy we can somehow be insulated or liberated from!

"Poor and forsaken mortal creatures whose defiance of the Almighty evokes His infinite pity, our actions which are contrary to our conscience are a serious enough breach of a divinely ordained code of conduct. This is so if only because they render us unworthy as God's place of abode - not to mention the fact that sins also make the world a very inhospitable place indeed. But when we do them in league with Diabolos, who unlike us has been God's sworn enemy from the very beginning unlike us, our intransigence takes on an entirely whole new dimension as a result.

"This happens because we freely decide to enlist the help of one who is the embodiment of evil, crafty and dead serious, and who has no remorse if he destroys creatures who were fashioned in the image of the Almighty and are actually now in line to fill those places in the divine mansion that had originally been reserved for him and his disgraced associates. Because of this, our own evil activity also automatically takes on the same gravity and becomes as deadly. We ourselves end up being little devils - in a sense.

"Like the archenemy, we have exulted when the Messiah's mission appeared doomed - as it did with His crucifixion and death on the cross, and as it still does with the continuing reign of evil. And we have beaten a retreat with the devil whenever the glory of God has become manifest - as it did on the day the Son of Man rose from the dead, and as it now does every hour of the day as His death and resurrection are re-enacted at Mass. And the description of Holy Mother the Church as the Mystical Body of Christ is very apt for precisely these reasons!

"In so doing, we in effect try to compel our Creator to take a dose of what we ourselves detest most - humiliation! Dead wood, we imagine that we can lecture Him on the purpose of creation, including our own *raison d'etre*!

"Prior to the fall, the Lord our God would undoubtedly smile when Adam or Eve, tripping over something, ended up with bruised knees or elbows. But He really pitied them - as he now pities us - when they had the gall to suggest that they did not have to live as befitted creatures fashioned in His image. He pities us when we express our desire to be rid of Him as our mentor - as if there were some other force which could sustain us and the rest of the universe! Offending God knowingly and wilfully is not only dumb but also suicidal, and demonstrates that we, indeed, do not know what we are doing when we start figuring that we could improve on His workmanship.

"We have lost all sense of our purpose in life, and even find it hard to believe that it transcends matter and is spiritual. Adam and Eve's last end had never been the morning glory, dahlias and roses, and the wild berries - or any of the Garden of Eden's other attractions. The whole idea of being fashioned in the image of the Non-Creature and Master Craftsman was that He also be our last end. We just do not seem to get it that Dante's Paradise Lost was a spiritual, not an earthly, paradise.

"We not only have conveniently forgotten that Man is created in God's image, but that this is the case whether the individual sees the light of day for the very first time in the shadow of the Himalayas, the Alps, Mt. Kilimanjaro, or in the shadow of Castel Gandolfo. We self-professed 'Christians' are the biggest offenders when it comes to segregation and other discriminatory practices. We even compete with everybody else as slave pushers.

"And we have taken to imagining that it is the mysterious peace of mind and serenity which canonized individuals exude even in death that marks out Man as being made in the image and likeness of God, instead of what happens at the moment of our creation.

"And, what is even worse, we tell our children that what we see when we look in a mirror is what we are! By suggesting to them that it is what they see in the mirror - flesh and blood - rather than the invisible soul that should be the focal point of their activities, we in effect suggest to them what the demon suggested to Adam and Eve in the Garden of Eden. He suggested to them that to be masters of their destiny, all they needed to do was concentrate on taking good care of those bodies by feeding well - on the forbidden fruit if necessary. They were to ignore the fact that munching on the forbidden fruit was going to compromise their spiritual relationship with their Maker.

"In our case we are telling our children that focusing their attention on what they see in the mirror - that indulging themselves instead of remaining disciplined and of good character - is what will both enrich their existence on earth and add longevity to their lives.

"They are to do as if they are prisoners of their bodies. As if their *élan vital* springs from their preoccupation with their physical selves. Because that is tantamount to self-indulgence, it actually saps their spiritual vitality and leaves them both physically and spiritually drained. But that is what we urge them to do - to concentrate on and pamper their bodies instead of concentrating on and pampering that which directly links them to the Author of Life - their souls.

"We human beings are so stupid, we even think that regimenting our self-indulgence is critical to maintaining an acceptable level of well-being. We imagine that we have to treat ourselves like automobiles - which have to be regularly refuelled to be of use - confirming that we human beings have ditched our lofty status of being children of God and have indeed sank to the level of *homines ex machina*.

"The evils we do to one another are, without exception, traceable to our attempts to act like automatons. And, in the meantime, we ridicule those who do not opt to live like automatons as simpletons and failures. And we fool ourselves into believing that

287

we were the ones who first conceived of the atrocious things we do to fellow humans. We even refuse to concede that we received inspiration of any kind from Diabolos or anyone else before we started down that path of self-destruction.

"We pride ourselves in living like automatons - as if devilishness itself was invented by us! We have become so brazen that we will even do daredevil things - as if the act of daring the Author of Life and Master Architect to try and stop us is a major accomplishment in itself! And, probably even worse, we lull ourselves into believing that we will always be able to get away with our stupidity.

"We are full of praise for those who act like machines, and we relish the sight of soldiers staging a match past or beating a retreat. We hail those countries that have the capability to deliver guided missiles and smart bombs at enemy targets with deadly accuracy as advanced, and have nothing but scorn for those countries which have outlawed armaments. We applaud those who exact revenge swiftly and efficiently, and we regard accommodation, tolerance and the readiness to forgive, not as virtues but as weaknesses if not outright stupidity. And it is, of course, savvy diplomacy not to interfere in global conflicts by way of condemning the aggressors, or siding with and providing assistance to the victims of aggressions.

"And, while the official representatives of foreign nations - the ambassadors - are guaranteed safety, the safety of anybody who takes it on himself/herself to communicate information that is deemed to be of any value to a foreign power is not, the sentence for any such action being execution by firing squad, hanging, lethal injection or other 'socially accepted' means. It is a good measure of the extent to which we human beings have turned against one another, and will do anything to destroy the 'bad guy' or anyone who happens to be different from us. The hatred between some nation states runs so deep, official communications between them have been severed for as long as their nationals can remember!

"Stealing, maiming and killing carried out by governments in the name of national security are accepted and 'legal'; and there is nothing wrong with robbery when undertaken by corporations - it is 'profit-taking'. Indecency has become 'sleekness' and is equated with 'open-mindedness', while decency is a sure sign that one is definitely thick between the ears.

"In the course of pandering to our bodies, we do the dumbest things conceivable. We are usually oblivious to what is good for one part of our constitution while indulging ourselves in ways we think are fulfilling to other parts of the body. We will try to recover from one addiction by getting latched onto some other addiction; and, knowing that time is not on our side, we often get stuck while attempting to satisfy our different appetites all at once! And instead of concluding that satisfying the bodily senses - be it the sense of hearing, sight, smell, taste or the sense of touch - individually or all of them together leads us nowhere at all, and that we should be looking for lasting happiness on a different level (the spiritual plane), we simply continue to act just like dogs do, namely keep trying to catch that tail until we are ready to drop down from exhaustion.

Fr. Raj: On death row...

"The mystery of it all is how creatures that are supposedly rational like ourselves succeed in reconciling all of this with the certain knowledge that we all are, without any exception, on death-row; that we are in the exact same boat as those awaiting the hangman's noose. Like those on death row in Japan, we in fact are completely in the dark as to the day or hour when the knock on the door of the holding cell will presage the end.

"Which is not to say that the human body isn't beautiful. It is without any doubt! There is something about human bodies that not only sets them aside from the bodies of birds, animals, reptiles, and other mammalian creatures, but makes them ultimately deserving of special deference from saints and angels alike. Of course, adjudged good and comely by the Master Craftsman Himself at creation, it is little wonder that when the prodigal son decided to return to his father's that son of his, who had been as good as dead and now here washed and dressed up in the finest robe, and after putting a ring on his finger and sandals, suitably feted.

"One reason providence let the contrite Mary Magdalene, that former *femme fatale* and Jezebel, into the company of the Holy Women was so she would be available to minister to the mother of the Deliverer in the days following the death, resurrection and ascension into heaven of her beloved Son. A bigger reason for celebrating the conversion of that former woman of the twilight was the fact that another creature that was created in the image and likeness of its Maker had resolved to live as befitted a child of God. But yet another reason for celebrating was the fact that Mary Magdalene will rise up body and soul on the last day in glory.

"Thanks to the fact that the Son of Man had condescended to take up our human nature when he agreed to take up our case with His Father, Mary Magdalene too was now destined to rise up on the last day. The fact that there was going to be an intervening period when Magdalene's body, along with those of the rest of mankind, would return to dust would not matter. That meant two things: the jewel, which would grace the heavenly mansion at the divine banquet, would come complete with a soul that was resplendent in God's grace and a body that was glorified! And, obviously something that can be glorified in the spiritual sense had to be adorable and beautiful.

"The human body, designed to facilitate our existence on this earth and also designed to be both a temple of God and a vessel of His grace, in fact *has* to be comely, fair and fascinating. For, if it were not, Mary Magdalene's subsequent act of consecrating herself body and soul to the Redeemer's Most Sacred

Heart would have been an empty gesture and a farce. And, by the same token, our divine Redeemer's self-immolation on the cross, an act of self-sacrifice which encompassed both His divine nature and also His human nature, would not have been the perfect sacrifice it was if that part of human nature wasn't beautiful and adorable. Our own self-denial, undertaken in imitation of our Lord and Savior, would likewise be ineffectual if the human body were not the wonderful piece of creation it is.

"The problem is with our appreciation of this bundle of beauty which is facile and often beguiling and banal, and also our notion of beauty. True appreciation of a beautiful object, whether it be physical or mystical, has to be preceded by an animated chant of the *Magnificat Anima Mea*, and end with a *Te Deum Laudamus* that is belted out with all one's guts. Selfishness cannot be a part of it. The bestiality and possessiveness which we earthlings equate with love and admiration are in fact things that have nothing in common with the profound reverence for what is good - reverence that takes full cognizance of the fact that beautiful things are beautiful only by virtue of being the work of one who is Himself not just charming and beautiful, but the embodiment of charm and beauty - the Supreme Good.

"Which only goes to emphasize the point regarding the image of ourselves which we see in the mirror. That image is nothing compared to something which, being a direct image of God, not only belongs naturally in the heavenly mansion, but is specifically designed to add a distinctive sparkle to it, namely the human soul. And the image in the mirror is also a far cry from the mystical image of a glorified body that will be reunited with the soul when the world comes to an end on the last day.

"In lusting after things of this world, we humans beings, starting with Adam and Eve, have always tried to pretend that the copyright for the masterful work of art represented by the human nature is ours and does not belong to the Master Architect. We spend tons of money keeping our noses - which are supposed to develop a sweat when the body is well exercised - permanently dusted and dry. We keep our naturally beautiful body skin permanently socked in all sorts of creams and lathers, and our lips painted in the strangest colors. We disfigure and permanently ruin the gorgeous hair on our crowns to the point to which it becomes totally unrecognizable.

"Even though it is well established that artificial creams, because they interfere with our immune systems, have a terrible toll on our health and life expectancy, we continue using these creams as if desisting from doing so is a sin against nature. We even refuse to accept scientific findings to the effect that using these artificial agents has the effect of accelerating the decomposition of our bodies when we eventually succumb.

"We tattoo our body parts and attach strange appendages like earrings, bracelets and things like that on them; surround our bodies with lots of jewellery and whatever else money can buy; force

293

ourselves to live through painful things like cosmetic surgery; take on heavy work-out schedules (while avoiding regular work or working to rule) supposedly to develop shapely or muscular bodies; and we then delude ourselves that we have made progress in establishing a right to the copyright. Preoccupied with looks, we cajole ourselves into believing that they are what matters, and that the soul exists only in our imagination - even though it is what informs the human body!

"Our reasoning is so convoluted, we frequently imagine that we have established a right to the copyright by the simple act of committing sins of the flesh; and that the more we do it, the more we own the body and can continue to misuse our God-given talents.

"Talking about misusing talents - any human being who decides to follow his/her reason in figuring out what it is that redounds best to his/her last end would be lucky not to find him/herself permanently restrained in a straight jacket - for his/her own good! Because those who have decided that they will not apply their minds to what really matters - their spiritual life - are in the majority, any move to do what behoves human beings to attain true self-actualization is not just viewed with suspicion. It is regarded as a very serious aberration with far reaching implications. And no wonder! For it is not just a question of priorities of the 'world' - and of those who try to put their 'spiritual salvation' first - being 'different' from those of Providence. They are at cross-purposes.

"We take unnecessary risks and do other outrageous things, and imagine that behaving like that promotes our cause. Even though we know, deep down in our hearts, that we do not have any right whatsoever to that copyright, we close our eyes and just go on doing our thing.

"We wish we owned that copyright for a variety of reasons. We have deluded ourselves into believing that ownership would impart to us the right to do whatever we fancy with the art-work - meaning with ourselves. We imagine, mistakenly, that ownership of that copyright would imply that we do not need the Master Architect, and would consequently absolve us from any sense of guilt for living in whatever way we pleased. We also believe, quite irrationally, that success in establishing ownership would mean that we human creatures can indeed lay a rightful claim to being like Him-Who-Is-Who-Is just as the temper suggested!

"But it is as well that we do not own the copyright; because if we did, we would probably have long ago pawned it to none other than Diabolos, our mortal enemy; and we likely would have done so with the same gusto with which we have been prepared to sell and resell our birthright for peanuts to the enemy. And he, in turn, would have been only too glad to preside over the final destruction of that great masterpiece. He likewise would have been only too glad to see the image of the Almighty One which is emblazoned thereon ripped out or otherwise destroyed to ensure that nothing at all of that art-work could ever be repossessed by the Master Architect.

Fr. Raj: At the height of their rebellion...

"When Adam and Eve, tricked by the fallen Lucifer, joined him and the other rebel spirits in the uprising against the Creator, they imagined, foolishly, that they had Him cornered. They were after all created in His image and likeness - just like the angels. But, unlike the angels, each of whom had a distinct nature and also formed a separate specie, Adam and Eve share this same human nature even while existing as individuals with different personalities. Adam and Eve were aware that the Prime Mover, His Divine Son, and the Spirit that united them in a perfect bond of love also shared the same divine nature even as they enjoyed each a separate existence as distinct persons.

"At the height of their rebellion, the first man and the first woman felt assured that, as the future father and mother of the human race, they were going to come out triumphant in their machinations against the Almighty One if only because He had no choice but to write off and deem as lost all their posterity as well in the event that he was going to hold them to account for eating of the fruit from the tree of knowledge. Adam and Eve could not imagine that their Creator, who was infinitely just, could condemn their wholly 'innocent' children and their children's children and cut them off simply because they, Adam and Eve, had staged a revolt.

"They thought that they had the Prime Mover and Almighty One cornered and that consequently He wasn't in a position to assert His authority over them to that extent, and to exact retribution from them for their sinful deed. It was quite plain that He could not move against them without ending the human race as a whole! If he did so, it would compromise His sense of justice, because they and their posterity were destined, in accordance with the divine plan, to share the same human nature. A curse on them would automatically be binding on their posterity as well for that reason!

"On the other hand, any 'punishment' that left their human nature unscathed would hardly be punishment at all - or so they reasoned. As Adam and Eve imagined it, their Creator was either going to tolerate their infidelity and in effect condone their evil doing or He was going to condemn humanity as a whole for their dastardly act. It, therefore, came as a great surprise when the first man and the first woman found themselves kicked out of the Garden of Eden and lost the sanctuary that had assured their safety from beasts of the wild, poisonous snakes, viruses, and other harmful creatures.

"And then the pendulum swung when, abandoned to an uncertain future on their own, Adam and Eve recanted and regretted their act. After imagining that their Creator was powerless to exact retribution from them for their sin of disobedience, the penitent Adam and Eve now imagined that, even though they were prepared to renounce Satan and his wiles and return to the fold, their situation was still completely hopeless.

"The fact was that it was not enough for them to just be ready to abandon their sinful ways. In order to become reconciled to their Divine Master, someone had to make up adequately for their misadventure that had cost them their friendship with a divinity. Someone had to pay the price for their affront to the Prime Mover; and that someone had to be a divinity if the recompense was to be acceptable!

"But where on earth were they going to get someone divine to intercede for them? Adam and Eve regarded their situation as quite hopeless, and were resigned to staying as captives - yes, lackeys - of Beelzebub. Mere humans, there was absolutely nothing that they themselves could do to make up adequately for injury to a God. And so, even though repentant, it was clear to Adam and Eve that they were doomed all the same. Despite the heartfelt remorse they felt, no amount of penance by them - or any creature for that matter - could be pleasing enough to the Almighty One and undo the damage caused by original sin and the effects thereof!

"And then there was the ever present danger that they could again succumb to the Evil One's temptations which were continuing. Noting that the fallen angels became lost forever as a result of their act of rebellion, Adam and Eve had every reason to fear that their own situation was likewise beyond remedy. Much as they were prepared to let the Almighty One have the 'pound of flesh' they knew was

His due, they could not figure out how that could ever come about.

"It caught them entirely by surprise when their Maker, in an unprecedented act of infinite mercy that also reflected a love that was infinite and unbounded, promised to send his only begotten Son to earth where, both as man and also as a member of the Godhead, He would be in a position to make amends on their behalf. Adam and Eve in fact never fully recovered from the shock they got when it was revealed to them that the Word, through whom everything that had come into being was made, had consented, in deference to the will of His Father, to pay the price exacted for their sins *and* the sins of their descendants!

"It was still up to men to accept the invitation to be reconciled with their Maker or to reject it. Adam and Eve were overwhelmed to learn that the relations between Man and his Maker, severed when they committed original sin, were going to be restored through the intervention of the divine Messiah. This would take effect as soon as the debt of sin was paid by the promised Redeemer and also 'Second Adam' in accordance with the promise made to them by the Father.

"Actually, the Word was going to 'become flesh' and was going to dwell among humans. In the Son of Man, as the Messiah would call Himself, the divine nature and the human nature were going to be united in one and the same Person. The Messiah, true God and true man, would then proceed to overcome sin with His death and His resurrection. Death itself, to which Adam and Eve became subject in the wake of their transgression would 'loose its sting'.

"Suddenly Adam and Eve - even though they once upon a time had cherished the fact that they had Lucifer as their ally and had lost their right to eternal life in the process, and were on the verge of despair even after they had decided to return to the fold - found that they could count on the Second Adam, who was none other than the Second Person of the Blessed Trinity, to intercede for them with His Father.

"But that was not all. He also was going to make recompense on their behalf - recompense that would be acceptable to a Divinity whose ire they had roused by entering into alliance with the Evil One. The first man and the first woman never forgave themselves for the fact that they had actually tried to blackmail their Maker and hold the infinite love He espoused for His creatures to ransom at the height of their rebellion.

Fr. Raj: In denial...

"The fact that we human beings were lost and had, in the process, allowed death to have mastery over us is evidence enough of the extent to which we had gone to subvert God's plan for us. It is incredible, but that is precisely what had happened. We even now still find the time to unashamedly celebrate it with great fanfare at the variety of carnivals that we observe regularly. We should know better, but we continue to be in denial regarding the impending doomsday at which we will be called upon to account for the manner in which we used the talents we have been entrusted with.

"We are so hopeless, we sometimes have a valid point to make - a point that might be good and positive for once - but we make it the wrong way and end up heaping blame on ourselves and feeling guilty as hell. And that sort of thing happens frequently too! We will, for instance, find ourselves staring adoringly at a person of the opposite sex; and, while genuinely admiring the work of God's creation, we might even mention it a passer-by, only to turn around and bash ourselves for revelling in unseemly talk or something like that. This is even though the encounter might end up causing end up causing those involved to wind up exchanging wedding vows at the altar! But we will in the meantime feel guilty for 'lusting' after a woman or a man, as the case may be.

"We forget that we are actually charged with a duty to admire the works of our good and loving Creator, albeit in a way that is prayerful and reverend or holy. On occasions like these, we fail to 'get it' that, as the sun was beginning to set again for the seventh consecutive time signaling the end of the seventh day of His labors of creation, our Maker Himself actually looked down and saw that what he had crafted was good not just in a metaphorical sense, but in a literal and concrete sense. We sometimes even completely forget that it is the intention behind the act that makes all the difference in matters of morality, and not the acts themselves.

"We end up trapping ourselves in our own arguments so to speak because, more often than not, we are really after sophistry, not just the simple truth. When it comes to our own lives, seconds, minutes, hours, days, months, years and decades all suddenly stop representing things that are real - perhaps because we cannot touch this thing called 'time'! This is even though those of us who work regularly lament that 'time isn't moving fast enough!' on Fridays and, come Saturday and Sunday, our tune changes to 'time is moving too fast'! Yes, 'moving' as if it was a piece of solid rock travelling down the slope of a hill!

"The only people who take time and death seriously seem to be lawyers who make a living from writing wills, funeral homes, and owners/managers of life insurance companies, banks and other investment firms which automatically inherit assets that are not claimed after people pass on. On the evidence, they are the only ones who believe that time really comes to an end for an individual at death, and that 'death' really means kicking the 'bucket' in one's path and moving on to some other place where things like time and worldly comfort no longer count. But they, obviously, believe it only in to the extent these things apply to their former clients and not to themselves - which leaves them also in the exact same boat as everybody else!

"Only a score of us have set our eyes on our great grandparents, and it must be a tiny number who have been so blessed as to be able to set their eyes on their great great grandparents. But we all continue to kid ourselves that the divine plan, under which sinners, their children and their children's children must die the death as a price for Man's intransigence is a tall tale.

"But what we all need is to take a walk, bump unexpectedly into friends we haven't seen in a long while, and then make the mistake of inquiring after some of our former mutual acquaintances. That might help us wake up to the reality of that thing called 'death'. Even though we human beings forget easily, it will be sometime before we forget the shock with which we learn that former associates we thought were doing very well (like ourselves if not better) and would, therefore, outlast everybody else - especially those former associates whose physical presence evoked visions of endless triumphs and continued prosperity - had indeed already passed on; and it will also be a while before we forgot that some former buddies we had written off and thought would be swept under and be gone and forgotten in a thrice were still going strong!

"Or, do we believe that it is not our God who created us, and is meting out the just punishment for our deliberate decision to stray from the right path, but someone else - Diabolos? Do we, perhaps, fantasize that everything that happens is the product of chance - yes, *chance* to which we should also credit the awesome symmetry and order in the universe, including the miracles of life *and*, I suppose, also death!

303

"Well, assume for a moment that we owe it all to this Diabolos. If Diabolos had been in the shoes of our Lord and Maker, he certainly wouldn't hesitate to mete out punishment to us *unjustly* - even if we had done no wrong! He would dole out the punishment *especially* if we were living righteously and shunning evil. No, it is not Diabolos who created us or ordained that we suffer for our sins. This is not because Diabolos is the embodiment of evil, but because he is a creature. He could never step into the shoes of our loving God for that reason. And we can rest assured that it is not Diabolos to whom we are due to render an accounting for the manner in which we used our God-given talents, because he himself is already in very big trouble for his failure to employ his own God-given talents in the proper manner.

"But why is it that we do as if we owe those among us who are Diabolos' minions apologies of any sort - especially when they seem determined to carry out the devil's bidding, treat us unjustly, and do everything they can to demoralize us? Or do we act like that because we ourselves are already like them in many respects!

Fr. Raj: God's love for humans...

"And that, unfortunately, clouds the situation somewhat, and makes it harder for us to appreciate the other and even more important fact. Which, namely, is that the Prime Mover 'so loved the world, He gave His only begotten Son; so that those who

304

would believe in Him would not perish...'

"We forget that Providence sent the Good Samaritan to the rescue even after first the priest and then the Levite avoided the traveler who had been brutalized by highway robbers and left there to die. That, similarly, the Deliverer heard the frantic cries and wailing of Peter and the other apostles in the sinking boat and calmed the seas so that they might survive to carry on His mission.

"And, again, when Lazarus passed the first time around - and even though his body had started to decompose - the Deliverer felt great sympathy for the distraught relatives, and caused the dead man to come alive and pick up where he had left off in his earthly life, a life that had obviously been lived to the full and that had been edifying to his contemporaries as well. And that was even though Lazarus had died for the reason we all die, namely because Man, following in the footsteps of Lucifer, had succumbed to sin.

"We also forget that, on hearing His mother whisper something to the effect that their hosts at the wedding of Canaan had run out of wine, the Son of Man immediately ordered the empty jars filled with water which he turned into refreshingly new wine.

"And again, in yet another example of an action that followed a pattern of behavior that couldn't be more consistent - even though the time was most inauspicious because He himself was under the gun and was greatly troubled in His mind - there the Messiah was, emerging from the secluded spot where

He had been praying to His Father. He was checking up on His disciples' well-being; and, seeing them struggling to keep their heavy eye-lids open and having a hard time trying to keep watch with Him, He 'had great pity on them'. Knowing that they felt very bad over it, He hastened to offer them words of encouragement saying: 'The spirit is willing, but the flesh is weak'!

"The same sentiments went for His Father. For, when the Maker of all things visible and invisible saw Adam and Eve disconsolate and distraught with shame after committing their original sin, He did not hesitate, as they hid in the bushes, to holler out to them saying 'Do not commit an act of despair now and make things worse...'

"They could not dare look Him in the eye, and they protested that He should leave them alone to pay the price for their intransigence. However, inclined to sin as a result of their rebellion, it was evident that they were going to seek solace from none other than the Tempter, and would almost certainly end up mired in unpardonable diabolical activity. Our Maker was not about to sit back and see that happen. And so, He had shouted out to them saying 'Do not be afraid. I will send my only Son to be your Redeemer...'

"And again, as the Messiah Himself faltered in His steps as He climbed Mount Calvary with His burden on behalf of all of us, Providence had this African by the name of Simon of Cyrene at the right spot and at the right time to help our Redeemer make it to the summit.

306

"Because we human beings find it hard to desist from dabbling in iniquity from time to time, we subsequently also find it hard to appreciate the fact that God will never abandon those in need. It is apparently quite difficult for us to put our hopes and dreams of fulfilment in the Almighty - we should in fact admit that it is impossible without the help of God's grace. With our attachment to material things remaining as strong as ever, we often even poke fun at God and ridicule the idea that He saves. We remain as faithless as those who thought they were being very witty when they mocked the Messiah saying 'He said that God was His Father. If He was indeed God's son, how come the father does not descend from heaven to rescue Him, now?'

"As long as this continues to be the case, our acceptance of the fact that human miseries and suffering - unpleasant things though they are - are beneficial to us in the new scheme of things will always elude us and appear a crazy thing to do. We won't quite be able to appreciate the fact that pain, both physical and mental, and things of that nature actual open up avenues that facilitate our participation in the work of redemption. Statements such as 'He sends sufferings to those He loves', or 'Take up your cross and follow me', or 'Blessed are those who weep and mourn, for the reward is theirs' will continue to make very little if any sense at all.

"That is also why pain and suffering will continue to be mysterious things, driving us to seek revenge, or otherwise do things which promise to 'bring closure' to our hurt feelings. And yet, doing these things is like telling the devil that someone is giving us trouble - perhaps God; and then immediately turning to God and telling Him that someone is proving a nuisance - the devil! But we have to choose who we wish to have as ally on the other hand - the devil or God. It cannot be both.

"Still, admonishing people to have God, and not the devil, as their ally is easier said than done. This is because there is another side to it. When you choose to have God as your ally and presume to accept the miseries He sends your way as things that are beneficial to you, you will also be expected, when your tormentors pounce, to 'turn the other cheek'! But your instinct will be urging you to prepare for the show down and warn: 'On my dead body'. And that is possible only when your 'tormentors' are not an 'act of God' and can be identified. So, the situation is quite complicated.

"But we are taught that God always 'intervenes' on our behalf To draw His compassion, the actions of others do not have to amount to 'sins that cry out to heaven'. He does not have to see 'the blood of Abel' flowing, or to see 'the sin of the Sodomites' or 'the injustice to the wage earner', or to hear 'the cry of the people oppressed in Egypt' or 'the cry of the foreigner, the widow, and the orphan', or to witness 'discrimination in all its ugly forms' before He is touched.

Fr. Raj: Second-guessing God...

"Talking about discrimination, God does not discriminate against us. And we certainly do not want to be discriminated against by fellow human beings or even by angels (who are made in God's image and likeness just like us). But, on the other hand, we ourselves seem unable to live without perpetuating discriminatory acts of one type or another against others and against God.

"Against others by treating them as though they are aliens who just masquerade as humans with no legitimate claim to their human nature, or else have come by their human nature in some felonious fashion, the greatest injustice being that wrought against those who are outside the purview of laws enacted by man and indefensible. And against God by acting as if He, being the Almighty, still got it all wrong when He set out the rules of the game the way He did, and ordained that we be wholly subject to His laws, both moral and natural.

"And the way we practice apartheid, segregation, tribalism and discrimination - the way we do these things, you would think that we are bewitched! The white people discriminate against both non-white people and against other white people; the black people discriminate against non-black people and against other black people; the yellow people discriminate against non-yellow people and against other yellow people; and the red people discriminate against non-red people and against other red people.

"And then the miscarriage of justice carried out in broad daylight and under the glare of television lights against perceived foes and in the absence of any proof of wrong-doing. The way we hound and cut down fellow humans, or otherwise treat them like creatures that had no inalienable rights. The way we love to demonstrate that might is right, and completely forget that any authority exercised by humans comes from God and is accountable.

"The way we do these things, you would think the gods in whose names we do these things were crazy - as they must be if, indeed, there are any such gods! And also there must be quite a bit of turmoil wherever those gods have their dwelling place. And we are so stupid we have no idea what kind of judgement we are soliciting when we purport to do them in the name of the God of Abraham and Isaac.

"In spite of all that and our stupidity, our good Lord and God, who is very concerned when a bird of the air loses a single feather and who, in addition to making us in his own image and likeness, has bestowed on us so many gifts, is attentive to each and all our cries. It goes without saying that He rushes to intervene especially when, seeing ourselves heading for the brink, we stop and, however reluctantly, pray for grace so we might at least be able to continue inching ahead hopefully in the right direction along the narrow path.

"And stopping to do that is hard enough, given all those conflicting and often also confusing messages which we, poor forsaken children of Adam and Eve, get from the different spiritual directors, some of whom advocate apartheid, segregation and discrimination - the very things they should be urging us to abhor - outright.

"The main point to be noted here is that God not only actually intervenes to prevent His people from being crushed by the enemy and those who are prepared to do his bidding, but even turns their miseries into good by using human suffering as a cleansing tool and also as a vehicle for unsolicited grace and other spiritual blessings.

"They are blessings that accrue to humans as Providence forges ahead with the implementation of His divine plan - something we short-sighted humans forget is on-going and unstoppable, and will continue regardless of what we do. Regardless, in fact, of what Diabolos, the embodiment of evil, and his lackeys do.

"This is no joking matter - it is very serious business we are discussing here. Yet, despite our avowals, we all continue, as one man, to act as if we are invincible - even though our own days are strictly numbered. And we forget, above all, that those who now weep will laugh with joy, and those who now laugh will weep and gnash their teeth.

Fr. Raj: Don't own copyright (to human nature)...

"If the Master Architect had made the mistake of letting us humans have the authority to determine how the human person, made in His own image and likeness, could be disposed of, our resurrection from the dead, and quite possibly the redemption of fallen Man, would likely have been put in great jeopardy. The way we discriminate and cheat each other, and ride roughshod over the rights of our fellow beings, there is no way God would have permitted us to fill the heavenly mansions with our cronies and to send his faithful servants to hell.

"And, in case you are wondering, the Master Architect and Craftsman could easily have entrusted us with the original portrait and the copyright to it by the simple act of giving each one of us at creation his or her own separate and distinct nature - as He did with the angels. But the angels who fell mucked it up even though they knew perfectly well that there was no hope of redemption for them if they strayed from the path of righteousness - if they allowed themselves to be locked in a mode that was incompatible with true self-actualization and their last end.

"Entrusting us with the copyright to our nature would almost certainly have complicated His plan of redemption in our case in the same way, possibly even rendering it impossible in practical terms. But we human beings show by the way we act that we have never stopped clamoring for the copyright. We wish that we could act God and dispose of fellow humans any way we chose. That is what we 'demand' when we ride roughshod over the rights of those who share our nature.

"But suppose we had been given the copyright!

312

Then, as and when we courted death through rebellion against our Maker and eventually "died" in both the spiritual *and* physical sense, our 'bodies' would promptly return to dust, never to see the light of day or to rise up again. And our unmanageable spirits would be consigned to a place where they would suffer ceaselessly from the thirst for their Maker whom they themselves, freely and knowingly, would have abjured in what was effectively an unpardonable act of sacrilege. And those sad and highly regrettable developments, which would signal the end of our impudence and cheek, would also unfortunately have heralded the end of the original and otherwise really excellent works of art - exactly as happened in the case of Lucifer and his band of rebel spirits.

"In the meantime, as we died and individually dispatched ourselves to heaven by remaining true to ourselves or to hell through our rebellion and intransigence, the Master Craftsman's responsibility for us individually would also end because, by being each one of us a separate and distinct specie just like angelic beings, we would constitute success stories or failures that were completely unrelated except for the fact that we were all of us original pieces of art that owed their existence from the same Master Craftsman.

"But, just because we do not own the copyright, it does not mean that the act of redemption does not require our cooperation. Indisputably, humans cannot attain salvation except by virtue of the graces that are dispensed through the Church's sacraments.

But, being free creatures, our individual salvation is also dependent on our cooperation with the graces that were earned for us by the Second Adam when He offered Himself as a 'Sacrificial Lamb' to His Father on our behalf, and permitted us sinful humans to visit death upon Him - a gruesome death on the cross. That is all the Deliverer asks of humans, namely cooperation with the divine grace by being faithful members of the Pilgrim Church. And that is not really asking too much when compared to the high price the Deliverer Himself paid to merit those graces with us in mind.

Just as the graces, that are dispensed to humans through the sacraments and act *ex opere operato*, are given to us freely by the Deliverer, being free creatures ourselves, we are expected to freely cooperate to attain their individual salvation. We are on trial and must stir to take advantage of the opportunity availed to us to prepare and pass what you called the Church Triumphant Entrance Test. We must adopt the position of 'willing spirits' that accept to be recipients of the redeeming grace and work with it to attain eternal life. There is no short cut.

Fr. Raj: The inhabitants of hell...

"Talking about angels - there is one question that is perfectly valid to ask, and an answer to which, while simple, seems particularly revealing with lots of implications for us human beings. The question itself is actually quite elementary and is as follows: 'How come that one perfectly sane and exceedingly gifted angelic being winds up in heaven and able to fill the role of God's messenger in our regard, while another also sane and also exceedingly gifted angelic being ends up, tragically, in hell and as a demon committed to both our physical and spiritual destruction? The answer is, of course, free will, which is indisputably an important part of their angelic nature.

"Regardless of the answer to the controversial question 'Are there human beings in hell?', we seem to have a clear and unambiguous answer to the equally valid question 'How come one perfectly sane and very gifted human creature might be lost and in hell, while another also perfectly sane human creature is saved and in heaven?'. Whereas one creature, angelic or human, exercises its right to freedom of choice in its best interests and winds up in heaven, apparently that does not stop another angelic or human creature from knowingly opting to go to hell!

"And, unfortunately, that gives the erroneous impression that the perennial conflict between the forces of good and the forces of evil is evenly matched! And erroneous for two reasons: Firstly, the free will and the ability of angelic beings and their fellow human creatures to exercise their right thereto are gifts and are, by definition, rooted in an act of charity on the part of our Maker - in other words, they are rooted in goodness. Up until that point, evil is not even in the picture. And secondly, heaven, the place where the Maker abides in the company of the triumphant angels and saints, is paradisiacal.

315

Whereas hell, the place of the damned, where Diabolos once kept Adam and Eve and other holy men and women captive until the Son of Man descended there after his death and rescued them, is a rotten place.

"In the one-sided contest between good and evil, good triumphed over the reign of evil long ago, as expected, with the resurrection from the dead of the Son of Man. The victory is so complete that Diabolos and his condemned lackeys cannot do anything to try and promote their lost cause without God's express permission. And that is in addition to the fact that they have been judged and cast into the fire that does not go out. Far from being evenly matched, the contest is already over and Diabolos, as expected, is the outright loser.

"As it is, we can use the talents we received *gratis* from our Maker - both physical talents or spiritual talents - for our self-actualization, and also remember to show that we are thankful for those gifts; or we can use them and forget that we owe anyone a 'thank you'; or, alternatively, we can misuse them and damn anyone who suggests that things do not quite seem right. For that matter, we even can go jump into the sea - as we, indeed, often do in our efforts to frustrate the divine plan. But that is all we can do. Our Maker has made certain that our human nature, like a work of art that is too valuable to be left on permanent display, stays well out of the reach of morons like ourselves. Oafs who have never had any scruples in allowing Diabolos to have his way with

316

these priceless prints from a masterpiece that is as singularly unique as the nature of man - prints we swore we would never part with at the time they were entrusted to us!

Fr. Raj: The prize (after fighting the good fight)...

"Because of the fact that we are created in the image of the Creator, and thanks to our spiritual nature and the role of the soul; thanks to the fact that, even though endowed with a free will, we were created to pay homage to the Lord our God and to serve Him with all our hearts and minds; and, of course, thanks to the fact that the Deliverer condescended to take on our human nature - human bodies now have a chance to add to the splendor in heaven; and to sparkle with a lustre so fulsome that the appreciation of the divine workmanship in bringing human beings into existence by the saints in heaven now completely transcends individual human relationships and the bonds between them.

"That is presumably why the Sacrament of Matrimony, so critical now to our survival as a human race on earth and, along with it, the marital bonds sanctified by it cease to be relevant. It is likely that even the distinction between human beings and the victorious spirits that came into existence without any bodily appendage is blurred, as all the victorious spirits, with or without a glorified body, join in anthem and glorify the Lord.

Fr. Raj: The real world: a ghostly world...

"Returning to the question of human souls versus human bodies, one preacher put it very succinctly. It was incorrect, in his words, to say that a human being had a soul. A human being *was* a soul and, according to him, only *had* a body, and a corruptible one at that!

"So, you can safely tell Fr. Cunningham, your Philosophy professor, that he is wrong when he says that Man is an *Animal Rationale* and things like that! We are not corporeal beings that are informed by the soul! It is a measure of our ignorance when we use the expression 'He/she gave up the ghost' in describing someone's 'demise'! One would have thought that it would be the ghost or soul that would shed the body when the latter became incapable of supporting the former in its temporal existence here on earth. And we certainly should start teaching our children that they we are spirits, and that they have bodies - bodies which they will eventually shed in the same way some reptiles shed their old skin even in mid-life.

"We who are baptized have even persuaded ourselves that we are better than those unbaptized folks who, unlike us, at least still try to practice fairness and equity in their dealings with fellow men. The paradox is that these other folks unwittingly end up bearing sterling witness to the unknown God in whose image they happen to be fashioned. As for those of us who have received formal invitations to the banquet, but think that baptism also confers on us the right to set our own rules of human conduct, the time is surely coming when we will find ourselves locked outside the banquet hall and vainly chanting 'Open, Lord! Open, Lord!'

"Let us face it. Every time we transgress, we essentially raise the same old issue relating to our commitment to conduct ourselves as behoves creatures that are made in the image of their Creator - and we should, of course, always remember that 'image of the Creator' and 'spiritual nature of human beings' are two ideas that are intrinsically the same. We raise that issue when we decide to be nasty to our neighbor, and do so each time we break any of God's other commandments. Looking at things from that angle certainly makes it easier to understand why mere intentions and thoughts may constitute sin. By the same token, it also becomes easier to understand why meritorious works may not necessarily be accompanied by deeds per se.

"I would go further and add that seeing things from that perspective also makes it easier to understand how people of goodwill, even though not members of the visible Church, may be headed for heaven, while those of us who have been specially invited to the banquet might be headed for some other place! And it makes it easier for all people of goodwill irrespective of religious affiliation to identify with our Savior who is also the Word through whom everything that is was made.

"It should not come as a surprise that it is children who have no difficulty accepting that they are spiritual beings, and understanding that it is not what is on the outside, but what is on the inside, that is of the essence. Until we start teaching them that material things matter, they typically subscribe to no such falsehoods. And until we adults impose ourselves on them and introduce them to all sorts of falsehoods, children, whether born in Mongolia, Peru, Siberia, California or Uganda, up until that time know that they are created in the image of their Maker. And they know, above all, that they are all brothers and sisters, until we start to teach them otherwise.

"Talking about teaching children, they are very easy to teach and learn easily, unlike us adults who have preconceived ideas; and hence their ability to absorb a great deal of material in a very short time. But, unfortunately, that is also why they are such easy prey - when we set upon them with our barrage of prejudiced notions about reality and the people around us. And, after we have done the devil's dirty work for him, we like to settle back and blame the mess in the world on 'Fate', by which we mean our Creator!

"I would even go further and say - at the risk of being excommunicated myself - that up until we adults begin to interfere with the attitudes and beliefs of children, all of them without any exception are members of both the visible and the invisible Church! And that is, perhaps, why our sacred Redeemer pleaded with His overzealous disciples that they let the children come to Him!

"It is clearly the failure to grasp that we human beings are spiritual beings which has resulted in so many people in the Church being scandalized by the recently promulgated dogmas to the effect that Adam and Eve had felt hunger and thirst, and had been no strangers to physical pain before their fall from grace, and also that it is spiritual death, not physical death, which is one of the consequences or by-products of sin. I suspect that it is also the reason the Pearl of Africa, as Churchill called it, has been receiving so many visitors since The Diaries and other artifacts were unearthed! Certainly looks like Churchill and British Intelligence came quite close to identifying the birthplace of Adam and Eve.

Fr. Raj: In sum...

"The Deliverer, as you call Him, saves us from ourselves and also from evil. He died to expiate for our failures; then, as he rose from the dead, He freed the souls of the just who had been held in bondage in the bowels. We are still inclined to sin; and we still die. The difference now, though, is that we are subject to the judgement of Him who has completely routed Satan and spelled doom for his evil empire. The same goes for those who will still be kicking at the end of time - they too will face judgement.

"To sum up, overestimating our strength and underestimating the power of Satan - the ringleader of those who would dethrone the Creator if they had the power to do so - does not at all help this situation. Neither does cavorting with Satan or anyone else who is in league with him. Just as playing sissy and suddenly pretending that we do not have the responsibility to exercise and diligently choose to follow our consciences isn't helpful either. These are very important points which cannot be overemphasized."

Father Oremus...

Father Oremus, a Canadian and the only North American on the seminary staff, taught Psychology. He had obviously been waiting patiently for the Indian to finish his lengthy harangue. As soon as Father Raj signaled that he was done, the Canadian was up on his feet. The last member of the panel to speak, Father Oremus did not waste any time getting to the point he had been dying to make.

"I will be quick and to the point, Reverend Mjomba. I am probably speaking for the distinguished members of this committee when I say that you deserve not just an 'A' but an 'A' Plus for the paper you have submitted. It is very well

reasoned, and for one it doesn't appear as if any of the material in was plagiarized.

"However, my commitment to give you an 'A' Plus, instead of an 'F', is conditional. You must agree to burn all the available copies of this thesis as soon as we are done. You will understand why in a minute.

"The greatest danger your paper presents in

my mind is this: for anyone to read and digest its contents and overall message, which is in fact orthodox by and large, it is necessary to spend a considerable time in what is effectively a prolonged chat with Beelzebub of all people! He is clearly the main character in this 'yarn' - that is what your paper, in spite of its merits, really is, isn't it!

"In the process of 'conversing' with Satan - there is no way that a thinking individual could just passively give him an ear. One inevitably starts to also place trust in him. There is, no doubt, a lot to be said for the bulk - if not all - of the arguments you have him verbalize. But I have to confess that you probably wouldn't have been able to make many of the points you have made as lucidly and eloquently as you did if you had not used the Evil One himself as the mouthpiece. I doubt very much if there is anybody else who could have. And so, as far as techniques go, you've certainly discovered one that is brilliant and, I dare say, also effective.

"Still, this relationship is not the kind we are supposed to have with the tempter! It might be permissible from the point of view of academic freedom and creativity. But from the point of view of the priestly ministry - from the point of view of pastoral work - that is certainly debatable. I myself would rather have the faithful miss Satan's exhortations, however inspiring, in their entirety than encourage them in any way to start communing with a creature who is committed to sowing the seeds of death.

"If there is one point which this 'Thesis on

Original Virtue' makes very clear, it is the fact that the devil is indeed very knowledgeable - that humans are well advised not to try and challenge him on that score; and thank God, because he is invisible, we humans generally do not get any opportunities to stare him down and try to argue with him. The thesis also makes it quite clear that we humans can beat him to it only when we put on the 'armor of Christ'!

"When the childhood innocence of a human is bolstered by the sacraments, then our ability to challenge the Prince of Darkness grows in leaps and bounds and soon eclipses the ability of *Sheitan* to tempt us. We are safe under the mantle of the Deliverer, the King of Kings and also Lord of Lords who nevertheless chose to be led away like a lamb to the slaughter, having agreed to pay the price for the decision of the first man and the first woman to ally themselves with Beelzebub, for the murderous conduct of humans against each other, the immorality, injustice, and for other transgressions that make humans look so hideous in the eyes of the Prime Mover. We are safe under the mantle of a Deliverer who, above all, deliverers the forsaken victims of a world out of control - a world that unjustly tramples on the innocent, and treats their cries and sufferings as if they are irrelevant and do not matter.

"And, by the way, you make the devil so believable, just to make sure that you are alright - that you have not ended up falling in his possession - it might be a good idea if we conducted a conditional exorcism. It is something I'm sure Father Cromwell covered in the Pastoral Theology Seminar.

"So, Sonny, do we have a deal?" Father Oremus asked in conclusion as his colleagues on the panel nodded in agreement.

"I think we can skip the conditional exorcism bit, Father Oremus" Mjomba quipped, to sustained applause and a nod of approval from Father Raj.

Father Oremus appeared to be mightily reassured that the man who heard Mjomba's weekly confessions did not consider a conditional exorcism necessary. And he was clearly relieved when Mjomba said: "Otherwise we have a deal!"

PART 7: WHAT MJOMBA ALSO WROTE (IN HIS THESIS)

It was typical of Mjomba, who was not one to shy away from a topic, either because it was involved or perhaps even a hard sell, to try and tackle as many of the topics bearing on the theme of his thesis as possible. The thesis accordingly included a discussion of what he referred to as the abundant testimony that acknowledgement of the Prime Mover's supremacy was inescapable.

Mjomba wrote that nothing testified to the power and might of the Prime Mover as much as did the phenomena of life and death. It had always been obvious that the involvement of humans in bringing about life or terminating it was only in their capacity as intermediaries, with what actually occurred in either instance remaining a riddle.

Ageing, dependence and dying...

Talking about death - that phenomenon which, by all counts, was so unsavory to humans it automatically evoked feelings of dread and terror - Mjomba wrote that it was preceded by another phenomenon that did not cause as much fear or anxiety in humans, but some nonetheless. This was the ageing process.

Growing old also evidenced the power and might of the Prime Mover even though perhaps to a lesser extent than death did, Mjomba wrote. Unlike conception or death, ageing used that real but intangible thing called time to achieve its end. Even though humans did all they could to ignore the ageing process and had huge programs going to assist them in perpetuating the charade, it did not really help. The ageing process, as it evolved and took hold with the passage of time, had a way of slowly chipping away the oftentimes quite unbelievable egotism, arrogance and cavalier attitudes of humans, and bringing them gradually to their knees as it were just before death inflicted the *coup de grace*.

The contrast occurred in the lower animal realm where, Mjomba claimed, the birds, beasts, reptiles and other so-called lower beings viewed ageing as a blessing, and patiently waited on death which, when it finally came, was also embraced courageously in abeyance to the will of their Creator who was Himself eternal and unchanging, and certainly didn't age as He didn't exist in time!

According to Mjomba, there was probably no significant correlation between the ageing process and immorality, contrary to the popular belief that the onset of puberty was accompanied by licentiousness and antipathy for authority both ecclesiastical and secular. He doubted that Adam and Eve's age bracket at the time they became so brazen as to dare the Prime Mover to act in the face of their intransigence would be indicative of any correlation between age and degeneracy - if their age at the time they fell from grace was known.

Mjomba wrote that it was a good thing it was

not, as the so-called scientific community would undoubtedly have latched on to the idea that, at that particular stage in their lives, humans were genetically prone to degeneracy and antisocial behavior - or some such foolish notion! But, all that notwithstanding, in the end every sign not just of life but of existence on earth or in the heavens, Mjomba wrote, proclaimed not just the existence of the Prime Mover, but His greatness as well.

Mjomba held the position that humans, even though free to choose between different alternatives and whims, were essentially dependent on the Prime Mover and on others from the time they were conceived in their mother's womb to the time they departed for the after-life. He suggested that the state of dependence underwent a decline as humans first grew older and became more capable of exercising personal autonomy only on the surface.

Humans, Mjomba wrote, continued to be dependent - indeed more so than before - even as they attained both physical and mental maturity. He argued that the reason for this lay in the fact that humans essentially began dying as soon as they were conceived in the womb!

Mjomba's argument that humans began dying as soon as they were conceived was based on the fact that cells in the embryo began dying at that time. Mjomba contended that if new cells did not develop quickly enough to replace the ones which were dying off, the newly conceived would not survive - and neither their owners.

To stave off death before birth, the unborn child had to strive to remain attached to its mother's umbilical cord. After birth, the baby strove to do whatever it took to suckle on its mother's breast and to take adequate rest just to keep death at bay. And when it started teething, the infant begun to supplement its intake of milk with solid foods that also required to be masticated, ingested and digested. It knew instinctively that it would die if it did not undertake those additional and obviously burdensome exercises - exercises that in turn caused muscles and bones in the infant to begin ageing earlier than they otherwise would and also faster.

Then, as soon as it became capable of moving on all its fours and of using its limbs, the little one made a strategic decision to put these and its other faculties to use in assisting adults to procure sustenance for the whole family and improve living conditions so everybody in the community could enjoy a longer life expectation.

And it would, of course, know by that time that it could not go on like that forever; and that, even though it had been reared up in society, it was essentially on its own and was in time going to pass from this life to another one in which its continued survival would not be contingent on its ability to provide or fend for itself in that fashion; and also that its dependence on its Prime Mover would actually be complete in that after-life.

Mjomba explained in a foot note that, contrary to popular belief, the performance of humans did not improve as they "grew up" or as they "developed" into adults, but it actually deteriorated. Mjomba argued that the human mind, for instance, did not start from a low point at birth and then improve as the human gained in "maturity" before declining with the on-set of old age. Rather, the performance of humans was at its peek at birth, as was evidenced by the speed of learning at that time, and began deteriorating steadily with the passage of time as humans "matured" - supposedly.

That also meant, contrary to popular myths, that human dependence, whether on the Prime Mover or on other humans, and already quite marked at birth, in fact increased as humans grew in years. Humans, faced with greater odds in infancy, employed more ingenuity in order to survive than they did in later life when they were clearly resigned to the fact that their days were numbered, Mjomba wrote. He added that children, knowing that they had to overcome greater challenges and eager to live life to the full, were more adept at coaxing their adult counterparts into assuming their responsibilities to society.

And that was due principally to the fact that children still enjoy their unadulterated innocence, and are unaccustomed to the ways of the world that are characterized by presumptiveness, a stubborn determination to have one's way and lord it over others folks, a reluctance to admit one's own faults, and most unfortunate of all a new found contempt by all adults so-called for the childlike simplicity that enables little children to recognize their dependence on the Prime Mover, and the critical role the recognition plays in the transition of humans from the state of being toddlers to the state of being young adults.

Mjomba added that it was this attribute of children that endeared them to the Deliverer, and that also guaranteed the Holy Innocents, whose lives were snuffed out prematurely by the brutal and wicked so-called Herod the Great, their crown.

Slower in their reflexes and in their ability to react inventively to unusual situations, adults - even though they did not like to admit it - were less capable of coping with the unknown and also felt much more insecure. Humans exercised more, not less, autonomy in their early years and became more dependent on the Prime Mover and on the rest of society as they grew older. And the craving to be "respected" that gripped individuals as they grew in years was reflective not of independence but of dependence. The desire to be hailed as "Sir" or "Madame" was really a disguised clamor for attention. And, according to Mjomba, the word "maturity" was a complete misnomer, and merely served to cloak the insecurity haunting the older generations.

He added that all the evils in the world, beginning with original sin, were perpetrated by humans who supposedly had come of age. When the so-called adults were not at the helm, on their own or conniving with others to engage in sins of omission or commission that were frequently disguised as good works, they typically were allowing themselves to be manipulated by others for selfish ends that were often passed off as patriotic deeds, simply because they lacked the moral fibre to conscientiously object to the obviously wicked schemes that were being hatched by their misguided compatriots who happened to be in positions of power.

The moment that the youth came of age, they found themselves ushered into a world in which nuts like Nerō Claudius Cæsar Drusus Germanicus, Gaius Julius Cæsar, and their modern equivalents whom Mjomba described as charlatans who try to outdo each other in masquerading as the "the Knight of the Wood" (Don Quixote), were running around killing people in the name of Empire, and others immersed in their own peculiar enterprises and schemes that anyone could see straight away were crooked to the hilt and left a lot to be desired in so far as virtue and integrity were concerned. It was just so ridiculous and of course also so scandalous.

Mjomba argued that recognition by humans of their dependence was what in turn induced in them the state of being child-like while they lived. But all too often humans deceived themselves that they had no need for either their Prime Mover or for anyone else, and that they were invincible and free to do as they wished with themselves. And they accordingly allowed themselves to slide into lives of fantasy, make believe and self-deception, eventually closing the door to true self-actualization.

That self-deception started, Mjomba claimed,

with the accession of humans from the status of being a juvenile, which also supposedly implied immaturity, to young adulthood, which was supposedly the state that marked the transition from immaturity to maturity, and was the point at which humans supposedly graduated into fully responsible individuals; and, barring a conversion of some kind, the self-deception or state of being deluded, persisted all through the lives of the individuals! It was just so ridiculous, Mjomba wrote.

This effectively meant, Mjomba went on, that the vast majority of humans, including those who were supposedly role models, stepped into positions of responsibility and/or positions of power just as they were starting to exhibit symptoms of what amounted to psychopathic behavior as a consequence of the persistent self-deception. This was the same behavior that was mistakenly viewed by the equally misguided talking heads around them as evidence of "leadership qualities.

It was that profound self-deception that, according to Mjomba, led humans to increasingly place their reliance on intrigues and so-called backroom deals and secrecy as the accepted methods of governance; and as a consequence of which the world was now effectively controlled by secret societies, led by the mafia in Italy and others around the world that went by the strangest acronyms, but were all licensed to kill: M16, DGSE, CIA, CIO, TC2, DAS, SSS, CSIS, PET, AISI, MOSSAD, JIC, FBI, IB, SB, ISI, KGB, ASIO, FSB, and so on. Conceding that one was dependent on the Prime Mover allowed one to give credit to Him for the blessings that came one's way during one's life-time without being the victim of a guilty conscience or losing one's self-respect in the process, Mjomba contended.

In the final analysis, it was really immaterial whether humans, made in the image and likeness of the Prime Mover Himself, acknowledged that they were dependent on Him or not. Unless and until humans found the one and the only object that comprised their last end, namely the Prime Mover, all their efforts in achieving fulfillment and actualization would go to waste. All humans without exception pined for those things and, of course, could only find them at the Prime Mover's pleasure, with the Prime Mover's help, and in the Prime Mover. This would always be so regardless of what humans themselves individually fancied. This was also dependence *par excellence*, Mjomba wrote.

Mystery of pain explained away...

Mjomba compared pain to the proverbial bitter pill that humans needed to take when they fell ill because of the ensuing benefits. He also suggested that what people really meant when they referred to the "mystery of pain" was the "mystery of life" which went hand in hand with burdens that people had to carry while they lived. And he went on that there was a direct relationship between the "mystery of

334

redemption" and the "mystery of life" with the principal actor being one and the same. Even though humanity had been redeemed and individual humans given a chance to mend fences with their Prime Mover, these humans found salvation when they *individually* agreed to bear the burdens He sent their way.

According to Mjomba's thesis, this was also evident from the manner in which little babies reacted to situations that caused them discomfort. As they matured and ceased being entirely dependent on the "adults" who had the responsibility of minding for them, they stopped whining and started using their heads to avoid getting into such situations, and they also instinctively got into the habit of practicing a little bit of patience seeing that some of the causes of pain were beyond their control. But that was also when they noticed that the adults were whining and complaining almost about everything all the time. Scandalized, they too started doing the same as they started maturing, and especially as they ceased being adolescents and begun to transition into adulthood!

To follow in the footsteps of the Deliverer, they were obliged to "take up their crosses" (which was another way of saying "bear their individual burdens patiently"), and then stagger after Him along the *Via Dolores* and up to the summit of Mt. Calvary. It was the only way humans could earn their crown.

By its very definition, "carrying one's cross" had to be a nasty thing - something that humans would shrink from instinctively and do their best to avoid. It fit the description "bitter pill" aptly.

Mjomba elaborated, in another foot note, that there was also a connection in his view between the dependence exhibited by humans - namely dependence on the Prime Mover and on other humans - and the so-called mystery of pain and suffering. According to Mjomba, the survival instinct of humans depended in large measure on the fact that they felt pain when something went wrong with their system. The pain could be physical or mental or a combination of both.

According to Mjomba, the pain felt by a human when a finger got stuck in a grinder for instance helped to ensure that the individual affected took quick and timely action to save whatever remained of the finger, and before the hand and perhaps even the rest of the arm also became wedged in the grinder to his or her great detriment. And if humans did not feel hunger when it began to gnaw in their middle, they would start to realize that there was something the matter with them when they were already a bag of bones or even too famished to recover.

Humans were in that sense very dependent on the Prime Mover for his foresight in making them susceptible to pain and suffering. Pain and suffering that was caused by other humans alerted the victims to the dangers lurking behind smiling faces and beguiling words uttered by those who led lives that were less than upright. And, of course, the fact that pain was a nasty thing which humans sought to avoid at all costs deterred them from doing things that were forbidden and the price for doing which included pain and suffering - when they could not be dissuaded otherwise.

Mjomba ascribed the mystery surrounding the phenomenon of pain and suffering to the fact that the Prime Mover was not in the habit of intervening to stop the pain and suffering just as He did not exercise His power to stop humans from knowingly choosing to do things that imperilled their eternal life. In the case of pain and suffering endured by the innocent at the hands of the wicked, the all loving and all-knowing Prime Mover permitted these things to take their toll - which was often quite unbearable - because He had decreed that He himself would take His revenge on the perpetrators in due course.

As far as those at the receiving end were concerned, putting up with undeserved pain and suffering had the immediate effect of driving home to them the fact that they were totally dependent on the Prime Mover, who also took care to ensure that they had the fibre to withstand what came their way, and also promised to reward them (in their afterlife) for joining the Deliverer in His atonement of the sins of men by putting up with the affronts of evil intentioned people.

As descendants of Adam and Eve, humans had after all been banished from the sight of the Prime Mover because of the original sin committed by the first man and the first woman. Nasty as pain and suffering (and, indeed, death itself) were, they did not compare with the fact that humans were the "poor, banished children of Adam". Whereas banishment was banishment and only the Deliverer, himself a member of the God-head, could reverse it, pain and suffering - and death - were a punishment for the rebellion of Adam and Eve, and allowed humans, none of whom (other than the Deliverer and His blessed mother) were altogether innocent in any case, to join with the Deliverer in atoning for sin.

It was really inconsequential whether the pain and suffering was caused by other wicked men or was attributable to "acts of God". It was the reason humans were expected to forgive fellow humans - and even "turn the other cheek" if necessary. Not doing so implied that they held a grudge against the Prime Mover also for natural disasters and things like that even if they did not say so. Thus, according to Mjomba, the fact that humans - and other living creatures - were capable of enduring pain only emphasized their dependence on the Prime Mover and His goodness.

Helpless in the face of pain and suffering on the one hand and the inclination to sin on the other, the obvious solution for humans in any part of the globe and in any epoch was to invoke the mercies of the Prime Mover. Mjomba commented that in this particular regard, a Masai peasant guarding his herd of cattle from marauding lions with a spear, and thankful to the Prime Mover for being cunning enough to outfox the predators in such an uneven match, was more prayerful than a preacher who relied on his rhetorical skills and a booming voice to attract and retain a core audience without which he would start operating at a loss and go out of business.

And, of course, there were those who thought that because they happened to live in these times - in the New Millennium - they had to be better than folks who inhabited Planet Earth in ages past, including the immediate descendants of Adam and Eve. Oblivious to the pollution all around them to which they individually contributed in no small measure daily, and also to the fact that Adam and Eve and their immediate descendants lived to be nine hundred plus years, many modern humans so-called believed that the world was itself a much better place to live in now than it would have been without them when the exact opposite was true! Mjomba pointed out that, rigged with nuclear bombs, the world of today was an unimaginable catastrophe waiting to happen!

Mjomba went on that while the path of righteousness was well marked and clearly identifiable, with the traffic on it heading in one direction, it had proved all too easy, judging from the record, for humans to stray from that path; and that humans found it really hard to resist joining the crowd on Broadway where the traffic headed in a thousand different directions all at once. It was, of course, not in their interest to walk on Broadway. But they were free and did it all the same.

Mjomba concluded with the comment that the mission of the Deliverer was to get the human traffic back on the path of truth. That was a daunting task humanly speaking. But, noted Mjomba, the Deliverer was not just human and a brother. He was one of the three persons constituting the Blessed Trinity in accordance with revelation.

The "contraption"...

Claiming that he was not exactly speaking from any sort of personal experience, Mjomba wrote that the human body as he saw it was no more than a contraption whose sole purpose was to facilitate the passage of the human soul through the first stage of its existence which was here on earth and temporal by design.

If the soured relations between the Prime Mover and humans had not been restored in the particular manner in which it had, involving as it did the Son of the Most High, the only thing that would have survived passage of the human from this life to the next would have been the soul, and the human body, or "casing" in which the soul had been "imprisoned" so to speak, would have been left to disintegrate into dust once and for all. And it would have been Beelzebub and his troops who would be lying in wait on the other side to "welcome" souls in a replay of what they did to Adam and Eve and others who must be very thankful that the Deliverer turned up there in "hell" and rescued them from their "captivity".

As it was, the involvement of the Man-God in the redemption of humans, Mjomba wrote, and specifically his triumph over death, resulted in a radically changed situation. Even though they did not really deserve it, humans not only could now look forward to resurrection at the end of time to the extent that the body was designed as a constituent part of human nature, but they along with their resurrected bodies, in the most extra-ordinary development of all, could likewise look forward to "beatific vision"!

Mjomba saw this as signifying a special kind of victory that only a divinity could pull off. Out of something as vile as sin, something inestimably good, which would otherwise not have been there or available, had directly ensued! Mjomba wrote that he could not help wondering at the number of times this had been replicated in the sinful world in which humans lived!

All these things notwithstanding, the fact that a sizeable chunk of earth consisting of the remains of humans will actually end up in heaven as glorified bodies of saints raised questions about what would become of the rest of the earth's crust. Mjomba wrote that he himself expected that too to be transformed into something useful at the very least even though the Prime Mover had the ability to return it to its pristine nothingness.

And that in turn raised questions about things like the Eternal City and other human artifacts like the pyramids, the Great Wall of China and things of that nature, not to mention marine, vegetative and animal life, and the galaxies. Mjomba was certain that if the Shroud of Turin was indeed the original parchment the holy women employed when embalming the lifeless body of the Deliverer after they succeeded in wresting it from His grieving mother, it too was going to survive Doomsday!

Mjomba was aware that it was common practice for artists to depict certain saints in poses that showed them communing with birds and animals or just clutching a twig. Mjomba had always thought that this was an excellent idea indeed, if only because these works of art highlighted the complementarity of sanctity and nature.

Mjomba also supposed that, after designing the earth and the interplanetary system, as well as plants, birds and animals, from scratch and causing them to spring into being, the Master Artist not only was capable of providing, but probably planned to provide these works of creation of His - works whose beauty He Himself lauded even before angels and after them humans were capable of doing so - with some role, and perhaps a significant role at that, come Doomsday.

The "universal" Church...

Mjomba went on to write that Christianity, rooted in Middle Eastern traditions rather than in European traditions as was widely assumed, was used by Westerners to condemn or even dismiss off hand religious beliefs and cultures that were not in conformance with their experience. Even though probably unavoidable because humans were humans, this was a tendency that, without a doubt, had grave consequences for the work of evangelization. According to Mjomba, the label "animism", itself a creation of Westerners, seemed designed to evoke in people's minds images of people who distastefully engaged in the "occult" so-called and whose worship and reverence for the Prime Mover was misplaced because they supposedly believed in "superstition", a phrase that was another Western creation!

Whatever was wrong with traditional African and other non-Western beliefs and religious practices was probably nothing or insignificant at the most, Mjomba asserted, compared with what was wrong or plain unacceptable in the traditional Western beliefs and religious practices, many of which exerted an inordinate influence in on Christianity. Mjomba wrote that the reverence for the earth in African and other societies did not have a place in Christianity except as something to be condemned.

At any rate, according to Mjomba, while they didn't see anything wrong with incorporating their own customs and traditions in the liturgy of the Church, Westerners apparently thought it was unimaginable that other cultures, with their treasured customs and traditions, could in some way be compatible with worship of the Prime Mover! The story of the Christmas tree that is traceable to the "Thunder Oak of mighty Thor" was a case in point. This was an oak tree, located in the village of Geismar in the vicinity of the Rhine, that was felled by the Benedictine monk Boniface on his first visit there and replaced by him with a little fir tree, the precursor to our present-day

Christmas trees, when he celebrated Holy Mass. Apparently it was around the Thunder Oak and other oak trees, dedicated to the pagan god Thor, that Europeans traditionally rallied in wintertime for annual events of worship to Thor. Those events were centered on sacrificing humans, usually small children, to that pagan deity!

In other words, people belonging to non-Western cultures were expected to do something quite preposterous, namely abandon their customs and traditions as a condition for becoming followers of the Deliverer! Westerners evidently interpreted the phrase "founded on a rock called Peter" to mean that the Deliverer founded a Church for some people and not for others, unless they were prepared to abandon their ways of life and started doing everything the way Palestinians did! And it was, even then, notable that Westerners themselves didn't follow their own maxims on converting to Christianity! Greeks, Romans, Gauls, Anglo Saxons, Huns, Celtics, Turks, Russians and other "Europeans" who embraced Christianity were not required to abandon their customs and traditions.

Giving an example of what might have been lost, Mjomba wrote that the languages of "pagans" in sub-Saharan Africa whose cultures have been under threat frequently included commonly used expressions that amounted to expressions of faith in the Prime Mover, like: "The Creator Himself alone knows!" and "Oh, God the Almighty One!". And, unlike similar expressions in Italian, English, French,

344

and other Western languages which made a practical joke of the Prime Mover, these were serious expressions which were uttered with due solemnity. In Mjomba's view, any loss in that regard had to be deemed a significant loss given the prevalent use of swearwords and other unacceptable epithets in Western societies today.

In Mjomba's view, the best way to approach differences in religious beliefs and practices was to follow the advice the Deliverer gave to his disciples when some of them reported that they had seen a stranger who did not belong to their group talking well about Him. Following that advice, they presumably ignored the negative in what that preacher who belonged to a different sect was saying and accepted him on the strength of the positive content of the message he was spreading about the Deliverer.

Mjomba did not recall the exact words that the Deliverer is quoted in the Gospels as using, and did not in any case think that the brief mention of that incident represented everything the Deliverer taught His disciples about religious tolerance. How to love one's enemies - and no doubt also how to accept fellow humans who espoused different views religious or otherwise - was after all what His teaching was all about. But the fact that He had to devote so much of His life to preaching love of the neighbor and tolerance also said something about the target of His message.

Mjomba wrote that the Deliverer obviously knew better than anyone else that those humans would ravenously hate and be intolerant as long as the Doomsday clock continued ticking, and that those who would try to love everyone they encountered in their lives, including those who were a nuisance or even an absolute menace, in the physical as well as the spiritual sense, would not find His act an easy one to follow.

It was not in doubt that the Deliverer established a "Church", founding it upon a rock called "Cephas" according to both tradition and the scriptures! Citing the famous passage from the Gospel According to St. Matthew that few disputed as authentic, but many apparently found hard to accept, Mjomba wrote: "*Et ego dico tibi, quia tu es Petrus, et super hanc petram ædificabo Ecclesiam meam, et portæ inferi non prævalebunt adversus eam. Et tibi dabo claves regni cælorum. Et quodcumque ligaveris super terram, erit ligatum et in cælis: et quodcumque solveris super terram, erit solutum et in cælis.*" (And I say to thee: That thou art Peter; and upon this rock I will build my church, and the gates of hell shall not prevail against it. And I will give to thee the keys of the kingdom of heaven. And whatsoever thou shalt bind upon earth, it shall be bound also in heaven: and whatsoever thou shalt loose upon earth, it shall be loosed also in heaven.) And, of course, if the powers of hell were not going to prevail against that Church because of the fact that it would be infused with the sanctifying power of the Holy Ghost, it did not at all mean that those powers would never succeed in prevailing against either its individual members or even its functionaries, Mjomba asserted.

And there was equally no doubt that the Deliverer and also High Priest empowered those he handpicked to be fishers of men with the laying on of hands in very specific ways, some of which we have knowledge of only thanks to something called "tradition", according to Mjomba. Those fishers of men or members of the hierarchy of what the Catechism referred to as the "Pilgrim Church" were empowered to "teach", and even to "tie" and to "loosen" whatever.

But while the Deliverer, the head of the "holy people of God" and also a member of the Godhead was perfect, and members of the Church could be called "saints" - even though "the Church was holy" - the sanctity of the Church, whilst real and not imaginary, was still lacking in perfection. Meaning that perhaps a case could be made that excommunication, while certainly justifiable in any instance in which the actions of a member threatened the Church's existence and excising or "cutting off" the member from the rest of the Church "in self-defense" was the only way to head off a catastrophe, at least in theory, could be based on faulty judgement.

And so, while effectual if carried out because of the specific nature of the empowerment, it seemed conceivable that an instance or instances of excommunication may well have been avoidable and to that extent unnecessary simply because of the fact that the decision to excommunicate or not to excommunicate was made by individuals from the body of saints and not the High Priest Himself.

But, leaving poor judgement and things like that aside, there certainly would be some among those who were called to minister to the holy people who, not unlike Judas like before them, would not shy away from betraying the master with a kiss even, according to Mjomba. Estimating that number at around a twelfth of the active ministry at any point of time during the life of the Church was probably conservative, Mjomba declared.

Mjomba even held the position that the Deliverer's warning about the false prophets who would descend on the world in the last days was really a warning that there would be a crop of new "churches" that would be founded by people claiming to be acting with His blessing or on His explicit orders, a situation that would make it really hard for souls to find their way past those "false prophets" into the Church. However well meaning, those who explicitly rejected the Church the Deliverer Himself founded could not be speaking for it at the same time, Mjomba asserted.

Ironically, Mjomba wrote, the reason many "believers" were attracted to the "new" churches and eschewed what Mjomba referred to as "the one, holy, Catholic Church", by which he meant the Church of Rome, was the genuine - but according to him groundless - fear that this so-called "traditional" Church had been taken over by the Antichrist and was now under the effective control of the prince of darkness! Terrible as disunity in God's Church was, the emergence of these "rival" churches fulfilled a prophecy - the prophecy regarding the ascendancy of false prophets, Mjomba asserted! And it naturally would not surprise him if some of these churches passionately espoused apartheid and other strange caste systems, or some other "doctrines" of that mold, while claiming to be divinely instituted. And if they murdered in the name of God, it wouldn't be the first time humans "sacrificed" fellow humans to pacify the strange divinities they worshipped!

Mjomba wrote that it was not at all surprising to him that, at a time when there was also this vast and ever growing number of biblical scholars who appeared to have complete mastery over the Gospels and even books of the Old Testament, there was now, all of a sudden and as never before in living memory, this proliferation of churches all of which claimed to be the one and only "true" Church founded by the Deliverer. And in the rush to establish churches, the fact that knowledge of the Prime Mover is revealed not to the "learned" but to little ones had pretty much been lost sight of.

Mjomba hoped that those who founded those churches had fully considered and thought through the fact that it was a grave matter indeed for an individual to set up oneself as the leader of a "church" that might be in competition with the Church founded by the Deliverer, whatever its apparent shortcomings. And, of course, any action of that nature was self-defeating in the final analysis, according to Mjomba, because the action to establish new churches suggested that the leaders of those new churches were sinless - or at least better than those the Deliverer Himself might have called to His ministry. It was all the more serious because those who did so could not guarantee that the doctrines that the newly founded church organizations spread were true or orthodox. And, unfortunately, the doctrines that were frequently misrepresented - presumably in good faith - pertained to the divinity of the Deliverer and the sanctifying power of the Deliverer's precious blood!

That was the problem with going off on a limb to try and change the world. In the absence of a special calling or vocation, Mjomba wrote, chances were that the individual would be really just playing out his/her fantasies, goaded on by misplaced zeal and a false sense of piety! The other problem was that pride in humans drove them to think that they, each individually, were not merely special, but extra-special and in fact more so than any other living being, as if that was possible - with everyone being more special than everyone else all at once! The fact, nonetheless, was that all humans not only liked to imagine that they were special messengers of the Prime Mover, but seemed to treat that as a condition for accepting that they were His creatures - as if *to believe* in the Prime Mover automatically entitled one to be the Prime Mover's *special* messenger!

Mjomba wrote that the temptation to use the "Word of God" to justify whatever one had a mind to do clearly had never been greater than in these times when, operating on purely business principles, one could "start a ministry" that was capable of raking in millions. These were the same principles that were being successfully used to start highly profitable "non-profit" organizations - non-profits to save the forests and the planet; non-profits to help business operators operate more profitably; non-profits to help one start a successful (or "profitable") non-profit venture - and what have you! Mjomba went on that it had become so difficult nowadays to differentiate between non-profit organizations and lobbyists, it had become standard practice for donors to clearly specify exactly what the gift or contribution may be used for.

Mjomba asserted that helping members of one's flock to rise to greater heights in the arena of money making had already become an important part of the pastor's job description in some "churches" and, consequently, nothing could really surprise him anymore!

The "Gospel of Creation"...

It was hard to find humans who were humble and truly "born again" who did not imagine that they were more special than other humans, Mjomba wrote. Yes, born again - by which he meant "becoming a child" like, say, St. Theresa of the Child Jesus or St. John the Baptist or Mary Magdalene after she had renounced her old ways. The key to "being born again", according to Mjomba, was acceptance that humans, on their own, were weaklings in the face of any temptation and that they were able to keep the commandments by cooperating with the graces of the Prime Mover which the Deliverer, a man-God and their brother, merited with His death on the tree and which were now in fact freely "available" to all humans who chose to play along.

Adam and Eve, Mjomba went on, thought that they were not just special but extra special, and therefore did not rest until they had tried to pull off their failed *coup de etat* against the Prime Mover. Judas Iscariot thought he was really special - more special than, say, Peter or Matthew; and he even imagined at one point that he was saving "progressive" folks who knew the value of money and other things of this world from a Deliverer who was not prepared to play by the rules of their game!

Judas Iscariot, a Christian, was in effect propagating his own Christian doctrine as all humans in fact try to do until such time as they become "converted" and start "living like little children". Mjomba wrote in his thesis that perhaps there was a lesson to be learnt from Judas Iscariot's own attempted *coup de etat* by those who walked in the footsteps of the Deliverer as leaders of the Church. Peter - the ever bumbling Peter who was Mjomba's usual culprit - had apparently mastered the lesson, but may be not so some of his successors who would have been inclined to "excommunicate" the betrayer and be done with him instead of continuing to encourage him to do better things as the Deliverer Himself did, wining and dining with Judas Iscariot to the very end and even allowing the man who would go down in history as the symbol of betrayal to embrace and kiss Him in the moments before He was led off to His ignominious death on the tree.

According to Mjomba, some popes thought they were so special they could use their sacred office to enjoy themselves with complete impunity! There were those in positions of authority who, like Pontius Pilate, thought they were *very* special - so special in fact that they could wage wars based on falsehoods and do other outrageous things that brought miseries to the innocent at whim without giving a thought to the fact that that authority came to them from above. Then there were those executives of greedy corporations who thought they were very special indeed and, even after they had had a whale of a time at the expense of the common man, imagined that they would - when the time came - prance, arm in arm with the likes of Mother Theresa and Francis of Assisi past St. Peter, into heaven!

And there were others who were laughing and making merry now and thought they were extra special, but whose turn to weep and gnash their teeth was around the corner. They were the citizens of some of the so-called "super powers" who were rolling in affluence thanks to the fact that their leaders, in furtherance of their "national interests" went out of their way to exploit the resources and wealth of the so-called "developing" nations. That exploitation took many forms, the most insidious of which was "bribery" that was touted as "economic aid", but invariably ended up in the pockets of a few individuals in leadership positions while the future of those developing nations ended up being mortgaged to the super powers in question.

Mjomba was thinking of the citizens of those nations whose economic power had been built on that sort of thievery and who had, in his view, to realize that "those who, directly or indirectly, have taken possession of the goods of another, are obliged to make restitution of them, or to return the equivalent in kind or in money, if the goods disappeared, as well as the profit or advantages their owner would have legitimately obtained from them", and that they accordingly had some making good to do if they did not want to be weeping and gnashing their teeth later. And those others who were now laughing and making merry at the expense of their fellow citizens in whatever nations they happened to live also needed to remember that "every offence committed against justice and truth entails the *duty of reparation*, even if its author has been forgiven".

Then there were those "messengers" of the Prime Mover, regardless of their religious persuasion, who thought they were so special they could "prey" on their gullible, if well intentioned, "flocks", feeding them with self-serving tidbits to make them feel good instead of the whole "bitter" or "unpleasant" truth, and giving them "false" hopes of redemption in the process. And then there were those others who had no scruples about "bending" the truth to increase their personal popularity with certain types of audiences or to get elected to office.

And, of course, the devil regarded himself as very special - so special, in fact, that he did not think that it was enough to be the marvel he had been created to be. And the devil, with one false step, lost his position as a gracious, highly respected headman among the choirs of angels and became a disgraced, good-for-nothing, hate-filled demon, who was now only fit for eternal punishment in that place of unquenchable fire which the Deliverer referred to as Gehenna.

According to Mjomba, when Diabolos confronted the Deliverer and suggested that the Deliverer, because He was "special", could inherit the earth's wealth if He desisted from carrying out His Father's will, the devil was in effect enunciating his own gospel, and one which went completely counter to the "word of the Living Prime Mover" and to the conscience. Mjomba went on that, since then, humans had come up with many variations of the "gospel according to the devil"; and that those targeted were actually taken in and fell for the empty promises of "salvation" from the lot of being a human. In fact, according to Mjomba, it had even become part and parcel of the human predicament to confront and have to deal with so many conflicting "messengers" of the Prime Mover, perhaps never quite knowing if one had already ruled out of consideration the true messenger of the Prime Mover and had whole-heartedly embraced the messenger who might turn out to be false!

Mjomba wrote that if there had not been any

false gospels in existence, and if the only thing out there had been the Gospel of Creation, humans who were hungry and thirsting for Truth (which they all admittedly were) would definitely have an easier time getting to it. He went on that those humans who had the cheek to knowingly enunciate false gospels tailored to their personal desires and who proceeded to live accordingly were in the same boat as Lucifer. Even though they were now laughing and making merry thanks to those "gospels", according to Mjomba, they now also were "having their fill", and that was going to come back in time to haunt them!

Mjomba continued that, like Diabolos, humans too were very clever and frequently put up a show of faithfulness to the Prime Mover as a way of masking their unfaithfulness! And they were always trying to "promote" themselves in the public eye; and these same people could not resist the temptation to try and "bring down" fellow humans by trumpeting the fact that humans generally could not engage in any meritorious activity on their own without the help of the Prime Mover's grace. It was as if they could not advance themselves except by dragging others down. In a way, fallen humans were like the devil - an extremely clever creature who understood better than humans did that humans - just like their angelic counterparts - could not accomplish any good save with the inspiration and assistance of the Prime Mover, and who accordingly took full advantage of that human predicament to bring down ruin upon humankind as well.

Lucifer, instead of ruining things for himself "in the beginning", would have been much better off spending his time praying and giving glory to his Creator, renewing his commitment to do the will of the Prime Mover who sustained him through each passing moment of his existence. But instead of "praying always" as he was supposed to, Lucifer started fancying that he could enunciate a new "gospel". That gospel, unlike the divine "Gospel of Creation" which took full cognizance of the fact that the Prime Mover was the Prime Mover and creatures were creatures, sought to turn the tables around so that Lucifer, a creature, would be equal to the Prime Mover without regard to the fact that the Prime Mover was the one and the only prime mover!

The fatal flaw in the gospel according to Lucifer was of course the underlying supposition that the Gospel of Creation was somehow lacking. And that presaged doom for any creature that attempted to live by any other gospel. And so, it came to pass that Lucifer and the host of angels who chose to follow the gospel according to Lucifer found themselves booted out of heaven. Their numbers and the fact that many of them, like Lucifer, had been destined, upon passing the Church Triumphant Entrance Test, to occupy lofty positions did not matter. They were all booted out of heaven - roughly half of the angels in existence at the "time".

According to Mjomba, the hosts of angels who fell from grace with Lucifer were very clever creatures - many times cleverer than humans! But they found out that they had acted "real foolish" the moment they turned their backs on Him-Who-Was-Truth and also undisputed Prime Mover. Because they were, strictly speaking, not living "in time" but "at the beginning" when the Prime Mover "decided" to share his *Esse* with "creatures" by bringing them into "being" and also because they were pure spirits, they couldn't have a second chance after flunking the Church Triumphant Entrance Test. And great was their fall, because they were such lofty creatures.

Everything similarly pointed to the importance of praying always for humans as well - praying to the Prime Mover who not only sustained humans from moment to moment, but kept them safe from themselves and also from the snares of the devil. But instead, and goaded on by the tempter, they wasted their time and energy trying fruitlessly to come up with good and effective substitute gospels for the Gospel of Creation - efforts that were intended to help them shirk their responsibilities as "children" of the Prime Mover and that would all eventually come to naught.

These "gospels", Mjomba wrote, were not gospels that had necessarily been committed to writing. They remained for the most part unwritten and inside the minds of humans. Some of the "gospels" were cast as interpretations of the Gospel of Creation, and others as philosophies of life that were supposedly unconcerned with the destiny of Spiritual Man. Others were cast as interpretations of the Sacred Scriptures that, Mjomba pointed out, were themselves only a tiny albeit important part of the

358

Gospel of Creation. But some of these "apocryphal" gospels, when not directly derived from the "gospel according to the devil", were based on personal, untested impressions of life, fantasies of individual humans, or even on wishful thinking by humans.

In the last analysis, if a variation of the Gospel of Creation was in error, it did not really matter whether it was depicted as a philosophy of life that claimed to be dissociated from religion, or as an interpretation of the "gospel according to the devil", or even as an interpretation of the Gospel of Creation; because the purpose of any gospel which contradicted the Gospel of Creation was the same - to define a new set of parameters for human existence that were according to an individual's personal liking and not parameters that were in conformity with the Gospel of Creation and will of the Prime Mover.

The most important thing to remember, Mjomba wrote, was that despite the rebellion of Lucifer and his cohorts, and that of humans, "Good" still reigned supreme, and the Gospel of Creation remained paramount. Mjomba added that there was no better rebuff to this "foolishness" (of enunciating new gospels) than the rebuff that Satan got when he unsuccessfully tempted the Deliverer, or the rebuke Peter received when he also tried to stop the Deliverer from proceeding to Jerusalem well-knowing that the purpose of that journey was to pay the price for the intransigence of men in fulfilment of the Prime Mover's promise to humans.

And it was a "good thing" that Beelzebub and also Peter were rebuffed, and that in the end the Deliverer opted for the company of Abraham and Moses at the transfiguration and not for the company of the tempter. It was good - very good - because the alternative in which the Son of Man would be in opposition to the Word through Whom all things were brought into existence was simply unthinkable! But that had been Satan's objective, and it also showed how supremely evil, wicked and dangerous Lucifer became when he fell from grace.

It was precisely for that reason that the Deliverer warned all to beware of the evil spirit, Mjomba asserted. But, unfortunately, humans calling the devil a variety of names engaged in what Mjomba claimed was condemnation that was for the most part a farce, completely meaningless, and useless. And many even did that while actually shielding the evil spirit and their own evil inclinations from exposure, according to Mjomba.

Because those working for the devil were also exploiting the fact that humans were now inclined to sin and simultaneously dependent on the Prime Mover's grace, they had to understand that doing so for their wicked ends was a very serious thing which made them as odious in the sight of the Prime Mover as the evil spirit himself. And yet, according to Mjomba, that was what almost everyone was busy doing.

But with the Reformation - which set the stage for the initial appearance of a multiplicity of "Christian" churches - a fact of history, Mjomba was of the view that everyone now, regardless of his/her traditional faith, had a responsibility to undertake whatever research was necessary to establish for him/herself the veracity of the claims of his/her "church" to being the "true" Church; and that included Catholics. And anyway, what "Catholic" could truthfully claim to be so "full of grace" that he/she had no room left to "grow' in his/her knowledge of as well as love for the Deliverer and His "Mystical Body". After all, the essence of "becoming like a child" or "being born again" was the recognition that one was totally dependent on the Prime Mover not only for the grace that enabled one to perform meritorious acts, but above all for the blessings that came one's way.

In the case of Catholics, a very important blessing consisted in being chosen by the Deliverer to be members, not just of the invisible Church, but to be members also of the visible Church set up by the Deliverer to guide the "believers" to guide to the New Jerusalem after He had fulfilled the Prime Mover's covenant with the nation of Israel. Chosen, Mjomba went on, to be not just coheirs and co-partners with the Jews in the promise, but to be the salt of the earth!

And certainly Catholics could not claim to be better than the man who had been blind from birth, and who had his sight restored by the Deliverer. Born blind like that man, they now see only thanks to the fact that the Deliverer came. If He had not come, Catholics wouldn't be seeing anything - just like everyone else. And to the extent Catholics claim that they do see, to that extent they too have become blind. And they certainly could not claim to be better than Peter who promptly deserted the Deliverer, even before the first cockcrow, after swearing that he would die rather than deny Him!

But was it not Catholics who prayed daily saying *"Quonian tu solus Sanctus"* (translated "For you alone are holy"? This was even though, added Mjomba laconically, it was only seminarians and the clergy who understood what was mumbled! And, indeed, the "Church of Rome", if it was indeed the "true" Church, had a very special responsibility to right whatever wrongs had given rise to this phenomenon of multiple "Christian" churches in the exact same way it had a very special responsibility to take the gospel to the ends of the earth.

When he was orally defending his thesis, Mjomba remembered that it was in fact a dogma of the Church that there was always scope for all members of the "apostolic Church" to grow in the knowledge and love of the Deliverer and His Mystical Body. Knowing that he had the full backing of the professors, Mjomba made the point about the responsibility of Catholics to undertake research to establish for themselves the veracity of the Church's claims to being the true Church even more forcefully - so forcefully in fact he upset a goodly number of his fellow seminarians, many of whom apparently imagined that they were in a sense "saved" (the very thing for which the "reformers" turned "heretics" stood condemned) and were inclined to the view that only the separated brethren and unbelievers needed to worry about that sort of thing!

Unfortunately, no individual in the Church, be it a member of the laity, a member of a religious order, a priest or a bishop, or even the Pontiff of Rome himself, could presume to undertake that task - the task of righting wrongs done by Catholics to one another and to others on his or her own accord, and without the help of divine grace. Which, according to Mjomba, effectively meant that, unless an individual was specifically called by the Deliverer and High Priest to undertake that important mission and equipped accordingly, there was nothing useful that anyone could accomplish on one's own!

Mjomba wrote that any attempt by self-appointed individuals to "reform" the Church or to "right wrongs" that had been committed by unworthy successors to the apostles carried with it the risk of making a situation that, humanly speaking, was already hopeless a great deal worse. Mjomba even mused aloud, as he defended his thesis, that if writing it had not been a requirement for going on to Major Orders, he would have personally preferred to remain noncommittal as far as discussing matters of his faith was concerned.

Individuals or groups of individuals going out on a limb to "fix things" in the Mystical Body of Christ were essentially acting like the apostle Peter who tried, on one occasion, to prevent the Deliverer from going to Jerusalem to die for the salvation of humans; and who tried, on another occasion, to prevent the constabulary of the Sanhedrin from laying their hands on His Master by striking out with his sword in a near successful attempt to change the course of history. Actions by self-appointed "reformers" were misguided, in Mjomba's view, and could also be likened to the attempt by the mother of two of the Deliverer's disciples to stake out a claim for the best "seats" in heaven, so one of them would sit on the victorious Deliverer's right, and another on His left! Mjomba added that the number of times that humans had been caught pining for a different kind of Deliverer *and* a different sort of Church was legion.

All of which, Mjomba conceded, left the question about how to go about righting wrongs committed by individuals in positions of authority in the "Prime Mover's Church" unanswered. And that was, perhaps, as it should be, he quipped! But that did not mean that Church leaders did not need to humble themselves and accept responsibility for the fact that some among them have sown and may be continuing to sow the seeds of disunity. They had to step up to the plate and at least take full responsibility for their actions, even if they were not up to the task of taking measures to correct the situation.

And again, *if* the Church of Rome was the successor to the Nation of Israel as the guardian of divine truth, *then* its responsibility with regard to the so-called "Separated Brethren" was automatically interwoven with its mission of spreading the message the Deliverer had entrusted it to the ends of the earth. And certainly those responsible, either now or in the future, for "ministering" to the faithful and for indirectly "administering" the Mystical Body of Christ, because they were quite capable of making erroneous administrative decisions just like any other "administering agency", had to now try and draw a lesson or two from any "errors" that the Church hierarchy at the time of the Reformation may have made.

Mjomba even then had a nagging feeling that there was something else afoot. Mjomba was writing his Thesis on Original Virtue almost two thousand after the Deliverer had established his Church and, addressing Peter, declared: "*Et ego dico tibi, quia tu es Petrus et super hanc petram aedificabo ecclesiam meam et portae inferi non praevalebunt adversum eam.*" (And I say to thee: That thou art Peter; and upon this rock I will build my church, and the gates of hell shall not prevail against it.) And yet, already ranged against the One True Church with its principal basilica constructed firmly over the tomb of Peter in Rome, were some thirty plus thousand competing and often also contradictory 'Christian' denominations, not to mention other religious groupings numbering in the thousands that were not affiliated to the visible *Sancta Ecclesia*.

Well, clearly the Deliverer must have anticipated moves by the powers of hell aimed at derailing His Church to make such a solemn promise to stand by his *Sancta Ecclesia* through the ages. And since Diabolos was powerful enough to given that keep Adam and Eve and the other "saints" captive in hell until they were liberated by the Deliverer when He himself resurrected from the dead, one couldn't gain say the power of the Evil One. Peter and his fellow apostles on their own were not going to be able to defend the Deliverer's *Sancta Ecclesia* from the powers of darkness. It needed the Deliverer Himself to make a solemn promise to them that He was not going to permit those powers to prevail against His Church in the same way He refused to allow Diabolos to keep the saints hostage in hell!

And, if there was one thing that was pretty evident and could not be disputed, it was that the good work undertaken by non-Catholic organizations and individuals, for example activities in pursuit of peace and justice and other good causes, had the blessing of the Prime Mover. According to Mjomba, this was so not just because the people involved were just people. But a prime reason could well be that the Prime Mover, in his infinite wisdom, knew what was lacking in the successors to the apostles and chose to complement the work they were doing in that way. The problem, according to Mjomba, was not that there were so many workers out there who were helping to reap the harvest; but that sinful, narrow-minded humans failed to see things from the perspective of the Him who was Infinite Wisdom, Infinite Love, and Infinite Mercy, and for Whom nothing - absolutely nothing - was impossible!

As for the "faithful" who were stuck with clergy who were unworthy of their calling in those circumstances, it was pretty much like being asked to turn the other cheek so it too *would* be smacked for the sake of the Deliverer - the Deliverer who *had* his side pierced at the behest of functionaries in the "church of the Old Testament". But while being stuck with the people who supposedly were not living up to their priestly vocation was one thing, it was another thing and a serious one too when people were baptized into the Catholic Church and remained Catholics only in name or considered it below their dignity to learn more about their faith, which included learning about their Church's history. According to Mjomba, increasing one's knowledge of the Mystical Body of Christ increased one's potential as an instrument of the Prime Mover's grace, something Catholics were urged to dedicate themselves for at the time of their baptism and confirmation.

Confessing that he would have been excited to see stuff he was being taught at St. Augustine's Senior Seminary address the subject of "Church unity" from the different angles he had outlined, Mjomba "clarified" that his position, which was admittedly radical by any stretch of the imagination, but apparently not entirely illogical (judging by the fact that he had not yet been lynched by his audience), was that the Prime Mover could very well turn human folly (such as that which drove people to found churches which specifically challenged the authority of His divine Church) to good; and that perhaps, unknown to humans, the Deliverer's prayer "that they may be one" was being answered even as there was this proliferation of new churches! And the same went

367

for anyone who was sincere in his/her observance of Islam, Buddhism, Hinduism, atheism, or any other belief. Created in the image of the Prime Mover, they were all His "temples" after all.

Mjomba stopped short of saying that Providence was using those churches and those other religions to prepare his "faithful" for the most important moment in their existence, namely that moment when they were leaving this world for the next. It seemed pretty obvious that it was a matter of time - perhaps years, months, days, or even hours – that all humans who were alive were going to "come face to face with the one who called Himself the Truth and the Light. With the fate of all those humans at stake, everybody needed to be praying that, just as the Prime Mover had already used the most unlikely situations in both the Old and in the New Testament to accomplish His designs, He would deign to do the same thing for the present "sinful" generation as well.

Mjomba wrote that, for all he knew, Providence was - not just probably but most certainly - using the most repressive regimes on earth where even church worship was outlawed to accomplish His divine plan and to save souls in the process - in the same way He used murderers to dispatch souls of the just to heaven! And similarly, Providence was using Diabolos himself to accomplish the divine plan. Which did not, of course, leave much room for comfort for those humans who had the opportunity to march with the Deliverer into the sanctuary of His *sancta ecclesia*, but were tardy in seizing it. First because there were so many others who would seize the opportunity if it were presented to them; but, perhaps even more importantly, humans being humans, the reasons for not seizing the opportunity presented would almost certainly be traceable to human frailties - prejudices and things of that nature - that cannot in and of themselves count as valid excuses.

But it was Mjomba's position that being a Catholic did not necessarily make one a better person than a "separated" brother or sister, a Buddhist, a Moslem, or even an agnostic living in Mongolia, America, or the South Sea Islands. Was it not a fact, after all, that "humans are sinful - all of them" Mjomba wrote, quoting Isaiah. That they had, all of them, become like unclean people, and all their good deeds were "like polluted rags"! Mjomba added the obvious, namely that all humans, with the exception of the Deliverer and His Blessed Mother who was sinless, were betrayers - just like Judas Iscariot - and equally in need of the mercies of the Prime Mover.

A member of a religious order was not better than an ordinary lay Christian, and a priest was not better than members of his flock. A prelate was not better than his priests, and the Holy Father was not better than the bishops and cardinals. They were all sinners, the only difference being that they each had a different calling. And then, if anything, membership in the Catholic Church carried with it the big risk of belonging to that group of "guests" who had been given a special invitation to attend the "Royal Wedding" in the parable, but declined. More so,

Mjomba supposed, than membership in any other religious organization because Catholics had the benefit of sacraments that non-Catholics did not have.

Thus, while not special, definitely more had been given to folks who were fortunate enough to count themselves as Catholics. Being extended a gratuitous offer of membership in an organization that the Word came all the way from heaven to establish for the salvation of men was definitely no small matter! The Word, through Whom everything that is came into existence, and also the Deliverer! Mjomba went on to point out the obvious, namely that this argument applied equally to whichever group out there had laid a claim to being the official guardian of revealed truths - unless the people making those claims were doing it as a joke!

Mjomba argued that the Church's action in paying special tribute to Catholics who led heroic lives as disciples of the Deliverer through canonization spoke volumes about the many Catholics, among them members of the Church's hierarchy, whose lives would never have been able to withstand scrutiny by the "Devil's Advocate". According to Mjomba's thesis, the "inquisitors" and other members of the Church's hierarchy like those who fought to keep Copernicus' theory from the public domain clearly fell in the latter category.

So, on the one hand, you had those heroic souls who led saintly if non-descript lives which the Church saw fit to hold up to the faithful for emulation, and then you had the vast majority of Catholics, among them many members of the clergy, who made blatant errors of judgement in decisions governing their personal lives and possibly others' spiritual lives as well. According to Mjomba, there was nothing to prevent them from making mistakes in their "administration of the Church" over time - mistakes that likely contributed to things like the Reformation!

If, in the sixteenth Century, Galileo's position on the center of the universe, which has since been vindicated, could be singled out by "Church folks" at the time and labeled as "heretical', it was quite likely that, at the time of the Reformation and at other times in the checkered history of the Church, some "sons and daughters of the Church" who were bent on seeing those they perceived as "heretics" excommunicated acted inadvertently, and were thus guilty in no small measure of contributing to disunity in Christendom themselves. And perhaps the Church really needed to "implore forgiveness" for the sins of its own as what Mjomba called "a lone voice in the Church" was suggesting.

Mjomba provoked an uproar, during his oral defense of the thesis, when he went on to suggest that, instead of working to heal existing breaches in the oneness of the Mystical Body of Christ, some members of the Church's hierarchy even now were probably in fact doing the opposite - that they were, God forbid, alienating multitudes who might otherwise have approached and embraced Catholicism; or, may be, doing more damage to Church unity than those among the separated brethren who, in good faith and without the benefit of the Church's guidance, now struggled, with only minimal guidance from the apostles' successors and without the benefit of the Church's sacraments, to lead lives that were worthy of the Deliverer's disciples and to help others do likewise. Mjomba added that referring to the separated brethren as "the *excommunicated* brethren" carried with it the risk of appearing even more condescending to the "brethren" all right, but would be more accurate and at least include an implicit acknowledgement of the grave responsibility of the Church's hierarchy for the lamentable situation that now prevailed in Christendom.

Regarding the "flowering" in modern times of Christian churches itself, Mjomba, not one to jump to quick conclusions, had ruled out the revolution in mass communications as a cause. Mjomba refused to fall for the temptation of making the simplistic assumption that living in a so-called age of mass communications automatically caused bogus "messengers" of the Prime Mover and "prophets" to spring up just so they might take advantage of the situation and exploit "God's Word" financially. Quoting one preacher he particularly admired, Mjomba asserted that there was no single incident or event that was a mere coincidence and was not provided for in the "divine plan". Mjomba wrote that, for all he knew, perhaps it was just as the Prime Mover wanted it: a flowering of church denominations occurring just as the revolution in mass communications was taking place!

This was even though Mjomba believed that some of the self-appointed messengers of God and prophets, wittingly or unwittingly, were exploiting the situation and making an extra buck for themselves in the process! But whether true or not, that by itself did not undermine his finding that the exponential growth in the number of Christian "churches" had coincided with the unprecedented growth in the number of theological colleges and, along with it, the number of those who considered themselves experts in biblical exegesis. And it did not particularly disturb him that the way the new crop of church leaders preached, led their "congregations" in prayer, and did other things was markedly different from the way Catholic priests delivered their sermons, administered the sacraments, or generally ministered to their folks. And Mjomba admitted that he probably would never have known that some of those new "churches" existed if it were not for television.

Mjomba supposed that the situation was somewhat analogous to that which existed at the time the Deliverer and His apostles criss-crossed Palestine witnessing to the Word, and their attention was drawn to the activities of a lone, almost independent exorcist. That exorcist likely led quite a different lifestyle from that of the twelve who, for one, had to travel light to keep up with the Deliverer as He went from place to place preaching and driving out evil spirits. Even though he was casting out devils in the Deliverer's name, that "strange" character about whom very little is known likely did not become aware of the inauguration of the sacrament of the Eucharist on the day before the Deliverer was crucified and of many other things that the Deliverer taught His disciples, according to Mjomba. Meaning that he probably was also ignorant about the special powers that the Deliverer gave the apostles - like the power to forgive sins and the power of ordination which would above all guarantee the unbroken exercise of Christ's priesthood through the ages - until, perhaps, well after the Day of Pentecost.

It was not as if the independent exorcist had anything against the Deliverer or the way He conducted himself. The exorcist's beef was with the Deliverer's band of followers. He did not particularly like the way the apostles acted as if they were the only ones who had been waiting for the promise of a deliverer to be fulfilled. And even if he did not have anything against their practice of following the Deliverer everywhere He went, he did not like the way they acted as if the Deliverer belonged to them and them alone!

The exorcist and his own band of followers would later contest many of the claims of the apostles and others who had lived and eaten with the Deliverer in the days leading up to His crucifixion and death on the cross, and in the intermediate period between His resurrection from the dead and subsequent ascension into heaven forty days later, regarding a special commission they said they had received from the Deliverer to carry on the mission he had started, and to travel to the ends of the earth as His official messengers. The independent exorcist, in particular, questioned the claims of the apostles to being given powers to forgive other people's sins in the Deliverer's name, to turn bread and wine into the body and blood of the Deliverer, to bless marriages, and anoint the sick and dying, and above all powers to lay hands on those they appointed as ministers in a new movement or "Mystical Body of the Deliverer" or "Church".

The independent exorcist even questioned the surviving apostles' claim that the new Church, which they also referred to as the "Universal Fellowship of the Risen Lord's Disciples" or "*Ecclesia Catholica*", now embodied a "New Testament" or promise that had replaced the Old Testament. The latter had, according to the self-proclaimed "Catholics", ceased to be when the curtain that previously screened the "Holy of Holies" in the temple in Jerusalem from public view was rent in two pieces after the Deliverer paid the price for the sins of men with his crucifixion and death on that "Good" Friday as they called it.

The independent exorcist said it was unimaginable that the Deliverer could empower a select few in that fashion when His message of salvation for the entire human race, and challenged the apostles to prove that the Deliverer had used the words "That which thou bindeth on earth shalt be bound in heaven, and that which thou looseth on earth shalt be loosed in heaven"! Claiming that he was acting to defend the memory of the Deliverer, the independent exorcist taught his own followers that the apostles were engaged in witchcraft and, possibly, even fraud!

Even for Mjomba, however, the similarities between the lone New Testament dissenter and the "Excommunicated Brethren" ended there. Citing evidence from the "Canadian Scrolls", Mjomba wrote that the "independent exorcist", as he was apparently known in Galilee and Judea, eventually came around and, in his own time, threw in his lot with the apostles. Identified as the Stephen of the Acts of the Apostles, the independent exorcist apparently grew tired of being treated as a "Separatist", and eventually abandoned his isolationist position, joining the main body of the Deliverer's followers shortly before Pentecost Day. Mjomba wrote that Stephen was actually received into the Universal Fellowship of the Risen Lord's Disciples" and baptized, along with his gaggle of followers, on the Day of Pentecost itself. Quoting from the Acts of the Apostles, Mjomba went on that the former independent exorcist embraced martyrdom at the hands of the Romans rather than renounce his new-found faith, not long after the apostles had elevated him to the rank of a Deacon and a "minister" in the "Catholic Church" with the laying on of hands.

Regarding the accusation of practicing witchcraft, many in Palestine were of the view that it was well grounded. That belief, Mjomba wrote, was reinforced by the official positions of the Roman authorities and their Jewish counterparts according to which followers of the "disgraced" Deliverer were into activities that were illegal and deserving of punishment. Instead of being cowed down and going into hiding, leaders of the infant "Church", led by Peter, the former fisherman the Deliverer had promised to turn into a fisher of men, not only stepped up the pace of "evangelization" in response, but went to great lengths to counter the accusations, issuing innumerable "communiqués" or "pastoral letters" in defense of the Church's orthodox position. Many of those Communiqués had survived and constituted what was now known as "Books of the New Testament", Mjomba wrote.

It was ironic, Mjomba wrote, that Stephen, who had earlier accused Christians of practicing witchcraft, died defending the early Church's right to administer the sacraments and to spread the good news of the New Testament. It served as a warning, Mjomba went on, for those in the Church who did not think that "separated" brothers or sisters could be of the calibre of St. Stephen the Martyr or Paul, the former persecutor of Christians who ended up as the Apostle of the gentiles - Paul, who even had to change his name just so that Christians would not turn and flee when he was introduced (as they in fact did instinctively before Paul got the presence of mind to adopt his new name, abandoning that of Saul and the notoriety it had raked up).

Not unpredictably, there was many a time when Mjomba, like the prisoner of his imagination that he was, wished that he would wake up one morning and find all the charismatic preachers he loved to watch on television as they expounded on the Word of God in front of delirious crowds of followers change the tune just a little, and cease contradicting each other and/or the original "gospel message" (whatever he meant by that). Mjomba imagined that to the extent they were all identifying with what was in effect the "Unknown Church" (more-or-less like the famous "Unknown God" of St. Paul's epistles), to that extent they had to be God-sent.

And so, switching from one religious channel on his TV set to another religious channel, Mjomba often did the unthinkable - certainly for someone of his education. He conveniently forgot that the preachers bore allegiance to specific Christian denominations, did not "hear" whatever they said that either contradicted the original "gospel message" (what that meant), and pretended that what he heard proclaimed from the different podiums in the glittering church edifices was actually the original, undiluted truth as taught by the Deliverer and faithfully preserved, even as it was being handed down from one generation to the next.

Neither did he notice the omissions that would have compromised the integrity of the sacred truths, the additions, or even the variations in interpretation of the controversial texts that had given rise to the historical "divisions" in the Church in the first place, variations that often seemed quite deliberate and merely convenient. Mjomba, in short, heard the speakers, many of whom were extremely gifted as orators, give voice to just one thing: the undiluted and unvarnished truth for which the Deliverer had given up his life on Mount Calvary! The same eternal truth to preserve which the Deliverer, triumphant even in death through His resurrection, had arranged for the Paraclete to come down from heaven on Pentecost Day and make sure that it would not be tampered with by the powers of the hell.

And so, there was Mjomba going again and seeing in his imagination the representatives of the different Christian denominations he saw represented there on "celluloid" mysteriously abandon their positions on the meaning of the previously controversial passages of the sacred scriptures and, without a single exception, embrace one unified interpretation of the scriptures and traditional practices of the Church. Nothing short of a dream in itself, that effort by Mjomba was akin to asking opposing foes in a bitter contest to suddenly discount the intense dislike they harbored for each other and, without any guarantees whatsoever for their safety, drop their guard and stay prostrate on their backs as they awaited deliverance from their "enemies" by some hitherto "unknown" divinity!

And this time, as those different preachers, talking in concert, said "The Lord this" or "It is written that", either all of them would be impostors in the eyes of the non-believers the TV broadcasts targeted or none of them. But each time, as Mjomba stopped imagining and returned to the reality of living in a world in which sin and shame reigned, he liked to think that letting his mind wander in that manner was never an entirely futile exercise.

Strange as it was, Mjomba believed that it was actually this practice that had helped him see the problem of disunity in the Church in what he now thought was the proper perspective. Unity among the "saints" clearly was a question that only the Prime Mover could successfully confront - just like the question of Man's original sin. Mjomba added that, in that sense, there was really no difference between them and adherents to other world religions with their own internal divisions - or even those who believed that they could not in good conscience subscribe to any religious belief.

This was even though many baptized Christians liked to think of themselves as special and even gave the impression that one had to be predestined in order to be saved - as if the precious blood of the Deliverer was shed, not for the sins of the world, but for the sins of only some special people! As if the Prime Mover, who loved the world so much that He gave his only begotten son in order that those who believe might be saved, did not really love everybody in that world! Instead of focusing on imagined privileges at a time the battle being fought during this period of trial on earth has not been won yet (which they do when they, of all people, ought to know that following faithfully in the Deliverer's footsteps is synonymous with self-denial and a readiness to suffer persecution for His sake), they needed to focus on the weighty obligations that baptism and the other sacraments of faith imposed on the recipients. It was important for them to realize that these were gifts for which a full accounting was expected in due course.

Notwithstanding the fact that the Deliverer had founded His Church with all the solemnity which the establishment of a divine institution deserved, Mjomba wrote, the mere fact that he had done so was apparently not going to force humans to change their ways. And according to him, it was very significant that the arguments one heard from those who cared to argue were not concerned with the sort of institution the Deliverer might have had in mind when He launched His Church, but with which of the innumerable churches that now existed inspired its adherents, killed enthusiasm - and things of that nature. Was it conceivable that the "Mystical Body of the Deliverer" might have faults that did not escape the sharp eye of observers in the past and today? Mjomba had no doubt that the Church, which included the Deliverer and imperfect men and women in its membership, had faults. And hence the need for the Paraclete who has the difficult job of fortifying humans who continue to sin even after they have been received in the Church.

And so, while many must indeed be commended for doing their research and finding the historical Church "lacking", their action in setting up competing "churches" which are supposed to provide them "satisfaction" might not be so commendable. According to Mjomba's thesis, membership in the Mystical Body of the Deliverer entailed all the things in life that left one "weeping" or "laughing", "hungry and thirsty" or "full", "reviled" or "the darling of whoever", *et cetera*. Mjomba's conclusion was that membership in churches in which one was enjoying the great feeling of being saved and always on top of things carried with it the risk that one could find oneself being told: "Don't you think you have already had your fill"! Mjomba stopped short of saying that justification, conditions in the next life or what we know as heaven and hell, and the last judgement were things that humans would find vastly different from what they now imagined.

Even as he was blasting those who were loath to entrust their salvation to the historical Church, Mjomba worried aloud at the vastly larger number of Catholics, including himself, who paraded themselves as staunch members of that Church, but were "lukewarm" in their observance of the Prime Mover's commandments. Declaring that it the actions of people like himself which caused many outside the Church to avoid becoming involved with an institution that *prime facie* was responsible for producing such uncouth characters, Mjomba went on that the intolerance by himself and those of his ilk of others' views and above all the self-righteousness, condemned by the Deliverer but embraced whole-heartedly by him and his fellow hypocrites who came in all shapes, sizes and shades, brought dishonor to the Mystical Body of Christ in the same way Judas Iscariot, a regular companion of the Deliverer and an apostle, did. Parading as "pro-life", they actually were the most uncompromising capital punishment advocates. And, claiming to be "peace-makers", they turned out to be rabid war mongers for whom unprovoked pre-emptive military strikes targeting weaker, but resource-rich nations were an acceptable option, and who were inclined to view any number of innocent casualties resulting there from as justifiable.

Disunity among the Deliverer's followers, already evident among the twelve even before the Son of Man, as He called Himself, laid down his life for men, was a human failing that apparently was not going to go away just like. And maybe it was a situation the Deliverer had very much on His mind when He made His position on tolerance clear - so clear it could even be said that He had actually over-articulated it to the discomfort of some of the disciples.

Granted that humans were primarily spiritual beings, perhaps the critical message the successors of the apostles needed to emphasize was not so much the fact that humans should become members of the *visible* Church in order that they may benefit from the sacramental grace that was readily available therein, as the fact that everyone should, like the Greeks whom the Apostle of the Gentiles found rendering homage to the "unknown" God, keep looking until they gained true knowledge of a God whom they publicly professed to know, but about whom they in fact knew next to nothing.

Or, perhaps, it was membership in the *Mystical Body of Christ* that preachers needed to exhort their audiences to seek over and above membership in an identifiable church organization, Catholic or otherwise. Mjomba wrote that it was quite conceivable that there might well be zealots in the Church who just either focused on putting up impressive church edifices or on the numbers of catechumens whom they "welcomed" into the Church, and were not really bothered if the new converts moved on to become true Christians or remained Christians only in name.

Mjomba suspected that the emphasis on church structures and church organizations had inevitably led to a tendency to emphasize externalities like "going to church" and "abstaining from eating meat on Friday", just as the priests and Pharisees who lived contemporaneously with the Deliverer did, at the expense of true spiritual holiness which consisted in being in constant communion with the Prime Mover.

The emphasis on externalities, which were not a reflection of true spiritual integrity or holiness, not only provided a good shield for hypocrisy but more often than not also signaled an absence of charity, according to Mjomba. Observance of precepts that was driven by faith alone was not good enough - even if it was faith that could move mountains. The observance of those precepts had also to be grounded in charity. However, according to Mjomba, it was the outward symbols of a supposedly "strong and immovable faith", and not love for God and for one another, which were usually in evidence when rules and regulations were being enforced.

Discussing the same topic (over-emphasis on externalities) from a somewhat different perspective, Mjomba wrote that it was admittedly not those who exclaimed "Lord, Lord!" who would be guaranteed a pass on the CTET; but those who kept the commandments. He went on to comment that love, or the virtue of charity, was illusory if it too did not go hand in hand with a commitment to keep the commandments.

The challenge, particularly for those who were called to be apostles or other Christs, was to be Christ-like. And the problem was that preachers, even when they did not openly claim to be Christ-like, invariably "acted" the part - all preachers except those who had actually come close to that ideal and, like the apostles Peter and Paul, were too modest for that very reason to trumpet their situation, that is.

Mjomba had added a rider to the effect that something like the Reformation would probably have occurred all the same even if the Holy See had had St. Peter as its incumbent with St. Paul as Secretary of State. And that was not because "people were free to walk away from what they did not like" as official Church history books implied. It was, Mjomba wrote, easy to blame everything on the reformers and say glibly that Luther and others had chosen to walk away from the truth and had only themselves to blame, just as it was easy to say that ecclesiastical officials in control of the See of Rome had compromised biblical truth and had even become mired in voodooism. The reformers on the one hand and those who believed that the way to settle the matter was through excommunication on the other all had (one) a conscience and (two) a free will to do as they chose.

The physical presence of St. Peter and St. Paul likely would not have changed the course of history. And, added Mjomba, posing the question "Who followed the dictates of his or her conscience and who didn't?" by anyone other than the particular individual involved a useless exercise. For, asking that question was the prerogative of the Prime Mover alone; and when it was asked by unscrupulous, devious humans (of whom there was no shortage), Church unity was hurt further. But, humans being humans, they apparently did not hesitate to usurp the Prime Mover's prerogative at the time of the Reformation as they had done throughout the ages, and would continue to do to the end of time, Mjomba wrote.

Regarding church edifices, was it not written that the Deliverer, referring to his own body, had dared his enemies (who, Mjomba added, were already bent on destroying Him at all costs) to tear down the "temple" promising to restore it in a matter of three days? This was despite the fact that nothing - not even the gates of Hades - had a chance of prevailing against the Church the Deliverer was establishing! That, Mjomba commented, appeared to suggest that it was membership in the Deliverer's *Mystical Body* rather than in the visible appendages that was really important.

Mjomba wrote that churches had often, indeed, undergone the same fate as the temple in Jerusalem, which was obviously quite regrettable. And, as if torching and burning churches to the ground weren't bad enough, Christians and others fleeing into them for safety had been slain. Besides, no one had ever said that the safety of the apostles' successors, just like that of the apostles, would be guaranteed either.

But, on the other hand, the emergence of Christendom as a major political force in the world had clearly been accompanied by the desire to build church edifices that reflected that power. While not a bad thing in itself, that development, Mjomba argued, might well have influenced the popular notion of membership in "churches" and might in the process have diluted the importance of membership in the "Mystical Body"!

Making reference in his thesis to the so-called "Secrets of the Lady of Fatima", Mjomba pointed out that the Third Secret envisioned roads littered with corpses of priests and bishops and even the corpse of a pope! Mjomba commented that the Lady of Fatima was undoubtedly aware that priests and bishops, and certainly the Pontiff of Rome, spent most of their time inside "churches". And he saw her reference to bodies being littered on "roads" instead of in "churches" as a possible attempt to de-emphasize the prevailing notion of "churches" and membership in them. After all, the place of the successors to the apostles was "on the road", spreading the good news, even though they too, like other humans, needed shelter and places where they could "break bread" and administer sacraments.

Mjomba wrote that he wondered about the origin of the word "church" and the original connotation of that word. Did "church" stand for a building, a bark similar to Noah's Ark, a corporate entity, a coming together of a relatively large number of people who shared similar or common beliefs to form a club or fellowship, or did it stand for a Deliverer on a mission, the gist of which was to lay down his life like the sacrificial lamb He was and, after dying, to rise again in victory over death and thereby save His poor and forsaken children who until then slaved away under the shadow of death?

Was "church" synonymous with "communion" - the union or oneness of Jesus Christ, its founder, with his followers? If this latter description was accurate, then *everybody* belonged to the Church, because Jesus Christ "exercises His kingship by drawing *all* men to Himself through His resurrection and death".

Mjomba wrote that until the Greeks Paul found worshipping the unknown God were recruited by him into the visible Church, they and their predecessors probably were members of the "invisible" Church. He could not imagine a stronger desire for baptism than that which drove these people in their fervent search for truth to admit that they had still to come upon the messengers of the Deliverer, and to recognize that the very best they could do in the interim period while they waited was to pay homage to the God whom they knew existed but did not have a name for!

Mjomba was quick to add that even after those Greeks had allowed Paul to get up on the podium in the Acropolis, heard him out and believed, the Deliverer's prayer that "they may be one" could only have meaning if there was a continuing threat of disunity in the Church fuelled presumably by egotism. Mjomba suggested that such a threat continued to be very much in evidence, and probably would be with humans to the end of time.

Talking about the threat to Church unity, Mjomba believed that a part of that threat was actually destined to emanate from within the Church itself. Pastors, like the flocks they ministered to, were human he argued. That being the case, there was, humanly speaking, a much greater chance of these "fishers of men" becoming more concerned with splitting hairs about some fine points of theology or philosophy, than with their own practice of the virtue of charity. Orthodoxy, in other words, likely was going to be valued more than neighborly love.

Mjomba wrote that he was not so sure that some Catholic clergy were not guilty of doing precisely that. He supposed that the few truly heroic priests and bishops would probably find themselves sidelined because they would be inclined to auction off treasures in St. Peter's Basilica in Rome and in churches around the world to feed the poor. Mjomba imagined that just a single fresco, if it could be removed from the ceiling of St. John Lateran and sold, or alternatively a stained-glass window diverted from the new Shrine to Our Lady at Catholic University in the U.S. capital, would each probably be capable of feeding thousands in drought prone Ethiopia or of providing shelter to hundreds in Bangladesh during the monsoon season.

But Mjomba did not fail to add, in the thesis, that ideas of that sort likely would not be popular with conservatives in the Church and particularly the Curia in Rome, and could even end up being ascribed to Satan; because, in the eyes of most people, ripping frescos and windows out of churches for any reason - the very things which drew worshippers and sightseers alike to these places signaled the beginning of the end for the Church in material terms, and could not possibly be in consonance with the Church's evangelizing mission for that "reason". In their eyes, adding to monuments (like St. Peter's Basilica in Rome and the Egyptian pyramids) that humans have constructed in the course of history in honor of the Prime Mover was something that was just as important as propagating the faith or feeding the hungry.

Disunity in the Church established by the Deliverer undoubtedly started with the confusion as between what was more important - Neighborly love or Orthodoxy? And it finally came down to numbers, Mjomba wrote, with the human factor deciding where the chips would fall. Even though the liberal faction lost over the conservative faction early on in the history of the Church, the attendant problems remained manageable until, like a cancer, the disagreements spilled over into other doctrinal areas, eventually resulting in a divorce of sorts.

Mjomba had, none-the-less, quipped during his

oral defense of the thesis: "Good thing the divine plan, after failing to be stymied by man's original sin and by the betrayal of one of the twelve whom the Deliverer had handpicked to be His apostles, was not about to be derailed by the failings of some members of the Church's hierarchy. And the Church's divine founder - who was also the Word - undoubtedly could also deal with all the fall-out from this; and it included the fact that many, for no fault of their own, now were never going to find their way into His visible Church all that easily or at all."

Mjomba, who was always at pains to depict the Church as something that was inclusive and not exclusive, and had no wish to say anything disparaging against other religions, was very sensitive to the fact that the position enunciated by him while discussing the "visible" Church appeared to be at variance with the position he laid out in his discussion of the "invisible" Church. But he believed that the two positions only *appeared* to contradict each other, and that they were in fact quite complimentary. But he admitted that this was not something that individuals who had been led by their consciences to remain outside the visible Church would find comforting, much less, acceptable.

But to the extent that those inside and outside the visible Church continued to be equally on trial during their sojourn on earth and were all going to face the Judge regardless of their religious affiliation, to that extent those inside the "visible" Church seemed to be at a distinct disadvantage. This was because, unlike those outside, they would have no excusing for not living aright given their access to the sacraments and the many opportunities for growing in holiness that were not available to humans outside the Church, Mjomba wrote.

Concluding his arguments regarding the universality of the Church, Mjomba stated that he did not believe that any of the foregoing "hogwash" clarified the meaning of the term "church". It likely would not, he wrote, because the Church the Deliverer established, denoted by the phrase "Mystical Body of Christ", involved more than a complex idea - in the realm of knowledge, it ranked as a mystery!

All of this underlined the important role of the Deliverer's forerunner who, Mjomba wrote, went knocking on people's doors urging them to come out with their implements and pave the roads and straighten the paths as part of the preparations to receive the Deliverer. To the ears of the inhabitants of the earth two thousand years ago, his message urging them to put their houses in order and generally begin to behave like rational creatures molded in the image of the Prime Mover sounded very novel. The situation, Mjomba wrote, was no different today. That was even though it should have sounded like music to the human ear.

And, referring to the Deliverer's own advice to the "sinful generation" to the effect that if it was a limb which was the cause of sin, humans should cut it off as it was better to go to Paradise without a limb rather than not get there at all, Mjomba commented that it was surprising that there were no humans who heeded the advice.

According to Mjomba, the evil deeds humans did were all part of what he called "one great fraud" perpetrated in a scheme that attempted to give respectability to pretense and make believe - when they were not acts that merely amounted to attempts to convert for their personal use things that were not rightfully theirs but the Prime Mover's. That was exactly what happened when humans destroyed rain forests.

When humans sinned, they were essentially stealing, Mjomba wrote. While every human could claim to possess an independent existence from any other creature human or otherwise, and along with it the nature or essence of an *animal rationale*, not only was the human nature and the existence enjoyed by individuals entirely gratuitously given, and along with them the specific responsibility of acknowledging the goodness of the Prime Mover; but humans forfeited any right to them when they chose - while knowing full well that it was wrong for them to do so - to act as if they were their own Creators and turned their relationship with the Prime Mover into one of outright enmity. Mjomba went on that to sin was to become a betrayer in the exact same way that Judas Iscariot betrayed the Deliverer to judges he knew were not interested in justice.

Sin, Mjomba wrote, was something every human, with the exception of the Deliverer who happened to be a God-head and his blessed mother through a special dispensation of grace, was blemished with either directly through individual conduct that fell short of upright behaviour, or by virtue of being descended from Adam and Eve who committed the original sin. And sin itself consisted in embracing a frame of mind that turned a human into an outlaw. In that frame of mind, any messenger of the Prime Mover and indeed the Prime Mover Himself was fair game - a *persona non grata* who would have to be neutralized or annihilated, or otherwise ejected from the world.

Still, this was all the more reason, now that the Prime Mover - who so loved the world that he was prepared to give his only begotten Son so that those who believed in Him would not perish - had kept his promise and sent the Deliverer, for humans, if they wanted to give themselves another shot at eternal life, to keep their part of the bargain by changing their ways.

Regarding the Adam and Eve, Mjomba wrote that, even though inclined to sin in the aftermath of the fall, by remaining focused on that promise (of a Deliverer) and by striving to be steadfast as the Prime Mover's faithful servants for the remainder of their days on earth, they hoped that they could still effectively hitch a ride into eternity that way. Once there, their reign with Him would be timeless, and their contentment permanently assured and no longer exposed to any kind of peril.

Until they succumbed to the artifices of Satan

and rebelled against their Maker, this was precisely the dream that the first Man and the first Woman had - up until the moment they began plotting their rebellion and got kicked out of Paradise. The dream of revelling in exaltation in timelessness in their after-life, and luxuriating in their new roles as veritable potentates in the Elysian Fields or Shangri-la!

As Mjomba saw it, good souls outside the visible Church for no fault of theirs were in the exact same boat as the repentant Adam and Eve - so long as they too strove to remain faithful to their consciences, that is.

The first humans: a close-up view...

To underline the point about immortality vis-a-vis a passing life of self-indulgence and debauchery, Mjomba described in great detail how Adam and Eve, recognizing that to enter into a marriage was good, but that it was better, and in that sense also more godly, to practice chastity, had both initially vowed to remain chaste throughout their sojourn on earth. He wrote that there had been no doubt in their minds that a state of chastity made them much more pleasing to the Prime Mover. Quite apart from the fact that they would have been more focused on their last end as a chaste couple, they were after all vessels of grace, and they regarded their bodies as temples of the Holy One!

In their perception, if it turned out that marriage was essential to the fulfilment of the divine plan, they would, of course, celebrate it; but in the afterlife and in triumph - when their trial on earth was over and done with. But for now, they were pledging to remain celibate, and to live as "spouses" of Him-Who-is-Who-is!

Mjomba suggested that Adam and Eve eventually took steps to wed only after they were specifically commanded a second time to do so by the Prime Mover in an episode on which the scriptures were silent. Quoting the Rwenzori Prehistoric Diaries, he wrote that Adam and Eve had indeed solemnly pledged to remain celibate, and to live as brother and sister, shortly after they ended their first and, as it would turn out, last tour of the world.

According to Mjomba, that was how Adam and Eve perceived things before they fell from grace. He suggested that Adam and Eve eventually took steps to wed only after they were specifically commanded to do so a second time by the Prime Mover in an episode on which the scriptures are silent. In the same episode to which there were supposedly were at least three clear references in the Rwenzori Prehistoric Diaries, the pair supposedly also received the explanation that marriages did not occur in the afterlife!

They looked different from each other to be sure. Black as coal, Adam was about seven feet tall, and had a physique that resembled that of an Inca prince. With the exception, that is, of his temples which looked like those of a Pharaoh, a nose which big and flat like that of Nubians, ear lobes which were medium sized, sturdy and swept back like those of a Karamojong, and small piercing eyes. His hair long and frizzy, and he was soft spoken just like Louis Armstrong. And when he walked or sprinted, it was with the firm gait of a buck in the prime of its life.

Eve, on the other hand, was slightly shorter - about six feet three inches. Fair-skinned, she was blessed with the body of a Mumtaz Mahal and a pair of adoring eyes which looked like those of a nymph. She had a facial outline of the Queen of Sheba, and she sported matted hair the color of cinnamon. She had the poise of the Statue of Liberty; and when she spoke, her voice sounded like a violin. When she walked or sprinted, it was with the gait of a Giraffe.

Adam also could not fail to notice that there existed between him and his "companion" from the very first a mutual attraction such as he had not thought possible before. According to Mjomba, Adam and the new addition to God's creatures whom the former was already referring to as "my other self" (because of the fact that they shared the exact same nature) easily recognized the bond of love existing between them as a mirror of the relationship existing between the Three Divine Persons or the so called Trinity.

Also, according to Mjomba, Adam and Eve would see their role in the divine plan and the reasons for being endowed with divergent but compatible gifts as man and woman defined very plainly in what next ensued. For, addressing both representatives of the human race, the Creator next commanded the couple to go, multiply and fill the earth!

In spite of their vastly different looks and despite the fact that they had been commanded by the Prime Mover to multiply and fill the earth, they not only preferred to regard each other like brother and sister, but the closeness they felt for each other and the strong spiritual bond between them which stemmed from the fact that both were equally children of the Prime Mover, made Adam and Eve believe that any relationship of a carnal nature between the two of them and hence also marriage were things which they had to regard as unsuitable and out of question. After the debacle of original sin, frivolous behavior of that sort certainly wasn't something that they were going to easily capitulate to - if they could help it!

Citing evidence from the Rwenzori Prehistoric Diaries, Mjomba wrote that it was not until they were specifically commanded by the Prime Mover for the second time - this time around in dreams - to marry and beget children that Adam and Eve buckled and took steps to get betrothed to each other as a prelude to exchanging wedding rings! And in any case Eve, whose character had demureness and modesty as its hallmark, would assuredly not have countenanced any permissive language from Adam, let alone permit him to touch her in any intimate way. Moreover, up until that point, both Adam and Eve placed emphasis on the fact that they were the Prime Mover's creatures and were made for Him rather than for each other.

The decision to marry was far more difficult for Adam and Eve's issue. The differences between them were less than those between their parents. For one, they were all half-castes, while at the same time, every one of them had facial and other characteristics that resembled Adam in part and Eve in part. According to Mjomba, it was only several centuries later, after the earth's population had expanded and some families had emigrated to parts of the continental shelf that had contrasting weather patterns, that humans begun developing distinctive facial and other characteristics as they became acclimatized to the vastly differing ecological systems. And then, growing up under the watchful gaze of Adam and Eve, they had learnt to respect each other and at all times to maintain suitable distance as befitted close kin.

Their parents clearly could be making an error of judgement in the counsel they were providing; and for a while the dilemma of the offspring of Adam and Eve was whether to listen and do the bidding of their parents or to disobey and precipitate a break with parents they otherwise held in the highest esteem, and who, besides, were the only mentors they knew. The fact, nonetheless, was that Adam and Eve had already saddled humanity with original sin and its dreadful consequences, and the young people felt that there was every reason to be cautious, and not to be gullible.

The siblings of Adam and Eve therefore needed a lot of reassurance before they could live with the fact that marriage and the associated conjugal relations between them were necessary both for the future of mankind and for the fulfilment of the divine plan. But, faced with a decision whose consequences were so far reaching, the young people, following in the example of Adam and Eve, made marriage a special subject of prayer and meditation as well.

In the end, the new generation along with the ageing Adam and Eve could not help discerning in all this the great mercies of the Prime Mover, particularly in light of the fact that even though sin had taken its toll, the Deliverer had already been promised. And they were mollified to think that His coming depended on the decisions they were even then making!

They were also well aware that, but for the goodness of the Prime Mover who kept plagues and accidents that might easily have wiped out that small pioneering band of humans, their own individual desire see humans multiply and fill all the corners of the earth were inconsequential. But even though they knew that no member of the human family lost even a single hair from their dome unless the loss was specifically permitted by the Prime Mover, they formed the habit of congregating as one human family to praise the Prime Mover and to pray that his will be done on earth just as it was in heaven.

And when an addition to the human family would occur, led by Adam and Eve, the entire population of earth, which was of course not very much at that time, would dutifully gathered together to give glory to the Prime Mover with feasting, solemn chants and prayer.

PART 8: SATANIC SCHEME

Christian Mjomba believed that his thesis would be incomplete if it did not include a recap of the first days on Earth of the first humans, and of the tragedy that befell the human race with the fall of Adam and Eve from grace. Quoting liberally from the Rwenzori Prehistoric Diaries, Mjomba wrote that, as time went by and Adam and Eve grew in the knowledge of "Him greater than which cannot be conceived" and in holiness, they started to hunger and yearn for the afterlife where they would be so much closer to the "Source". The lives they led in those first days before their fall from grace were spiritual, and far removed from the mundane. Consequently, they often went for days without thinking of themselves, eating or sleeping. While praying and meditating, their love for and longing to be with the Prime Mover frequently caused them to experience levitation that came on spontaneously, Mjomba wrote.

It was, according to Mjomba's thesis, obvious that Lucifer and his host worked hard and skillfully to try and get Adam and Eve to change course to no avail. Even though the powers of the Underworld planned their moves carefully and in detail, including timing, they did not succeed in derailing Adam and Eve a second time. Mjomba had Mephistopheles, in his disguise as a serpent, confront Adam and Eve time and again, especially on those occasions when they were relaxing and enjoying a well-deserved respite from hours of meditation, or when they were almost starved to death after long bouts of fasting, with the wicked suggestion that they would be like God if they ate of the "forbidden fruit".

But if Satan did not succeed in ensnaring Adam and Eve, it was a different story with their issue, particularly the later generations who did not have the benefit of learning about the dangers he posed - and his wicked schemes - first hand from the first Man and Woman.

Surprise in this matter, according to Mjomba, was everything; because if those good people were alerted to the fact that the Evil One was up and about and plotting furiously to permanently derail their almost certain union with the Almighty One, they would always be on their guard even during the moments they were relaxing and idle just like Adam and Eve - and the archenemy knew it!

It was, according to Mjomba, not surprising that Adam and Eve were forgiven by the infinitely merciful Prime Mover when, on coming to after they fell from grace and caused the fortunes of mankind to be bedevilled by original sin, they realized their folly and renounced Satan and all his wiles. For Adam and Eve, the life-long lesson they learnt from that dastardly and most unfortunate event in human history was that, however advanced in holiness, without the grace of God, on their own they were as nothing.

Be that as it may, while, for one reason or another, the descendants of Adam and Eve would find it hard to grasp that earthly bliss, whether engendered by material well-being or physical and mental accomplishments, fell far short of what the human person ultimately deserved, namely bliss in eternity, it would not be so with the first Man and Woman.

According to Mjomba, the attempt by Adam and Eve to seize what looked like an excellent opportunity to take over Planet Earth and the surrounding galaxies and expropriate everything in them from the Creator and rightful owner had been intended only as a means to a definite end. That end was to preside over their "conquest" or "spoils of war" in eternity, and that was what the act of disobedience of Adam and Eve was all about. If they indulged themselves along the way - as they had seen animals and other lower creatures appear to do - that was only incidental to it. Anything less than that was unacceptable and would, as indeed happened, cause Adam and his companion to back off.

At one point, during his oral defense of his thesis before the panel of professors and classmates at St. Augustine's Seminary, Mjomba would suggest that around that time Adam, for some inexplicable reason, adopted the second name of Tuntah while Eve called herself Nkhamoun! Mjomba cited the Rwenzori Prehistoric Diaries as his authority and added that, generations later, an Egyptian prince, believing that his newborn son might succeed where Adam and Eve failed, groomed his son whom he called Tuntahkhamoun for the undertaking. True to the promise he made to his father at the time he came of age, Tuntahkhamoun, as is now well known, did try to attain life everlasting here on earth.

That stance of Adam and Eve on the question of material happiness and its temporal nature, which appeared to have been firm and unyielding, meant that none of their descendants, even though tainted with the original sin committed by their forefathers, would have any excuse for not staying on the path of righteous living in accordance with their consciences. Their descendants' obligation to do precisely that was sealed when the Prime Mover not only forgave Adam and Eve, but also delivered on His promise of a Redeemer, according to Mjomba.

Mjomba went out of his way to suggest that many blundered and failed to see the role of Israel in its proper perspective. The role of Israelites as a chosen people was, he wrote, meaningless unless it was seen in relation to mankind as a whole. The Prime Mover's promise of a Deliverer, made to Adam and Eve, was a promise to all descendants of Adam and eve, he argued; and it stood to reason that the Deliverer had to be born of one or other descendant of Adam and Eve if he was going to be a true human and not something else. That individual happened to be an Israelite. But the purpose of his sojourn on earth remained the redemption of all humans from the scourge of sin.

It was typical of human beings that there would be complaints all around about the way the Prime Mover hired workers for his vineyard, Mjomba wrote. The Israelites, who were hired by the "Landowner" to work in the vineyard at dawn and who subsequently bequeathed to the world Mary, Queen of Apostles, as well as the Deliverer Himself, would be upset when they found out that they were receiving the same wage for a day's work as the Italians who would join the labor gang in the vineyard at nine O'clock and give the world the likes of Francis of Assisi. And the Italians would be upset to find that they were receiving the same wage as the Gauls who would start work in the vineyard at mid-day and give the world their own crop of saints. And the Gauls would in turn be upset to find that their wages and the wages of the Anglo-Saxons who would report for work in the vineyard as late as three O'clock in the afternoon and give to the world the likes of Mark Edmund and Thomas Moore were exactly the same.

And everybody, including the Anglo-Saxons, would grouse that they were apparently working for the exact same pay as the Ugandans whom the "Landowner" would recruit to work in His vineyard at five O'clock in the evening and who would bequeath to the world the Blessed Martyrs of Uganda! Mjomba did not fail to point out that the Ugandans would also be in for a shock on finding out that the wages of the "Separated Brethren", Moslems, Hindus, and others who had conscientious objections to the role of the Pontiff of Rome in spiritual matters and other aspects of Catholic doctrine and lived accordingly, and of "non-believers" who, like the Greeks before them, worshiped the "Unknown God" because they did not know better and their own wages were identical wages!

It was, Mjomba added, a measure of the extent to which the human family had strayed from the path of righteousness that the biblical phrase "eating of the fruit" was now interpreted and understood as being banal.

This had in turn resulted in moralists portraying a whole array of physical acts as being evil in and of themselves and, only when it was convenient, making an about-turn and acknowledging that it was always the intention, not the physical acts per se, that constituted sin with the latter representing what Mjomba called mere occasions of sin. In the process, they had vilified some of man's most important physical endowments and along with them entire traditions, customs and cultures that had sustained communities through times of calamity.

They had consequently played into the hands of Beelzebub and inadvertently paved the way for the rise of cults and other aberrations, and also unwittingly given impetus to the very things they would have the world believe that they were seeking to prevent from happening. But worse than that, by suggesting that an ordinary act on which the survival of the human race depends was evil in and of itself for instance, they were thereby providing those who abused the rights and privileges associated with such an act the excuse to claim that those who were supposedly the defenders of morality had got it all wrong, and to argue that it was they - namely the abusers - who had refused to bury their heads in sand in the manner of ostriches!

Instead of hailing the debut of all men and women into the world of created things as humans with full rights to the inheritance promised to Adam and Eve, some preachers, according to Mjomba, impugned the fact that the earth's current inhabitants were descended from Adam and Eve and laid the blame for the effects of original sin at the door of their flocks as if those poor souls could have stopped the first Man and Woman from straying from the path of righteousness!

The fact that the present generation of humans were also inclined to sin as a natural consequence of original sin was blamed on the people who were not even there when Adam and Eve abused their rights and privileges by choosing to disobey their heavenly Father and Lord of all! The Earth's present inhabitants were blamed for the fact that the first Man and the first Woman eons ago failed to make the grade!

The distinction between acts of free will and the consequences thereof and actions over which men had no control for one reason or another had been blurred. But these self-same moralists, Mjomba wrote, had found ways not only of exonerating themselves from these supposed evils but also of holding themselves harmless from their effects!

Mjomba went on that it was clear to Adam and Eve, as they reflected on the singular poise and the aplomb, and the august and quite exquisite comportment with which the lower creatures carried themselves while allowing the brilliance of the Creator to radiate glow and shine forth in them, that they themselves could in fact attain to a higher - much higher - state of holiness, and one in which the brilliance of the Creator would burst forth in an even more telling way if allowed to. And it was, of course, also clear that their reward would not only be far greater, but enduring in a real sense of that word. The way they were constituted - of an incorruptible soul that informed a physical, earthly frame - guaranteed that.

Mjomba wrote that in spite of all that, it was very tempting for Adam and Eve, seeing the harmony in the universe, the flawless, almost dizzying symmetry in physical substances - or dead matter as they preferred to regard it - and observing the way the birds, the animals, the reptiles, and even the insects together matched, danced and sang, each species in its own unique way, to the original, hallowed and regal score composed by the Grand Master on the one hand, and the halting steps they themselves were taking as they proceeded to discover and map out the strange surroundings in which they had found themselves on the other, to think that the brilliance of the Prime Mover was potentially less evident in their own human nature.

Mjomba noted in his thesis that the eventual decision of Adam and Eve to join the fallen angels in challenging the authority of the Prime Mover would spring from a stubborn determination to break not just the moral law but the natural law governing the universe as well. They would do this even though they understood that such a course of action would not be without consequences.

Mjomba argued that the mere fact that life had to go on after the original sin - that humans still had the obligation to seek and achieve self-actualization, that Adam and Eve were still obligated to multiply and fill the earth, and so on and so forth - would make a situation that was already complicated even more so. And the fact that it would mostly be the old and wizened who would be the first to pass from this world to the next for their rendezvous with the Prime Mover, thus depriving the world of the most valued mentors, would definitely not auger well for the future of mankind.

Reincarnated devils...

Mulling over that fateful decision of the father and mother of mankind, Mjomba, who was also seeking an explanation for the fact that pain, suffering and death to all appearances had been a normal and accepted feature of life among birds, animals, reptiles, fishes and insects even before sin came into the world through the transgression of Adam and Eve, had on a number of occasions flirted with the idea that there had to be some connection between the act of disobedience of Lucifer and his lackeys and the condition of these lower life forms.

On one occasion, after meditating on the subject late into the night, Mjomba had woken up in the morning convinced that those earthly creatures were actually reincarnated devils; and it had taken some doing for him to discard that silly idea. But, as the sweat in which his whole person was soaked suggested, he had felt very perturbed indeed while he clung to that idea.

Mjomba had assumed that Adam and Eve, whilst equipped with that same information, had proceeded to break the Prime Mover's commandments all the same - something he regarded as completely unthinkable! How could they do it knowing that they could end up meeting the same fate! If those lower life forms were really incarnated devils as he thought, but Adam and Eve and their descendants were not privy to that information, then in reality humans were in much greater danger than they suspected, surrounded as they were by so many animals they thought were domesticated, good company and harmless. They were rearing, pampering and fondling those innocent looking household pets without the slightest idea that they were dealing with devils.

While his dream lasted, Mjomba wrestled with the frightening thought that so many folks believed that it was not just safe, but a good thing for their children to play with puppies, cats, and the other exotic animals that people were in the habit of adopting and turning into household pets! Believing that he had an obligation to alert the world of the immense danger those "household pets" and the other domesticated animals and poultry posed to them and their loved ones, Mjomba tried to start with a neighbor who had several cats and a dog. He was surprised that despite his efforts to hurry up and get going, his feet initially refused to move. He felt like someone in a straitjacket. Even though it wasn't the first time he had found himself in that sort of situation, he didn't have any idea how it came about that he couldn't get his legs moving in the normal manner.

And then, as he approached his neighbor's front door after exerting so much of his energy to overcome the strange "inertia", another problem cropped up and caused him to turn and head back - he could not believe it, but he was very scantily dressed - too scantily dressed to be outside and knocking on people's doors. It was completely unbelievable! Before he awoke, Mjomba, who was convinced that he knew why some pets - pit bulls for example - remained dangerous and vicious in spite of years of grooming as household pets, suspected that it was Satan who was behind his inability to move quickly at will, and also behind his memory loss which he blamed for leaving his house undressed.

Mjomba was very relieved when he awoke up and realized that he had just been dreaming - that he wasn't running around outside without his clothing on. His first instinct was to jump to the conclusion that everything else in the dream was also pure fantasy. And for a moment or so, while he was reeling from the fact that it would have been disastrous for someone of his standing to be outdoors naked without realizing it, he thought that was the case. When it dawned on him that it wasn't - that for weeks now he in fact had been examining the response of humans to the Prime Mover's invitation to them to attend the divine banquet and had accordingly been busy crafting his thesis on "Original Virtue", he felt very disappointed and angry with himself for being one of them.

Later that day, when his thoughts were composed and he was feeling at ease and much more settled that he had felt in the hours following his nightmarish dream, Mjomba was surprised that he was in fact still reliving the dream in his subconsciousness and that he was actually worried about Beelzebub and what he could do. It might be far-fetched to imagine that the lower life forms were reincarnated demons. But, as he surveyed the scene in chapel at Benediction and scrutinized the pious faces of the seminarians closest to him, it struck Mjomba that there was really nothing to prevent the devil from masquerading as a human - perhaps as a seminarian or even as a priest - and then taking advantage of the gullibility of Christians to pass himself off as a messenger of the Prime Mover or something like that.

Mjomba recalled at least one occasion on which one fellow appeared on the premises of St. Augustine's Seminary and passed himself off as a priest who was stranded. The "priest", using the names of a real priest who served in a remote parish, had succeeded in hoodwinking the Rector and the other members of the seminary faculty into believing that he was indeed a priest who needed assistance.

412

It was not until early the next morning when the cover of the "priest" was blown by an alert seminarian who had noticed that the fellow "bungled" instead of reciting Mass in the same order as other priests did.

The "priest", believed to be a former member of the seminary brotherhood, because he seemed to be conversant with the set up in the rectory, had made his getaway before he could be apprehended. Still, the joke for a long time among the students was that may be quite a few of the many "visiting" clergy who dropped in periodically while en route to their destinations on previous occasions - and some of whom had even been permitted to hear confessions – were really frauds! Well, if humans could pull things like that off, Mjomba had no doubt that the devil also could.

And may be there indeed were hordes of such "priests" out there - like the one who nearly got caught - manning entire "parishes" and doing everything from gathering in funds for Peter's pence to "ministering" to unsuspecting folk! And what was there to prevent such devilish "priests" from abandoning their "allegiance" to the Catholic Church and claiming that they belonged to a different denomination altogether if it suited them to do that! Since their objective would not be to "preach" the truth, but to mislead their unsuspecting "flocks" and make it as difficult as possible for those souls to find the truth, those priests, because they would be devoted to promoting the agenda of Diabolos, would certainly not be the kind who would hesitate to change their church

413

allegiances on the spur of the moment and especially if doing so would serve that purpose.

Diabolos was, of course, in all probability a lot smarter than that, and he was consequently not in the least surprised at the fact that the number of Christian denominations was very large and growing by the day. Mjomba believed that this state of affairs was of concern to the Deliverer precisely because Diabolos was behind it. If he wasn't - if the divisions in Christendom were merely "accidental" - there wouldn't be any grounds for concern. It would all be accidental and by implication an integral part of the divine plan.

It just so happened that it was the Deliverer's express desire from the beginning that all his human brothers and sisters - Catholic and non-Catholic, and Christian and non-Christian - come under the mantel of the apostolic Church he founded on the "rock called Peter". Mjomba was therefore certain that the divine plan had no provision for a world in which individuals for reasons best known to themselves promoted competing (and contradictory) religious beliefs. That being the case, Mjomba did not doubt that those humans who were responsible for creating divisions among men, regardless of whether they were acting on their own, in tandem with others, or in league with Diabolos, would be held to account if for no other reason than that unity and love, in the Deliverer's view, are synonymous. Mjomba wrote that the Deliverer made it crystal clear when as He prayed to His Father in the Garden of Gethsemane that

414

restoring unity to humankind was what His passion and death were all about.

Even though Mjomba did eventually succeed in putting that dream behind him, it was not until after it had left its indelible mark on him. That dream, combined with the knowledge that the devil had been so brazen as to try and neutralize the Author of Life, left Mjomba unsure about the exact extent to which the Evil One could go to try and ruin things for humans. In other words, the dream left Mjomba with the kind of respect for the devil's ambitions and capabilities it clearly had not been in his (Mjomba's) nature to entertain.

Mjomba did not think that there were any devils masquerading as humans and much less as pastors and ministers. But he told himself that if it ever happened that some of the individuals who passed themselves off as "ministers" in the Church or Mystical Body of the Deliverer were in reality not humans but demons in disguise, he wouldn't be surprised. In a world in which lying and deception had become equated with being diplomatic or savvy, and in which bribery and extortion were legal, and also a world in which daylight murder, the senseless destruction of property, and other practices that were unbecoming of humans were increasingly gaining acceptance as a way of settling scores, and almost anything went, it would not at all have surprised Mjomba if such devilishness was found to permeate the ministry as well.

The fall from grace...

In his account of the rebellion of the first Man and Woman, Mjomba described how a teary Eve aroused Adam one night and informed him that she was intending to exercise her right to choose, not with regard to a method of exploiting the earth's rich resources or anything like that, but with respect to the ultimate object of their existence. Up until that moment, whatever she had done, she had done it to the greater honor and glory of the Prime Mover. She now informed Adam that she for her part intended, come daylight, to shift the focus away from the Prime Mover to herself - and him, if he cared to join her in her diabolic plan.

Eve knew that she was engaging in something that was against common sense and wrong. But, to her surprise, Adam responded that he not only respected her right to choose, but that he himself had been thinking very much along those same lines, and that he welcomed her bold initiative which admittedly required a lot of courage.

Mjomba actually had Adam quip: "Eve, you've obviously been talking to Beelzebub", adding with a shrug that so had he himself. But Eve let him know that she had been prepared to go off and live by herself someplace else if it had turned out that he wasn't ready to join her in her scheme. Adam had recoiled instinctively at Eve's statement. Still, he had noted in a whisper in the darkness that the Prime Mover was invisible anyway, adding that even though they did not actually have to do what they planned to do, he himself was curious about the effect of going that route, especially in view of the fact that their right to choose was actually God-given.

Whereupon Eve announced with a sneer that everything would be OK. She had, she revealed, been secretly conducting an experiment with a diet she was certain could prolong human life indefinitely. The diet she had discovered, which included a special "miracle" fruit cocktail, would assure an uninterrupted supply in the right quantities of the red blood cells that the atoms and molecules of the human body needed to regenerate themselves continuously and at a constant pace. She added with a snicker that all they now needed to do was feast on that fruit cocktail.

"By the way", Eve added, a wicked smile enveloping her face; "Have you noticed that you have been losing some of the gray hairs around your temple lately?"

When Adam replied in the affirmative, Eve informed him that she had been using him as a guineapig to ensure the formula of their medicinal diet worked, and hoped that he did not mind the role.

Adam let her know that he minded. But, now that they were in this thing together, he had no choice but to forgive her everything, he declared. He also acknowledged, besides, that he admittedly owed her a bundle for proving that she herself could fill the role of a scientific genius - a Dr. Life of sorts - when they needed one.

Pointing to a three-legged stool on which Adam

417

loved to relax, Eve said: "The life of that settee of yours is ten years or so. Now, anything that we didn't find here - everything that we have ourselves fabricated - has a life of only so many years. We can even decide to trash or recycle these wares before their time is up! Actually everything we see, the crust of the earth included, has only a limited life..."

"Darling", Adam had reportedly interjected; "To the extent that created matter is changing all the time, I am sure this marvelous planet of ours including everything on it - the elephants, giraffes, crocodiles, *et cetera* - has only a short lease of life. What exactly are you trying to say?"

"That is exactly the point I am trying to make, my dear" Eve retorted. "All matter, including the stuff our bodies are made of, changes and is therefore finite. But - and note this - the diet formula I have discovered will help assure that our physiques will keep reinventing themselves. That is the power of a special diet of broccoli served raw, and boiled maize washed down with passion fruit juice!"

"Now you are talking" Mjomba quoted Adam as interjecting, and then adding with a sigh of relief: "This topic was otherwise becoming really depressing!"

Adam went on to inform Eve that he also happened to know that apples were rich in Vitamin C that in turn spurred the body to produce red blood cells in large quantities. He agreed that, with the atoms and molecules of their bodies being thus regenerated continuously, they would not grow old or die! And to make doubly sure about their eternity on this earth, they would also develop concoctions that would render their systems immune from malaria which they apparently could contract from mosquito bites, rabies in the event that they got bitten by some wild animal with that disease, the flu, and from any other diseases and viruses.

And they, of course, knew that in addition to all of the above, they would need to exercise - by working the fields, hewing logs, or even just jogging - to ensure arthritis and other diseases of old age would not catch up with them as the years went by.

Adam and Eve had both already guessed or knew that their days on earth were numbered under the existing order and that, even as faithful servants of the Creator, they were destined to pass from this world to the next all the same. The only difference between now and the situation after their rebellion would be that their transition as disloyal creatures would conceivably be accompanied by trauma and grief, especially as it would presage their judgement day.

It was while they were discussing their satanic scheme that Eve surprised Adam with a revelation of a somewhat different even though related sort. She said it was her intuitive feeling that if they had not moved quickly to wrap up the matter concerning the diet, it was Adam who most certainly would die first. She added that her intuition had been confirmed by what she had noticed in the animal kingdom - animals of the female gender consistently outlived their male counterparts!

The reference to dying had shaken Adam, not so much because he was the one who was likely to be the first human being to die, but because of the implied suggestion that he might in fact "die the death" as he put it whilst he was unrepentant after they disobeyed the Prime Mover. It was a prospect that Adam, even with all the macho he commanded, could not countenance, and certainly wasn't prepared for. If they were going to proceed with their wicked scheme, they had also to make damn certain that they did not die. Because on leaving their earthly paradise for a different realm, there wouldn't be any place in which to hide.

Voicing that fear, Adam accordingly declared somberly: "I see! The poor devil couldn't hide, and that is why he had it!"

Mjomba added that, clearly and very unfortunately, instead of dissuading him, Eve's revelation about the likelihood of Adam being the first one to kick the bucket only served to sway him to Eve's position regarding the diet. Mjomba went on to write, with respect to dying, that it was evident that Lucifer had actually died the death, albeit a purely spiritual death. That Satan was really "dead" - kaput! But that, in the spiritual realm in which creatures created in the image of the Prime Mover existed, "death" really meant condemnation and not annihilation.

Adam, who had no reason not to believe Eve, was persuaded by her views regarding the diet and the important role it was going to play in what they were plotting to do. Reasoning somewhat like Lucifer and the other fallen spirits had done, Adam and Eve felt that they had to choose now if they preferred independence to the rewards of continuing as faithful servants of the Prime Mover. The course of action they were choosing would make them independent of the Prime Mover; and they, of course, had no intention of ever wanting to confront Him after such an act of apostasy.

Before the fall from grace, Eve, like Adam, was shrewd and sharp to a degree that would have been regarded as quite astounding by their progeny. Sullied as they would be by original sin from birth (with the notable exception of the immaculate Mary and the Deliverer Himself), Adam and Eve's descendants simply could never have attained to that sort of sharpness or shrewdness - at least while they lived. Mjomba accordingly argued that it would be a combination of the sharp intelligence enjoyed by those first humans and the powerful bond of mutual respect between them that, in the end, would ultimately also prove to be man's undoing!

Adam and Eve easily appreciated the fact that, without their cooperation, the divine plan, which envisaged an expanded Garden of Eden brimming with animal and vegetative life and generations of human beings created in the Prime Mover's image, was doomed. According to Mjomba, the reference in the bible to a forbidden fruit was only allegorical; "fruit" being the term coined by either Adam or Eve to refer to the betrayal of the trust and confidence the

421

Almighty had placed in them both.

In his thesis, Mjomba actually had Eve coin that term in what he described as an ultimate act of self-debasement. Prior to that moment in human history, when either Adam or Eve munched on apples or any of the many other types of fruit that were in abundant supply in the Garden of Eden, they had done so not out of need or for the purpose of personal self-gratification, but strictly for the greater glory of God. From now on, not only did they intend to use the act of eating as a symbolism for defiant behavior, but they were also determined to go out of their way to pluck and eat these fruits to appease what was essentially imagined hunger - which, of course, proved to be very real indeed when they stumbled out of Paradise in shame with an invisible host of God's faithful angels on their heels.

Mjomba supposed that by that time Adam was already acting as if Eve, along with the rest of created earthly beings, both animate and inanimate, was personal property he was free to use for his personal aggrandizement in a scheme that practically had Adam himself enthroned as Lord of the Universe.

Mjomba also had Eve acting similarly - as if Adam, in spite of his marvelous nature, was more the result of unspectacular natural evolution and less a product of the Creator's crafting genius. He even had her forgetting - at least for the moment - that she herself had been formed out of Adam's rib, and believing a tall tale to the effect that it was as a result of the natural forces of evolution that she had become the incarnation of entrancing womanhood and pristine beauty!

According to Mjomba's thesis, in a typical instance of "group think" which may not of itself have constituted a sin, Adam agreed with Eve that with their superior instincts they were quite capable of fending for themselves, and of taking measures to keep lions, alligators and other dangerous creatures at bay. It was, to say the least, a miscalculation on the part of the first Man and Woman to suppose that their instincts were superior to those of lower creatures just because those creatures, unlike them, did not enjoy the benefit of the faculties of reason and will.

But, as Mjomba pointed out, pride came before the fall! Pride was effectively the sin Adam and Eve committed, he wrote. It blinded them to the fact that they needed the Prime Mover, and it also caused their egos to be inflated to the point to which common sense ceased being common.

In the transformed Garden of Eden, or the Valley of Tears as it would be known thence forward, they not only would never be able to think clearly because of one distraction or another, but they would also frequently be unable to summon the will power required to take the necessary steps to accomplish a desired goal even when everything else was in place. This would be because, with their fall from grace, Adam and Eve would become inclined to evil rather than to godly things. The antidote or remedy for that condition would be to remain as close as possible to the Prime Mover by praying at all times and thus continually grow in the knowledge of "that greater than which nothing can be thought". But it would be a remedy the patient rarely wanted to take.

All of that, Mjomba wrote, would in time translate into a lethargy of sorts that would accompany every activity they engaged in even when it might look like there was some hope on the horizon. And the situation would of course be much worse if, instead of encouragement and hope, things looked all gloomy with no reprieve in sight. Given the potential for rivalries, jealousies, prejudices, and intrigues, and with hate among men likely to wind up as the rule rather than the exception, accomplishing anything that was positive and virtuous would end up being a tough sell indeed - and almost impossible when the machinations of the devil, temptations of the flesh, the widespread penchant to glorify evil and promote materialism, escapism and debauchery and make them socially acceptable, and so on and so forth were figured in.

According to Mjomba, Adam and Eve would have no reason to believe that the laws of nature would suddenly change and incorporate miracles as a part of the natural order, especially after they had sinned. Without any doubt, therefore, Adam and Eve and their descendants would be in for a pretty rough time thanks to the folly of the first Man and Woman.

But that was not all. Mjomba argued in his thesis that the mere fact that life had to go on after the original sin - the fact that humans still had the obligation to seek and achieve self-actualization, and the fact that Adam and Eve were themselves still obligated to multiply and fill the earth, etc. - would make a situation that was already complicated even more so. And the fact that it would be mostly the old and wizened who would pass from this world to the next first for their rendezvous with the Prime Mover would definitely not auger well for the future of mankind.

With the errors of Adam and Eve being repeated over and over by succeeding generations, and with history - the history of professed transgressors - repeating itself all along, time would come, Mjomba wrote, when things would be really hard for humanity.

Reflecting further on the changed reality after the fall of Adam and Eve from grace, Mjomba would write, regarding the condition of the human intellect, that instead of being the powerful instrument for anticipating the face-to-face vision of the Prime Mover in eternity as it had originally been intended, the mind had ended up being what Thomas Aquinas and others would describe as "a feeble instrument which man would untiringly endeavor to apply to that most exalted of objects", namely the Almighty One.

But Mjomba would note that even then, because of the operation of the mercy of God, man's most confused knowledge of that perfect of all beings - knowledge hardly deserving the name (as the philosopher put it) as was evident from the many forms of religious worship that were themselves as contradictory as they were confusing - would nevertheless cease to be despicable so long as it had as its object the infinite essence of God. In his thesis, Mjomba would attribute to Adam a remark to the effect that everything that had been legitimate to do before had become a virtual trap that goaded one to commit sin all over again - if one was presumptuous and did not stay close to the Prime Mover.

Mjomba would confide to a fellow seminarian at St. Augustine's that he saw one very important analogy in all of this. Just as the actions of Adam and Eve, who were representatives of mankind, had definitive consequences for their descendants, the actions of Nkharanga and Mvyengwa, the parents of Innocent Kintu who were also the first members of the Welekha tribe to be baptized into the Church, would also have definitive consequences for those who would come under their sway.

The "evil genius"...

In the meantime, as he went about re-enacting scenarios of biblical events for his thesis, Mjomba sometimes wondered if the original writers of the books of the old and new testaments did not go about their tasks in much the same way as he himself was doing. With a lot of modesty, Mjomba silently acknowledged that he himself was of a vastly different metal from those who wrote the sacred texts. He had made a habit of reminding himself that, if he was receiving any inspiration, it had to be coming from the devil; and he felt at times as if he was enunciating an apocryphal gospel for that reason!

What made him certain that he was also being inspired was the fact that the ideas inundating his mind, and which he was clandestinely converting into material for the book he was writing, were coming in from the outside - he would have been the first to admit that he was actually involved in plagiarism in this particular regard. And what was more, he could not control the rate at which they came; and the one thing he had learnt was that, when they slowed to a trickle or simply dried up, the sensible thing was to simply bide his time.

He had also noticed that, when he did not jot down the ideas his mind received quickly - which was usually on any piece of paper that was within his reach, including old newsprint which had bits of space here and there wherein he could scribble the ideas as fast as they were invading his mind - they went right back whence they came. If they returned, they sometimes did so in their entirety. But, more often, only portions of the original ideas came back; and when they did, they hovered on the edge of his mind apparently in readiness to slip back into oblivion if again ignored for any length of time.

If they vanished and retreated back into the impenetrable void - which Mjomba had always identified with the habitat of the supra natural and which seemed patently out of bounds for mortal creatures like himself - he just wrote them off along with those ideas which did not return after their first call, because he knew that there was nothing he could do about it. But even then, he always had this feeling that when ideas thronged into his mind and then disappeared like that, it was not without a reason. He had no doubt that they left an imprint which, though imperceptible, subsequently either affected the way he assembled the material which he succeeded in capturing and committing down to paper, or perhaps even the substance of what he was in the process of communicating by way of his pen. Perhaps they even affected decisions he made in his life - decisions that were completely unrelated to his efforts at being creative. After all, Mjomba always reminded himself, committing something down to paper was in and of itself a wholly unproductive activity.

And, in what appeared to be a sure sign that he was receiving inspiration that he was always more inclined to blame on the Evil One, sometimes ideas Mjomba thought were really fabulous just kept coming and coming, even as he was looking for a way to conclude the story. Because each one of them had the potential of making his final product unique in yet another way, Mjomba usually found himself compelled to jot down and incorporate the new stream of ideas just as he had the others.

But Mjomba sometimes wondered whether, despite his assertions about being inspired, it was not true that it was he himself, not Satan or for that matter anyone else, who was coming up with the ideas for his masterpiece. Even though it was possible that such a stance sprang from modesty, he wondered if he was not just looking out for a scapegoat to blame in case those ideas turned out to be awry and not quite to his liking. Assuming that was the case, he certainly also knew that he was not the first human to demonize the archenemy and make him out to be worse than he really was. And, anyway, who could possibly blame him for making Beelzebub look bad. From what he knew, it was the duty of everybody to do just that, if only because Lucifer and his cohorts were also busy doing precisely that not just to humans but to the Prime Mover Himself!

And so now, if it happened that his thesis - which he always likened to a masterpiece - turned out to be below standard and he received an "F" for his pains, there was no doubt that he would blame his misfortunes in that regard on Beelzebub. Mjomba even imagined a scenario in which the devil decided, on second thoughts, that the masterpiece could not possibly be in his interest and, changing from being his chum to being his nemesis, embarked on an all-out mission to frustrate his efforts in that regard. That possibility scared the hell out of Mjomba, because he just could not imagine himself pitted single-handedly against Beelzebub!

Still, Mjomba, unlike many believers, liked to kid himself that he wasn't really scared of the devil. He frequently reassured himself that he might even be superior to the archenemy in some respects. He could for one claim that he himself had brains in addition to an intellect, whereas Lucifer only had an intellect, albeit a sharp one!

429

The devil really could never be demonized enough, according to Mjomba. Here, after all, was a creature that, though intelligent in a most extraordinary way, had himself abused his intelligence to the fullest by trying to impersonate the Prime Mover!

Mjomba confessed that he got the idea of demonizing the devil from the scores of preachers who blamed him (the devil) for all the bad things humans did, and provided guidance to their flocks accordingly. "He made me do it" was a refrain Mjomba had heard time and again as he mingled with Christians.

Until he decided to join them and set the stage for blaming Beelzebub for any sloppiness on his part as he worked on his so-called masterpiece, he in fact had a mind to devote a paragraph or two explaining the stupidity of those who seemed to take delight in transferring blame for all the sins they committed to the Evil One and who actually made it appear that it was a good thing that Satan's following, consisting of other disgraced spirits and perhaps also humans among them, was large. Because then, these supposedly devout Christians would always have someone to blame for the slips, big and small, for which they themselves would otherwise have to assume full responsibility.

Mjomba had a lingering thought that many a smart preacher also used the devil to scare the hell out of their flock so that those poor people who did not know any better could part with their wealth in the belief that they were buying a ticket to heaven!

Mjomba also pointed out that preachers, perhaps because they did not want to offend their congregations, appeared reluctant to admit that humans, the preachers themselves not excepted, were quite capable of filling the devil's role perfectly. Mjomba wrote that humans in fact frequently "played the devil", just as they frequently "played God", and preyed on each other accordingly. Mjomba cited as an example the attempt by Peter to (as he called it) subvert the divine plan by suggesting to the Deliverer that he not proceed to Jerusalem and risk being killed in fulfilment of prophecies to that effect. Apparently wanting to drive the point home, the Deliverer, according to the evangelist, had called Peter "Satan" and ordered him to get back and out of His way so He could press on with His journey. And, of course, nothing could be more devilish than misleading an assembly of people while posing as a leader and a teacher, particularly with regard to any "special mandate" to speak for the Deliverer.

And if humans could tempt fellow humans, there was little doubt that they could also inspire themselves to do evil, which they in fact frequently did, with the evil thoughts emanating from within exactly as the Deliverer said. And, Mjomba wrote, it was in fact evil thoughts originating from within that drove many a human to wage wars and kill or otherwise make the lives of their fellow men miserable while asserting that they were rooting out evil from society! It was evidently also why there were so many religions on earth, each one claiming to be the true

431

one.

Then, the most hypocritical humans appeared to be also the most adept at exploiting the bible and things like that for their personal ends! Mjomba added that writing the thesis he was writing was, unfortunately, a requirement that now made him look like he was doing exactly that, namely exploiting the bible for personal gain! But, in his particular case, he was at least pointing out the evil and even admitting to the possibility that he might be hoodwinking other humans with an eye to making an extra buck or two, or benefiting from the exercise in some other way.

But Mjomba still recognized the devil as the evil genius *par excellence* nonetheless. A pure spirit, with not an ounce of matter or even a drop of water in his constitution, the adversary had proved that he was capable of successfully infiltrating the world of humans and planting his evil ideas. That was in addition to his ability to lull other lesser endowed, albeit intelligent creatures like himself nonetheless, into believing that he had a good cause in trying to unseat the Prime Mover.

Mjomba asserted that although brainless because he was a pure spirit, Lucifer had been very handsomely endowed with all sorts of spiritual gifts at creation, and that he was very clever indeed. So clever in fact, he had been able to trick fellow spirits that were also endowed with exceedingly sharp intellects into doing the most foolish thing, namely launch an assault on the Prime Mover! Before becoming a devil, Mephistopheles stood out among the created spiritual essences as a particularly radiant jewel that was not lacking in any way and possessed all the attributes a created being could possess. Mjomba supposed that the only thing the future Satan did not possess was a super nature!

And, operating from the bottomless pit in the bowels of the earth, the disgraced Beelzebub, even though now completely incapable of doing anything that could be classified as useful, good or meritorious, had shown that he still had the gall - and indeed also ability - to wreck untold havoc in the world of humans in spite of his own down-fall. The wicked genius had succeeded in toppling Adam and Eve from their elevated pedestal as the unchallenged Masters of the Universe using a ruse that was not even that original or brilliant in conception - as it would turn out. And the clever Satan had brought this off, Mjomba lamented, even while the minds of the first Man and Woman, still unsullied by concupiscence and the other effects of original sin, were still razor sharp!

A prisoner of his imagination, Mjomba worried, that just as the angels that fell for Lucifer's ruse had fallen and turned into devils, there probably were also humans who had become veritable devils after turning their backs on the Prime Mover. This was even though, prior to becoming devils, they too were essences that had been spectacularly endowed at creation and that, like the fallen spirits, were molded in the image of Him-Who-is-Who-is! Yes, human devils, Mjomba had repeated to the laughter of his fellow students, adding that they too deserved to be demonized. But, unfortunately, instead of being demonized, many ended up being glorified!

Mjomba claimed that he could give many examples of human devils who had actually been canonized by "history". According to him, they included historical figures whose actions had given rise to evils like colonialism, imperialism, and other "isms" which were equated in their time to biblical truth! Mjomba asserted that the human "devils" included "war mongers" whose inflated egos drove them to do things that could be classified as crimes against humanity. They included dictators who did not have the welfare of their subjects at heart and whose actions brought ruin and unspeakable miseries upon their subjects. Also included were slave dealers, pimps and others who made their livelihood from the shameless exploitation of fellow humans.

And, as if glamorizing historical characters who were responsible for causing their fellow men and women unspeakable misery was not bad enough, human beings - strange creatures that they were - went on to create fictional devils whom they then promptly canonized. An example of such a character - which Mjomba loved to cite - was Robin Hood, the heartless robber and terrorist whom literary scholars fondly referred to none-the-less as the "Prince of Thieves".

Returning to the main subject of his discourse, Mjomba went on that, in his relationship with "willing" humans - which was just about the same as saying all humans, Diabolos, who symbolized everything that was wicked, had proved very adept at suggesting that they might be able to get away with their evil intentioned actions simply because actions in and of themselves could not be properly designated as sinful! And humans, even though quite capable, with the help of the Prime Mover's grace, of frustrating the machinations of the archenemy, had shown that they could be fooled - just like the fallen angels before them.

Yes! An evil genius in every sense of that word, and very deserving of the capital sentence he had received for his pains too, Mjomba wrote. As was well-known, the Prime Mover, on that figurative seventh day following his labors had declared that everything he had designed and brought into existence, including the devil before he attempted the coup d'etat, was noble and worthy of admiration.

Explaining his use of the term "figurative" in a foot note, Mjomba wrote that back then, "days" might have meant "hours", and "hours" might actually have meant "minutes" and so on; and he also submitted that, even if Adam and Eve, the first people on earth, had had a glimpse of the time sheet completed by the Prime Mover after his labors and had been successful in translating its contents into human lingo which was itself just evolving, there was every likelihood that their translation was itself figurative since the Prime Mover's "minute", "hour" and "day" in eternity could not in any case have meant the same thing as "minute", "hour" and "day" in the lives of earth-bound creatures. And arguably the likelihood that those terms, after they had been coined by Adam and Eve (or by whoever did it), changed meaning over time as spoken tongues evolved lent weight to his point regarding the figurative use of those terms in the scriptures. And, talking about languages and the scriptures, Mjomba did not doubt that the original inspired text of the Book of Genesis was originally scripted in Ge-ez, the first human "lingo".

For good measure, Mjomba wrote, nobody can tell you who the author of the Book of Genesis was, or the language in which that "book" was originally written. Which left one to conjecture that the Book of Genesis was scripted in Ge-ez, the world's oldest known lingo that Zinjatropus most likely spoke.

According to Mjomba's thesis, neither the Israelites as a distinct people, nor "Hebrew" as a language, existed when the original Book of Genesis came into being. It was his position that Hebrew first came into use approximately one hundred thousand years later, after that divinely inspired work had been translated into other languages which themselves subsequently went out of use. And it was a position that was gaining increasing acceptance in the scientific community. It was, thus, only much later that the Book of Genesis was translated into Hebrew. Mjomba did not fail to point out that Ge-ez, unlike so many other ancient languages that had "died" or became extinct, had surmounted a variety of obstacles and refused to "die" like Latin and those other languages.

According to Mjomba, the original "Book of Genesis", a self-published work that was presented to the world by its inspired author as an "original, unedited, and unabridged story" of the creation of the world and all that was in it, probably differed very substantially from the stylishly written "Book of Genesis" that has been bequeathed to us in many important respects. For one thing, Mjomba doubted very much if the original Book of Genesis had any of the "biblical clarity" which the present version boasted. He suspected that as the sacred text was translated from one language into another, and as it was touched and re-touched by well-meaning but over-zealous scribes during the four hundred thousand-year history of mankind, it underwent editorial and perhaps even substantive changes, and also acquired the "biblical clarity" along the way. The well-meaning scribes had even chopped up the holy book into chapters and verses - following their own whims obviously!

In support of his contention, Mjomba made reference to the fact that thousands of books - many of them several times as long as the books of scripture they supposedly were expounding on, and a good number of which even contradicted one the other despite being held up by their authors as the authoritative interpretation of the inspired works - had been written. With the recent discovery of the cave where Adam and Eve had lived, and along with it, the Rwenzori Prehistoric Diaries, Mjomba was one of the hordes of people who were now eagerly praying and hoping that someone would stumble upon the scrolls containing the original, unembellished, Book of Genesis.

Mjomba went on that, through his machinations and God-given creative ability, Lucifer, after he turned against his Prime Mover, had effectively succeeded in creating vacuums where good had previously reigned supreme. In the process, he had also succeeded in persuading humans to abandon common sense itself, and in confusing them to the point where everything they would normally do to survive had now become treacherous. While he had apparently been unable to cause any problems in the purely physical realm, the devil, a pure spirit, had succeeded in planting chaos in the spiritual realm to boot.

Also, even a beautiful creature like a snake, so poised and captivating, now evoked the image of trickery and evil! And, instead of simply being regarded as the delectable produce of Mother Earth, good old-fashioned apples were now also suspect, just because of their association in people's minds with the fall of Adam and Eve from grace.

Thanks to Satan - although, admittedly, desires of the flesh also played their part - an ordinary, well-meaning folk could now not contemplate doing simple things like taking sustenance without being enticed either to pander to the pallet for its own sake or to capitulate to gourmandism. As things stood, enjoying a glass of fine wine with the intention of celebrating life easily led to intoxication.

It did not take much for relaxing or a well-deserved rest to translate into indolence and idolatry. Unless one was fortified with grace when one stopped to admire anything, there was every chance that one's innocent admiration of an object would quickly start to degenerate into covetousness.

Literature, the arts, and the media were all now employed to promote causes that were largely shady instead of being used to inform and educate. The distinction between those activities that were intimate by design and those that were not was, for all practical purposes, lost and forgotten. The reproductive act, so vital to the survival of the human race, had become equated with indecency and depravity. Already the idea of "dressing up", when considered in isolation from fashions and fads, had lost meaning.

Mjomba wrote that the reproductive act had evidently become one aspect of human life about which almost everyone liked to moralize. The innumerable spins on the interpretation of the sixth commandment in particular were proof enough of that. But, by the same token, it was also an aspect of human life that was ideal for illustrating the principle that it was not the act but the intention that comprised sin. As happened in other areas in which humans started tampering with the Prime Mover's original purpose for making things the way he had done, to the extent humans had removed sexuality from its original context in the Divine Plan, to that extent this precious part of human nature had lost its ability to fulfil humans the way it was intended to do.

How could humans ever hope to achieve self-actualization if they were unable to use the gifts they had received from the Prime Mover the way those gifts were meant to be used? In the final analysis humans, as creatures who were endowed with reason and a free will, did things the way they did because they chose to. This was so despite the wish of some that, just because the Deliverer had come, the choices they made now didn't really matter, and that the only thing that did was "faith in Jesus"! Yeah, only "faith in Jesus" even if you reviled the Church He established and empowered to carry on His mission, as well as its teachings!

The fact was that the Evil One, even though a master of shrewdness, did not have the power to compel humans to follow his vile and contemptible insinuations. Just imagine what things would be like if Beelzebub had that power, Mjomba quipped! Perhaps if the tempter had not been there to beguile humans with counsel that was less than honest, humans might very well have taken on that role and done the dirty work themselves. Mjomba added that, by the look of it, some humans, not caring a hoot if the devil existed or didn't exist, were already doing precisely that, to the obvious delight of the Prince of Darkness no doubt!

They would essentially have their fellow humans believe that self-actualization and escapism were synonymous. Mjomba likened escapism to seeking total or lasting fulfillment from appreciating the everchanging face of the pop charts' top ten

440

numbers. And he proceeded to comment that this was what actually happened when talents and other endowments that humans had received from the Prime Mover were treated as if they were just accidents of nature with no place in the divine plan. With their original purpose in that plan thwarted, their use for transitory satisfaction could no longer lead to actualization that, in the case of humans, had to be permanent to be effectual.

Because humans were spiritual beings, one's chances for achieving self-actualization were enhanced by self-abnegation or the giving of oneself particularly in relation to one's neighbor, according to Mjomba's thesis. In other words - making sacrifices or loving the neighbor above oneself as commanded by the Prime Mover, and preparing oneself in that way to receive the Ultimate Good, which can only be received entire and not piece-meal. An important implication of this was that individuals who did that were unencumbered by any worldly possessions when the time came for them to depart this life for the next one, and that their self-actualization was assured even when they left this world before they reached the "prime" of their life in the worldly sense.

Mjomba advanced the strange argument that it was the self-immolation that counted most when trying to determine how close one was to self-actualization, and that material success was entirely irrelevant. The enjoyment of a fleeting moment of satisfaction in this life was certainly not a prerequisite for achieving true self-actualization. According to his thesis, the exposure to suffering and pain, deprivation, and things of that nature, according to Mjomba's thesis, predisposed humans to fulfillment.

To be a celebrity author in the next life, one did not have to be a published author or to have "authored" anything, Mjomba wrote. In fact not publishing anything even helped ensure that the merits from one's potential as an author were not reduced to naught or damaged as one basked in the glow of being a best-seller or a Nobel Laureate and things like that.

To be an accomplished and superb preacher, one did not need to step inside a pulpit or to give a homily, and even less a rousing one. They did not even have to be ordained ministers, and it was unimportant that they might not have once opened their mouths - like the Holy Innocents whose suffering and premature death for the sake of the Holy Child are things that will continue to resound in the ears of believers and non-believers all over the world to the last day.

What was more, to be "something" in the eyes of the Prime Mover, one did not even have to grow up and become "mature" in anything in the worldly sense. One did not even need to develop to the point where one could eat with a fork and knife. Mjomba quipped that if the ability to feed oneself using chopsticks had been a prerequisite for any celestial accomplishment, most people including himself, would probably be disqualified.

To be a "Doctor of the Church", St. Theresa of

Lisieux did not have to be appointed to an endowed professorship at some funny place where the ivory tower mentality was the hype first. She accomplished that by leading the life of a recluse, shirking publicity, and making certain that she did not break the rules of her monastery, especially the ones other nuns regarded as unimportant.

To qualify as a celestial "Beauty Queen", it was not necessary for one to become a maiden first, according to Mjomba. And there was, of course, no age limit for entering the "Beauty Queen' contest. Mjomba added that to be a member of the Mystical Body of Christ, it was not even necessary for one to complete the journey of groping one's way into the visible Church the Deliverer founded - so long as one was doing one's best to find the "unknown" God. According to Mjomba, the Sermon on the Mount made perfect sense and was apparently backed by solid reasons too!

According to Mjomba's thesis, the real and the only determinant of self-actualization for humans was the degree to which they embraced the state of being childlike, and consequently were prepared to give the full credit for actual or potential achievements to the Prime Mover ungrudgingly. That was also the state in which all humans started off at birth, but which they strove to abandon as they lost their innocence, grew in selfishness, and stopped being childlike as they supposedly "matured". And it was a state, Mjomba asserted, which was also the hallmark of humility.

Using the pop charts to illustrate the short-sightedness of humans with regard to happiness and self-actualization, Mjomba wrote that, after embracing the pop chart's top ten numbers as the very best there ever could be in one week, and after taking the necessary action to gain possession of them, those humans who were given to adoring pop music - and Mjomba readily admitted that he was one of them - soon found they had to start all over again when the new top of the pop charts popped up in the next week without ever learning from their experience! As Mjomba liked to put it, the difference between self-deception and escapism was the same!

Mjomba went on that because escapism did not have reason as its basis, the tendency for those mired in it to "push the envelope" to its limits was strong. Escapism undermined self-discipline; and those caught up in its clutches often even risked severe bodily harm in their misguided quest for material happiness.

Lucifer was thus, not just the evil genius *par excellence*, but verily the prince of darkness, and humans ignored him at their peril, according to Mjomba. To drive the point home, he wrote that the Deliverer took pity over those whom he found languishing under the spell of Beelzebub and immediately went to their aid. But even after the Evil One had been rebuked times and again, he had kept up with his harassment, not even sparing the Deliverer himself.

Mjomba suggested that the devil was particularly active on those occasions when the

444

Deliverer performed miracles, and that he must have done everything in his power to diminish their efficacy. Mjomba accordingly imagined gluttonous individuals, at the miracle of the multiplication of loaves and fishes, consuming food far in excess of their needs, as they were wont to do. And he also imagined habitual drunks among the wedding guests at Canaan, who probably had been responsible for the wine shortage in the first place, drinking to an unprecedented excess, when the Deliverer changed water into wine to alleviate the shortage they had caused.

But in truth, Mjomba wrote, the devil, while not harmless, was finished after he failed to make the grade. According to the seminarian, Satan was finished in the exact same way his lackeys among humans become finished when they find themselves locked in the pursuit of temporal, completely transient happiness or fulfillment - as they invariably discover upon leaving this life for the after-life. The bitterness they now harbored from knowing that others would in time move on to occupy the elevated places in heaven they themselves had forfeited was a sure sign that they knew they had been written off for good. Satan's fate was sealed, and he knew it.

But, a big time liar and a spoiler, he was out to try and ruin things for others despite the fact that he himself had been fashioned in the image and likeness of the Prime Mover. The Evil One was now ceaselessly haunted by thoughts of what he would have been had he not wilfully deviated from the path

445

of truth.

As far as being vanquished went, Mephistopheles had been defeated and was completely powerless. This was clear from the fact that he could only tempt individuals to a certain extent; and, even then, he could not coerce the target of his entrapment to fall for his bait however alluring or to capitulate to his insinuations however slick and beguiling.

Emphasizing the archenemy's powerlessness, Mjomba, ever the pro-life advocate, wrote that the most fragile human, even when still in the form of a foetus that was on the verge of being expelled from its mother's womb accidentally or deliberately, wielded far more power and clout than the devil.

But being completely vanquished also meant being dangerous beyond imagination, Mjomba argued. While a jailbird could afford to relax and rest on his or her laurels (at least during the intervals he or she was not incarcerated), it was not so with the mighty Prince of the Underworld. The devil did not have any laurels on which he could rest; and he wasn't in a position to enjoy even one single moment of peace during which he could contemplate things that were good or worthwhile either. And that, according to Mjomba, made him one really mad, and exceedingly dangerous creature that was on the loose nonetheless.

Because it was not in his nature to spare himself any pains born of the fear of failure, the devil worked ceaselessly; and his persistence had paid off.

As a result of his machinations, humans - the vast majority of them at any rate - were for all practical purposes oblivious of their last end as they went about their daily business. And this, Mjomba quipped, just when you thought that humans would be absorbed with preparations for something as critically important as their after-life!

To the extent that those humans who acknowledged that they had an after-life in practice now paid only lip service to that fact, with an ever increasing number more inclined to ridicule the very notion of an after-life and to equate themselves to lower creatures that were not endowed with the faculties of the intellect and free will, to that extent the prince of darkness could claim unqualified success for his endeavors as a spoiler. And, what was more, he consequently could claim that humans were vanquished while he himself was at least still kicking - in an ironic and, indeed, altogether unexpected reversal of the situation!

And, assuming for the sake of argument, that humans were right, the devil would be able to say that humans themselves had to admit that they were finished in the true sense of that word, especially since creatures that were created with an intellect and a free will, and for that reason ranked as spiritual beings, could not be more "finished" or as Mjomba loved to put it more "kaput" than that!

A shameless liar but no blithering idiot, he had succeeded in convincing humans that worldly glamour - rather than human suffering, self-denial, mortification and penance in the aftermath of original sin - signaled beauty in the human person. And stupid, idiotic humans had gone on to make that tall tale an article of faith and a guiding principle of their lives! And then, not content with permitting Beelzebub to dictate to them on such a vital matter, humans took it upon themselves to celebrate - yes, celebrate - that "sacred" truth regularly with festivals in places like Rio, Cancun, Tampa Bay, Miami, and now even on the worldwide Web!

Evolution and Man...

Mjomba, who had once upon a time confided to Primrose that he was both a creationist and an evolutionist, had allowed in his thesis that, around the fifth or sixth century, a large proportion of the earth's population, which was, undoubtedly much smaller than today's population, likely consisted of individuals who were either transsexual or bisexual, the result supposedly of inter-marriages between individuals who were close kin. Mjomba went as far as suggesting that in those early years of human history, conjugal relations between blood brothers and sisters were even regarded as the ideal - until it was discovered that the preponderance of the evidence pointed in the opposite direction.

Mjomba hypothesized that, with the number of transvestites and hermaphrodites together constituting roughly two thirds or thereabout of the earth's population, being a transvestite or a hermaphrodite was, Mjomba claimed, socially acceptable. And - what was more - their lifestyles were even coveted, Mjomba wrote. The number of people who were born with regular male and female features was in the minority, and it was considered very much a blessing in those days to be born with bisexual features. For most people, heterosexual relations were thus not a practical proposition.

According to Mjomba's thesis, marriages between heterosexual partners at that time in history were not regarded as highly as they would by later generations. Heterosexual relations resulted in childbirth; and the associated burdens, specifically the work involved in rearing children, made the marriages unpopular. Mjomba wrote that the preoccupation with bringing up children was looked down upon partly because it imposed restrictions on things like migration and adventurous travel for its own sake, which was a very popular pastime in those days. The situation was exacerbated by the fact that people lived to be three - and sometimes even four - hundred years! Consequently, couples often ended up with as many as fifty children from the same union, making it difficult for the parents to go anywhere!

And even as the population was thus exploding, the explorers, single men and women who were more often than not transsexuals, returned to regale those who had been left behind with tales of adventure and captivating accounts of conditions in distant exotic lands. Treated as heroes, the returnees automatically went on to enjoy a high social status, much of it at the expense of those who had stayed on to rear their families and were sometimes looked down on and despised as unadventurous and "sissy" moms and pops.

Mjomba posited that the coveted position of transvestites in the society of those days was bolstered by the general belief that bisexual and transsexual individuals were more fully developed. There was also the fact, he pointed out, that they had physiques that tended to be more robust and athletic than average, and that supposedly made them exceedingly handsome and the envy of everyone.

Mjomba contended that it was only much later, as the number of bisexual and transsexual persons dwindled with the passage of time and they became a tiny minority, that the tables completely turned in favor of the segment of the population that was hetero-sexual, allowing moms and pops to once again enjoy self-esteem in their own right. It was thus that being born an ordinary man or woman - like Adam and Eve of old - on the gender continuum eventually stopped being regarded as a bane, and again became respectable, taking on the noble image it has continued to enjoy to this day.

Mjomba credited the changes in the demographic makeup of the earth's human population at that time to the natural forces of evolution, and argued that creationism and evolution were ideas that, far from being incompatible, were in fact complementary. But there were also diseases that plagued humans during this period - diseases

450

that, according to Mjomba, singled out transsexual and bisexual couples. He argued that those diseases played an important part in bringing about the fundamental changes in the population pattern, and also in changing people's attitudes towards sexual relations between individuals of the same sex.

Mjomba believed that there was a great deal of controversy among moralists of that epoch regarding the part(s) of the gender or sexual continuum that supposedly represented the norm. He suggested that there likely was even greater controversy regarding the types of sexual relations - and the form(s) of sexual activities - that could be considered legitimate. In the absence of formal books of scriptures and organized church groups, those moralists could not themselves escape being characterized as self-proclaimed and self-serving, and their exhortations went largely unheeded.

Also, according to Mjomba, contrary to popular belief, all human beings throughout the ages had enjoyed an equal opportunity for salvation. Humans did not choose their race, their gender, the epoch in which they came into existence, and even less whether to come into being at all or not. Any human, Mjomba himself included, theoretically could have come into the world as Adam, Eve, Judas Iscariot, or as some other shady character that had already lived or whose time was still to come.

Conceived in original sin (with the exception of Mary and her divine Son), they all started out as innocent individuals nonetheless; and it was only

451

subsequently that they succumbed voluntarily to venial and/or mortal sin, and in some instances sacrilegious sins as well - depending on the extent to which they were determined to thwart the divine plan also known as providence. The mystery of it all was that humans, led by Adam and Eve, chose to disobey the Prime Mover at all! It was a mystery because, first, they were not under any compulsion to go off and sin against their Creator. Secondly, when they did so, their chosen course of action did not even guarantee any happiness. They were in fact taking a gamble.

And then they also knew that they were abandoning the sure path to fulfilment - fulfilment guaranteed them by none other than the Prime Mover Himself. When humans sinned, they were in that sense committing what they knew to be a folly. In the case of Adam and Eve, it was (as it turned out) an insane, irrational, act that they immediately regretted!

Mjomba conceded that many moralists thought otherwise. But that was because they confused physical actions that were in themselves neither good nor bad with human intent. That confusion, according to Mjomba, had also caused many present-day moralists to arrive at the erroneous conclusion that there was an intrinsic correlation between the state of technological development and immorality.

It was, of course, Mjomba's firm position that the act of disobedience to the Creator, rather than being found on the lower subliminal level of their human nature, primarily involved the higher faculties of the intellect and the will, and accordingly was to be

452

found in the spiritual realm.

To further illustrate that point, Mjomba had detailed how, every time the First Man allowed his gaze to fall upon the only other human in the universe (who after all owed her existence to the fact that, in the Creator's view, it was not good for Man to be alone!), Adam had developed the tendency to become absorbed by Eve's womanly nature from time to time. Adam had easily guessed that he felt overwhelmed in her presence because her physique and temperament had been designed to be different from and yet at the same time complimentary to his own manly nature.

Citing evidence in the Rwenzori Prehistoric Diaries, Mjomba wrote that Adam often wondered whether Eve was encountering the same problem, but could not marshal the courage to ask her! As far as Mjomba was concerned, it was quite normal for Adam and Eve to experience those feelings; and the fact that both Adam and Eve had come into being as grown-ups, and did not have the benefit of experiencing what early childhood and normal adolescence were like, had nothing at all to do with those feelings. According to Mjomba's thesis, there was at least no evidence in either the Diaries or the Book of Genesis to suggest that there was anything abnormal about the attitudes and temperament of the first Man and Woman in those respects.

Mjomba even argued that there would have been a much greater likelihood of that happening had Adam and Eve come into the world as little babies and then developed in stages, including the stage of puberty, before they reached adult-hood - as normally occurred in the case of their posterity. With no earthly dad and/or mom to wean and guide them through those critical stages in life, and without the sort of animal instinct that would have made up for the absence of a dad and mom to cuddle them, Adam and Eve would almost certainly have ended up as imbeciles who were unable to take care of themselves, let alone bring up their own issue in a culture that stressed lofty ideals and service to each other and above all to the Prime Mover - or worse!

Adam, Mjomba wrote, proceeded as a matter of course to join Michael the Arch-angel and the rest of the heavenly host in praising the Prime Mover for that new marvel in his creation, and to deride Lucifer and the other fallen angels for imagining that they could derive anything but illusory satisfaction from refusing to pay the Creator homage as the Almighty One - and, as well, a Prime Mover who had not stopped at fashioning cherubs, and seraphs and the members of the other choirs of angels in His own image and likeness, but had proceeded to mold humans likewise in His divine image! That was even though the heavenly host were invisible to the naked eye, and could only be discerned through the eyes of their faith.

Parallel between humans and devils...

And, in a bold and wholly unprecedented move,

454

Mjomba had gone on to describe how Adam and Eve, using the immense clout they wielded over other forms of life on earth and with remarkable ingenuity, successfully coaxed the beasts of the earth, the birds of the air, fishes and other creatures of the sea, along with the other life forms on earth - even including inanimate objects - to participate in festivals that brought out the best in them for the greater glory of the Prime Mover.

Mjomba contended that those festivals, celebrating as they did not only the sublime nature of the Prime Mover but also His boundless wisdom, power and love, were a major irritant to Lucifer and the other inhabitants of the under-world; and that one especially powerful suggestion advanced by Beelzebub during the temptation of Adam and Eve in the Garden of Eden, was that instead of celebrating the somewhat prosaic fact that the Creator was a genius of sorts, celebrating the ingenuity with which they laid on those festivals and their own innate genius, promised to be so much more exciting and fun!

Satan reportedly emphasized that all he was suggesting was that Adam and Eve focus less on the genius that God obviously was, and more on their own innate, less celebrated ingenuity and their other talents! As if that was not bad enough, Satan had further argued that the shift was in fact necessary to redress the imbalance in the order of nature - or something to that effect!

Noting that the seed of rebellion sown by the

455

Evil One in the minds of the first Man and the first Woman did indeed result in sin, Mjomba had proceeded to depict Eve as suggesting to the man out of whose rib she had been formed that everything seemed to be set for them to assume the roles of Supreme King and Supreme Queen of a world that was entirely independent of the invisible Prime Mover! Eve had found her not-so-secret admirer – who, like her, assumed at that point that the authority they wielded over other creatures of the universe could be taken completely for granted - as interested as ever in the idea of being at the top of an eternal tree of the human family and exercising absolute reign over generations of human creatures. That was something that would make them divine in all but name!

Yes, she (Eve) would be the definitive Queen Bee while Adam, whom she was now anxiously waiting to welcome and embrace as her "royal" consort, was going to be the King Bee! And they thought that, by elbowing the Prime Mover to the side and out of their direct vision, they would themselves become virtual divinities - somewhat like Him! And, yes - people would die! Anyone who would refuse to pay them homage or to toe the line in other respects would be straightened up. They were not going to brook any nonsense from any one. Their imperial status would not be negotiable.

After all, their subjects would be descended from their own royal stock. And, while they would indeed be offspring of royalty, the fact would remain that they would owe it all to the Queen Bee and the

King Bee! That is why stern action would be taken against anyone who would have the cheek to display a "bad attitude".

According to Mjomba's thesis, Adam and Eve resolved well before they were themselves cast out from the Garden of Eden that they would be "bad" when it came to dealing with their disloyal subjects. There would be jails in which to confine the most "unruly" elements. And, yes! Adam and Eve would also institute detentions without trial. Quoting from the Rwenzori Prehistoric Diaries, Mjomba wrote that at one point, Adam, who was really just following Eve's lead in all this, was horrified when he caught Eve giggling mirthfully and excited at the thought of "prisoners" in leg chains! Mjomba went on that Eve, that matronly mother of the human race who owed her own existence to the fact that Adam had been willing to donate one of his ribs so the Prime Mover could use it to form her, apparently even relished visions of piles of human skulls on the edge of some killing fields - skulls of those "subjects" who did not heed warnings to toe the line or be destroyed!

And even though Adam told himself many times that he was going to walk away and leave Eve to her strange devices, he could not muster the courage to do so. He could not imagine leaving the only other living person he had known, even though she was degenerating into something of a sub-human. Because, even when Eve was acting like a devil, there was something about her that mesmerized him and held him completely captive!

And it was not long before he surrendered to the woman's overwhelming magnetism and mysterious power.

In fact, after a while, Adam himself begun to relish the "cool manner" in which Eve described the fate that awaited anyone who would suddenly "turn up with an attitude" as she liked to put it. Eve was apparently elated when Adam suggested that any of their descendants who qualified as a "very bad character", according to their definition, would deserve to be "drawn, hanged, and quartered"! But Eve thought that it would be more fun to execute - or, as she liked to put it, "neutralize" - such characters by stoning them to death with the help of rocks or whatever method came in handy.

Whereupon Adam, whose "conversion" was now complete, chimed in saying that they could organize and "crush" such folks if they could develop catapults and other devices for delivering rocks and other missiles that shattered on impact in what he described as "shock and awe" operations!

Citing what he referred to as incontrovertible "evidence" in the Rwenzori Prehistoric Diaries, Mjomba wrote that Adam, in his eagerness to reassure Eve that he intended to go with her all the way in their burgeoning rebellion against the Prime Mover, actually conducted some experiments in a nearby jungle and reported back to Eve something Mjomba thought was quite astounding. He informed Eve that it would not be long before they were actually able to fabricate what he called "nuclear" and "hydrogen" contraptions that could be detonated over concentrations of hostile forces. Adam explained that to use those contraptions or "bombs" effectively without compromising their own safety, they would have to deliver the "bombs" by catapult or some similar conveyance and ignite in-built fuses by remote control from a safe distance.

According to Mjomba's thesis, Adam let Eve know that once developed, an arsenal of those nuclear and hydrogen bombs would serve as a deterrent and ensure that their subjects, wherever they were, toed the line. Adam, according to Mjomba, regretted that they could not employ those weapons of mass destruction or "WMD" as he fondly referred to the "bombs" to knock the daylights out of beings that were pure spirits, like Diabolos for instance!

But it was evident that Adam, a coward, was mindful of the possibility of uprisings and revolutions whose objective would be the overthrow of the "imperial rule" they were even now planning to impose on their as yet unborn descendants. It meant that they had to be prepared to be ruthless and merciless in dealing with any dissent! It would be necessary to resort to those types of things in the New Order in which the offspring of Adam and Eve would automatically become subjects who would be expected to pay the duo homage in the same way they themselves now paid homage to the Prime Mover!

Mjomba wrote that it was a mark of the extent to which human creatures, even though created in the image of the Prime Mover, could be bad that Adam and Eve could plot harm to their own kind even before the target of their vitriol had come into the world. That Adam and Eve could stand there in the Garden of Eden (where they themselves were still virtual guests) and do such a thing defied comprehension in Mjomba's view. They were doing so in the absence of any perceived threat of any kind to themselves and while they were simultaneously plotting to break their own covenant with the Prime Mover! Mjomba wondered how the first Man and the first Woman could do those sorts of things and still sleep soundly when night fell. And it wasn't as if they had nothing to do!

All the while that Adam and Eve were busy plotting against the Prime Mover and planning harm to their own progeny - and also eyeing the ripening fruits on the Tree of Knowledge which they knew was out of bounds - they were supposed to be working the fields to grow their own food so that they would be self-reliant. Mjomba noted that the first Man and the first Woman had really committed not one but a string of sins, including the original sin. He commented that if the first couple had not allowed themselves to be idle - if they had remained at their post tilling the soil, hewing logs, harvesting the crops, and doing the other things they needed to do to meet their needs - even though they might still have failed the Prime Mover and committed sins, they likely would have been what he (Mjomba) called "unoriginal sins"; and the human race would have been spared the dreadful and debilitating consequences of the original sin. In other words, "original virtue" would have triumphed!

But Adam and Eve chose to be idle, and to abandon themselves to scheming evil on a magnitude that came close to rivalling the scheming by Diabolos himself! It was simply incomprehensible - Adam and Eve who were beneficiaries of such largess from the Prime Mover not just plotting to do harm to the unborn and the innocent who were moreover their own kind, but also plotting against their Creator! Not even beasts did that sort of thing.

Or, perhaps, it was more appropriate to say that it was only humans (who were blest with a free will and also with faculties of the intellect and the imagination) who could misuse their talents to that extent and in that fashion! Mjomba noted that Adam and Eve were planning to disobey a Being that, far from threatening them in any way, had in fact brought them into existence out of nothing, endowed them with immense and incredible gifts, and had in addition promised to be their mainstay throughout all eternity.

It did not in the end surprise Mjomba at all that humans, who would have been quite happy (or so they stupidly imagined) to be completely rid of their Prime Mover in league with Diabolos, had all too often proved to be so cruel to their own kind. It distressed Mjomba to think that Lucifer, who had set things in motion with his act of intransigence, had not had any scruples about targeting beings that were pure spirits like himself, and that he had eventually succeed in tricking numbers of them into following him into perdition. Mjomba did not doubt that Satan started hatching his schemes against his fellow angels well before they too had come into existence.

It distressed Mjomba to think that Diabolos, apparently the first creature to be brought into being, fell from grace in the very beginning - before any other creatures (both angels and humans) had been brought into being. It was a horrible thought that the very first creature to exist could betray the Creator so early on in the divine plan - just as it was a horrible thought that Adam and Eve, the very first Man and Woman, had betrayed their Prime Mover so soon after they had been brought into being and before any other humans had been created. That - and the fact that Beelzebub did not respect any boundaries and eventually drew humans as well into his dastardly schemes and rebellion against the Prime Mover - spoke volumes about his evil mind.

As Adam and Eve would both discover later to their utter dismay in the wake of their rebellion, the "satisfaction" which their cunning archenemy lead them to believe would be theirs for the asking on attaining independence from the Prime Mover would in fact be a sham. It would be entirely transitory, and unlike the satisfaction they now got from serving the Almighty One whose divine nature was synonymous with perfect goodness, perfect wisdom and perfect love. And there would be no guarantee that they wouldn't lose their hard won "independence" to some ambitious or plainly greedy members of the human family!

Luckily for Adam and Eve and their posterity, it required no more than an acknowledgement by Adam and Eve that they had sinned to get Satan off their backs. For one, that admission was in itself evidence that the first Man and Woman had finally succeeded in seeing through the lies of Diabolos. It also predisposed them for the divine act of mercy that would in time translate in the advent into the world of their God and Redeemer.

This was even though Adam and Eve, who had still to exchange married vows, were not yet husband and wife at the time of their rebellion. It is also thus noteworthy and to the credit of Adam and Eve that, even though not yet husband and wife, they both responded to the Prime Mover's promise of a Deliverer in way that reflected great statesmanship on the part of Adam and great statesmanship on the part of Eve.

Pulling together and letting bygones be bygones, they were able to steer clear of the trap laid by Diabolos and avoided being drawn into the blame game to his great disappointment. And, even though they continued to be pummelled by the effects of original sin, including the threat of physical death which was now very real, Adam and eve, almost miraculously succeeded in working their way back into good books with their Prime Mover, holding fort until their liaison was finally blessed by the infinitely loving - and forgiving - Creator.

Judgement...

In Adam and Eve's terminology, death occurred when the body became separated from the soul. What happened to the lower animals - or "brutes", as Adam and Eve referred to the animals, reptiles, and fishes - and other "living" creatures and plants when they expired and ceased to exist did not rise to anything approximating death, because divine grace did not come into the picture. These lower beings came into the world and departed there from at the pleasure of the Creator so to speak.

According to the thesis, when the lower creatures expired, that was not really *death* because it was not a penalty for disobedience to the Creator. Mjomba supposed that the transition of these lower animals from the *state of being* back to the *state of non-being* looked like it was traumatic all right. And who knows! Perhaps at that point in time, everything they too had ever done in their animal lives returned to haunt them even if only momentarily - before the lower creatures slipped back into nothingness and oblivion!

Mjomba wrote that perhaps it was during that same moment - a final moment in time so to speak - during which they too got a chance to acknowledge Him-Who-Is-Who-Is for one last time as the Almighty One who brought them into being gratuitously out of nothingness, albeit not in His own image and likeness as in the case of their "masters" back on earth! A final moment, Mjomba added, during which *dying* beasts were also afforded what might be described as a *glimpse* of sorts of the Omnipotent before their "egos", consumed by their love and adoration for their Maker, caused them to burn out and return to nothingness!

Mjomba was convinced that something like that probably occurred especially since back on earth these same beasts *saw* things with their eyes and *sensed* the reality around them in very much the same way as humans did. Still, that transformation, according to Mjomba, remained very much akin to the chemical transformation that vegetative creatures under-went when they too "died" and became recycled.

Egos being consumed by love and adoration for the Omnipotent - that was especially true for dying humans, according to Mjomba. In their case, and because they were made in the image and likeness of the Prime Mover, the mere act of facing the Judge - after leaving behind a world which they had left better or worse than they had found it - had to be traumatic of and in itself. It had to be a frightful experience for humans, who were endowed with both reason and a free will, to come face to face with their self-deception and to finally accept that when they did things that were proscribed during their "time of trial" on earth, they did those things, not because they themselves *were humans* or because they *were made* in a certain way, but because they *were capable* of doing them and *chose* to so act. And, pertaining to eternal life, that period of trial on earth, which in modern times sometimes stretched to thirty thousand days for the "unlucky" ones, was still a relatively short one!

Mjomba wrote that, like a diamond in a pile of trash, the beauty in humans seemed to sparkle even more when they were indulging in filth. But, conversely, the ugliness of sin was also more revolting when, with worldly trappings that had served to cloak it swept away, the naked human soul suddenly found itself in the Divine Presence. It had to be even more devastating for souls of the damned to suddenly discover that after living the lie, the propensity to continue lying stayed with them right there in the presence of the Living Truth as undeniable evidence of their malfeasance, making them absolutely loathsome.

And it had to be a dreadful feeling for those souls to find they now had to own up to the fact that back on earth they really were just *servants* who decided to bury the talents they had been entrusted with by their *Master*. Mjomba wrote that it had to be really heart-breaking for those souls to admit at that late stage that they should have known that their protestations about the Deliverer being a mean and exacting Master - who "reaped where He did not saw" - could not possibly wash. It had to be a most pitiful sight as those who, up until that moment had been laughing and making merry, all of a sudden started to weep and gnash their teeth in a belated act of remorse. And it had to be a horrible spectacle indeed as those same souls, realizing that they did not now belong there in the Divine Presence by their own choosing, made a stampede for exists that were not there!

Mjomba imagined the really incorrigible, for whom time to make amends and become cleansed from the guilt of their sins with fire in *Purgatory* - or whatever you may wish to call it - did not look like something they would welcome, making a rather reckless, if instinctive, stampede towards earth which they had just vacated. According to him, they did that instinctively when it dawned on them that they had squandered their time on earth on pipe dreams instead of working on their self-actualization as the children of the Prime Mover they were - time during which they had absolutely defied the clamor of their consciences and refused to accept that they could not serve two masters - the Prime Mover and mammon. That they had refused to heed the Deliverer's advice that they sell all their possessions, give the proceeds, not to Judas Iscariot, the Deliverer's purse bearer, or (by extension) to "churches" (which with one single exception were "bogus" anyway), but to the poor and go follow Him. And that, having adamantly refused to detach themselves from temporal things in order to afford themselves the opportunity to dwell on the more important things pertaining to their eternal life, they had indeed flunked the Church Triumphant Entrance Test!

Mjomba clarified that because they possessed the *knowledge* that they were supposed to walk the walk, they no longer had a valid excuse for not walking that walk. That was even though, knowledge was only the start, and to walk that walk successfully also required *cooperation* with the grace of the Prime Mover.

Mjomba supposed that the decision of souls of the damned to take flight was induced by their hatred for those other souls of the just who were headed for Purgatory and eventually heaven where they would exult in the Divine Presence for eternity - and their enormous pride.

Mjomba imagined them breaking out from the Divine Presence all right, but not quite succeeding in quelling their craving for fulfilment, a craving that only their Maker could give. Some, according to Mjomba, headed blindly for earth in hopes of being able to repossess their bodies and to perchance resume leading their ungodly lives of lies and self-deception. But instead, they all found themselves deep inside the earth's crust in the company of demons and other lost souls!

Mjomba had no doubt that that was where hell was located - deep in the crust of the earth. It was there, after all, that Adam and Eve and the souls of all their descendants had ended up as captives of Diabolos - until rescue came on that *Good* Friday two thousand years ago when the Deliverer descended into hell in person. And it was there, as a matter of fact, that the Deliverer spent three days and three nights, communing with the spirits of His human ancestors before He *freed* them on the day of His resurrection.

Mjomba wrote that in the case of Lucifer and

468

his following, their expulsion from the heavenly paradise could not be described as "dying" in the physical sense for the simple reason that the constitution of angels did not contain bodily matter. According to Mjomba's thesis, they "died" spiritually nevertheless, and underwent something that was completely unknown in the world of matter. The human concept of death consisting in the separation of the soul from the human body pales when compared to spiritual death, which consists in the inability of an unrepentant creature that happens to be fashioned in the image and likeness of the Prime Mover to hide and escape "damnation". Like the fallen angels, upon leaving the plane of matter and entering the spiritual plane, "death", consisting in the flight of the "damned" soul from the presence of the Prime Mover and Source of Life, became imminent. With absolutely nowhere to hide, the unrepentant soul, standing condemned for its acts of commission and omission, had to make an exit of sorts from the face of the Prime Mover, and typically ended up in a real place called "hell" (because of the very unpleasant conditions there) located in the bowels of the earth.

The Forbidden Fruit...

When they disobeyed, Adam and Eve found that they could hide only for so long, and they quickly realized that they would also end up really "dead" likewise, absent an act of divine mercy and their own willingness to be redeemed. And so, strictly speaking, Adam and Eve were slated to die twice after their own sin of disobedience: physically upon their transition to the after-life and also spiritually, if they did not return to the fold. Mjomba argued that, until their sin in the Garden of Eden, "death" as we now know it existed for Adam and Eve only as an idea, and a very unimportant one. He even went on to suggest that what probably came to their mind when thinking about their "physical" death or transition to the after-life was really "life" and not "death". This was because that transition, following their "trial" on earth, presaged even better things for them as faithful servants of the Prime Mover. And, unlike the lower beings whose "transformation" effectively meant the end of the road, physical death was something they looked forward to - until they decided to become rebels.

Mjomba had Adam and Eve thinking, mistakenly as it would turn out, that the chance of anything like the painless "death" of lower beings ever befalling them - let alone a torturous transformation from life on this earth to something else as punishment for disloyalty to the Prime Mover - appeared very remote, if for no other reason than that, up until this time, it had never crossed their minds that this could happen to them! It was inconceivable that anyone of them could end up in a bottomless pit in the bowels of the earth as a punishment for disloyal conduct, and they were effectively blinded by the fact that such a thing had never happened to humans before and was completely foreign to human experience!

In the days leading up to the rebellion, they had even calculated the probability of "dying" and leaving this world for the next. Using advanced calculus, the first couple reckoned that they could regard a one way ticket to hell as an improbable event, and they accordingly wrote it off as a possibility. That was even though they knew that Satan and the other renegade spirits were already there. In any event, they would in time develop the technology that would effectively transfer the decision to "die" or not to die from nature (representing the Prime Mover) to themselves! It was a matter of carrying out the necessary research; and, brilliant creatures, they regarded it as doable.

Adam and Eve allowed themselves to revel in the silly notion that their rule over a mighty, earthly kingdom, because it would be subject to materialistic determinism, would be unchallenged and everlasting. But to work, the scheme also called for Adam and Eve to conceal from their subjects the original purpose of creation, and to usurp the original Creator's role by acting as if it was they who were conferring existence upon their human subjects through parentage! Their claim to being the Majestic King and Queen of the universe would otherwise indeed ring hollow, and their dream of a perpetual reign over humankind would be frustrated thereby.

The first Man and Woman had not yet cohabited, and they certainly had not yet conceived a child, as they considered the choices confronting

471

them. Fair skinned and blond because she had been fashioned out of Adam's rib, Eve had initiated the conversation as a part of her bid to interest Adam in procreation. But, following her womanly instincts and using the gift of intuition with which she was richly endowed, she had continued to maintain her distance from Adam, nonetheless, and to give herself time to study him and weigh her options.

Tanned and boasting a thick mane of hair the color of clay from which he originally came, Adam showed himself as keen as ever to do whatever it would take to ensure that Eve agreed to accept his hand in matrimony. Anxious to show that he was valiant and a man of metal, he had responded that he concurred with everything she was saying and could not wait to see her enthroned as Queen of their earthly kingdom and himself as King. According to Mjomba, he had even suggested that he would use the occasion to solemnize the first royal wedding ever.

Even though they had been commanded by the Creator to multiply and fill the earth, it was not a command that was intended to abrogate their God-given right to decide and choose. Adam and Eve were well aware of that. They, indeed, knew that not everything their God-given nature permitted them to do was necessarily righteous. They could choose to commit suicide, frightful though such a thing was to imagine if only because a pact between the first man and the first woman to end their earthly existence would have automatically resulted in the end of the world as far as the human race was concerned. Or they could opt to just become iconoclasts. The ability to choose represented the one aspect of their nature that distinguished them from mammals, birds, vegetation and physical matter.

Emboldened, Eve had gone on to announce that nothing - absolutely nothing - could stop them from proceeding to create their progeny in their own image and likeness, if they wanted to so proceed. "It is so ordered" Adam, in a clumsy effort to prove his manliness, had replied. He knew that he and his companion had the where-with-all to beget children. And even though his progeny would come into the world programmed to grow and develop into autonomous individuals, he believed that he could manipulate his offspring to his own and Eve's advantage. That was what they planned on doing in complete disregard for the fact that their own human nature, which was itself fashioned in the Creator's image, had been made the way it had been made for the sole purpose of enabling them to do God's bidding - which was to multiply and fill the earth. And so, lamentably, Adam and Eve found themselves tempted to see what would happen if they usurped powers that belonged only in the divine realm!

Mjomba had Adam and Eve realizing, virtually immediately, that their scheme was going to result in their being cast out from the Garden of Eden. They must also have understood that they would not be guaranteed the protective mantle which had hitherto kept at bay everything from the crafty Lucifer and his legion of fallen angels to animals of the wild and other creatures, big and small and visible and invisible, that were certain to turn hostile. Mjomba presumed that they had initially balked.

But, unfortunately for the human race, Adam and Eve were perceiving themselves already at that point as virtual prisoners who were expected to enjoy the comforts of the Garden of Eden, the boundaries of which extended and encompassed the whole universe, provided whatever they did redounded to the greater glory of the Creator and Him alone. In other words, they were free to do absolutely anything, but only if they did it selflessly. Adam was also in full agreement with Eve that being able to choose one way or the other was a challenge they could not imagine away and had to face up to.

When the crafty Beelzebub, sneaking past a band of guardian angels and up into the branches of the tree under which the two-some stood in the guise of a reptile, suggested that it wasn't their fault that they were created with the faculties of reason and free will; and that, unlike lower forms of life, they were now obligated to make a choice one way or the other; they had found to their surprise that their God-given common sense did not contradict his point. They did, indeed, feel as if they were on trial and in a limbo of some kind, awaiting an unknown fate.

Whereupon the archenemy, eager to see the rebellion against the Creator expand, had goaded them on, pointing out that it behoved them to do something, outrageous or otherwise, before they could attain any form of self-actualization! Because he had happened on to the earth before Eve, Adam had found himself stung by his conscience and had recoiled at the idea of turning against the Prime Mover, even though he seemed prepared to do virtually anything to please his companion.

In response to the disappointed Adam's reasoned objections, Eve, who had started it all in a veiled effort to draw Adam's interest to herself and shore up their relationship, had thereupon suggested that they cut a deal with the Prime Mover! Under the agreement, which would not qualify as a rebellion, their offspring would be fashioned not in His image but their own. Under the deal, the original divine plan would thus be only slightly modified to allow Adam and Eve to represent themselves to their progeny as gods, the fact that they were themselves creatures notwithstanding.

Looking Eve in the eye, Adam had immediately realized that she was determined to win his love at all costs, which had caused him to mutter something like "Look at you!" He had also established as fact that she was the embodiment of spousal beauty and charm. On the spur of the moment, he had decided that he and Eve would fall from grace or stay in the Prime Mover's favor together.

Eve had convinced Adam that it was quite feasible to cut such a deal with the Prime Mover whose mistake it was to bestow upon both of them such high intelligence and the right to choose. Knowing quite well that it wasn't in the Prime Mover's nature to go back on his word and take those gifts away from them, Adam had agreed with Eve that they seemed to be in a particularly strong bargaining position.

The alternative to the deal was obvious. Adam and Eve would be at liberty to exercise their God-given right to choose. And they would dutifully make choices, some of which, if followed through, could frustrate the original divine plan. For one, they could decide to change the purpose of sexuality making it primarily for recreation rather than procreation. In the process, they could decide to forego bearing any children, to slow the growth of the human race to a rate they and they themselves alone would determine, or to multiply and fill the earth - but only for their own self-aggrandizement.

Even though that was the current game plan, at the time the idea of a revolt against the Prime Mover got into Eve's head at the very start and she for her part made up her mind to "play along", the situation had looked decidedly trickier than that. The woman who was destined to be the mother of the human race had not just assumed that Adam, her God-given companion and consort, would also play along.

It was quite conceivable that the future father of the human race could refuse to do so; and then there was the off chance, in the event Adam decided that he didn't want to have any part in the rebellion, that he might try to talk her out of it - and succeed! It just so happened that, after she got the evil idea from Satan, Eve had been successful in persuading Adam to join her in the wicked scheme. But it wasn't completely unimaginable that, even then, Adam could chicken out along the way and leave her to her own devices.

It wasn't that Eve was paranoid or anything like that. It seemed to her a sensible thing to prepare herself to deal with all those possibilities and plan her moves accordingly.

Eve of course knew that Adam and herself had been fashioned the way they had been for a reason, namely so that they would be able to procreate. But, while she took it that this had not been intended to signify that her role would merely be that of a "courtesan", if Adam approached her with the suggestion that they start begetting children, she understood that, everything being equal, she would be at fault by being needlessly averse to the idea. In other words, she would "submit" to him. And, of course, Adam also would be under a similar obligation if she approached him with the same intention.

But now, as Eve was considering the different ways in which she could thwart the divine plan, it struck her that one way would be to rebuff Adam's approaches in the event that he decided not to join the rebellion. In other words, she would refuse to submit to him in the above regard. Citing Eve's diaries as his authority, Mjomba wrote that Eve told herself that, if she was prepared to stand up to the Prime Mover, who was Adam any way!

Eve reasoned that, even if Adam agreed to stick with her as a co-conspirator, there would almost certainly be occasions when "the lout" would be tempted to refuse to submit himself to her for his own selfish reasons. To deter him from doing that to her, she herself was going to think of clever ways of bluffing him, and pretending that she herself had valid reasons for not "submitting" to him. She considered herself a good actor, a much better one than Adam, for one; and she thought she was quite capable, for instance, of successfully feigning illness, or of making it appear as though it was an inopportune time for them to make love each time he made the "unwanted" approaches.

Adam was undoubtedly going to be a very disappointed man if he was going to take her for granted. There was absolutely nothing Adam could do, short of raping her, if she did not want to have his baby! And if he laid a hand on her with that intention, she would poison him. After administering "the portion" to him, she would then take her own life by drinking some of it herself so she would be all by herself on earth. Eve reasoned that, if 'it was not good that the man should be alone', by the same token it would not be good that she should remain in the world all by herself after she had played her part to getting rid this fellow who had described her (patronizingly in her view) as 'bone of my bones, and flesh of my flesh' in that fashion!

But she could also use a different tack to frustrate the divine plan. She could decide to have all the babies Adam wanted, but deliberately refuse to give them a good upbringing. She could in that way use her offspring as proxies through whom she would achieve the same end of derailing the divine plan! She noted that she had a whole range of options, and wondered if Adam, unpredictable man that he was, knew it too!

And so now, as if on cue, Eve had proceeded to outline to the man she very much wanted to be her consort many ingenious ways of avoiding conception, including the use of the chastity belt, as well as many ways of enhancing or alternatively permanently undermining the human reproductive process. Adam was not just impressed with Eve's arguments. He was surprised that Eve and himself commanded such clout regardless of whether they were going to continue to do everything to the Creator's greater honor and glory or otherwise.

Adam even noted that, unlike Lucifer and his band of fallen angels for whom actions and intentions comprised one and the same thing, their human nature allowed for a distinction. Indeed, the future of their relationship with the Creator depended not so much on the nature of their individual actions as on the intentions behind them. And it was precisely this aspect of their human nature that gave the couple apparent room for bargaining. Adam and Eve even had a lingering feeling that if their plan ever went awry, there just might be a chance to recant and quickly get back into the Creator's good books before it was too late.

Unlike the angelic beings that were all created in one and the same moment in eternity, humans could procreate and multiply over time. Adam and Eve accordingly thought they could justify relegating their issue to a secondary position under the new order they were proposing. It did not seem unreasonable or too far-fetched for them to contemplate setting themselves up as gods of some kind, and having their heirs venerate them as such. Mjomba had, accordingly, argued that sexuality featured in the eventual act of rebellion as Adam and Eve finally moved to consummate their diabolic plan even though the sinful act occurred in the spiritual realm.

It was as though the first couple did not foresee the serious consequences of their action, including the Creator's intention to stop restraining his other creatures ranging from lions, crocodiles and other mammals to reptiles and, more ominously, minute creatures like germs, viruses, and other parasites which were invisible to the naked eye and which could turn particularly deadly at a command from the Creator.

They also had to know that there could even be subsequent challenges to their own authority from within the family of human beings, as well as from other unknown dangers inherent in their decision to travel a route that no man before them had ever travelled. They could not be entirely sure, for instance, that in some corner of the universe, creatures of comparable or perhaps even superior intelligence existed that might attempt to flush them from the face of the earth on the orders of their Maker or for their own selfish ends, assuming they too were in revolt!

While Mjomba supposed that the faculty of reason of the first Man and Woman, unfettered as it was by concupiscence and other effects of sin, was indescribably sharp, making them incredibly smart and supremely intelligent, he also believed that they must have been an especially thick-skinned, obstinate and obdurate pair to have proceeded with the rebellion given what they knew. He also depicted them as daring, reckless and shortsighted in a most curious way. Citing "incontrovertible" evidence in the Rwenzori Prehistoric Diaries, Mjomba wrote that in their foolishness, Adam and Eve, discussed how, as free creatures, it would not be the last time they would reach out, pluck and eat fruit from the Tree of Knowledge.

Adam and Eve had every intention of making a habit of it, and they deluded themselves that they would silence their consciences thereby forever. To maximize and prolong the "happiness" and gratification they expected to derive from challenging the Prime Mover's authority, after plucking the fruit from the Tree of Knowledge, they planned to withdraw to a secluded place in the Garden of Eden - preferably some distance from the shrine which they had built in honor of the Creator in the days when their friendship with Him was strong and their faith in Him was rock solid - and they would take their time to enjoy it. They were, of course, determined not to waste any of the forbidden fruit's nourishing juices and especially its vaunted life giving plasma as they fed on it. And they were not going to let anything or anyone, be it a guardian angel or even the Prime Mover Himself, spoil their fun.

Yes, fun because everything they were going to do was really legitimate apart that is from their motives, which were wicked! The act of munching on the forbidden fruit was itself neither good nor bad. It was quite conceivable for Eve to mistakenly pluck fruit from the Tree of Knowledge, and to share it with her companion (Adam) without the latter suspecting that it was the forbidden fruit he was sampling. In the event, the Prime Mover would just have smiled and let it go. Their action would not have constituted a sin - not even a venial sin! Adam and Eve knew that much.

Their real intention was to counter the will of the Omnipotent and establish themselves as a viable alternative to Him in creation; and that spelled lots of fun. They were essentially planning to hijack the agenda of the Prime Mover and to make it their own; and how could that not be fun! But even though their sinful act would arise out of sordid scheming and was going to be premeditated in every way, they for their part were going to pretend, as they carried out their sordid act of defiance, that they were doing so in all innocence and without any ill intentions! And to make matters worse, they intended to do it in the name of humanity!

According to the Rwenzori Prehistoric Diaries, it was as Adam and Eve were contemplating their options that Lucifer suggested that there couldn't possibly be any harm in trying. Moreover, they would be like the Prime Mover. The suggestion by Beelzebub that they would be like the Prime Mover caused visions of invincible humans who could do virtually anything the Prime Mover did to invade their imagination. Humans who could also cause other humans to come into existence out of nothing even as the Prime Mover had caused them both to bounce into life out of the blue, and who could perhaps even successfully challenge the Prime Mover to a contest or a dual in which the winner took all! They certainly were capable of multiplying. The animals, birds, mammals, insects, and even vegetative life - in fact all the living things they had encountered during their short life spans - were capable of doing it! That would be a good start!

Of course, as rational beings, Adam and Eve now imagined that they could challenge the Prime Mover in a much more effective way by doing what the lower beings did instinctively in a more deliberate fashion and in accordance with their own plan, albeit a wicked plan that would be at cross purposes with the divine plan.

That would constitute a definite challenge to the Prime Mover! It was very tempting for Adam and Eve to start imagining that they not only would do a better job of imitating the Prime Mover than the lower creatures, but they could pose a real challenge to Him - or whatever force it was that had caused them and everything they saw around them to spring into existence out of nothing! Along with the idea that the Prime Mover could be effectively challenged, the devil had apparently instilled in Adam and Eve the idea that perhaps the idea of a Prime Mover only existed in their imagination, and that it might be possible that there was no such Being! Of course if it turned out that the Prime Mover only existed in their imagination, that would spoil the fun they definitely were looking forward to having as they kicked off their own homegrown rebellion.

Adam and Eve thought it was good thing that they did not yet have any issue because they could not be sure that the "louts" would join them in their plot. Since they were the sole representatives of the human race, their posterity did not have a choice in this matter - and that meant every one of their children and their children's children without any exception. It appeared as though everything was going to work to Adam and Eve's advantage.

To get a bigger kick out of their act of defiance, Adam and Eve intended to bring their faculty of the imagination to bear so that they would derive any amount of pleasure they wanted from feeding on the forbidden fruit. Actually, with the help of that faculty and the faculty of the will, they could literally do anything they fancied. And they could also create any amount of chaos on earth to make things hard for the Prime Mover - or so they thought! That was certainly going to entail lots of fun!

But that was not all - Adam and Eve went as far as imagining that every time they would sample the forbidden fruit, their experience on those later occasions would be as gratifying and "uplifting" as it would be the first time around! That would make their sin a real coup with an immortal dimension, and it would be a reward of sorts for the gamble they were taking - or so they thought. Mjomba wrote that they even joked that they were wasting time and needed to get going immediately - if for no other reason than that each time they sinned, it would be like they were doing it the first time. They imagined that their act of stealing fruit from the Tree of Knowledge and eating it would thus always be a delightful, fresh, and energizing experience they would never be bored with.

Foolishly, Adam and Eve imagined, according to Mjomba's thesis, that there would be no consequences for their despicable act in those circumstances. That, on the contrary, the successful act of sinning - or challenging the authority of the Prime Mover - would itself amount to a well-earned reward. They simply refused to heed their consciences which, according to Mjomba, were even then sending all sorts of signals to the effect that the first Man and Woman would be literally stung with guilt and shame in the aftermath of their ignoble deed.

What they did not suspect was that while a life of make believe and fantasy was possible during the time of their pilgrimage on earth, the self-deception could not be perpetuated indefinitely, and certainly not beyond the grave. Yes, grave! Adam and Eve knew that it was matter - changing matter - that informed their souls. That being the case, their "pilgrimage" on earth had to be subject to certain limitations, one of which was that they would move on to an afterlife! And, however that transition (from earth to the afterlife) was viewed, it still marked a very grave moment in their existence - a moment that ordinarily was going to see them ushered into the presence of the Prime Mover and a permanent, unchanging afterlife - what their descendants would refer to as "life beyond the grave".

There, stripped of the trappings of matter that made it possible for humans on earth to perpetuate the self-deception, they would be literally assailed by the realization that it was all a mirage. It definitely was going to come back to haunt Adam and Eve, perhaps even before they were ushered into their afterlife, that the preoccupation by humans that wasn't geared to their last end, had a definite price - a price not unlike that which an unfaithful spouse stood to pay at the end of time. In this particular case, Adam and Eve's acknowledgement memory of their inconstancy would itself become transformed into an unbearable scourge. It would be the driving force behind the clamor by their whole being for the permanent, unchanging and Perfect Good!

Autonomous individuals who suddenly found themselves scorned by the one and the only true and perfect lover they knew should have been theirs if they had not sought their satisfaction elsewhere and betrayed His trust in that way, they would now be more than glad to endure any amount of spiritual sufferings and misery - and, if possible, also physical pain - if that could distract them enough and ease their sense of loss and deprivation. Adam and Eve would realize that, in the afterlife, nothing could be more painful, humiliating and unsettling than to be taunted by a yawning emptiness that only the Perfect One could fill. If only they knew what would be in store for them if they ended up in a place where, deprived of the Perfect Good they knew was meant for them, they would be overwhelmed by a dreadful and unquenchable thirst that made one crave for the harshest self-punishment for not having focused on their last end during their earthly pilgrimage!

Just as Lucifer and his legion of disobedient angels fell for the temptation to be like gods who would hold sway in the ethereal world, Adam and Eve, according to Mjomba's thesis, thought that they could somehow get away with a challenge to the Creator's position in the earthly universe. If anything, the fact that the angels had already staged a rebellion before them made it even more tempting for Adam and Eve to try the same thing one more time. The sharp wit and intelligence Adam and Eve commanded made them capable of being really dare-devilish, Mjomba wrote.

Because they themselves were fashioned in the Creator's image, they were supposed to apply their exceptional grasp of philosophical and scientific ideas in the service of the Creator. But they were now involved in a plot to use these gifts in reaching out and harnessing the riches, not just of Planet Earth, but also of the myriad constellations of the planets and stars in ways that would make it possible for them to cut their losses on their certain eviction from the Garden of Eden.

They had to know that their action was going to leave them thus exposed in all sorts of ways, if only because both of them knew clearly that they owed their existence to the Prime Mover's selfless love. But the prospect of being regarded as gods to whom everything was owed by their offspring had apparently proved too much of a temptation! Mjomba also argued that, with their superior intelligence, the first Man and the first Woman imagined that they might be able to devise ways and means of neutralizing the dangers the lower animal species, reptiles, germs and viruses might pose.

Mjomba, letting his imagination run a little wild, had theorized that the faithlessness of Adam and Eve had finally reached its peak and that the father and mother of mankind had "crossed the Rubicon" just as they were consummating their marriage. Coinciding with her first "dark night of the soul" ever, Eve's wedding night had been anything but blissful. A rebel, both *de facto* and *de jure*, she had suddenly found herself stripped and deprived of the grace into which she had been "born" and of the benefits ensuing there from. In the immediate aftermath of her act of rebellion and her determination to put not God but her own self-love first in whatever she did, Eve had suddenly found herself vulnerable and exposed to the intrigue of both Satan and Man, not to mention the elements. And, for the first time ever, she had seen a need to cover her delicate figure with apparel of some kind.

As Mjomba described it, Eve and her second half knew the instant they lost their innocence that they were going to "die the death"! But that was not all. As the light of God's grace faded away, they saw that they could not face the Creator against whom they had sinned. They had accordingly stumbled blindly for the exits from the Garden of Eden only to find none existed.

They should have known better because the Garden of Eden, within whose confines they had made their abode until hitherto and the scene of their original sin, continued to be a part of Planet Earth and unchanged. What had changed was Man who had tried to usurp the power of the Prime Mover. And it was also then that they realized that their faculties of the will and the intellect, which had played key roles in their act of rebellion, and on which they had banked so much for implementing their evil scheme had they succeeded in pulling off the ill-fated deal, were irrevocably blunted and crippled, victims of the shock waves of their falling out with their Creator.

The first Man and Woman were shocked to discover that their mental impairment was permanent. In addition to the fact that logical acts by man could not be guaranteed, there was now also no guarantee that humans could be counted on to think logically. That was because man was now inclined to give precedence to thoughts that promoted self-interest as

489

opposed to thoughts that were objectively sound, sensible and sublime. In practical terms, that translated in the pursuit of things that were *gratifying* over things reason suggested were *legitimate* regardless of the benefits in the short, or even long, term. Even though man's survival depended on the amount of knowledge that he accumulated and applied, the sad fact was that the human learning process itself was now introverted.

As Mjomba noted in his thesis, these were developments that would for one snarl the fostering of many a human child in the days to come. Many descendants of Adam and Eve would grow up impaired and suffering from all sorts of neuroses as a direct result. Hovering on the verge of lunacy themselves, it gave Eve and her consort little consolation to know that their ever-forgiving Creator would not hold them to any irresponsible deeds committed by them from that moment on by virtue of insanity.

To cut a long story short, Eve had realized that there were inherent risks in putting all her trust and confidence in Adam. She knew full well that she herself had just cheated on her Creator by vowing to leave open the possibility of using the faculties she was endowed with - the intellect, the faculty of the will and the faculty of the imagination, the sense faculties and, of course, her carnal feelings as well - for her own exaltation rather than the Creator's. And she was of course aware that Adam, acting in concert, had also betrayed Him in a similar manner. She quickly concluded that she could not really trust Adam all that much after that.

And now, suddenly prone to misunderstand, she thought that she observed in Adam's gestures evidence of a nature that had suddenly turned mean and cruel. She could have sworn that her second half would probably go chasing other dames and cheating on her were it not for the fact that she was the only woman around. His tendency to look the other way and avoid her gaze seemed to be evidence enough of that. And perhaps worst of all, Eve was already harboring genuine fears to the effect that her "husband" could even kill her on some pretext, an act that, Mjomba noted, would have been tantamount to genocide.

Adam, in Eve's view, no longer seemed to be the congenial and tender loving man to whom she had pledged her loyalty in the moments before they fell from grace as everlasting wife. Wondering if she could ever be delivered from the beast into which Adam appeared to have turned in the twinkling of an eye, she frequently found herself lost in her thoughts and did not even bother to hide her state of mind from Adam who caught her in her reverie on more than one occasion.

Before they fell from grace, Eve had been sure that if they made love, it would be a sacred act performed without any self-interest. Adam had felt the same way. Their act of love would have mirrored the Prime Mover's selfless act of creation. And now, with their fall from grace, their perception of the world,

491

previously unfettered and unadulterated as well as objective, had become narrow and limited; and, apart from suggestions of the devil, it was only what appealed to their lower instincts that caught their attention.

Adam and Eve were now inclined to sin, and could not act guilelessly or innocently. The realization that they were incapable of doing anything on their own that could be characterized as good came as a terrible shock and made Adam and Eve cringe. They blamed each other for their terrible mistake.

The world as they had known it up until then vanished from before their eyes, replaced by something that was entirely novel. Everything about it was intriguing, if only because, with their ties to the only Creator they had known and to whom they owed everything including their very existence cut and permanently severed, they now felt quite lonely and isolated. Stripped of the Prime Mover's grace, they now also felt exposed and naked both spiritually and physically. The Garden of Eden, which had up until then been synonymous with the universe, suddenly no longer appeared so. Mjomba had both Adam and Eve now imagining that there could be enemies lurking out there both in the bowels of earth and in the skies yonder. But, seeing themselves unfit and unworthy to be in the Creator's presence, their first impulse, according to the thesis, was to flee.

Mjomba, accordingly, had Adam and Eve stampeding for what they thought were the exits from the transformed Garden of Eden, albeit only in their imagination. This was even though everything pointed to the fact that the original Garden of Eden was anything but a gated community. Deep down in their hearts, they not only wished they had not exercised their freedom of choice as a result of which they had gone against the will of their Creator, but they even wished that they had been created without their gifts of the intellect and the will and only with instincts, like the lower animals.

In the meantime, overwhelmed with disgust and disbelief, Eve had cut herself loose from Adam's grip and accused him of being a selfish, dissembling and wretched man and a crook who was out to exploit her for his own ends. For his part, Adam had recoiled at the treachery and cunning that, according to him, Eve had employed to draw him into an irrevocable marriage bond, only to deny him the satisfaction she had lead him to believe was going to be his for the asking. According to Mjomba's expose, the seeds for infidelity, marriage break-ups, prostitution, rape, incest, and other evils like hypocrisy were also sown at that truly tragic moment in the tempestuous history of humankind.

Mjomba had concluded his thesis with two quite astounding suggestions. One was to the effect that the Creator's promise of redemption played a critical part in helping the father and mother of the human race to remain sane and not succumb to the traumatic experience of being banished from the Garden of Eden. The other was to the effect that, notwithstanding that demonstration of the Creator's infinite love and mercy, Adam and Eve frequently chose to overlook the Prime Mover's promise of a Savior and, in the ensuing frustration, threw all caution to the wind and betrayed Him time and again by doing things not to His greater glory and honor, but their own.

It all tragically started, according to Mjomba, with Adam and Eve feeling very self-confident, and thinking that they could trust themselves rather than the grace of the Prime Mover to stay out of trouble. Mjomba wrote that Adam and Eve found themselves betraying the Prime Mover again and again as a result of being too trustful of themselves, and neglecting things like prayer and mortification; and that it was only after they had indulged themselves and discovered - too late - that temporal joys were indeed ephemeral and passing that they would nudge themselves back into the realization that it was unwise to be too trustful of themselves or to neglect prayer and fasting.

Mjomba wrote that Adam and Eve committed sins all over again even though they had both "accepted" the promised Deliverer in the exact same way Simeon, John the Baptist, Simon Peter, and others would accept Him and had promised full cooperation. According to Mjomba's thesis, they certainly knew that they would be deceiving themselves if they started imagining that they were safe from the Evil One, let alone "saved". And any suggestion that one became "saved" merely by "accepting" the Deliverer however firmly would have been rebuffed by the first couple.

PART 9: THE SEMINARY BROTHERHOOD

Reflecting back on life at St. Augustine's Seminary, Christian Mjomba could not help marvelling at the fact that that was indeed the place to which he had been attracted as a young man, and to which he had even grown endeared. He was surprised that his mental journey not only was transcending time and space, but was also occurring in what appeared to be the twinkling of an eye.

The strange spell, under which he was labouring and which was undoubtedly also responsible for the sudden onslaught of sullenness and gloom, now steered his attention into a slightly different direction. Without electing to do so, Mjomba found himself focusing his attention on the fact that at the time he commenced work on his book, he and his class were at an advanced stage in their preparations for the subdeaconate and the deaconate, the "major" orders that preceded ordination to the holy priesthood.

Mjomba noted with a faint but discernible smile that, amid all that, he had harbored the rather weird notion that he had made an important discovery pertaining to the phenomenon of insanity. He had succeeded in doing so while working secretly but persistently on the dossier on Innocent Kintu, a fellow seminarian and also tribesman who had been taken ill with a strange ailment. Mjomba actually believed that his discovery was likely to make psychiatry turn a new leaf!

Frowning, Mjomba thought about his earlier years as a junior seminarian and recalled with nostalgia that he had been determined from his earliest days to carefully nurture his vocation to the priesthood, and that he had easily found seminary life fascinating. Later, when the opportunity to contribute to human knowledge came beckoning, he had taken it in stride just as easily. With plenty of time allotted to such things as study and meditation at the senior seminary, enabling him to mature relatively quickly in those favorable surroundings, it did indeed appear as if everything had been mapped out in advance by Providence.

In the junior seminary, Mjomba, the son of simple Welekha peasants, had received what amounted to a classic education as he progressed from Preparatory Class (or Prep as it was called) to Low Figures, High Figures, and onto Grammar, Syntax, Poetry and finally Rhetoric. That education included world history, European literature, Latin and even some Greek. Mjomba particularly enjoyed Julius Caesar's *De Bello Gallico* and, of all things, Ovid. In the senior seminary, as he was introduced, along with his compatriots, to Scholastic Philosophy, Canon Law, Moral and Dogmatic Theology, and Biblical Exegesis amongst others at the senior seminary, the speed with which Mjomba grew in self-actualization had actually known no bounds.

Mjomba had always felt fortunate that his ambition to serve God had put him in line for what amounted to a first class education. He had been

497

particularly happy that the rector at St. Augustine's, to assure his candidates for the priesthood a well-rounded education, on a regular basis invited religious scholars of other schools of thought to address the student body. The visiting scholars included Buddhists, Hindus, Moslems, and even followers of Confucius.

Ever a keen participant in the ensuing discussions, Mjomba had been struck by the profound insights that this dialogue afforded any one who was eager to expand his knowledge. As a result of the exposure to the wider metaphysical realms, he had developed a special interest in the unique and rather extensive collection of materials on world philosophies and religions in the seminary library. The availability of those materials enabled him to pursue his own independent investigation of various theories propagated by the philosophers of the orient and the premises underlying those theories.

But Mjomba had not been entirely happy in certain other respects. Although he kept mum about it, he had gradually begun to lament, albeit in silence, the fact that the seminary's own contemplative practices did not incorporate things like Yoga and the techniques of Transcendental Meditation as taught by the great Maharishi - at least not directly. And while he, like everyone else in the seminary, believed that the writings of thinkers and philosophers of the orient contained many erudite things, it seemed to him, in so far as oriental wisdom went, that non-Christian faiths, Islam for example, had incorporated more of it than had Christianity.

Mjomba was further disappointed that the Church's definition of Christian did not include Moslems, although they accepted much of the Old Testament, including the vast majority of the prophets referred to therein, and even though they revered the Lord Jesus as Messiah and Savior of the world. In any event, since Christ came to save all men, such a narrow definition seemed hopelessly out of sync with the thrust of the message of redemption.

It bothered Mjomba that the Catholic Church went on to count members of many other groups whose doctrines were admittedly outlandish among the world's body of Christians. And even then, he himself wasn't so sure how an "outlandish" doctrine might be defined. He sometimes wondered what Buddhists, Moslems, Hindus and others thought of the Catholic Church's doctrines!

Actually, since all religions were God-given by definition, Mjomba thought the notions of true and false or outlandish religions, and the distinctions made by preachers between different faiths on those grounds, themselves had a ring of untruth, certainly unreality, about them. Mjomba sometimes wondered what things would be like in this former Garden of Eden if everybody woke up one morning to discover that there was actually one single, acknowledged True Religion to which every soul on the earth subscribed without question.

He noted that, by implication, every member of the human race would either be living in Elysium or in the New Jerusalem, and would accordingly not be in need of salvation. Or, as the banished but incorrigible descendants of Adam and Eve, they would all, without a single exception, be living lives that put them beyond the pale of salvation in that imaginary Utopia, as would be evident from the level of interest in the subject of religion. But it would also be a Utopia that also assumed that humans had a nature that was completely different from their present one - the nature of either angels (sinless beings) or of demons (long lost souls)!

The absence of a multiplicity of religions would in effect make all these bickering preachers redundant! Mjomba's conclusion was that it was important that all religions, without exception, were treated as God-given and fully respected by everyone. Actually, with the exception of the few individuals whose practice of religion was truly heroic, all other so-called believers or supposedly God-fearing people, regardless of their religious persuasion, in Mjomba's view worshipped mere personalized images of the Deity they were supposed to worship, and could therefore be said to be idolaters.

The fact that most people's idea of the Supreme Being was so hazy seemed to be proof enough of that. But the many heinous crimes committed through the ages in the name of religion represented, for Mjomba, an even more compelling reason for his conclusion that these people, despite what they said, actually worshipped something other than the Supreme Being, and consequently laid a false claim on being godly people.

Noting that preachers liked to brag about being in the "business of saving souls", Mjomba wrote that by far the vast majority were in that business for the money - period. And they wanted the *status quo* in the Church to continue because it served their purposes quite well. In order to rake in the money faster, they went to great pains to show how their "ministry" was so unique! In the process, they had diversified and tailored the highly marketable product called "Key to Heaven" to suit the whims and desires of every Dick and Harry - as if that were possible!

Mjomba decried the fact that many unwary souls in search of the Truth invariably became ensnared in the schemes of those marketing geniuses. But in their haste to use "Peter's Pence" to enrich themselves, those who "owned" those "ministries" and the preachers whose job was to attract and retain a large following, all forgot something.

According to Mjomba, while all sorts of people had set up ministries to "preach the Word" and had established churches for the purpose of "ministering to their flocks", they all conveniently forgot that the first question they themselves would be asked on exiting this life for the afterlife would be: "You and others in your profession - why did you, if you were genuinely interested in saving souls through preaching the Word - not begin by sitting down, not just with your 'Christian' buddies, but with Hindus,

Buddhists, Moslems and others, and agreeing or at least attempting to agree on the one most fundamental thing, namely what that Word was. Did you find that hard to do because it would have inevitably meant sacrificing your money-spinning machine or so-called 'ministry' in the process? And you claim that you actually performed so many 'miracles' in my name. Did it not strike you that the very first miracle you needed to *pray* for, especially given your unflinching faith in me according to your own avowals, ought to have been that you - despite your totally wrong motives - might get to know me and also get to understand that the Word or Truth is indivisible? Or did you - and your buddies - look upon this as just another way of making a living? *Diversifying* the Gospel message and *marketing* it to different audiences *using tips you picked up in Biz School*? And now, tell Me - would you go back and do what you did all over again if you were given an opportunity?"

As he worked through his thesis, Mjomba wondered if there was some way of putting it that would jolt the world's religious leaders to some action in that regard and save them face on Judgement Day in the process!

But Mjomba acknowledged that, a dissembling lot, it was not entirely inconceivable that if the Deliverer were to suddenly appear in person in their midst, these selfsame preachers would do everything within their power to keep Him out of the *Church* He Himself founded and over which they claimed to be guardians! Mjomba clarified what he meant by "Church" in that context, namely the Mystical Body of Christ, which included the crowds those preachers claimed as their "flock"...yes, their flock, and theirs alone!

Mjomba wrote that this, sadly, was well within the realm of possibilities, particularly given the fact that many Christian "churches" had already decided to have no place in their liturgy for some of the sacraments the Deliverer instituted with such solemnity, among them the Sacrament of the Blessed Eucharist. Mjomba lamented that humans had not stopped at distorting the nature of the Church, herself a sacrament of the Deliverer's action at work in her through the mission of the Holy Ghost, in their perception of it and, after discarding some of the sacraments themselves, could be counted on to try to get rid of His messengers as well as Himself as the end drew near.

Mjomba could not think of a Christian denomination that could claim unequivocally that the Church it represented had always been "a place of prayer for all nations" (Isaiah 56:7). Perhaps no individual church denomination was meant to be "a place of prayer for all nations" in the same way the temple in Jerusalem had been at the time the Deliverer walked in and over-turned the tables of the merchants who operated from there, Mjomba wrote!

Obviously a believer in the existence of God, Mjomba thought that the most potent argument for His existence related to the Last Judgement. In Mjomba's perception, given the evils humans did to one another, nothing would make sense if there were no Supreme Being who would avenge the miseries suffered by people at the hands of others. Even so, Mjomba had been tempted on more than one occasion to suppose that there not only had to be many gods, but also many heavens to accommodate the many self-proclaimed prophets who were irreconcilable when the world, exactly as in the beginning, finally came to an end with a big bang! It would actually have made a lot of sense, he once told himself, if someone had come forward to point out that an important text, essential to understanding the nature of humans, had for some reason been eliminated from the Book of Genesis in the course of the centuries: "And God said: Let there be many gods - and also many heavens!"

A heaven for the wicked...

As if the attempt to make the all good and all-knowing Prime Mover responsible for putting the idea of idolatry in the heads of humans was not atrocious enough, Mjomba, a virtual slave of his own imagination, also concocted the notion of a "hell in heaven"! He even told himself that it wasn't an entirely implausible idea. Given the fact that every generation without exception had had its peculiar crop of self-justified but decidedly sick people who claimed a monopoly on heaven for themselves and their followers, Mjomba thought the notion of a "hell in heaven" made a lot of sense. And that was even before the myriad truly evil characters responsible for the many crimes committed against humanity in the course of human history, and many of whom were even glorified as heroes in history books, were brought into the picture.

Mjomba imagined that these "dissembling" individuals, when they finally departed this world for the next, went to the "heaven of their dreams" all right; a heaven that, in these cases, also had a provision for the hell these folks so richly deserved! When thinking about this particular category of people, the contrasting images which crowded Mjomba's mind ranged from government functionaries and their lackeys who maltreated others under the guise of performing a public service to hypocritical members of religious orders whose deeds of commission and omission caused others severe mental anguish.

A heaven for the wicked! The idea was not really as asinine as it sounded at first. Satan, clever devil that he (or she) was, surely would not leave those who had faithfully done his bidding in this life completely in the lurch in the next. In Mjomba's view, the idea of a heaven for the wicked - albeit one that ultimately was hellish - was a difficult one to dismiss as completely preposterous.

That was not to say it wasn't a frightening thought! It rankled Mjomba to think that the wicked might indeed have a place of refuge where they could find solace of some kind. That in turn raised the possibility, even though remote, that conditions in the hellish heaven just might be tolerable; and, perhaps, even tolerable enough to enable the wicked to gloat with pleasure over their wicked deeds through all eternity! It was like giving them the last laugh.

Mjomba wished that his imagination didn't devise notions of that sort. But he could not stop the grotesque images from invading his mind, and taking note of them at least allowed new ones to take the place of old ones, a circumstance which made it possible for him to avoid being overly engrossed by any individual image.

Even though he did not use it much, Mjomba just loved the expression "devil incarnate" very much, and he believed that many of the characters that would end up in the "hellish heaven" generally fit the bill pretty well. But especially, he thought, the following classes of people. Those unscrupulous and usually also invisible power brokers in government administrations around the world who were primarily responsible for putting in place inequitable policies that violated the rights of those in society not in a position to defend themselves; merchants and the hired guns of greedy corporations who had no scruples whatsoever about using the so-called corporate clout of their clients to blackmail members of the public into parting with their hard-earned cash and other possessions; and preachers who went out of their way to hood-wink the gullible members of their congregations by scaring the hell out of them while enriching their coffers.

Having noted that the idea of a "hellish heaven"

was indeed plausible, Mjomba had inevitably stopped to consider a different but related idea, namely the idea of a "heavenly hell". Unlike the former idea which was merely plausible, the latter notion seemed a given. As Mjomba imagined it, after enduring what was mostly a hell-on-earth in resignation, good men and women departed this world only to find themselves unexpectedly propelled into a place that defied description - truly a heavenly hell! Wondering, as he often did, about which heaven would be more crowded, Mjomba had little doubt that it was the former, and he sometimes worried that, while he had the free exercise of his will, he could easily find himself consigned to the camp of the devils incarnate on Judgement Day. And that genuine fear prevented him from laughing off the idea of a hellish heaven and its parallel notion of a heavenly hell every time he felt like doing so.

Mjomba dearly wished that he was wrong - that his reading of the situation couldn't possibly be correct! That, after all was said and done, the bad guys received their just punishment, and the good guys their just reward, and the bad guys the punishment they so richly deserved. It would be just dreadful if there was even the remotest possibility of an order in which evil was rewarded. That would be an order in which the Diabolos, not the Prime Mover, effectively called the shots instead of being punished. That was a situation that was plain unacceptable - a contradiction in terms. And if that were the case, it would mean that devilish humans would not get what they deserved upon their departure for the afterlife.

The fact was that evil people themselves had a way of making it appear as if they were the wizened ones and couldn't therefore have it wrong. They had a way of making it appear as if the good guys were the stupid ones and, as such, were wasting the precious time they had on their hands - the time they could be using to fulfil themselves even at the expense of others and become actualized. And then there was the fact that Adam and Eve had demonstrated so early on in the history of humankind that one could do as one pleased, and still thrive in this world. Indeed, if you looked around, you were much more likely to find that it was the bad guys who were enjoying and in control, and that it was the good guys who were being exploited and at the receiving end.

But if it were to happen that it was the bad guys, not the good guys, who would end up as the ultimate winners, it would first of all make a complete mockery of the good old maxim that *charity was capable of concealing a multitude of sins* - the maxim that was supposed to demonstrate that there was some benefit to remaining decent or the good guy. But that adage itself implied, Mjomba noted, that charity or plain decency was a rare commodity, since the saying would otherwise be of no value. Mjomba felt a measure of relief as he noted that the first human beings had been thrown out of the Garden of Eden for acting atrociously. It wouldn't have been right if they had done what they did and just got away scot-free.

Even so, such sentiments seemed right on and logical, Mjomba wasn't sure that he wouldn't get into trouble for suggesting that human beings deserved everything they got for deviating from the path of righteousness. Mjomba could not help shuddering at the thought that his ideas, if expressed by him publicly, would put him at loggerheads with his Church. This was because his Church, in step with other denominations, taught that it alone was the official custodian of revealed Truth. And, here he was, confusing the situation by suggesting that the Diabolos might have a role in determining events that would transpire on the last day.

There were other aspects of Catholic doctrine that also riled the former seminarian. A keen student of Church History, Mjomba was actually scandalized by what he regarded as an impious sense of self-righteousness on which he blamed the desire of many in Christendom in the Middle Ages to see foes excommunicated and barred from activities of the so-called visible Church.

It was his expectation that sometime in the future, perhaps even in his lifetime, his Church would come around and apologize for its role in the break-up of Christendom, among other things! He thought such a development was inevitable for a number of reasons. After Adam and Eve had been cast out from the Garden of Eden after they had sinned, it simply did not make any sense, now that the Redeemer had come as promised, for anybody to claim that the Church was for some people and not for others.

Even though the Messiah condemned the actions of Judas Iscariot, the man who betrayed him to his enemies, in the strongest terms, there was no evidence that even he was excommunicated from the visible Church. But could it be that Judas was in fact excommunicated, but it just happens to be one of the many things that the scriptures, which were not intended to include all revealed truth, skipped?

While Mjomba admired Peter for being such a natural turncoat, eager to demonstrate his loyalty by striking out with his sword and cutting off the ear of Malchus, a servant of Caiaphas, the high priest, ear one moment and emphatically denying that he was one of the Savior's disciples in another, he found a lot to admire in the betrayer.

Here was a man who had, first of all, left all to follow in the foot-steps of the Messiah, volunteered to risk his life by being the one to keep the group's purse, and who was so filled with anguish over his role in the fate of the Savior he not only hastened to return to those who were actually guilty of handing Him over to the Roman imperialists the proceeds of his crime; and who deemed his own life not worth living after failing to persuade them not to proceed as they planned. Mjomba also thought that Judas was very much on the Savior's mind when He prayed to His heavenly Father for the forgiveness of His enemies, affirming that they did not, indeed, know what they were doing.

But Mjomba was forced to acknowledge, that the rampant prejudices that prevented the descendants of Adam and Eve, regardless of the

510

peculiar circumstances of their birth, from recognizing the Deliverer of humankind and also finding their way into his *Ecclesia* – the present-day Arch of Noah – were also responsible for preventing humans to see that all sinners, not just the Judas Iscariot, were betrayers of the Deliverer along with Judas Iscariot just as they all sinners, just the Jews, had a hand in sending the Deliverer to His grisly death on the cross.

With regard to the original matter under discussion, Mjomba noted that rifts in matters of doctrine in fact abounded in the early Church, and that they never deteriorated into any excommunications"! But perhaps at a certain point in time "charity", that virtue that (according to Peter) "covereth a multitude of sins", did in fact become rarer and rarer among churchmen, making the Reformation inevitable. Talking about charity, Mjomba often wondered how a person like Peter who was so prone to bungling would have fared at the hands of churchmen of a later age!

Given what befell Joan of Arc, it wasn't difficult for Mjomba to imagine what might have been the fate of Peter had he been a contemporary of the Spanish saint. And there would have been less likelihood for a person who had participated in the incarceration and murder of Christians like Saul making a mark as an Apostle of the Gentiles or anything else. With respect to people like Mary Magdalene and her likes, Mjomba wondered if any amount of public penance could have been enough in a different age to persuade anyone that they no longer posed a danger to society.

It did not really surprise Mjomba that, on their arrival in Africa, Christian missionaries had promptly denounced the ancient beliefs of his people as satanic. If they believed in the supernatural and in *Katonda*, *Were*, *Mwenyezi Mungu* or in a Creator who went by some other name, that was automatically witchcraft. Any belief that recognised the after-life was *animism* - and, of course, infinitely worse than the worship by Romans and Greeks of statues, when they were not actually treating the dictators loading over them as divinities. And if demons had been human, it would undoubtedly have been Africa from where they would have emerged.

What surprised Mjomba, above all, was the particularly virulent manner in which Westerners regarded Africa as the source of all bad things! Mjomba also made reference to a later generation of "scholars" who usually hailed from segregated America, and for whom all things African proved just ideal for airing racially biased views. Mjomba wrote that it was especially the latter who seemed bent on tracing weird practices prevailing in "advanced" societies like mass suicides, human sacrifices, and all manner of cults, *et cetera* to Africa. Mjomba wrote that these creative and rather uncanny individuals, following their treks through Africa on foot and on camel, produced best sellers in which their historic "discoveries", suitably embellished with some of the most interesting anecdotes, were laid out.

It was clearly a magnificent way of becoming

an instant authority on Africa that people like Dr. Livingstone and others set in motion! A trek through that "dark continent" on foot and camel! Mjomba added that, with travel made easier with the invention of air planes, it was no wonder that all the deadly diseases that afflicted Europe and America like Malaria (as if there were no Malaria carrying mosquitoes on other continents), the West Nile virus (which was evident from the name given to that virus), the AIDS virus and others had been traced back to Africa.

Mjomba worried that may be the Mad Cow disease discovered in Europe would also eventually be traced back to the "Dark Continent" as Africa was, apparently, still regarded by some folks in Europe and America on the sly. It was, according to him, quite possible that there might be some people who might try, even at that late stage, to re-write history and place the origins of the black plague which ravaged Europe in those olden times in places in Africa that Westerners of that era did not know existed.

Given the extent of the misinformation, the outright ignorance and the deep-seated prejudices, Christians in the new world in particular, Mjomba wrote, had reason to be apprehensive about the integrity of the "Church's teachings". It was prudent to be apprehensive because, since the Church's inauguration on the day of Pentecost, its teachings had been manipulated and exploited for personal ends by all manner of people with all sorts of motives, Mjomba declared. There was the fact that Christians the world over were now permanently burdened with the cost of Christmas trees, a relic from Europe's idolatrous past, to cite just one example. But, according to him, the fact that some of the worst human rights abusers in human history not only had burst in on the world scene equipped with ideologies that were firmly rooted in Christianity and who were themselves Christians appeared to confirm his view that it was critically important to be apprehensive on that score.

While admitting that unity among the Prime Mover's chosen people (by which Mjomba understood everyone whom the Prime Mover had chosen to bring into being) was a major concern even before the Deliverer left Mother Earth to return to His Father on Ascension Day, Mjomba wrote that, in addition to having to contend with divisiveness in their local churches, Christians in the New World had also to deal with divisions that had been originally fomented in the West, and had now become a permanent feature of Christendom. He claimed that the Church in Africa was saddled with the cumulative consequences of Western schisms and heresies - schisms and heresies that might not have arisen in a different cultural and/or social setting.

Noting that the apostles, including Peter who had denied the Deliverer several times when He needed the support of his band of disciples most, were human, Mjomba supposed that the successors to the twelve apostles also were human. That was why they had evidently made mistakes in judgement

514

over time throughout the Church's history. Mjomba wrote that some of those "apostles", from time immemorial, have exuded an aura of self-importance and outright arrogance - as if they were co-judges with the Deliverer, not people who were sent to minister. And when they were not involved in scandal, they acted so self-righteously, you would think that they themselves did not need to be forgiven seven times seven times a day like everyone else.

Others brooked no criticism - as if they too were infallible, not just the Pontiff of Rome when he was speaking *ex cathedra*! Mjomba hastened to add, with emphasis, that the purpose of his analysis was not to lay blame for human errors contributing to disunity in God's Church, but rather to throw additional light on the specific nature of that problem and to trace it back to its source, namely the Evil Genius.

On the question of beliefs being satanic, Mjomba argued in his thesis that, throughout the ages, Africans seemed better informed than, say, the Greeks who used to fabricate idols from stone only to quickly turn around and venerate them! That was a world of a difference from making a hypothesis that spirits survived upon the death of humans, and that they might be lurking in trunks of two hundred year old trees or in the vicinity of graveyards, and acting accordingly!

Mjomba wrote that even though he still considered himself a Christian and a Catholic at that, he did not really see very much difference between the Deity worshipped in the West and the Deity his

515

Wazunda ancestors worshipped. May be it all boiled down to labels: Were, the all-knowing, life-giving Wind for whom the people of Zunda-land reserved the greatest respect and honor, versus the Trinity of the Western world for instance!

When the Wazunda went hunting in the forest, planted crops, celebrated a good harvest or the coming of age of their youth with feasting and dancing, or did anything involving two or more members of the community, they did it to the greater glory of the life-giving Wind. Now, that seemed a distinctly more impressive form of worship than the Christian worship that, for the most part, started and ended at the church doorstep. That was what missionaries in their ignorance no doubt regarded as diabolic. And they had unfortunately succeeded in persuading everyone, including the Wazunda themselves, that this was in fact the case!

With theology textbooks making only negative references to animism, as the religion of his forefathers was now officially labeled, the fact that it was pregnant with many erudite things had been lost sight of. The doctrines of Buddhism, Islam and Hinduism fared distinctly better in this regard even though they too were regarded by Westerners as outlandish. The fact that the latter religions one and all still boasted followers whose numbers run into the millions did not seem to matter in the least.

Mjomba had often let his imagination run wild as he pondered these things, and he had at times wondered if Christianity would not one day be completely eclipsed by these other religions as the number of their followers grew and multiplied! And, talking about being eclipsed, Mjomba would have vouched that the number of practicing Christians in the West had already been eclipsed by the number of Europeans and Americans who professed agnosticism!

But it had been with respect to African customs and traditions that Mjomba had found most fault with his Church. Whereas Christianity in general seemed to operate on the premise that native customary practices in Africa, when not steeped in animism - and "debased" thereby - were good for nothing, Islam, for one, held many of those practices in esteem, its positions on the role of women in society and on polygamy being cases in point.

And then, even though Islam made more rather than less demands on its African converts in other respects than did Christianity, it was a religion that was, surprisingly, well regarded on the African continent. That Christianity continued, despite the odds stacked against it, to draw into its fold the number of followers it did, was certainly something that could be said in its favor on the other hand. But it still remained inexplicable.

Far from quenching Mjomba's thirst for knowledge about the strange world in which he had found himself, these excellent opportunities for discovery apparently only kindled it. This was particularly so with regard to the effect of the new social order on the lives of individuals in his Wazunda tribal society.

PART 10: UNKNOWN DISEASE WITH NO KNOWN CURE

The changes just then sweeping the region, far from being confined to the religious sphere alone, were having a far-reaching impact in the cultural, political, and economic spheres as well. An offspring of a generation whose lives straddled the pre-colonial and post-colonial era himself, Mjomba could not really help being curious about the way people on the continent were adapting to the stupendous changes which seemed to be taking place around them all the time.

Even though the changing social infrastructure seemed to be working to the advantage of the populace at large - at least to the extent that East Africans were being introduced to things like a money economy and modern industrialization, Mjomba had no doubt about the fact some sections of the populace were being adversely affected. There was of course the tiny but powerful elite - the "black Europeans" - for whom the new social order was a boon of untold proportions. It was also pretty obvious which grouping he himself belonged to.

One development which Mjomba found particularly unsettling pertained to "Brain Death", the mysterious disease which was responsible for reducing, first, Andrea Mkicha, a childhood friend, and then Innocent Kintu, a fellow member of the seminary brotherhood at St. Augustine's, to "vegetables". It was the strangest disease ever to strike sub-Saharan

Africa. After it struck, in addition to transforming its victims such that he or she could no longer recognize previous acquaintances, it also caused them to completely disregard everything from the need for nourishment to the importance of personal hygiene.

And then this hitherto unknown disease with no known cure targeted the "most promising" folks, which meant the so-called "best and brightest" members of society's tiny elite. Because it was these who also usually scooped up the available scholarships and fellowships to study abroad when they did not take up the few available places at institutions of higher learning in the region, there was a growing suspicion that the dread disease was in fact being "imported" from Europe and America! The fact that the disease's victims were mostly members of well-to-do families who had the most contact with Westerners appeared to confirm that suspicion.

It seemed such a waste that the victims of the disease tended to be individuals who were close to completing advanced studies in their specialization or at the apex of successful academic careers. And as some of those who had gone off to study in Europe and America returned "brain dead" - that was how ordinary Wazunda folks described the strange disease and also how it got its name - young people, in a new and extraordinary development, had begun to shirk overseas study opportunities.

Mjomba had been very much aware of the fact that he himself belonged to the country's emerging elite. But the other and, perhaps even more important fact, that he had grown up surrounded by illiteracy on a monumental scale, had never been lost on him. In spite of it, or perhaps even because of it, apart from his desire to succeed in life, his next most pressing ambition which he had developed along the way was to learn as much as possible about other people, especially those the society he lived in now tended to marginalize.

Mjomba had always suspected that it was this strange combination of his desire to succeed in life on the one hand and his desire to understand the plight of the disadvantaged members of society that had eventually landed him in the seminary. But he could not rule out other motives, like for instance his desire to meet the challenge which seminary life posed, including things like life-long celibacy. He had often wondered if there was any difference between a yearning to prove one-self and striving to learn something for learning's sake.

Talking about yearning for knowledge for its own sake, Mjomba sometimes longed that he had lived at the time of St. Augustine when, so it was said, earning the qualification of Doctor of Philosophy meant you actually knew everything there was to be known about everything that had been discovered! The fact that this eminent "father of the Church" hailed from Hippo, the ancient North African city, made him more than a father of the Church. It automatically made the "Doctor of the Church", as Augustine was also known, Mjomba's mentor as well!

It was, in a way, funny that the phrase "Doctor

of Philosophy" also summed up, and rather succinctly for that matter, what the words "traditional medicine man" conveyed to Mjomba. "PhD" seemed to epitomize everything that a medicine-man in traditional African society was supposed to be. In addition to practicing the art of healing, he too was expected to know everything that there was to be known about everything that had been discovered!

Mjomba had often come close to agreeing with those who thought that there was something definitely suspect with Western education, and who accordingly argued that being under the tutelage of the medicine men was a far better proposition than going off to Europe or America in pursuit of "paper" qualifications.

While he had been aware that those who went to study abroad invariably developed "ivory tower" mentalities as they were called, he was not aware that those who pursued traditional wisdom got into any sort of mental fixations; and certainly none approximating an "ivory tower" mentality! Still, even though Mjomba was concerned at the time about the possibility that Westerners might actually not be as sophisticated and erudite as they looked on the surface, his thoughts in that regard remained just that - thoughts - and did not at all affect his deep-seated love of knowledge in the Western sense.

Mjomba did not care if it sometimes appeared as if he was yearning for knowledge for its own sake. Since the very definition of the word "philosophy" implied a love of knowledge for its own sake, it seemed unlikely that he could go wrong on that score.

With respect to the real matter at issue - whether he should don his traditional "toga" and begin an apprenticeship under the direction of the village seers or continue with his Western education in the classics, fate clearly appeared to have determined for him in advance the route to take; and Mjomba thought travelling along that predetermined route spelled lots of fun too.

It could very well be that growing up with one leg in a tradition-bound society and the other in a modern, fast changing environment actually fuelled his thirst for learning. Whatever it was, Mjomba could not help being troubled by the notion that, somehow, too much knowledge occasionally killed the brain!

Mjomba got a premonition of things to come when he was in his third year in the senior seminary. That was when Andrea Mkicha, Mjomba's childhood friend who had gone off to study in America on an "IIE scholarship" (whatever that meant!), returned prematurely showing symptoms of "brain death". The experience had been shattering to Mkicha's relatives who had expected him to come home loaded with degrees. Mkicha had been one of the first victims to fall prey to the strange malady. The doctors had not detected anything wrong with him physically; but he had continued to act funny, as if he was possessed.

Even though no blood relation of Mkicha's, Mjomba had always considered himself a member of the extended family of his pal; and the news about his old chum's condition had left him thoroughly dejected and disheartened. The fact that his interest in the general subject of mental health had already been building up for some time mattered very little since the diagnosis of his friend's illness by experts had turned up nothing. What mattered was that the "brain killer" had again proved that it could strike and vanish without a trace.

In point of fact, Mjomba who was already quite concerned that the populace at large was having to own up to the reality of a fast-changing social, economic and political environment, now also had a growing interest in the mental well-being of those members of his tribe who happened to be well schooled. He had always supposed that it was they who would be at the vanguard of progress in the modern sense and, as such, were the hope of his tradition-bound tribesmen.

And then, while interested in the lot of his countrymen, he also had to contend with the fact that he himself belonged to the group most at risk from "brain death". This was no idle threat from the hitherto unknown disease with no known cure, given the fact that some of his closest buddies had already fallen prey to it! It was, indeed, a combination of all those things that caused any mention of the word "bookish" at this time to send jitters down his spinal cord!

On the other hand, Mjomba's interests had been expanding imperceptibly and on the point of encompassing the general question of how peoples of Africa - and of the rest of the world, for that matter - reconciled their traditional beliefs with foreign ideologies.

Up until then, Christian Mjomba had held the view that the peculiar codes of conduct in force in seminaries, particularly the near monastic regime of life at St. Augustine's, made those institutions unlikely places for breeding characters "on the lunatic fringe".

But that started to change the moment Innocent Kintu, a first year Philosophy student, lapsed into a condition that seemed identical in almost every respect to that of Mkicha and then, lo and behold, failed to come out of it! To his disappointment, some of his fellow seminarians described what overtook Brother Kintu somewhat differently, saying he had simply "gone off the rails". But since those who traditionally "went off the rails" had never been known to get back on, that characterization of the situation had brought Mjomba little comfort.

Up until that point in time, Mjomba had not taken any particular interest in the behaviour of Brother Kintu. But now, he began quite involuntarily to feel a measure of concern that grew and eventually became comparable to that of a doctor for his/her patient.

He had, in any event, by that time already resolved to devote not just the periods allotted for meditation but the great bulk of his regular study time as well to exploring - and trying in general to grapple with - the subject of psychosis, even though he did not initially know the difference between that and "neurosis". He would actually have readily admitted at that time that he was not in a position to tell the behaviour of someone who was a moron, a nincompoop, or just a dunce from that of a miscreant - or even from that of some individual who just chose to play a role in society which amounted to simple mischief.

However, with *Logica Minor*, *Logica Major*, Psychology, Biblical Exegesis, and above all Metaphysics behind him, Mjomba clearly savored the idea that he was initiating a real life case study of a truly mysterious subject. The expression "mysterious disease" would in a way have captured very well whatever Westerners meant or purported to mean by "insanity". In the experience of the Welekha, there was no such a thing as "insanity". And Mjomba did not quite understand why the West did not embrace the position of the Welekha on "insanity"; because, even though they referred to it as a disease, by their own admission, they did not know what it was, with Freud, their foremost scholar on the subject, using another meaningless term to describe it, namely "neurosis"! And the only thing they definitively knew about the different types of neuroses apparently being that they were caused by misguided folk suppressing some other mysterious thing that they labeled the "libido"!

Mjomba found it a very exciting prospect that he, Mjomba, was in effect embarking on research into something that was entirely mysterious - insanity, schizophrenia, lunacy, neurosis, mischief, or whatever label you used to describe the "unknown disease with no known cure"! "Insanity" or "mysterious disease with no known cure" was a subject that Mjomba, fresh from investigating those other abstract subjects, imagined would be extremely fascinating and engaging.

It was thus that the Reverend Mjomba, while seeking answers to questions relating to the psychotic condition of religious types like Brother Kintu, had found himself pursuing questions relating to the phenomenon of insanity as it affected not just the elite in his society but everybody in general almost as a matter of course.

In the meantime, as Mjomba went about these activities, new problems arose. He had, for one, found himself almost constantly nagged by his conscience for ignoring the maxim that obedience was better than virtue! For obvious reasons, he had decided to go about his research quietly, and had avoided letting anyone his spiritual director included get wind of it. And for that - for breaking that cardinal rule - his feelings of guilt would haunt him for the remainder of his days at St. Augustine's!

Mjomba was understandably also badgered, during that period, by the fearsome thought that he ran the gauntlet of catching the strange disease and would almost certainly succumb to it unless he succeeded in the research he had started. But these very pursuits, because they were intellectual, likely were enhancing his chances of falling prey to the strange malady! These were irrational fears to be sure. But, try as he might to cast them off, he never succeeded in shrugging off the idea that he was on a perilous course.

Racked by these fears on the one hand, and tormented by his conscience on the other, Mjomba sometimes wondered if his efforts in the direction he had chosen to take were of any worth. The two, like a double-edged sword, worked away at him persistently and at times very nearly caused him to lose his nerve.

To make things even worse, and particularly because there was nothing Mjomba would have liked more than a tranquil, recollected state of mind, he had found his mind constantly besieged throughout that time by a train of disquieting thoughts. One numbing thought which had kept recurring suggested that the miseries he endured were, one and all, a well-deserved punishment for allowing himself to capitulate to the wiles of Satan and to personal pride!

Still, none of these things succeeded in deflecting Mjomba from his course. He had continued throughout his ordeals to associate the full attainment of his self-actualization with success in his self-imposed mission, which he likened to redemption. He had likewise refused to be intimidated by the widespread reports that the dread disease, now dubbed the "the disease of the mentally active" by the village folk, had broken its boundaries and no longer appeared to be confined to returning intellectuals from Europe and America. Well, given the evidence, it indeed had begun to affect locally bred intellectual types as well!

Some unscrupulous members of the seminary brotherhood had begun suggesting, much to

Mjomba's chagrin, that it was something other than insanity that was sweeping the region and the rest of the world. They claimed that these were simply symptoms of a metaphysical condition engendered by the *"Devil's Claw"*, a phrase they used to denote possession by Beelzebub!

There were still others who went even further. Taking their cue from the Western characterization of Animism, the traditional religion of people in the region, as a wayward and ungodly enterprise, they declared that the peculiar lapses of the mind that had been observed were also typical cases of possession by ancestral spirits in the service of the Evil One!

It was around this time that Mjomba - of all things - met and fell headlong in love with Jamila. And in a way, he owed it all to Brother Innocent Kintu. With the latter's problem refusing to go away of its own, the seminary authorities had eventually decided to entrust the stricken brother to the care of a Dr. Claus Gringo, a leading psychiatrist at the National Medical Teaching Hospital, or NMTH as it was popularly known.

The campus of the NMTH, the country's only teaching hospital, had changed the western skyline of Dar es Salaam. The beauty of the metropolis to the west had suffered near irrevocable damage as some ten thousand hectares of high ground on the city's western perimeters were systematically turned into a veritable forest of high rises for the university campus. To make things worse the campus, which some locals erroneously considered to be an exact replica of

Oxford University, was fenced in - suitably others believed. It looked entirely out of place in the sedate surroundings of the "Heaven of Peace"!

It was not uncommon to hear talk to the effect that the "people on the hill" lived in an "Ivory Tower" and out of touch with reality as a result, adding to the mystique surrounding the NMTH. What was more, the university's residents had demanded - and had, indeed, been allowed to enjoy - something the rest of the populace did not enjoy, some thing called academic freedom!

The seminary authorities were hopeful that the well-known and undoubtedly brilliant academic, a native of neighboring Uganda, could nudge Brother Kintu back into his usual senses by applying a dose of the wisdom he had acquired at the illustrious Makerere University, and sharpened over the additional period of twelve years or so that Dr. Gringo had spent at Stanford University in America where he specialized in Psychiatric Medicine.

St. Augustine's entire student body had been hopeful likewise, if only because it clearly took longer to become a psychiatrist than to become a priest! Mjomba, for his part, had believed that such an outcome, while unlikely in the normal course of events, came well within the realm of possibilities with himself in the picture. On the day Mjomba met and fell in love with Jamila, he had come to NMHT's Psychiatric Department, which also happened to be Jamila's place of work, to volunteer that critical assistance.

Approximately a year had passed since he had commenced his research on Kintu with the specific objective of resolving the issue regarding the exact nature of the strange malady. And now, on the verge of completing the equally exacting task of documenting details of his "discovery", the Rev. Mjomba was keeping his appointment with Prof. Gringo when he accosted the then Jamila Kivumbi in the latter's office.

The seminarian, who had been brought up to admire women only as God's creatures, had been swept off his feet at the sight of the ravishing Jamila, a quadroon whose maiden name meant "awesome beauty"!

Jamila had been swept off her own feet simultaneously. No sooner had she set her sight on the charming young man in a cleric's garb than she had decided, in her innocence, that the only way of paying adequate tribute to his good looks and charm was to look him straight in the eye and not say quits until his gaze met hers.

It would probably have ended disastrously for both of them had it not for the fact that the Rev. Mjomba was required to retreat behind the confining walls of St. Augustine's Seminary, a good half day's journey away, immediately his consultation with the psychiatrist concluded.

By the time he made his appearance at the National Medical Teaching Hospital's Psychiatric Unit, the wily churchman had taken great pains to learn first-hand the personal history of his fellow seminarian. He had been steadfast, and as diligent as anyone could be, in his application of the Thomist Method to the analysis required to unlock the secrets behind the phenomenon of insanity and in the process uncover the real causes of Brother Kintu's psychotic condition. He had left no stone unturned as he delved into Kintu's background in search of clues, working away at it during the school term and his vacations alike.

The seminarian had intended to come for his appointment with the professor armed with a dossier on Brother Kintu. But it just so happened that he had not been able to transcribe his notes into something more legible in time for his trip to Dar es Salaam. He had come armed instead with confidence that he had enough mastery of his pet subject as well as the ability to expound on the subject of insanity to the professor's satisfaction if not awe. And, above all, he was determined to take the lid off the mystery surrounding the plague known throughout the region as "brain death" once and for all!

With unbounded imagination and great tenacity, in addition to documenting Brother Kintu's "psychic roots" - Mjomba's favorite term for describing Kintu's checkered background - in great detail, Mjomba had succeeded in envisioning and portraying the Church as a major player in the downfall of the likes of Brother Innocent Kintu. And he had even gone on to effectively depict the quiet corridors of St. Augustine's Seminary as a potential breeding ground for the mentally deranged! Strangely, he did not feel any scruples for using his inside knowledge of the Catholic Church in making his point.

In the immediate aftermath of his highly successful session with Prof. Gringo, the seminarian had been somewhat surprised to find that the "dossier" contained the ingredients of a first class novel - the sort of novel that would, he had no doubt, set trends in addition to leaving fame as well as fortune to its author! A maverick in a world he believed was largely governed by group-think, Mjomba apparently resolved at that time not to allow himself to be circumscribed by rules of any sort as he went about writing his "best seller".

A non-conformist *par excellence*, he even set down his own rules. He would aim, first and foremost, to produce something good! In the process of doing so, he would not write for any specific audience. In his view, that sort of thing created unnecessary obligations that interfered with people's freedom of expression and which, in the final analysis, imposed unnecessary limits on an individual's fling at creativity!

His novel would, likewise, not be structured. He frowned on the very notion of doing things to form, and would have argued that the very next step in that direction was to do things to form for form's sake.

Mjomba had heard about writers' forums, and believed that the so-called literary conventions had been formulated in those forums for a reason. He in fact had a lingering notion that it was the most unworthy members of this league who were behind those conventions for their own benefit no doubt. And it did not surprise him that the league in question also constituted what was possibly the most exclusive club!

Mjomba frowned upon what he considered unfortunate restrictive rules on how to express one-self. He could not see any purpose for them other than that of protecting the monopoly of a few. He hated to think that other well-meaning authors indirectly supported a scheme that infringed on the right of all citizens to free expression in such an obvious manner! He was certainly determined not to allow any of that nonsense to influence his literary venture.

At one time, Mjomba even entertained the somewhat strange idea that his book would be a better work if it had no introduction or conclusion! And he wanted his work to be "original", by which he also meant unedited! He would even have preferred that his book was title-less; although he finally wavered in that respect and allowed that a best seller had to have a title of some kind.

Trying to think of one, an almost endless flood of possible titles for his book had filed through his mind. They included some really strange ones like "The Bombshell", "The Bomb", "On a Shuttle to Whiteman's Heaven", "Discourse with Madmen", "The Thesis, Antithesis and Synthesis", "The Madman", "Psychic Wars", "The Devil's Claw", "Blockbuster", "On the Invisible Trail", "The Vatican Tape", "On the Lunatic Fringe", "The Disease", "Crazy", "Weird Cure", "Hell in Heaven", "Heaven in

Hell", "The Millennium Book", "A Trip to Mjomba-land", "Rap Book", "And the Ancestral Spirits Go Matching On" and, perhaps the strangest of them all, "In Search of the Chigoe"!

Indeed "In Search of the Chigoe" had sounded just right. Mjomba would never forget the advice that his great grandfather, who lived to be a hundred and one years of age and was highly respected by all for his intellectual prowess right up to the time he departed to join the ancestral spirits, used to dispense to young people in the village. "If you allow the chigoe to get embedded in your brain, it will drive you mad the same way it drives cattle mad when it gets lodged in a spot that lay midway between the horns! You start that process when you give chiggers a home in your feet. So root them out at the first available opportunity!" he had admonished.

It was typical of Mjomba that if he became involved in an activity, his involvement became a real obsession, and he usually did not quit until he had endeavoured to fathom each and every angle of the activity or subject. A virtual captive of his own imagination on this occasion as on other similar occasions, Mjomba wasn't about to quit until he had checked out the most unlikely titles as well. One such title, which he regretted not being able to include in his short list, was *The Gospel According to Iscariot*. Even so, it was not before he had tried to think of something that would have justified its inclusion.

But on one thing, Mjomba adamantly refused to compromise, namely the idea of book reviews.

Mjomba derided the very idea. He argued that the writings that together constituted what was now known as the Bible, having been rejected by the major publishers of the day, ended up being self-published and never got the opportunity to be reviewed in any literary journal. But according to Mjomba, reviewing forthcoming book titles was really a cheap sales gimmick designed to promote selected authors' writings regardless of their true literary merit.

Besides, the problem with "marketing", according to Mjomba, was that it appealed, not to the higher faculties, but to man's base instincts. Mjomba claimed that marketing techniques mimicked the highly successful but questionable methods employed by Beelzebub in tempting Adam and Eve and their descendants! He, thus, not only didn't have any intention of seeking reviews for his "Masterpiece", but he was prepared to take any prospective "book reviewer" to task for trying to reduce his masterpiece to something that was cheap and run-of-the-mill.

It must be noted, to Mjomba's credit, that he even considered modifying the plot of his book slightly so that "Father Campbell", his novel's principal character whom he had also cast as Father Rector at the institution that was going to play the role of St. Augustine's Senior Seminary in the book, would preside over a staff of eleven. That would in turn have made for a realistic scenario in which the priests would have been nicknamed by the seminary's student body after the apostles, with the name of the betrayer being reserved for the rector.

With the main spokesperson for Catholicism in the book going by the name of Iscariot, it would have been in order for the fictitious author to entitle his work *The Gospel According to Judas Iscariot*. Mjomba regretted that he did not have the gall to publish a book with such a title. He simply could not predict what people's emotions on seeing such a book on the bookstand might be. It would, of course, be fine with him if that title led them to buy the book. But Mjomba feared that it could just as easily cause them to boycott it.

It always sounded so exciting to be a best-selling author. Mjomba thought he just could not wait to savor the joys of being one. But, despite the fact that he himself often dreamed of a great windfall from sales of his book, Mjomba would still have contended that it was intrinsically wrong for anyone to write for money.

These views did not prevent him from interrupting his chores ever so often to imagine long queues of eager buyers lining up to snap up copies of "The Bombshell" from book-shelves in faraway places like Paris, London, Los Angeles, Toronto, and even Moscow! Mjomba would certainly have argued that his book, by the very way it was conceived, guaranteed that kind of interest around the globe as well as the associated financial gain; but that these things did not in themselves form what could be characterized as a *raison de tre* for his fling at being an author. That, at any rate, was how he now liked to view himself and his book venture.

In the years that followed his original encounter with Prof. Gringo, the maverick Mjomba had allowed his ideas an almost limitless period to hibernate, moving to complete the expansion of material into a full-fledged historical novel nearly a decade later.

During the intervening period, a lot of things had taken place, most notably Mjomba's "conversion" to Islam and subsequent marriage to the woman of his dreams. Mjomba had at one time discarded his old given name and adopted the name of Ibrahim to emphasize the importance he placed on his new circumstances and the change of his awareness of reality. But he had reverted to using his original given name soon after at the urging of Jamila who confessed to being quite fond of the name Christian.

And while he hardly observed any teachings of his newfound faith, he revelled in the notion that he was a "born again" person, even though not in the Christian Evangelical sense. He had also subsequently attended the elitist Makerere University whence, following in the footsteps of his friend and mentor in the person of Professor Gringo, he had proceeded to the Leland Stanford, Jr. University in California where he studied Management and Finance.

Already a father of two now, the liberated Mjomba was determined to complete the book before their third child was born. But he was also just as determined to keep the project concealed from Jamila until its completion. Since he could not do any script-writing at home for that reason, he had found it necessary to use the luncheon periods for that purpose, affording himself a sandwich for lunch instead of the usual three course lunch his wife insisted was essential to maintain his health.

Christian Mjomba's thoughts were far from all that - and the book - now as he reflected on his domestic life. He felt he had to admit to a kind of fear that the sight of his pregnant wife had of late begun to arouse in him. He had already become so prone to it that he now recoiled instinctively whenever she came into view. Even so, he had not imagined that his face could be a mask of fear as Jamila's reaction that morning had appeared to suggest.

As he sat there slumped in thought, a tiny part of his brain seemed to twitch, and then without as much as a warning, his spirits started to rise. He was beginning to straighten up in his seat when he felt a twitch in a different part of his brain. It was at that point that, with the shattering speed of lightening accompanied by what sounded like a clap of thunder, the cause of his fear suddenly became obvious.

This was followed by something that was even stranger. Mjomba's mind, acting impulsively, refused to let itself be confronted with the subject. He was loath to admit that he had not been paying enough attention to his wife's needs even though the size of her tummy indicated that she could have a baby at any time.

It was precisely during the previous week that work on the book had been most demanding. After chronicling all the events that led to his hero's mental collapse, Mjomba had found himself faced with the almost impossible task of reconciling certain obvious formal conclusions with some of the pet theories on the causes of insanity as enunciated by the character in the book personifying himself. These theories, while not so compelling in themselves, were already so interwoven with the rest of the story, any move to discard any one of them threatened to result in a story so diluted as to make it worthless altogether. To retain them intact, on the other hand, seemed to spell inconsistency of such a magnitude, his own credibility as an author would be at stake!

Thoroughly flustered, Mjomba was very nearly driven at one stage to destroy in one stroke of the pen the mannequin representing himself in the person of Moses Kapere - his alter ego in the book. He faulted this facsimile of himself now for being too unwieldy and headstrong, and for preventing him from modifying the roles of his characters to accommodate his pet theories. He also saw this character, whose only distinction consisted of the fact that it was his very own creation, as the biggest threat to the project to which he had devoted so much of his life. He felt that if he had been in a position to do so without bringing irreparable ruin to his project and consequently also to himself, he would have been glad to expunge it from existence and start creating another one all over. It still remained that he had painstakingly created that likeness of himself over a period of many months, and it would in fact break his heart if he went that route.

Mjomba felt helpless and cornered. He felt, on the one hand, that he could not really countenance the thought that his own creation somehow was turning out to be not so terrific after all, and that it had become necessary to consider whether or not it should continue to exist. But he considered it out of question, on the other hand, for him to capitulate to pressure of any kind from any quarter, and certainly not to pressure from a jerk that owed its very existence to him!

That sort of pressure, which seemed calculated to cause Mjomba to circumscribe his freedom of expression, was unacceptable. It was still his intention to see his book gain instant and universal acclaim as an immortal work, and it was completely unthinkable that he could give in to blackmail emanating from any quarter, the mannequin he had created of himself included.

Too vain to concede defeat to his own effigy in that very unusual battle of wits, Mjomba had refused to yield. Suffice it to say that it had only been through some of the most excruciating and exacting of efforts at concentration that he had succeeded in balancing his arguments in favor of Theory "R", the theory he hoped would advance medical science and seal his fate as a celebrated author and thinker.

PART 11: PRIMROSE

After a good deal of soul searching, Mjomba had decided that both Jamila and himself were fairly worried - as indeed they were entitled to be. Following the months and finally weeks of waiting, it had begun to look as if the baby really could come any time!

Mjomba felt slightly unnerved as he recalled that his wife no longer ventured outdoors as often as she used to or might have wished, He shied at the idea that while he himself still went to work as usual, he was visibly weighed down with anxiety for Jamila and the unborn infant without being conscious of it.

The previous evening Mjomba, the less worried of the two no doubt despite his appearance, had reluctantly agreed that he would arrange to take his accumulated leave - thirty or so days in all - without further delay. He had taken leave on the occasion of the birth of Kinte two years earlier. If the circumstances had permitted him to do so when Kunta, now four, was born, he would probably have done the same thing.

On the present occasion, he had yet to observe signs of childbirth and consequently was inclined to maintain a wait-and-see attitude. He would accordingly have preferred to go on his vacation when signs showed that childbirth was imminent. Although he loved his wife dearly, he also regarded his job highly and was not the sort of person to walk away from his desk - and stay away for a whole month at that - lightly!

Mjomba let his mind wander back to the time, four years earlier, when he had sat through his Winter Quarter examinations at Stanford while Jamila was being prepared for the theatre at the nearby Stanford Medical Center. Almost exactly two and a half years before, he had arrived here on a scholarship awarded by the Institute of International Education. He had decided to come along with his spouse of three months at his own expense.

It stood out as the only time he had felt doubts about the wisdom of having Jamila accompany him on the overseas trip. After sitting what later turned out to be among his best exam papers, the youthful scholar from the Third World had jumped on his bicycle and had made it to the maternity ward barely in time to embrace the still bloodstained and slimy little Kunta as he was being transferred to the nursery in a nurse's arms.

Mjomba's mental processes were accustomed to revert to the family's sojourn in America whenever an occasion presented itself. He beamed with pleasure at the thought that Kunta, a United States citizen by birth, would always be an ever-present symbol of the happy days he and Jamila spent in California, as would also be the passport Kunta would carry, with the picture of a wide-eyed eagle on its cover. More so, he had once confided to a friend, than the coveted MBA he had bagged for his academic endeavors!

More than at any time before, Mjomba was

nonplussed that the Americans, with all their gadgetry, had failed in their attempt to pin-point his wife's exact due date! It did not surprise him when on their return to Africa, Kinte's expected date of birth as forecast by the doctor at the National Medical Teaching Hospital had also turned out to be wrong.

We've at least leant not to bank too much on doctors' forecasts, thought Mjomba, slightly bemused. They might be fonts of life-saving knowledge, he told himself mentally; but their knowledge had proved deficient when it came to forecasting the birth dates of Kunta and Kinte at any rate. He was in jitters as he wondered what doctors two hundred years from now would think about the latest gadgets in use at the Stanford Medical Center - some of them so top-of-the-line they were, he suspected, unavailable anywhere else outside of Stanford University's boundaries!

Mjomba reflected ruefully that neither his wife nor himself seemed to have learnt from their experiences how to control their anxiety. Just as on the occasion of Kinte's birth, Jamila was registered at both Dr. Mambo's private maternity clinic and the National Medical Teaching Hospital as well for her prenatal care. He vividly recalled that he was the one who had insisted that she receive her prenatal treatment at both places on both occasions. The idea that Jamila had been visiting two hospitals for the same thing now looked decidedly crazy.

Not unlike many of the supposedly moneyed city folk of Dar es Salaam, Mjomba had a bias for the treatment private clinics dispensed, and accordingly preferred them to the Government hospitals in spite of the added cost which went with it.

He made a half-hearted attempt to justify his previous insistence that his wife see the doctors at both places, and he abandoned it almost as soon as he had begun. As if in confirmation of the stupidity of his action, it suddenly dawned on him that Dr. Mambo had given February 26, three days away, as the expected date of delivery while, according to the doctor at the "NMTH", the due date was February 29!

Attired in a close fitting, lilac coloured Kaunda suit and rocking gently in the swivel chair, Mjomba buzzed his secretary. He felt a great deal more upbeat than he had felt at any time since reporting to work that morning.

"Primrose, kindly get me a leave form" he said in a husky voice.

A typical "siren" and still single at twenty-seven, Prim, as she was known among her friends, apparently deemed it permissible whenever she addressed her young but fairly highly educated boss on the intercom to put on her "charm".

And, predictably, there had never been any doubt in her mind regarding the fact that Mjomba took delight in listening to her affected tones. The sharp-witted Primrose, besides, took full advantage of whatever information came her way in her capacity as his confidential secretary to deliver her point home in that regard. Her tendency to do this had increased sharply since her recent discovery that in addition to being a Stanford alumnus, Mjomba had also studied at St. Augustine's Seminary.

Like most informed people in the region, Primrose knew that those who went to St. Augustine's Seminary studied Philosophy and Theology, abstract subjects that, at least in the view of the majority, did not appear to have any real relevance to ordinary life and were consequently regarded as esoteric. It was precisely for that reason that St. Augustine's Seminary was held in such high regard by many people, some of whom would remark that it could not possibly be called "Major" for nothing.

Regarding Mjomba's attendance at St. Augustine's Seminary Primrose was certain that if she had not been involved in helping him to prepare his book manuscript for publication, she would not have come by that valuable information. She had a lingering suspicion that it was one aspect of Mjomba's life he didn't really want every Dick and Harry to know about - in the exact same way he did not want any Dick and Harry to know about his literary project. This was despite the fact that St. Augustine's was a well-known, universally respected center of learning. Her own feeling on first learning that Mjomba was an ex-seminarian was that her boss had quit the seminary because he had a special fondness for women. That was what everyone said about ex-seminarians.

Primrose knew that it was an unfair conclusion about people who decided for reasons best known to themselves that they did not have a calling for the Catholic priesthood. But, as a woman, Primrose sometimes thought that as far as stereotypes went, this one was just fine. She even wondered why, in their defense, ex-seminarians did not advance the argument that they adored women very much. As the current date she hoped to marry was always saying, women were second only to angels in loveliness as creatures of the Almighty, and she did not understand why he kept repeating it. She loved her date so much she often told herself that she would not have doubted his words even if he had said it just once!

Primrose adored Mjomba openly. But that did not in any way appear to affect the respect she felt for her boss or, indeed, her loyalty to him. The language of the material she typed for him had tended to be of a standard that put the proper appreciation of her boss's work beyond her general capabilities; but she had been content to regard it as her privilege to be able to help in bringing his dream of becoming an illustrious author closer to reality.

While he enjoyed the treat all right, Mjomba had long ago decided that it would serve him best in the long run if he gave the appearance of "tolerating" his secretary's behaviour without either openly approving or disapproving it.

Primrose knew that Mrs. Mjomba was close to delivery, and she decided to use that knowledge to the fullest. "Yeah, maternity leave!' she crooned, her lyrical voice reverberating with mirth. "I will take care of the formalities for the leave. How long - a month...month and a half? That should be enough for you. According to your last pay-stub, you have forty-five days unused, Sir."

For reasons best known to herself, Primrose seemed more inclined to use the formal address when joking around with her boss. And she was usually much more informal when serious business being conducted.

"First of all, I know you would very much like to knight me!" Mjomba retorted in his usual, jocular manner. "But, quite frankly, I am still very keen to give the real thing a shot. There is a slim chance I could get the Knighthood from Her Majesty the Queen herself; and I would therefore appreciate it very much if you would keep 'Sir' in reserve for now!"

Ignoring his secretary's sidesplitting laughter at the other end of the intercom, he continued: "But you are otherwise right regarding maternity leave. I only need one month - should be fully recovered in that time. See! We men are different from you women - when it is your turn, we will be talking the standard six month's maternity leave, won't we? You take a little longer to recover..."

His finger still on the buzzer, he added tauntingly: "As a true African, I do not actually believe in the equality of the sexes. And I'm sure you do not disagree with me on that! Isn't it the reason you've never invited me to join the Feminist Movement?" He was referring to the fact that Primrose was the elected head of the union of secretarial staff at the Port Authority.

"You are useless" Primrose chortled amid giggles.

Mjomba was capable of sounding infinitely flattering. And he sounded at his best as he added: "Sweetheart, make my leave effective tomorrow."

With that, he was about to break off the conversation when, her voice as affected as ever, Primrose hissed from her end of the line: "Do not pretend. You are envious!"

"By the way, Chief, you could use my entitlement of four months' maternity leave..." she added with a triumphant giggle.

Even after his phone set had gone dead, the sound of her titter continued to seep into Mjomba's office through the wall separating the two sections of his *office en suite*.

Mjomba was engrossed with his tête-à-tête with his secretary only very briefly after it ended. He typically never allowed himself to be preoccupied with the frequent tête-à-têtes he had with Primrose for any length of time after they ended. He did not do so on this occasion either. But he felt a sting of guilt for allowing himself to enjoy the chat with his secretary. He did not understand why he felt like that. It was something that had never happened before.

Even though there did not appear to be any logic to it, Mjomba just felt that he was being unfair to his beloved Jamila by enjoying these light-hearted moments with Prim. And it was not because Jamila would have disliked the idea of him joking around in that fashion with other women. He knew his spouse too well to suspect her of that sort of thing. He wondered if his feelings of guilt arose from the fact that he was laughing and smiling so soon after fretting over Jamila's condition.

But Mjomba's conscience continued to badger him with the "fact" that he had allowed himself to indulge in that manner. It made him feel that his concern for Jamila moments earlier had not been really genuine. This was even though he was convinced that this was not so. He was, therefore, glad to put the banter he had just indulged in behind him quickly.

Jerking himself to attention, he looked like the typical young-and-upcoming executive as he steered his medium-sized hulk the few inches it had strayed from the flat-topped mahogany desk. But his mind was still wandering, as he turned to survey the contents of his In-Tray; and it took the wail of the siren announcing the twelve o'clock shift at the Docks to bring him to.

PART 12: THE COUNTDOWN

The whine of the siren was at its highest pitch when the buzzer went off. With a practiced movement of the arm, Mjomba picked up the telephone receiver and listened to Primrose's affected, almost lyrical voice.

After announcing that a Mrs. Killian was on the line, his secretary deliberately took time to replace her receiver and was able in the process to catch the words: "*Mama Kunta anaumwa vibaya sana...*" (Translated: "the Mother of Kunta is in labor...").

It was, perhaps, the pay. But the glamour associated with working in the Port Authority's Accounting and Finance Department undoubtedly had something to do with it, as was also the fact that the concentration of people with professional designations in that department was second only to that in the Engineering Department. In any event, over the years, these various factors had led to a conspicuous cluster of top-flight secretaries on the two floors of the Trade Center occupied by Accounting and Finance.

That had in turn assured that communications between the different finance sections, whose heads apparently shared a common passion for top-of-the-line telephone sets, was almost as good as it could be and easily the most efficient compared with inter-office communication in other departments.

Within minutes following Mjomba's conversation with his secretary, telephones in the department and elsewhere were buzzing with the news that the wife of the Deputy Controller Finance, regarded by all the female members of the department's staff without exception as a stunning beauty and a model of comeliness and charm, was in labor!

Mjomba was on his legs when Mrs. Killian, a neighbor, rang off with a click. He felt an irresistible urge to bolt, and was surprised that he remained stationary. His hands were groping about in his pockets for his car's ignition keys at the same time as he was trying to figure out in his mind if there wasn't anything else of importance that he was about to forget in the rush. He had completely forgotten that on his way to the office, as he drove past the Ocean View Motor Garage, he had decided to leave the car there for routine maintenance in view of his leave plans, and that he had been given a lift to the Trade Center in the auto repair shop's courtesy shuttle.

It was then that his eyes alighted on the blue binder that was lying next to the In-Tray. In spite of his quickening pulse, Mjomba seemed in absolute control of his reflexes as he snatched it up, and then proceeded to carefully place the pages of his manuscript in the binder. Shoving the binder under his left armpit, he reached for his attaché case and was making a dash for the doorway when he stopped in his tracks. Mjomba's recollection that he had checked the car in at the Ocean View Motor Garage that morning for routine maintenance in view of his leave plans could not have been more timely. Without a prior booking, his Ford Cortina would not normally be ready for collection until at least three in the afternoon!

Christian Mjomba sat himself down heavily and dialled Office Services. Finding the number engaged, he hesitated, then persuaded himself that it might be worthwhile to give it another try after a couple of seconds. But before he could try the number a second time, he decided that it was crazy of him to expect to get a staff car at that short notice from the "bunch" on the ninth floor!

Unlike the brass of Accounting and Finance who had received their education mostly in elite institutions in the West and were given to swaggering, the Chief of Office Services had received his Management diploma in Communist Russia, and his reticent deportment was oftentimes the object of muted wisecracks by junior Accounting and Finance staff with what appeared to be the tacit approval of the department's senior staff. Even though, because of the enormous power he wielded which was exemplified by the extensive demand for office services throughout the Port Authority, it was rumoured that he had once used the shoe in a Chief Officers' meeting after the manner of a former Chairman of the Union of the Soviet Socialist Republics at the United Nations in New York!

Not surprisingly, over time, Office Services in general had been typecast in an image that hinted at bungling and mismanagement. Actually, that department's problems stemmed from the fact that the Port Authority's Chief Accountant and Financial Controller, with a deft hand at figures, succeeded expertly year in and year out in getting the lion's share of corporate funds at budget time mostly at the expense of Office Services which, consequently, never managed to haggle for enough to enable it to purchase the automotive and other equipment it needed to do a good job.

And when the amiable Czar of Office Services would lament, in conversations with Accounting and Finance division chiefs at parties thrown in honor of Members of the Board in the aftermath of the Budget sessions, at the paucity of funds in his approved Budget, pointing as he usually did to the double-digit figures the Board authorized for Accounting and Finance which were in stark contrast to the mostly single-digit figures authorized for his department, some of them found enormous pleasure in drawing attention to the fact that it the incumbent of that position was out of town. This was supposed to imply that he shouldered considerably more responsibilities and consequently deserved a bigger budget for that reason!

Barricaded in his office, the Deputy Controller Finance was beside himself. The idea crossed his mind that he would deserve to be damned if he put any reliance on the people of Office Services in an emergency such as this one. He had always had the distinct feeling that they did not work for money. Since they certainly did not work for the sake of it, he often times wondered what it was they had on their minds each morning when they set out from their homes for the Trade Center. And then it suddenly occurred to him that there was probably no need for the rush any way; the earliest due date was, as he recalled, a clear three days off!

Mjomba was more composed now as he stuffed the manila envelope into his brief case. His face was expressionless, nonetheless, as he bade his secretary a hearty farewell and set off from the Trade Center. It was unusual for a Port Authority official of his standing to be seen heading for the bus stage. Inexplicably, he declined numerous offers of lifts by Port Authority employees who drove up to him and volunteered to drive him to his destination in their personal autos. It was as if he preferred to roast in the Dar es Salaam sun rather than inside those cars, none of which had air-conditioning.

It did not take long for a wobbly "DTC" bus, as residents of the sprawling metropolis referred to buses operated by the government owed Dar es Salaam Transport Corporation, to come chugging along, a cloud of dust trailing it. It was a while since Mjomba had last used public transportation. The lone passenger boarding the DTC bus at that "stage", he was curious about the conditions inside. Hoping to use the opportunity to "practice his psychology", he looked for a back seat from where he could observe the demeanor of the bus's other passengers. Once inside, however, a dockworker who had promptly recognized him jumped up and offered his seat.

Mjomba knew at once that it would be remiss

for him to decline the offer. If he had tried to decline the offer, the dockworker would simply have insisted that he take it - that was how respectful Tanzanians were. Even though he would have enjoyed the ride standing, Mjomba thanked the dockworker and eased his frame onto the metal seat.

The combination of being located close to the Equator and also being at Sea Level sometimes caused Dar es Salaam to literally sizzle in the hot sun - exactly like North America during the summer. The only difference was that here, unlike in America, the buses did not have air-conditioning. Imports from the Peoples' Socialist Republic of China, which was one the few countries with which Socialist Tanzania enjoyed cordial relations, they were equipped with metal seats as opposed to rubber cushioned seats, perhaps because the former tended to have a longer life. But those metal seats, particularly those that were directly exposed to the sun, could also get pretty hot. With respect to the particular seat that Mjomba was offered, it was the metal used as the back rest which had been directly exposed to the sun's naked rays and which made him feel as though the skin on his back was being peeled off.

Mjomba remained seated because that was the only way he would avoid offending the polite dockworker. At one point, he thought that he wouldn't survive the short ride to the Old Post Office, which was his destination. But he bit his lips and pretended that he was enjoying the ride. In the meantime, anyone could easily have told those passengers who recognized the boss of Accounting and Finance and those who didn't by the way they either showed deference for his presence by relapsing into an awkward silence or ogled at him because he seemed in obvious discomfort.

The journey over the short distance in the squelching heat seemed to take forever, and caused Mjomba to re-live his memories of the rides he had enjoyed in ultra-modern air-conditioned buses on many an occasion in America! Ever since Mjomba enjoyed his very first such ride in the airport bus from JFK International Airport to New York's Central Station when he and Jamila arrived in America, he had become inclined to feel that distances did not seem to matter anymore! Because of this, he would almost certainly have reacted with ambivalence if, for example, he had been asked to trade his low rise apartment in Escondido Village on the Stanford campus for married quarters in the nearby City of Palo Alto, Menlo Park or some other place requiring him to commute to the School of Business by some other means.

An even more enjoyable way of getting to school would have been on bicycle. Palo Alto, Menlo Park and the neighboring cities had special bicycle lanes, which eliminated all danger from vehicular traffic. Moreover, Mjomba needed the exercise and would have been happy to commute to the "GSB" in that manner. Thinking about the options he had in America, Mjomba had to stifle a giggle when he tried to imagine what would be on the minds of dockworkers in Dar es Salaam if they saw him one day cruising to work on a bicycle! They definitely would think he had gone bonkers or something. Only the poorest of the poor exposed themselves to the dangers of riding bicycles here. Just as cars were status symbols differentiating the elite from the rest of the populace, bicycles too were status symbols of sorts demarcating the "have-nots" from those who were affluent or on the road to achieving that status. You could not be affluent and go anywhere on a bicycle!

And if there was one thing about life in America that Mjomba thought was on the downside, it was that the well-to-do rubbed shoulders with the "ordinary" folks on the "BART" in San Francisco and subway systems in other cities, and even on buses, nobody was considered special. Americans did not recognize status symbols, and that took the fun out of life. It took Mjomba a while to get used to the fact that travelling to America had caused him to lose his "elite" status. But he never got used to the idea that he was a member of a "minority" simply because he was black! Anyway, how on *earth* could one talk of "whites" or people of European ancestry being in the majority when there were all those Chinese who numbered in the billions! That was unless one was really parochial in one's outlook and was unable to see beyond the borders of one's country - or if one decided that Chinese also were "white" after all and not something else!

Mjomba wasn't surprised that everybody on

that bus was staring at him as if his face matched one of those on the FBI's Ten Most Wanted list. As if by coincidence, a privately operated mini-bus sporting a faded poster of the FBI's Ten Most Wanted list just then whizzed past his bus and sped on ahead so it would be first in line to pick up passengers at the next Bus stop. The mini-bus, reeling under its load of passengers, careened so dangerously close to pedestrians crowding the walk-way on the far side of the road as it overtook the DTC vehicle, Mjomba found himself cursing under his breath, and wondering if that offending driver did not qualify to be on the FBI's Ten Most Wanted list!

Disembarking from the DTC at the Old Post Office, Mjomba found himself momentarily caught up in the maddening pace set by ordinary Dar es Salaamites as they went about their business. Whereas everybody talked about the pace of life in Europe and America being fast, it had never really occurred to Mjomba until that time that the pace of life in Dar es Salaam might also be fast. He was ready to concede that he himself had been living in an ivory tower and detached from the ordinary Dar es Salaamites - the real people!

He now realized that Dar es Salaam's impoverished residents had actually set a pace that, in many respects, was even faster than the pace of life in the West. Because there were no queues at bus stops, everybody scrambled to be first on the bus and get a seat. And the way the buses, the mini-buses particularly, were crammed with people, they

559

might have been tins of sardines. Mjomba sympathized with the women and children who were at a distinct disadvantage in obtaining seating.

He thought it was very funny that a virtual stranger had offered him a seat; but then he realized that it was probably because that "polite" individual knew that the gesture was really nothing compared to a favor(s) someone in Mjomba's position could do. Imagining himself in the shoes of the "polite" dockworker, Mjomba agreed that, indeed, one never knew when one might be in need of such a favor.

Mjomba persuaded himself to "get a move on" as a colleague of his liked to say. After disembarking from the DTC bus, the bustle around him had caused him to stop and stare at the concourse of men, women and children as they went about their business.

Ocean View Garage was less than a mile from the Old Post Office. Even though DTC buses bound for a variety of destinations including places with such exotic sounding names as "Mwanyanamala", "Kinondoni" and "Karioko" by-passed it, Mjomba, who was glad to escape the gawking eyes of fellow passengers on the DTC bus from which he had disembarked, opted for a stroll along Ocean Drive.

He was obviously "spoilt" and did not think he could withstand the scotching heat *inside* those crowded buses anymore. The cool breeze blowing inland from the direction of Zanzibar made the walk a much more pleasant experience than the bus ride. But he could not help wondering how Dar es Salaam's poor survived those dreadful conditions. He did not at first understand why the authorities did not make any effort to import air-conditioned buses equipped with upholstered seats rather than hard, metal seats that heated so easily in the scotching sun.

The overflowing number of Dar es Salaamites who packed the existing DTC buses and the few privately owned mini-buses, which had been previously banned under the Government's socialist policies and had only recently been permitted to operate in the city, were certainly enough to keep double that number of DTC buses and mini-buses overloaded most of the time. Mjomba, therefore, initially figured that the Government had everything to gain by importing or itself assembling double that number of buses.

He was also sure that, even though poor, the people would be only too glad to dish out a little more in bus fare for a comfortable seat - if things came to that. The most important thing was that, in a stroke, the quality of life of so many people would be affected for the better. But then, Tanzania was the only African country with free universal primary school education and also free universal health care, which called for the construction and staffing of a vast number of schools and health clinics in a matter of months. Certainly ambitious policies; but Tanzanians, led by the Oxford educated *Mwalimu* or, as Westerners would have put it, *Professor* Nyerere, appeared quite determined to back them up with action.

It occurred to Mjomba that the inconvenience of the Dar es Salaamites just might be the price that had to be paid to get the rest of the country - in fact the heart of the nation also on its feet and moving! Moreover, in the eyes of the Western world, Tanzania was essentially a rogue state, because of its socialist leanings. Which meant that the people of that country did not have full and free access to the assistance that would normally have been available from institutions like the World Bank and the International Monetary Fund. With the Cold War still raging, that was the cold reality.

As he ambled along the elegant Nkrumah Boulevard past the State House, a demure building that had previously belonged to an Asian trader, and the debonair Aga Khan Hospital close by, the thought kept occurring to him that he ought to have telephoned the garage to confirm that work on his car was proceeding on schedule. Even though he made it to the garage in forty-five minutes, which was just about the same length of time it would have taken him if he had waited and caught the next DTC bus going in that direction, the fact he hadn't phoned prevented him from fully enjoying his stroll.

At the garage, Mjomba's heart sank and he was temporarily paralyzed by a lump in his throat on learning that the car had in fact been ready for release to him for some hours, having been attended to in double-quick time in deference to his entreaty early that day. He was agitated for no apparent reason and found himself struggling vainly to refrain from making comparisons between the performance of the garage and performance of Office Services or the city's DTC that day. He did not want to believe that there could be such a stark contrast between the performance of a small, privately managed enterprise and the performance of a whole department of the Port Authority or that of one of the largest corporations in the country!

Before jumping into the driver's seat, Mjomba tossed the envelope containing the manuscript into the front passenger seat, its usual place. He seemed to like having the manuscript in sight as much as possible as though it was by a process of osmosis that he received the inspiration he needed for developing his dossier on Innocent Kintu into a full-fledged, best-selling novel!

With his briefcase in its usual place on the back seat, he steered the sedan into Umoja wa Wanawake Way to head home. He could not fail to notice the improved performance brought on by the new tyre-rod ends and the wheel alignment. Mjomba had already driven past the Kanji Sulemani Stores on the final homeward stretch when he remembered the Baby Oil!

He made a U-turn at the Kaunda/Msasani Roads junction and raced back towards the Kanji Sulemani Stores. As he did so, his mind suddenly became besieged with images of the assortment of baby items that he and his wife had been "showered" with by their newfound friends in America on the occasion of Kunta's birth four years earlier.

Although neither Jamila nor himself were white - or perhaps because of it and their distinctive British accent - they had made many friends in the relatively short period they had been in America; and the baby shower, which came as a complete surprise, had turned out to be quite a shower! As he thought about the many items they had had to exchange at the nearby Macy's and the Emporium, a vein in his right cheek-bone began twitching at a rapidly accelerating pace, triggered no doubt by the flood of images.

Mjomba had been dismayed on at least one other occasion - the occasion of Kinte's birth two years before - that baby showers as an institution did not figure in his own tribal customs! He shut his eyes briefly, as if in admission of the immutability of that situation, opening them just in time to avoid a head-on collision with an approaching vehicle. But there was no way he could stop his mind wandering now!

Mjomba again felt a lump rise to his throat as he turned to consider the results of his efforts of the past several days which were intended to make up for what the couple missed by being in Africa instead of America. Armed with a list of baby items prepared by Jamila on the one hand and a purse that was far from adequate on the other, he had done the rounds of shops in the teaming capital, buying an item here and noting the price of another there.

Heralding the seasonal rains, the heat and the accompanying humidity had been unbearable and inhibiting. Then there was the fact that since the socialist revolution, and particularly when the country adopted the "glorious" *Ujamaa* doctrine or African Socialism, most items that had previously flooded the local markets had disappeared from the shelves.

And, when they happened to be available, they were so expensive, even for someone of his station, it had stopped being an exaggeration to use terms like "paying through the nose" or "paying dearly" for a commodity. Plagued with that combination of troubles, the results of his mission had been decidedly poor as a consequence.

While a newborn babe, in the view of the Mjombas, could do without such things as pants and coats in the less than friendly weather of the "Heaven of Peace", Baby Oil was considered indispensable - a veritable soothing balm in Dar es Salaam's nigh permanent heat wave. Kanji Sulemani Stores did not have Baby Oil in stock, and the revelation left Mjomba feeling like a dumbbell!

If you missed an item at the Kanji Sulemani Stores for which they were stockists, it was usually a safe bet that the whole town had run out of it. The very idea now made him feel exasperated and steamed up. The previous day, the Asian attendant had shaken her head from side to side and advised her eager customer to "make another try tomorrow". The sight of the same attendant shaking her head from side to side in her accustomed manner caused him to splutter on his way out: "What the heck...shortages! As if it wasn't bad enough paying out a fortune when something happened to be available!"

In spite of his woes, Mjomba made it home in time to take Jamila to hospital. In the general anxiety, everybody there had ignored Kunta and Kinte. They were in the lounge by themselves, their attention riveted to a solitary bag stuffed with baby things, some of them leftovers from Kunta's epoch as a tot.

Mjomba bounded past them into the hallway leading to the master bedroom only to be met by his wife in the narrow passage. Waited on by women-folk from adjoining homes, Jamila had bathed and donned her favorite maternity outfit - a light green pleated blouse worn over a chestnut spotted *Kanga*.

Minutes later, outside the beach bungalow, Jamila hesitated as her husband swung the Ford's doors open. It was common knowledge that few owners of cars with low suspensions in this former British possession could afford to maintain the shock absorbers in anything approximating a good state of repair. Ocean View Motor Garage had only that afternoon attached, for the fifth consecutive time, a note on the Ford's repair bill advising that the shock absorbers needed attention! Jamila seemed to guess as much.

At the behest of Mrs. Killian, the hospital-bound retinue piled into her Volkswagen - Jamila, Mjomba, Kunta, Kinte, Mrs. Killian herself and Priscilla, her two-year-old daughter. Mrs. Killian, who was expecting - and whose tummy made her look eight rather than five months pregnant - had stopped driving as a precaution and easily prevailed on Mjomba to take the wheel.

566

They made it to Dr. Mambo's Clinic with considerable aplomb, thanks to the performance the kids put up along the way. His wife's labour pains notwithstanding, Mjomba could not resist the laughter each time one of them pointed to the bulging tummy of either Mrs. Killian or of Jamila and, with childlike simplicity and grief-stricken voice, intoned: "Painful?"

When they had filed out of the *Beetle*, Kunta, ebullient as ever, led the column to the hospital's Reception Desk, followed by Mrs. Killian who had Jamila in tow. Mjomba brought up the rear with Priscilla and Kinte swinging under his arms. As they trooped in, two smiling nurses surrounded Mrs. Killian and began to steer her towards a wheelchair! Watching the scene from the back of the queue, Mjomba could not help laughing - indeed not even his wife was able not to laugh despite the labor pains.

The place, a favorite haunt for patients with middle-class incomes, was buzzing with activity. Doctors' paths criss-crossed and nurses, bursting with mysterious enthusiasm, darted here and there. As soon as several of their number laid their hands on Jamila, they whisked her away into an Examination Room and out of sight.

About fifteen minutes or so after his abrupt and all too sudden separation from his wife, Mjomba, anxiety written all over his face, busied himself with the children in an effort to hide his own strangely sharp feelings of expectancy. Jamila's regular doctor, an Oxford educated obstetrician of half-Asian and half-Arab heritage, spied him and made a beeline for him.

"Your wife's almost ready now," she whispered in his ear.

"Is it a boy or a girl?" Mjomba asked, excited. He was convinced that he had noticed a reassuring smile flash on her face. It was an oval, Semitic face that struck Mjomba as being very sensual. The facial features of the doctor, a close family friend, had always reminded him of those of Jamila who, like the doctor, boasted a mixed African, Arab and European ancestry.

Jamila's maternal great grandmother was a slave woman her great grandfather, a former slave trader, had added to his harem just before that dreadful institution was outlawed. That was also before the ageing slave trader turned to the lucrative spice trade and settled down in Zanzibar off mainland Tanganyika, as Tanzania was then known. Jamila's paternal grandfather on the other hand was a native of the Seychelles islands which lie smack in the middle of the Indian Ocean. Like most native sons of those islands, his family tree included people of combined African, Arab, French, Indian and Chinese descent. It did not, therefore, surprise Mjomba that his wife still retained Semitic features amongst others. For some reason, though, his focus had always been on her Arab ancestry.

Still, a favorite joke of his was that his flame was the incarnation of everything that was desirable in a woman by virtue of her lineage - just like Eve of the Old Testament! But he sometimes also claimed, when it suited him, that his wife's comeliness owed more to the fact that the old slave trader apparently had still got an eye for original beauty and charm when he added Jamila's grandmother to his flock of wives.

Mjomba, who had on one occasion been forced by Jamila to confess that he was a secret admirer of her doctor, thought it a strange coincidence that his wife's paediatrician not only bore a great deal of likeness to her, but also apparently had Arab blood in her. He sometimes wondered whether her descendants were slaves, or slave merchants, or both.

"Jamila is almost ready to start delivering the baby," volunteered Mrs. Killian in explanation. She had over-heard the exchange and had concluded that she stood considerably less chance of being misunderstood by the distracted Mjomba than did the doctor.

The doctor's reassuring smile was still playing on her face and the laughter was restrained as she said: "Next time, make it the hospital a little earlier or it might be in the taxi!"

The doctor's warning caused memories of an incident to which he had been witness about a year or so before to come tumbling back into his brain. He had given a lift to a neighbor at early dawn to Dr. Mambo's Clinic and was waiting by the clinic's entrance, located not far from where they were, for the neighbor to emerge from the wards when a taxicab appeared from nowhere and pulled up next to his battered Ford.

The cab driver had scarcely brought his weather-beaten Peugeot 404 station wagon, with its complement of two female passengers and a worried looking man roughly Mjomba's own age, to a standstill when he leapt out and scrambled for the Reception Desk. But by the time the cabbie emerged from the building with a nursing sister close on his heels, the number of his passengers had grown to four!

It was a painful sight which met Mjomba's eyes when, ambling out of the Ford like someone in a stupor, he stood helplessly by and watched the nursing sister sever the umbilical cord joining mother and babe using what looked like a common pair of scissors right there in the taxi!

Recalling the incident, he found himself re-living the experience all over again, and struggling to contain his sharp feelings of anger at the adult passengers in that vehicle and anxiety for the child which the sight of the naked and crying babe being rushed up the hospital's stairway in a nurse's arms had evoked in him at the time. It suddenly seemed to Mjomba an appropriate time to relate the incident. But the doctor was gone before he could engage her in further dialogue.

Mjomba had a mind to maintain a vigil at the hospital for at least those crucial final hours of the countdown. As the entourage, consisting now of Mrs. Killian, her daughter Priscilla, Kunta, Kinte and himself, headed off towards Msasani Peninsula in the *Beetle* with himself at wheel, Mjomba after due consultations with Mrs. Killian, made a detour allowing him to call on his in-laws to request help for little Kunta and Kinte. Thrilled to learn that another grand-child was on the way, the senior Kivumbis were only too glad to let Fatuma, a seventeen-year-old cousin of Jamila's and a favorite with the kids, join the entourage for the rest of its journey.

Later that evening, the seven O'clock news was being announced over the National Broadcasting Service when, leaving the children in the competent hands of Fatuma, Mjomba jumped into the Ford and headed for Dr. Mambo's Clinic, heart pounding.

Jamila and her husband openly dreaded caesarean sections despite the fact that a section probably saved Kunta's life at birth. From what Jamila had been able to piece together later from her fragmentary memory of the events of that afternoon at the Stanford Medical Center, the team of distinguished doctors had initially let her attempt natural delivery.

The baby's head had apparently started to appear when readings on the battery of scientific instruments there by her bedside started to signal danger with regard to the baby's condition. The readings, which only days before had magically established the child's gender, were none-too-encouraging for a little while, a reflection on the unprecedented level of hypertension to which Jamila was an unfortunate prey. That had prompted the doctors to transfer her to the operating table right there and then.

571

Mjomba had been informed in advance of his wife's confinement at the Medical Center that he not only was free to attend delivery, but could also photograph the proceedings if he so wished. It had predictably taken some persuading to get Jamila to agree to be photographed while giving birth; but, as usual, she had acquiesced to her husband's will and consented to his plan to capture on film the different stages of their child's development starting right from the moment of his birth.

The couple already owned a variant of the famous Polaroid Land camera which Mjomba had bought as a present for his wife at Orley Airport during their stop-over in Paris on their San Francisco bound flight a year earlier. But Mjomba was so consumed by the idea of recording their child's history that he even deemed it worthwhile to invest in a reasonably good movie camera. In that way they would be able in their old age to sit back and view daylong movies featuring their kid, so Mjomba imagined, instead of having to flip through hundreds of still photos! He had accordingly proceeded to the Emporium and procured a Kodak XL 360 camera, and a Kodak Movie-Deck 435 to go with it, charging the cost against his student Triple 'E' Account.

The knowledge that he could not be permitted inside the operating theatre in the event of his wife's delivery by caesarean section had laid the ground for Mjomba's somewhat irrational aversion for that form of childbirth, an aversion that was reinforced by the fact that medical operations in Africa and elsewhere in the third world were fraught with danger for obvious reasons.

In the course of time, the disappointed Mjomba had gradually lost track of the fact that his examinations schedule had in any case already precluded him from picture taking. And so, his pathological dislike for operations, coupled with his natural dread for blood-letting in general, made a caesarean section the last thing he could wish for his wife.

Jamila, for her part, had a longstanding dread for delivery by caesarean section, stemming from an incident that occurred while she was still a child. A woman who was their distant relation had died while giving birth and, although the cause of death had nothing to do with caesarean sections, Jamila's grandmother, discussing the dangers of childbirth in general with other women while the wake was still under way, had said that a woman could not very safely bear a second child if she had had her first through the caesarean method. She had said this within earshot of her granddaughter!

Caesarean sections were, of course, virtually unknown during the old lady's time; but her words, which were regarded by her audience as words that were pregnant with wisdom, had left a lasting impression on the young Jamila.

To the couple's immense relief, despite the section Jamila had had for Kunta's birth, Jamila gave birth to Kinte three years later through natural, uncomplicated delivery. Taking place in Socialist

Tanzania which was regarded by Westerners as a typical basket case and a banana republic, it came as a bit of a surprise. And one would accordingly have expected Mjomba to rise to the occasion and give the Cuban doctors who were the mainstay of his country's health system some credit. But this had instead provided Mjomba an excuse to shower more praise on the Americans who "had done it again"!

Many of Mjomba's friends, a good number of whom had received their education in the Soviet Union and Communist China, would in any case have sworn that they had it on good authority that if a child was delivered by caesarean section in any hospital in that former British trust territory, the chances of the child's mother subsequently having another baby by natural birth were nil. Bolstered by the popular myths, they would even have happily wagered everything they were worth that such a mother could never live through two more childbirths!

On the present occasion, the doctors had said that the odds against a caesarean outweighed those against a trouble-free natural childbirth. In spite of the assurances, the couple's anxiety had remained boundless. Not even the growing excitement, as the days of Jamila's confinement wore on, had seemed able to affect the gloom that characterized everything they did.

All that notwithstanding, Mjomba's mind, as he sauntered casually into the desolate reception area of Dr. Mambo's Clinic, had somehow already ruled out the prospects for a caesarean section. At that

574

juncture, he merely expected a nurse to emerge from one of the corridors and overwhelm him with the news that his wife had delivered a baby, preferably a girl this time, and that both mother and child were doing fine.

He met with unexpected disappointment, though for a different reason. The nurse who approached, as he stood erect in the center of the hallway, belonged to a new shift; and her gaze told him before she even spoke that he looked very much like an intruder. And it also occurred to him just then that visiting time had in fact expired hours earlier!

The nurse allowed the inevitable smile to form on her face as she confronted him. "Good evening. What can I do for you, Sir?"

Mjomba initially felt like telling the nurse to stop "Sirring" him and to do what he imagined nurses were expected to do first and foremost, namely to empathize with everybody both infirm and able bodied. (You really could never tell if the ones who looked able bodied were not sick in other ways!) Instead, he faltered repeatedly as he struggled to explain himself.

He had hardly concluded when she vanished into a corridor, only to return shortly afterward intoning from the distance: "*Bado ... bado kidogo.*" Even though most spoke English very well, Tanzanians just loved to speak Swahili, their national language.

And one thing that could be said about Swahili was that it was serving as a bridge uniting the vastly diverging peoples of a country the size of Texas and with a population that was twice that of France! And it also seemed to be true that "speaking the national language" was often used as an excuse to engage strangers one would not otherwise be able to approach in conversation. And that was especially so if you had some inkling that they were not particularly fluent in it.

None of this was the case here, however. With just a hint of sympathy in her voice, the nurse added: "Could take another hour!"

"Fine! I will call later" Mjomba said, his manner business-like now. And as he did so, he turned and set out purposelessly down the darkened street.

Mjomba's throat was scorched and he felt badly in need of a drink. But, on a strange impulse, he fought to keep thoughts relating to his own comfort from his head. Summoning all his will power, he tried to restrict the meanderings of his faculties of the intellect and imagination to considerations that strictly pertained to the welfare of Jamila and nothing else! Like a mystic contemplating the sufferings of a divinity, he even attempted putting himself mentally in his wife's position and enduring the labor pains with her! But the result, perhaps predictably, was total confusion.

Mjomba regained control of himself presently however and, turning left into India Street, quickened his steps in the direction of the Solar Clock in the heart of downtown Dar es Salaam. He was hoping, as he approached Independence Avenue, that he could kill time window-shopping along the famous tree-lined thoroughfare.

Mjomba found that he was the only one dawdling about on the street. It was then that, bewildered and confused as ever, he considered downing a beer or two at the rooftop Moonlite Bar down the road. The red and blue lights of the establishment cast an enigmatic pall over the street and the surroundings as he approached.

He climbed wearily to the top of the dingy stairway. The bar chatter, a mere distant hum of voices when he began the ascent, was now a thunderous drone that invaded his ears from all sides. Intending to pause only briefly in front of the swing doors before gaining entrance, he took in his breath and readied to brush them aside with his arms. He even allowed himself the indulgence of letting his imagination run ahead of him, so that he now already saw himself occupying a high stool at the bar and a suitably cold, if unlabeled, bottle of Kilimanjaro Beer and a large glass before him. He had filled the glass - in his mind - and was all but feeling the cold beer trickle down his parched throat when he came out of his doldrums.

Regaining his presence in front of the swing doors of the bar, Mjomba could not help wondering why the thought had not crossed his mind earlier than that! How on earth could he possibly be thinking of revelling in booze, and on an empty stomach at that, just as his wife was in labor!

He did not stop to consider the possibility of treating himself to a Fanta or a Coke, both of which were a rarity at drinking places and unlikely to be in stock at the Moonlite anyway. Turning away from the hubbub, he made straight for his car in the parking lot of Dr. Mambo's Clinic. He jumped in and, adjusting the reclining angle of the driver's seat, he lowered it to its extremity. He eased himself into it, determined as ever to complete his vigil as planned.

It was forty minutes or so later when, blinking wearily and looking thoroughly flustered, Mjomba once more sauntered into the clinic's reception hall. Several nurses, including the one who had interviewed him earlier, were relaxing on a bench.

They all seemed to stare at him with knowing looks. But it was their colleague who spoke: "Mr. Christian Mjomba?"

Her voice and face were familiar enough and her manner was polite, if cautious.

A casual glance at the girls and, in particular, the speaker and he became convinced that he had been the subject of their chatter shortly, if not immediately, before he made his reappearance. Staring back at them, he imagined their countenances, so prim and un-demeaning now, enveloped in giggles; and he thought: "How pert of them!"

Aloud, Mjomba replied, "Yes" and waited for the news he had already sensed would not be forthcoming.

"I'm sorry," the nurse went on after the pause. "But we don't have any news for you yet. In fact, as it is already pretty late... "

"I know…I know", Mjomba cut in. With full anticipation of what she had been about to say, he continued: "Think I will be better off waiting at home."

"Would you like us to telephone you if there is news?" she piped in his general direction. Her tone was rhetorical and she seemed to expect no more than a nod. But Mjomba raised his voice and began thanking her profusely for the idea.

"Oh, we will be glad to do that" the nurse said cheerily, her mates nodding approval the while. Another nurse consulted a chart she took from a shelf and read out Mjomba's residential telephone number inquiringly.

"That's it, that's it" he said with a wan smile.

Before retracing his steps to the car, Mjomba turned to the first nurse and, wringing his hands, said: "I will be most grateful indeed!"

The hands of Jamila's Omega watch, which he had borrowed, indicated the time as 10:00 O'clock sharp as he started the car's engine to drive away. He half expected to find a message at home instructing him to head back to the clinic on arrival home, but none had been received.

The children were comfortably in bed. Provided with ample warning of her uncle's arrival by the Ford's head lamps, which illuminated the dimly lit living-room as Mjomba was negotiating the last bend in the winding stretch of dirt road leading up to the gates of the bungalow, Fatuma started to lay out his dinner on the table even before the sound of the doorbell, a near perfect facsimile of the purr of a nightingale, tingled overhead.

Mjomba left the dinner untouched for lack of appetite. He took a "cold" shower instead and stepped out of it without noticing that the water, which was hot enough to kill a fly because of exposure to muggy temperatures earlier on in the day, put it in a different class of shower altogether.

After that he selected a seat by the telephone, tuned his Satellite receiver into the Voice of America, and settled back to listen to the African Panorama Show.

As he recalled later, a male announcer on the "show" had given the time as "Thirty minutes past the hour", which Mjomba had interpreted as 11:30 p.m. Then a sprightly female voice had come on the air to announce: "'Tis Request Time!"

Apparently, weariness had overcome him in the moments that followed, sending him into a deep slumber. For beyond that, his mind registered nothing - apart, that is, from the dream.

When the telephone rang, the fifteen-minute programme was still continuing. But in that short space of time, he not only had travelled in his dream to far away California and back, but he had also made it to the near-by National Medical Teaching Hospital and back, the places of birth of Kunta and Kinte respectively.

At the Stanford Medical Center off the panoramic High Way One, Mjomba found himself gazing through a glass partition at his day-old son. Freshly circumcised and naked, poor little Kunta had his tiny legs held apart to allow the bulb's heat to dry the wound. And now he whimpered ever so piteously as if to say that no more and no less than the return of his foreskin could persuade him to make a truce with the world!

The only one of African stock among the nursery's occupants on the day in question, Kunta was possessed of a hue that made him appear no different nonetheless from his white and yellow comrades. He was recognizable only by the name plate which was pinned to his crib and by his wonderfully rich crop of hair - Mjomba had it on good authority that African babies typically arrived with lots more hair on their crown than babies of other ethnic groups!

Closer home at the NMTH where Mjomba was transported in his sleep for the final leg of his phenomenal trip, he had slipped into the nursery disguised as Jamila so he could take a stealthy look at the day old Kinte.

Although the necessity of the disguise was not immediately apparent, his action would be fully justified by what transpired next in the dream.

Mjomba was shocked to discover that two, and in some cases three, infants were being made to share a crib! However, before he could recover from his shock or locate the boy in the crowd of the nursery's wailing in-mates, the plot was discovered.

The guard, a wretched looking old man who had initially pretended to be fast asleep, had in fact been awake and quite alert. But, apparently also a deaf mute, he proved impervious to the intruder's pleas and even offer of a bribe, and proceeded to set off the alarm!

Even before the old guard's emasculated hands had found a proper grip on the mechanism's lever, there was a pealing sound not unlike that of a fire alarm. The sound promptly merged with the telephone's muffled purr as Mjomba, his forehead ringed with beads of sweat, awoke.

If the anxiety precipitated by the neighbor's telephone call that afternoon, and the exhaustion from the subsequent events had dulled the expectant Mjomba's mental faculties, the events of the dream, so nightmarish and livid, had tended to sharpen them. But his wits were still a shade blunted as he stirred to answer the telephone. His bruised nerves were screaming for more relaxation; and it was not until he heard the faintly familiar voice of a girl talking that he completely awoke to reality, which now burst in on him like a clap of thunder.

Even though, when the nurse's voice came crackling through the ear-piece with the news that his wife had just given birth to a baby boy, the Mjombas' third, it all sounded like another dream to the awaking man. Bubbling faster than Mjomba could follow, the nurse said he weighed seven pounds - a giant of a baby, Mjomba thought, considering his mother's size.

The nurse had added: "A beautiful, chocolate coloured little thing with an ample tuft of Negroid hair on his dome!"

As with Kunta and Kinte, the new arrival's hue

apparently took after that of their mom, a ravishing bronze beauty herself. The clear tone of Jamila's skin combined with the classic dimensions of her head, body, and legs, and the tantalizing natural grace she exuded to make her a veritable lily in Mjomba's life. But, strangely, it was upon a black and white photograph acquired during their courtship that Mjomba frequently gazed to keep himself reminded of his "lily flower".

To his artistic mind, the abstractness of a black and white portrait of his enchantress, because it left more to the imagination, was more preferable to the brightness of a colored portrait!

Christian Mjomba fancied the picture of his then smiling bride-to-be so much that he continued to carry the old picture with him everywhere he went inside the covers of a note-book long after they had been wedded.

Standing there shouting excitedly into the telephone, Mjomba scarcely noticed the figure of Fatuma who had been aroused from her sleep by the commotion, and now looked on from the passage-way, her complexion wrapped up in glee.

A strange elation took hold of her when she noticed that his gaze concentrated on a faded but still expressive black and white photograph of her aunt.

Setting down the receiver, Mjomba nearly ran into Fatuma. But he realized almost at once that the Ford's ignition keys were in his trouser pocket, and made an about-turn which prevented a collision but left her dazed all the same. With gestured hand signals and muttered words that fell far short of a comprehensible manner of speech, he attempted, as he backed out of the house, to direct her to lock the door after him. He bolted for the garage door before he could finish.

Outnumbered three to one...

The pains and pangs of childbirth behind her, Jamila was nestled contentedly in the trim hospital bed and sipping tea to quell her rising desire for food when her husband came swaying into the recovery room. Mjomba could see that she was thrilled and utterly mirthful. He flopped down by his wife's bedside and hugged her vigorously.

In reply to his "Hurray!" she plunged into a vivid description of the ordeal she had been through only minutes before - how she had "pushed and pushed" and come close to giving up in her exhaustion! She had scarcely finished when he too began to describe how he had kept vigil, and how he had come close to abandoning it in despair!

When he had finished, Jamila revealed that the child had really started to come as her husband took off in their battered Ford less than an hour earlier! She not only had overheard the conversations in the reception hall, but could tell when he drove off because the Ford's exhaust pipe had a defective muffler.

Their chatter, seemingly endless, did not appear as if it was about to bore them in any way.

They continued to vie with one another in recalling anecdotes from the day's huge store of events. Mjomba, bubbling with joy, had all but forgotten about the other hero of the day in the course of the chatter. But now, as the nurse who had broken the good news to him over the telephone appeared in the doorway, a small bundle balanced between her arms, the atmosphere in the room changed visibly.

"Flora, this is Christian, my husband," Jamila said as the nurse walked into the room.

"We've already met" Mjomba interposed as he gingerly took the "bundle" in his arms and stared down at the pink, round face. Still wrapped up in his swaddling clothes, the newborn babe looked like an angel and far from being battle-scarred, despite his gruelling and traumatic entry into the world.

Flora watched on as Mjomba turned to his wife and, eyebrows up-raised, said half in jest: "Love, one more perhaps-not-so-tough job this time for you. Will you choose the name by which this young chap shall be known?"

"Kintu!" The syllables seemed to come automatically from Jamila's lips, and for a long moment seemed to hold Mjomba dumbfounded. The previously garrulous executive made no effort to hide his surprise. And, all this while, his wife was grinning; a taut, waspish grin, as if she were intent on hiding something from him - which she evidently was.

That very week, Jamila had seen her husband do some thing that had caused her to ponder many things. She had seen him sleep walking, pacing to and fro in his sleep in their master bedroom, like someone deep in thought. She had also noticed that he kept repeating the words "Kunta, Kinte, Kintu... Gunta, Ginte, Gintu" as he did so!

The meanderings of her thoughts, subsequently, as she sought to put what she had heard in some kind of perspective, had initially led her to ROOTS, Alex Haley's bestseller which had a prominent place on the mantle above the fireplace! But that famed masterpiece had failed to adequately explain the name "Kintu".

The passage of time had completely erased from her memory anything that might have connected "Kintu" with the patient Prof. Gringo had treated and, as far as she knew, subsequently discharged almost a decade before. She would not even have cared to know that Innocent Kintu, who now went by the names of Justice Innocent Maramba and who was a celebrated libertine, had taken the advice of Prof. Gringo seriously and had used Theory "R" both to understand his distorted psychological make-up and to correct his flawed view of the world.

Jamila herself had never really shown much interest in the so-called Theory "R", or in the fact that it might have the potential for inducing the cure of mentally deranged persons who felt that the rest of the world, rather than themselves, had got their act wrong! It was doubtful that she would even have cared to know that it was that same Innocent Kintu who was currently her country's Acting Chief Justice - Justice Innocent Maramba - and who was likely to be confirmed in that elevated position, with powers to send people to their deaths, by His Excellency the President!

No interpreter of dreams, Jamila had nonetheless settled on one thing - if the new baby would turn out to be a boy as the ultra-sound scan at the NMTH was suggesting, she would not mind calling him Kintu, Gintu, Gunta or whatever! They all sounded good enough and even an improvement on Haley's "Gunte" anyway - as long it was going to make Mjomba happy. But, having attained her ambition, she now felt either too shy or thought it would be too much of an embarrassment to her idol to explain what had transpired! And even though she was already on first name terms with Flora, she did not consider it proper to bring up such a matter in front of the nurse!

Black as coal and some ten years or so Jamila's junior, Flora was spectacularly formed and quite a stunning beauty herself. She observed the goings-on with what appeared, at first, to be detached concern.

The daughter of a Baptist minister, Flora had been brought up to see only good in people. But now, confronted with what she thought was mischief on an imaginable scale, she found herself empathising with Mjomba and almost hating the woman she had up until now shown so much respect and esteem.

Flora had come to Dr. Mambo's Clinic straight from nursing school. And Mrs. Mjomba, whom she greatly admired above all for her grace, loomed up in her perception as just the right sort of role model for her. It was precisely because of her high expectations of the woman she was already proud to refer to as "My patient" that she now felt such enormous disappointment. She could not bring herself to believe that people of her gender could actually be so impish.

Staring wideeyed at Jamila, Flora was now convinced that under the mask of that awesome beauty lay a nefarious and cruel nature. She had reached that conclusion sorely from surveying the shape of Jamila's mouth at the height of her fleeting standoff with her handsome hubby. Flora even stopped concealing the fact that she was finding him enormously attractive, and began to gawk idolizingly at the man she did not have any scruples about nagging scarcely an hour before.

Staring straight into Mjomba's eyes, and her comely face a mirror of concern for her newfound idol, Flora now flexed the muscles of her well-rounded curves.

When she was sure that her movement had attracted his attention, she took her time to brush aside imaginary dust from her satin-white skirt; and she did not at all seem bothered by the fact that Jamila saw and noted both the eager expression on her face and the mischievous grin accompanying it!

In normal circumstances, nothing would have sounded more familiar to Mjomba than the syllables that formed the name "Kintu". And yet, coming from his wife's mouth at that moment, those syllables sounded so unfamiliar, they might as well have been a different set of syllables altogether! Following a strange law of nature, "Kintu" had taken on a completely different ring in Mjomba's ears.

Mjomba urged himself to calm down and remain that way for a while. This wasn't the first time this kind of thing had happened to him. He was aware that when composing an essay involving ideological conflict, the characters sometimes tended almost naturally to withdraw to the background in the mind of the essayist to allow the ideas attributed to them to get the prominence they deserved. He tried to reassure himself that, perhaps, in this particular instance something was causing the name "Kintu" to pale into something that sounded only remotely familiar to Mjomba to allow a different side to the story to get the prominence it deserved?

Like so many things about which one has only half a recollection, the name continued to defy association with every object his groping mind resurrected. During the minute or so which followed (a minute that looked more like a decade to the embattled Mjomba), "Kintu" remained a little more than a mere sound with no apparent meaning to it.

Or was it that Kintu, the principal character in Mjomba's book, had now assumed a nature all of its own - a nature that perhaps was so complex it had become a puzzle that could elude its own inventor's efforts to solve it! Mjomba smiled at the thought that someone who was responsible for bringing an object into life could in fact end up being rebuffed by his own invention in that fashion! He thought about the innumerable number of times he had painstakingly developed ideas for his "masterpiece" in his mind only to see them slip from his memory and, recede beyond his powers of recall and become lost forever!

Instead of helping Mjomba to nail down the original source of the name Jamila had picked for their son, these thoughts, as they churned through his mind, only caused him to become increasingly depressed. Even though something told him that the obvious solution to his problem was to stop getting mired in thoughts of that kind and to assume a more relaxed stance, he was unable to abandon the subject at that juncture now that he had become so involved with it.

Instead, he now recalled how, at an earlier time, he had been about to lose a battle of wits - or so he then thought - in somewhat similar circumstances between himself and a character he had created for a special role in his "masterpiece" and had to retreat in shame! As he recalled it, he had suddenly found himself at loggerheads on some point with the character in question, and had begun recoiling in fear, because the character, which had taken on a life all of its own, refused to take any nonsense or to budge from the position it had taken. That had caused Mjomba to decide that it was better to throw in the towel.

To allay his mounting fears and lay them to rest on that occasion, he had gradually succeeded in persuading himself that it was all a figment of his imagination - probably due to fatigue - and that there was really nothing amiss between himself and the fictional character in the "masterpiece"! To be fair to Mjomba, his day had been a full one, to be sure; and it could well be that the pressures he was under were intense and enough to drive any average person nuts in very much the same way.

"Honey" Mjomba said finally, his mind still swimming in the world of imagery; "If I had been the one searching for a name for the baby and had come across this one, my choice would have been no different!"

As he spoke, Flora, who had been holding her breath and had also been praying that he would come up with a response that was adequate, emptied her lungs of the stale air with an audible hiss. Visibly relieved and relaxed, she turned and faced him without bothering to conceal the fondness with which she now regarded him. She did this just as Jamila's long eyelashes flickered up and down in quick succession as she on her part shed imaginary tears of joy!

Blushing, Mjomba was surprised that Flora had been inching ever closer to the spot where he had retreated while trying to solve the "Kintu" puzzle, and now stood practically facing him with only a foot or so between them!

Even before the nurse advanced that close, Mjomba was already finding it hard to hide the fact that he was feeling awkward, not just because of the silence which had followed his meaningless utterance, but even more so because of Flora's presence and peculiar demeanor.

He told himself that he should become annoyed with the nurse for getting a kick out of making him feel so uncomfortable. Secretly, he felt exhilarated by her chicanery, however, and wondered why.

Flora was clearly envious of her patient, and appeared to be interested in drawing Mjomba's attention away from Jamila as much as possible, and she did not seem to care a hoot how either of them took it.

Mjomba hardly felt relieved when Jamila, her eyes misty and heart-beat racing, rested her hand on his lap and then, her gaze intent on him, said: "Darling, you must find Kintu a middle name so he will be just like his buddies!"

He felt a lump suddenly form in his throat, and breathing became difficult as he tried to think of a name - any well sounding name - only to find himself stuck!

He could not believe what was happening. He, Christian Mjomba, who bragged about one day being able to bequeath to the world a masterpiece that likely would also get into the Guinness's Book of Records as the best-selling literary work of all time, and who was so confident about his ability to send shock waves into the scientific community by explaining away madness, could not come up with a middle name for his son? A son, moreover, so beloved he had gladly stayed up all night so he could snuggle and hug him and welcome him into the world as soon as possible after his arrival?

Mjomba stole a quick look at the nurse. A thought - although only a thought - had just occurred to him that it was perhaps her presence, which was rendering his vaunted mental faculties suddenly so ineffectual! He looked away swiftly, hoping to thereby prevent Jamila from catching him at it. But it was too late. His wife, who was wide-eyed, not only noticed everything, but had obviously been anticipating Mjomba's move. She threw a glance first in his direction and then in the direction of Flora who herself had been on the alert and had not failed to return Mjomba's glance.

At that point in time, Flora reminded Mjomba of his secretary. The nurse's seductive posture as she stood there in front of them was clearly enough evidence, if any evidence was necessary, that the minister's daughter had taken out all the stops in a deliberate attempt to both tease and harass him.

Mjomba shut his eyes and paused to think about Innocent Kintu, the central character of his "masterpiece". As images of the nurse's beguiling manner came flocking back, he came close to concluding that a non-fictional character like Kintu could in fact be considered fictional when contrasted with a character like Flora!

Although sure that the worst was about to happen, miraculously it did not. Jamila, hiding the fact that he had just been a witness to her own hubby's cheating eyes - or something approximating it - behind a mask of blind selfless love, merely edged closer to him so that their cheeks all but touched.

That is not to say this was something Mjomba would have liked to see happen to him. At that particular moment, there was nothing Mjomba would have wanted more than to be many miles away from Jamila!

Severely embarrassed by both women, Mjomba wished that Flora's attitude to him was different or at least cold - just like the attitude she had displayed earlier on that evening when the very tone of her voice seemed hostile. He would have gladly turned to face her now as a way of appeasing his indignant wife.

Mjomba was on the point of despair when an idea that was as strange as it was outlandish suggested itself. Here he was, being treated like oaf by the two women! The conclusion that another woman might have a hand in it, even though remote, was suddenly appealing. And the most likely suspect was Primrose, no doubt, he told himself. After a short while, he was convinced that it had to be his secretary who had set him up!

And with that, Mjomba was soon quite agitated as he tried to figure out exactly how Primrose had gone about letting his wife in on the secret pertaining to the book project. Mjomba was overwhelmed with emotion at the thought that Primrose, while physically distant, could be involved in his miseries. He also began to wonder, even though in a somewhat fuzzy way at this point, what it was Primrose expected to obtain from being a traitor to him in that fashion.

Almost overwhelmed by his feelings of antipathy for women in general at that juncture, Mjomba could not resist putting the rhetorical question to himself. Well, if it was not his secretary who was behind this, who else could it possibly be? How could Jamila otherwise ever have come up with the name Kintu! Mjomba was certain that Jamila had no personal recollection of anything that had occurred during those early days of their courtship relating to the case of Innocent Kintu.

Mjomba felt certain that it was Primrose who had to be the missing link his groping mind had been trying to nail down. At that moment, as he reached the conclusion that Jamila and Primrose had been in secret communication regarding his literary project, the single word he had been attempting to pin down in his mind's inner-most recesses - before he made the mistake of trying to steal a glance at Flora - materialized from out yonder and settled on the edge of his mind.

To Mjomba's weary mind, the naked 40-watt bulb lighting up his wife's recovery room, had it been lighting up his inner sanctum, might as well have been replaced by the sun itself in that fraction of a second as the word "masterpiece" formed in his thought processes!

The unbroken silence persisted for another uneasy second. And then it was promptly shattered as Mjomba announced triumphantly: "He will just be known as Kintu Gunte wa Mjomba - That is what he is going to be called" he said with finality.

Aside and out of ear-shot, he mumbled: "Kintu Gunte wa Mjomba...doesn't sound bad at all - they actually even rhyme! Kintu Gunte wa Mjomba...Kintu Gunte wa Mjomba!"

Jamila's face registered some puzzlement; and, as if in sympathy, the dimples that were playing on Flora's cheeks also vanished.

"OK! Honey," said Mjomba, brightening. "I guess I cannot keep the secret to myself any longer...!"

"Secret! What secret?" Jamila asked methodically. Her quizzical expression was shared by Flora.

"Guess what! 'Tis yourself who led me to it with your very appropriate choice of name for this guy!"

Slowly he added: "Although I now also know very well the tricks you have all been up to, don't you think?"

Then, as nothing appeared to register - nothing at all, he went on: "Over the past nine months, I have been engaged in writing a book...a masterpiece!"

"A book...a masterpiece? You don't say?" Jamila intoned, a look of disbelief in her eyes.

"Yes, and wait - 'Tis going to be quite a book! I have decided to dedicate it to you and the children. It is designed, naturally, to be a best seller...!"

"Best seller!" Jamila echoed, cutting him short.

"Yes, it will top the best seller lists." Mjomba's voice was vibrant and a shade emphatic.

"And, here - just listen to the title: *The Psychic Roots of a Nut!*" he said, his gaze transfixed to a dot in the ceiling.

"'Tis leaden with stuff every literate person just has to know!" he went on. "And although it is about madmen, it will appeal likewise to ordinary folk struggling to stay on the rails - like us here!"

As Jamila and Flora broke out into a laugh, Mjomba continued: "I predict that Kintu, the book's hero, will become an even greater celebrity than Gunte. And I am not talking about our Kintu here. Gunte of ROOTS, Alex Haley's immortal work!"

Jamila recovered from her laughter in time to say, "What is all this nonsense, Christian?"

In response, Mjomba snapped his fingers. "Hey, hold it!" He said, half shouting. "I think I've got the manuscript in the car!"

He scrambled off the edge of the bed and, thrusting the little "bundle" he held into Flora's waiting arms, scampered off towards the parking lot. The laughter was mildly restrained when he whizzed back into the room seconds later, flourishing a small blue folder bulging with neatly typed pages.

"Here it is" Mjomba said, breathless. "You see, not many books have been written about nut cases, let alone the mental roots of..."

"Darling" Jamila cut in, an expression of obviously contrived earnestness enveloping her face; "Are you sure you are not going haywire yourself?"

When she saw that he remained unmoved, she feigned an exaggerated appearance of despair and cast an awkward glance in Flora's direction.

"The narrative is fairly adequate as it stands

597

now" Mjomba pursued, when Jamila and Flora stopped giggling. "I still have to find a publisher; but even so I do not expect he will edit away very much..."

"Now you are talking!" Jamila interjected. "First get a publishing house to accept your manuscript for publication, and stop counting the chicks before they are hatched - or is it Flora here whom you are trying to impress?"

The nurse, whose participation in the proceedings, had so far been confined to giggles and diffident eye winks, broke herself-imposed silence: "Your husband has already won me over as his literary fan" she said, her tone subdued. Then, her eyes full upon Mjomba, she continued: "It sounds a very interesting book you are writing; and, though I am no great reader of books, you can already be sure of at least one customer...!"

Following the burst of energy Mjomba had expended dashing to and fro to get the manuscript and his subsequent verbal exchange with Jamila, the sound of Flora's voice made him feel a good deal more relaxed. He took the opportunity afforded by the pause in her address to take in her figure, which he suddenly found to be strikingly well proportioned and captivating. He did not wait for his newly found fan to finish.

"Not a bit of it, Flora" he chortled; "I believe I can safely promise you a free autographed copy."

Dragging his gaze away from the large shadowy eyes, he added: "I can't even believe I have finally succeeded in pulling off something so...so ingenious! Until this moment, only my secretary knew I was preoccupied with this project. I gave myself a deadline to accomplish the task as part of the fun, and all the time I had to keep Mama Kunte here - well, also Mama Kintu Gunte wa Mjomba now - in the dark about what probably is my life's most important single achievement. I cannot recall the number of revisions I made. Actually, especially of late, I have often been scared to turn over a page for fear I would start re-writing some paragraph all over again...!"

In a voice that was devoid of all reticence, Flora cut him short: "Would you mind telling me what *The Psychic Roots of a Nut* is about, Mr. Mjomba?"

Mjomba thought he noticed something intriguing about Flora's manner, particularly her decision to address him as "Mr. Mjomba" as opposed to something else. In any case her dark handsome features now loomed up in his mind as a devastating contrast to his wife's and, funnily, also as a challenge! He was bugged by the fact that she had looked just like any other ordinary plain girl in a nurse's uniform when they first accosted each other just hours before!

With Jamila momentarily preoccupied with Kintu, he allowed himself a quick probing stare at Flora only to be met with a direct electrifying gaze. In that instant, he almost forgot himself. His eyes shut as he realized that he was again the object of Flora's intense, and quite unabashed scrutiny. But, even with the image of the girl shut out, he still found himself only partially in control of his emotions. He felt like a spell was being unleashed on him. In an attempt to conceal the effect all that was having on him, Mjomba backed to the edge of the bed and, clasping his sweating hands together, seated himself down by his wife's side.

As Mjomba was beginning uncertainly to give a condensed version of the material of his forthcoming book, Jamila nudged him in the side with a forefinger to draw his straying attention.

Feeling a good deal steadier after that treatment, Mjomba went on: "Kintu - not our Kintu but the book's hero - is born into a land where animism reigns supreme, and of parents who are among the territory's very first converts to Christianity, Innocent Kintu sets out to observe the precepts he is taught strictly from the very beginning. He is determined to pursue the dictates of his faith to their logical conclusion - never mind that the tenets of the strange new religion are in apparent and fairly outrageous conflict with the traditional beliefs and customs of his people.

"For a time, he succeeds in fulfilling his heart's wish, and is even regarded as his tribe's standard bearer. Then the unexpected occurs - Innocent Kintu is taken ill!

"But just as Kintu, a senior seminarist now and a favored candidate for the priesthood, is sliding into what members of the seminary faculty suppose is insanity, one Moses Kapere - a fellow seminarian and a tribesman of Kintu's - also finds himself all of a sudden fighting to keep his own scruples and misgivings from driving him off the rails!

"The 'Rod', as Kapere has been nicknamed by his brethren, avoids a crushing depression only to land in a baffling triple dilemma. If his tribesman's brand of Christianity is the right one, then his own practice of religion, which supposedly is liberal and unpretentious in contrast to the blind, almost impulsive spirituality of his brother-in-Christ, is ill founded and sham! But the realization that Brother Innocent and himself could still both be fakes leaves him in a trap.

"Thus, unless and until he resolves the mystery surrounding the brother's behaviour, there may well be little likelihood that he himself will ever fully realize his own identity in the mystifying circumstances of the New World!

"It is this equally strange set of circumstances which prepares the ground for a giant step for science - the discovery by the 'Rod' of Theory "R"! That theory not only solves the mystery of Brother Innocent's malady, but also helps medicine and in particular psychiatry turn a completely new leaf!"

At the end of Mjomba's exposition, all three, oblivious of their individual problems at the start, burst out into a merry laugh. Mjomba's guffaw was a low-pitched, sonorous affair, exaggerated to camouflage the fact that it was all feigned. And it contrasted with the thrill, child-like tantrums of the women, who appeared genuinely impressed by the presentation.

Mjomba stopped "laughing" a little earlier than the others and intoned: "But there is a catch! Moses Kapere, the Rod, is actually me. The true life

601

'Innocent' is another story altogether...!"

Mjomba waited for the wail of laughter to recede before launching himself into the story from a completely different angle: "The perfect madman who can only exist in the figment of the mind, the Innocent Kintu you will discover between these pages is a completely reinvented character who, I dare say, owes everything to my imagination and ingenuity. A one-faced character, incapable by definition of leading a double life, he still ends up living two lives all the same - and to the full, actually!"

Mjomba was very well aware that there had been a time when the original Innocent Kintu, now Acting Chief Justice Maramba and a respected member of the bench, fitted that description to the letter. The only other person who was aware of that fact was Prof. Gringo, now a Professor Emeritus and also Vice Chancellor of the prestigious Julius Nyerere University, They also both knew how Judge Maramba's cure had come about, namely with the assistance of Theory "R".

But the special bond of friendship that had formed between the three men in the aftermath of the landmark "cure" had foreshadowed everything else, including what they might have jointly reaped materially from it. They had come to an agreement that the reputation and future career of their beloved friend and confidant would be at stake if it were revealed that "His Honor" had at one time suffered from one of the most terrible form of insanity; and Prof. Gringo had immediately moved to alter the medical records of his former patient to make it look as if he had just been misunderstood and that there hadn't been anything wrong with his "patient".

With Maramba's stellar performance at Oxford and Yale from where he had earned advanced law degrees in succession, and his appointment almost immediately upon his return to the plum job on the bench, neither Prof. Gringo nor Mjomba had felt any regrets about their action. And, needless to say, it did not surprise them that things turned out the way they did for their friend. As far as they were concerned, if you borrowed a leaf from the Psychic Roots of Innocent Kintu as Dr. Maramba had done and reorganized your life accordingly especially in the world of academia where success depended entirely on one's ability to think right, the sky would be the only limit in a literal sense.

In return, Dr. Maramba had used his influence with the republic's President, an Oxford alumnus like himself, to get Prof. Gringo where he now was. As for Mjomba, the rumours were already rife that he might become the country's deputy Minister of Finance. It was precisely because of these machinations that Prof. Gringo had made little progress in persuading the scientific community that Theory "R" worked.

A practicing psychiatrist still and professor emeritus at Julius Nyerere University, Prof. Gringo now viewed the problem differently. He needed patients who were capable of digesting the theoretical part of Theory "R", and who could then proceed to also use it as a tool for self-therapy, following in

Maramba's footsteps, and eventually induce their own cure that way. Experience had taught him that those types of patients were not easy to come by.

The professor sometimes wished that he himself had heard about theory 'R' earlier than he did. As a research fellow at the Hoover Institution during his final year at Stanford, he had been commissioned by the think tank to develop psychological profiles of the new crop of military leaders in Africa, following the wave of coup d'états in the early sixties. He was now of the firm belief that his profiles would have been much more precise if he had had the benefit of Mjomba's discovery.

The professor, who happened to belong to the same clan as that to which the King of Buganda belonged and considered himself a member of royalty for that reason, would have been very delighted if his scope of work had included profiles for the world's so-called democratic leaders as well. A rank conservative, he was inclined to the view that they too were usurpers driven by a yearning to fill the role of royalty, and he would have welcomed an opportunity to probe their mental processes.

He wondered what went on in their minds as they went about their business as heads of state in their respective countries! He tried and failed to understand how politicians in the West could ever justify the actions that had led to the two world wars, for instance! Certainly individuals who could produce and go on to employ weapons of mass destruction of kind that brought death and ruin to the cities of

Hiroshima and Nagasaki, and then continue with their lives as if nothing had happened, did not just deserve to have their heads examined, in Mjomba's view they deserved to be confined in a maximum security detention center for the rest of their lives and denied any opportunity to harm their fellow humans in such a senseless fashion ever again.

As far as the professor was concerned, so called democratic leaders, be it in the West or the East, were really no different from the crop of coup leaders whose turn it now was to hit the headlines. In his view, to accede to the lofty places politicians in those "democracies" occupied, they had merely employed a different method, namely a popular revolution that went by the more dignified name of the popular ballot. Prof. Gringo knew all too well that, in the majority of cases, those so-called popular revolutions had initially been supported by the now rather unpopular bullet in any case.

In the opinion of the man of letters, the exercise of territorial rule was a form of reigning. If a common man who was not representing royalty was allowed to reign, there were no grounds to stop any other common man from doing the same by one method or another. The solution seemed obvious to the professor. The business of governing was better left to those who were born to govern!

He had no doubt in his mind that Theory "R" would have been not only helpful but critical in proving his point in all these cases of what he regarded as "usurped power". And, with respect to the wider applicability of the theory, there was in Prof. Gringo's estimation, no question whatsoever concerning its potential with regards the theory's wider applicability.

And when, as happened from time to time, feelings of guilt for not doing everything in his power to popularise the cure and demonstrate to the world that the end was in sight for one of the most pernicious conditions ever to plague man threatened to overwhelm him, he always had what he considered to be a very good ready excuse: He would have to first of all persuade the world that Theory "R" really worked in the judge's case - something he was not at all prepared to do. But he still dreamed of the day when he might be in a position to show conclusively that the theory worked using other cases.

And now that Innocent Kintu, aka Justice Maramba, was on the verge of becoming his adopted country's Chief Justice, Prof. Gringo even felt that he had a duty to the Tanzania people to keep the medical history of the Acting Chief Justice under wraps forever. Prof. Gringo agreed with Mjomba that, before his cure, Justice Maramba fit the description of the "perfect madman". But even though he now considered Kintu one of the most predictable individuals alive, he knew he could not under any circumstances reveal that Justice Maramba had been down that road - the perfect madman, and even less a one-faced character "incapable by definition of leading a double life" as Prof. Gringo always liked to add!

Mjomba had been fully supportive of the

professor in this matter from the start. Accordingly, as the two women gasped with laughter over his description of the hero of his book, Mjomba stood back and, inside, enjoyed a laugh of his own, sure that his lie had carried the day.

And he did not wait to give them a break in their laughter either, for he presently added: "Dr. Claus Gringo, Kintu's psychiatrist had an assistant...a quadroon! Flora, do I need to say the rest?"

The fresh burst of laughter petered out only to become thunderous once more as he added: "I'm sure you already recognize it - the old story of the scramble for Africa! It started off as scramble for Africa's wealth; then it became a scramble for our bodies with slavery. The advent of the churches turned it into a scramble for our souls!"

He had hardly finished talking when Jamila, still jittery with laughter, said haltingly: "Flora, I should have warned you not to encourage him in this ... the next thing we are going to hear is that he is offering to be nominated for the Nobel Prize for Literature or something!"

It was Mjomba's turn now to explode with laughter. In the meantime Flora, whose adulation of Mjomba at this point, made her a reluctant party in anything which even remotely threatened to diminish his stature, found herself interjecting: "Medicine! Psychiatry! He should go for the Nobel Prize for Medicine."

She saw Jamila react to her suggestion with a start, but continued with a lofty indifference: "Unless you think he is a mad author who has gone out of his way to explain away insanity as a joke!"

The drone of bells, as a distant clock struck mid-night, brought everyone to attention and averted what might have turned out to be an ugly incident, with Jamila apparently inclined to say disparaging things about her husband on the one hand, and Flora all too keen to glorify everything about him on the other.

Mjomba, who had cut his own concocted spasms of laughter short in the meantime, had his mind elsewhere. This being his first real opportunity to demonstrate that the course of the world was about to be changed by the Psychic Roots of a Nut, he was considering recounting what the book was about all over again, although from a completely different angle this time - the same angle he had used when he scribbled his suggested blurb the day before. But before he could barge in with the modified summary of the book, the already ugly mood in the room changed for the worse.

Just then, little Kintu Gunte wa Mjomba fell into a violent temper, and dramatically started waving his tiny but tight-fisted hands in the air, in an apparent effort to connect to Flora's head! He tried to kick the sides of his captor, but only caused his unpracticed legs to become entangled in the web of swaddling bands enfolding him.

As if determined to exercise his autonomy and personal freedom, he began to scream in his tiny, squeaky voice that was not unlike a kitten's. Finally, defeated, Flora bade the couple good-morning and reluctantly retreated with her charge into the sanctuary of the nursery.

As soon as he was left alone in the room with his wife, the senior Mjomba kissed her on the cheek before dropping the blue folder carefully in her lap.

"Put it away until tomorrow, Honey" he said, turning his own cheek. "You need all your rest as of now - and, besides, my book is really meant to be read in perfect peace by the fireside!"

Jamila fell into a deep slumber almost as soon as Mjomba departed.

Fiend in Flora...

Flora was not expecting to find Mjomba around when she finished putting her charge to bed and returned five minutes or so later. Thinking that Jamila would be delighted to know that her baby was comfortably in bed, especially in view of the maelstrom her husband had generated, the nurse headed for Jamila's room.

Flora's mind was otherwise set on getting back to her associates in the nurses' Common Room as fast as her legs could carry her there. She had no doubt that her experiences during the half hour or so that she had been away, contained abundant material to keep her friends on the shift entertained and cheered up until morning. Telling each other yarns from their experiences was an established way of killing time on that dull shift. Stories involving love affairs fascinated the girls the most, and Flora could not wait to carp about how she had come close to "overthrowing a government", the expression they used to refer to any action that caused an existing love relationship to break-up! It was not unusual for the storyteller to stretch the facts of a case, if necessary, to make the story more interesting. Flora did not feel that it would be necessary to resort to that in this particular case, however.

She could not wait to get back to the Common Room with her hot tale, and she quickened her steps accordingly. One thing she could, however, not entirely erase from her memory, as she closed in on the sick bay where Jamila's room was located, was the way she had conducted herself in front of Jamila and her husband.

But her mind was, even though, not entirely wanting in so far as laying blame was concerned. If there was one thing Flora was ready to swear to, Mjomba was completely to blame for whatever had transpired and, indeed, almost pushed her over the brink! It was undoubtedly all his fault, she told herself!

On her lips as she prepared to announce her arrival to Jamila was the single word "Men"!

"Men!" she was also in fact ready to exclaim as soon as she came within earshot of her waiting pals; "They all are the same."

It was after all Mjomba who, with his singular charm and allure, had encroached on her space there within the precincts of Dr. Mambo's Clinic. Her colleagues could have vouched that it was completely

610

out of character for her to behave as she had done in front of Jamila and her hubby without prodding of some kind. Well, had he not been a good man, she would be thinking of suing just now - for sexual abuse! Lucky for him that she now only proposed to make that curious and somewhat unseemly encounter the main subject of their chatter there within the confines of the Common Room.

The light in Jamila's room was still on. The recent rivalry already apparently forgotten, Flora slowed her pace so she would have more time to be recollected before announcing her arrival. After all she did not have any beef against her genteel patient, she told herself.

She was able to make out Jamila's form from a distance. Slouched against her pillow and clasping the blue folder close to her breast, Jamila appeared to be engrossed in her husband's work. It was only after Flora approached the bed and was about to address her mentor turned rival that she realized that Jamila was asleep. Slumped to one side, Jamila was sound asleep and snoring fitfully. At that moment, a thought as absurd as it was reckless thrust itself into her mind. She could almost hear the fiend in her whisper that this was the time to get even with Jamila and also her chance - perhaps the only one she would ever get - to beat Jamila to it by filching the manuscript from the sleeping woman, withdrawing to a secluded spot, and being the first to peruse the work of the man she had fallen for!

Flora strove to stifle a mischievous smile that

had begun to envelope her face. She chastised her inner-self and even closed her eyes as she struggled to avoid giving the wicked proposition any consideration. Flora felt a deep sense of guilt for what struck her as a diabolical idea. She could have sworn that it wasn't her idea at all.

She did not stop to reflect if the "weird" notion sprung from that frail part of her which her own dad used to refer to as the flesh - the part of human nature which, according to what she had been taught, had been irrevocably sullied by concupiscence after the fall of Adam and Eve; or if the wicked scheme was an idea that Beelzebub (whoever he was!), taking advantage of her feeble nature, was attempting to plant in her mind; or if the whole thing was just another side of her good-natured old self and did not merit any further thought for that reason. But, for certain, it was less likely, she thought, to be a case of possession by that cryptic and formless archenemy of humankind who sometimes also went by the name of Mephistopheles - she could not see any reason why the archenemy would choose her of all people for any wicked scheme he might have in mind!

And, no believer in animism, she would have scorned the suggestion that the spirits of her ancestors had something to do with it. If there was another thing Flora was again ready to swear to, it was that Christian Mjomba, by thrusting himself unannounced into her life, was completely to blame for whatever was going on!

Flora believed in miracles, but could not bring

herself to accept that one happened just as she was fretting over the wicked ideas which were descending on her out of nowhere. But, in a split second, the mischievous ideas were gone, making her start to wonder if her fears were all imaginary! There was no mischievous smile for Flora to suppress, and no urge to snicker either! All the naughty ideas were gone in an instant.

Assuming a businesslike air on what seemed like an impulse, Flora stepped inside the room, smoothed the bedding methodically and, finding a pillow, tucked it carefully under Jamila's head. Then, stepping back, she surveyed the scene one more time before reaching for the light switch. Finally, satisfied that her patient was comfortably asleep, Flora dimmed the lights and slid noiselessly out of Jamila's room into the brilliance of the brightly lit hallway. But she made an about-turn almost instantaneously, and slipped back inside the darkened sick bay.

Then, moving stealthily, Flora just let her feet bear her along noiselessly like a snake gliding over bushy ground. As she approached Jamila's bedside, she resembled a leopard that was about to prance on its prey, and did not once take her eyes off the blue folder that the sleeping Jamila seemed to be hugging as never before. Then gently, very gently, Flora extricated the blue folder from Jamila's clasp. She was surprised at the firm hold that the sleeping woman maintained on the folder, and in the end found that she had to yank it away from Jamila's grip with a certain amount of force.

Clutching her prize close to her own breast now and her heart beating wildly, Flora hastened out of the room. She headed for the administrative wing without stopping once to think. The place was deserted and looked forbidding at that time of night. Her quick steps brought her presently to the Matron's office located in the Maternity Wing's interior.

Once inside, Flora closed the door behind her and switched on the lights. She was already turning the manuscript's pages over even as she skirted the ornate, flat-topped desk used by the Matron. Her face buried in the papers now, she made for the photocopier at the far end of the room almost blindly. She mechanically reached for the "ON" switch on the underside of the apparatus and depressed it without looking.

Flora did not wait and started to extricate the single pink sheet that lay ineptly among the manuscript's pages like a page marker. The "marker" stood out clearly from among the rest of the manuscript's pages, which were milky white. On inspection, the "marker" turned out to be the blurb in draft - or so it's two-letter header **"Suggested Blurb"** in bold face proclaimed it to be. Just what she needed, she whispered to herself, before reverting her attention to the copier, which remained silent. Setting the blurb and the rest of the manuscript down on the matron's desk while taking care not to throw the neat but loose bundle of papers into disarray, Flora checked to make certain that she had depressed the right button on the copier.

She was clearly relieved to discover that the cause of the machine's failure was the fact that its power cable was unplugged. Snatching up the blurb, she started reading it silently to herself even as she was fumbling with the power cable. She somehow succeeded in getting the cable in its socket on the wall at the first try even though she did it blindly without looking.

Flora was well aware that her presence in the area at that hour would raise eyebrows if discovered. But she also knew that the chances of any one observing her were very slim. Even so, the whine of the machine's compressors as the copier began to warm up sent a chill down her spine. To her ears, the whine of the Xerox copier as it broke the deadening silence sounded like the noise of a garbage truck in gear, and nearly caused her to flee. But she recovered quickly and continued to pore over the blurb.

When Flora snatched the manuscript from Jamila's unrelenting grip, her intention had been to photocopy the approximately two hundred pages or so making it up for her own use and then quietly slip the original manuscript back into Jamila's waiting arms. Although that was still Flora's intention, there were already signs that there was something in the offing that was likely to alter the course of events.

The first thing that had caught Flora's attention when the lights in the Matron's office came on was the pink coloured sheet which had obviously been shoved into the folder at the last minute. It was this sheet that

615

Flora now gingerly clasped between her thumb and pointing finger as she readied the photocopying machine.

The nurse stood there motionless, her eyes glued to the page with the blurb, while the photocopying machine warmed up. She continued to do so even after the erratic drone of the copier gave way to a smooth whirr, signaling that the copier was all ready and set to do its job at the touch of the button. Flora remained transfixed in the same spot as her eyes darted first from one side of the yellow page to the other, and then up and down the page as she perused the text of the blurb several times over.

If Mjomba's smooth talk earlier on had already sold the story of Innocent Kintu to the nurse, the catchy blurb now nailed the deal, if any nailing was necessary. Her scrutiny of the blurb drafted by Mjomba, the man who had proved to be such a fatal attraction before little Kintu Gunte wa Mjomba spoilt everything for her by getting into a sudden fit, convinced her that she had not been entirely out of her senses to fall for him. And all the while, as she gradually absorbed the message contained in the blurb's five odd sentences, she wondered what the rest of the manuscript might have in store!

While perusing the blurb, Flora felt as though Mjomba was verily present; and she decided to prolong that feeling by reading it slowly and several times over. The five odd sentences making up the blurb also sparked in her something else. It was a sudden interest in the book's subject matter!

Her mind, already in turmoil because she knew very well that "overthrowing the government of Jamila" was not a practical proposition for her at this time, and because of her suspicion that Jamila would in any case put up the stiffest fight to keep Mjomba all for herself, began to swarm with images of a cast of immortal characters who were ready to act out Innocent Kintu's story at the word "go". It did not matter that the blurb was as brief as it was. What really mattered was its theme, which seemed to be simply loaded - just like a sparkling model of a new line of automobiles!

Flora was already thinking that the story about Innocent Kintu was likely only a smoke screen for an autobiographical work. The blurb itself referred to "the dramatic story of an aspiring author who had seen his friends fall prey, one by one, to a hither-to unheard of brain condition". Flora was convinced that the fictitious author had to be Mjomba himself! For a minute or so she stood there, immobile; like someone who had become paralysed in her tracks and had turned into a statue. She was helpless as more images suggested by the blurb continued to stream through her mind.

Flipping over the pages, she stopped at the "foreword" and buried her head inside once more. The fact that the foreword run into three pages rather than half a page as she had noticed with some of the novels she recalled reading didn't seem to matter to her at all. Then, even though she was just perusing through text, she felt as though she was watching a

617

James Bond movie with Mjomba playing the part of that famous actor. In her mind's eye, she saw Mjomba setting out on his long journey of discovery, which easily fit into her idea of a "mission impossible". She believed that, after seeing Innocent Kintu fall prey to the hitherto unheard-of disease, her idol, fearful for himself, had set out to gain insight into the disorder - the only way out of his bind.

According to the blurb, the strange disease appeared to single out intellectuals! With a certain amount of temerity, she followed Mjomba's trail as he grappled with the immediate problem faced by his pal and himself, and then as he battled to simultaneously establish himself as a writer of consequence.

The nurse's compassion was bottomless as the "fictitious" author began to show signs that he might himself be going crazy. But her sorrow for him was balanced by the fact that he already believed, at that early stage, that he had stumbled onto a remarkable scientific discovery. But even then, it was the researcher, rather than the discovery, that was the primary focus of her attention.

Flora's obsession with the fictitious author hit a bump when the blurb went on to declare that all of this transpired as the troubled but handsome essayist, a member of the seminary brotherhood who had been on the verge of taking the perpetual vow of chastity at the time, met and wed a dazzling beauty. There was no doubt in Flora's mind that this dazzling beauty was Jamila.

But, instead of dissuading her from reading

further, that part of the foreword whose veracity Mjomba himself had confirmed only minutes earlier, simply propelled her to read on. If anything, she now felt that she had no choice but to finish reading the rest of the manuscript right there and then, at least so she would know the odds against her!

A full three hours later, when the sounds of day break brought her to, Flora would be unable to explain how she had switched off the photocopier, found her way to the matron's desk, and settled down in the matron's cozy chair to finish reading Christian Mjomba's "masterpiece". It was because she did those things completely instinctively.

Once in the Matron's seat, Flora had apparently begun to read the manuscript to herself aloud. Starting with the page of contents, she had eagerly delved into the rest of the material and become so carried away with the story, she had felt just like someone who was watching a motion picture. It was when the "movie" concluded around dawn that she had risen up to leave the "theatre" and had been surprised to discover herself in the matron's office!

PART 13: MJOMBA'S "DEATH AND RESURRECTION"

His demeanor looking steely in the glimmer of the streetlights dotting the hospital grounds, Christian Mjomba made for the spot where he had parked the Ford as if drawn there by a magnet. For all practical purposes, his mind was blank and free of all concerns as he steered into *Umoja wa Wanawake* Drive to head home.

It was as he approached the house and was guiding the car into the lock-up garage that something really strange happened. It started with a cock's crow which sounded just like a bugle as it rose from a neighbor's poultry shed that backed up to his garage and shattered the silence. That was immediately followed by the squeaking of a partridge awakening with a stir in nearby bushes, which must have awoken the entire population of bird-life inhabiting trees in the area causing, and which in turn proceeded to serenade him with a majestic cacophony of melodies.

All might have been well had the welcoming not reminded him of the one morning he had arrived home from a night of debauchery. The evening before, a couple of people he barely knew had persuaded him to join them for what they described as a light social evening; and, before he knew it, the group, including himself, had found itself at this place called Hannibal's Cove.

Once the group had settled down to the roast meat and booze, which included exotic cocktails such as Africoco and Red Top, it had proved impossible for

620

Mjomba to tear himself away from the company. Dead drunk and ill with a splitting headache, he had staggered from the joint when it was already daybreak, miraculously guided the Ford home without any incident along the way, only to crash it into his garage door! That had apparently startled the single cock that shared quarters with the chickens in the poultry shed, and got it crowing perhaps a little earlier than usual. What then followed was the exact same welcome from the bird realm, triggered no doubt by the rooster's crow. But it had, naturally, been quite a different story when he confronted Jamila in the house. Although all was now long forgotten - and forgiven, that episode of all things was the last thing Mjomba would have wanted to be reminded of on this particular morning as he arrived home from Dr. Mambo's Clinic.

There was no undoing what had come to pass, however. But, even though he did not anticipate a dressing down of any sort on this particular occasion, he was unable to erase from his head the feeling that the serenade might be a bad omen. Inside the house, Mjomba hurried to bed and closed his eyes in an attempt to shut out memories of his fling at wanton living - the only one he recalled ever having! The attempt appeared to succeed as he rolled over and, with a loud snore, fell asleep. But it was also then that he started to dream.

Free from the shackles of his terrestrial existence, Mjomba easily travelled back, in the illusory world of dreams, to Dr. Mambo's Clinic. Even though not something he did often, Mjomba felt very much at home pursuing his adventures in the nether world and gave the impression that he was as practiced in matters of that world as anyone else fortunate enough to belong there.

And so, there he was, gliding effortlessly in the hallway through which, utterly exhausted as a result of going non-stop since emerging from his office at the Trade Center early the previous day and in a virtual stupor, he had wearily trudged scarcely a half hour earlier, careful not to trip and find himself sprawling on the floor. He had not been prepared to risk making himself a laughing stock in front of Flora and her work-mates then. But now, the glorious state that came with his new predicament precluded any such misadventure.

Like the good devoted husband he was, Mjomba's thoughts immediately turned to his wife. "You need all your rest as of now" he recalled saying to her not long before. He had not doubted that Jamila, his beloved, would do as behoved a loving wife and take her much needed rest in response to his plea. He only needed to shift his head in her direction from wherever he was to see if she had followed his advice. As he did so, he observed that his belle had, indeed, fallen into a deep slumber. He noticed in an instant that, even as she lay sleeping, Jamila was still clutching the manuscript for his forth-coming best seller with both hands as if reading from it.

The light in her room was still on. Suddenly

Mjomba appeared visibly agitated, in spite of the fact that he was living in a cosmic world, as he spied Flora saunter into Jamila's recovery room. He observed with keen interest as the girl, a comely figure of enormous beauty even by cosmic standards, looked over his wife. Apparently satisfied that her patient was comfortably in bed, Flora reached out for the light switch on the table lamp by the bedside.

Mjomba noted that the light in the room dimmed very gradually, in the exact same way the lights in some theatres still did, until the room in which his dear Jamila lay asleep was finally enveloped in near total darkness. But it was not before something else transpired.

Even though enjoying an existence on a plane that, for all practical purposes, was hallowed, Mjomba, his exalted state notwithstanding, could not suppress a giggle as he watched the still earth-bound Flora, a wicked grin on her face, do something really funny.

He saw the nurse stoop low over the sleeping Jamila to kiss her on the cheek; but in the same movement, the girl also peeped inside the open covers of the manuscript, which remained in his wife's firm grip and close to her bosom - at least for now. Then, moving gracefully, Flora stepped out of the darkening room and into the brilliance of the brightly lit hallway. But she had scarcely done that when she suddenly made an about turn. She moved stealthily now and just let her feet bear her along noiselessly as if she were a snake. Inside the darkened room and as she approached Jamila's bedside, she resembled a leopard that was about to pounce on its quarry. Then, gently, very gently, Flora attempted to extricate the manuscript from his wife's grasp. She seemed surprised at the firm hold that the sleeping woman maintained on the blue binder. In the end, Flora found she had to yank the manuscript away forcibly from Jamila's firm grip.

Finally, clutching her prize close to her own breast now, and her heart visibly beating wildly, Flora hastened out of the room. Without stopping to think, she made her gate-away at a quickening pace and, wheeling round a corner, momentarily vanished from Mjomba's view.

It was Mjomba's turn to get on the move now. He spun around and then, gliding along like a seraph himself, sped after her. He easily caught up with the nurse, but decided to follow her at a safe distance instead. He could see that she was heading for the clinic's administrative wing. The place, normally abuzz with activity, was deserted and looked forbidding at that time of the night even to Mjomba. Flora's quick steps brought her presently to the matron's office located in the administrative wing's interior. Once inside, she closed the door behind her.

All Mjomba had to do to gain entrance was to incline his frame slightly to one side, eyeball the part of the door or wall he intended to penetrate and then will himself through it by virtue of being a spiritual or incorporeal being first and foremost, and a corporeal or physical entity only in an ancillary sense. And sure enough, that puissant combination of will power and faith in himself saw him materialize instantaneously on the other side of the door as if he were a spook. Because he wasn't used to doing that sort of thing, Mjomba shut his eyes instinctively as he approached the door and opened them when he realized that he was safely inside.

He got there in time to see Flora switch on the lights. She stared around her, clearly pleased that she was now all by herself, or so she thought! With a fleeting glance, she quickly noted the different items in the office, among them the matron's work desk, the Xerox copier, and a bookshelf that held imposing medical tomes.

There appeared to be something spellbinding about the photocopier, because her eyes lingered on it for a while before they moved on to survey the other items in the room. She did not see the ghost of Mjomba perched atop the bookshelf, although her eyes rested briefly on two wooden carvings that depicted Masai warriors and were literally framing his face. But she could not help noting that, after the matron's desk, the bookshelf was the most prominent item in the room.

Mjomba watched idly as the girl skirted the matron's ornate, flat-topped mahogany desk while turning over the pages of the manuscript at the same time, and head straight for the copier at the far end of the office almost blindly. He looked astonished and intrigued, observing Flora perform what he regarded as an interesting feat without incident - and then he immediately checked himself. For here he was, relishing the joys of the supra-natural realm, and at the same time indulging in mundane things like the display of emotion. It was in fact the second time he had caught himself displaying his feelings, the first time being the giggle he failed to suppress when he saw Flora plant a kiss on Jamila's cheek.

As he was well aware, the ground rules of his existence in the enchanted realm of pure spirits did not permit one to feel "intrigued" or "fascinated", or anything of that sort. Such states of mind, because they were originally designed to satisfy the lower needs of human beings, could never be agreeable with the lofty nature that people in the dream world enjoyed!

Like the rest of the mystic creatures that dwelt in the fantasy world in which he now found himself, Mjomba had a pretty clear perception of the consequences of violating the mystic cannons of behaviour. Discernment of the precepts that were in force moreover came naturally to the dream world's subjects, and not through studying legal manuals or handbooks as was the case back on Earth. Knowledge of such things came to them through introspection. Awareness of the self automatically triggered a thorough comprehension of the basic rules governing one's mystic environment. There was therefore no excuse for not knowing what one was supposed to know, and certainly no excuse for breaking any mystic cannon of conduct.

Mjomba thus also knew well enough that the

penalty for violating a rule, although always commensurate with the gravity of the transgression, tended to be severe at least in human terms. (Talking about seeing things in human terms, Mjomba had no inkling as to how he had come by the undoubtedly canny ability to see things in that dimension!) The reason infractions of the rules attracted severe punishment was because they were always accompanied by full knowledge that they were misdeeds. Additionally, the misdeeds were always done without any coercion whatsoever, be it moral or mystical.

Another point to be noted was the fact that the sinners or transgressors themselves invariably conceded on their own volition that the punishment meted out was well earned. Mjomba understood introspectively that this had something to do with the fact that mystic creatures, because of the manner in which their cognitive faculties worked, never needed reminders that their existence in that realm was entirely gratuitous, a pure favor or gift attributable to the action of His Mystic Majesty which some, somewhat gamely, referred to as the Big Bang.

And so, just as Mjomba was starting to feel fascinated by what he was seeing, he froze in his tracks, as a result of which his boyish face was left wrapped up in a half smile. His near fatal error clearly told on his demeanor, which immediately changed from frivolous to somber. His quick action had averted retribution from His Mystic Majesty. But even though well pleased with himself for acting promptly and averting calamity, he now desisted from showing it, because that too would be in violation of the rules!

Flora, her face completely buried in his manuscript and obstructed from view, was preparing to switch on the photocopier when the draft blurb, which was typed on the only colored sheet in the sheath of papers, caught her attention. The pink sheet lay ineptly and shriveled inside the otherwise neat bundle of papers, and caused her to conclude that it had been shoved into the original batch of papers at the last moment. She reached out mechanically for the power switch on the side of the copier and depressed it without taking her eyes off the blurb.

With Mjomba watching intently, the nurse came to with a start when the copier failed to react. She looked up from the papers for the first time and was clearly relieved to discover that the copier's power cable had been unplugged from its wall socket. But her gaze immediately dipped, and her attention again became focused on the blurb as she reached out with her right arm and plugged the copier's power cord into the wall socket.

Mjomba observed all this from his vantage point atop the matron's bookshelf and did not miss any detail. In his supra-natural state, even though he may not have been able to do things like forecast the future or anticipate each and every act of individuals from studying their habits, he was certainly capable of making out what was on their minds by just observing their actions. And when an individual was reading

628

from a book or from a piece of paper, it was quite easy for Mjomba to scrutinize the same material and to make his own conclusions about it by just observing movements of the reader's eyelids.

Mjomba could therefore tell that Flora was apprehensive that her presence in the area at that hour would raise eyebrows if discovered. He also knew from studying her demeanor her thoughts about the chances of anyone observing her there being very slim. And when the nurse depressed the copier's "ON" button the second time, it did not come as a complete surprise to him when the whine of the machine's compressors, as it sprung to life and begun to warm up, sent a chill down her spine.

Mjomba's own reaction at that stage was completely cool for once - as it was expected to be. He would ordinarily have found it hard to hide the empathy he felt for Flora. He was, however, determined this time not to allow his feelings to ruin things for him, and he succeeded, although not without a struggle, in suppressing them.

Something in his psyche caused him to focus on Flora's thoughts earlier when she snatched the manuscript from Jamila's unrelenting grip. Her intention had been to obtain her own photocopy of each one of its two hundred or so odd pages, and then quietly slip the original manuscript back into Jamila's waiting arms. She, of course, knew nothing at that juncture regarding the blurb.

While the photocopying machine warmed up, Flora, who was also fairly exhausted by the evening's events, sat herself down at the matron's desk and started reading the proposed blurb for Mjomba's masterpiece. She sat there motionless, her eyes glued to the pink sheet. She continued to do so even after the loud drone of the copier ceased, signaling that it was all ready and set to do her bidding at the touch of a button if she chose to proceed with her plan.

If Mjomba's smooth talk earlier on had already sold the story of Innocent Kintu to Flora, the catchy blurb now nailed the deal, if any nailing was still necessary. And as Flora's eyes darted from the blurb to the first page of the manuscript and then to the second and so on, occasionally reading a paragraph several times over, the smile on her impish face became more and more bemused. It became clear before long that she was unable to interrupt the enjoyment she was deriving from perusing the material for Mjomba's masterpiece for any reason whatsoever.

But while Flora was preoccupied thus and obviously enjoying what she was reading, the opposite appeared to be true for Mjomba. With each sentence she read, Mjomba's demeanor, hitherto so remarkable for the serenity and calm it enthused, began to change, until finally, irate with no one in particular but nonetheless bursting with feelings of anger and disappointment, Mjomba began to flay his arms from side to side like earthlings sometimes did when they were in great distress.

Mjomba could not imagine that the world

around him could be so dreamlike and unreal. The material Flora had filched from his wife had turned out, inexplicably, to be so radically different from his original manuscript, it could not even have qualified as apocryphal. As he followed the movement of Flora's eyelids and translated them into the words she was reading, he noticed that it was not just the story line that was completely uninteresting and dull. The expressions employed to describe scenes in the story were so poorly chosen, they could not possibly have been his! What was more, he wouldn't have liked someone like Flora, whom he wanted to impress, to associate material that was so poorly conceived and written with him. How the phony material came to be in the same binder in which his manuscript had been was a complete mystery, and he also could not understand how Flora could enjoy reading a piece of work that was so poorly conceived and written.

As the indignant Mjomba stood there swaying from side to side and beating his breast with his fists in exasperation, he saw that his reaction to the unfolding events was going to add to the problem, but he had already made up his mind that he couldn't care less now. The outrage induced by the turn of events had caused him to overlook the fact that, in the mystic domain to which he still belonged, the essences there were not permitted to behave like the lower earthly beings. You allowed yourself to be drawn out of your element in any manner at your peril. But here he was, indulging in subliminal feelings, although he was supposed to be enjoying an existence that was well above, and indeed beyond, the influences of things that pampered to temporal appetites or the flesh! But even though he saw his mistake, there was no turning back now. And so, visibly jarred by what he had witnessed, he allowed himself to completely wallow in self-pity.

To add to the confusion, Mjomba now noticed that Flora had proceeded to the copier in what appeared to be a flash. At her touch, the Xerox came alive and begun churning out copies of the phony work that still sported his name as its author. Observing Flora's strange antics, which he found to be very hurtful and chastening, he literally gagged at the thought that spurious copies of his manuscript might already be in circulation around the globe!

Mjomba was in a virtual daze as he watched the copier churn out a complete set of the "manuscript". It seemed a little far-fetched to suppose at that juncture that thieves had somehow succeeded in stealing his life's work, and had replaced it with a substitute that was so substandard; and he decided that it was, indeed, a little far-fetched to imagine that there were any thieves at work here. But this was just because the prospect of that happening was something he would not have been able to stomach!

The whole world around him looked decidedly different now and indeed appeared to be sinking. He could not contain himself, and was soon audibly castigating himself for having trusted Flora from the beginning. He had no doubt that she had a major role in whatever had happened to his manuscript, and wished he had stopped her in her tracks or even raised an alarm when he witnessed the theft of his manuscript from Jamila's recovery room.

Flora turned off the copier's power and the apparatus's mechanical life came to an abrupt end, its work done. But this apparently also coincided with the fall of the dreaming Mjomba from mystic grace. He watched helplessly as his ghost plunged from its mysterious and elevated plane of existence to an earthly one in that same fraction of time.

Mjomba had by now already written off any chances of continuing on as a respectable member of the mystic realm, and knew that his banishment from that realm was imminent. He had successfully stood up to His Mystic Majesty by breaking the rules and regulations that governed the mystic realm. But, surprisingly, he now felt relief of sorts. This was even though many questions regarding the whereabouts of his original manuscript remained unanswered. He thought it was nice to be free from those burdensome mystic canons; and for a moment he positively relished the feeling of being autonomous and answerable to no other being. He had no illusions about the fact that he was about to face judgement for his intransigence, but even that did not seem to matter - for now!

Mjomba was still in that ambivalent state of mind when he noticed the change that had started to come over the proceedings. It was in the form of music that caught his ear and gradually grew in volume. Mjomba began to discern the sounds of a chorale being performed by a choir, or what sounded like one, in the background. It took a while before the noise from Flora's activities in the matron's office and the distant sounds of the night were completely drowned out by the recital by what, without a doubt, was one of the most accomplished choirs Mjomba had ever heard.

He recognised the chant as Gregorian even before the voices themselves were completely audible. The chorale's phrases were already quite distinct and Mjomba could make them out even as he was still struggling to trace and locate the source of the music. It was the famous Canticle of Mary that was being sung to an ancient tune - one that had been Mjomba's favorite during his seminary days. He felt an awesome, almost unbearable, feeling of nostalgia well up inside of him as he listened to the cantors intone the first lines of each stanza, followed immediately by a fitting bellow executed by the main body of the choir singing the rest of the stanza in chorus.

Captivated by the beautiful sounds, Mjomba seemed completely oblivious to his impending metamorphosis. He noted the brief pause as members of the disciplined choir took in a breath; and then, in breach of normal practice, he did something seminarians never did. He began to sway to the music!

The fact that Mjomba's movements were almost imperceptible was immaterial. The theological position regarding "sacred" music was that to sing it was to pray twice. And "swaying" to the music, because it was suggestive of sentimentalism, was something that just wasn't done. It was completely anathema. It was actually standard practice for seminarians the world over not to display any kind of emotion when at worship. They didn't even close their eyes when saying their prayers. They just stared in the distance and kept mumbling whatever petitions they were presenting to the Prime Mover.

And, of course, it was not just seminarians who practiced these habits which many, the separated brethren who belonged to the Evangelical confession in particular, found very "strange"; it was an established fact, that went back to the time when Latin was the Church's official language, that Catholics did not have to understand what they were even saying when praying. And that had also popularized the notion that Catholics typically acted as if they were already assured of salvation by the mere fact of being Catholics, and did not feel obligated to put their faith "on show" as appeared to be the case with members of other faiths.

Mjomba, in contravention of those well-established and tested traditions, continued swaying to the beat of the chorale when the cantors chanted the next stanza, which began with the words "And His mercy is from age to age, on those who fear Him". Something told him that a choir that was capable of such an accomplished performance had to be hailing from the "New Jerusalem".

It was as the rest of the choir from the New

Jerusalem or wherever rejoined with "He puts forth His arm in strength and scatters the proud-hearted" with another fitting bellow that Mjomba became engulfed in the chilling transformation. His feelings of nostalgia were already quite severe as the cantors intoned the next stanza. But they suddenly changed to feelings of extreme dread and then became overwhelming as the cantors' subdued chant was replaced by the roaring refrain from the rest of the choir!

And then, instead of the cantors resuming with "He casts the mighty from their thrones and raises the lowly" as Mjomba expected, it was the entire choir which now pressed on with the chant, yelping out those words in an ever rising crescendo.

Even at that late stage, Mjomba longed for some respite that he hoped would come with a decrescendo. He was surprised that the choir - that choir which had already impressed him so with its flawless delivery of the Canticle of Mary and which he had already grown to cherish so much - was preparing to press on with yet another crescendo for the very next stanza. He could tell because of the intervening pose that was longer than usual, and by the fact that everyone in the choir was taking advantage of it to take in a really deep breath - or so he imagined. Having sang the *Magnificat* a countless number of times himself during the years he was first a minor and then a major seminarian, Mjomba knew exactly what the words of that next stanza were even before members of the choir from the New Jerusalem resumed the chant.

The din accompanying the rendition of the expression "He fills the starving with good things, and sends the rich away empty" initially suggested some kind of rally. But instead of one rally, there was wave upon wave of echoing sound, as the words making up that expression were sung with slow and carefully measured articulation! The clarity and decisiveness with which they were sung appeared designed to move the haughtiest of the haughty to humble compunction.

And then there came this one final, absolutely colossal and shattering babel of voices as the celestial choir, evidently comprising of thousands upon thousands of souls, uttered the words "And He sends the rich away empty". Those final words of the canticle were sung to a crescendo so powerful that objects on the mantel and on the top-most bookshelf began to plunge to the floor. That was immediately followed by what looked and sounded like a powerful earthquake. The walls of the matron's office began to cave in and to tumble to the ground.

Mjomba did not know what had happened to Flora in the meantime. He was so engrossed in his own uncertain fate, he had neither the time nor, indeed, the liberty to think about the well-being of others. He suspected, in any case, that it was Flora who had set him up after allowing herself to be used as a ruse to lure him into the situation in which he now found himself.

Mjomba knew instinctively at that time that the

end was near. He also knew without a doubt that at the gates of paradise where he had found himself - a nirvana where things that were impossible on earth were possible - that sort of finale presaged sentencing by His Mystic Majesty. In his particular case, since he had already fallen from grace, this could only be a prelude to banishment to the bottomless pit.

The odds of escaping damnation - and the fires of hell that accompanied such sentencing - were clearly stacked against him. And, as if to seal his fate, he now recalled in vivid detail the events of the day that he, Mjomba, a cradle Catholic whose baptismal name "Christian" was derived from the name of His Deliverer which meant "the anointed one", had discarded that beautiful name in a pointless effort to endear himself to his Muslim wife and stopped going to church to receive the sacraments!

Mjomba stood convicted because, when he stopped going to church and receiving the sacraments, he turned his back on the Deliverer who was quoted by Luke as saying in no unmistakable words: "Watch ye, therefore, praying at all times, that you may be accounted worthy to escape all these things that are to come, and to stand before the Son of man." How could he now expect to be on the Prime Mover's guest list for the divine banquet when he hadn't as much as tried to put on what the Apostle of the Gentiles called "the armor of light"!

Just as the Sadducees had the wrong ideas about marriage and were chided by the Deliverer for not understanding either the scriptures or the power of God, Mjomba clearly did not understand reality and had his priorities wrong when he sought to please Jamila at the expense of his eternal life. Now that he had crossed to the other side of the gulf that separated the living from the dead where upon rising from the dead humans were as the angels in heaven who neither wed nor become wedded, there was no question that it would have augured much better for both of them if he, Mjomba, had put his eternal life first.

The sentence that was about to be meted out to him was analogous to death, because that was what losing the fight against His Mystic Majesty in reality amounted to. He had crossed the Prime Mover in a manner that was so inexcusable he himself had already lost all hope that forgiveness by the Almighty One could ever come his way. He knew, in a word, that his final damnation was at hand!

Mjomba began to experience "death" first hand as he felt what he thought were pieces of rubble from the ceiling falling on him. He went numb, and then instantaneously began to feel an overpowering, searing and cruel thirst. He wished in vain for a drop of some liquid - any liquid - to use to soothe his parched throat. But in the midst of all that, there was one thing, Mjomba felt certain, was contributing most to his final demise. It was the pitiless searing that enveloped his entire person. He felt as though his body had been lowered into a pool of boiling oil and was being kept there while it vaporized.

Mjomba recalled the time when, chatting about

the unknown in general and about death in particular with Primrose, they had jokingly "promised" each other in a "pact" that whoever died first would return and let the survivor know, in a dream or even in an apparition, what exactly happened when people passed away, and what was on the "other side"! Even though everything that was happening was taking place in a dream, Mjomba not only found himself recalling the "pact" he had made with his secretary, but felt he had a binding obligation to fulfill its terms. But he was now dismayed to discover that a gulf was starting to form between himself and the folks he had left behind, and that even though he would have liked to pay the folks he had left behind a visit for the purpose of informing them about his terrible agony of death and the judgement that was about to get under way, there really was no way to turn back, once one had started out on the one way trip to the next life. He was, accordingly, very sorry that he could not keep his part of the bargain in that matter.

And it was also as he was thinking about his pact with Primrose that he was given to understand that he was dying in mortal sin with no time to go to confession, and was accordingly being denied any chance of expiating his sins in Purgatory. That news was really disappointing because he would have been glad to spend a thousand years in Purgatory rather than continue to endure what he was enduring forever and ever.

As has already been stated, Mjomba had known very well that moody or spirited episodes, whether joyous or saturnine, were incompatible with the contemplation of His Mystic Majesty. One reason for that was that the source of sentimental feelings lay outside of the mystic splendor. But the truth of the matter was that one could not fulfil the grave duty of contemplating the Mystic Being while allowing one's attention to be deflected by evanescent or other emotion arousing objects. Mjomba now hated himself for having allowed himself to fall for the subterfuge which, without a doubt, had been engineered by the mystic essences that had been disgraced for similar reasons before him and wanted company. He felt an overpowering feeling of guilt that was, however, shorn of all remorse.

Well-knowing that he was accursed and on the road to damnation, Mjomba could not desist from uttering what he expected to be his own last curse as an inhabitant of the mystic realm. He accordingly devised a plan to utter a general curse - one that would not be directed at any particular individual or object. He no longer felt any concern about the consequences of his actions. Mjomba felt that his impiety would suit the present occasion better if it had a pervasiveness about it rather than if the impiety was narrowly directed. He was already resigned, after all, to the seemingly obvious fact that he was a sinner whose despicable act of sacrilege had now put him beyond the pale of redemption. At this particular stage, he was, indeed, supposed to be incapable of the very act of repentance, and it was only God who knew if his present determination to do the very worst by uttering a curse was likely to bode better or worse for him at his final judgement which he knew was now imminent.

And the heck! Like the souls of those who were already damned, he didn't have anything to lose. On the point of death, he was about to leave behind all his meagre possessions, and he was moreover headed to hell. He was dying a pauper; but it of course wouldn't have made any difference if he was leaving behind billions or even gazillions of whatever, like those greedy owners of banks and other business corporations, who didn't have any scruples about squeezing the last pennies from working class folks and even widows, did up until they kicked the bucket.

Mjomba chuckled at the thought that his rendezvous in hell with folks who had been filthy rich and never had any qualms about exploiting poor souls like himself was now certain! And if it felt natural for him to utter a curse in the circumstances he had found himself in, it undoubtedly was even more true in the case of those other penny-pinching fools at the time they discovered that they were actually headed that same route! With all of these chaps in the same boat as himself, he sure was in good and also fairly interesting company. And there sure had to be lots of cursing going on there in hell.

Like the suicidal person who was desperate to cut it all short in one stroke but was lacking the where-with-all or the will to bring about his end, Mjomba opened his mouth - or what remained of it after the battering it had received during the continuing earthquake - in readiness to commit that final act of sin. He seemed sinfully delighted as he got ready to swear the name of His Mystic Majesty in vain.

Before he could formulate the appropriate words for the much-anticipated curse - what he would have liked to call the mother of all curses - the moment he had been waiting for arrived. This was the moment during which he expected to be ushered into the presence of His Mystic Majesty. Mjomba was struck by the fact that the events taking place appeared to be following a designated pattern.

Mjomba was totally resigned to the fact that the time for him to die was finally at hand. He believed, up until that moment, that he was just about as ready for the final separation of his mystic soul from its physical habitat as anyone could possibly be. He knew that it was going to be a nerve wrenching experience, but he was ready - or so he thought.

For a fleeting moment, he even felt like a traveler on a homeward stretch. And in that fleeting moment - a mere fraction of a second which he would have liked to see stretch into infinity - everything around him suddenly appeared quaintly familiar as if his journey, which was about to conclude, had begun right there. His composure came close to being shattered in that fraction of a second as it occurred to him that this might in fact be the place where he had first learnt to discern right from wrong and where his conscience had been formed, and that the figure of the Judge, whom he had still to meet in person, might likewise turn out to be a very familiar one, particularly as the Judge also happened to be his Creator!

Indeed, the thought that his recollection of these surroundings dated back to the moment he, Mjomba, was created wasn't very distant from his mind. He imagined that it was also the time when his conscience was formed - as His Mystic Majesty gazed knowingly upon him after willing him out of nothingness and even endowing him with a free will out of His boundless generosity.

Mjomba did not have the slightest doubt in his mind that the period starting from the moment his conscience was formed, giving him a road map for his sojourn on earth, to the time of his homecoming had been solely intended for making preparations for his reunion with His Mystic Majesty. It effectively meant that he was supposed to grow and wax strong, in the intervening period, and bedeck himself with virtues in readiness for his final rendezvous with His Mystic Majesty at the divine banquet. He could, indeed, sense that there was partying and revelry going on somewhere in the vicinity, and had no doubt that it was the divine banquet taking off. The sounds that caught his ear included recitations of psalms and chants in praise of His Mystic Majesty.

Talking about sounds catching the ear - it was plain to Mjomba, as the seconds leading up to his last judgement ticked away, that whereas one could talk about silence here in the afterlife, there really was no such a thing on the other side of the Gulf on "earth". Creatures there just imagined it. The reality was that when humans were born and embarked on the process of adapting to the environment, their eardrums selectively recognized certain noises as "sound" - specifically the noises whose sources they could identify. Humans then typically chose to completely ignore the noises that did not make any sense to them. Those were the noises that the eardrums filtered out - because humans and other creatures refused to recognize them as "sound".

When "sleeping" babies smiled and grinned, they were not really asleep, even though the adults around thought so. They were wide awake and, with their eye-lids barely closed, were busy trying to differentiate between the noises which made sense and which they were going to recognize as sounds, and deciding on which ones they were going to ignore for the rest of their lives in the "realm of the living".

The same was true for people who were "unconscious" or "brain dead". Mesmerized by things of the senses, folks on earth were prone to jump to the conclusion that everything was lost when their dear ones who were "unwell" stopped physical activity. Doctors and others at the bedside of "the dying" were typical. The problem was really not with those who were "unconscious' or "comatose", but with the folks who were supposedly "well" and in good health. Because they were earth-bound and regarded the five senses as indispensable, they mistakenly equated "physical activity" with "well-ness", and clung to the erroneous notion that loved ones who felt "unwell" were "slipping away" and possibly receding into a state of inertness and virtual non-existence the moment they stopped "registering a pulse" or showing other "signs of life" like dilated pupils and the apparent inability to react to pinpricks and things of that nature.

In such situations people, who were unable to discern the patient's ability to use his/her senses, typically started hunkering to disconnect essential life-support systems for the individual who was comatose or supposedly "brain-dead". They were unable to get away from the notion that physical (as opposed to spiritual) activity was indicative of good health and wellbeing, and were consequently prone to misreading the real "signs of life".

When an individual stopped acting in the way folks around him/her were used to, instead of humbly accepting the fact that there are plenty of things that they know next to nothing about, those stupid fools usually start to place the blame for their inability to make heads or tails of the situation on the poor outgunned and outmanned individual instinctively, and are quick to conclude that the "poor chap" (who is displaying the "puzzling" behavior) must be developing a mental abnormality of some kind. When a good natured, normally talkative, individual suddenly loses his/her voice, the fruitless attempts of that individual to regain his/her vocal expression will tend to be viewed as a sign that he/she was now deliberately acting funny and in the process of "losing it" or "going off his/her rocker"! That was how really stupid and crazy people were!

An unconscious or comatose person was

actually very much awake and conscious. Those who were certified as "brain dead" were in the exact same boat as sleeping infants. They might appear to be oblivious to their surroundings; but they were very much "awake" in point of fact, and much more conscious of the goings-on in the room far more than the distracted doctors and grieving "loved ones" present at their bedside. Even without batting an eye, they usually discerned the intentions of the folks in the vicinity as they prepared to disconnect their life support systems and effectively kill them.

And it was of course quite clear that the driving motive behind the actions of those who were supposedly "alright", but were gearing to cut short their lives, was impatience and frustration. In the end it translated down to an unwillingness to sacrifice more of their comforts and time to continue providing the "palliative" care the patients required to continue living. It was an irony of fate that in the early and final phases of life, when infants and folks on their deathbeds were so close to their Maker and were in fact more alert to their surroundings and spiritually more active than at any other time in their lives, those around them became prone to misconstrue the situation and to regard them as completely inert, unconscious or brain dead, and "unresponsive".

Here, in the "realm of the dead", it was all silence, except for the sounds of praise and adoration that came from the redeemed souls as they exalted in the presence of His Mystic Majesty, and the shouts - or more precisely screams - of desperation and mourning as the damned which arose from the Pit or hell.

One other thing: the "appearance" of creatures here in the afterlife did not even come close to what they looked like back in the realm of the living. If you had tried your best not to hurt anyone while you lived, you looked handsome; and you looked even more so if you had also led an ascetic life. But if you had murdered, stolen or hurt others in some way - and especially if you had combined that with a life of debauchery - you came out looking so evil and so unlike His Mystic Majesty, the last thing you wanted to do was be seen in His presence.

And, instead of belching out sounds of praise and adoration from your guts, the only noises you would be capable of producing would be desperate cries amid what sounded like the gnashing of teeth. Those were the sorts of noises that could not be allowed to disturb the peace and tranquility that reigned in "heaven"; and hence His Mystic Majesty's decision to banish all those who ended up like that from His sight.

And one thing was absolutely clear to Mjomba, now that he was far removed from the realm of the living: if you were not absolutely perfect - that is, if you were not entirely focused both on the Prime Mover who was the last end of all creatures that were fashioned in the image of the Prime Mover, and were still attached in some way to any "worldly" pleasure or distraction - there was no way you could survive the radiance of His Mystic Majesty! You would even have enough trouble trying to hang around in the glitter of those who had just emerged from Purgatory after finally atoning for sins committed by them over the course of their lifetime.

The litmus test was that if you were afforded the opportunity of a second lifetime back "on earth", you not only would be prepared to have as your preferred bed-fellows those you previously deemed your nemesis or worst enemies the first time around, but would also be prepared to lay down your life for them! And, while at it, should it happen that someone misunderstood you and decided to slap you on the cheek, you perforce would have to ask for his pardon and then turn the other cheek as well.

And you, of course, would also be at pains to ensure that you remained "detached" from all temporal things, including the desire to "save your life" and all the different forms that took! Thus, if you had previously allowed lukewarmness to govern your relations with the Prime Mover, in your second lifetime, you would say Bye Bye to all that and, rather than make a living in an occupation that involved betraying your trust in Him in any manner, knowing that you are weak and your own efforts ineffectual in these matters, you would spend all your time beseeching the Prime Mover for the strength to unhesitatingly opt to die a pauper or even starve to death rather than sin against your Maker.

That, combined with unceasing prayers and contemplation, including attendance at daily Mass and devotions to the saints - and particularly devotions to the Mother of the Deliverer - in addition to selfless service to the poor and a sustained regime of acts of self-immolation and penance should guarantee you a pass on the Church Triumphant Entrance Test and a modest mansion in heaven.

Devotions to the woman whom the evangelist describes as "having the sun itself for her raiment" cannot be overemphasized. For, even though a creature, her glitter in heaven which far exceeds the glitter of all the angels and saints combined, would be particularly punishing for the unworthy. And it so happened that, by the same token, it was through her incessant pleas to her Divine Son and Judge that time served by souls in Purgatory was reduced often by as much as a half and their entry into paradise was speeded up.

Any way - to return to the subject under discussion - your inability or unwillingness to do those things would be proof that you never had any love for your neighbors and avowals by you to the effect that you loved the Prime Mover in your first life were all a bunch of lies!

Mjomba saw more clearly than ever before that it indeed was easier for the proverbial camel to pass through the eye of a needle than for a rich man to negotiate his way through the gates of heaven.

Humans were so dumb, Mjomba reminisced. Some who killed even thought they could cover their tracks by being careful not to leave behind any tell-tale evidence trying them to the ghastly act. Others even made things worse by trying to cloak the fact that they were "partners with the Evil One" in sin behind a facade of piety and self-righteousness. They thought they could hoodwink everybody in the process, including the Prime Mover Himself, by committing murder and other "mortal" sins in that fashion.

They were dumb because the "hypocrites" forgot that any mortal sin - and certainly any act of murder - itself represented by its nature an indelible mark that became etched on the conscience of the sinner, setting the perpetrator apart from "God's chosen"! The act of sinning in itself constituted genetic evidence (for the misdeed) that could not be obliterated without "destroying" the offender - something the Prime Mover had said He would never do and that was, certainly, beyond the power of evil doers themselves.

And that led Mjomba to note one additional thing which, namely, was that some humans who murdered believed, quite mistakenly, that they were despatching their victims to an early miserable end. In reality, their actions resulted in the very opposite - the murderers were despatching those they hated to a blissful afterlife and guaranteeing themselves an ignominious end in the Pit in the company of demons and other murderers.

After electing to do the opposite of what he himself had been expected to do in life, Mjomba now could not bring himself to approach that banquet table (wherever it was) in his present forlorn shape. And he knew that it was far too late now to do anything about it; and, even worse, that it was all his fault!

Mjomba even succeeded, in that short space of time, in reflecting on the fact that it was undoubtedly his conscience, coupled with his proximity to the Prime Mover, which caused him to accept his fate, dreadful and awesome though it was, as something he entirely deserved. If he had been in a position to do so now, he would have willingly cut off any offending limb in addition to punishing himself in all sorts of ways to atone for his sins. But it was too late now. He understood that he now had to steel himself for the ultimate punishment, which would consist in knowing that for all eternity he was going to have fiends for company and would not be able to see his Creator face to face! The pain from knowing that he had allowed himself to sink so low and to identify with the fiends and others who were enemies of everything that was noble and wholesome in the period he had been a member of the Pilgrim Church was already quite intolerable.

It struck Mjomba that if he had neglected to acknowledge his Creator in the way he had been expected to during his sojourn in the mystic realm, it was highly unlikely that he had accorded his fellow humans the attention, respect and love they were entitled to. He thought of the turmoil in which much of the "world" was usually gripped practically all the time and which made the lives of innumerable souls absolutely miserable, and shuddered at the thought that most of the human suffering was avoidable because the wars and other causes of human misery were the work of humans who acted irrationally and were selfish and despicable like himself.

Even with the devil and his lieutenants swarming the mystic realm at any given time and making all sorts of wicked suggestions, it was very clear and unequivocal that those humans who were responsible for the sufferings of others, because they were endowed with the faculties of reason and free will, could not escape "judgement". They couldn't even plead incapacity because there was no such a thing as insanity in the afterlife! The fools had doomed themselves - period. Mjomba, who was already grieving the fact that he had squandered his own blessings as a member of the Pilgrim Church in the mystic realm, didn't feel that he himself deserved any pity and found that he wasn't feeling any pity for them either.

Mjomba entered into the final throes of his death. He could not help noticing, as he did so, that they coincided with the fact that his soul, which normally informed his body, was now finding the conditions of that "habitat" increasingly incapable of sustaining it for any further length of time. Mjomba was astounded by the fact that his "preparedness" added up to naught virtually!

He knew it wasn't just a coincidence that he was finding himself overwhelmed, as he entered that phase, by a numbing feeling that effectively shut out all pain, physical and mental. But then, contrary to what he had been expecting, his "vision", hitherto blurry and pretty much a drag by reason of having to constantly touch base with his cognitive faculties, suddenly became transformed into a sharp stinging activity that appeared to draw on some kind of prescience or divination that emanated from his inner core. First of all, he had never suspected before that he had any capacity for prescience or divination, let alone to that degree! And secondly, it had never dawned on him that there was anything to such things as "prescience", "clairvoyance" or "psychic powers". He always imagined that these were catchwords that individuals claiming to be in touch with the occult employed to hoodwink their unsuspecting clients.

These developments, which were entirely unforeseen, had the effect of both disarming Mjomba and making his responses to events from then on "typical" of persons in their death throes. He reflected on the conventional depictions of individuals in their demise that employed terms such as "painful", "silent" and "painless" to describe the phenomenon of dying. He would have vouched, with the sharp presence of mind that he now commanded, that the media types and all the other so-called experts who pontificated on matters of death back on the other side of the "gulf" were way off the mark.

If his experience up until that moment were anything to go by, no amount of pain, physical or otherwise, could be compared to the distress faced by a solitary soul that was awaiting judgement - and especially that soul which knew well enough that instead of coming out of it shining, it faced the inevitable, thoroughly merited, reproach by His Mystic

Majesty for having had the audacity to suggest that the "Master" was the type who reaped what He did not sow, and then gone on to "bury" the talents that the Master had entrusted to him for safe-keeping! It weighed heavily on Mjomba to think that he had dissipated, not a few, but an untold number of opportunities to bloom in sanctifying grace, and thus fortified, proceed to shape up in mystic blessedness and in the likeness his soul bore to his Mystic Majesty!

And here he now was, awaiting the damning sentence and denunciation by His Mystic Majesty. It was the kind of denunciation that unrepentant sinners, aware that they fully deserved it, pined for. But it was one they dreaded at one and the same time and would have wished to avoid at all costs because of the indescribable mental agony accompanying it! Being spiritual essences, that agony dwarfed any physical pain that humans could endure without passing out!

Not surprisingly, the suffering and agony that Mjomba himself had felt as the bricks from the walls of the matron's office plummeted on top of him reducing him to granules amounted in retrospect to a painless scratch compared with the grief with which he was smitten as his now certain encounter with His Mystic Majesty approached and, along with it, the looming prospect of being banished forever from His majestic presence for what he now saw as the vile life he had led.

If it had been possible to choose between living a thousand distressingly drab lives which entailed dying a thousand excruciatingly painful deaths, and standing there contemplating the mirrored image of his unworthy self as he awaited his final judgement, with hind sight he unhesitatingly would have chosen the former.

It was clearly too late to do anything about his fate now. Like the rich man, in the bible story, who would have loved to sneak back to earth to alert his kinsmen about their eventual fate if they did not mend their ways, Mjomba wished for the impossible as he pondered his impending damnation. He would have loved to be allowed just a few moments during which he would slip back into the realm he had just left so he could at least warn Jamila and, perhaps Primrose and even Flora, as well as Prof. Gringo, his good friend and mentor, about what lay beyond the grave.

And he, of course, would not forget his former schoolmate who now sat on the Bench back in Tanzania and routinely sent others to their death because they were supposedly "criminals". Mjomba vowed that if he were given an opportunity, he would successfully persuade Justice Maramba to use his powers as the nation's chief justice not just to stay all executions in the country and pardon everyone on death row, but also to arrange to send home all the folks who were now incarcerated in jails with no more than a warning that they conduct themselves lawfully, making sure that they did not allow themselves to be brought before any court ever again. A recital of his experiences "on the other side of the gulf" to an assembly of the ex-convicts would, Mjomba felt certain, convince them to stay out of trouble with the law.

Talking about death row and the so-called capital "punishment", it was obvious to Mjomba, now that he was minutes - or rather moments - away from his judgement, that taking away the life of a human, or killing under any pretext, was so totally wrong. He could not believe that the current, supposedly enlightened, generation of humans back on earth not only still had "death chambers" and things of that sort, but frequently pursued scorched earth policies to "liquidate" enemies.

Or was it perhaps this tendency on his part and that of other humans, when rationalizing about anything, to seek to establish "the logical conclusion" to arguments. That was, after all, something that no one, including the most illogical, could ever really "wish away" as Mjomba put it. It was a fact of life that those who killed did so to inflict hurt. Since it would be illogical to knowingly seek to dispatch your enemy to heaven by visiting upon him/her death prematurely, you would not do it. One logical conclusion, therefore, was that people killed enemies with the intention of dispatching them to hell!

Now, that was the very opposite of what humans were commanded to do, namely love one another. You could not possibly love someone and be praying at the same time that the object of your love should disappear in hell! And you, of course, could not get a better example of a mortal sin than desiring, not just to cut short the life of another human, but to do so with the specific aim of causing that human, who was created in the image of the Prime Mover just like yourself, to forfeit heaven. That was a very pathetic situation in which humans, already under the death sentence because of their rebellion against the Prime Mover, self-righteously turned on fellow humans and put them to death on what was really a pretext!

Mjomba quipped that it was not all that rare to find that the "death sentence" hanging over the heads of members of the bench as a result of being the poor and forsaken children of Adam and Eve being carried out long before the "death sentences" passed by those self-same justices on so-called convicts were carried out.

Given his own situation which was already hopeless, Mjomba did not wish to make it worse by appearing to be doing the very thing he was condemning, namely passing his own "capital sentence" on those capital punishment advocates back on earth, including his dear friend Justice Maramba, by emphasizing that their refusal to forgive their enemies effectively made them unworthy of forgiveness.

And so, instead of making his argument compelling by pursuing it to its logical conclusion, and showing that capital punishment advocates were themselves in the same if not worst situation as the "criminals" they were so quick to condemn, he tampered it by supposing that when the time came for these "stupid fools" to themselves die, the prospect of giving up their own ghosts (which would be in the exact same manner as their victims had done before them) *most likely* caused these folks to wake up to the reality of their situation, and to regret their error - just before it became their turn to confront the Judge. As if to mitigate the sentence he was facing, Mjomba allowed himself to regret aloud that he unfortunately could not do more than that for the earthlings who were bent on revenge.

Knowing that the professor was a person of great means, Mjomba would have particularly welcomed the opportunity to try and convince the man of letters to give it all away to the poor.

Recalling that the Deliverer had urged the rich man who came to him seeking advice to sell all his possession all and give the proceeds, not to Judas Iscariot, his purse bearer or treasurer, but to the poor, Mjomba made a point of reminding himself that, if he were to get the opportunity to return to earth, he would caution his friend, after he got rid of his rental properties and especially his considerable interests in corporations, to distribute the money to the homeless in Calcutta, Nairobi, New York, and other places like that directly and not to churches or so-called charities that were likely to use most of it on "staff salaries" and "bonuses" and other things like that.

It seemed patently absurd for anyone in the mystic realm - the realm in which creatures that had been cast in the image of the Prime Mover at creation spent were "on trial" before going to their reward in their afterlife, to be acquisitive or possessive. He, indeed, could not recall any instance in which anybody gave a thought to keeping cash handy so that the individual in question could take it along to heaven or hell when one died! Reflecting on his own past, Mjomba thought he himself must have been stark mad to aspire to riches and fame the way he used to! Suffice it to say that he would now have welcomed the opportunity to travel back to the earth and confront Prof. Gringo with these obvious facts.

Mjomba also would, if he were allowed to cross the Gulf and return to earth, approach the Holy Father with one simple request: he would ask that he, Mjomba, be allowed to lead an army of Capuchin monks to Hollywood. Their objective would be to persuade the people there to use "show biz" so-called to heighten general awareness for the fact that the human body was the temple of the Prime Mover and the dwelling of the Word through Whom the universe came into being; that it was subsequently the Spirit of the God the Father, and not humans who had ownership over the human body; and that immorality was consequently self-defeating. Mjomba was quite confident that the world's capital of showbiz, hosting a delegation that was led by someone who had come back from the dead, would be persuaded to change its ways.

Mjomba would, likewise, seek the pope's permission to head a delegation of Carmelite nuns to the capitals of the world in order to dissuade governments from starting wars. That mission would be even more important than the mission to convert

Hollywood, because while His Mystic
majesty found immorality despicable and repulsive,
He did not easily forgive the sin of starting a war in
which people went out and killed each other,
regardless of the way it was justified, because He
created humans to live as family and love one
another!

Still, Mjomba had this gnawing feeling that his
message, like the divine messages transmitted to
earthlings through prophets, would also go
unheeded; and, in any case, the chances of his being
allowed to be such a messenger, given the vile life he
himself had led, were pretty slim. Still, he hankered,
vainly as it would turn out, for the chance to just give
it a try - to go through the motions. And should the
kindred and friends whose hearts he would be trying
to change turn on him and cause him to suffer
martyrdom like the prophets did, he would appreciate
that even more.

These thoughts made Mjomba envious of
martyrs and others whose upright lives, empathy for
the downtrodden and the helpless, and determination
to do what was right according to their consciences
caused them to suffer in silence for the cause of
justice. He regretted that he could not manage a
laugh now. But reflecting back on the fact that he
himself used to regard individuals with those kinds of
ideas as damn fools, he sincerely wished he could
open his mouth and laugh lustily at himself for ever
having entertained thoughts like those and, alas,
making such a damn fool of himself in the process.

661

Mjomba was still fully conscious and alert, the excruciating mental and physical pain plaguing him notwithstanding; and he could sense it when the scales finally fell from his eyes. They were the scales that had continued to provide a shield of sorts from the radiance of His Mystic Majesty. He could tell that this also signaled the final separation of his mystic soul from his earth-bound body. He, of course, also knew that this unique event was touched off by the failure of his heart, that extra-ordinary organ which had served both as the seat of love and also as the wellspring from which had flowed an unending stream of life-giving "plasma" from the moment he had graduated in his mother's womb to a hatched egg, or fetus, from one that hadn't been!

At that particular point in time and in the situation in which he had found himself, Mjomba would not have cared less as to which of those two milestones - his first heart beat or the final rapture as he went into cardiac arrest and died - deserved more attention. All he was really concerned about was that the great moment for his rendezvous with His Mystic Majesty was at hand and, for all practical purposes, had sneaked in on him like a thief in the night.

Mjomba kept repeating to himself that he should have known better than to trade in his birthright to eternal glory in the presence of His Mystic Majesty for terrestrial happiness. But he was still reeling from his realization that he was now doomed and "lost" in the true sense of that word when, with a quiver, his cardiovascular organ, throbbed its last and final time, and then he immediately began returning, along with whatever remained of his physical frame, to the dust from which they had originally been fashioned in the first place. His breast, already battered by the bricks and mortar and nearly unrecognizable, heaved, allowing him to hear and witness that definitively final and distinctive heartbeat for himself.

Mjomba imagined that this was the routine that applied in each and every instance of demise among humans. He was amazed that the unspeakable agony that had characterized his wait subsided just enough to allow him to focus on those climactic events. While listening to his last heartbeat, Mjomba had also steeled himself for the separation of his soul from the body. Intent on hearing the last heartbeat and on getting a feel for that final rapture as well, he had been comfortable dividing his attention in that fashion. But there was no doubt that he had expected to find the latter more entrancing. For, even though he had envisioned it coming on the heels of his heart stoppage, the pain he felt had caused him to begin anticipating the separation well before it was due - at least two or, may be, even three heartbeats earlier.

Even though he knew that he was headed for damnation, Mjomba could not help taking in the sight of his spiritual self as he floated across the gulf that separated the realm of the living from that of the departed. It was as if his soul had been reduced to an icon in one directory of a personal computer where it didn't now belong, and was being imported into a completely different directory where it now belonged using an invisible mouse. Mjomba could almost trace the path of his soul as it was "physically" dragged there and then released into an empty niche in the new directory where it now belonged with a single, expert click of the mouse.

Yes, expert click of the mouse. It was pretty clear to Mjomba by now that, in the mystic realm, everything was done "expertly". Mystic creatures did not fumble. And certainly, of course, not His Mystic Majesty! Mjomba had not failed to notice that the fellow guarding the entrance to heaven (through which the just went in single file after being commended by the His Mystic Majesty for their faithfulness to Him and for passing the Church Triumphant Entrance Test with flying colors) was St. Peter. He was easily recognizable by his bold head, which was partly concealed by a white skull cap or mitre, and his tall walking cane, undoubtedly one of many he had used to lean on as he went from place to place in what was then known as Asia Minor preaching the Gospel of the Deliverer.

It was a mystery to Mjomba how Peter's rugged hiking staff and the skull cap had found their way into the mystic realm just as his own presence there in the mystic realm was a total mystery. But it was no mystery that Peter, who had "fumbled" so many times as an earthling (particularly in the period before the Paraclete came down from heaven as promised and buffed up his faith) now radiated anything but faithlessness, uncertainty or an inclination to "bumble". Now a living symbol of faith in the mystic realm, Peter, the first Bishop of Rome who had the power to "excommunicate" but had always thought the better of using it at least compared to some of his successors in the See of Rome, was a picture of calm, preciseness, and of course "expertness".

It was revealed to Mjomba while he was up there in the mystic realm that excommunicating someone was analogous to killing in self-defense; and that while Peter could have excommunicated "dissidents" in the early Church, particularly those who were insistent that only Jews could be Christians, he chose instead to embark on an all-out crusade to educate and enlighten people both in Palestine, Asia Minor, and in Italy - or Italia as it was then know - about the truth. Not one to be stopped by anything when the truth was at stake, Peter even took writing lessons from Luke and one Josephus so he too could communicate by means of epistles like John and Paul were doing.

Everything that took place around the man who had also been known as "the Rock" was done very efficiently; and there was absolutely no possibility of some unworthy soul sneaking past him into heaven. Even if some sinful earthling, arriving here without enough *spiritual* possessions to merit a place in heaven, were still bent on trying to bribe his/her way past St. Peter into heaven, that option was effectively closed. Firstly, *spiritual* possessions just did not lend themselves to that sort of thing. Secondly, souls arrived here for their judgement without any *material* possessions (and you could not *bribe* with nothing). And, thirdly, there was just that one "Gate of Heaven", and no other.

It struck Mjomba as something of great moment to live to see his own soul take on the shape of a kite, to follow its flight as it floated gradually and unhindered over the gulf separating the realm of the living from that of the dead, and to observe it landing gently in its allocated spot on the other side of the Gulf within sight of the Gate of Heaven. Mjomba was beginning to think that there actually might be nothing more to it than that. But he soon realized in that timeless second that things were otherwise.

It at first sounded as though it was Mjomba's last heartbeat that was being amplified in an inexplicable fashion and was coming across as a loud "twang". Mjomba realized, too late, that the "twang" was accompanied by what felt like a brick landing on his head. It was all the more terrifying because he knew that he did not have a body. But he still made up his mind that it was do or die, as he "scrambled" to avoid additional "blows" he imagined were now going to follow fast and furious, and rain down on him. Or perhaps it was his fearfulness that had transformed his last heartbeat into what now came across as blows to his "body".

Mjomba assumed that it was because he was a hardened sinner that he failed to realize what the blows signified until almost the very end. As it turned out, for every mortal sin he had committed, he received a blow to the head. The blows for the venial sins he had committed were administered to other less vital parts of his body. The blows to the head were obviously intended to be mortal blows just as the vices they were intended to avenge were deadly vices. Even though the blows representing his lesser sins were not as deadly in their force as they landed on various parts of his body, they were unbearable all the same.

Mjomba thought that the whole spectrum of physical pain that humans anywhere ever endured was represented in the variety of pain he was enduring. The pain inflicted differed according to the size and shape of the "brick", and he could tell from the way they landed that they seemed to come in all sorts of shapes and sizes, and also from the speed at which they hurtled to his body from wherever they came from. He was made to understand that the pain from the blows he received for venial sins were tempered somewhat by any good turns he had done to anyone during his sojourn on earth. But, to the extent that he had been either vengeful or unforgiving to others, to that extent any relief he would otherwise have received was denied.

The relief he received notwithstanding, Mjomba had no doubt that he should have died from any single one of those blows - and he would have preferred to die rather than continue to endure the blows the bricks were inflicting on him. Because they were bricks and not living things, he could not really implore them to finish him off quickly - even if that had been possible - or to spare him. Even though he knew that much, the pain made him delirious and incapable of thinking straight, and he soon found himself mumbling things to that effect all the same. It was all to no avail because, to all intents and purposes, he had already kicked the bucket!

He decided that there was no point in trying to make out at that juncture if what was happening pertained to the heartbeat or if it was directly related to his transition from the realm of the living to that of the departed. Even though in turmoil, he urged himself to just be content with acknowledging that whatever it was, it was utterly phenomenal! The sheer terror it was inspiring in him made it so. And since there was now no stopping what had been decreed to transpire as of that moment, Mjomba resigned himself to his fate, even though his survival instinct, which was now entirely out of control, continued to battle on.

Then for an instant, but a very brief instant indeed, it appeared to Mjomba as if there might not be anything at all to all that had transpired from the time he had found himself in the mystic realm as he sprang into action and pursued the nurse in his eagerness to see the fate of the manuscript she had filched from Jamila's recovery room up until that moment. He was beginning to think that it might all thankfully be a dream - and that included what was looking more and more like his certain damnation - when, lo and behold, all hell broke loose! And this was the real, not figurative, hell.

It began with a shattering sound not unlike that

of a mammoth herd comprising hundreds of thousands of wild buffalo approaching at a gallop. It was a sound that was utterly unfathomable, and the same applied to the sight that met Mjomba's gaze when he plucked the gaze to look. Mjomba had less than a split second to grasp what was afoot, namely that an army of demons headed by none other than Lucifer himself was charging him, and that those diabolical creatures were about to sweep him away and into the infernal pit with them. This was evidently what the Gospels meant by "perdition" and, as Mjomba quickly sensed, it wasn't going to be pleasant at all.

The creature that was at the head of the forces of evil that were descending on him was hideous and loathsome in the extreme, not to mention menacing. It was clear that Mjomba had been courting danger in a most reckless manner when he engaged the services of the devil in the production of his thesis, and let the evil one be his virtual advisor. The devil's involvement with his book project could not possibly bode well for anyone who picked it up to read, Mjomba now admitted; and he resolved that, beginning that moment, the purpose for pursuing Flora into the mystic realm was going to be to stop the manuscript from falling into the hands of any human of good will. And he noted, in that regard, that Flora, even though her own intention wasn't above board, was inadvertently helping to assure the salvation of the soul of his own beloved Jamila by her act of theft.

Seeing that it was of the utmost importance

now more than ever before to try and stop Flora from disseminating the contents of his manuscript, Mjomba attempted to get up and resume his pursuit of the girl only to discover that he couldn't muster the strength to even as much as stand upright. It was so frustrating not to be able to get up and speed after the girl when so much was at stake. Mjomba attributed his inability to do so to the approaching Enemy, the church's official name for Beelzebub, and one Mjomba agreed was appropriate and right on.

Mjomba realized that it was the intention of the nondescript creatures that were charging at him to not only crush him and then bury him in the hell where they themselves belonged, but to do to him something that was even worse. Fashioned in the image of His Mystic Majesty, by virtue of which he could invoke the assistance of the Almighty One and Prime Mover if he chose to if he ever found himself in the midst of adversity, Mjomba's condition as a damned soul was not going to permit him ever to say the Our Father or to even as much as wish to be shielded by His Mystic Majesty against the invectives of his enemies.

Even though Mjomba had crossed His Mystic Majesty almost as soon as he had stepped into the mystic realm, and had seemed prepared to accept the consequences for his indiscretions, that (he now realized) was vastly different from being damned in the same way Satan and the host of demons that had opted to do his bidding had been damned and cast into hell. That was not at all what Mjomba had in mind when he decided to cross His Mystic Majesty. And it wasn't what he had in mind when he decided to use the Evil One as his mouthpiece for expounding on the Church's doctrines either. When he fell for the temptation to get a helping hand from Old Scratch so that he might be able to turn in a winning thesis, he had been thinking of Lucifer the Archangel, who with Michael the Archangel had ministered to the Prime Mover before Lucifer chose to go his own ways.

Mjomba's reaction to his now impending damnation was instinctive. Totally mollified, Mjomba found himself doing something he had been used to doing often during his years in Minor and Major Seminary, but hadn't done in a long time. He found himself reciting the Aspirations to the Holy family; and he recited them slowly and deliberately, almost as if determined to defy Satan and the army of totally enraged demons that was bearing down upon him: "*Jesus, Mary and Joseph, I give you my heart and my soul. Jesus, Mary and Joseph, assist me in my last agony. Jesus, Mary and Joseph, may I breathe forth my soul in peace with you…*"

And as he prayed, the advance of the demons that had appeared unstoppable started to show signs that it might slow down just enough to enable him to complete the invocation. And that was when the pain from being buffeted by the falling bricks and debris from the earthquake became completely unbearable.

The Demoniac...

Mjomba, who believed that he had already

breathed his last and was well on his way to join his ancestors, had concluded that the bedlam and chaos that reigned all around was evidence that he had died in the state of mortal sin, and probably had been adjudged as even unworthy to be ushered into the presence of His Mystic Majesty. He even acknowledged that the supreme self-confidence, cheek and bravado that somehow had taken control of him in the moments leading to his death had dissolved so that he now couldn't hurt a fly even if he wanted to! Whatever lingering doubt Mjomba may have had that the prophetic words of the Canticle of Mary that 'His Mystic Majesty scatters the proud in their conceit' applied to *all* conceited humans, he himself included, was now quickly dispelled. And, Yes - Mjomba now finally also admitted that there was no doubt whatsoever that when His Mystic Majesty showed the strength of His arm, that was all there was to it. There was no creature whatsoever that could gainsay or challenge the outcome, and that included the Ruler of the Underworld!

In a complete reversal of his attitude, Mjomba now wished that he had hearkened to his professors who were for the most part set against his dilly-dallying with Old Scratch, and to people like St. Francis De Sales who advised that it should be the principal business of humans "'to conquer themselves and, from day to day, to go on increasing in strength and perfection", and Catherine of Siena who wrote: "Our captain on this battlefield is Christ Jesus. We have discovered what we have to do. Christ has bound our enemies for us and weakened them that they cannot overcome us unless we so choose to let them. So we must fight courageously and mark ourselves with the sign of the most Holy Cross."

He now realized, too late, that they were all echoing the Deliverer Himself who told His disciples in Luke 21:36: "Watch ye, therefore, praying at all times, that you may be accounted worthy to escape all these things that are to come, and to stand before the Son of man." And Mjomba finally also admitted, again too late, that he had failed to pay heed to the Deliverer's admonition that it was easier for a camel to pass through the eye of a needle, than for a rich man to enter into the kingdom of God.

Before he died, Mjomba, as a member of the seminary brotherhood, had had far more exposure to the doctrines of the Church than most other folks, had been fully aware of these things. He regretted that he had not made it a habit while he lived to invoke the names of the Deliverer, His virgin mother, and the Deliverer's foster father at least mentally every day; and he definitely should have been in the habit of reading selections from folks like St. John Chrysostom and St. Ignatius Loyola who all emphasized the importance of constant prayer and meditation. But Mjomba readily conceded as he strained to withstand the relentless assault by the elements on his person, that this was now not the time to dwell on those things.

Mjomba was quick to note that the severe "blows" raining down on him were accompanied by what he could only describe as bedlam of a really massive order. It was as if all the lost souls were gathered in one giant pit and that, even though they were damned and written off, after a break or pause had succeeded in mustering fresh energy and were resuming their dejected, yet bawdy, howl of eternal despair from their location at the bottom of the cavernous - and needless to add also hellish - sink hole which was now their home. As before, the tremendous roar also caused him to experience a searing sensation - as if he still had his body with him and it was again being doused with sulphuric acid or some other such flaming liquid.

It was then that the strangest thing of all occurred. The imaginary blows to his body stopped as suddenly as they had begun. That was, however, followed by a silence so numbing and ominous, Mjomba immediately began to wish that the pandemonium had not stopped. His "wish" for something to break the silence was granted, although not in the manner he had expected.

It started off like the clangor of a thousand hammers invading the stillness; and as the unexpected, totally awesome and terrifying sound broke the deafening silence, the caricature of the Evil One materialized from nowhere and inserted itself between Mjomba and St. Peter, completely blocking from view the shimmering Gate of Heaven that St. Peter was guarding. Mjomba had seen Hollywood's portrayal of Beelzebub in the Lord of Darkness, and remembered being freaked out the first time he saw that movie. Confronted by the creature that was referred to in the sacred scriptures as the Ruler of the Underworld, Mjomba gasped at how far short of the devil's real appearance the depiction of Satan in that flick came. The fiend's appearance (his caricature came complete with a bloodstained pitch folk, two enormous wings, seven heads, ten menacing horns and a fearsome tail exactly as described in Revelation 12:3-4) was so grotesque and revolting, Mjomba swore that he would have passed out and died if he had still been on Earth. His instinctive reaction was to make the sign of the cross so that Satan would keep his distance. And, finding that he was not in control of his limbs and did not have the wherewithal to get up and take flight as the advancing Adversary approached, he tried vainly to mutter a prayer; but discovered that even that was denied.

Mjomba freaked out as the Ruler of the Underworld, his unsightly face enveloped in a devilish giggle, quickened his steps and closed in on him. "Hee, hee, haaaaaa! Finally Gotcha!" the Father of Death and also Father of Lies croaked.

The devil was grinning wickedly as he continued: "You fool! If you thought that I was in the business of helping nuts like you write winning *theological* treatises, you were seriously mistaken. And I am not in the business of helping humans conform their consciences to the teachings of the Sancta Ecclesia either, damn you!

"I, Mephistopheles, am in the business of leading souls astray and getting them damned. And yes, in our pact, I pledged to shine as much light on Truth as possible. But it wasn't so that *humans* would not have any excuses on their day of reckoning. Look, every human has a conscience, an inner guide to determining right from wrong. As the Second Vatican Council clearly stated, every human has in his heart a law inscribed by God. Deep within their consciences, humans discover a law which humans have not laid upon themselves, but which they must obey. Look here, you! I took it upon myself to shine as much light on Truth as possible so that *you* wouldn't have any excuse whatsoever on this your day of reckoning!"

"That thesis of yours on Original Virtue" Diabolos continued, "is destined, as you should have already noticed, for the trash heap. A Thesis on Original Virtue! No one would be interested in reading it; and it would be a money loser for any publisher who thought of getting it in print. It is going to be read by no one… Hee, hee, haaaaaa! And, anyway - it would be a bonus if some humans picked it up, and read it so they too wouldn't have any excuse on their judgement day either.

"I have to be nice to humans while they are still on the other side of the gulf that separates the living from the dead. But when they kick the bucket and get to this side of the gulf that separates the living from the dead, they discover soon enough that my official role is that of Accuser. I now have the great pleasure of ushering you to your dungeon in hell. Yeah, hell! This is the place regarding which St. Chrysostom cautioned that folks must not ask where it is, but how they are to escape it!

"At the time you kicked the bucket, you had not been to confession in a long while. Jamila would have been happy to convert; but you didn't even bother to try to evangelize her at all. You didn't love her...you were just infatuated with her good looks! You also leave behind your very own offspring who are unbaptized and do not, therefore, belong in the Mystical Body of the Deliverer! And the same applies to your 'sweetheart' Jamila.

"Through Adam, the first human, death entered into all. Unless humans be born again of water and the Holy Ghost, they cannot get past Peter over there and enter into the kingdom of heaven. As for you yourself, fashioned in the Prime Mover's image, you crossed the gulf that separates the living from the dead whilst in mortal sin. Without sanctifying grace, you are exactly like the fellow who did not have on the wedding garment in the parable of the marriage feast you jackass, and you must now reap what you sowed! Come with me..."

It was then that, without any warning whatsoever, a pack of growling demons, frightful in the extreme in their demeanor and also unimaginably ugly, appeared from nowhere, and started charging him. Judging by the zeal with which they did so, he knew that he would not be recognizable after they were done with him. These fallen angels that had forfeited heaven as a result of joining the former Angel of Light in his dastardly rebellion against the Prime

Mover were definitely up to no good!

Up until that moment, Mjomba, goaded on by his fertile imagination, had from time to time toyed with the idea that perhaps one could actually be resigned to one's fate as a lost soul. But now, with the menacing and totally hideous spirits bearing down on him with none other than Mephistopheles himself at the head of the column, he was jolted from the spiritual malaise that had caused him to entertain that silly notion. He immediately saw that the reality was otherwise. He had no doubt whatsoever that those demons were jostling to get to him in order to take out their own individual frustrations on him.

Mjomba recalled the words of the Catechism to the effect that, after the Deliverer had come and paid the price of sin with His death on the cross, the destiny of humans remained largely in their own hands. It, in fact, stated unambiguously that the dignity of humans was rooted in their creation in the image and likeness of God; and that it was fulfilled in their vocation to divine beatitude. It was essential to humans freely to direct themselves to that fulfillment; and humans, by their deliberate actions, conformed or did not conform to the good promised by God and attested by moral conscience. The Catechism made it quite clear that humans made their own contribution to their interior growth; and they made their whole sentient and spiritual lives into means of that growth. With the help of grace they grew in virtue, avoided sin; and, if they sinned, they entrusted themselves, as did the prodigal son, to the mercy of their Father in heaven. It was thus that they attained to the perfection of charity.

In contrast, the fallen angels were never afforded a second chance after they fell from grace and forfeited the opportunity to minister to the Prime Mover. It was no wonder they hated humans to the extent they did.

And now here he was, a poor mortal who had passed on and was facing off, all by himself, against the Ruler of the Underworld and his minions, and on the verge of being shuttled off against his will to a dungeon in hell by raucous, almost deranged pack of demons. Only God knew what they were going to do to him, after they succeeded in pinning him down, before carting him off to his assigned dungeon in the belly of hell!

Mjomba had no illusion about the evil intentions of these unclean spirits. For one, these malignant spirits that, in the words of St. Augustine of Hippo, "begrudge the whole human race an eternal dwelling place" and for whom "the eternal happiness of humans is punishment", were going to make damn sure that he endured the spiritual deprivation, and other miseries that had been their lot from the moment they were cast into hell, to at least the same extent as they themselves did!

His drooping eyelids shut briefly when it crossed his mind that things were going to be really bad for him precisely because he was a human. There was every chance that these crazed creatures were going to use this opportunity to avenge the fact that other humans who had lived their lives aright, like the Blessed Virgin Mary and St. Joseph for instance, were already enjoying beatific vision, whilst they themselves, having been disgraced and disowned by their Maker except to the extent He permitted them to continue to exist, were destined to languish in hell for all eternity! This hell was shaping up to be one that Mjomba had not bargained for at all!

This was also the very first time that Mjomba had come face to face with the Evil One; and also with the "legion of demons" that Mark and Luke had referred to in their evangelical narratives (Mark 5:1-20 and in Luke 8:26-39). Yes, Lucifer had been instrumental in helping him craft his "winning theological thesis" all right. But Mjomba should have suspected that the devil had something else up his sleeve!

He could not believe that he, Christian Mjomba, like the proverbial prodigal son, had fritted away the innumerable opportunities to grow in the knowledge and love of Him who had told Moses "I am who am" (Exodus 3) and in holiness. As a creature that was fashioned in the Image (something that the Ruler of the Underworld had made a point of alluding to just moments earlier) and whose happiness and fulfillment accordingly could only be found in the Prime Mover Himself, his "hell" was going to consist first and foremost in his inability to find any measure of self-actualization outside of the Prime Mover. And that was undoubtedly the lot of the fallen angels as well.

But, wait! It really wasn't like him to do what the

Accuser was suggesting he had done - namely rebel, on his own volition, against the Prime Mover; and to choose temporal happiness over his eternal happiness! It took a mere split second for Christian Mjomba to wake up to reality, and to admit that something had gone seriously wrong!

The realization that these were all the machinations of the devil, and were the result of unwittingly allowing the Evil One to gain full control over his humanity, came as a complete shock! Probably starting from the time he had worked on his thesis whilst at St. Augustine's seminary, he, Christian Mjomba, in all likelihood had become possessed by evil spirits! Mjomba winced at his discovery. All the alleged sins of omission and commission that the Accuser was endeavoring to pin on him were committed by him all right, but probably not willfully! He, Christian Mjomba, was a demoniac who clearly had done whatever he had done whilst under the total influence and full control of Beelzebub, and while possessed by the legion of demons!

In his eagerness to excel and turn out a winning thesis when he was a member of the seminary brotherhood, Mjomba had allowed himself to flirt with Satan, something they had been warned against doing on innumerable occasions, during retreats and the weekly spiritual conferences at St. Augustine's Seminary. And, before long, he had found himself at the service of the Evil One, and acting as the Adversary's scribe, and was committing to paper everything that the Ruler of the Underworld was dictating. Satan had just admitted that he was not in the business of helping chaps like him produce winning theology dissertations. The realization that he had allowed himself to get too close to the Evil One and that it was big mistake to dillydally with the devil hit him in that split second.

At a certain point while in the service of the Evil One, he, Mjomba, had evidently become possessed by the "Legion"! How otherwise could it be that, knowing what he knew, he had become an apostate upon leaving St. Augustine's Seminary, and had even stopped going to church altogether! This was unbelievable! The crafty devil had been busy dangling before his eyes the prospects of a thesis that was a winner while biding his time to allow his Legion to gain a foothold and possess him! This was utterly incredible - except that it was no laughing matter.

Mjomba saw clearly that he had indeed been very presumptuous to imagine that he could trick Satan into working for the salvation of souls instead of their damnation. That was tantamount to dreaming that he could get the devil to drive out his fellow demons from demoniacs the way the Deliverer did on so many innumerable occasions as He went about the business of His Father in Judea, Galilee and Samaria! It had been so reckless of him to do that, and he should have known better than to even try.

He had gone out on a limb and, just as in the case of the seven sons of Sceva who, along with other vagabond exorcists (as Luke calls them in Acts 19:13-19), went about and attempted to invoke the

682

name of the Deliverer over those that had evil spirits, saying: "I conjure you by Jesus, whom Paul preacheth", the Evil One had unmistakably decided to make an example of him. It wasn't hard for Mjomba now to imagine the wicked Diabolos delirious with laughter and mocking him with the words: "Jesus I know, and Paul I know; but who are you, nincompoop?"

It was, of course, too late now because he had already crossed the gulf that separates the living from the dead. But he vowed all the same that if he were back on earth and still kicking, the right thing for him to do at that juncture was to burn his supposedly "winning theological thesis", preferably in front of his fellow seminarians, in the same way many of the fools "who had followed curious arts, brought together their books, and burnt them before all" as described by Luke in his *Āctūs Apostolōrum*.

Mjomba had no doubt that right up until the time he started work on his theological thesis - when pride got the better of him and he started fantasizing about crafting a winning thesis with a little help from the Ruler of the Underworld - he had been just fine. He had in fact caused one demon that was proving to be quite irritating to take flight – he hoped for good – by being extra attentive at Holy Mass each morning at St. Augustine's, not missing out on any occasion to receive the sacraments, including weekly confession, and through prayer and fasting. But he had now ended up like this because of cozying up with Beelzebub.

Mjomba sobbed uncontrollably as he tried to imagine how things had unraveled. The first thing that came to his mind was that, at some point, the unclean spirit in the person of Lucifer conceivably did leave him - in response to his feeble efforts at staying true to his vocation and close to his Maker. But then, going through arid places seeking rest and finding none, the demon alerted to what he could do to remain free and unfettered by evil, almost certainly had sought out perhaps up to a dozen other demons that were at least as wicked as himself; and, entering him again under the ruse of shining light on truth and assisting him thereby with his project, he had turned him into a dwelling place that, for all practical purposes, was permanent now; and it was not just for himself but for those other evil demons as well! Mjomba owned up to the fact that the last state in which he had previously languished had consequently become a lot worse - in fact as bad as it could possibly be!

It was evident from the words of the Deliverer found in the Gospels of Matthew (Matthew 12:43) and Luke (Luke 11:24) that that was how the devil operated. Mjomba had no doubt whatsoever about that.

This also explained Mjomba's otherwise inexplicable descent into apostasy upon leaving the seminary; and it also showed that a human could look fine and dandy - and even saintly - on the outside when everything was completely rotten on the inside! Mjomba gasped at the realization that someone of his stature at the Port Authority could actually be possessed and good for nothing!

And if he, Mjomba, had been demon-possessed whilst back on earth, there sure had to be many other folks in the same boat. Mjomba had himself admittedly gotten some things wrong, and provided Satan a loophole in the process; and, of course, the life he had been leading right up until he kicked the bucket had not been exactly exemplary. But it didn't compare with the lives that a lot of folks he knew lead. Mjomba started to suspect that at least some of these people - and he had in mind in particular the folks who seemed to delight in doing or saying things that were calculated to upset others all the time - had to be possessed just like he himself had been until he kicked the bucket! And that was not mentioning folks who were into really uncouth things - oppressive dictators who were a law unto themselves and didn't give a damn about the inalienable rights of their subjects, corrupt cops and judges who used their positions to promote their agendas, crooked politicians who portrayed themselves as angels, preachers who spewed out hate in the name of the Prime Mover, to name just a few!

The Ruler of the Underworld must have been reading Mjomba's mind. And if he (Mjomba) was still having any misgiving about the fact that he might be possessed by Legion, these too were quickly dispelled as the Evil Ghost croaked: "Hee, hee, haaaaaa! Haaaaaa! Yeah, that is how I deal with stupid fools like you! When they give me an opening, I do not hesitate to send Legion to possess them, and that is exactly what I did. Hee, hahahaa! Goddamn fool! There is nothing that can save you now…"

That was the last thing Mjomba wanted to hear. This was ridiculous! And, as if on cue, the Accuser croaked: "Remember what Paul wrote in his missive to the Philippians concerning the sin of pride? 'Let nothing be done through contention, neither by vain glory: but in humility, let each esteem others better than themselves: Each one not considering the things that are his own, but those that are other men's.' Those are Paul's words not mine! Hee, hee, ha, haaaaaa! Lout that you are, you thought you could use me to turn in a winning thesis and use it to show that you were better than your fellow seminarians, eh? Hee, hee, ha, haaaaaa! This was a classic case of pride coming before the fall…Damn you!"

"When you were embarking on the class assignment which required you to write the thesis on 'Original Virtue', you should have stopped to reflect on the words of the *Pater Noster* (the Lord's prayer); and also on the advice that St. Paul gave to the Corinthians when he wrote "*Sive ergo manducatis, sive bibitis, sive aliud quid facitis: omnia in gloriam Dei facite*" (Therefore, whether you eat or drink, or whatsoever else you do, do all to the glory of God)! It was an occasion for you to recall that Ignatius of Loyola turned those words of wisdom into the motto "*Ad maiorem Dei gloriam inque hominum salute*" (For the greater glory of God and the salvation of humanity)! But No! Willful and headstrong as ever, all you were concerned with was how to impress not just the community at St. Augustine's but the whole world with a 'winsome thesis'!

"And then you had the gall to imagine that you could trick me, Beelzebub, into working for the salvation of souls by getting me involved in your cockeyed project. Where on earth did you get such an idea, you idiot and deluded numbskull?"

Mjomba mustered the courage to look up and stare Satan in the eye, and he immediately regretted doing so. It felt like staring into the bloodshot eyes of a riled black-neck spitting cobra just as the creature was aiming its venom into your own!

Briefly regaining his wits about him, Mjomba swore that he was not going to let Diabolos have his way. He tried to get up and take flight from the menacing pack of demons that was now barely feet away, only to discover that he was not in control of his limbs and could not move his legs. The crafty Satan had obviously anticipated his reaction and had done something to immobilize him - probably some magic spell similar to those wizards and witches cast over their unwitting victims!

But Mjomba was undaunted. And, moreover, desperate times called for desperate measures! He decided that he was going to scream for help. If he yelled loudly enough, there was the outside chance that St. Peter would hear him and do something to distract the advancing pack of demons, if nothing else. And it was do or die now as the demons, led by the Prince of Hades, closed in on him.

Flailing his arms about like a battered pugilist who was hoping to be saved by the bell, Mjomba succeeded in opening his mouth. He was relieved to hear the reverberating echo of his voice as he hollered: "Saint Peter…Saint Peter…Saint Peter… help…help…help!" But that was also when he felt the searing pain about his head, neck and middle. Beelzebub now had him in a headlock, while the faceless demons were dutifully gnawing away at other parts of is torso to the accompaniment of sounds akin to those of a pack of hungry wolves battling over the fast dwindling carcass of a kill.

The experience was jarring; and the breaking point was not long in coming. Jolted out of his slumber, Christian Mjomba lunged forward, his face a twisted mask that spoke volumes about the mystifying experience he had just been through as he lay dreaming on his coach.

Even after he had awakened, Mjomba apparently still imagined that he was in the strange mystic world, and not far from the abominable pit and its accursed population. He was now awake; but the sounds of the accursed spirits, as some shouted and screamed curses directed at His Mystic Majesty in their loathsome place of abode and others snarled and growled over the sudden loss of their quarry, broke through the stillness, and started ringing in his ears all over again almost as if they were real.

To counter them, Mjomba opened his own mouth and began screaming out aloud for all he was worth. The result was some sort of primal scream the like of which only a few living creatures could parody. It was a howl that would have caused a charging buffalo to halt its tracks. The deafening screams that followed did more than that to Fatuma who had been in the process of laying the table for breakfast. Terrified to the bone by Mjomba's shouts, and convinced that he was deranged, she dropped the tray that was loaded with the various items she had hoped would make a nice breakfast for him smack on top of his head, and turned to flee.

Mjomba continued to holler: "Hooo! Hooo! Hooo! The world is coming to an end..."

As he did so, the terrified Fatuma barged out of the room and raced round the corner toward the phone, with Mjomba hard on her heels. It appeared as if he wanted her out of his bedroom as soon as possible and at any cost.

"Oh! What are you also doing here?" he roared as he took after her. He was, for all practical purposes, still living in his dream. Meanwhile, during her flight, Fatuma dropped the empty tray in Mjomba's path hoping that it would slow him just enough to allow her to punch the numbers "911" into the dial.

"Oh! The devil...the demons...the demons! So, so many of them! What is that?" Mjomba was roaring even as he missed his step and landed head first on the hard cement floor.

For her part, Fatuma was convinced that her uncle had gone bananas and was trying to kill her. When she got to the children's bedroom, she headed straight for the cute little telephone set on the dressing table.

"Oh, I'm sorry, Fatuma. I was dreaming...!" Mjomba gasped as he finally caught up with her. Panting and still quite distracted, he made a beeline for Ali's bedroom chair and slumped into it. He had apparently come to when he stumbled and fell. Fatuma, who had already picked up the phone and was trying frantically to punch in the emergency number, stood there paralyzed.

"Uncle, are you alright? It was my fault. I'm sure I hurt you!" she mumbled apologetically. A short while earlier, she had actually been praying that he would trip and hurt himself so badly he would have no choice but to abandon his pursuit. But, seeing him dishevelled and in a sorry state, she now felt that she was partly responsible for his plight, and blamed herself for over-reacting. She could see that he was still frightened, but did not quite understand why.

"Where are the children?" Mjomba asked, noting that their beds were empty.

"In the basement, watching TV," Fatuma replied.

"Oh, yes of course," he rejoined, remembering that Musa and Ali always got out of bed very early and headed to the basement to enjoy their favorite cartoons.

Although still reeling from the terrifying experience of being pursued by her uncle, Fatuma managed a big broad smile that Mjomba found very comforting.

A stubborn piece of bacon and the yoke from the fried eggs she had prepared for him still dangled from his greying hair. Otherwise, nothing of his breakfast which she had carefully arranged on the tray and was in the process of delivering to him in his bed - the pot of hot black coffee, the cup and its saucer, a large slice of pawpaw, etc. - had survived.

Fatuma's enthusiasm evaporated as she recounted how she had accidentally splashed the coffee over her uncle's face as she was leaning forward to check if he really was talking in his sleep or was awake and addressing her. And she now confessed that she had not been prepared for his reaction and, in particular, his resonating screams. Mjomba fought to suppress laughter, and Fatuma herself could not help sniggering as she remarked that he had really terrified her when he lunged from his bed and started after her. Although the thought that the lovely china she had carefully laid out on the tray shortly before the misadventure lay in fragments either on the bed or on the floor of the master bedroom had a dampening effect on her exuberance at this time, that would not be the case that evening when she would relate the incident to Jamila.

"I wasn't sure if you were asleep, and was checking when..."

Mjomba stopped her with a wave of his hand, upon which they both exploded in laughter.

None of them had noticed Ali and Musa who were smiling at them from the hallway. Still clad in their sleeping gowns, they had overheard the pandemonium and had dashed upstairs to find out what the heck was going on. Ali and Musa had found Fatuma wonderful and they, accordingly, had not really missed their mom. But the thought on their minds, as they were scurrying upstairs, had been that their mom was back with the baby! They were evidently disappointed that nothing really exciting had happened to justify the bedlam that had sent them charging upstairs. And now, as they turned to head back to the basement and the world of cartoons, they did not hide their obvious disappointment.

Fatuma must have read their minds, and was starting after them when Mjomba reached out and grabbed her hand to stop her exit.

"I'm sorry for all this," he murmured. "Don't worry about my room. I'll clean up."

"No, it's all my fault. I want to make sure Ali and Musa are OK, and I will be right back."

Fatuma decided on the spur of the moment that the kids were fine. It would not have done any good reminding them of the unexplained commotion upstairs, which would be the case if she turned up in the basement at that time. She, accordingly, headed instead for the kitchen where she picked up a mop and a towel.

The circumstances in which she had aborted her earlier mission to deliver breakfast to her uncle had left her feeling that she had turned her aunt's elegant bedroom into one that was topsy-turvy and an utter wreck. She, accordingly, couldn't wait to get there and clean up. When she did, she was somewhat surprised that it wasn't in such a terrible mess after all. But she was still glad that Mjomba was there to help her tidy the place up. When she had packed up the cleaning items to return to the kitchen to continue with her early morning chores, she noticed that Mjomba was retrieving some writing materials from a drawer.

With pen and paper in hand, Mjomba, who was feeling as if he had not had an ounce of sleep, slipped into his bed with the intention of jotting down details of his nightmarish dream before they evaporated. Very much to his amazement, he found that the only thing he could recall was the fact that he was on his deathbed - yes, his deathbed - and bound for hell! He, Mjomba, on a deathbed bound for hell! It was unbelievable!

He had a faint recollection about being ushered into the presence of a stately, and rather awesome Being with the unlikely title of His Mystic Majesty, and also about Purgatory and the reason why it wasn't among the stops he had been scheduled to make en route to his afterlife. But when he endeavored to commit to writing his fragmentary recollection of these things, his recollection of them faded as soon as he began scribbling on his writing pad.

Mjomba's memory of the gates of hell, which came in fits and starts but was still petrifying all the same, was even more elusive. After about twenty minutes of that game of hide and seek, Mjomba stared at the pad and was shocked to see that he had filled an entire sheet with incomplete words and otherwise meaningless phrases that he had scrawled on the pad in a fruitless attempt to reduce his feelings to written expressions.

Fifteen minutes later, Mjomba was still smarting from the fact that he was having a serious lapse of memory at precisely the time he needed it most to record what he saw as an incredible and extremely absorbing story when Fatuma cautiously walked in with a tray loaded with freshly made coffee, and egg and bacon on toast.

When Mjomba saw her, the dream's very subject matter vanished from his mind. He was animated as he flung the pad and the pen into a corner and did not seem concerned about the effect of that clearly irrational act on the girl.

Fatuma's instinct was to hand over the breakfast tray to her uncle, and then proceed to retrieve the items he had so carelessly tossed on the floor with the intention of placing them neatly on one of the bedside tables or on the dresser. But, recalling what had transpired earlier that morning, she decided to take the cue from his action and to retreat from the bedroom as quickly as possible - after making sure that the tray was in his firm grip.

Perhaps it was his disappointment with himself for being unable to remember details of his nightmarish dream. Or maybe it was the fact that he was genuinely starving and the aroma of the coffee was inviting. Whatever it was, it caused Mjomba to reach out eagerly for the tray and to belatedly set about enjoying his breakfast. He took a big bite into the toast with its load of scrambled eggs and bacon, sipped coffee from the slender, hand engraved china, and then sank back into the cushion and closed his eyes to enjoy what he considered to be the fruit of his sweat.

PART 14: THE "MASTERPIECE"

Jamila felt well enough to go home the next day. There was, moreover, nothing she wished for so much as to be reunited with her family and be able to share her joy with her neighbors, relatives and friends in the snug comfort of her home. She was therefore heavily disappointed when Dr. Mambo, doing the rounds himself at dawn, insisted on detaining her for at least another twelve hours in a different and also more comfortable room. Dr. Mambo had no reason to doubt that Jamila's personal physician would not concur with his decision to keep her there a little while longer - "just to be sure" as he was wont to say to his own patients.

Jamila, who still clung to the idea she had got from her great grandmother many years earlier that hospitals were places where people went to die, thought that Dr. Mambo had to be kidding when he uses the same phrase to her. Since there was nothing wrong with her baby either, she really wanted out of there as soon as possible.

In the wake of Dr. Mambo's departure, she was disconsolate - and all the more so for want of something active to do. As always happened at such times, she felt irritable. And, rather strangely, it was her husband, not her condition or Dr. Mambo, who loomed up in her mind as the apparent cause of her misery! She ate her breakfast, consisting of a slice of pawpaw, scrambled eggs on toast, bacon and tea, in sullen silence. Even though she had a dislike for

Flora, she began to wish that the girl, whom she now merely saw as chatty and fun to have close by, were around to help her focus her mind on anything but Mjomba whom she literally hated now. And even as she was being transferred to her new room and a different bed with fresh linen not long afterward, her charm and good looks were overshadowed by her moroseness.

About an hour later, she was all but resigned to her gloom when the blue folder on the stool by her bedside caught her gaze. The ordeal of the previous day and everything else that had happened, including her husband's late night visit - and the manuscript - had gone out of her mind, wiped out by her uninterrupted five hour slumber and the morning's events. But now, everything came tumbling back.

The Psychic Roots of a Nut! The idea of her husband writing a book now, all of a sudden, seemed so plausible! Yes, for all the bustle and activity that characterised his everyday schedule - for all his inexhaustible fountain of love for her - Mjomba was, she clearly realized now, the "thinking" type of a man! That was the impression he had given her years before when their paths first crossed, and it now seemed to find confirmation in his fling at being an author!

For some reason, Jamila's memory of that first meeting remained amazingly fresh, almost as if it all had taken place months rather than years before - eight years to be exact! She still could have told, even after all those years, the exact type of attire he wore,

697

including the color and the shape of his shoes. The picture of him in his majestic apparel of a travelling clergyman had stuck fast in her imagination, seemingly not to be erased by even the passage of time.

Although she had been brought up in the Moslem tradition as befitted the daughter of an Al Hajj, the ascendancy of Christianity in the region and the growing impact of foreign cultural influences on the land had caused her adherence to the Moslem faith to gradually wear off.

She had been prepared to become a Christian for his sake and as a prelude to exchanging their marriage vows. She had been pleasantly surprised to find him keen to embrace Islam. But the adoption of Islam by the former Reverend Christian Mjomba had meant little in practice, apart from his subsequent change of name from Christian to Ibrahim, and the fact that he stopped going to church.

Secretly she had been happy that Ibrahim, or "Ib" as she sometimes called him for short, continued to collect and read scholarly works on Christianity in general and Catholicism in particular, and generally kept away from religious gatherings of Christians and Moslems alike.

Jamila had always felt a little shy about extolling her husband's intellectual endowments. But there had perpetually lain at the back of her mind, nonetheless, the thought that he was potentially if not actually a genius. If he were writing a book, she now reflected, he would of course use the opportunity to delve into the most obscure subject of them all - namely insanity! Indeed she could not think of a better sounding title for a book dedicated to herself and her children than that which her husband, staring fixedly at an imaginary point in the ceiling of her recovery room, had announced. *The Psychic Roots of a Nut*!

She suddenly felt that she had to read the manuscript and hopefully finish doing so before facing Ib later that day. All signs of dejection were gone as Jamila settled back between the fresh linen and began leafing through the leaves of Mjomba's "masterpiece".

She found the material, which was split into four main sections and numerous sub-sections, gripping from the very first. In a clear departure from the usual manner in which novels were written, her husband had employed the present tense throughout to put his message across. Kintu's psychological development comprised the first and second parts of the "novel", and they were replete with interesting twists and turns.

There was some similarity between *The Psychic Roots of Innocent Kintu* and Alex Haley's *Roots*. In contrast to Alex Haley's famous work that sought to establish the ancestral roots of Gunte, her husband's study went all out to establish the mental roots of Kintu, his unsung hero. It was a formidable task that, she finally admitted, he had acquitted himself of most admirably nonetheless.

The third section, in contrast to the first two,

was abstract and full of philosophical erudition. As if that were not enough, the rhetoric in that part of the "masterpiece" was at times so thick, she could hardly see the wood for the trees as they say. But it contained the biggest stock of surprises - she, Jamila, indeed featured in it!

In the fourth and also final section, her husband simply went crazy as he cast her former boss in the role of someone who was harassed by the ancestral spirits. Although she would have wanted to wipe all memories of Flora from her mind, she could not help recalling Flora's last words the previous night - words that had implied that her husband was not a mad author.

The Psychic Roots of a Nut certainly did not suggest that its author was the kind who would vanish in the main stream. She mused that he was destined to be either a best seller or a worst seller, but not one belonging to the run-of-the-mill. But she was, of course, more inclined to the view that it was just a matter of time - as a matter of fact weeks if not days - before he became a celebrity. At one point, her face aglow with excitement, Jamila peered at an invisible dot in the ceiling and wondered how she would make out as the spouse of a famous author.

Quite early on as she devoured the paragraphs, then pages and eventually sections of her husband's work, something rather uncharacteristic of novels begun to unveil, and to suggest that this was the most unusual one she had ever read and probably would ever read.

Although the characters in the first and second parts of the book were mute and spoke not a word, her husband had somehow succeeded in ascribing to them thoughts in a way that stripped all mystery from their actions. Although she had heard before this the truism popularized by Darwin that actions spoke louder than words, she had never imagined that it could all be so true!

Then, the "novel" aimed surely enough at explaining the unexplainable - insanity! But could Ibrahim Mjomba, the man she had known as her husband for a full six years now, really unravel the mysterious subject as she had earlier been inclined to think? She remembered how incredulous she had felt eight years before when Ib and Professor Claus Gringo were in consultation with herself in attendance, and had begun to discuss precisely that same subject. She did not recall anything beyond that because, after concluding shortly thereafter that the man in the attire of a travelling cleric was the handsomest person she had ever seen, she had immediately lost all interest in the substance of their discussion from there on. Little did she suspect at the time that she would be faced with the same question at a later date and that she would have to answer it one way or another.

Jamila's incredulity in turn gave rise to suspicions that, apart from the section of the manuscript in which she herself featured, the accounts she was perusing were possibly entirely fictitious in character! And, as she delved deeper and

701

deeper into the material, she gradually began to realize that it was indeed a question she had to answer one way or another before the day was out - and on the basis of the account before her rather than her wifely feelings for Ib.

As the morning wore on, Jamila begun discovering to her amazement, as she delved further into the material, that the more she doubted her husband's ability to explain the unexplainable, the more the material impressed her with its realism and logic! It seemed as if her husband's work was designed to arouse scepticism in the reader - in the same way a good story caused anticipation to build up in the mind of a reader - only to turn around and use the scepticism to take the reader a few more steps towards the book's climactic point.

The biblical clarity of the first two sections of the "novel" caused her lurking suspicion that the work might have been intended as some sort of joke by her husband to remain at bay. But, as Jamila finally turned to the book's final section in which she herself was featured, the pieces of the puzzle began to fall in place all at once.

Nudging herself into a comfortable seating position on the bed as her wandering eyes picked her name from a page, she quickly became engrossed with her part in the book at the same time. Memories of the events of that morning, almost a decade earlier, when Professor Gringo, her boss, and the brash young cleric were locked in an abstract discussion revolving around one of the professor's patients, came tumbling back into her mind. She easily recalled how their voluble chatter had aroused in her a strange curiosity, causing her at one point to abandon her post at the secretarial desk so that she could indulge in eavesdropping.

Observing the performance of the young "padre" through the keyhole had suddenly evoked in her the most unimaginable, altogether wanton, feelings of lust. Bewildered, she had slunk back to her workstation and attempted in vain to banish memories of the experience from her mind by banging away at her electric typewriter.

Jamila was light-hearted and curiously happy as she came to the concluding pages of the "masterpiece". Turning over the last leaf, she kidded herself that, for all its rhetoric and abstruseness, the final section was the best by far. And it all seemed so much evidence, if indeed she needed any more, of Ib's complicated nature; and she found her husband all the more worthy of her admiration.

While the former Jamila Kivumbi's mind was preoccupied with the sagacious material in the closing pages of her husband's work, not many blocks away events, which might have come straight from a James Hadley Chase thriller, were unfolding with Ibrahim Mjomba at their center!

The "Clown"...

The needle of the Ford Cortina's speedometer seemed to be jammed at the forty kilometre mark as the battered car roared along past the new Post Office and approached the Askari Monument in downtown Dar es Salaam. The din caused by the absence of the silencer was now supplemented by a rattling sound not unlike the clatter produced by a quartet of belled cows moving at a canter.

In his final bid to get baby oil following a tip-off volunteered by a neighbor's domestic worker, Mjomba had spent most of the morning searching for a backyard store on the southern outskirts of the city. He had had to motor over roads which, while listed on the map as major thoroughfares, had turned out to be rough tracks filled with potholes big enough in a few instances to conceal a four-year old - and which, he discovered to his horror, they often did.

Mjomba's inability to skirt all the potholes in his path had proved rather telling on the Ford Cortina's low-lying suspension. His sympathy for the machine, as its under-carriage again and again scraped the road surface, had in time given way to gloomy resignation.

The auto must have shed the rubber bushes as he approached the shack where the baby oil was sold. Mjomba, who intended to purchase all the stock of baby oil on hand, learnt to his surprise that it was actually one of the store's slowest moving items in that store's wares. Unmoved by that information, he had proceeded all the same to snap up the store's remaining stock of baby oil - a measly five cartons, in his eyes, each of which contained no less than a dozen bottles of the imported product.

704

As he set off on the journey down-town, which also felt like a journey back to civilization, the lower ends of the vehicle's rear shock absorbers, no longer insulated from their metal housing, had started beating out their strange new rhythm with a mercilessness which caused him to soon forget his newly acquired taste of sweet success. The taste, derived from his knowledge that nothing on the list of baby items that Jamila had given him a couple of days earlier remained to be bought, had turned to instant bitterness as Mjomba tried to imagine what it would cost him to get the car fixed.

Even though he enjoyed driving autos, he didn't have a clue about how they operated - he considered that to be the job of vehicle mechanics. And he believed that the more shattering the noise an auto produced when one or more of its parts begun malfunctioning, the more expensive it would be to fix the problem causing the noise! In some ways he was right because some auto repair garages used all sorts of excuses to inflate the repair bill including billing for imaginary defects; and that was not taking into account the likelihood of the establishment's underpaid employees, operating on their own, making off with some of the vehicle's working parts.

Mjomba had listened in confusion to the violent and, as it turned out, non-stop clanking noise originating from the auto's rear; and, after deciding that he had enough problems and could not risk being stranded in an unfamiliar part of the sprawling city, he had fought the temptation to stop the vehicle and seek

705

out the cause of the noise and assess the extent of the damage to his beloved Ford Cortina with a stubborn determination. He, however, had not failed to notice the strange fact that the medley of jangling sounds increased in their intensity as the speed of the auto decreased - and vice versa!

The city sounds in the vicinity of the Askari Monument were drowned out completely by the noise as the Ford Cortina slowed down behind a queue of cars. One and all, the milling crowds stopped to stare. Disappointment became registered on the faces of the majority of onlookers as the source of the din turned out to be a slow moving, if somewhat battered, family sedan and not a fire engine in full throttle. Mjomba, his form rigid in the driver's seat, seemed unconcerned by all the attention.

Next to him on the front seat was a gigantic bouquet of flowers neatly wrapped up in gift paper. In the back seat, Fatuma struggled to keep Kunta and Kinte in check. An unusually joyous and expectant atmosphere prevailed; and it received a periodic boost from Mjomba's ingratiating backward glances, which revealed a broad smile.

Every time he looked back over his shoulder, the children ogled at the image of a crested crane emblazoned just below the knot of the blue-grey tie.

If Ali and Musa had seen their dad in a tie before, they evidently no longer had any recollection of it. Unlike the climate inland, the weather conditions in Dar es Salaam were typical of those that prevailed along Africa's coastline and included a dose of humidity that could be quite inhibiting. This was a function of being on or near the Equator and at sea level all at once. Consequently, in Dar es Salaam's year-round sweltering heat, only magistrates and advocates donned ties; and Mjomba, like all other right-thinking city folk, had never had any reason to go against that sensible tradition.

Indeed, apart from an odd collection of ties and western suits that were leftovers from his grad-school days in America, his wardrobe consisted mostly of "Kaunda" suits complete with matching scarves, fancy Afro shirts and jeans.

Mjomba looked manifestly like some old-time clown with the noose-like object around his neck. The picture of a bird just below the knot now made him look all the more clownish, the fact that it constituted the emblem of his Alma Mater notwithstanding. Fatuma blushed many times, even Mjomba himself choked repeatedly with laughter seeing Ali and Musa bursting with infectious joy

As he turned into the driveway of Dr. Mambo's Clinic, the thought crossed his mind that the drive from their bungalow to the Clinic, normally a twenty-five minute drive, had been accomplished in something like the twinkling of an eye. It was not that his mind had been preoccupied with anything in particular. On the contrary, it had in fact been as close to the proverbial *tabula rasa* as it possibly could have been without actually being a "smoothed tablet".

He had made a desperate, woefully futile effort to get his mind attuned to the clangor produced by the

Ford Cortina as he set out from home that afternoon, but had decided that he wouldn't allow anything whatsoever to disturb his hard-earned peace of mind at least for the rest of that afternoon - except for the attention he was receiving from Ali and Musa, that is. With his reason relieved of its usual guiding role, his automatic reflexes had taken over charge; and so he came to, now a full twenty-five minutes later, to find himself guiding the ageing auto into the crowded parking lot instinctively!

To all appearances, Mjomba's mind was far away as he snatched up the flowers and banged the car's door behind him. He strode along, head held high and the bouquet, which he gripped with both hands abreast of him, looking very much like a fixed bayonet in a soldier's arms. Perhaps because he knew he could trust Fatuma to take care of Ali and Musa as the party headed for the wards, Mjomba matched on oblivious, for all practical purposes, to the fact that he had been travelling in their company.

He suddenly had the sensation of walking into someone! The next moment he was nagged by an overwhelming sense of being off balance, and he instinctively shut his eyes to prevent them from being poked by whatever he was walking into. He tried to bring himself to a halt as best he could while still clutching onto the flowers, but instead felt his legs tripping each other. He was all but resigned to the fact that there was going to be an ensuing thud and all that it would entail when he became conscious of something very strange. He was enveloped in, of all things, the fragrance of a perfume, the scent from which was simply stunning!

Mjomba was still expecting to hit the pavement and was wondering if he would break any bones during the fall when he felt someone seize and steady him. He simultaneously heard the words "Oh, excuse me!", or something to that effect. They were spoken in the barest whisper and came from a female voice that sounded faintly familiar! He heard them at the same time as he was feeling the provocatively soft touch of fingertips he imagined were suitably long and slender about his loins.

Flora's hands were still flailing helplessly for support when Mjomba opened his eyes. In the same split second, he flung the flowers out of the way to one side and then shot out his right hand, just in time to stop the nurse from striking the paved ground.

After clambering out of the auto, Ali and Musa had merely skirted the colliding pair and raced on, unconcerned, towards the Reception in their haste to rejoin their mom. Fatuma, trailing behind them, had stopped in her tracks and stared with open mouth as the nurse's white uniform blew up a cloud of dust. She had scarcely closed her mouth when, certain that the nurse who had walked into her uncle from nowhere was going to end up sprawled on the floor, she clutched her chin and braced for worst - almost as if she were the one who was plummeting to the ground.

But even before she could finish sighing with relief that an awkward situation had been averted by her uncle's quick action, she found herself watching with her heart literally in her mouth as Mjomba and the nurse first exchanged glances which indicated that they knew each other, and then broke out into a merry laugh!

All three were jolted to attention by shouts that emanated from a nearby hallway and filled the air. Two plaintive voices were screaming: "*Mama! Mtoto, Mama, Mtoto...!*"

Mjomba, Flora and Fatuma were drawn to Jamila's room as if by a magnet. Jamila and little Kunta were being mobbed by Ali and Musa when Mjomba, clutching the bouquet of flowers that had somehow survived the collision and was undamaged, stepped inside the box-like recovery room. Flora and Fatuma, their faces all giggles, closed in around the berth. Jamila took in the bouquet of flowers and the Stanford tie in a glance, and tried to conceal her obvious pleasure at seeing the room filled with all the smiling faces.

For a moment, Kunta's wellbeing seemed in jeopardy as Jamila left Ali and Musa who were still mobbing Kunta to their own devices to give Mjomba his due attention. Luckily for Kunta, Flora did not waste any time taking over control of the situation and installing herself as overseer of Kunta's first encounter with his astute if over-eager siblings. Unlike Flora, who couldn't resist stealing a glance, Fatuma, standing at a respectable distance near a window, turned to admire a nearby rose bush as husband and wife embraced and their lips sought out

710

each other. Almost immediately afterward, Jamila's lips were heard making tiny little noises and giving the impression that she was struggling to free herself from Mjomba's grip! She suddenly did, but just long enough to enable her to hiss: "Oh, I love you...and *The Psychic Roots of a Nut* - it is the best novel I've ever read! But it has the wrong title. Darling, promise that you will change it to *The Masterpiece*!"

Jamila's gleaming eyes looked like a pair of diamonds as they sought out the blue folder that now lay on the nightstand. They seemed to derive similar satisfaction from lingering over the folder to that which their owner was deriving from the man's embrace.

Made in the USA
Middletown, DE
17 April 2022

64358364R00411